IMPERIUM

"Harris's zest for political machinations serves the material well."
—*The Washington Post*

"A minutely observed political novel . . . set during the most poignant era in ancient Roman history." —*Newsday* (New York)

"In Harris's hands the great game [of politics] becomes a beautiful one." —*The Times* (London)

"Excellent. . . . Full of back-biting and double-dealing, compromise and intrigue." —*Time Out*

POMPEII

"Terrific . . . gripping . . . a literally shattering climax."
—*The New York Times Book Review*

"A meticulously researched, beautifully written historical thriller of extraordinary breadth and depth." —*The Miami Herald*

"The blast from Vesuvius kicks ash." —*People*

"Immediately engrossing." —*San Francisco Chronicle*

"Harris garnishes the action with seductive period detail, and the novel comes alive in the main event, a cataclysmic explosion with a thermal energy equal to a hundred thousand Hiroshimas."
—*The New Yorker*

ALSO BY ROBERT HARRIS

FICTION

Imperium

Pompeii

Archangel

Enigma

Fatherland

NONFICTION

Selling Hitler: The Story of the Hitler Diaries

THE
GHOST
WRITER

This book was previously published with the title *The Ghost*

Robert Harris

G

Gallery Books

New York   London   Toronto   Sydney

Gallery Books
A Division of Simon & Schuster, Inc.
1230 Avenue of the Americas
New York, NY 10020

This Gallery Books trade paperback edition March 2010

GALLERY BOOKS and colophon are trademarks of Simon & Schuster, Inc.

For information about special discounts for bulk
purchases, please contact Simon & Schuster Special Sales at
1-866-506-1949 or business@simonandschuster.com.

The Simon & Schuster Speakers Bureau can bring authors to your
live event. For more information or to book an event contact the
Simon & Schuster Speakers Bureau at 1-866-248-3049
or visit our website at www.simonspeakers.com.

Designed by Suet Y. Chong

Manufactured in the United States of America

10   9   8   7   6   5   4   3   2

Library of Congress Cataloging-in-Publication Data
is available for the hardcover edition.

ISBN 978-1-4391-9055-5
ISBN 978-1-4165-7147-6 (ebook)

This book was previously published with the title *The Ghost*

To Gill

AUTHOR'S NOTE

I would like to thank Andrew Crofts for permission to use the quotes from his excellent handbook, *Ghostwriting* (A & C Black, 2004). Two other successful ghostwriters, Adam Sisman and Luke Jennings, were kind enough to share their experiences with me. Philippe Sands, QC, generously provided advice about international law. Rose Styron spent several days showing me round Martha's Vineyard: I could not have had a more gracious and well-informed guide. My publisher, David Rosenthal, and my agent, Michael Carlisle, were even more helpful and encouraging than usual—although each is as unlike his fictional counterpart as it is possible to be.

Robert Harris
Cap Bénat, July 26, 2007

I am not I: thou art not he or she:
they are not they.

Evelyn Waugh,
Brideshead Revisited

THE
GHOST
WRITER

ONE

———— ★ ————

> Of all the advantages that ghosting offers, one of the
> greatest must be the opportunity that you get to meet
> people of interest.
>
> Andrew Crofts,
Ghostwriting

THE MOMENT I HEARD how McAra died, I should have
walked away. I can see that now. I should have said, "Rick, I'm
sorry, this isn't for me, I don't like the sound of it," finished my
drink, and left. But he was such a good storyteller, Rick—I often
thought *he* should have been the writer and I the literary agent—
that once he'd started talking there was never any question I
wouldn't listen, and by the time he had finished, I was hooked.

The story, as Rick told it to me over lunch that day, went like
this:

McAra had caught the last ferry from Woods Hole, Massachusetts, to Martha's Vineyard two Sundays earlier. I worked out afterward it must have been January the twelfth. It was touch-and-go whether the ferry would sail at all. A gale had been blowing since midafternoon and the last few crossings had been canceled. But toward nine o'clock the wind eased slightly, and at nine forty-five the master decided it was safe to cast off. The boat was crowded; McAra was lucky to get a space for his car. He parked belowdecks and then went upstairs to get some air.

No one saw him alive again.

The crossing to the island usually takes forty-five minutes, but on this particular night the weather slowed the voyage considerably: docking a two-hundred-foot vessel in a fifty-knot wind, said Rick, is nobody's idea of fun. It was nearly eleven when the ferry made land at Vineyard Haven and the cars started up—all except one: a brand-new tan-colored Ford Escape SUV. The purser made a loudspeaker appeal for the owner to return to his vehicle, as he was blocking the drivers behind him. When he still didn't show, the crew tried the doors, which turned out to be unlocked, and freewheeled the big Ford down to the quayside. Afterward they searched the ship with care: stairwells, bar, toilets, even the lifeboats—nothing. They called the terminal at Woods Hole to check if anyone had disembarked before the boat sailed or had perhaps been accidentally left behind—again: nothing. That was when an official of the Massachusetts Steamship Authority finally contacted the Coast Guard station in Falmouth to report a possible man overboard.

A police check on the Ford's license plate revealed it to be registered to one Martin S. Rhinehart of New York City, although Mr. Rhinehart was eventually tracked down to his ranch in California. By now it was about midnight on the East Coast, nine p.m. on the West.

"This is *the* Marty Rhinehart?" I interrupted.

"This is he."

Rhinehart immediately confirmed over the telephone to the police that the Ford belonged to him. He kept it at his house on Martha's Vineyard for the use of himself and his guests in the summer. He also confirmed that, despite the time of year, a group of people were staying there at the moment. He said he would get his assistant to call the house and find out if anyone had borrowed the car. Half an hour later she rang back to say that someone was indeed missing, a person by the name of McAra.

Nothing more could be done until first light. Not that it mattered. Everyone knew that if a passenger had gone overboard it would be a search for a corpse. Rick is one of those irritatingly fit Americans in their early forties who look about nineteen and do terrible things to their body with bicycles and canoes. He knows that sea: he once spent two days paddling a kayak the entire sixty miles round the island. The ferry from Woods Hole plies the strait where Vineyard Sound meets Nantucket Sound, and that is dangerous water. At high tide you can see the force of the currents sucking the huge channel buoys over onto their sides. Rick shook his head. In January, in a gale, in *snow*? No one could survive more than five minutes.

A local woman found the body early the next morning, thrown up on the beach about four miles down the island's coast at Lambert's Cove. The driver's license in the wallet confirmed him to be Michael James McAra, age fifty, from Balham in south London. I remember feeling a sudden shot of sympathy at the mention of that dreary, unexotic suburb: he certainly was a long way from home, poor devil. His passport named his mother as his next of kin. The police took his corpse to the little morgue in Vineyard

Haven and then drove over to the Rhinehart residence to break the news and to fetch one of the other guests to identify him.

It must have been quite a scene, said Rick, when the volunteer guest finally showed up to view the body: "I bet the morgue attendant is still talking about it." There was one patrol car from Edgartown with a flashing blue light, a second car with four armed guards to secure the building, and a third vehicle, bombproof, carrying the instantly recognizable man who, until eighteen months earlier, had been the prime minister of Great Britain and Northern Ireland.

THE LUNCH HAD BEEN Rick's idea. I hadn't even known he was in town until he rang me the night before. He insisted we meet at his club. It was not *his* club, exactly—he was actually a member of a similar mausoleum in Manhattan, whose members had reciprocal dining rights in London—but he loved it all the same. At lunchtime only men were admitted. Each wore a dark blue suit and was over sixty; I hadn't felt so young since I left university. Outside, the winter sky pressed down on London like a great gray tombstone. Inside, yellow electric light from three immense candelabra glinted on dark polished tables, plated silverware, and rubied decanters of claret. A small card placed between us announced that the club's annual backgammon tournament would be taking place that evening. It was like the changing of the guard or the houses of parliament—a foreigner's image of England.

"I'm amazed this hasn't been in the papers," I said.

"Oh, but it has. Nobody's made a secret of it. There've been obituaries."

And, now I came to think of it, I *did* vaguely remember seeing something. But I had been working fifteen hours a day for a month to finish my new book, the autobiography of a footballer, and the world beyond my study had become a blur.

"What on earth was an ex–prime minister doing identifying the body of a man from Balham who fell off the Martha's Vineyard ferry?"

"Michael McAra," announced Rick, with the emphatic delivery of a man who has flown three thousand miles to deliver this punch line, "*was helping him write his memoirs.*"

And this is where, in that parallel life, I express polite sympathy for the elderly Mrs. McAra ("such a shock to lose a child at that age"), fold my heavy linen napkin, finish my drink, say good-bye, and step out into the chilly London street with the whole of my undistinguished career stretching safely ahead of me. Instead I excused myself, went to the club's lavatory, and studied an unfunny *Punch* cartoon while urinating thoughtfully.

"You realize I don't know anything about politics?" I said when I got back.

"You voted for him, didn't you?"

"Adam Lang? Of course I did. Everybody voted for him. He wasn't a politician; he was a craze."

"Well, that's the point. Who's interested in politics? In any case, it's a professional ghostwriter he needs, my friend, not another goddamned politico." He glanced around. It was an iron rule of the club that no business could be discussed on the premises— a problem for Rick, seeing as he never discussed anything else. "Marty Rhinehart paid ten million dollars for these memoirs on two conditions. First, it'd be in the stores within two years. Second, Lang wouldn't pull any punches about the war on terror.

From what I hear, he's nowhere near meeting either requirement. Things got so bad around Christmas, Rhinehart gave him the use of his vacation house on the Vineyard so that Lang and McAra could work without any distractions. I guess the pressure must have gotten to McAra. The state medical examiner found enough booze in his blood to put him four times over the driving limit."

"So it was an accident?"

"Accident? Suicide?" He casually flicked his hand. "Who'll ever know? What does it matter? It was the book that killed him."

"That's encouraging," I said.

While Rick went on with his pitch, I stared at my plate and imagined the former prime minister looking down at his assistant's cold white face in the mortuary—staring down at his ghost, I suppose one could say. How did it feel? I am always putting this question to my clients. I must ask it a hundred times a day during the interview phase: How did it feel? *How did it feel?* And mostly they can't answer, which is why they have to hire me to supply their memories; by the end of a successful collaboration I am more them than they are. I rather enjoy this process, to be honest: the brief freedom of being someone else. Does that sound creepy? If so, let me add that real craftsmanship is required. I not only extract from people their life stories, I impart a shape to those lives that was often invisible; sometimes I give them lives they never even realized they had. If that isn't art, what is?

I said, "Should I have heard of McAra?"

"Yes, so let's not admit you haven't. He was some kind of aide when Lang was prime minister. Speechwriting, policy research, political strategy. When Lang resigned, McAra stayed with him, to run his office."

I grimaced. "I don't know, Rick."

Throughout lunch I'd been half watching an elderly television actor at the next table. He'd been famous when I was a child for playing the single parent of teenage girls in a sitcom. Now, as he rose unsteadily and started to shuffle toward the exit, he looked as though he'd been made up to act the role of his own corpse. That was the type of person whose memoirs I ghosted: people who had fallen a few rungs down the celebrity ladder, or who had a few rungs left to climb, or who were just about clinging to the top and were desperate to cash in while there was still time. I was abruptly overwhelmed by the ridiculousness of the whole idea that I might collaborate on the memoirs of a prime minister.

"I don't know—" I began again, but Rick interrupted me.

"Rhinehart Inc. are getting frantic. They're holding a beauty parade at their London office tomorrow morning. Maddox himself is flying over from New York to represent the company. Lang's sending the lawyer who negotiated the original deal for him—the hottest fixer in Washington, a very smart guy by the name of Sidney Kroll. I've other clients I could put in for this, so if you're not up for it, just tell me now. But from the way they've been talking, I think you're the best fit."

"Me? You're kidding."

"No. I promise you. They need to do something radical—take a risk. It's a great opportunity for you. And the money will be good. The kids won't starve."

"I don't have any kids."

"No," said Rick with a wink, "but I do."

WE PARTED ON THE steps of the club. Rick had a car waiting outside with its engine running. He didn't offer to drop me anywhere, which made me suspect he was off to see another client, to whom he would make exactly the same pitch he had just made to me. What is the collective noun for a group of ghosts? A train? A town? A haunt? At any rate, Rick had plenty of us on his books. Take a look at the bestseller lists: you would be amazed how much of it is the work of ghosts, novels as well as nonfiction. We are the phantom operatives who keep publishing going, like the unseen workers beneath Walt Disney World. We scuttle along the subterranean tunnels of celebrity, popping up here and there, dressed as this character or that, preserving the seamless illusion of the Magic Kingdom.

"See you tomorrow," he said, and dramatically, in a puff of exhaust fumes, he was gone: Mephistopheles on a fifteen percent commission. I stood for a minute, undecided, and if I had been in another part of London it is still just possible things might have gone differently. But I was in that narrow zone where Soho washes up against Covent Garden: a trash-strewn strip of empty theaters, dark alleys, red lights, snack bars, and bookshops—so many bookshops you can start to feel ill just looking at them, from the tiny little rip-off specialist dealers in Cecil Court to the cut-price behemoths of Charing Cross Road. I often drop into one of the latter, to see how my titles are displayed, and that was what I did that afternoon. Once inside, it was only a short step across the scuffed red carpet of the "Biography & Memoir" department, and suddenly I had gone from "Celebrity" to "Politics."

I was surprised by how much they had on the former prime minister—an entire shelf, everything from the early hagiography, *Adam Lang: Statesman for Our Time*, to a recent hatchet job titled *Would You Adam and Eve It? The Collected Lies of Adam Lang*, both by the same author. I took down the thickest biography and opened it at the photographs: Lang as a toddler, feeding a bottle of milk to a lamb beside a drystone wall, Lang as Lady Macbeth in a school play, Lang dressed as a chicken in a Cambridge University Footlights revue, Lang as a distinctly stoned-looking merchant banker in the nineteen seventies, Lang with his wife and young children on the doorstep of a new house, Lang wearing a rosette and waving from an open-topped bus on the day he was elected to parliament, Lang with his colleagues, Lang with world leaders, with pop stars, with soldiers in the Middle East. A bald customer in a scuffed leather coat browsing the shelf next to me stared at the cover. He held his nose with one hand and mimed flushing a toilet with the other.

I moved around the corner of the bookcase and looked up McAra, Michael in the index. There were only five or six innocuous references—no reason, in other words, why anyone outside the party or the government need ever have heard of him, so to hell with you, Rick, I thought. I flicked back to the photograph of the prime minister seated smiling at the cabinet table, with his Downing Street staff arrayed behind him. The caption identified McAra as the burly figure in the back row. He was slightly out of focus—a pale, unsmiling, dark-haired smudge. I squinted more closely at him. He looked exactly the sort of unappealing inadequate who is congenitally drawn to politics and makes people like me stick to the sports pages. You'll find a McAra in any country, in any system, standing behind any leader with a political machine to operate: a greasy engineer in the boiler room of power. And this was the man who had been entrusted to ghost a ten-million-dollar memoir? I felt professionally affronted. I bought myself a small pile of research material and headed out of the bookshop with a growing conviction that maybe Rick was right: perhaps I was the man for the job.

It was obvious the moment I got outside that another bomb had gone off. At Tottenham Court Road people were surging up above ground from all four exits of the tube station like storm water from a blocked drain. A loudspeaker said something about "an incident at Oxford Circus." It sounded like an edgy romantic comedy: *Brief Encounter* meets the war on terror. I carried on up the road, unsure of how I would get home—taxis, like false friends, tending always to vanish at the first sign of trouble. In the window of one of the big electrical shops, the crowd watched the same news bulletin relayed simultaneously on a dozen televisions: aerial shots of Oxford Circus, black smoke gushing out of the underground station, thrusts of orange flame. An electronic ticker running across the bottom of the screen announced a suspected suicide bomber, many dead and injured, and gave an emergency number to call. Above the rooftops a helicopter tilted and circled. I could smell the smoke—an acrid, eye-reddening blend of diesel and burning plastic.

It took me two full hours to walk home, lugging my heavy bag of books—up to Marylebone Road and then westward toward Paddington. As usual, the entire tube system had been shut down to check for further bombs; so had the main railway stations. The traffic on either side of the wide street was stalled and, on past form, would remain so until evening. (If only Hitler had known he didn't need a whole air force to paralyze London, I thought, just a revved-up teenager with a bottle of bleach and a bag of weed killer.) Occasionally a police car or an ambulance would mount the curb, roar along the pavement, and attempt to make progress up a side street.

I trudged on toward the setting sun.

It must have been six when I reached my flat. I had the top two floors of a high, stuccoed house in what the residents called Notting Hill and the post office stubbornly insisted was North Kensington. Used syringes glittered in the gutter; at the halal butchers opposite they did the slaughtering on the premises. It was grim. But from the attic extension that served as my office I had a view across west London that would not have disgraced a skyscraper: rooftops, railway yards, motorway, and sky—a vast urban prairie sky, sprinkled with the lights of aircraft descending toward Heathrow. It was this view that had sold me the apartment, not the estate agent's gentrification patter—which was just as well, as the rich bourgeoisie have no more returned to this area than they have to downtown Baghdad.

Kate had already let herself in and was watching the news. Kate: I had forgotten she was coming over for the evening. She was my—? I never knew what to call her. To say she was my girlfriend was absurd; no one the wrong side of thirty has a *girlfriend*. Partner wasn't right either, as we didn't live under the same roof. Lover? How could one keep a straight face? Mistress? Do me a favor. Fiancée? Certainly not. I suppose I ought to have realized it was ominous that forty thousand years of human language had failed to produce a word for our relationship. (Kate wasn't her real name, by the way, but I don't see why she should be dragged into all this. In any case, it suits her better than the name she does have: she looks like a Kate, if you know what I mean—sensible but sassy, girlish but always willing to be one of the boys. She worked in television, but let's not hold that against her.)

"Thanks for the concerned phone call," I said. "I'm dead, actually, but don't worry about it." I kissed the top of her head, dropped the books onto the sofa, and went into the kitchen to pour myself a whiskey. "The entire tube is down. I've had to walk all the way from Covent Garden."

"Poor darling," I heard her say. "And you've been shopping."

I topped up my glass with water from the tap, drank half, then topped it up again with whiskey. I remembered I was supposed to have reserved a restaurant. When I went back into the living room, she was removing one book after another from the carrier bag. "What's all this?" she said, looking up at me. "You're not interested in *politics*." And then she realized what was going on, because she was smart—smarter than I was. She knew what I did for a living, she knew I was meeting an agent, and she knew all about McAra. "Don't tell me they want *you* to ghost his book?" She laughed. "You cannot be serious." She tried to make a joke of it—"You *cannot* be serious" in an American accent, like that tennis player a few years ago—but I could see her dismay. She hated Lang, felt personally betrayed by him. She used to be a party member. I had forgotten that, too.

"It'll probably come to nothing," I said and drank some more whiskey.

She went back to watching the news, only now with her arms tightly folded, always a warning sign. The ticker announced that the death toll was seven and likely to rise.

"But if you're offered it you'll do it?" she asked, without turning to look at me.

I was spared having to reply by the newsreader announcing that they were cutting live to New York to get the reaction of the former prime minister, and suddenly there was Adam Lang, at a podium marked "Waldorf-Astoria," where it looked as though he had been addressing a lunch. "You will all by now have heard the tragic news from London," he said, "where once again the forces of fanaticism and intolerance . . ."

Nothing he uttered that night warrants reprinting. It was almost a parody of what a politician might say after a terrorist attack. Yet, watching him, you would have thought his own wife and children had been eviscerated in the blast. This was his genius: to refresh and elevate the clichés of politics by the sheer force of his performance. Even Kate was briefly silenced. Only when he had finished and his largely female, mostly elderly audience was rising to applaud did she mutter, "What's he doing in New York, anyway?"

"Lecturing?"

"Why can't he lecture here?"

"I suppose because no one here would pay him a hundred thousand dollars a throw."

She pressed Mute.

"There was a time," said Kate slowly, after what felt like a very long silence, "when princes taking their countries to war were supposed to risk their lives in battle—you know, lead by example. Now they travel around in bombproof cars with armed bodyguards and make fortunes three thousand miles away, while the rest of us are stuck with the consequences of their actions. I just don't understand you," she went on, turning to look at me properly for the first time. "All the things I've said about him over the past few years—'war criminal' and the rest of it—and you've sat there nodding and agreeing. And now you're going to write his propaganda for him, and make him richer. Did none of it ever mean anything to you at all?"

"Hold on a minute," I said. "You're a fine one to talk. You've been trying to get an interview with him for months. What's the difference?"

"What's the difference? Christ!" She clenched her hands—those slim white hands I knew so well—and raised them in frustration, half claw, half fist. The sinews stood out in her arms. "*What's the difference?* We want to hold him to account—that's the difference! To ask him proper questions! About torturing and bombing and lying! Not 'How does it feel?' *Christ!* This is a complete bloody waste of time."

She got up then and went into the bedroom to collect the bag she always brought on the nights she planned to stay. I heard her filling it noisily with lipstick, toothbrush, perfume spray. I knew if I went in I could retrieve the situation. She was probably expecting it; we'd had worse rows. I'd have been obliged to concede that she was right, acknowledge my unsuitability for the task, affirm her moral and intellectual superiority in this as in all things. It needn't even have been a verbal confession; a meaningful hug would probably have been enough to get me a suspended sentence. But the truth was, at that moment, given a choice between an evening of her smug left-wing moralizing and the prospect of working with a so-called war criminal, I preferred the war criminal. So I simply carried on staring at the television.

Sometimes I have a nightmare in which all the women I have ever slept with assemble together. It's a respectable rather than a huge number—were it a drinks party, say, my living room could accommodate them quite comfortably. And if, God forbid, this gathering were ever to occur, Kate would be the undisputed guest of honor. She is the one for whom a chair would be fetched, who would have her glass refilled by sympathetic hands, who would sit at the center of a disbelieving circle as my moral and physical flaws were dissected. She was the one who had stuck it the longest.

She didn't slam the door as she left but closed it very carefully. That was stylish, I thought. On the television screen the death toll had just increased to eight.

TWO

———————— ★ ————————

A ghost who has only a lay knowledge of the subject
will be able to keep asking the same questions as the
lay reader, and will therefore open up the potential
readership of the book to a much wider audience.

Ghostwriting

RHINEHART PUBLISHING UK CONSISTED of five ancient
firms acquired during a vigorous bout of corporate kleptomania in
the nineteen nineties. Wrenched out of their Dickensian garrets in
Bloomsbury, upsized, downsized, rebranded, renamed, reorga-
nized, modernized, and merged, they had finally been dumped in
Hounslow, in a steel-and-smoked-glass office block with all its
pipes on the outside. It nestled among the pebble-dash housing
estates like an abandoned spacecraft after a fruitless mission to find
intelligent life.

I arrived, with professional punctuality, five minutes before noon, only to discover the main door locked. I had to buzz for entry. A notice board in the foyer announced that the terrorism alert was ORANGE/HIGH. Through the darkened glass I could see the security men in their dingy aquarium checking me on a monitor. When I finally got inside I had to turn out my pockets and pass through a metal detector.

Quigley was waiting for me by the lifts.

"Who're you expecting to bomb you?" I asked. "Random House?"

"We're publishing Lang's memoirs," replied Quigley in a stiff voice. "That alone makes us a target, apparently. Rick's already upstairs."

"How many've you seen?"

"Five. You're the last."

I knew Roy Quigley fairly well, well enough to know he disapproved of me. He must have been about fifty, tall and tweedy. In a happier era he would have smoked a pipe and offered tiny advances to minor academics over large lunches in Soho. Now his midday meal was a plastic tray of salad taken at his desk overlooking the M4, and he received his orders direct from the head of sales and marketing, a girl of about sixteen. He had three children in private schools he couldn't afford. As the price of survival he'd actually been obliged to start taking an interest in popular culture, to wit, the lives of various footballers, supermodels, and foul-mouthed comedians whose names he pronounced carefully and whose customs he studied in the tabloids with scholarly detachment, as if they were remote Micronesian tribespeople. I'd pitched him an idea the year before, the memoirs of a TV magician who had—of course!—been abused in childhood but who had used his skill as an illusionist to conjure up a new life, etc., etc. He'd turned it down flat. The book had gone straight to number one: *I Came, I Sawed, I Conquered*. He still bore a grudge.

"I have to tell you," he said, as we rose to the penthouse, "that I don't think you're the right man for this assignment."

"Then it's a good job it's not your decision, Roy."

Oh, yes, I had Quigley's measure right enough. His title was UK Group Editor in Chief, which meant he had all the authority of a dead cat. The man who really ran the global show was waiting for us in the boardroom: John Maddox, chief executive of Rhinehart Inc., a big, bull-shouldered New Yorker with alopecia. His bald head glistened under the strip lighting like a massive, varnished egg. As a young man he'd acquired a wrestler's physique in order (according to *Publishers Weekly*) to tip out the window anyone who stared too long at his scalp. I made sure my gaze never rose higher than his superhero chest. Next to him was Lang's Washington attorney, Sidney Kroll, a bespectacled fortysomething with a delicate pale face, floppy raven hair, and the limpest and dampest handshake I'd been offered since Dippy the Dolphin bobbed up from his pool when I was twelve.

"And Nick Riccardelli I think you know," said Quigley, completing the introductions with just a hint of a shudder. My agent, who was wearing a shiny gray shirt and a thin red leather tie, winked up at me.

"Hi, Rick," I said.

I felt nervous as I took my seat beside him. The room was lined, Gatsby-like, with immaculate unread hardcover books. Maddox sat with his back to the window. He laid his massive, hairless hands on the glass-topped table, as if to prove he had no intention of reaching for a weapon just yet, and said, "I gather from Rick you're aware of the situation and that you know what we're looking for. So perhaps you could tell us exactly what you think you'd bring to this project."

"Ignorance," I said brightly, which at least had the benefit of shock value, and before anyone could interrupt I launched into the little speech I'd rehearsed in the taxi coming over. "You know my track record. There's no point my trying to pretend I'm something I'm not. I'll be completely honest. I don't read political memoirs. So what?" I shrugged. "Nobody does. But actually that's not my problem." I pointed at Maddox. "That's *your* problem."

"Oh, please," said Quigley quietly.

"And let me be even more recklessly honest," I went on. "Rumor has it you paid ten million dollars for this book. As things stand, how much of that d'you think you're going to see back? Two million? Three? That's bad news for you, and that's especially bad news," I said, turning to Kroll, "for your client. Because for him this isn't about money. This is about reputation. This is Adam Lang's opportunity to speak directly to history, to get his case across. The last thing he needs is to produce a book that nobody reads. How will it look if his life story ends up on the remainder tables? But it doesn't have to be this way."

I know in retrospect what a huckster I sounded. But this was pitch talk, remember—which, like declarations of undying love in a stranger's bedroom at midnight, shouldn't necessarily be held against you the next morning. Kroll was smiling to himself, doodling on his yellow pad. Maddox was staring hard at me. I took a breath.

"The fact is," I continued, "a big name alone doesn't sell a book. We've all learned that the hard way. What sells a book—or a movie, or a song—is *heart*." I believe I may even have thumped my chest at this point. "And that's why political memoir is *the* black hole of publishing. The name outside the tent may be big, but everyone knows that once they're inside they're just going to get the same old tired show, and who wants to pay twenty-five dollars for that? You've got to put in some heart, and that's what I do for a living. And whose story has more heart than the guy who starts from nowhere and ends up running a country?"

I leaned forward. "You see, here's the joke: a leader's autobiography ought to be *more* interesting than most memoirs, not *less*. So I see my ignorance about politics as an advantage. I *cherish* my ignorance, quite frankly. Besides, Adam Lang doesn't need any help from me with the politics of this book—he's a political genius. What he does need, in my humble opinion, is the same thing a movie star needs, or a baseball player, or a rock star: an experienced collaborator who knows how to ask him the questions that will draw out his heart."

There was a silence. I was trembling. Rick gave my knee a reassuring pat under the table. "Nicely done."

"What utter balls," said Quigley.

"Think so?" asked Maddox, still looking at me. He said it in a neutral voice, but if I had been Quigley, I would have detected danger.

"Oh, John, *of course*," said Quigley, with all the dismissive scorn of four generations of Oxford scholars behind him. "Adam Lang is a world-historical figure, and his autobiography is going to be a world publishing event. A piece of history, in fact. It shouldn't be approached like a"—he ransacked his well-stocked mind for a suitable analogy but finished lamely—"a feature for a celebrity magazine."

There was another silence. Beyond the tinted windows the traffic was backing up along the motorway. Rainwater rippled the gleam of the stationary headlights. London still hadn't returned to normal after the bomb.

"It seems to me," said Maddox, in the same slow, quiet voice, his big pink mannequin's hands still resting on the table, "that I have entire warehouses full of 'world publishing events' that I somehow can't figure out how to get off my hands. And a heck of a lot of people read celebrity magazines. What do you think, Sid?"

For a few seconds Kroll merely carried on smiling to himself and doodling. I wondered what he found so funny. "Adam's position on this is very straightforward," he said eventually. (*Adam*: he tossed the first name as casually into the conversation as he might a coin into a beggar's cap.) "He takes this book very seriously—it's his testament, if you will. He wants to meet his contractual obligations. And he wants it to be a commercial success. He's therefore more than happy to be guided by you, John, and by Marty also, within reason. Obviously, he's still very upset by what happened to Mike, who was irreplaceable."

"Obviously." We all made the appropriate noises.

"Irreplaceable," he repeated. "And yet—*he has to be replaced*." He looked up, pleased with his drollery, and at that instant I knew there was no horror the world could offer—no war, no genocide, no famine, no childhood cancer—to which Sidney Kroll would not see the funny side. "Adam can certainly appreciate the benefits of trying someone entirely different. In the end, it all comes down to a personal bond." His spectacles flashed in the strip lights as he scrutinized me. "Do you work out, maybe?" I shook my head. "Pity. Adam likes to work out."

Quigley, still reeling from Maddox's put-down, attempted a comeback. "Actually, I know quite a good writer on the *Guardian* who uses a gym."

"Maybe," said Rick, after an embarrassed pause, "we could run over how you see this working practically."

"First off, we need it wrapped up in a month," said Maddox. "That's Marty's view as well as mine."

"A month?" I repeated. "You want the book in a month?"

"A completed manuscript does exist," said Kroll. "It just needs some work."

"A lot of work," said Maddox grimly. "Okay. Taking it backward: we publish in June, which means we ship in May, which means we edit and we print in March and April, which means we have to have the manuscript in-house at the end of February. The Germans, French, Italians, and Spanish all have to start translating right away. The newspapers need to see it for the serial deals. There's a television tie-in. Publicity tour's got to be fixed well in advance. We need to book space in the stores. So the end of February—that's it, period. What I like about your résumé," he said, consulting a sheet of paper on which I could see all my titles listed, "is that you're obviously experienced and above all you're fast. You deliver."

"Never missed once," said Rick, putting his arm round my shoulders and squeezing me. "That's my boy."

"And you're a Brit. The ghost definitely has to be a Brit, I think. To get the jolly old tone right."

"We agree," said Kroll. "But everything will have to be done in the States. Adam's completely locked in to a lecture tour there right now, and a fund-raising program for his foundation. I don't see him coming back to the UK till March at the earliest."

"A month in America, that's fine—yes?" Rick glanced at me eagerly. I could feel him willing me to say yes, but all I was thinking was: a month, they want me to write a book in a month . . .

I nodded slowly. "I suppose I can always bring the manuscript back here to work on."

"The manuscript stays in America," said Kroll flatly. "That's one of the reasons Marty made the house on the Vineyard available. It's a secure environment. Only a few people are allowed to handle it."

"Sounds more like a bomb than a book!" joked Quigley. Nobody laughed. He rubbed his hands unhappily. "You know, I will need to see it myself at some point. I am supposed to be editing it."

"In theory," said Maddox. "Actually we need to talk about that later." He turned to Kroll. "There's no room in this schedule for revisions. We'll need to revise as we go."

As they carried on discussing the timetable, I studied Quigley. He was upright but motionless, like one of those victims in the movies who get stuck with a stiletto while standing in a crowd and die without anyone noticing. His mouth opened and closed ever so slightly, as if he had a final message to impart. Yet even at the time I realized he'd asked a perfectly reasonable question. If he was the editor, why shouldn't he see the manuscript? And why did it have to be held in a "secure environment" on an island off the eastern seaboard of the United States? I felt Rick's elbow in my ribs and realized Maddox was talking to me.

"How soon can you get over there? Assuming we go with you rather than one of the others—how fast can you move?"

"It's Friday today," I said. "Give me a day to get ready. I could fly Sunday."

"And start Monday? That would be great."

Rick said, "You won't find anyone who can move quicker than that."

Maddox and Kroll looked at one another and I knew then that

I had the job. As Rick said afterward, the trick is always to put yourself in their position. "It's like interviewing a new cleaner. Do you want someone who can give you the history of cleaning and the theory of cleaning, or do you want someone who'll just get down and clean your fucking house? They chose you because they think you'll clean their fucking house."

"We'll go with you," said Maddox. He stood and reached over and shook my hand. "Subject to reaching a satisfactory agreement with Rick here, of course."

Kroll added, "You'll also have to sign a nondisclosure agreement."

"No problem," I said, also getting to my feet. That didn't bother me. Confidentiality clauses are standard procedure in the ghosting world. "I couldn't be happier."

And I couldn't have been. Everyone except Quigley was smiling, and suddenly there was a kind of all-boys, locker-room-after-the-match kind of feeling in the air. We chatted for a minute or so, and that was when Kroll took me to one side and said, very casually, "I've something here you might care to take a look at."

He reached under the table and pulled out a bright yellow plastic bag with the name of some fancy Washington clothes store printed on it in curly black copperplate. My first thought was that it must be the manuscript of Lang's memoirs and that all the stuff about a "secure environment" had been a joke. But when he saw my expression, Kroll laughed and said, "No, no, it's not *that*. It's just a book by another client of mine. I'd really appreciate your opinion if you get a chance to look at it. Here's my number." I took his card and slipped it into my pocket. Quigley still hadn't said a word.

"I'll give you a call when we've settled the deal," said Rick.

"Make them howl," I told him, squeezing his shoulder.

Maddox laughed. "Hey! Remember!" he called as Quigley showed me out of the door. He struck his big fist against his blue-suited chest. "Heart!"

As we went down in the lift, Quigley stared at the ceiling. "Was it my imagination, or did I just get fired in there?"

"They wouldn't let you go, Roy," I said with all the sincerity I could muster, which wasn't much. "You're the only one left who can remember what publishing used to be like."

" 'Let you go,' " he said bitterly. "Yes, that's the modern euphemism, isn't it? As if it's a favor. You're clinging to the edge of a cliff and someone says, 'Oh, I'm terribly sorry, we're going to have to let you go.' "

A couple on their lunch break got in at the fourth floor and Quigley was silent until they got off to go to the restaurant on the second. When the doors closed, he said, "There's something not right about this project."

"Me, you mean?"

"No. Before you." He frowned. "I can't quite put my finger on it. The way no one's allowed to see anything, for a start. And that fellow Kroll makes me shiver. And poor old Mike McAra, of course. I met him when we signed the deal two years ago. He didn't strike me as the suicidal type. Rather the reverse. He was the sort who specializes in making other people want to kill themselves, if you know what I mean."

"Hard?"

"Hard, yes. Lang would be smiling away, and there would be this thug next to him with eyes like a snake's. I suppose you've got to have someone like that when you're in Lang's position."

We reached the ground floor and stepped out into the lobby.

"You can pick up a taxi round the corner," said Quigley, and for that one small, mean gesture—leaving me to walk in the rain rather than calling me a cab on the company's account—I hoped he'd rot. "Tell me," he said suddenly, "when did it become fashionable to be stupid? That's the thing I really don't understand. The Cult of the Idiot. The Elevation of the Moron. Our two biggest-selling novelists—the actress with the tits and that ex-army psycho—have never written a word of fiction. Did you know that?"

"You're talking like an old man, Roy," I told him. "People have been complaining that standards are slipping ever since Shakespeare started writing comedies."

"Yes, but now it's really happened, hasn't it? It was never like this before."

I knew he was trying to goad me—the ghostwriter to the stars off to produce the memoirs of an ex–prime minister—but I was too full of myself to care. I wished him well in his retirement and set off across the lobby swinging that damned yellow plastic bag.

IT MUST HAVE TAKEN me half an hour to find a ride back into town. I had only a very hazy idea of where I was. The roads were wide, the houses small. There was a steady, freezing drizzle. My arm was aching from carrying Kroll's manuscript. Judging by the weight, I reckoned it must have been close on a thousand pages. Who was his client? Tolstoy? Eventually I stopped at a bus shelter in front of a greengrocer's and a funeral parlor. Wedged into its metal frame was the card of a minicab firm.

The journey home took almost an hour and I had plenty of time to take out the manuscript and study it. The book was called *One Out of Many*. It was the memoir of some ancient U.S. senator, famous only for having kept on breathing for about a hundred and fifty years. By any normal measure of tedium it was off the scale—up, up, and away, beyond boring into some oxygen-starved stratosphere of utter nullity. The car was overheated and smelled of stale takeaways. I began to feel nauseous. I put the manuscript back into the bag and wound down the window. The fare was forty pounds.

I had just paid the driver and was crossing the pavement toward my flat, head down into the rain, searching for my keys, when I felt someone touch me lightly on the shoulder. I turned and walked into a wall, or was hit by a truck—that was the feeling—some great iron force slammed into me, and I fell backward, into the grip of a second man. (I was told afterward there were two of them, both in their twenties. One had been hanging round the entrance to the basement flat, the other appeared from nowhere and grabbed me from behind.) I crumpled, felt the gritty wet stone of the gutter against my cheek, and gasped and sucked and cried like a baby. My fingers must have clasped the plastic bag with involuntary tightness, because I was conscious, through this much greater pain, of a smaller and sharper one—a flute in the symphony—as a foot trod on my hand, and something was torn away.

Surely one of the most inadequate words in the English language is "winded," suggestive as it is of something light and fleeting—a graze, perhaps, or a touch of breathlessness. But I hadn't been winded. I had been whumped and whacked and semiasphyxiated, knocked to the ground, and humiliated. My solar plexus felt as though it had been stuck with a knife. Sobbing for air, I was convinced I had been stabbed. I was aware of people taking my arms and pulling me up into a sitting position. I was propped against a tree, its hard bark jabbing into my spine, and when at last I managed to gulp some oxygen into my lungs, I immediately started blindly patting my stomach, feeling for the gaping wound I knew must be there, imagining my intestines strewn around me. But when I inspected my moist fingers for blood, there was only dirty London rainwater. It must have taken a minute for me to realize that I wasn't going to die—that I was, essentially, intact—and then all I wanted was to get away from these good-hearted folk who had gathered around me and were producing mobile phones and asking me about calling the police and an ambulance.

The thrill of having to wait ten hours to be examined in casualty, followed by half a day spent hanging around the local police station to make a statement, was enough to propel me out of the gutter, up the stairs, and into my flat. I locked the door, peeled off my outer clothes, and went and lay on the sofa, trembling. I didn't move for perhaps an hour, as the cold shadows of that January afternoon gradually gathered in the room. Then I went into the kitchen and was sick in the sink, after which I poured myself a very large whiskey.

I could feel myself moving now out of shock and into euphoria. Indeed, with a little alcohol inside me I felt positively merry. I checked my inside jacket pocket and then my wrist: I still had my wallet and my watch. The only thing that had gone was the yellow plastic bag containing Senator Alzheimer's memoirs. I laughed out loud as I pictured the thieves running down Ladbroke Grove and stopping in some alleyway to check their haul: *"My advice to any young person seeking to enter public life today . . ."* It wasn't until I'd had another drink that I realized this could be awkward. Old Alzheimer might not mean anything to me, but Sidney Kroll might view matters differently.

I took out his card. Sidney L. Kroll of Brinkerhof Lombardi Kroll, attorneys, M Street, Washington, DC. After thinking about it for ten minutes or so, I went back and sat on the sofa and called his cell phone. He answered on the second ring: "Sid Kroll."

I could tell by his inflection he was smiling.

"Sidney," I said, trying to sound natural using his first name, "you'll never guess what's happened."

"Some guys just stole my manuscript?"

For a moment I couldn't speak. "My God," I said, "is there nothing you don't know?"

"What?" His tone changed abruptly. "Jesus, I was kidding. Is that *really* what happened? Are you okay? Where are you now?"

I explained what had happened. He said not to worry. The manuscript was *totally* unimportant. He'd given it to me only because he thought it might be of interest to me in a professional capacity. He'd get another sent over. What was I going to do? Was I going to call the police? I said I would if he wanted, but as far as I was concerned bringing in the police was generally more trouble than it was worth. I preferred to view the episode as just another round on the gaudy carousel of urban life: "You know, *que sera, sera*, bombed one day, mugged the next."

He agreed. "It was a real pleasure to meet with you today. It's great that you're on board. Cheerio," he said, just before he hung up, and there was that little smile in his voice again. *Cheerio.*

I went into the bathroom and opened my shirt. A livid red horizontal mark was branded into my flesh, just above my stomach and below my rib cage. I stood in front of the mirror for a better look. It was three inches long and half an inch wide, and curiously sharp edged. That wasn't caused by flesh and bone, I thought. I'd say that was a knuckle-duster. That looked *professional*. I started to feel strange again and went back to the sofa.

When the phone rang, it was Rick, to tell me the deal was done. "What's up?" he said, interrupting himself. "You don't sound right."

"I just got mugged."

"No!"

Once more I described what had happened. Rick made appropriately sympathetic noises, but the moment he learned I was well enough to work, the anxiety left his voice. As soon as he could, he brought the conversation round to what really interested him.

"So you're still fine to fly to the States on Sunday?"

"Of course. I'm just a bit shocked, that's all."

"Okay, well, here's another shock for you. For one month's work, on a manuscript that's supposedly already written, Rhinehart Inc. are willing to pay you two hundred and fifty thousand dollars, plus expenses."

"What?"

If I hadn't already been sitting on the sofa I would have fallen onto it. They say every man has his price. A quarter of a million dollars for four weeks' work was roughly ten times mine.

"That's fifty thousand dollars paid weekly for the next four weeks," said Rick, "plus a bonus of fifty if you get the job done on time. They'll take care of airfares and accommodation. *And* you'll get a collaborator credit."

"On the title page?"

"Do me a favor! In the acknowledgments. But it'll still be noticed in the trade press. I'll see to that. Although for now your involvement is strictly confidential. They were very firm about that." I could hear him chuckling down the phone and imagined him tilting back in his chair. "Oh, yes, a whole new wide world is opening up for you, my boy!"

He was right there.

THREE

$\star$

If you are painfully shy or find it hard to get others
into a relaxed and confident state, then ghosting might
not be for you.

Ghostwriting

AMERICAN AIRLINES FLIGHT 109 was due to leave Heathrow for Boston at ten-thirty on Sunday morning. Rhinehart biked
round a one-way business-class ticket on Saturday afternoon, along
with a contract and the privacy agreement. I had to sign both
while the messenger waited. I trusted Rick to have got the contract straight and didn't even bother to read it; the nondisclosure
undertaking I scanned quickly in the hall. It's almost funny in retrospect: *"I shall treat all confidential information as being strictly
private and confidential, and shall take all steps necessary to prevent
it from being disclosed or made public to any third party or relevant
person . . . I shall not use or disclose or permit the disclosure by any*

person of the confidential information for the benefit of any third party . . . Neither I nor the relevant persons shall by any means copy or part with possession of the whole or any part of the confidential information without prior permission of the Owner . . ." I signed without a qualm.

I've always liked to be able to disappear quickly. It used to take me about five minutes to put my London life into cold storage. All my bills were paid by direct debit. There were no deliveries to cancel—no milk, no papers. My cleaner, whom I hardly ever saw in any case, would look in twice a week and retrieve all the mail from downstairs. I had cleared my desk of work. I had no appointments. My neighbors I had never spoken to. Kate had likely gone for good. Most of my friends had long since entered the kingdom of family life, from whose distant shores, in my experience, no traveler e'er returned. My parents were dead. I had no siblings. I could have died myself and, as far as the world was concerned, my life would have gone on as normal. I packed one suitcase with a week's change of clothes, a sweater, and a spare pair of shoes. I put my laptop and mini–disk recorder into my shoulder bag. I would use the hotel laundry. Anything else I needed I would buy on arrival.

I spent the rest of the day and all that evening up in my study, reading through my books on Adam Lang and making a list of questions. I don't want to sound too Jekyll and Hyde about this, but as the day faded—as the lights came up in the big tower blocks across the railway marshaling yard, and the red, white, and green stars winked and fell toward the airport—I could feel myself beginning to get into Lang's skin. He was a few years older, but apart from that our backgrounds were similar. The resemblances hadn't struck me before: an only child, born in the Midlands, educated at the local grammar school, a degree from Cambridge, a passion for student drama, a complete lack of interest in student politics.

I went back to look at the photographs. *"Lang's hysterical performance as a chicken in charge of a battery farm for humans at the 1972 Cambridge Footlights Revue earned him plaudits."* I could imagine us both chasing the same girls, taking a bad show to the Edinburgh Fringe in the back of some beat-up Volkswagen van, sharing digs, getting stoned. And yet somehow, metaphorically speaking, I had stayed a chicken, while he had gone on to become prime minister. This was the point at which my normal powers of empathy deserted me, for there seemed nothing in his first twenty-five years that could explain his second. But there would be time enough, I reasoned, to find his voice.

I double-locked the door before I went to bed that night and dreamed I was following Adam Lang through a maze of rainy, redbrick streets. When I got into a minicab and the driver turned round to ask me where I wanted to go, he had McAra's lugubrious face.

HEATHROW THE NEXT MORNING looked like one of those bad science fiction movies "set in the near future" after the security forces have taken over the state. Two armored personnel carriers were parked outside the terminal. A dozen men with Rambo machine guns and bad haircuts patrolled inside. Vast lines of passengers queued to be frisked and X-rayed, carrying their shoes in one hand and their pathetic toiletries in a clear plastic bag in the other. Travel is sold as freedom, but we were about as free as lab rats. This is how they'll manage the next holocaust, I thought, as I shuffled forward in my stockinged feet: they'll simply issue us with air tickets and we'll do whatever we're told.

Once I was through security, I headed across the fragrant halls of duty-free toward the American Airlines lounge, intent only on a courtesy cup of coffee and the Sunday morning sports pages. A satellite news channel was burbling away in the corner. No one was watching. I fixed myself a double espresso and was just turning to the football reports in one of the tabloids when I heard the words "Adam Lang." Three days earlier, like everyone else in the lounge, I would have taken no notice, but now it was if my own name was being called out. I went and stood in front of the screen and tried to make sense of the story.

To begin with, it didn't seem that important. It sounded like old news. Four British citizens had been picked up in Pakistan a few years back—"kidnapped by the CIA," according to their lawyer—taken to a secret military installation in eastern Europe, and tortured. One had died under interrogation, the other three had been imprisoned in Guantánamo. The new twist, apparently, was that a Sunday paper had obtained a leaked Ministry of Defence document that seemed to suggest that Lang had ordered a Special Air Services unit to seize the men and hand them over to the CIA. Various expressions of outrage followed, from a human rights lawyer and a spokesman for the Pakistani government. File footage showed Lang wearing a garland of flowers round his neck on a visit to Pakistan while he was prime minister. A spokeswoman for Lang was quoted as saying the former prime minister knew nothing of the reports and was refusing to comment. The British government had consistently rejected demands to hold an inquiry. The program moved on to the weather, and that was it.

I glanced around the lounge. Nobody else had stirred. Yet for some reason I felt as if someone had just run an ice pack down my spine. I pulled out my cell phone and called Rick. I couldn't remember whether he had gone back to America or not. It turned out he was sitting about a mile away, in the British Airways lounge, waiting to board his flight to New York.

"Did you just see the news?" I asked him.

Unlike me, I knew Rick was a news addict.

"The Lang story? Sure."

"D'you think there's anything in it?"

"How the hell do I know? Who cares if there is? At least it's keeping his name on the front pages."

"D'you think I should ask him about it?"

"Who gives a shit?" Down the line I heard a loudspeaker announcement howling in the background. "They're calling my flight. I got to go."

"Just before you do," I said quickly, "can I run something past you? When I was mugged on Friday, somehow it didn't make much sense, the way they left my wallet and only ran off with a manuscript. But looking at this news—well, I was just wondering—you don't think they thought I was carrying Lang's memoirs?"

"But how'd they know that?" said Rick in a puzzled voice. "You'd only just met Maddox and Kroll. I was still negotiating the deal."

"Well, maybe someone was watching the publishers' offices and then followed me when I left. It *was* a bright yellow plastic bag, Rick. I might as well have been carrying a flare." And then another thought came to me, so alarming I didn't know where to begin. "While you're on, what do you know about Sidney Kroll?"

"Young Sid?" Rick gave a chuckle of admiration. "My, but he's a piece of work, isn't he? He's going to put honest crooks like me out of business. He cuts his deals for a flat fee rather than commission, and you won't find an ex-president or a cabinet member who doesn't want him on their team. Why?"

"It's not possible, is it," I said hesitantly, voicing the thought more or less as it developed, "that he gave me that manuscript because he thought—if anyone was watching—he thought it would look as though I was leaving the building carrying Adam Lang's book?"

"Why the hell would he do that?"

"I don't know. For the fun of it? To see what would happen?"

"To see if you'd get mugged?"

"Okay, all right, it sounds mad, but just think it through for a minute. Why are the publishers so paranoid about this manuscript? Even Quigley hasn't been allowed to see it. Why won't they let it out of America? Maybe it's because they think someone over here is desperate to get hold of it."

"So?"

"So perhaps Kroll was using me as bait—sort of a tethered goat—to test who was after it, find out how far they'd be willing to go."

Even as the words were leaving my mouth I knew I was sounding ridiculous.

"But Lang's book is a boring crock of shit!" said Rick. "The only people they want to keep it away from at this point are their shareholders! *That's* why it's under wraps."

I was starting to feel a fool. I would have let the subject go, but Rick was enjoying himself too much.

" 'A tethered goat'!" I could have heard his shout of laughter from the other terminal even without the phone. "Let me get this straight. According to your theory, someone must have known Kroll was in town, known where he was Friday morning, known what he'd come to discuss—"

"All right," I said. "Let's leave it."

"—*known* he might just give Lang's manuscript to a new ghost, known who you were when you came out of the meeting, known where you lived. Because you said they were waiting for you, didn't you? Wow. This must've been some operation. Too big for a newspaper. This must've been a *government*—"

"Forget it," I said, finally managing to cut him off. "You'd better catch your flight."

"Yeah, you're right. Well, you have a safe trip. Get some sleep on the plane. You're sounding weird. Let's talk next week. And don't worry about it." He rang off.

I stood there holding my silent phone. It was true. I was sounding weird. I went into the men's room. The bruise where I'd been punched on Friday had ripened, turned black and purple, and was fringed with yellow, like some exploding supernova beamed back by the Hubble Telescope.

A short time later they announced that the Boston flight was boarding, and once we were in the air my nerves steadied. I love that moment when a drab gray landscape flickers out of sight beneath you, and the plane tunnels up through the cloud to burst into the sunshine. Who can be depressed at ten thousand feet when the sun is shining and the other poor saps are still stuck on the ground? I had a drink. I watched a movie. I dozed for a while. But I must admit I also scoured that business-class cabin for every Sunday newspaper I could find, ignored the sports pages for once, and read all that had been written about Adam Lang and those four suspected terrorists.

WE MADE OUR FINAL approach to Logan Airport at one in the afternoon, local time.

As we came in low over Boston Harbor, the sun we had been chasing all day seemed to travel over the water alongside us, striking the downtown skyscrapers one after the other: erupting columns of white and blue, gold and silver, a fireworks display in glass and steel. O my America, I thought, my new-found-land—my land where the book market is five times the size of the United Kingdom's—shine thy light on me! As I queued for immigration I was practically humming "The Star-Spangled Banner." Even the guy from the Department of Homeland Security—embodying the rule that the folksier an institution's name, the more Stalinist its function—couldn't dent my optimism. He sat frowning behind his glass screen at the very notion of anyone flying three thousand miles to spend a month on Martha's Vineyard in midwinter. When he discovered I was a writer he couldn't have treated me with greater suspicion if I had been wearing an orange jumpsuit.

"What kind of books you write?"

"Autobiographies."

This obviously baffled him. He suspected mockery but wasn't quite sure. "Autobiographies, huh? Don't you have to be famous to do that?"

"Not anymore."

He stared hard at me, then slowly shook his head, like a weary St. Peter at the pearly gates, confronted by yet another sinner trying to wheedle his way into paradise. "Not anymore," he repeated, with an expression of infinite distaste. He picked up his metal stamp and punched it twice. He let me in for thirty days.

When I was through immigration, I turned on my phone. It showed a welcoming message from Lang's personal assistant, someone named Amelia Bly, apologizing for not providing a driver to collect me from the airport. Instead she suggested I take a bus to the ferry terminal at Woods Hole and promised a car would meet me when I landed at Martha's Vineyard. I bought the *New York Times* and the *Boston Globe* and checked them while I waited for the bus to leave to see if they had the Lang story, but either it had broken too late for them or they weren't interested.

The bus was almost empty, and I sat up front near the driver as we pushed south through the tangle of freeways, out of the city, and into open country. It was a few degrees below freezing and the sky was clear, but there had been snow not long before. It was piled in banks next to the road and clung to the higher branches in the forests that stretched away on either side in great rolling waves of white and green. New England is basically Old England on steroids—wider roads, bigger woods, larger spaces; even the sky seemed huge and glossy. I had a pleasing sense of gaining time, imagining a gloomy, wet Sunday night in London, in contrast to this sparkling afternoon winterland. But gradually it began to darken here as well. I guess it must have been almost six when we reached Woods Hole and pulled up at the ferry terminal, and by then there were a moon and stars.

Oddly enough, it wasn't until I saw the sign for the ferry that I remembered to spare a thought for McAra. Not surprisingly, the dead-man's-shoes aspect of the assignment wasn't one I cared to dwell on, especially after my mugging. But as I wheeled my suitcase into the ticket office to pay my fare, and then stepped back out again into the bitter wind, it was only too easy to imagine my predecessor going through similar motions a mere three weeks earlier. He had been drunk, of course, which I wasn't. I looked around. There were several bars just across the car park. Perhaps he had gone into one of those? I wouldn't have minded a drink myself. But then I might sit on exactly the same bar stool as he had, and that would be ghoulish, I thought, like taking one of those tours of murder scenes in Hollywood. Instead I joined the passenger queue and tried to read the *Times* Sunday magazine, turning to the wall for protection from the wind. There was a wooden board with painted lettering: CURRENT NATIONWIDE THREAT LEVEL IS ELEVATED. I could smell the sea but it was too dark to see it.

The trouble is, once you start thinking about a thing, you can't always make yourself stop. Most of the cars waiting to board the ferry had their engines running so the drivers could use their heaters in the cold, and I found myself checking for a tan-colored Ford Escape SUV. Then, when I actually got on the boat, and climbed the clanging metal stairwell to the passenger deck, I wondered whether this was the way McAra had come. I told myself to leave it, that I was working myself up for nothing. But I suppose that ghosts and ghostwriters go naturally together. I sat in the fuggy passenger cabin and studied the plain, honest faces of my fellow travelers, and then, as the boat shuddered and cast off from the terminal, I folded my paper and went out onto the open top deck.

It's amazing how cold and darkness conspire to alter everything. The Martha's Vineyard ferry on a summer's evening I imagine must be delightful. There's a big stripy funnel straight out of a storybook, and rows of blue plastic seats facing outward, running the length of the deck, where families no doubt sit in their shorts and T-shirts, the teenagers looking bored, the dads jumping about with excitement. But on this January night the deck was deserted, and the north wind blowing down from Cape Cod sliced through my jacket and shirt and chilled my skin to gooseflesh. The lights of Woods Hole slipped away. We passed a marker buoy at the entrance to the channel swinging frantically this way and that as if trying to free itself from some underwater monster. Its bell tolled in time with the waves like a funeral chime and the spray flew as vile as witch's spit.

I jammed my hands in my pockets, hunched my shoulders up around my neck, and crossed unsteadily to the starboard side. The handrail was only waist-high, and for the first time I appreciated how easily McAra might have gone over. I actually had to brace myself to keep from slipping. Rick was right. The line between accident and suicide isn't always clearly defined. You could kill yourself without ever really making up your mind. The mere act of leaning out too far and imagining what it might be like could tip you over. You'd hit that heaving icy black water with a smack that would take you ten feet under, and by the time you came up the ship might be a hundred yards away. I hoped McAra had absorbed enough booze to blunt the horror, but I doubted if there was a drunk in the world who wouldn't be sobered by total immersion in a sea only half a degree above freezing.

And nobody would have heard him fall! That was the other thing. The weather wasn't nearly as bad as it had been three weeks earlier, and yet, as I glanced around, I could see not a soul on deck. I really started shivering then; my teeth were chattering like some fairground clockwork novelty.

I went down to the bar for a drink.

WE ROUNDED THE WEST Chop Lighthouse and came into the ferry terminal at Vineyard Haven just before seven, docking with a rattle of chains and a thump that almost sent me flying down the stairs. I hadn't been expecting a welcoming committee, which was fine, because I didn't get one, just an elderly local taxi driver holding a torn-out page from a notebook on which my name was misspelled. As he heaved my suitcase into the back, the wind lifted a big sheet of clear plastic and sent it twisting and flapping over the ice sheets in the car park. The sky was packed white with stars.

I'd bought a guidebook to the island, so I had a vague idea of what I was in for. In summer the population is a hundred thousand, but when the vacationers have closed up their holiday homes and migrated west for the winter, it drops to fifteen thousand. These are the hardy, insular natives, the folks who call the mainland "America." There are a couple of highways, one set of traffic lights, and dozens of long sandy tracks leading to places with names like Squibnocket Pond and Jobs Neck Cove. My driver didn't utter a word the whole journey, just scrutinized me in the mirror. As my eyes met his rheumy glance for the twentieth time, I wondered if there was a reason why he resented picking me up. Perhaps I was keeping him from something. It was hard to imagine what. The streets around the ferry terminal were mostly deserted, and once we were out of Vineyard Haven and onto the main highway, there was nothing to see but darkness.

By then I'd been traveling for seventeen hours. I didn't know where I was, or what landscape I was passing through, or even where I was going. All attempts at conversation had failed. I could see nothing except my reflection in the cold darkness of the window. I felt as though I'd come to the edge of the earth, like some seventeenth-century English explorer who was about to have his first encounter with the native Wampanoags. I gave a noisy yawn and quickly clamped the back of my hand to my mouth.

"Sorry," I said to the disembodied eyes in the rearview mirror. "Where I come from it's after midnight."

He shook his head. At first I couldn't make out whether he was sympathetic or disapproving; then I realized he was trying to tell me it was no use talking to him: he was deaf. I went back to staring out the window.

After a while we came to a crossroads and turned left into what I guessed must be Edgartown, a settlement of white clapboard houses with white picket fences, small gardens, and verandas, lit by ornate Victorian street lamps. Nine out of ten were dark, but in the few windows that shone with yellow light I glimpsed oil paintings of sailing ships and whiskered ancestors. At the bottom of the hill, past the Old Whaling Church, a big misty moon cast a silvery light over shingled roofs and silhouetted the masts in the harbor. Curls of wood smoke rose from a couple of chimneys. I felt as though I was driving onto a film set for *Moby-Dick*. The headlights picked out a sign to the Chappaquiddick ferry, and not long after that we pulled up outside the Lighthouse View Hotel.

Again, I could picture the scene in summer: buckets and spades and fishing nets piled up on the veranda, rope sandals left by the door, a dusting of white sand trailed up from the beach, that kind of thing. But out of season the big old wooden hotel creaked and banged in the wind like a sailing boat stuck on a reef. I suppose the management must have been waiting till spring to strip the blistered paintwork and wash the crust of salt off the windows. The sea was pounding away nearby in the darkness. I stood with my suitcase on the wooden deck and watched the lights of the taxi disappear around the corner with something close to nostalgia.

Inside the lobby, a girl dressed up as a Victorian maid with a white lace mobcap handed me a message from Lang's office. I would be picked up at ten the next morning and should bring my passport to show to security. I was starting to feel like a man on a mystery tour: as soon as I reached one location, I was given a fresh set of instructions to proceed to the next. The hotel was empty, the restaurant dark. I was told I could have my choice of rooms, so I picked one on the second floor with a desk I could work at and photographs of Old Edgartown on the wall: John Coffin House, circa 1890; the whale ship *Splendid* at Osborn wharf, circa 1870. After the receptionist had gone, I put my laptop, list of questions, and the stories I had torn out of the Sunday newspapers on the desk and then stretched out on the bed.

I fell asleep at once and didn't wake until two in the morning, when my body clock, still on London time, went off like Big Ben. I spent ten minutes searching for a minibar before realizing there wasn't one. On impulse, I called Kate's home number in London. What exactly I was going to say to her I had no idea. In any case there was no answer. I meant to hang up but instead found myself rambling to her answering machine. She must have left for work very early. Either that, or she hadn't come home the night before. That was something to think about, and I duly thought about it. The fact that I had no one to blame but myself didn't make me feel any better. I took a shower and afterward I got back into bed, turned off the lamp, and pulled the damp sheets up under my chin. Every few seconds the slow pulse of the lighthouse filled the room with a faint red glow. I must have lain there for hours, eyes wide open, fully awake and yet disembodied, and in this way passed my first night on Martha's Vineyard.

THE LANDSCAPE THAT DISSOLVED out of the dawn the next morning was flat and alluvial. Across the road beneath my window was a creek, then reed beds, and beyond those a beach and the sea. A pretty Victorian lighthouse with a bell-shaped roof and a wrought-iron balcony looked across the straits to a long, low spit of land about a mile away. That, I realized, must be Chappaquiddick. A squadron of hundreds of tiny white seabirds, in a formation as tight as a school of fish, soared and flicked and dived above the shallow waves.

I went downstairs and ordered a huge breakfast. From the little shop next to reception I bought a copy of the *New York Times*. The story I was looking for was entombed deep in the world news section and then reinterred to ensure maximum obscurity far down the page:

> LONDON (AP)—Former British prime minister Adam Lang authorized the illegal use of British special forces troops to seize four suspected Al Qaeda terrorists in Pakistan and then hand them over for interrogation by the CIA, according to newspaper reports here Sunday.
>
> The men—Nasir Ashraf, Shakeel Qazi, Salim Khan, and Faruk Ahmed—all British citizens, were seized in the Pakistani

city of Peshawar five years ago. All four were allegedly transferred out of the country to a secret location and tortured. Mr. Ashraf is reported to have died under interrogation. Mr. Qazi, Mr. Khan, and Mr. Ahmed were subsequently detained at Guantánamo for three years. Only Mr. Ahmed remains in U.S. custody.

According to documents obtained by the London *Sunday Times*, Mr. Lang personally endorsed "Operation Tempest," a secret mission to kidnap the four men by the UK's elite Special Air Services. Such an operation would have been illegal under both UK and international law.

The British Ministry of Defence last night refused to comment on either the authenticity of the documents or the existence of "Operation Tempest." A spokeswoman for Mr. Lang said that he had no plans to issue a statement.

I read it through three times. It didn't seem to add up to much. Or did it? It was hard to tell anymore. One's moral bearings were no longer as fixed as they used to be. Methods my father's generation would have considered beyond the pale, even when fighting the Nazis—torture, for example—were now apparently acceptable civilized behavior. I decided that the ten percent of the population who worry about these things would be appalled by the report, assuming they ever managed to locate it; the remaining ninety would probably just shrug. We had been told that the free world was taking a walk on the dark side. What did people expect?

I had a couple of hours to kill before the car was due to collect me, so I took a walk over the wooden bridge to the lighthouse and then strolled into Edgartown. In daylight it seemed even emptier than it had the previous night. Squirrels chased undisturbed along the sidewalks and scampered up into the trees. I must have passed two dozen of those picturesque nineteenth-century whaling captains' houses, and it didn't look as if one was occupied. The widow's walks on the fronts and sides were deserted. No black-shawled women stared mournfully out to sea, waiting for their menfolk to come home—presumably because the menfolk were all on Wall Street. The restaurants were closed, the little boutiques and galleries stripped bare of stock. I had wanted to buy a windproof jacket but there was no place open. The windows were filled with dust and the husks of insects. "Thanks for a great season!!!" read the cards. "See you in the spring!"

It was the same in the harbor. The primary colors of the port were gray and white—gray sea, white sky, gray shingle roofs, white clapboard walls, bare white flagpoles, jetties weathered blue-gray and green-gray, on which perched matching gray-and-white gulls. It was as if Martha Stewart had color coordinated the whole place, Man and Nature. Even the sun, now hovering discreetly over Chappaquiddick, had the good taste to shine pale white.

I put my hand up to shield my eyes and squinted at the distant strand of beach with its isolated holiday houses. That was where Senator Edward Kennedy's career had taken its disastrous wrong turn. According to my book, the whole of Martha's Vineyard had been a summer playground for the Kennedys, who liked to sail over for the day from Hyannisport. There was a story of how Jack, when he was president, had wanted to moor his boat at the private jetty of the Edgartown Yacht Club but had decided to sail away when he saw the massed ranks of the members, Republicans to a man, lined up with their arms folded, watching him, daring him to land. It was the summer before he was shot.

The few yachts moored now were shrouded for winter. The only movement was a solitary fishing boat with an outboard motor heading for the lobster traps. I sat for a while on a bench and waited to see if anything would happen. Gulls swooped and cried. On a nearby yacht the wind rattled the cables against a metal mast. There was hammering in the distance as property was renovated for the summer. An old guy walked a dog. Apart from that, nothing occurred in almost an hour that could possibly have distracted an author from his work. It was a nonwriter's idea of a writer's paradise. I could see why McAra might have gone insane.

FOUR

★

The ghost will also be under pressure from the
publishers to dig up something controversial that they
can use to sell serial rights and to generate publicity at
the time of publication.

Ghostwriting

IT WAS MY OLD friend the deaf taxi driver who picked me up
from the hotel later that morning. Because I'd been booked into a
hotel in Edgartown, I'd naturally assumed that Rhinehart's property must be somewhere in the port itself. There were some big
houses overlooking the harbor, with gardens sloping down to private moorings, that looked to me to be ideal billionaire real estate—which shows how ignorant I was about what serious wealth
can buy. Instead, we drove out of town for about ten minutes, following signs to West Tisbury, into flat, thickly wooded country,

and then, before I'd even noticed a gap in the trees, swung left down an unmade, sandy track.

Until that moment I was unfamiliar with scrub oak. Maybe it looks good in full leaf. But in winter I doubt if nature has a more depressing vista to offer in its entire flora department than mile after mile of those twisted, dwarfish, ash-colored trees. A few curled brown leaves were the only evidence they might once have been alive. We rocked and bounced down a narrow forest road for almost three miles and the only creature we saw was a run-over skunk, until at last we came to a closed gate, and there materialized from this petrified wilderness a man carrying a clipboard and wearing the unmistakable dark Crombie overcoat and polished black oxfords of a British plainclothes copper.

I wound down my window and handed him my passport. His big, sullen face was brick colored in the cold, his ears terra-cotta: not a policeman happy with his lot. He looked as if he'd been assigned to guard one of the Queen's granddaughters in the Caribbean for a fortnight, only to find himself diverted here at the last minute. He scowled as he checked my name against the list on his clipboard, wiped a big drop of clear moisture from the end of his nose, and walked around inspecting the taxi. I could hear surf performing its continuous, rolling somersault on a beach somewhere. He returned and gave me back my passport, and said—or at least I thought he said: he muttered it under his breath—"Welcome to the madhouse."

I felt a sudden twist of nerves, which I hope I concealed, because the first appearance of a ghost is important. I try never to show anxiety. I strive always to look professional. It's dress code: chameleon. Whatever I think the client is likely to be wearing, I endeavor to wear the same. For a footballer, I might put on a pair of trainers; for a pop singer, a leather jacket. For my first-ever meeting with a former prime minister, I had decided against a suit—too formal: I would have looked like his lawyer or accountant—and selected instead a pale blue shirt, a conservative striped tie, a sports jacket, and gray trousers. My hair was neatly brushed, my teeth cleaned and flossed, my deodorant rolled on. I was as ready as I would ever be. *The madhouse?* Did he really say that? I looked back at the policeman, but he had moved out of sight.

The gate swung clear, the track curved, and a few moments later I had my first glimpse of the Rhinehart compound: four wooden cube-shaped buildings—a garage, a storeroom, and two cottages for the staff—and up ahead the house itself. It was only two stories high but as wide as a stately home, with a long, low roof and a pair of big square brick chimneys of the sort you might see in a crematorium. The rest of the building was made entirely of wood, but although it was new it had already weathered to a silvery-gray, like garden furniture left out for a year. The windows on this side were as tall and thin as gun slits, and what with these, and the grayness, and the blockhouses farther back, and the encircling forest, and the sentry at the gate, it all somehow resembled a holiday home designed by Albert Speer; the Wolf's Lair came to mind.

Even before we drew up, the front door opened and another police guard—white shirt, black tie, zippered gray jacket—welcomed me unsmilingly into the hall. He quickly searched my shoulder bag while I glanced around. I'd met plenty of rich people in the course of my work, but I don't think I'd ever been inside a billionaire's house before. There were rows of African masks on the smooth white walls and lighted display cabinets filled with wood carvings and primitive pottery of crude figures with giant phalluses and torpedo breasts—the sort of thing a naughty child might do while the teacher's back was turned. It was entirely lacking in any kind of skill or beauty or aesthetic merit. (The first Mrs. Rhinehart, I discovered afterward, was on the board of the Museum of Modern Art. The second was a Bollywood actress, fifty years his junior, whom Rhinehart had been advised by his bankers to marry in order to break into the Indian market.)

From somewhere inside the house I heard a woman with a British accent shouting, "This is absolutely bloody *ridiculous*!" A door slammed and then an elegant blonde in a dark blue jacket and skirt, carrying a black-and-red hardcover notebook, came clicking down the corridor on high heels.

"Amelia Bly," she said with a fixed smile. She was probably forty-five but at a distance could have passed for ten years younger. She had beautiful large, clear blue eyes but wore too much makeup, as if she worked at a cosmetics counter in a department store and had been obliged to demonstrate all the products at once. She exuded a sweetly opulent smell of perfume. I presumed she was the spokeswoman mentioned in that morning's *Times*. "Adam's in New York, unfortunately, and won't be back till later this afternoon."

"Actually, forget I said that: it's *fucking* ridiculous!" shouted the unseen woman.

Amelia expanded her smile a fraction, creating tiny fissures in her smooth pink cheeks.

"Oh, dear. I'm so sorry. I'm afraid poor Ruth's having 'one of those days.'"

Ruth. The name resonated briefly like a warning drumbeat or the clatter of a thrown spear among the African tribal art. It had never occurred to me that Lang's wife might be here. I had assumed she would be at home in London. She was famous for her independence, among other things.

"If this is a bad time—" I said.

"No, no. She definitely wants to meet you. Come and have a cup of coffee. I'll fetch her. How's the hotel?" she added over her shoulder. "Quiet?"

"As the grave."

I retrieved my bag from the Special Branch man and followed Amelia into the interior of the house, trailing in her cloud of scent. She had very nice legs, I noticed; her thighs swished nylon as she walked. She showed me into a room full of cream leather furniture, poured me some coffee from a jug in the corner, then disappeared. I stood for a while at the French windows with my mug, looking out over the back of the property. There were no flower beds—presumably nothing delicate would grow in this desolate spot—just a big lawn that expired about a hundred yards away into sickly brown undergrowth. Beyond that was a pond, as smooth as a sheet of steel under an immense aluminum sky. To the left, the land rose slightly to the dunes that marked the edge of the beach. I couldn't hear the ocean: the glass doors were too thick—bulletproof, I later discovered.

An urgent burst of Morse from the passage signaled the return of Amelia Bly.

"I'm so sorry. I'm afraid Ruth's a little busy at the moment. She sends her apologies. She'll catch you later." Amelia's smile had hardened somewhat. It looked as natural as her nail polish. "So, if you've finished your coffee, I'll show you where we work."

She insisted that I go first up the stairs.

The house, she explained, was arranged so that all the bedrooms were on the ground floor, with the living space above, and the moment we ascended into the huge open sitting room, I understood why. The wall facing the coast was made entirely of glass. There was nothing man-made within sight, just ocean, pond, and sky. It was primordial: a scene unchanged for ten thousand years. The soundproofed glass and under-floor heating created the effect of a luxurious time capsule that had been propelled back to the Neolithic age.

"Quite a place," I said. "Don't you get lonely at night?"

"We're in here," said Amelia, opening a door.

I followed her into a big study, adjoining the sitting room, which was presumably where Marty Rhinehart worked on holiday. There was a similar view from here, except that this angle favored the ocean more than the pond. The shelves were full of books on German military history, their swastikaed spines whitened by exposure to the sun and the salt air. There were two desks: a little one in the corner at which a secretary sat typing at a computer, and a larger one, entirely clear except for a photograph of a powerboat and a model of a yacht. The sour old skeleton that was Marty Rhinehart crouched over the wheel of his boat—living disproof of the old adage that you can't be too thin or too rich.

"We're a small team," said Amelia. "Myself, Alice here"—the girl in the corner looked up—"and Lucy, who's with Adam in New York. Jeff the driver's also in New York—he'll be bringing the car back this afternoon. Six protection officers from the UK—three here and three with Adam at the moment. We badly need another pair of hands, if only to handle the media, but Adam can't bring himself to replace Mike. They were together so long."

"And how long have you been with him?"

"Eight years. I worked in Downing Street. I'm on attachment from the Cabinet Office."

"Poor Cabinet Office."

She flashed her nail-polish smile. "It's my husband I miss the most."

"You're married? I notice you're not wearing a ring."

"I can't, sadly. It's far too large. It bleeps when I go through airport security."

"Ah." We understood one another perfectly.

"The Rhineharts also have a live-in Vietnamese couple, but they're so discreet you'll hardly notice them. She looks after the house and he does the garden. Dep and Duc."

"Which is which?"

"Duc is the man. Obviously."

She produced a key from the pocket of her well-cut jacket and unlocked a big gunmetal filing cabinet, from which she withdrew a box file.

"This is not to be removed from this room," she said, laying it on the desk. "It is not to be copied. You can make notes, but I must remind you that you've signed a confidentiality agreement. You have six hours to read it before Adam gets in from New York. I'll have a sandwich sent up to you for lunch. Alice, come on. We don't want to cause him any distractions, do we?"

After they'd gone, I sat down in the leather swivel chair, took out my laptop, switched it on, and created a document titled "Lang ms." Then I loosened my tie and unfastened my wristwatch and laid it on the desk beside the file. For a few moments I allowed myself to swing back and forth in Rhinehart's chair, savoring the ocean view and the general sensation of being world dictator. Then I flipped open the lid of the file, pulled out the manuscript, and started to read.

ALL GOOD BOOKS ARE different but all bad books are exactly the same. I know this to be a fact because in my line of work I read a lot of bad books—books so bad they aren't even published, which is quite a feat, when you consider what is published.

And what they all have in common, these bad books, be they novels or memoirs, is this: they don't ring true. I'm not saying that a good book *is* true necessarily, just that it *feels* true for the time you're reading it. A publishing friend of mine calls it the seaplane test, after a movie he once saw about people in the City of London that opened with the hero arriving for work in a seaplane he landed on the Thames. From then on, my friend said, there was no point in watching.

Adam Lang's memoir failed the seaplane test.

It wasn't that the facts in it were wrong—I wasn't in a position to judge at that stage—it was rather that the whole book somehow felt false, as if there was a hollow at its center. It consisted of sixteen chapters, arranged chronologically: "Early Years," "Into Politics," "Challenge for the Leadership," "Changing the Party," "Victory at the Polls," "Reforming Government," "Northern Ireland," "Europe," "The Special Relationship," "Second Term," "The Challenge of Terror," "The War on Terror," "Sticking the Course," "Never Surrender," "Time to Go," and "A Future of Hope." Each chapter was between ten and twenty thousand words long and hadn't been written so much as cobbled together from speeches, official minutes, communiqués, memoranda, interview transcripts, office diaries, party manifestos, and newspaper articles. Occasionally, Lang permitted himself a private emotion *("I was overjoyed when our third child was born")* or a personal observation *("the American president was much taller than I had expected")* or a sharp remark *("as foreign secretary, Richard Rycart often seemed to prefer presenting the foreigners' case to Britain rather than the other way round")* but not very often, and not to any great effect. And where was his wife? She was barely mentioned.

"A crock of shit," Rick had called it. But actually this was worse. Shit, to quote Gore Vidal, has its own integrity. This was a crock of nothing. It was strictly accurate and yet overall it was a lie—it had to be, I thought. No human being could pass through life and feel so little. Especially Adam Lang, whose political stock-in-trade was emotional empathy. I skipped ahead to the chapter called "The War on Terror." If there was going to be anything to interest American readers it must surely be here. I skimmed it, searching for words like "rendition," "torture," "CIA." I found nothing, and certainly no mention of Operation Tempest. What about the war in the Middle East? Surely some mild criticism here of the U.S. president, or the defense secretary, or the secretary of state; some hint of betrayal or letdown; some behind-the-scenes scoop or previously classified document? No. Nowhere. Nothing. I took a gulp, literally and metaphorically, and began reading again from the top.

At some point the secretary, Alice, must have brought me in a tuna sandwich and a bottle of mineral water, because later in the afternoon I noticed them at the end of the desk. But I was too busy to stop, and besides I wasn't hungry. In fact, I was beginning to feel nauseous as I shuffled those sixteen chapters, scanning the sheer white cliff face of featureless prose for any tiny handhold of interest I could cling to. No wonder McAra had thrown himself off the Martha's Vineyard ferry. No wonder Maddox and Kroll had flown to London to try to rescue the project. No wonder they were paying me fifty thousand dollars a week. All these seemingly bizarre events were rendered entirely logical by the direness of the manuscript. And now it would be *my* reputation that would come spiraling down, strapped into the backseat of Adam Lang's kamikaze seaplane. I would be the one pointed out at publishing parties—assuming I was ever invited to another publishing party—as the ghost who had collaborated on the biggest flop in publishing history. In a sudden shaft of paranoid insight, I fancied I saw my real role in the operation: designated fall guy.

I finished the last of the six hundred and twenty-one pages (*"Ruth and I look forward to the future, whatever it may hold"*) in midafternoon, and when I laid down the manuscript I pressed my hands to my cheeks and opened my mouth and eyes wide, in a reasonable imitation of Edvard Munch's *The Scream*.

That was when I heard a cough in the doorway and looked up to see Ruth Lang watching me. To this day I don't know how long she'd been there. She raised a thin black eyebrow.

"As bad as that?" she said.

SHE WAS WEARING A man's thick, shapeless white sweater, so long in the sleeves that only her chewed fingernails were visible, and once we got downstairs she pulled on top of this a pale blue hooded windbreaker, disappearing for a while as she tugged it over her head, her pale face emerging at last with a frown. Her short dark hair stuck up in Medusa-like spikes.

It was she who had proposed a walk. She said I looked as though

I needed one, which was true enough. She found me her husband's windproof jacket, which fitted perfectly, and a pair of waterproof boots belonging to the house, and together we stepped out into the blustery Atlantic air. We followed the path around the edge of the lawn and climbed up onto the dunes. To our right was the pond, with a jetty, and next to that a rowboat that had been hauled above the reed beds and laid upside down. To our left was the gray ocean. Ahead of us, bare white sand stretched for a couple of miles, and when I looked behind, the picture was the same, except that a policeman in an overcoat was following about fifty yards distant.

"You must get sick of this," I said, nodding to our escort.

"It's been going on so long I've stopped noticing."

We pressed on into the wind. Close up, the beach didn't look so idyllic. Strange pieces of broken plastic, lumps of tar, a dark blue canvas shoe stiff with salt, a wooden cable drum, dead birds, skeletons, and bits of bone—it was like walking along the side of a six-lane highway. The big waves came in with a roar and receded like passing trucks.

"So," said Ruth, "how bad is it?"

"You haven't read it?"

"Not all of it."

"Well," I said, politely, "it needs some work."

"How much?"

The words "Hiroshima" and "nineteen forty-five" floated briefly into my mind. "It's fixable," I said, which I suppose it was: even Hiroshima was fixed eventually. "It's the deadline that's the trouble. We absolutely have to do it in four weeks, and that's less than two days for each chapter."

"Four weeks!" She had a deep, rather dirty laugh. "You'll never get him to sit still for as long as that!"

"He doesn't have to write it, as such. That's what I'm being paid for. He just has to talk to me."

She had pulled up her hood. I couldn't see her face; only the sharp white tip of her nose was visible. Everyone said she was smarter than her husband and that she'd loved their life at the top even more than he had. If there was an official visit to some foreign country, she usually went with him: she refused to be left at home. You only had to watch them on TV together to see how she bathed in his success. Adam and Ruth Lang: the Power and the Glory. Now she stopped and turned to face the ocean, her hands thrust deep in her pockets. Along the beach, as if playing Grandma's footsteps, the policeman also stopped.

"You were my idea," she said.

I swayed in the wind. I almost fell over. "I was?"

"Yes. You were the one who wrote Christy's book for him."

It took me a moment to work out who she meant. Christy Costello. I hadn't thought of him in a long while. He was my first bestseller. The intimate memoirs of a seventies rock star. Drink, drugs, girls, a near-fatal car crash, surgery, and finally rehab and redemp in the arms of a good woman. It had everything. You could give it at Christmas to your grungy teenager or your churchgoing granny, and each would be equally happy. It sold three hundred thousand copies in hardcover in the UK alone.

"You know *Christy*?" It seemed so unlikely.

"We stayed at his house on Mustique last winter. I read his memoirs. They were by the bed."

"Now I'm embarrassed."

"No. Why? They were brilliant, in a horrible kind of a way. Listening to his scrambled stories over dinner and then seeing how you'd turned them into something resembling a life—I said to Adam then: 'This is the man you need to write your book.' "

I laughed. I couldn't stop myself. "Well, I hope your husband's recollections aren't quite as hazy as Christy's."

"Don't count on it." She pulled back her hood and took a deep breath. She was better looking in the flesh than she was on television. The camera hated her almost as much as it loved her husband. It didn't catch her amused alertness, the animation of her face. "God, I miss home," she said. "Even though the kids are away at university. I keep telling him it's like being married to Napoleon on Saint Helena."

"Then why don't you go back to London?"

She didn't say anything for a while, just stared at the ocean, biting her lip. Then she looked at me, sizing me up. "You did sign that confidentiality agreement?"

"Of course."

"You're sure?"

"Check with Sid Kroll's office."

"Because I don't want to read about this in some gossip column next week, or in some cheap little kiss-and-tell book of your own a year from now."

"Whoa," I said, taken aback by her venom. "I thought you just said I was your idea. I didn't ask to come here. And I haven't kissed anyone."

She nodded. "All right then. I'll tell you why I can't go home, between you and me. Because there's something not quite right with him at the moment, and I'm a bit afraid to leave him."

Boy, I thought. This just gets better and better.

"Yes," I replied diplomatically. "Amelia told me he was very upset by Mike's death."

"Oh, did she? Quite when *Mrs. Bly* became such an expert in my husband's emotional state I'm not sure." If she had hissed and sprung claws she couldn't have made her feelings plainer. "Losing Mike certainly made it worse, but it isn't just that. It's losing power—that's the real trouble. Losing power, and now having to sit down and relive everything, year by year. While all the time the press are going on and on about what he did and didn't do. He can't get free of the past, you see. He can't move on." She gestured helplessly at the sea, the sand, the dunes. "He's stuck. We're both stuck."

As we walked back to the house, she put her arm through mine. "Oh, dear," she said. "You must be starting to wonder what you've let yourself in for."

THERE WAS A LOT more activity in the compound when we got back. A dark green Jaguar limousine with a Washington license plate was parked at the entrance, and a black minivan with darkened windows was drawn up behind it. As the front door opened, I could hear several telephones ringing at once. A genial gray-haired man in a cheap brown suit was sitting just inside, drinking a cup of tea, talking to one of the police guards. He jumped up smartly when he saw Ruth Lang. They were all quite scared of her, I noticed.

"Afternoon, ma'am."

"Hello, Jeff. How was New York?"

"Bloody chaos, as usual. Like Piccadilly Circus in the rush hour." He had a crafty London accent. "Thought for a while I wouldn't get back in time."

Ruth turned to me. "They like to have the car ready in position when Adam lands." She began the long process of wriggling out of her windbreaker just as Amelia Bly came round the corner, a cell phone wedged between her elegant shoulder and her sculpted chin, her nimble fingers zipping up an attaché case. "That's fine, that's fine. I'll tell him." She nodded to Ruth and carried on speaking—"On Thursday he's in Chicago"—then looked at Jeff and tapped her wristwatch.

"Actually, I think *I'll* go to the airport," said Ruth, suddenly pulling her windbreaker back down. "Amelia can stay here and polish her nails or something. Why don't you come?" she added to me. "He's keen to meet you."

Score one to the wife, I thought. But no: in the finest traditions of the British civil service, Amelia bounced off the ropes and came back punching. "Then I'll travel in the backup car," she said, snapping her cell phone shut and smiling sweetly. "I can do my nails in there."

Jeff opened one of the Jaguar's rear doors for Ruth, while I went round and nearly broke my arm tugging at the other. I slid into the leather seat and the door closed behind me with a gaseous thump.

"She's armored, sir," said Jeff into the rearview mirror as we pulled away. "Weighs two and a half tons. Yet she'll still do a hundred with all four tires shot out."

"Oh, do shut up, Jeff," said Ruth, good-humoredly. "He doesn't want to hear all that."

"The windows are an inch thick and don't open, in case you were thinking of trying. She's airtight against chemical and biological attack, with oxygen for an hour. Makes you think, doesn't it? At this precise moment, sir, you're probably safer than you've ever been in your life, or ever will be again."

Ruth laughed again and made a face. "Boys with their toys!"

The outside world seemed muffled, distant. The forest track ran smooth and quiet as rubber. Perhaps this is what it feels like being carried in the womb, I thought: this wonderful feeling of complete security. We ran over the dead skunk, and the big car didn't register the slightest tremor.

"Nervous?" asked Ruth.

"No. Why? Should I be?"

"Not at all. He's the most charming man you'll ever meet. My own Prince Charming!" And she gave her deep-throated, mannish laugh again. "God," she said, staring out of the window, "will I be glad to see the back of these trees. It's like living in an enchanted wood."

I glanced over my shoulder at the unmarked minivan following close behind. I could see how this was addictive. I was getting used to it already. Being forced to give it up after it had become a habit would be like letting go of mommy. But thanks to terrorism, Lang would never have to give it up—never have to stand in line for public transport, never even drive himself. He was as pampered and cocooned as a Romanov before the revolution.

We came out of the forest onto the main road, turned left, and almost immediately swung right through the airport perimeter. I stared out of the window in surprise at the big runway.

"We're here already?"

"In summer Marty likes to leave his office in Manhattan at four," said Ruth, "and be on the beach by six."

"I suppose he has a private jet," I said in an attempt at knowingness.

"Of course he has a private jet."

She gave me a look that made me feel like a hick who'd just

used his fish knife to butter his roll. *Of course he has a private jet.* You don't own a thirty-million-dollar house and travel to it by bus. The man must have a carbon footprint the size of a yeti's. I realized then that just about everybody the Langs knew these days had a private jet. Indeed, here came Lang himself, in a corporate Gulfstream, dropping out of the darkening sky and skimming in low over the gloomy pines. Jeff put his foot down and a minute later we pulled up outside the little terminal. There was a self-important cannonade of slamming doors as we piled inside—me, Ruth, Amelia, Jeff, and one of the protection officers. Inside, a patrolman from the Edgartown police force was already waiting. Behind him on the wall I could see a faded photograph of Bill and Hillary Clinton being greeted on the tarmac at the start of some scandal-shrouded presidential vacation.

The private jet taxied in from the runway. It was painted dark blue and had HALLINGTON written in gold letters by the door. It looked bigger than the usual CEO's phallic symbol, with a high tail and six windows either side, and when it came to a stop and the engines were cut the silence over the deserted airfield was unexpectedly profound.

The door opened, the steps were lowered, and out came a couple of Special Branch men. One headed straight for the terminal. The other waited at the foot of the steps, going through the motions of checking the empty tarmac, glancing up and around and behind him. Lang himself seemed in no hurry to disembark. I could just about make him out in the shadows of the interior, shaking hands with the pilot and a male steward, then finally—almost reluctantly, it seemed to me—he came out and paused at the top of the steps. He was holding his own briefcase, which was not something he had done when he was prime minister. The wind lifted the back of his jacket and plucked at his tie. He smoothed down his hair. He glanced around as if he was trying to remember what he was supposed to do. It was on the edge of becoming embarrassing when suddenly he caught sight of us watching him through the big glass window. He pointed and waved and grinned, exactly the way he had in his heyday, and the moment—whatever it was—had passed. He came striding eagerly across the concourse, transferring his briefcase from one hand to the other, trailed by a third Special Branch man and a young woman pulling a suitcase on wheels.

We left the window just in time to meet him as he came in through the arrivals gate.

"Hi, darling," he said and stooped to kiss his wife. His skin had a slightly orange tint. I realized he was wearing makeup.

She stroked his arm. "How was New York?"

"Great. They gave me the Gulfstream Four—you know, the transatlantic one, with the beds and the shower. Hi, Amelia. Hi, Jeff." He noticed me. "Hello," he said. "Who are you?"

"I'm your ghost," I said.

I regretted it the instant I said it. I'd conceived it as a witty, self-deprecatory, break-the-ice kind of a line. I'd even practiced my delivery in the mirror before I left London. But somehow out there, in that deserted airport, amid the grayness and the quietness, it hit precisely the wrong note. He flinched.

"Right," he said doubtfully, and although he shook my hand, he also drew his head back slightly, as if to inspect me from a safer distance.

Christ, I thought, he thinks I'm a lunatic.

"Don't worry," Ruth told him. "He isn't always such a jerk."

FIVE

It is essential for the ghost to make the subject feel
completely comfortable in his or her company.

Ghostwriting

"BRILLIANT OPENING LINE," SAID Amelia as we drove back
to the house. "Did they teach you that at ghost school?"

We were sitting together in the back of the minivan. The secretary who'd just flown in from New York—her name was Lucy—
and the three protection officers occupied the seats in front of us.
Through the windscreen I could see the Jaguar immediately ahead
carrying the Langs. It was starting to get dark. Pinned by two sets
of headlights, the scrub oaks loomed and writhed.

"It was particularly tactful," she went on, "given that you're
replacing a dead man."

"All right," I groaned. "Stop."

"But you do have one thing going for you," she said, turning her large blue eyes on me and speaking quietly so that no one else could hear. "Almost uniquely among all members of the human race, you seem to be trusted by Ruth Lang. Now why's that, do you suppose?"

"There's no accounting for taste."

"True. Perhaps she thinks you'll do what she tells you?"

"Perhaps she does. Don't ask me." The last thing I needed was to get stuck in the middle of this catfight. "Listen, Amelia—can I call you Amelia? As far as I'm concerned, I'm helping write a book. I don't want to get caught up in any palace intrigues."

"Of course not. You just want to do your job and get out of here."

"You're mocking me again."

"You make it so easy."

After that I shut up for a while. I could see why Ruth didn't like her. She was a shade too clever and several shades too blonde for comfort, especially from a wife's point of view. In fact it struck me as I sat there, passively inhaling her Chanel, that she might be having an affair with Lang. That would explain a lot. He'd been noticeably cool toward her at the airport, and isn't that always the surest sign? In which case, no wonder they were so paranoid about confidentiality. There could be enough material here to keep the tabloids happy for weeks.

We were halfway down the track when Amelia said, "You haven't told me what you thought of the manuscript."

"Honestly? I haven't had so much fun since I read the memoirs of Leonid Brezhnev." She didn't smile. "I don't understand how it happened," I went on. "You people were running the country not that long ago. Surely one of you had English as a first language?"

"Mike—" she began, then stopped. "But I don't want to speak ill of the dead."

"Why make them an exception?"

"All right, then: Mike. The problem was, Adam passed it all over to Mike to deal with right at the beginning, and poor Mike was simply swamped by it. He disappeared to Cambridge to do the research and we barely saw him for a year."

"Cambridge?"

"Cambridge—where the Lang Papers are stored. You've really done your homework, haven't you? Two thousand boxes of documents. Two hundred and fifty yards of shelving. One million separate papers, or thereabouts—nobody's ever bothered to count."

"McAra went through all that?" I was incredulous. My idea of a rigorous research schedule was a week with a tape recorder sitting opposite my client, fleshed out by whatever tissue of inaccuracies Google had to offer.

"No," she said irritably. "He didn't go through every box, obviously, but enough so that when he finally did emerge, he was completely overwrought and exhausted. I think he simply lost sight of what he was supposed to be doing. That seems to have triggered a clinical depression, though none of us noticed it at the time. He didn't even sit down with Adam to go over it all until just before Christmas. And of course by then it was far too late."

"I'm sorry," I said, twisting in my seat so that I could see her properly. "You're telling me that a man who's being paid ten million dollars to write his memoirs within two years turns the whole project over to someone who knows nothing about producing books and who is then allowed to wander off on his own for twelve months?"

Amelia put a finger to her lips and gestured with her eyes to the front of the car. "You're very loud, for a ghost."

"But surely," I whispered, "a former prime minister must recognize how important his memoirs are to him?"

"If you want the honest truth, I don't think Adam ever had the slightest intention of producing this book within two years. And he thought that that would be fine. So he let Mike take it over as a kind of reward for sticking by him all the way through. But then, when Marty Rhinehart made it clear he was going to hold him to the original contract, and when the publishers actually read what Mike had produced . . ." Her voice trailed off.

"Couldn't he just have paid the money back and started all over again?"

"I think you know the answer to that question better than I do."

"He wouldn't have got nearly such a large advance."

"Two years after leaving office? He wouldn't have got even half."

"And nobody saw this coming?"

"I raised it with Adam every so often. But history doesn't really interest him—it never has, not even his own. He was much more concerned with getting his foundation established."

I sat back in my seat. I could see how easily it all must have happened: McAra, the party hack turned Stakhanovite of the archive, blindly riveting together his vast and useless sheets of facts; Lang, always a man for the bigger picture—"the future not the past": wasn't that one of his slogans—being feted around the American lecture circuit, preferring to live, not relive, his life; and then the horrible realization that the great memoir project was in trouble, followed, I assumed, by recriminations, the sundering of old friendships, and suicidal anxiety.

"It must have been rough on all of you."

"It was. Especially after they discovered Mike's body. I offered to go and do the identification, but Adam felt it was his responsibility. It was an awful thing to go through. Suicide leaves everyone feeling guilty. So please, if you don't mind, no more jokes about ghosts."

I was on the point of asking her about the rendition stories in the weekend papers when the brake lights of the Jaguar glowed, and we came to a stop.

"Well, here we are again," she said, and for the first time I detected a hint of weariness in her voice. "Home."

It was fairly dark by this time—half past five or thereabouts—and the temperature had dropped with the sun. I stood beside the minivan and watched as Lang ducked out of his car and was swept through the door by the usual swirl of bodyguards and staff. They had him inside so quickly one might have thought an assassin with a telescopic sight had been spotted in the woods. Immediately, all along the façade of the big house, the windows started lighting up, and it was possible, briefly, to imagine that this was a focus of real power and not merely some lingering parody of it. I felt very much an outsider, unsure of what I was supposed to do and still twisting with embarrassment over my gaffe at the airport. So I lingered outside in the cold for a while. To my surprise, the person who realized I was missing and who came out to fetch me was Lang.

"Hi, man!" he called from the doorway. "What on earth are you doing out here? Isn't anybody looking after you? Come and have a drink."

He touched my shoulder as I entered and steered me down the passage toward the room where I'd had coffee that morning. He'd already taken off his jacket and tie and pulled on a thick gray sweater.

"I'm sorry I didn't get a chance to say hello properly at the airport. What would you like?"

"What are you having?" Dear God, I prayed, let it be something alcoholic.

"Iced tea."

"Iced tea would be fine."

"You're sure? I'd sooner have something stronger, but Ruth would kill me." He called to one of the secretaries: "Luce, ask Dep to bring us some tea, would you, sweetheart? So," he said, plonking himself down in the center of the sofa and flinging out his arms to rest along its back, "you have to be me for a month, God help you." He swiftly crossed his legs, his right ankle resting on his left knee. He drummed his fingers, wiggled his foot and inspected it for a moment, then returned his cloudless gaze to me.

"I hope it will be a fairly painless procedure, for both of us," I said, and hesitated, unsure how to address him.

"Adam," he said. "Call me Adam."

There always comes a moment, I find, in dealing with a very famous person face-to-face, when you feel as if you're in a dream, and this was it for me: a genuine out-of-body experience. I beheld myself as if from the ceiling, conversing in an apparently relaxed manner with a world statesman in the home of a media billionaire. He was actually going out of his way to be nice to me. He *needed* me. What a lark, I thought.

"Thank you," I said. "I have to tell you I've never met an ex–prime minister before."

"Well," he said with a smile, "I've never met a ghost, so we're even. Sid Kroll says you're the man for the job. Ruth agrees. So how exactly are we supposed to go about this?"

"I'll interview you. I'll turn your answers into prose. Where necessary, I might have to add linking passages, trying to imitate your voice. I should say, incidentally, that anything I write you'll be able to correct afterward. I don't want you to think I'll be putting words in your mouth that you wouldn't actually want to use."

"And how long will this take?"

"For a big book, I'd normally do fifty or sixty hours of interviews. That would give me about four hundred thousand words, which I'd then edit down to a hundred thousand."

"But we've already got a manuscript."

"Yes," I said, "but frankly, it's not really publishable. It's research notes, it's not a book. It doesn't have any kind of voice." Lang pulled a face. He clearly didn't see the problem. "Having said that," I added quickly, "the work won't be entirely wasted. We can ransack it for facts and quotations, and I don't mind the structure, actually—the sixteen chapters—although I'd like to open differently, find something more intimate."

The Vietnamese housekeeper brought in our tea. She was dressed entirely in black—black silk trousers and a collarless black shirt. I wanted to introduce myself, but when she handed me my glass, she avoided meeting my gaze.

"You heard about Mike?" asked Lang.

"Yes," I said. "I'm sorry."

Lang glanced away, toward the darkened window. "We should put something nice about him in the book. His mother would like it."

"That should be easy enough."

"He was with me a long time. Since before I became prime minister. He came up through the party. I inherited him from my predecessor. You think you know someone pretty well and then—" He shrugged and stared into the night.

I didn't know what to say, so I didn't say anything. It's in the nature of my work to act as something of a confessor figure, and I have learned over the years to behave like a shrink—to sit in silence and give the client time. I wondered what he was seeing out there. After about half a minute he appeared to remember I was still in the room.

"Right. How long do you need from me?"

"Full time?" I sipped my drink and tried not to wince at the sweet taste. "If we work really hard we should be able to break the back of it in a week."

"A week?" Lang performed a little facial mime of alarm.

I resisted the temptation to point out that ten mllion dollars for a week's work wasn't exactly the national minimum wage. "I may need to come back to you to plug any holes, but if you can give me till Friday, I'll have enough to rewrite most of this draft. The important thing is that we start tomorrow and get the early years out of the way."

"Fine. The sooner we get it done the better." Suddenly Lang was leaning forward, a study in frank intimacy, his elbows on his knees, his glass between his hands. "Ruth's going stir-crazy out here. I keep telling her to go back to London while I finish the book, see the kids, but she won't leave me. I love your work, I have to say."

I almost choked on my tea. "You've read some of it?" I tried to imagine what footballer, or rock star, or magician, or reality game show contestant might have come to the attention of a prime minister.

"Sure," he said, without a flicker of doubt. "There was some fellow we were on holiday with—"

"Christy Costello?"

"Christy Costello! Brilliant. If you can make sense out of his life, you might even be able to make sense out of mine." He jumped up and shook my hand. "It's good to meet you, man. We'll make a start first thing tomorrow. I'll get Amelia to fix you a car to take you back to your hotel." And then he suddenly started singing:

> *"Once in a lifetime*
> *You get to have it all*
> *But you never knew you had it*
> *Till you go and lose it all."*

He pointed at me. "Christy Costello, 'Once in a Lifetime,' nineteen seventy"—he wobbled his hand speculatively, his head cocked, his eyes half closed in concentration—"seven?"

"Eight."

"Nineteen seventy-eight! Those were the days! I can feel it all coming back."

"Save it for tomorrow," I said.

"HOW DID IT GO?" inquired Amelia as she showed me to the door.

"Pretty well, I think. It was all very friendly. He kept calling me 'man.' "

"Yes. He always does that when he can't remember someone's name."

"Tomorrow," I said, "I'll need a private room where I can do the interviewing. I'll need a secretary to transcribe his answers as we go along—every time we break I'll bring the fresh tapes out to her. I'll need my own copy of the existing manuscript on disk—yes, I know," I said, holding up my hand to cut off her objections, "I won't take it out of the house. But I'm going to have to cut and paste it into the new material, and also try to rewrite it so that it sounds vaguely like it was produced by a human being."

She was writing all this down in her black and red book. "Anything else?"

"How about dinner?"

"Good night," she said firmly and closed the door.

One of the policemen gave me a ride back to Edgartown. He was as morose as his colleague on the gate. "I hope you get this book done soon," he said. "Me and the lads are getting pretty brassed off stuck out here."

He dropped me at the hotel and said he'd pick me up again in the morning. I had just opened the door to my room when my cell phone rang. It was Kate.

"Are you okay?" she said. "I got your message. You sounded a bit . . . odd."

"Did I? Sorry. I'm fine now." I fought back the impulse to ask her where she'd been when I called.

"So? Have you met him?"

"I have. I've just come from him."

"And?" Before I could answer, she said, "Don't tell me: charming."

I briefly held the phone away from my ear and gave it the finger.

"You certainly pick your moments," she went on. "Did you see yesterday's papers? You must be the first recorded instance of a rat actually boarding a sinking ship."

"Yes, of course I saw them," I said defensively, "and I'm going to ask him about it."

"When?"

"When the moment arises."

She made an explosive noise that somehow managed to combine hilarity, fury, contempt, and disbelief. "Well, yes, *do* ask him. Ask him why he illegally kidnaps British citizens in another country and hands them over to be tortured. Ask him if he knows about the techniques the CIA uses to simulate drowning. Ask him what he plans to say to the widow and children of the man who died of a heart attack—"

"Hold on," I interrupted. "You lost me after drowning."

"I'm seeing someone else," she said.

"Good," I said and hung up.

After that there didn't seem much else to do except go down to the bar and get drunk.

It was decorated to look like the kind of place Captain Ahab might fancy dropping into after a hard day at the harpoon. The seats and tables were made out of old barrels. There were antique seine nets and lobster traps hanging on the roughly planked walls, along with schooners in bottles and sepia photographs of deep-sea anglers standing proudly beside the suspended corpses of their prey: the fishermen would now all be as dead as their fish, I thought, and such was my mood that the notion pleased me. A big television above the bar was showing an ice hockey game. I ordered a beer and a bowl of clam chowder and sat where I could see the screen. I know nothing about ice hockey, but sport is a great place to lose yourself for a while, and I'll watch anything available.

"You're English?" said a man at a table in the corner. He must have heard me ordering. He was the only other customer in the bar.

"And so are you," I said.

"Indeed I am. Are you here on holiday?"

He had a clipped, hello-old-chap-fancy-a-round-of-golf sort of a voice. That, and the striped shirt with the frayed collar, the double-breasted blazer, the tarnished brass buttons, and the blue silk handkerchief in the top pocket, all flashed bore, bore, bore as clearly as the Edgartown Lighthouse.

"No. Working." I resumed watching the game.

"So what's your line?" He had a glass of something clear with ice and a slice of lemon in it. Vodka and tonic? Gin and tonic? I was desperate not to be trapped into conversation with him.

"Just this and that. Excuse me."

I got up and went to the lavatory and washed my hands. The face in the mirror was that of a man who'd slept six hours out of the past forty. When I returned to the table, my chowder had arrived. I ordered another drink but pointedly didn't offer to buy one for my compatriot. I could feel him watching me.

"I hear Adam Lang's on the island," he said.

I looked at him properly then. He was in his middle fifties, slim but broad shouldered. Strong. His iron-gray hair was slicked straight back off his forehead. There was something vaguely military about him but also unkempt and faded, as if he relied on food parcels from a veterans' charity. I answered in a neutral tone, "Is he?"

"So I hear. You don't happen to know his whereabouts, do you?"

"No. I'm afraid not. Excuse me again."

I started to eat my chowder. I heard him sigh noisily and then the clink of ice as his glass was set down.

"Cunt," he said as he passed my table.

SIX

---- ★ ----

I have often been told by subjects that by the end of
the research process, they feel as if they have been in
therapy.

Ghostwriting

THERE WAS NO SIGN of him when I came down to breakfast
the next morning. The receptionist told me there was no other
guest apart from me in residence. She was equally firm that she
hadn't seen a British man in a blazer. I'd already been awake since
four—an improvement on two, but not much—and was groggy
enough and hungover enough to wonder if I hadn't hallucinated
the whole encounter. I felt better after some coffee. I crossed the
road and walked around the lighthouse a couple of times to clear
my head, and by the time I returned to the hotel the minivan had
arrived to take me to work.

I'd anticipated that my biggest problem on the first day would be physically getting Adam Lang into a room and keeping him there for long enough to start interviewing him. But the strange thing was that when we reached the house, *he* was already waiting for *me*. Amelia had decided we should use Rhinehart's office, and we found the former prime minister, wearing a dark green tracksuit, sprawled in the big chair opposite the desk, one leg draped over the arm. He was flicking through a history of World War Two that he'd obviously just taken down from the shelf. A mug of tea stood on the floor beside him. His trainers had sand on their soles: I guessed he must have gone for a run on the beach.

"Hi, man," he said, looking up at me. "Ready to start?"

"Good morning," I said. "I just need to sort out a few things first."

"Sure. Go ahead. Ignore me."

He went back to his book while I opened my shoulder bag and carefully unpacked the tools of the ghosting trade: a Sony Walkman digital tape recorder with a stack of MD-R 74 minidisks and a mains lead (I've learned the hard way not to rely solely on my batteries); a metallic silver Panasonic Toughbook laptop computer, which is not much larger than a hardcover novel and considerably lighter; a couple of small black Moleskine notebooks and three brand-new Jetstream rollerball pens, made by the Mitsubishi Pencil Co.; and finally two white plastic adapters, one a British multipoint plug and one a converter to fit an American socket. It's a superstition with me always to use the same items, and to lay them out in the proper sequence. I also had a list of questions, culled from the books I'd bought in London and my reading of McAra's first draft the previous day.

"Did you know," said Lang suddenly, "that the Germans had

jet fighters in 1944? Look at that." He held up the page to show the photograph. "It's a wonder we won."

"We have no floppy disks," said Amelia, "only these flash drives. I've loaded the manuscript onto this one for you." She handed me an object the size of a small plastic cigarette lighter. "You're welcome to copy it onto your own computer, but I'm afraid that if you do, your laptop must stay here, locked up, overnight."

"And apparently Germany declared war on America, not the other way round."

"Isn't this all a bit paranoid?"

"The book contains some potentially classified material that has yet to be approved by the Cabinet Office. More to the point, there's also a very strong risk of some news organization using unscrupulous methods to try to get hold of it. Any leak would jeopardize our newspaper serialization deals."

Lang said, "So you've actually got my whole book on that?"

"We could get a hundred books on that, Adam," said Amelia, patiently.

"Amazing." He shook his head. "You know the worst thing about my life?" He closed the book with a snap and replaced it on the shelf. "You get so out of touch. You never go in a shop. Everything's done for you. You don't carry any money—if I want some money, even now, I have to ask one of the secretaries or one of the protection boys to get it for me. I couldn't do it myself, anyway, I don't know my—what're they called?—I don't even know that—"

"PIN?"

"You see? I just don't have a clue. I'll give you another example. The other week, Ruth and I went out to dinner with some people in New York. They've always been very generous to us, so I say, 'Right, tonight, this is on me.' So I give my credit card to the manager and he comes back a few minutes later, all embarrassed, and he shows me the problem. There's still a strip where the signature's supposed to be." He threw up his arms and grinned. "The card hadn't been activated."

"This," I said excitedly, "is exactly the sort of detail we need to put in your book. Nobody knows this sort of thing."

Lang looked startled. "I can't put that in. People would think I was a complete idiot."

"But it's human detail. It shows what it's like to be you." I knew this was my moment. I had to get him to focus on what we needed right from the start. I came round from behind the desk and confronted him. "Why don't we try to make this book unlike any other political memoir that's ever been written? Why don't we try to tell the truth?"

He laughed. "Now that would be a first."

"I mean it. Let's tell people what it really feels like to be prime minister. Not just the policy stuff—any old bore can write about that." I almost cited McAra but managed to swerve away at the last moment. "Let's stick to what no one except you knows—the day-to-day experience of actually leading a country. What do you feel like in the mornings? What are the strains? What's it like to be so cut off from ordinary life? What's it like to be hated?"

"Thanks a lot."

"What fascinates people isn't policy—who cares about policy? What fascinates people is always people—the detail of another person's life. But because the detail is naturally all so familiar to you, you can't sort out what it is the reader wants to know. It has to be drawn out of you. That's why you need me. This shouldn't be a book for political hacks. This should be a book for every-one."

"The people's memoir," said Amelia dryly, but I ignored her, and so, more important, did Lang, who was looking at me quite differently now: it was as if some electric lightbulb marked "self-interest" had started to glow behind his eyes.

"Most former leaders couldn't get away with it," I said. "They're too stiff. They're too awkward. They're too *old*. If they take off their jacket and tie and put on a"—I gestured at his out-fit—"put on a tracksuit, say, they look phony. But you're different. And that's why you should write a different kind of political mem-oir, for a different age."

Lang was staring at me. "What do you think, Amelia?"

"I think you two were made for each other. I'm beginning to feel like a gooseberry."

"Do you mind," I asked, "if I start recording? Something use-ful might come out of this. Don't worry—the tapes will all be your property."

Lang shrugged and gestured toward the Sony Walkman. As I pressed Record, Amelia slipped out and closed the door quietly behind her.

"The first thing that strikes me," I said, bringing a chair round from behind the desk so that I could sit facing him, "is that you aren't really a politician at all, in the conventional sense, even though you've been so amazingly successful." This was the sort of tough questioning I specialized in. "I mean, when you were grow-ing up, no one would have expected you to become a politician, would they?"

"Jesus, no," said Lang. "Not at all. I had absolutely no interest in politics, either as a child or as a teenager. I thought people who were obsessed by politics were weird. I still do, as a matter of fact. I liked playing football. I liked theater and the movies. A bit later on I liked going out with girls. I never dreamed I might become a politician. Most student politicians struck me as complete nerds."

Bingo! I thought. We'd been working only two minutes and already we had a potential opening of the book right there:

> When I was growing up, I had no interest in politics. In fact, I thought people who were obsessed by politics were weird.
> I still do . . .

"So what changed? What turned you on to politics?"

"Turned on is about right," said Lang with a laugh. "I'd left Cambridge and drifted for a year, hoping that a play I'd been involved in might get taken up by a theater in London. But it didn't happen and so I ended up working in a bank, living in this grotty basement flat in Lambeth, feeling very sorry for myself, because all my friends from Cambridge were working in the BBC, or getting paid a fortune to do voice-overs on adverts, or what have you. And I remember it was a Sunday afternoon—raining, I was still in bed—and someone starts knocking on the door . . ."

It was a story he must have told a thousand times, but you wouldn't have guessed it, watching him that morning. He was sitting back in his chair, smiling at the memory, going over the same old words, using the same rehearsed gestures—he was miming knocking on a door—and I thought what an old trouper he was: the sort of pro who'd always make an effort to put on a good show, whether he had an audience of one or one million.

". . . and this person just wouldn't go away. Knock knock

knock. And, you know, I'd had a bit to drink the night before and what have you, and I'm moaning and groaning. I've got the pillow over my head. But it starts up again: knock knock knock. So eventually—and by now I'm swearing quite a bit, I can tell you—I get out of bed, I pull on a dressing gown, and I open the door. And there's this girl, this gorgeous girl. She's wringing wet from the rain, but she completely ignores that and launches into this speech about the local elections. Bizarre. I have to say I didn't even know there *were* any local elections, but at least I have the sense to pretend that I'm very interested, and so I invite her in, and make her a cup of tea, and she dries off. And that's it—I'm in love. And it quickly becomes clear that the best way of getting to see her again is to take one of her leaflets and turn up the next Tuesday evening, or whenever it is, and join the local party. Which I do."

"And this is Ruth?"

"This is Ruth."

"And if she'd been a member of a different political party?"

"I'd have gone along and joined it just the same. I wouldn't have *stayed* in it," he added quickly. "I mean obviously this was the start of a long political awakening for me—bringing out values and beliefs that were already present but were simply dormant at that time. No, I couldn't have stayed in just *any* party. But everything would have been different if Ruth hadn't knocked on that door that afternoon, and kept knocking."

"And if it hadn't been raining."

"If it hadn't been raining I would have found some other excuse to invite her in," said Lang with a grin. "I mean, come on, man—I wasn't *completely* hopeless."

I grinned back, shook my head, and jotted "opening??" in my notebook.

WE WORKED ALL MORNING without a break, except for when a tape was filled. Then I would briefly hurry downstairs to the room that Amelia and the secretaries were using as a temporary office and hand it over to be transcribed. This happened a couple of times, and always on my return I'd find Lang sitting exactly where I'd left him. At first I thought this was a testament to his powers of concentration. Only gradually did I realize it was because he had nothing else to do.

I took him carefully through his early years, focusing not so much on the facts and dates (McAra had assembled those dutifully enough) as on the impressions and physical objects of his childhood: the semidetached home on a housing estate in Leicester; the personalities of his father (a builder) and his mother (a teacher); the quiet, apolitical values of the English provinces in the sixties, where the only sounds to be heard on a Sunday were church bells and the chimes of ice cream vans; the muddy Saturday morning games of football at the local park and the long summer afternoons of cricket down by the river; his father's Austin Atlantic and his own first Raleigh bike; the comics—the *Eagle* and the *Victor*—and the radio comedies—*I'm Sorry, I'll Read That Again* and *The Navy Lark*; the 1966 World Cup Final and *Z Cars* and *Ready, Steady, Go!*; *The Guns of Navarone* and *Carry On, Doctor* at the local movie theater; Millie singing "My Boy Lollipop" and Beatles singles played at forty-five RPM on his mother's Dansette Capri record player.

Sitting there in Rhinehart's study, the minutiae of English life nearly half a century earlier seemed as remote as bric-a-brac in a Victorian trompe l'oeil—and, you might have thought, about as relevant. But there was cunning in my method, and Lang, with his genius for empathy, grasped it at once, for this was not just his childhood we were itemizing but mine and that of every boy who was born in England in the nineteen fifties and who grew to maturity in the seventies.

"What we need to do," I told him, "is to persuade the reader to identify emotionally with Adam Lang. To see beyond the remote figure in the bombproof car. To recognize in him the same things they recognize in themselves. Because if I know nothing else about this business, I know this: once you have the readers' sympathy, they'll follow you anywhere."

"I get it," he said, nodding emphatically. "I think that's brilliant."

And so we swapped memories for hour after hour, and I will not say we began to *concoct* a childhood for Lang, exactly—I was always careful not to depart from the known historical record—but we certainly pooled our experiences to such an extent that a few of my memories inevitably became blended into his. You may find this shocking. I was shocked myself, the first time I heard one of my clients on television weepily describing a poignant moment from his past that was actually from *my* past. But there it is. People who succeed in life are rarely reflective. Their gaze is always on the future: that's why they succeed. It's not in their nature to remember what they were feeling, or wearing, or who was with them, or the scent of freshly cut grass in the churchyard on the day they were married, or the tightness with which their first baby squeezed their finger. That's why they need ghosts—to flesh them out, as it were.

As it transpired, I collaborated with Lang for only a short while, but I can honestly say I never had a more responsive client.

We decided that his first memory would be when he tried to run away from home at the age of three and he heard the sound of his father's footsteps coming up behind him and felt the hardness of his muscled arms as he scooped him back to the house. We remembered his mother ironing, and the smell of wet clothes on a wooden frame drying in front of a coal fire, and how he liked to pretend that the clotheshorse was a house. His father wore a vest at table and ate pork dripping and kippers; his mother liked the occasional sweet sherry and had a book called *A Thing of Beauty* with a red-and-gold cover. Young Adam would look at the pictures for hours; that was what first gave him his interest in the theater. We remembered Christmas pantomimes he had been to (I made a note to look up exactly what was playing in Leicester when he was growing up) and his stage debut in the school nativity play.

"Was I a wise man?"

"That sounds a little smug."

"A sheep?"

"Not smug enough."

"A guiding star?"

"Perfect!"

By the time we broke for lunch, we had reached the age of seventeen, when his performance in the title role of Christopher Marlowe's *Doctor Faustus* had confirmed him in his desire to become an actor. McAra, with typical thoroughness, had already dug out the review in the *Leicester Mercury*, December 1971, describing how Lang had "held the audience spellbound" with his final speech, as he glimpsed eternal damnation.

While Lang went off to play tennis with one of his bodyguards, I dropped by the downstairs office to check on the transcription. An hour's interviewing generally yields between seven and eight thousand words, and Lang and I had been at it from nine till nearly one. Amelia had set both secretaries on the task. Each was wearing headphones. Their fingers skimmed the keyboards, filling the room with a soothing rattle of plastic. With a bit of luck I would have about a hundred double-spaced pages of material to show for that morning's work alone. For the first time since arriving on the island, I felt the warm breath of optimism.

"This is all new to me," said Amelia, who was bent over Lucy's shoulder, reading Lang's words as they unfurled across the screen. "I've never heard him mention any of this before."

"The human memory is a treasure-house, Amelia," I said, deadpan. "It's merely a matter of finding the right key."

I left her peering at the screen and went into the kitchen. It was about as large as my London flat, with enough polished granite to furnish a family mausoleum. A tray of sandwiches had been laid out. I put one on a plate and wandered around the back of the house until I came to a solarium—I suppose that's what you would call it—with a big sliding glass door leading to an outside swimming pool. The pool was covered with a gray tarpaulin depressed by rainwater, on which floated a brown scum of rotting leaves. There were two silvered wooden cube-shaped buildings at the far end, and beyond those the scrub oak and the white sky. A small, dark figure—so bundled up against the cold he was almost spherical—was raking leaves and piling them into a wheelbarrow. I presumed he must be the Vietnamese gardener, Duc. I really must try to see this place in summer, I thought.

I sat down on a lounge, releasing a faded odor of chlorine and suntan lotion, and called Rick in New York. He was in a rush, as usual.

"How's it going?"

"We had a good morning. The man's a pro."

"Great. I'll call Maddox. He'll be glad to hear it. The first fifty thousand just came in, by the way. I'll wire it over. Speak to you later." The line went dead.

I finished my sandwich and went back upstairs, still clutching my silent phone. I had had an idea, and my newborn confidence gave me the courage to act on it. I went into the study and closed the door. I plugged Amelia's flash drive into my laptop, then I attached a cable from my computer to the cell phone and dialed up the internet. How much easier my life would be, I reasoned—how much quicker the job would be done—if I could work on the book in my hotel room each night. I told myself I was doing no harm. The risks were minimal. The machine rarely left my side. If necessary, it was small enough to fit under my pillow while I slept. The moment I was online, I addressed an email to myself, attached the manuscript file, and pressed Send.

The upload seemed to take an age. Amelia started calling my name from downstairs. I glanced at the door and suddenly my fingers were thick and clumsy with anxiety. "Your file has been transferred," said the female voice that for some reason is favored by my internet service provider. "You have email," she announced a fraction later.

Immediately I yanked the cable out of the laptop, and I had just removed the flash drive when somewhere in the big house a klaxon started. At the same time there was a hum and a rattle above the window behind me and I spun round to see a heavy metal shutter dropping from the ceiling. It descended very quickly, blocking first the view of the sky, then the sea and the dunes, flattening the winter afternoon to dusk, crushing the last sliver of light to blackness. I groped for the door and when I flung it open the unfiltered sound of the siren was strong enough to vibrate my stomach.

The same process was happening in the living room: one, two, three shutters falling like steel curtains. I stumbled in the gloom, cracking my knee against a sharp edge. I dropped my phone. As I stooped to retrieve it, the klaxon stalled on a rising note and died with a moan. I heard heavy footsteps coming up the steps, and then a saber of light flashed into the big room, catching me in a furtive crouch, my arms flung up to shield my face: a parody of guilt.

"Sorry, sir," came a policeman's puzzled voice from the darkness. "Didn't realize there was anyone up here."

IT WAS A DRILL. They held it once a week. "Lockdown," I think they called it. Rhinehart's security people had installed the system to protect him against terrorist attack, kidnap, hurricanes, unionized labor, the Securities and Exchange Commission, or whatever passing nightmare currently stalked the restless nights of the *Fortune* 500. As the shutters rose and the pale wash of Atlantic light was released back into the house, Amelia came into the living room to apologize for not having warned me. "It must have made you jump."

"You could say that."

"But then I did rather lose track of you." There was an edge of suspicion to her manicured voice.

"It's a big house. I'm a big boy. You can't keep an eye on me all the time." I tried to sound relaxed, but I knew I radiated unease.

"A word of advice." Her glossy pink lips parted in a smile, but her big, clear blue eyes were as cold as crystal. "Don't go wandering round too much on your own. The security boys don't like it."

"Gotcha." I smiled back.

There was a squeak of rubber soles on polished wood and Lang came hurtling up the stairs at a tremendous rate, taking them two or three at a time. He had a towel around his neck. His face was flushed, his thick and wavy hair damped and darkened by sweat. He seemed angry about something.

"Did you win?" asked Amelia.

"Didn't play tennis in the end." He blew out his breath, dropped into the nearby sofa, bent forward, and started vigorously toweling his head. "Gym."

Gym? I looked at him in amazement. Hadn't he already been for a run before I arrived? What was he in training for? The Olympics?

I said, in a jovial way, designed to show Amelia how unfazed I was, "So, are you ready to get back to work?"

He glanced up at me furiously and snapped, "You call what we're doing *work*?"

It was the first time I'd ever seen a flash of bad temper from him, and it struck me with the force of a revelation that all this running and pressing and lifting had nothing whatever to do with training; he wasn't even doing it for enjoyment. It was simply what his metabolism demanded. He was like some rare marine specimen fished up from the depths of the ocean, which could live only under extreme pressure. Deposited on the shore, exposed to the thin air of normal life, Lang was in constant danger of expiring from sheer boredom.

"Well, I certainly call it work," I said stiffly. "For both of us.

But if you think it's not intellectually demanding enough for you, we can stop now."

I thought I might have gone too far, but then with a great effort of self-control—so great, you could practically see the intricate machinery of his facial muscles, all the little levers and pulleys and cables, working together—he managed to hoist a tired grin back onto his face. "All right, man," he said tonelessly. "You win." He flicked me with his towel. "I was only kidding. Let's get back to it."

SEVEN

--- ★ ---

Quite often, particularly if you are helping them write a memoir or autobiography, the author will dissolve into tears when telling the story . . . Your job under these circumstances is to pass the tissues, keep quiet and keep recording.

Ghostwriting

"WERE YOUR PARENTS AT all political?"

We were once again in the study, in our usual positions. He was sprawled out in the armchair, still wearing his tracksuit, the towel still draped round his neck. He exuded a faint aroma of sweat. I sat opposite with my notebook and list of questions. The minirecorder was on the desk beside me.

"Not at all, no. I'm not sure my father even voted. He said they were all as bad as one another."

"Tell me about him."

"He was a builder. Self-employed. He was in his fifties when he met my mother. He'd already got two teenage sons by his first wife—she'd run off and left him some while before. Mum was a teacher, twenty years younger than him. Very pretty, very shy. The story was he came to do some repair work on the school roof, and they got talking, and one thing led to another, and they got married. He built them a house and the four of them moved in. I came along the following year, which was a shock to him, I think."

"Why?"

"He thought he was through with babies."

"I get the impression, reading what's already been written, that you weren't that close to him."

Lang took his time before answering. "He died when I was sixteen. He'd already retired by then, because of bad health, and my stepbrothers had grown up, married, moved out. And so that was the only time I remember him being around a lot. I was just getting to know him, really, when he had his heart attack. I mean, I got on all right with him. But if you're saying was I closer to my mother—then yes, obviously."

"And your stepbrothers? Were you close to them?"

"God, no!" For the first time since lunch, Lang gave a shout of laughter. "Actually, you'd better scrub that. We can leave them out, can't we?"

"It's your book."

"Leave them out, then. They both went into the building trade, and neither of them ever missed an opportunity to tell the press they wouldn't be voting for me. I haven't seen them for years. They must be about seventy now."

"How exactly did he die?"

"Sorry?"

"Your father. I wondered how he died. Where did he die?"

"Oh. In the garden. Trying to move a paving slab that was too heavy for him. Old habits—" He looked at his watch.

"Who found him?"

"I did."

"Could you describe that?" It was hard going, far harder than the morning session.

"I'd just come home from school. It was a really beautiful spring day, I remember. Mum was out doing something for one of her charities. I got a drink from the kitchen and went out into the back garden, still in my school uniform, thinking I'd kick a ball around or something. And there he was, in the middle of the lawn. Just a graze on his face where he'd fallen. The doctors told us he was probably dead before he hit the ground. But I suspect they always say that, to make it easier for the family. Who knows? It can't be an easy thing, can it—dying?"

"And your mother?"

"Don't all sons think their mothers are saints?" He looked at me for confirmation. "Well, mine was. She gave up teaching when I was born, and there was nothing she wouldn't do for anyone. She came from a very strong Quaker family. Completely selfless. She was so proud when I got into Cambridge, even though it meant she was left alone. She never once let on how ill she was— didn't want to spoil my time there, especially when I started acting and was so busy. That was typical of her. I'd no idea how bad things were until the end of my second year."

"Tell me about that."

"Right." Lang cleared his throat. "God. I knew she hadn't been well, but . . . you know, when you're nineteen, you don't take much notice of anything apart from yourself. I was in Footlights. I had a couple of girlfriends. Cambridge was paradise for me. I used to call her once a week, every Sunday night, and she always sounded fine, even though she was living on her own. Then I got home and she was . . . I was shocked . . . she was . . . a skeleton basically—there was a tumor on her liver. I mean, maybe now they could do something, but then . . ." He made a helpless gesture. "She was dead in a month."

"What did you do?"

"I went back to Cambridge at the start of my final year and I . . . I lost myself in life, I suppose you could say."

He was silent.

"I had a similar experience," I said.

"Really?" His tone was expressionless. He was looking out at the ocean, at the Atlantic breakers rolling in, his thoughts seemingly far away over the horizon.

"Yes." I don't normally talk about myself in a professional situation, or in any situation, for that matter. But sometimes a little self-revelation can help to draw a client out. "I lost my parents at about that age. And didn't you find, in a strange way, despite all the sadness, that it made you stronger?"

"Stronger?" He turned away from the window and frowned at me.

"In the sense of being self-reliant. Knowing that the worst thing that could possibly happen to you had happened, and you'd survived it. That you could function on your own."

"You may be right. I've never really thought about it. At least not until just lately. It's strange. Shall I tell you something?" He leaned forward. "I saw two dead bodies when I was in my teens and then—despite being prime minister, with all that entails: having to order men into battle and visit the scene of bomb blasts and what have you—I didn't see another corpse for thirty-five years."

"And who was that?" I asked stupidly.

"Mike McAra."

"Couldn't you have sent one of the policemen to identify him?"

"No." He shook his head. "No, I couldn't. I owed him that, at least." He paused again, then abruptly grabbed his towel and rubbed his face. "This is a morbid conversation," he declared. "Let's change the subject."

I looked down at my list of questions. There was a lot I wanted to ask him about McAra. It was not that I intended to use it in the book, necessarily; even I recognized that a postresignation trip to the morgue to identify an aide's body was hardly going to sit well in a chapter entitled "A Future of Hope." It was rather to satisfy my own curiosity. But I also knew I didn't have the time to indulge myself; I had to press on. And so I did as he requested and changed the subject.

"Cambridge," I said. "Let's talk about that."

I'd always expected that the Cambridge years, from my point of view, were going to be the easiest part of the book to write. I'd been a student there myself, not long after Lang, and the place hadn't changed much. It never changed much: that was its charm. I could do all the clichés—bikes, scarves, gowns, punts, cakes, gas fires, choirboys, riverside pubs, porters in bowler hats, fenland winds, narrow streets, the thrill of walking on stones once trodden by Newton and Darwin, etc., etc. And it was just as well, I thought, looking at the manuscript, because once again my memories would have to stand in for Lang's. He had gone up to read economics, briefly played football for his college's second eleven, and had won a reputation as a student actor. Yet although McAra had dutifully assembled a list of every production the ex–prime minister had ever appeared in, and even quoted from a few of the revue sketches Lang had performed for Footlights, there was—again—something thin and rushed about it all. What was missing was passion. Naturally, I blamed it on McAra. I could well imagine how little sympathy that stern party functionary would have had with all these dilettantes and their adolescent posturings in bad productions of Brecht and Ionescu. But Lang himself seemed oddly evasive about the whole period.

"It's so long ago," he said. "I can hardly remember anything about it. I wasn't much good, to be honest. Acting was basically an opportunity to meet girls—don't put that in, by the way."

"But you *were* very good," I protested. "When I was in London I read interviews with people who said you were good enough to become a professional."

"I suppose I wouldn't have minded," Lang conceded, "at one stage. Except you don't change things by being an actor. Only politicians can do that." He looked at his watch again.

"But Cambridge," I persisted. "It must have been hugely important in your life, coming from your background."

"Yes. I enjoyed my time there. I met some great people. It wasn't the real world, though. It was fantasyland."

"I know. That was what I liked about it."

"So did I. Just between the two of us: I *loved* it." Lang's eyes gleamed at the memory. "To go out onto a stage and pretend to be someone else! And to have people applaud you for doing it! What could be better?"

"Great," I said, baffled by his change of mood. "This is more like it. Let's put that in."

"No."

"Why not?"

"Why not?" Lang sighed. "Because these are the memoirs of a *prime minister*." He suddenly pounded his hand hard against the side of his chair. "And all my political life, whenever my opponents have been really stuck for something to hit me with, they've always said I was a *fucking actor*." He sprang up and started striding up and down. " 'Oh, Adam Lang,' " he drawled, performing a pitch-perfect caricature of an upper-class Englishman, " 'have you noticed the way he changes his voice to suit whatever company he's in?' 'Aye' "—and now he was a gruff Scotsman—" 'you can't believe anything the wee bastard says. The man's a performer, just piss and wind in a suit!' " And now he became pompous, judicious, hand-wringing: " 'It is Mr. Lang's tragedy that an actor can only be as good as the part he is given, and finally this prime minister has run out of lines.' You'll recognize that last one from your no doubt extensive researches."

I shook my head. I was too astonished by his tirade to speak.

"It's from the editorial in the *Times* on the day I announced my resignation. The headline was 'Kindly Leave the Stage.' " He carefully resumed his seat and smoothed back his hair. "So no, if you don't mind, we won't dwell on my years as a student actor. Leave it exactly the way that Mike wrote it."

For a little while neither of us spoke. I pretended to adjust my notes. Outside, one of the policemen struggled along the top of the dunes, headfirst into the wind, but the soundproofing of the house was so efficient he looked like a mime. I was remembering Ruth Lang's words about her husband: *"There's something not quite right about him at the moment, and I'm a bit afraid to leave him."* Now I could see what she meant. I heard a click and leaned across to check the recorder.

"I need to change disks," I said, grateful for the opportunity to get away. "I'll just take this down to Amelia. I won't be a minute."

Lang was brooding again, staring out of the window. He made a small, slightly dismissive gesture with his hand to signal that I should go. I went downstairs to where the secretaries were typing. Amelia was standing by a filing cabinet. She turned around as I came in. I suppose my face must have given me away.

"What's happened?" she said.

"Nothing." But then I felt an urge to share my unease. "Actually, he seems a bit on edge."

"Really? That's not like him. In what way?"

"He just blew up at me over nothing. I guess it must be too much exercise at lunchtime," I said, trying to make a joke out of it. "Can't be good for a man."

I gave the disk to one of the secretaries—Lucy, I think it was— and picked up the latest transcripts. Amelia carried on looking at me, her head tilted slightly.

"What?" I said.

"You're right. There is something troubling him, isn't there? He took a call just after you finished your session this morning."

"From whom?"

"It came through on his mobile. He didn't tell me. I wonder . . . Alice, darling—do you mind?"

Alice got up and Amelia slipped into position in front of the computer screen. I don't think I ever saw fingers move so rapidly across a keyboard. The clicks seemed to merge into one continuous purr of plastic, like the sound of a million dominoes falling.

The images on the screen changed almost as quickly. And then the clicks slowed to a few staccato taps as Amelia found what she was looking for.

"Shit!"

She tilted the screen toward me, then sat back in her chair in disbelief. I bent to read it.

The web page was headed "Breaking News":

> January 27, 2:57 PM (EST)
>
> NEW YORK (AP)—Former British Foreign Secretary Richard Rycart has asked the International Criminal Court in The Hague to investigate allegations that the former British prime minister Adam Lang ordered the illegal handover of suspects for torture by the CIA.
>
> Mr. Rycart, who was dismissed from the cabinet by Mr. Lang four years ago, is currently United Nations special envoy for humanitarian affairs and an outspoken critic of U.S. foreign policy. Mr. Rycart maintained at the time he left the Lang government that he was sacked for being insufficiently pro-America.
>
> In a statement issued from his office in New York, Mr. Rycart said he had passed a number of documents to the ICC some weeks ago. The documents—details of which were leaked to a British newspaper at the weekend—allegedly show that Mr. Lang, as prime minister, personally authorized the seizure

of four British citizens in Pakistan five years ago.

Mr. Rycart went on: "I have repeatedly asked the British government, in private, to investigate this illegal act. I have offered to give testimony to any inquiry. Yet the government have consistently refused even to acknowledge the existence of Operation Tempest. I therefore feel I have no alternative except to present the evidence in my possession to the ICC."

"The little shit," whispered Amelia.

The telephone on the desk started ringing. Then another on a small table beside the door chimed in. Nobody moved. Lucy and Alice looked at Amelia for instructions, and as they did, Amelia's own mobile, which she had in a little leather pouch on her belt, set up its own electronic warble. For the briefest of moments I saw her panic—it must have been one of the very few occasions in her life when she didn't know what to do—and in the absence of any guidance, Lucy started reaching for the phone on the desk.

"Don't!" shouted Amelia, then added, more calmly: "Leave it. We need to work out a line to take." By now a couple of other phones were trilling away in the recesses of the house. It was like noon in a clock factory. She took out her mobile and examined the incoming number. "The pack is on the move," she said and turned it off. For a few seconds she drummed her fingertips on the desk. "Right. Unplug all the phones," she instructed Alice, with something of her old confidence back in her voice, "then start surfing the main news sites on the web to see if you can discover anything else Rycart is saying. Lucy, find a television and monitor all the news channels." She looked at her watch. "Is Ruth still out walking? Shit! She is, isn't she?"

She grabbed her black-and-red book and clattered off down the corridor on her high heels. Unsure of what I was supposed to do, or even exactly what was happening, I decided I'd better follow her. She was calling for one of the Special Branch men. "Barry! Barry!" He stuck his head out of the kitchen. "Barry, please find Mrs. Lang and get her back here as soon as you can." She started climbing the stairs to the living room.

Once again, Lang was sitting motionless, exactly where I had left him. The only difference was that he had his own small mobile phone in his hand. He snapped it shut as we came in.

"I take it from all the telephone calls that he's issued his statement," he said.

Amelia spread her hands wide in exasperation. "Why didn't you tell me?"

"Tell you before I'd told Ruth? I don't think that would have been very good politics, do you? Besides, I felt like keeping it to myself for a while. Sorry," he said to me, "for losing my temper."

I was touched by his apology. That was grace in adversity, I thought. "Don't worry about it," I said.

"And have you?" asked Amelia. "Told her?"

"I wanted to break it to her face-to-face. Obviously, that's no longer an option, so I just called her."

"And how did she take it?"

"How do you think?"

"The little shit," repeated Amelia.

"She should be back any minute."

Lang got to his feet and stood looking out of the window with his hands on his hips. I smelled again the sharp tang of his sweat. It made me think of an animal at bay. "He wanted very much to let me know there was nothing personal," said Lang, with his back to us. "He wanted very *very* much to tell me that it was only because of his well-known stand on human rights that he felt he couldn't keep quiet any longer." He snorted at his own reflection. "His 'well-known stand on human rights' . . . Dear God."

Amelia said, "Do you think he was taping the call?"

"Who knows? Probably. Probably he's going to broadcast it. Anything's possible with him. I just said, 'Thank you very much, Richard, for letting me know,' and hung up." He turned round, frowning. "It's gone unnervingly quiet down there."

"I've had the phones unplugged. We need to work out what we're going to say."

"What did we say at the weekend?"

"That we hadn't seen what was in the *Sunday Times* and had no plans to comment."

"Well, at least we now know where they got their story." Lang shook his head. His expression was almost admiring. "He really is after me, isn't he? A leak to the press on Sunday, preparing the ground for a statement on Tuesday. Three days of coverage instead of one, building up to a climax. This is straight out of the textbook."

"Your textbook."

Lang acknowledged the compliment with a slight nod and returned his gaze to the window. "Ah," he said. "Here comes trouble."

A small and determined figure in a blue windbreaker was striding down the path from the dunes, moving so rapidly that the policeman behind her had to break into an occasional loping run to keep up. The pointed hood was pulled down low to protect her face, and her chin was pressed to her chest, giving Ruth Lang the appearance of a medieval knight in a polyester visor, heading into battle.

"Adam, we've really got to put out a statement of our own," said Amelia. "If you don't say anything, or if you leave it too long, you'll look—" She hesitated. "Well, they'll draw their own conclusions."

"All right," said Lang. "How about this?" Amelia uncapped a small silver pen and opened her notebook. "Responding to Richard Rycart's statement, Adam Lang made the following remarks: When a policy of offering one hundred percent support to the United States in the global war on terror was popular in the United Kingdom, Mr. Rycart approved of it. When it became unpopular, he disapproved of it. And when, due to his own administrative incompetence, he was asked to leave the Foreign Office, he suddenly developed a passionate interest in upholding the so-called human rights of suspected terrorists. A child of three could see through his infantile tactics in seeking to embarrass his former colleagues.' End point. End paragraph."

Amelia had stopped writing midway through Lang's dictation. She was staring at the former prime minister, and if I didn't know it was impossible, I'd swear the Ice Queen had the beginnings of a tear in one eye. He stared back at her. There was a gentle tap on the open door and Alice came in, holding a sheet of paper.

"Excuse me, Adam," she said. "This just came over AP."

Lang seemed reluctant to break eye contact with Amelia, and I knew then—as surely as I had ever known anything—that their relationship was more than merely professional. After what seemed an embarrassingly long interlude he took the paper from Alice and started to read it. That was when Ruth came into the study. By this time I was starting to feel like a member of an audience who has left his seat in the middle of a play to find a lavatory and somehow wandered onto the stage: the principal actors were pretending I wasn't there, and I knew I ought to leave, but I couldn't think of an exit line.

Lang finished reading and gave the paper to Ruth. "According to the Associated Press," he announced, "sources in The Hague—whoever they may be—say the prosecutor's office of the International Criminal Court will be issuing a statement in the morning."

"Oh, Adam!" cried Amelia. She put her hand to her mouth.

"Why weren't we given some warning of this?" demanded Ruth. "What about Downing Street? Why haven't we heard from the embassy?"

"The phones are disconnected," said Lang. "They're probably trying to get through now."

"Never mind *now*!" shrieked Ruth. "What fucking use is *now*? We needed to know about this a week ago! What are you people doing?" she said, turning her fury on Amelia. "I thought the whole point of *you* was to maintain liaison with the Cabinet Office? You're not telling me they didn't know this was coming?"

"The ICC prosecutor is very scrupulous about not notifying a suspect if he's under investigation," said Amelia. "Or the suspect's government, for that matter. In case they start destroying evidence."

Her words seemed to stun Ruth. It took her a beat to recover. "So that's what Adam is now? A suspect?" She turned to her husband. "You need to talk to Sid Kroll."

"We don't actually know what the ICC are going to say yet," Lang pointed out. "I should talk to London first."

"Adam," said Ruth, addressing him very slowly, as if he had suffered an accident and might be concussed, "if it suits them, they will hang you out to dry. You need a lawyer. Call Sid."

Lang hesitated, then turned to Amelia. "Get Sid on the line."

"And what about the media?"

"I'll issue a holding statement," said Ruth. "Just a sentence or two."

Amelia pulled out her mobile and started scrolling through the address book. "D'you want me to draft something?"

"Why doesn't *he* do it?" said Ruth, pointing at me. "He's supposed to be the writer."

"Fine," said Amelia, not quite concealing her irritation, "but it needs to go out immediately."

"Hang on a minute," I said.

"I should sound confident," Lang said to me, "certainly not defensive—that would be fatal. But I shouldn't be cocky, either. No bitterness. No anger. But don't say I'm pleased at this opportunity to clear my name, or any balls like that."

"So," I said, "you're not defensive but you're not cocky, you're not angry but you're not pleased?"

"That's it."

"Then what exactly are you?"

Surprisingly, under the circumstances, everybody laughed.

"I told you he was funny," said Ruth.

Amelia abruptly held up her hand and waved us to be quiet. "I have Adam Lang for Sidney Kroll," she said. "No, I won't hold."

I WENT DOWNSTAIRS WITH Alice and stood behind her shoulder while she sat at a keyboard, patiently waiting for the ex–prime minister's words to flow from my mouth. It wasn't until I started contemplating what Lang should say that I realized I hadn't asked him the crucial question: had he actually ordered the seizure of those four men? That was when I knew that of course he must have done, otherwise he'd simply have denied it outright at the weekend, when the original story broke. Not for the first time, I felt seriously out of my depth.

"I have always been a passionate—" I began. "No, scrub that. I have always been a strong—no, *committed*—supporter of the work of the International Criminal Court." Had he been? I'd no idea. I assumed he had. Or, rather, I assumed he'd always pretended he had. "I have no doubt that the ICC will quickly see through this politically motivated piece of mischief making." I paused. I felt it needed one more line, something broadening and statesmanlike. What would I say if I were him? "The international struggle against terror," I said, in a sudden burst of inspiration, "is too important to be used for the purposes of personal revenge."

Lucy printed it, and when I took it back up to the study I felt a curious bashful pride, like a schoolboy handing in his homework. I pretended not to see Amelia's outstretched hand and showed it first to Ruth (at last I was learning the etiquette of this exile's court). She nodded her approval and slid it across the desk to Lang, who was listening on the telephone. He glanced at it silently, beckoned for my pen, and inserted a single word. He tossed the statement back to me and gave me the thumbs-up.

Into the telephone he said, "That's great, Sid. And what do we know about these three judges?"

"Am I allowed to see it?" said Amelia, as we went downstairs.

Handing it over, I noticed that Lang had added "domestic" to the final sentence: "The international struggle against terror is too important to be used for the purposes of *domestic* personal revenge." The brutal antithesis of "international" and "domestic" made Rycart appear even more petty.

"Very good," said Amelia. "You could be the new Mike McAra."

I gave her a look. I think she meant it as a compliment. It was always hard to tell with her. Not that I cared. For the first time in my life I was experiencing the adrenaline of politics. Now I saw why Lang was so restless in retirement. I guessed this was how sport must feel, when played at its hardest and fastest. It was like tennis on Centre Court at Wimbledon. Rycart had fired his serve low across the net, and we had lunged for it, got our racket to it, and shot the ball right back at him, with added spin. One by one the telephones were reconnected and immediately began ringing, demanding attention, and I heard the secretaries feeding my words to the hungry reporters: *I have always been a committed supporter of the work of the International Criminal Court.* I watched my sentences emailed to the news agencies. And within a couple of minutes, on the computer screen and on television, I started seeing and hearing them all over again ("In a statement issued in the last few minutes, the former prime minister says . . ."). The world had become our echo chamber.

In the middle of all this, my own phone rang. I jammed the receiver to one ear and had to put my finger in the other to hear who was calling. A faint voice said, "Can you hear me?"

"Who is this?"

"It's John Maddox, from Rhinehart in New York. Where the hell are you? Sounds like you're in a madhouse."

"You're not the first to call it that. Hold on, John. I'll try to find somewhere quieter." I walked out into the passage and kept following it round to the back of the house. "Is that better?"

"I've just heard the news," said Maddox. "This can only be good for us. We should start with this."

"What?" I was still walking.

"This war crimes stuff. Have you asked him about it?"

"Haven't had much chance, John, to be honest." I tried not to sound too sarcastic. "He's a little tied up right now."

"Okay, so what've you covered so far?"

"The early years—childhood, university—"

"No, no," said Maddox impatiently. "Forget all that crap. *This* is what's interesting. Get him to focus on this. And he mustn't talk to anyone else about it. We need to keep this absolutely exclusive to the memoirs."

I'd ended up in the solarium, where I'd spoken to Rick at lunchtime. Even with the door closed I could still hear the faint noise of the telephones ringing on the other side of the house. The notion that Lang would be able to avoid saying anything about illegal kidnapping and torture until the book came out was a joke. Naturally I didn't put it in quite those terms to the chief executive of the third largest publishing house in the world. "I'll tell him, John," I said. "It might be worth your while talking to Sidney Kroll. Perhaps Adam could say that his lawyers have instructed him not to talk."

"Good idea. I'll call Sid now. In the meantime, I want you to accelerate the timetable."

"Accelerate?" In the empty room my voice sounded thin and hollow.

"Sure. Accelerate. As in speed things up. Right at this moment, Lang is hot. People are starting to get interested in him again. We can't afford to let this opportunity slip."

"Are you now saying you want the book in *less* than a month?"

"I know it's tough. And it'll probably mean settling for just a polish on a lot of the manuscript rather than a total rewrite. But what the hell. No one's going to read most of that stuff anyway. The earlier we go, the more we'll sell. Think you can do it?"

No, was the answer. No, you bald-headed bastard, you psychopathic prick—have you seriously read this junk? You must be out of your fucking mind. "Well, John," I said mildly, "I can try."

"Good man. And don't worry about your own deal. We'll pay you just as much for two weeks' work as we would for four. I tell you, if this war crimes thing comes off, it could be the answer to our prayers."

By the time he hung up, two weeks had somehow ceased to be a figure plucked at random from the air and had become a firm deadline. I would no longer conduct forty hours of interviews with Lang, ranging over his whole life. I would get him to focus specifically on the war on terror, and we would begin the memoir with that. The rest I would do my best to improve, rewriting where I could.

"What if Adam isn't keen on this?" I asked, in what proved to be our final exchange.

"He will be," said Maddox. "And if he isn't, then you can just remind *Adam*"—his tone implied we were just a pair of faggoty Englishmen—"of his contractual obligation to produce a book that gives us a full and frank account of the war on terror. I'm relying on you. Okay?"

It's a melancholy place to be, a solarium when there's no sun.

I could see the gardener in exactly the same spot where he had been working the day before, stiff and clumsy in his thick outdoor clothes, still piling leaves in his wheelbarrow. No sooner had he cleared away one lot of detritus than the wind blew in more. I permitted myself a brief moment of despair, leaning against the wall, my head tilted to the ceiling, pondering the fleeting nature of summer days and of human happiness. I tried to call Rick, but his assistant said he was out for the afternoon, so I left a message asking him to ring me back. Then I went in search of Amelia.

She wasn't in the office, where the secretaries were still fielding calls, or the passage, or the kitchen. To my surprise, one of the policemen told me she was outside. It must have been after four by now and getting cold. She was standing in the turning circle in front of the house. In the January gloom, the tip of her cigarette glowed bright red as she inhaled, then faded to nothing.

"I wouldn't have guessed you were a smoker," I said.

"I only ever allow myself one. And then only at times of great stress or great contentment."

"Which is this?"

"Very funny."

She had buttoned her jacket against the chilly dusk and was smoking in that curious noli me tangere way that a certain kind of woman does, with one arm held loosely against her waist and the other—the one with the hand holding the cigarette—slanted across her breast. The fragrant smell of the burning tobacco in the open air made me crave a cigarette myself. It would have been my first in more than a decade, and it would have started me back on forty a day for sure, but still, at that moment, if she'd offered me one, I would have taken it.

She didn't.

"John Maddox just called," I said. "Now he wants the book in two weeks instead of four."

"Christ. Good luck."

"I don't suppose there's the faintest chance of my sitting down with Adam for another interview today, is there?"

"What do you think?"

"In that case, could I have a lift back to my hotel? I'll do some work there instead."

She exhaled smoke through her nose and scrutinized me. "You're not planning to take that manuscript out of here, are you?"

"Of course not!" My voice always rises an octave when I tell a lie. I could never have become a politician: I'd have sounded like Donald Duck. "I just want to write up what we did today, that's all."

"Because you do realize how serious this is getting, don't you?"

"Of course. You can check my laptop if you want."

She paused just long enough to convey her suspicion. "All right," she said, finishing her cigarette. "I'll trust you." She dropped the stub and extinguished it delicately with the pointed toe of her shoe, then stooped and retrieved it. I imagined her at school, similarly removing the evidence: the head girl who was never caught smoking. "Collect your stuff. I'll get one of the boys to take you into Edgartown."

We walked back into the house and parted in the corridor. She headed back to the ringing telephones. I climbed the stairs to the study, and as I came closer, I could hear Ruth and Adam Lang shouting at one another. Their voices were muffled, and the only words I heard distinctly came at the tail end of her final rant:

". . . spending the rest of my bloody life here!" The door was ajar. I hesitated. I didn't want to interrupt, but on the other hand I didn't want to hang around and be caught looking as if I were eavesdropping. In the end I knocked lightly, and after a pause I heard Lang say wearily, "Come."

He was sitting at the desk. His wife was at the other end of the room. They were both breathing heavily, and I sensed that something momentous—some long-pent-up explosion—had just occurred. I could understand now why Amelia had fled outside to smoke.

"Sorry to interrupt," I said, gesturing toward my belongings. "I wanted to—"

"Fine," said Lang.

"I'm going to call the children," said Ruth bitterly. "Unless of course you've already done it?"

Lang didn't look at her; he looked at me. And, oh, what layers of meaning there were to be read in those glaucous eyes! He invited me, in that long instant, to see what had become of him: stripped of his power, abused by his enemies, hunted, homesick, trapped between his wife and mistress. You could write a hundred pages about that one brief look and still not get to the end of it.

"Excuse me," said Ruth and pushed past me quite roughly, her small, hard body banging into mine. At the same moment, Amelia appeared in the doorway, holding a telephone.

"Adam," she said, "it's the White House. They have the president of the United States on the line for you." She smiled at me and ushered me toward the door. "Would you mind? We need the room."

IT WAS PRETTY WELL dark by the time I got back to the hotel. There was just enough light in the sky to show up the big, black storm clouds massing over Chappaquiddick, rolling in from the Atlantic. The girl in reception, in her little lace mobcap, said there was a run of bad weather on the way.

I went up to my room and stood in the shadows for a while, listening to the creaking of the old inn sign and the relentless *boom-hiss, boom-hiss* of the surf beyond the empty road. The lighthouse switched itself on at the precise moment when the beam was pointing directly at the hotel, and the sudden eruption of red into the room jerked me out of my reverie. I turned on the desk lamp and took my laptop out of my shoulder bag. We had traveled a long way together, that laptop and I. We had endured rock stars who believed themselves messiahs with a mission to save the planet. We had survived footballers whose monosyllabic grunts would make a silverback gorilla sound as if he were reciting Shakespeare. We had put up with soon-to-be-forgotten actors who had egos the size of a Roman emperor's, and entourages to match. I gave the machine a comradely pat. Its once shiny metal case was scratched and dented: the honorable wounds of a dozen campaigns. We had got through those. We would somehow get through even this.

I hooked it up to the hotel telephone, dialed my internet service provider, and, while the connection was going through, went into the bathroom for a glass of water. The face that stared back at me from the mirror was a deterioration even on the specter of the previous evening. I pulled down my lower eyelids and examined the yolky whites of my eyes, before moving on to the graying teeth and hair, and the red filigrees of my cheeks and nose. Martha's Vineyard in midwinter seemed to be aging me. It was Shangri-La in reverse.

From the other room I heard the familiar announcement: "You have email."

I saw at once that something was wrong. There was the usual queue of a dozen junk messages, offering me everything from penis enlargement to the *Wall Street Journal*, plus an email from Rick's office confirming the payment of the first part of the advance. Just about the only thing that wasn't listed was the email I had sent myself that afternoon.

For a few moments, I stared stupidly at the screen, then I opened the separate filing cabinet on the laptop's hard drive that automatically stores every piece of email, incoming and outgoing. And there, sure enough, to my immense relief, at the top of the "Email you have sent" queue was one titled "no subject," to which I had attached the manuscript of Adam Lang's memoirs. But when I opened the blank email and clicked on the box labeled "download," all I received was a message saying, "That file is not currently available." I tried a few more times, always with the same result.

I took out my mobile and called the internet company.

I shall spare you a full account of the sweaty half hour that followed—the endless selecting from lists of options, the queuing, the listening to Muzak, the increasingly panicky conversation with the company's representative in Uttar Pradesh or wherever the hell he was speaking from.

The bottom line was that the manuscript had vanished, and the company had no record of its ever having existed.

I lay down on the bed.

I am not very technically minded, but even I was beginning to grasp what must have happened. Somehow, Lang's manuscript had been wiped from the memory of my internet service

provider's computers, for which there were two possible explana-
tions. One was that it hadn't been uploaded properly in the first
place, but that couldn't be right, because I had received those two
messages while I was still in the office: "Your file has been transferred" and "You have email." The other was that the file had since
been deleted. But how could that have happened? Deletion would
imply that someone had direct access to the computers of one of
the world's biggest internet conglomerates and was able to cover
his tracks at will. It would also imply—had to imply—that my
emails were all being monitored.

Rick's voice floated into my mind—*"Wow. This must've been
some operation. Too big for a newspaper. This must've been a* government"—followed swiftly by Amelia's—*"You do realize how serious
this is getting, don't you?"*

"But the book is crap!" I cried out loud, despairingly, at the
portrait of the Victorian whaling master hanging opposite the bed.
"There's nothing in it that's worth all this trouble!"

The stern old Victorian sea dog stared back at me, unmoved.
I had broken my promise, his expression seemed to say, and something out there—some nameless force—knew it.

EIGHT

★

Authors are often busy people and hard to get hold of;
sometimes they are temperamental. The publishers
consequently rely on the ghosts to make the process of
publication as smooth as possible.

Ghostwriting

THERE WAS NO QUESTION of my doing any more work that
night. I didn't even turn on the television. Oblivion was all I
craved. I switched off my mobile, went down to the bar, and,
when that closed, sat up in my room emptying a bottle of scotch
until long past midnight, which no doubt explains why for once I
slept right through the night.

I was woken by the bedside telephone. The harsh metallic tone
seemed to vibrate my eyeballs in their dusty sockets, and when I
rolled over to answer it I felt my stomach keep on rolling, wobbling away from me across the mattress and onto the floor like a

taut balloon full of some noxious, viscous liquid. The revolving room was very hot; the air-conditioning turned up to maximum. I realized I'd gone to sleep fully dressed and had left all the lights burning.

"You need to check out of your hotel immediately," said Amelia. "Things have changed." Her voice pierced my skull like a knitting needle. "There's a car on its way."

That was all she said. I didn't argue; I couldn't. She'd gone.

I once read that the ancient Egyptians used to prepare a pharaoh for mummification by drawing his brain out through his nose with a hook. At some point in the night a similar procedure had seemingly been performed on me. I shuffled across the carpet and pulled back the curtains to unveil a sky and sea as gray as death. Nothing was stirring. The silence was absolute, unbroken even by the cry of a gull. A storm was coming in all right; even I could tell that.

But then, just as I was about to turn away, I heard the distant sound of an engine. I squinted down at the street beneath my window and saw a couple of cars pull up. The doors of the first opened and two men got out—young, fit looking, wearing ski jackets, jeans, and boots. The driver stared up at my window and instinctively I took a step backward. By the time I risked a second look, he had opened the rear of the car and was bent over it. When he straightened he took out what at first, in my paranoid state, I took to be a machine gun. Actually it was a television camera.

I started to move quickly then, or at least as quickly as my condition would allow. I opened the window wide to let in a blast of freezing air. I undressed, showered in lukewarm water, and shaved. I put on clean clothes and packed. By the time I got down to reception it was eight forty-five—an hour after the first ferry from the mainland had docked at Vineyard Haven—and the hotel looked as though it was staging an international media convention. Whatever you might say against Adam Lang, he was certainly doing wonders for the local economy: Edgartown hadn't been this busy since Chappaquiddick. There must have been thirty people hanging around, drinking coffee, swapping stories in half a dozen languages, talking on their mobiles, checking equipment. I'd spent enough time around reporters to be able to tell one type from another. The television correspondents were dressed as though they were going to a funeral; the news agency hacks were the ones who looked like gravediggers.

I bought a copy of the *New York Times* and went into the restaurant, where I drank three glasses of orange juice straight off, before turning my attention to the paper. Lang wasn't buried in the international section any longer. He was right up there on the front page:

WAR CRIMES COURT
TO RULE ON BRITISH
EX-PM

~

ANNOUNCEMENT
DUE TODAY

~

Former Foreign Sec.
Alleges Lang OK'd
Use of Torture by CIA

Lang had issued a "robust" statement, it said (I felt a thrill of pride). He was "embattled," "coping with one blow after another"—beginning with "the accidental drowning of a close aide earlier in the year." The affair was "an embarrassment" for the British and American governments. "A senior administration official" insisted, however, that the White House remained loyal to a man who was formerly its closest ally. "He was there for us and we'll be there for him," the official added, speaking only after a guarantee of anonymity.

But it was the final paragraph that really made me choke into my coffee:

> The publication of Mr. Lang's memoirs, which had been scheduled for June, has been brought forward to the end of April. John Maddox, chief executive of Rhinehart Publishing Inc., which is reported to have paid $10 million for the book, said that the finishing touches were now being put to the manuscript. "This is going to be a world publishing event," Mr. Maddox told *The New York Times* in a telephone interview yesterday. "Adam Lang will be giving the first full inside scoop by a leader on the West's war on terror."

I rose, folded the newspaper, and walked with dignity through the lobby, carefully stepping around the camera bags, the two-foot zoom lenses, and the handheld mikes in their woolly gray windproof prophylactics. Between the members of the fourth estate, a cheerful, almost a party atmosphere prevailed, as might have existed among eighteenth-century gentlefolk off for a good day out at a hanging.

"The newsroom says the press conference in The Hague is now at ten o'clock Eastern," someone shouted.

I passed unnoticed and went out onto the veranda, where I put a call through to my agent. His assistant answered—Brad, or Brett, or Brat: I forget his name; Rick changed his staff almost as quickly as he changed his wives.

I asked to speak to Mr. Ricardelli.

"He's away from the office right now."

"Where is he?"

"On a fishing trip."

"Fishing?"

"He'll be calling in occasionally to check his messages."

"That's nice. Where is he?"

"The Bouma National Heritage Rainforest Park."

"Christ. Where's that?"

"It was a spur-of-the-moment thing—"

"Where is it?"

Brad, or Brett, or Brat, hesitated. "Fiji."

THE MINIVAN TOOK ME up the hill out of Edgartown, past the bookshop and the little cinema and the whaling church. When we reached the edge of town, we followed the signs left to West Tisbury rather than right to Vineyard Haven, which at least implied that I was being taken back to the house, rather than straight to the ferry to be deported for breaching the Official Secrets Act. I sat behind the police driver, my suitcase on the seat beside me. He was one of the younger ones, dressed in their standard nonuniform uniform of gray zippered jacket and black tie. His eyes sought mine in the mirror and he observed that it was all a very bad business. I replied briefly that it was, indeed, a bad business, and then pointedly stared out of the window to avoid having to talk.

We were quickly into the flat countryside. A deserted cycle track ran beside the road. Beyond it stretched the drab forest. My frail body might be on Martha's Vineyard but my mind was in the South Pacific. I was thinking of Rick in Fiji and all the elaborate and humiliating ways I could fire him when he got back. The rational part of me knew I would never do it—why shouldn't he go fishing?—but the irrational was to the fore that morning. I suppose I was afraid, and fear distorts one's judgment even more than alcohol and exhaustion. I felt duped, abandoned, aggrieved.

"After I've dropped you off, sir," said the policeman, undeterred by my silence, "I've got to pick up Mr. Kroll from the airport. You can always tell it's a bad business when the lawyers start turning up." He broke off and leaned in close to the windscreen. "Oh, fuck, here we go again."

Up ahead it looked as though there had been a traffic accident. The vivid blue lights of a couple of patrol cars flashed dramatically in the gloomy morning, illuminating the nearby trees like sheet lightning in a Wagner opera. As we came closer I could see a dozen or more cars and vans pulled up on either side of the road. People were standing around aimlessly, and I assumed, in that lazy way the brain sometimes assembles information, that they had been in a pileup. But as the minivan slowed and indicated to turn left, the bystanders started grabbing things from beside the road and came running at us. "Lang! Lang! Lang!" a woman shouted over a bullhorn. "Liar! Liar! Liar!" Images of Lang in an orange jumpsuit, gripping prison bars with bloodied hands, danced in front of the windscreen. "WANTED! WAR CRIMINAL! ADAM LANG!"

The Edgartown police had blocked the track down to the Rhinehart compound with traffic cones and quickly pulled them out of the way to let us through, but not before we'd come to a stop. Demonstrators surrounded us, and a fusillade of thumps and kicks raked the side of the van. I glimpsed a brilliant arc of white light illuminating a figure—a man, cowled like a monk. He turned away from his interviewer to stare at us, and I recognized him dimly from somewhere. But then he vanished behind a gauntlet of contorted faces, pounding hands, and dripping spit.

"They're always the really violent bastards," said my driver, "peace protesters." He put his foot down, the rear tires slithered uselessly, then bit, and we shot forward into the silent woods.

AMELIA MET ME IN the passage. She stared contemptuously at my single piece of luggage as only a woman could.

"Is that really everything?"

"I travel light."

"Light? I'd say *gossamer*." She sighed. "Right. Follow me."

My suitcase was one of those ubiquitous pull-alongs, with an extendable handle and small wheels. It made an industrious hum on the stone floor as I trailed after her down the passage and around to the back of the house.

"I tried to call you several times last night," she said without turning round, "but you didn't answer."

Here it comes, I thought.

"I forgot to charge my mobile."

"Oh? What about the phone in your room? I tried that as well."

"I went out."

"Until midnight?"

I winced behind her back. "What did you want to tell me?"

"This."

She stopped outside a door, opened it, and stood aside to let me go in. The room was in darkness, but the heavy curtains didn't quite meet in the middle, and there was just enough light for me to make out the shape of a double bed. It smelled of stale clothes and old ladies' soap. She crossed the floor and briskly pulled back the curtains.

"You'll be sleeping in here from now on."

It was a plain room, with sliding glass doors that opened directly onto the lawn. Apart from the bed, there was a desk with a gooseneck lamp, an armchair covered in something beige and thickly woven, and a wall-length closet with mirrored doors. I could also see into a white-tiled en suite bathroom. It was neat and functional, and dismal.

I tried to make a joke of it. "So this is where you put the granny, is it?"

"No, this is where we put Mike McAra."

She slid back one of the doors to the closet, revealing a few jackets and shirts on hangers. "I'm afraid we haven't had a chance to clear it yet, and his mother's in a home for the elderly so she doesn't have the space to store it. But as you say yourself, you travel light. And besides, it will only be for a few days, now that publication has been brought forward."

I've never been particularly superstitious, but I do believe that certain places have an atmosphere, and from the moment I stepped into that room, I didn't like it. The thought of touching McAra's clothes filled me with something close to panic.

"I always make it a rule not to sleep in a client's house," I said, attempting to keep my voice light and offhand. "I often find, at the end of a working day, it's vital to get away."

"But now you can have constant access to the manuscript. Isn't that what you want?" She gave me her smile, and for once there was genuine merriment in it. She had me exactly where she wanted me, literally and figuratively. "Besides, you can't keep running the media gauntlet. Sooner or later they'll discover who you are, and then they'll start pestering you with questions. That would be horrid for you. This way you can work in peace."

"Isn't there another room I could use?"

"There are only six bedrooms in the main house. Adam and Ruth have one each. I have one. The girls share. The duty policemen have the use of one for the overnight shift. And the guest block is entirely taken over by Special Branch. Don't be squeamish: the sheets have been changed." She consulted her elegant gold watch. "Look, Sidney Kroll will be arriving any minute. We're due to get the ICC announcement in less than thirty minutes. Why don't you settle in here and then come up and join us. Whatever's decided will affect you. You're practically one of us now."

"I am?"

"Of course. You drafted the statement yesterday. That makes you an accomplice."

After she'd gone, I didn't unpack. I couldn't face it. Instead I sat gingerly on the end of the bed and stared out of the window at the wind-blasted lawn, the low scrub, and the immense sky. A small blaze of brilliant white light was traveling quickly across the gray expanse, swelling as it came closer. A helicopter. It passed low overhead, shaking the heavy glass doors, and then, a minute or two later, reappeared, hovering a mile away, just above the horizon, like a sinister and portentous comet. It was a sign of how serious things had become, I thought, if some hard-pressed news manager on a trimmed budget was willing to hire a chopper in the hope of catching a fleeting shot of the former British prime minister. I pictured Kate, smugly watching the live coverage in her office in London, and was seized by a fantastic desire to run out and start twirling, like Julie Andrews at the start of *The Sound of Music*: Yes, darling, it's me! I'm here with the war criminal! I'm an *accomplice*!

I sat there for a while, until I heard the noise of the minivan pulling up to the front of the house, followed by a commotion of voices in the hall, and then a small army of footsteps thudding up the wooden staircase: I reckoned that must be the sound of a thousand dollars an hour in legal fees on the hoof. I gave Kroll and his client a couple of minutes for handshakes, condolences, and general expressions of confidence, then wearily left my dead man's room and went up to join them.

KROLL HAD FLOWN IN by private jet from Washington with two young paralegals: an exquisitely pretty Mexican woman he introduced as Encarnacion and a black guy from New York called Josh. They sat on either side of him, their laptops open, on a sofa that placed their backs to the ocean view. Adam and Ruth Lang had the couch opposite, Amelia and I an armchair each. A cinema-size flat-screen TV next to the fireplace was showing the aerial shot of the house, as relayed live from the helicopter we could hear buzzing faintly outside. Occasionally

waiting journalists in the large cha

where the press conference was

the empty podium with its ICC lo

boughs and scales of justice—I felt a littl

But Lang himself seemed cool. He was jacketless,

shirt and a dark blue tie. It was the sort of high-pressure

his metabolism was built for.

"So here's the score," said Kroll, when we'd all taken our places. "You're not being charged. You're not being arrested. None of this is going to amount to a hill of beans, I promise you. All that the prosecutor is asking for right now is permission to launch a formal investigation. Okay? So when we go out of here, you walk tall, you look cool, and you have peace in your heart, because it's all going to be fine."

"The president told me he thought they might not even let her investigate," said Lang.

"I always hesitate to contradict the leader of the free world," said Kroll, "but the general feeling in Washington this morning is they'll have to. Our Madam Prosecutor is quite a savvy operator, it seems. The British government has consistently refused to hold an investigation of its own into Operation Tempest, which gives her a legal pretext to look into it herself. And by leaking her case just before going into the Pre-Trial Chamber, she's put a lot of pressure on those three judges to at least give her permission to move to the investigation stage. If they tell her to drop it, they know damn well that everyone will just say they're scared to go after a major power."

"That's crude smear tactics," said Ruth. She was wearing black leggings and another of her shapeless tops. Her shoeless feet were

...eath her on the sofa; her back was turned to her hus-

...ng shrugged. "It's politics."

"Exactly my point," said Kroll. "Treat it as a political problem,
...t a legal one."

Ruth said, "We need to get out our version of what happened.
Refusing to comment isn't enough anymore."

I saw my chance. "John Maddox—" I began.

"Yeah," said Kroll, cutting me off, "I talked to John, and he's
right. We really have to go for this whole story now in the memoirs. It's the perfect platform for you to respond, Adam. They're
very excited."

"Fine," said Lang.

"As soon as possible you need to sit down with our friend
here"—I realized Kroll had forgotten my name—"and go over the
whole thing in detail. But you'll need to make sure it's all cleared
with me first. The test we have to apply is to imagine what every
word might sound like if it's read out while you're standing in the
dock."

"Why?" said Ruth. "I thought you said none of this was going
to amount to anything."

"It won't," said Kroll smoothly, "especially if we're careful not
to give them any extra ammunition."

"This way we get to present it the way we want," said Lang.
"And whenever I'm asked about it, I can refer people to the account
in my memoirs. Who knows? It might even help sell a few copies."
He looked around. We all smiled. "Okay," he said, "to come back
to today. What am I actually likely to be investigated for?"

Kroll gestured to Encarnacion.

"Either crimes against humanity," she said carefully, "or war crimes."

There was a silence. Odd the effect such words can have. Perhaps it was the fact that it was she who had said them: she looked so innocent. We stopped smiling.

"Unbelievable," said Ruth eventually, "to equate what Adam did or didn't do with the Nazis."

"That's precisely why the United States doesn't recognize the court," said Kroll. He wagged his finger. "We warned you what would happen. An international war crimes tribunal sounds very noble in principle. But you go after all these genocidal maniacs in the third world, and sooner or later the third world is going to come right back after you; otherwise it looks like discrimination. They kill three thousand of us, we kill one of them, and suddenly we're all war criminals together. It's the worst kind of moral equivalence. Well, they can't drag America into their phony court, so who can they drag? It's obvious: our closest ally—you. Like I say, it's not legal, it's political."

"You should make exactly that point, Adam," said Amelia, and she wrote something in her black-and-red notebook.

"Don't worry," he said grimly, "I will."

"Go ahead, Connie," said Kroll. "Let's hear the rest of it."

"The reason we can't be sure which route they'll choose at this stage is that torture is outlawed both by Article Seven of the 1998 Rome Statute, under the heading of 'Crimes against humanity,' and also under Article Eight, which is 'War crimes.' Article Eight also categorizes as a war crime"—she consulted her laptop—"'wilfully depriving a prisoner of war or other protected person of the rights of fair and regular trial' and 'unlawful deportation or transfer or unlawful confinement.' Prima facie, sir, you could be accused under either Seven or Eight."

"But I haven't ordered that anyone should be tortured!" said Lang. His voice was incredulous, outraged. "And I haven't deprived anyone of a fair trial, or illegally imprisoned them. Perhaps—*perhaps*—you could make that charge against the United States, but not Great Britain."

"That's true, sir," agreed Encarnacion. "However, Article Twenty-five, which deals with individual criminal responsibility, states that"—and once again her cool dark eyes flickered to the computer screen—"'a person shall be criminally responsible and liable for punishment if that person facilitates the commission of such a crime, aids, abets, or otherwise assists in its commission or its attempted commission, including the means for its commission.' "

Again there was a silence, filled by the distant drone of the helicopter.

"That's rather sweeping," said Lang quietly.

"It's absurd, is what it is," cut in Kroll. "It means that if the CIA flies a suspect for interrogation somewhere in a private plane, the owners of that private plane are technically guilty of facilitating a crime against humanity."

"But legally—" began Lang.

"It's not legal, Adam," said Kroll, with just a hint of exasperation, "it's political."

"No, Sid," said Ruth. She was concentrating hard, frowning at the carpet and shaking her head emphatically. "It's legal as well. The two are inseparable. That passage your young lady just read out makes it perfectly obvious why the judges will have to allow an investigation, because Richard Rycart has produced documentary evidence that suggests that Adam did in fact do all those things: aided, abetted, and facilitated." She looked up. "That is legal jeopardy—isn't that what you call it? And that leads inescapably to political jeopardy. Because in the end it will all come down to public opinion, and we're unpopular enough back home as it is without this."

"Well, if it's any comfort, Adam's certainly not in jeopardy as long as he stays here, among his friends."

The armored glass vibrated slightly. The helicopter was coming in again for a closer look. Its searchlight filled the room. But on the television screen all that could be seen in the big picture window was a reflection of the sea.

"Wait a minute," said Lang, raising his hand to his head and clutching his hair, as if he were glimpsing the situation for the first time. "Are you saying that I can't leave the United States?"

"Josh," said Kroll, nodding to his other assistant.

"Sir," said Josh gravely, "if I may, I would like just to read you the opening of Article Fifty-eight, which covers arrest warrants. 'At any time after the initiation of an investigation, the Pre-Trial Chamber shall, on the application of the Prosecutor, issue a warrant of arrest of a person if, having examined the application and the evidence or other information submitted by the Prosecutor, it is satisfied that there are reasonable grounds to believe that the person has committed a crime within the jurisdiction of the Court, and the arrest of the person appears necessary to ensure the person's appearance at trial.' " He fixed his solemn gaze on Adam Lang.

"Jesus," said Lang. "What are 'reasonable grounds'?"

"It won't happen," said Kroll.

"You keep saying that," said Ruth irritably, "but it could."

"It won't but it could," said Kroll, spreading his hands. "Those two statements aren't incompatible." He permitted himself one of his private smiles and turned to Adam. "Nevertheless, as your attorney, until this whole thing is resolved, I do strongly advise you not to travel to any country that recognizes the jurisdiction of the International Criminal Court. All it would take is for two of these three judges to decide to grandstand to the human rights crowd, go ahead and issue a warrant, and you could be picked up."

"But just about every country in the world recognizes the ICC," said Lang.

"America doesn't."

"And who else?"

"Iraq," said Josh, "China, North Korea, Indonesia."

We waited for him to go on; he didn't.

"And that's *it*?" said Lang. "Everywhere else *does*?"

"No, sir. Israel doesn't. And some of the nastier regimes in Africa."

Amelia said, "I think something's happening." She aimed the remote at the television.

AND SO WE WATCHED as the Spanish chief prosecutor—all massive black hair and bright red lipstick, as glamorous as a film star in the silvery strobe of camera flashes—announced that she had that morning been granted the power to investigate the former British prime minister, Adam Peter Benet Lang, under Articles Seven and Eight of the 1998 Rome Statute of the International Criminal Court.

Or rather, the others all watched her, while I watched Lang. *"AL—intense concentration,"* I jotted in my notebook, pretending to take down the words of the chief prosecutor but really studying my client for any insights I could use later. "*Reaches hand out for R: she doesn't respond. Glances at her. Lonely, puzzled. Withdraws hand. Looks back at screen. Shakes head. CP says 'was this just single incident or part of systematic pattern of criminal behavior?' AL flinches. Angry. CP: 'justice must be equal for rich & poor, powerful & weak alike.' AL shouts at screen: 'What about the terrorists?'*"

I had never witnessed any of my authors at a real crisis in their lives before, and scrutinizing Lang, I gradually began to realize that my favorite catchall question—"How did it feel?"—was in truth a crude tool, vague to the point of uselessness. In the course of those few minutes, as the legal procedure was explained, a rapid succession of emotions swept across Lang's craggy face, as fleeting as cloud shadows passing over a hillside in spring—shock, fury, hurt, defiance, dismay, shame . . . How were these to be disentangled? And if he didn't know precisely what he felt now, even as he was feeling it, how could he be expected to know it in ten years' time? Even his reaction at this moment I would have to manufacture for him. I would have to simplify it to make it plausible. I would have to draw on my own imagination. In a sense, I would have to lie.

The chief prosecutor finished her statement, briefly answered a couple of shouted questions, then left the podium. Halfway out of the room, she stopped to pose for the cameras again, and there was another blizzard of phosphorus as she turned to give the world the benefit of her magnificent aquiline profile, and then she was gone. The screen reverted to the aerial shot of Rhinehart's house, in its setting of woods, pond, and ocean, as the world waited for Lang to appear.

Amelia muted the sound. Downstairs, the phones started ringing.

"Well," said Kroll, breaking the silence, "there was nothing in *that* we weren't expecting."

"Yes," said Ruth. *"Well done."*

Kroll pretended not to notice. "We should get you to Washington, Adam, right away. My plane's waiting at the airport."

Lang was still staring at the screen. "When Marty said I could use his vacation house, I never realized how cut off this place was. We should never have come. Now we look as though we're hiding."

"Exactly my feeling. You can't just hole up here, at least not today. I've made some calls. I can get you in to see the House majority leader at lunchtime and we can have a photo op with the secretary of state this afternoon."

Lang finally dragged his eyes away from the television. "I don't know about doing all that. It could look as though I'm panicking."

"No, it won't. I've already spoken to them. They send their best wishes; they want to do everything they can to help. They'll both say the meetings were fixed weeks ago, to discuss the Adam Lang Foundation."

"But that sounds false, don't you think?" Lang frowned. "What are we supposed to be discussing?"

"Who cares? AIDS. Poverty. Climate change. Mideast peace. Africa. Whatever you like. The point is to say: it's business as usual, I have my agenda, it's the big stuff, and I'm not going to be diverted from it by these clowns pretending to be judges in The Hague."

Amelia said, "What about security?"

"The Secret Service will take care of it. We'll fill in the blanks in the schedule as we go along. The whole town will turn out for you. I'm waiting to hear back from the vice president, but that would be a private meeting."

"And the media?" said Lang. "We'll need to respond soon."

"On the way to the airport, we'll pull over and say a few words. I can make a statement, if you like. All you have to do is stand next to me."

"No," said Lang firmly. "No. Absolutely not. That really will make me look guilty. I'll have to talk to them myself. Ruth, what do you think about going to Washington?"

"I think it's a terrible idea. I'm sorry, Sid, I know you're working hard for us, but we've got to consider how this will play in Britain. If Adam goes to Washington, he'll look like America's whipping boy, running crying home to Daddy."

"So what would you do?"

"Fly back to London." Kroll began to object but Ruth talked over him. "The British people may not like him much at the moment, but if there's one thing they hate more than Adam, it's interfering foreigners telling them what to do. The government will have to support him."

Amelia said, "The British government are going to cooperate fully with the investigation."

"Oh, really?" said Ruth, in a voice as sweet as cyanide. "And what makes you think that?"

"I'm not thinking it, Ruth, I'm reading it. It's on the television. Look."

We looked. The headline was running across the bottom of the screen: "BREAKING NEWS: BRITISH GOVT 'WILL COOPERATE FULLY' WITH WAR CRIMES PROBE."

"How dare they?" cried Ruth. "After all we've done for them!"

Josh said, "With respect, ma'am, as signatory to the ICC, the British government has no choice. It's obliged under international law to 'cooperate fully.' Those are the precise words of Article Eighty-six."

"And what if the ICC eventually decides to arrest me?" asked Lang quietly. "Do the British government 'cooperate fully' with that as well?"

Josh had already found the relevant place on his laptop. "That's covered by Article Fifty-nine, sir. 'A State Party which has received a request for a provisional arrest or for arrest and surrender shall immediately take steps to arrest the person in question.' "

"Well, I think that settles it," said Lang. "Washington it is."

Ruth folded her arms. The gesture reminded me of Kate: a warning of storms to come. "I still say it will look bad," she said.

"Not as bad as being led away in handcuffs from Heathrow."

"At least it would show you had some guts."

"Then why the hell don't you just fly back without me?" snapped Lang. Like his outburst of the previous afternoon, it wasn't so much the display of temper that was startling as the way it suddenly erupted. "If the British government want to hand me over to this kangaroo court, then fuck them! I'll go where people want me. Amelia, tell the boys we're leaving in five minutes. Get one of the girls to pack me an overnight bag. And you'd better pack one for yourself."

"Oh, but why don't you share a suitcase?" said Ruth. "It will be so much more convenient."

At that, the very air seemed to congeal. Even Kroll's little smile froze at the edges. Amelia hesitated, then nervously smoothed down her skirt, picked up her notebook, and rose in a hiss of silk. As she walked across the room toward the stairs, she kept her gaze fixed straight ahead. Her throat was flushed a tasteful pink, her lips compressed. Ruth waited until she had gone, then slowly uncoiled her feet from beneath her and carefully pulled on her flat, wooden-soled shoes. She, too, left without a word. Thirty seconds later, a door slammed downstairs.

Lang flinched and sighed. He got up and collected his jacket from the back of a chair and shrugged it on. That was the signal for us all to move. The paralegals snapped their laptops shut. Kroll stood and stretched, spreading his fingers wide: he reminded me of a cat, arching its back and briefly unsheathing its claws. I put away my notebook.

"I'll see you tomorrow," said Lang, offering me his hand. "Make yourself comfortable. I'm sorry to abandon you. At least all this coverage should improve sales."

"That's true," I said. I cast around for something to say that would lighten the atmosphere. "Perhaps Rhinehart's publicity department have arranged the whole thing."

"Well, tell them to stop it, will you?" He smiled, but his eyes looked bruised and puffy.

"What are you going to say to the media?" asked Kroll, putting his arm across Lang's shoulders.

"I don't know. Let's talk about it in the car."

As Lang turned to leave, Kroll gave me a wink. "Happy ghosting," he said.

NINE

---- ★ ----

What if they lie to you? "Lie" is probably too strong a word. Most of us tend to embroider our memories to suit the picture of ourselves that we would like the world to see.

Ghostwriting

I COULD HAVE GONE down to see them off. Instead I watched them leave on television. I always say you can't beat sitting in front of a TV screen if you're after that authentic, firsthand experience. For example, it's curious how helicopter news shots impart to even the most innocent activity the dangerous whiff of criminality. When Jeff the chauffeur brought the armored Jaguar round to the front of the house and left the engine running, it looked for all the world as if he were organizing a Mafia getaway just before the cops arrived. In the cold New England air, the big car seemed to float on a sea of exhaust fumes.

I had the same disorientating feeling that I'd experienced the previous day, when Lang's statement started pinging back at me from the ether. On the television I could see one of the Special Branch men opening the rear passenger door, and standing there, holding it open, while down in the corridor I could hear Lang and the others preparing to leave. "All right, people?" Kroll's voice floated up the staircase. "Is everybody ready? Okay. Remember: happy, happy faces. Here we go." The front door opened, and moments later on the screen I glimpsed the top of the ex–prime minister's head as he took the few hurried steps to the car. He ducked out of sight, just as his attorney scuttled after him, round to the Jaguar's other side. At the bottom of the picture it said, "ADAM LANG LEAVES MARTHA'S VINEYARD HOUSE." They know everything, I thought, these satellite boys, but they've never heard of tautology.

Behind them, the entourage debouched in rapid single file from the house and headed for the minivan. Amelia was in the lead, her hand clutched to her immaculate blonde hair to protect it against the rotors' downdraft; then came the secretaries, followed by the paralegals, and finally a couple of bodyguards.

The long, dark shapes of the cars, their headlights gleaming, pulled out of the compound and set off through the ashy expanse of scrub oak toward the West Tisbury highway. The helicopter tracked them, whirling away the few winter leaves and flattening the sparse grass. Gradually, for the first time that morning, as the noise of its rotors faded, something like peace returned to the house. It was as if the eye of a great electrical storm had finally moved on. I wondered where Ruth was, and whether she was also watching the coverage. I stood at the top of the stairs and listened for a while, but all was quiet, and by the time I returned to the television, the coverage had shifted from aerial to ground level, and Lang's limousine was pulling out of the woods.

A lot more police had arrived at the end of the track, courtesy of the Commonwealth of Massachusetts, and a line of them was keeping the demonstrators safely corralled on the opposite side of the highway. For a moment the Jaguar appeared to be accelerating toward the airport, but then its brake lights glowed and it stopped. The minivan swerved to a halt behind it. And suddenly, there was Lang, coatless, seemingly as oblivious to the cold as he was to the chanting crowd, striding over to the cameras, trailed by three Special Branch men. I hunted around for the remote in the chair where Amelia had been sitting—her scent still lingered on the leather—pointed it at the screen, and pumped up the volume.

"I apologize for keeping you waiting so long in the cold," Lang began. "I just wanted to say a few words in response to the news from The Hague." He paused and glanced at the ground. He often did that. Was it genuine, or merely contrived, to give an impression of spontaneity? With him, one never knew. The chant of "Lang! Lang! Lang! Liar! Liar! Liar!" was clearly audible in the background.

"These are strange times," he said and hesitated again, "strange times"—and now at last he looked up—"when those who have always stood for freedom, peace, and justice are accused of being criminals, while those who openly incite hatred, glorify slaughter, and seek the destruction of democracy are treated by the law as if *they* are victims."

"Liar! Liar! Liar!"

"As I said in my statement yesterday, I have always been a strong supporter of the International Criminal Court. I believe in its work. I believe in the integrity of its judges. And that is why I do not fear this investigation. Because I know in my heart I have done nothing wrong."

He glanced across at the demonstrators. For the first time he appeared to notice the waving placards: his face, the prison bars, the orange jumpsuit, the bloodied hands. The line of his mouth set firm.

"I refuse to be intimidated," he said, with an upward tilt of his chin. "I refuse to be made a scapegoat. I refuse to be distracted from my work combating AIDS, poverty, and global warming. For that reason, I propose to travel now to Washington to carry on my schedule as planned. To everyone watching in the United Kingdom and throughout the world, let me make one thing perfectly clear: as long as I have breath in my body, I shall fight terrorism wherever it has to be fought, whether it be on the battlefield or—if necessary—in the courts. Thank you."

Ignoring the shouted questions—"When are you going back to Britain, Mr. Lang?" "Do you support torture, Mr. Lang?"—he turned and strode away, the muscles of his broad shoulders flexing beneath his handmade suit, his trio of bodyguards fanned out behind him. A week ago I would have been impressed, as I had been by his speech in New York after the London suicide bomb, but now I was surprised at how unmoved I felt. It was like watching some great actor in the last phase of his career, emotionally overspent, with nothing left to draw on but technique.

I waited until he was safely back in his gas- and bombproof cocoon, and then I switched off the television.

WITH LANG AND THE others gone, the house seemed not merely empty but desolate, bereft of purpose. I came down the stairs and passed the lighted showcases of tribal erotica. The chair by the front door where one of the bodyguards always sat was vacant. I reversed my steps and followed the corridor round to the secretaries' office. The small room, normally clinically neat, looked as if it had been abandoned in a panic, like the cipher room of a foreign embassy in a surrendering city. A profusion of papers, computer disks, and old editions of *Hansard* and the *Congressional Record* were strewn across the desk. It occurred to me then that I had no copy of Lang's manuscript to work on, but when I tried to open the filing cabinet, it was locked. Beside it, a basket full of waste from the paper shredder overflowed.

I looked into the kitchen. An array of butcher's knives was laid out on a chopping block; there was fresh blood on some of the blades. I called a hesitant "Hello?" and stuck my head round the door of the pantry, but the housekeeper wasn't there.

I had no idea which was my room, and I therefore had no option but to work my way along the corridor, trying one door after another. The first was locked. The second was open, the room beyond it exuding a rich, sweet odor of heavy aftershave; a tracksuit was thrown across the bed: it was obviously the bedroom used by Special Branch during the night shift. The third door was locked, and I was about to try the fourth when I heard the sound of a woman weeping. I could tell it was Ruth: even her sobs had a combative quality. *"There are only six bedrooms in the main house,"* Amelia had said. *"Adam and Ruth have one each."* What a setup this was, I thought as I crept away: the ex–prime minister and his wife sleeping in separate rooms, with his mistress just along the corridor. It was almost French.

Gingerly, I tried the handle of the next room. This one wasn't locked, and the aroma of worn clothes and lavender soap, even more than the sight of my old suitcase, established it immediately as McAra's former berth. I went in and closed the door very softly. The big mirrored closet took up the whole of the wall dividing my room from Ruth's and when I slid back the glass door a fraction, I could just make out her muffled wailing. The door scraped on its runner, and I guess she must have heard, for all at once the crying stopped, and I imagined her startled, raising her head from her damp pillow and staring at the wall. I drew away. On the bed I noticed that someone had put a box, stuffed so full the top didn't fit. A yellow Post-it note said, "Good luck! Amelia." I sat on the counterpane and lifted the lid. *"MEMOIRS,"* proclaimed the title page, *"by Adam Lang."* So she hadn't forgotten me after all, despite the exquisitely embarrassing circumstances of her departure. You could say what you liked about Mrs. Bly, but the woman was a pro.

I recognized I was now at a decisive point. Either I continued to hang around at the fringes of this floundering project, pathetically hoping that at some point someone would help me. Or—and I felt my spine straightening as I contemplated the alternative—I could seize control of it myself, try to knock these six hundred and twenty-one ineffable pages into some kind of publishable shape, take my two hundred and fifty grand, and head off to lie on a beach somewhere for a month until I had forgotten all about the Langs.

Put in those terms, it wasn't a choice. I steeled myself to ignore both McAra's lingering traces in the room and Ruth's more corporeal presence next door. I took the manuscript from its box and placed it on the table next to the window, opened my shoulder bag, and took out my laptop and the transcripts from yesterday's interviews. There wasn't a lot of room to work, but that didn't bother me. Of all human activities, writing is the one for which it is easiest to find excuses not to begin—the desk's too big, the desk's too small, there's too much noise, there's too much quiet, it's too hot, too cold, too early, too late. I had learned over the years to ignore them all and simply to start. I plugged in my laptop, switched on the lamp, and contemplated the blank screen and its pulsing cursor.

A book unwritten is a delightful universe of infinite possibilities. Set down one word, however, and immediately it becomes earthbound. Set down one sentence and it's halfway to being just like every other bloody book that's ever been written. But the best must never be allowed to drive out the good. In the absence of genius there is always craftsmanship. One can at least try to write something that will arrest the readers' attention, that will encourage them, after reading the first paragraph, to take a look at the second, and then the third. I picked up McAra's manuscript to remind myself of how not to begin a ten-million-dollar autobiography:

CHAPTER ONE

Early Years

> Langs are Scottish folk originally, and proud of it.
> Our name is a derivation of "long," the Old English
> word for "tall," and it is from north of the border
> that my forefathers hail. It was in the sixteenth cen-
> tury that the first of the Langs . . .

God help us! I ran my pen through it, and then zigzagged a thick blue line through all the succeeding paragraphs of Lang ancestral history. If you want a family tree, go to a garden center—that's what I advise my clients. Nobody else is interested. Maddox's instruction was to begin the book with the war crimes allegations, which was fine by me, although it could serve only as a kind of long prologue. At some point, the memoir proper would have to begin, and for this I wanted to find a fresh and original note, something that would make Lang sound like a normal human being. The fact that he wasn't a normal human being was neither here nor there.

From Ruth Lang's room came the sound of footsteps, and then her door opened and closed. I thought at first she might be coming to investigate who was moving around next door, but instead I heard her walking away. I put down McAra's manuscript and turned my attention to the interview transcripts. I knew what I wanted. It was there in our first session:

> I remember it was a Sunday afternoon. Raining. I
> was still in bed. And someone starts knocking on
> the door . . .

If I tidied up the grammar, the account of how Ruth had canvassed Lang for the local elections and so drawn him into politics would make a perfect opening. Yet McAra, with his characteristic tone deafness for anything of human interest, had failed even to mention it. I rested my fingers on the keys of my laptop, then started to type:

CHAPTER ONE

Early Years

> I became a politician out of love. Not love for any
> particular party or ideology, but love for a woman

who came knocking on my door one wet Sunday afternoon . . .

You may object that this was corny, but don't forget (A) that
corn sells by the ton, (B) that I had only two weeks to rework an
entire manuscript, and (C) that it sure as hell was a lot better than
starting with the derivation of the name Lang. I was soon rattling
away as fast as my two-finger typing would permit me:

> She was wringing wet from the pouring rain, but she
> didn't seem to notice. Instead, she launched into a
> passionate speech about the local elections. Until
> that point, I'm ashamed to say, I didn't even know
> there were any local elections, but I had the good
> sense to pretend that I did . . .

I looked up. Through the window I could see Ruth marching determinedly across the dunes, into the wind, on yet another of her brooding, solitary walks, with only her trailing bodyguard for company. I
watched till she was out of sight, then went back to my work.

I CARRIED ON FOR a couple of hours, until about one o'clock
or so, and then I heard a very light tapping of fingertips on wood.
It made me jump.

"Mister?" came a timid female voice. "Sir? You want lunch?"

I opened the door to find Dep, the Vietnamese housekeeper,
in her black silk uniform. She was about fifty, as tiny as a bird. I felt
that if I sneezed I would have blown her from one end of the
house to the other.

"That would be very nice. Thanks."

"Here, or in kitchen?"

"The kitchen would be great."

After she'd shuffled away on her slippered feet, I turned to face my room. I knew I couldn't put it off any longer. Treat it like writing, I said to myself: go for it. I unzipped my suitcase and laid it on the bed. Then, taking a deep breath, I slid open the doors to the closet and began removing McAra's clothes from their hangers, piling them over my arm—cheap shirts, off-the-peg jackets, chain store trousers, and the sort of ties you buy at the airport: nothing handmade in *your* wardrobe, was there, Mike? He had been a big fellow, I realized, as I felt all those supersize collars and great, hooped waistbands: much larger than I am. And, of course, it was exactly as I'd dreaded: the feel of the unfamiliar fabric, even the clatter of the metal hangers on their chrome-plated rail, was enough to breach the barrier of a quarter of a century's careful defenses and plunge me straight back into my parents' bedroom, which I'd steeled myself to clear three months after my mother's funeral.

It's the possessions of the dead that always get to me. Is there anything sadder than the clutter they leave behind? Who says that all that's left of us is love? All that was left of McAra was *stuff.* I heaped it over the armchair, then reached up to the shelf above the clothes rail to pull down his suitcase. I'd expected it would be empty but, as I took hold of the handle, something slid around inside. Ah, I thought. At last. The secret document.

The case was huge and ugly, made of molded red plastic, too bulky for me to manage easily, and it hit the floor with a thud. It seemed to reverberate through the quiet house. I waited a moment, then gently laid the suitcase flat on the floor, knelt in front of it, and pressed the catches. They flew up with a loud and simultaneous snap.

It was the kind of luggage that hasn't been made for more than a decade, except perhaps in the less fashionable parts of Albania. Inside it had a hideously patterned, shiny plastic lining, from which dangled frilly elastic bands. The contents consisted of a single large padded envelope addressed to M. McAra Esq., care of a post office box number in Vineyard Haven. A label on the back showed that it had come from the Adam Lang Archive Centre in Cambridge, England. I opened it and pulled out a handful of photographs and photocopies, together with a compliments slip from Julia Crawford-Jones, PhD, Director.

One of the photographs I recognized at once: Lang in his chicken outfit, from the Footlights Revue in the early nineteen seventies. There were a dozen other production stills showing the whole cast; a set of photographs of Lang punting, wearing a straw boater and a striped blazer; and three or four of him at a riverside picnic, apparently taken on the same day as the punting. The photocopies were of various Footlights programs and theater reviews from Cambridge, plus a lot of local newspaper reports of the Greater London Council elections of May 1977, and Lang's original party membership card. It was only when I saw the date on the card that I rocked back on my heels. It was from 1975.

I started to reexamine the package with more care now, beginning with the election stories. At first glance I thought they'd come from the London *Evening Standard*, but I saw they were from the news sheet of a political party—Lang's party—and that he was actually pictured in a group as an election volunteer. It was hard to make him out in the poorly reproduced photocopy. His hair was long, his clothes were shabby. But that was him, all right, one of a team knocking on doors in a council estate. "Canvasser: A. Lang."

I was more irritated than anything. It certainly didn't strike me as sinister. Everybody tends to heighten his own reality. We start with a private fantasy about our lives and perhaps one day, for fun, we turn it into an anecdote. No harm is done. Over the years, the anecdote is repeated so regularly it becomes accepted as a fact. Quite soon, to contradict this fact would be embarrassing. In time, we probably come to believe it was true all along. And by these slow accretions of myth, like a coral reef, the historical record takes shape. I could see how it would have suited Lang to pretend he'd gone into politics only because he'd fancied a girl. It flattered him, by making him look less ambitious, and it flattered her, by making her look more influential than she probably was. Audiences liked it. Everyone was happy. But now the question arose: what was I supposed to do?

It's not an uncommon dilemma in the ghosting business, and the etiquette is simple: you draw the discrepancy to the author's attention and leave it up to him to decide how to resolve it. The collaborator's responsibility is not to insist on the absolute truth. If it were, our end of the publishing industry would collapse under the dead weight of reality. Just as the beautician doesn't tell her client that she has a face like a sack of toads, so the ghost doesn't confront the autobiographer with the fact that half his treasured reminiscences are false. Don't dictate, facilitate: that is our motto. Obviously, McAra had failed to observe this sacred rule. He must have had his suspicions about what he was being told, ordered up a parcel of research from the archives, and then removed the ex–prime minister's most polished anecdote from his memoirs. What an amateur! I could imagine how well that must have been received. No doubt it helped explain why relations had become so strained.

I turned my attention back to the Cambridge material. There was a strange kind of innocence about these faded jeunesse dorée, stranded in that lost but happy valley that lay somewhere between the twin cultural peaks of hippiedom and punk. Spiritually, they looked far closer to the sixties than the seventies. The girls had long lacy dresses in floral prints, with plunging necklines, and big straw hats to keep off the sun. The men's hair was as long as the women's. In the only color picture, Lang was holding a bottle of champagne in one hand and what looked very much like a joint in the other; a girl seemed to be feeding him strawberries, while in the background a bare-chested man gave a thumbs-up.

The biggest of the cast photographs showed eight young people grouped together under a spotlight, their arms outstretched as if they had just finished some show-stopping song and dance routine in a cabaret. Lang was on the far right-hand side, wearing his striped blazer, a bow tie, and a straw boater. There were two girls in leotards, fishnet tights, and high heels: one with short blonde hair, the other dark frizzy curls, possibly a redhead (it was impossible to tell from the monochrome photo): both pretty. Two of the men apart from Lang I recognized: one was now a famous comedian, the other an actor. A third man looked older than the others: a postgraduate researcher, perhaps. Everyone was wearing gloves.

Glued to the back was a typed slip listing the names of the performers, along with their colleges: G. W. Syme (Caius), W. K. Innes (Pembroke), A. Parke (Newnham), P. Emmett (St. John's), A. D. Martin (King's), E. D. Vaux (Christ's), H. C. Martineau (Girton), A. P. Lang (Jesus).

There was a copyright stamp—*Cambridge Evening News*—in

the bottom left-hand corner, and scrawled diagonally next to it in blue ballpoint was a telephone number, prefixed by the international dialing code. No doubt McAra, indefatigable fact hound that he was, had hunted down one of the cast, and I wondered which of them it was and if he or she could remember the events depicted in the photographs. Purely on a whim, I took out my mobile and dialed the number.

Instead of the familiar two-beat British ringing tone, I heard the single sustained note of the American. I let it ring for a long while. Just as I was about to give in, a man answered, cautiously.

"Richard Rycart."

The voice, with its slight colonial twang— *"Richard Roicart"*— was unmistakably that of the former foreign secretary. He sounded suspicious. "Who is this?" he asked.

I hung up at once. In fact, I was so alarmed that I actually threw the phone onto the bed. It lay there for about thirty seconds and then started to ring. I darted over and grabbed it—the incoming number was listed as "withheld"—and quickly switched it off. For half a minute I was too stunned to move.

I told myself not to rush to any conclusions. I didn't know for certain that McAra had written down the number, or even rung it. I checked the package to see when it had been dispatched. It had left the United Kingdom on January the third, nine days before McAra died.

It suddenly seemed vitally important for me to get every remaining trace of my predecessor out of that room. Hurriedly, I stripped the last of his clothes from the closet, upending the drawers of socks and underpants into his suitcase (I remember he wore thick knee-length socks and baggy white Y-fronts: this boy was old-fashioned all the way through). There were no personal papers that I could find—no diary or address book, letters, or even books—and I presumed they must have been taken away by the police immediately after his death. From the bathroom I removed his blue plastic disposable razor, toothbrush, comb, and the rest of it, and then the job was done: all tangible effects of Michael McAra, former aide to the Right Honourable Adam Lang, were crammed into a suitcase and ready to be dumped. I dragged it out into the corridor and around to the solarium. It could stay there until the summer, for all I cared, just as long as I didn't have to see it again. It took me a moment to recover my breath.

And yet, even as I headed back toward his—my—our—room, I could sense his presence, loping along clumsily at my heels. "Fuck off, McAra," I muttered to myself. "Just fuck off and leave me alone to finish this book and get out of here." I stuffed the photographs and photocopies back into their original envelope and looked around for somewhere to hide it, then I stopped and asked myself why I should want to conceal it. It wasn't exactly top secret. It had nothing to do with war crimes. It was just a young man, a student actor, more than thirty years earlier, on a sunlit riverbank, drinking champagne and sharing a spliff with his friends. There could be any number of reasons why Rycart's number was on the back of that photo. But still, somehow, it demanded to be hidden, and in the absence of any other bright idea, I'm ashamed to say I resorted to the cliché of lifting the mattress and stuffing it underneath.

"Lunch, sir," called Dep softly from the corridor. I wheeled round. I wasn't sure if she'd seen me, but then I wasn't sure it mattered. Compared to what else she must have witnessed in the house over the past few weeks, my own strange behavior would surely have seemed small beer.

I followed her into the kitchen. "Is Mrs. Lang around?" I said.

"No, sir. She go Vineyard Haven. Shopping."

She had fixed me a club sandwich. I sat on a tall stool at the breakfast bar and compelled myself to eat it, while she wrapped things in tinfoil and put them back in one of Rhinehart's array of six stainless steel fridges. I considered what I should do. Normally I would have forced myself back to my desk and continued writing all afternoon. But for just about the first time in my career as a ghost, I was blocked. I'd wasted half the morning composing a charmingly intimate reminiscence of an event that hadn't happened—*couldn't* have happened, because Ruth Lang hadn't arrived to start her career in London until 1976, by which time her future husband had already been a party member for a year.

Even the thought of tackling the Cambridge section, which once I'd regarded as words in the bank, now led me to confront a blank wall. Who was he, this happy-go-lucky, girl-chasing, politically allergic, would-be actor? What suddenly turned him into a party activist, trailing around council estates, if it wasn't meeting Ruth? It made no sense to me. That was when I realized I had a fundamental problem with our former prime minister. He was not a psychologically credible character. In the flesh, or on the screen, playing the part of a statesman, he seemed to have a strong personality. But somehow, when one sat down to think about him, he vanished. This made it almost impossible for me to do my job. Unlike any number of show business and sporting weirdos I had worked with in the past, when it came to Lang, I simply couldn't make him up.

I took out my cell phone and considered calling Rycart. But the more I reflected on how the conversation might go, the more reluctant I became to initiate it. What exactly was I supposed to say? "Oh, hello, you don't know me, but I've replaced Mike McAra as Adam Lang's ghost. I believe he may have spoken to you a day or two before he was washed up dead on a beach." I put the phone back in my pocket, and suddenly I couldn't rid my mind of the image of McAra's heavy body rolling back and forth in the surf. Did he hit rocks, or was he run straight up onto soft sand? What was the name of the place where he'd been found? Rick had mentioned it when we had lunch at his club in London. Lambert something-or-other.

"Excuse me, Dep," I said to the housekeeper.

She straightened from the fridge. She had such a sweetly sympathetic face. "Sir?"

"Do you happen to know if there's a map of the island I could borrow?"

TEN

★

It is perfectly possible to write a book for someone,
having done nothing but listen to their words, but
extra research often helps to provide more material
and descriptive ideas.

Ghostwriting

IT LOOKED TO BE about ten miles away, on the northwestern
shore of the Vineyard. Lambert's Cove: that was it.

There was something beguiling about the names of the loca-
tions all around it: Blackwater Brook, Uncle Seth's Pond, Indian
Hill, Old Herring Creek Road. It was like a map from a children's
adventure story, and in a strange way that was how I conceived of
my plan, as a kind of amusing excursion. Dep suggested I borrow
a bicycle—oh yes, Mr. Rhinehart, he keep many, many bicycles, for
use of guests—and something about the idea of that appealed to
me as well, even though I hadn't ridden a bike for years, and even

though I knew, at some deeper level, no good would come of it. More than three weeks had passed since the corpse had been re-covered. What would there be to see? But curiosity is a powerful human impulse—some distance below sex and greed, I grant you, but far ahead of altruism—and I was simply curious.

The biggest deterrent was the weather. The receptionist at the hotel in Edgartown had warned me that the forecast was for a storm, and although it hadn't broken yet, the sky was beginning to sag with the weight of it, like a soft gray sack waiting to split apart. But the appeal of getting out of the house for a while was overpowering and I couldn't face going back to McAra's old room and sitting in front of my computer. I took Lang's windproof jacket from its peg in the cloakroom and followed Duc the gar-dener along the front of the house to the weathered wooden cubes that served as staff accommodation and outbuildings.

"You must have to work hard here," I said, "to keep it looking so good."

Duc kept his eyes on the ground. "Soil bad. Wind bad. Rain bad. Salt bad. Shit."

After that, there didn't seem much else to say on the horticul-tural front, so I kept quiet. We passed the first two cubes. He stopped in front of the third and unlocked the big double doors. He dragged back one of them and we went inside. There must have been a dozen bicycles parked in two racks, but my gaze went straight to the tan-colored Ford Escape SUV, which took up the other half of the garage. I had heard so much about it, and had imagined it so often when I was coming over on the ferry, that it was quite a shock to encounter it unexpectedly.

Duc saw me looking at it. "You want to borrow?" he asked.

"No, no," I said quickly. First the dead man's job, then his bed, then a ride in his car—who could tell where it might end? "A bike will be fine. It will do me good."

The gardener wore an expression of deep skepticism as he watched me go, wobbling off uncertainly on one of Rhinehart's expensive mountain bikes. He obviously thought I was mad, and perhaps I *was* mad—island madness, don't they call it? I raised my hand to the Special Branch man in his little wooden sentry's hut, half hidden in the trees, and that was very nearly a painful mistake, as it made me swerve toward the undergrowth. But then I somehow steered the machine back into the center of the track, and once I got the hang of the gears (the last bike I'd owned had only three, and two of those didn't work) I found I was moving fairly rapidly over the hard, compacted sand.

It was eerily quiet in that forest, as if some great volcanic catastrophe had bleached the vegetation white and brittle and poisoned the wild animals. Occasionally, in the distance, a wood pigeon emitted one of its hollow, klaxon cries, but that served more to emphasize the silence than to break it. I pedaled on up the slight gradient until I reached the T-junction where the track joined the highway.

The anti-Lang demonstration had dwindled to just one man on the opposite side of the road. He had obviously been busy over the past few hours, erecting some kind of installation—low wooden boards on which had been mounted hundreds of terrible images, torn from magazines and newspapers, of burned children, tortured corpses, beheaded hostages, and bomb-flattened neighborhoods. Interspersed among this collage of death were long lists of names, some handwritten poems, and letters. It was all protected against the elements by sheets of plastic. A banner ran across the top, as over a stall at a church jumble sale: FOR AS IN ADAM ALL DIE, EVEN SO

IN CHRIST SHALL ALL BE MADE ALIVE. Beneath it was a flimsy shelter made of wooden struts and more plastic, containing what looked like a card table and a folding chair. Sitting patiently at the table was the man whom I'd briefly glimpsed that morning and couldn't remember. But I recognized him now, all right. He was the military type from the hotel bar who'd called me a cunt.

I came to an uncertain halt and checked left and right for traffic, conscious all the while of him staring at me from only twenty feet away. And he must have recognized me, because I saw to my horror that he had got to his feet. "Just one moment!" he shouted, in that peculiar clipped voice, but I was so anxious not to become embroiled in his madness that, even though there was a car coming, I teetered out into the road and began pedaling away from him, standing up to try to get up some speed. The car hit its horn. There was a blur of light and noise, and I felt the wind of it as it passed, but when I looked back the protester had given up his pursuit and was standing in the center of the road, staring after me, arms akimbo.

After that, I cycled hard, conscious I would soon start to lose the light. The air in my face was cold and damp, but the pumping of my legs kept me warm enough. I passed the entrance to the airport and followed the perimeter of the state forest, its fire lanes stretching wide and high through the trees like the shadowy aisles of cathedrals. I couldn't imagine McAra doing this—he didn't look the cycling type—and I wondered again what I thought I would achieve, apart from getting drenched. I toiled on past the white clapboard houses and the neat New England fields, and it didn't take much effort to visualize it still peopled by women in stern black bonnets and by men who regarded Sunday as the day to put on a suit rather than take one off.

Just out of West Tisbury I stopped by Scotchman's Lane to check directions. The sky was really threatening now, and a wind was getting up. I almost lost the map. In fact, I almost turned back. But I'd come so far, it seemed stupid to give up now, so I eased myself back onto the thin, hard saddle and set off again. About two miles later the road forked and I parted from the main highway, turning left toward the sea. The track down to the cove was similar to the approach to the Rhinehart place—scrub oak, ponds, dunes—the only difference being that there were more houses here. Mostly, they were vacation homes, shuttered up for the winter, but a couple of chimneys fluttered thin streamers of brown smoke, and from one house I heard a radio playing classical music. A cello concerto. That was when it started to rain at last—hard, cold pellets of moisture, almost hail, that exploded on my hands and face and carried the smell of the sea in them. One moment they were plopping sporadically in the pond and rattling in the trees around me, and the next it was as if some great aerial dam had broken and the rain started to sweep down in torrents. Now I remembered why I disliked cycling: bicycles don't have roofs, they don't have windshields, and they don't have heaters.

The spindly, leafless scrub oaks offered no hope of shelter, but it was impossible to carry on cycling—I couldn't see where I was going—so I dismounted and pushed my bike until I came to a low picket fence. I tried to prop the bike against it, but the machine fell over with a clatter, its back wheel spinning. I didn't bother to pick it up but ran up the cinder path, past a flagpole, to the veranda of the house. Once I was out of the rain, I leaned forward and shook my head vigorously to get the water out of my hair, and immediately a dog started barking and scratching at the door behind me. I'd assumed the house was empty—it certainly looked it—but a hazy white moon of a face appeared at the dusty window blurred by the screen door, and a moment later the door opened and the dog flew out at me.

I dislike dogs almost as much as they dislike me, but I did my best to seem charmed by the hideous, yapping white furball, if only to appease its owner, an old-timer of not far off ninety to judge by the liver spots, the stoop, and the still-handsome skull poking through the papery skin. He was wearing a well-cut sports jacket over a buttoned-up cardigan and had a plaid scarf round his neck. I made a stammering apology for disturbing his privacy, but he soon cut me off.

"You're British?" he said, squinting at me.

"I am."

"That's okay. You can shelter. Sheltering's free."

I didn't know enough about America to be able to tell from his accent where he was from, or what he might have done. But I guessed he was a retired professional and fairly well-off—you had to be, living in a place where a shack with an outside lavatory would cost you half a million dollars.

"British, eh?" he repeated. He studied me through rimless spectacles. "You anything to do with this feller Lang?"

"In a way," I said.

"Seems intelligent. Why'd he want to get himself mixed up with that damn fool in the White House?"

"That's what everyone would like to know."

"War crimes!" he said, with a roll of his head, and I caught a glimpse of two flesh-colored hearing aids, one in either ear. "We could all have been charged with those! And maybe we ought to have been. I don't know. I guess I'll just have to put my trust in a higher judgment." He chuckled sadly. "I'll find out soon enough."

I didn't know what he was talking about. I was just glad to be standing where it was dry. We leaned on the weathered handrail and stared out together at the rain while the dog skittered dementedly on its claws around the veranda. Through a gap in the trees I could just make out the sea—vast and gray, with the white lines of the incoming waves moving remorselessly down it, like interference on an old black-and-white TV.

"So what brings you to this part of the Vineyard?" asked the old man.

There seemed no point in lying. "Someone I knew was washed up on the beach down there," I said. "I thought I'd take a look at the spot. To pay my respects," I added, in case he thought I was a ghoul.

"Now *that* was a funny business," he said. "You mean the British guy a few weeks ago? No *way* should that current have carried him this far west. Not at this time of year."

"What?" I turned to look at him. Despite his great age, there was still something youthful about his sharp features and keen manner. His thin white hair was combed straight back off his forehead. He looked like an antique Boy Scout.

"I've known this sea most of my life. Hell, a guy tried to throw *me* off that damn ferry when I was still at the World Bank, and I can tell you this: if he'd succeeded, I wouldn't have floated ashore in Lambert's Cove!"

I was conscious of a drumming in my ears, but whether it was my blood or the downpour hitting the shingle roof I couldn't tell.

"Did you mention this to the police?"

"The police? Young man, at my age, I have better things to do with what little time I have left than spend it with the police! Anyway, I told all this to Annabeth. She was the one who was dealing with the police." He saw my blank expression. "Annabeth Wurmbrand," he said. "Everybody knows Annabeth—Mars Wurmbrand's widow. She has the house nearest the ocean." At my failure to react, he became slightly testy. "She's the one who told the police about the lights."

"The lights?"

"The lights on the beach on the night the body was washed up. Nothing happens round here that she doesn't see. Kay used to say she was always happy leaving Mohu in the fall, knowing she could be sure Annabeth would keep an eye on things all winter."

"What kind of lights were these?"

"Flashlights, I guess."

"Why wasn't this reported in the media?"

"In the media?" He gave another of his grating chuckles. "Annabeth's never spoken to a reporter in her life! Except maybe an editor from the *World of Interiors*. It took her a decade even to trust Kay, because of the *Post*."

That started him off talking about Kay's big old place up on Lambert's Cove Road that Bill and Hillary used to like so much, and where Princess Diana had stayed, of which only the chimneys now remained, but by then I had stopped listening. It seemed to me the rain had eased somewhat and I was eager to get away. I interrupted.

"Do you think you could point me in the direction of Mrs. Wurmbrand's house?"

"Sure, but there's not much point in going there."

"Why not?"

"She fell downstairs two weeks ago. Been in a coma ever since. Poor Annabeth. Ted says she's never going to regain consciousness. So that's another one gone. Hey!" he shouted, but by then I was halfway down the steps from the veranda.

"Thanks for the shelter," I called over my shoulder, "and the talk. I've got to get going."

He looked so forlorn, standing there alone under his dripping roof, with the Stars and Stripes hanging like a dishrag from its slick pole, that I almost turned back.

"Well, tell your Mr. Lang to keep his spirits up!" He gave me a trembling military salute and turned it into a wave. "You take care now."

I righted my bike and set off down the track. I wasn't even noticing the rain anymore. About a quarter of a mile down the slope, in a clearing close to the dunes and the pond, was a big, low house surrounded by a wire fence and discreet signs announcing it was private property. There were no lamps lit, despite the darkness of the storm. That, I surmised, must be the residence of the coma-tose widow. Could it be true? She had seen *lights*? Well, it was certainly the case that from the upstairs windows one would have a good view of the beach. I leaned the bike against a bush and scrambled up the little path, through sickly, yellowish vegetation and lacy green ferns, and as I came to the crest of the dune the wind seemed to push me away, as if this too were a private domain and I had no business trespassing.

I'd already glimpsed what lay beyond the dunes from the old guy's house, and as I'd cycled down the track, I'd heard the boom of the surf getting progressively louder. But it was still a shock to clamber up and suddenly be confronted by that vista—that seam-less gray hemisphere of scudding clouds and heaving ocean, the waves hurtling in and smashing against the beach in a continuous, furious detonation. The low, sandy coast ran away in a curve to my right for about a mile and ended in the jutting outcrop of Makonikey Head, misty through the spray. I wiped the rain out of my eyes to try to see better, and I thought of McAra alone on this immense shore—facedown, glutted with salt water, his cheap winter clothes stiff with brine and cold. I imagined him emerging out of the bleak dawn, carried in on the tide from Vineyard Sound, scraping the sand with his big feet, being washed out again, and then returning, slowly creeping higher up the beach until at last he grounded. And then I imagined him dumped over the side of a dinghy and dragged ashore by men with flashlights, who'd come back a few days later and thrown a garrulous old witness down her architect-designed stairs.

A few hundred yards along the beach a pair of figures emerged from the dunes and started walking toward me, dark and tiny and frail amid all that raging nature. I glanced in the other direction. The wind was whipping spouts of water from the surface of the waves and flinging them ashore, like the outlines of some amphibious invasion force: they made it halfway up the beach and then dissolved.

What I ought to do, I thought, staggering slightly in the wind, is give all this to a journalist, some tenacious reporter from the *Washington Post*, some noble heir to the tradition of Woodward and Bernstein. I could see the headline. I could write the story in my mind.

> WASHINGTON—The death of Michael McAra, aide to former British prime minister Adam Lang, was a covert operation that went tragically wrong, according to sources within the intelligence community.

Was that so implausible? I took another look at the figures on the beach. It seemed to me they had quickened their pace and were heading toward me. The wind slashed rain in my face and I had to wipe it away. I ought to get going, I thought. By the time I looked again they were closer still, stumbling determinedly up the expanse of sand. One was short, the other tall. The tall one was a man, the short one a woman.

The short one was Ruth Lang.

I WAS AMAZED THAT she should have turned up. I waited until I was sure it was her, then I went halfway down the beach to meet her. The noise of the wind and the sea wiped out our first exchanges. She had to take my arm and pull me down slightly, so that she could shout in my ear. *"I said,"* she repeated, and her breath was almost shockingly hot against my freezing skin, *"Dep told me you were here!"* The wind whipped her blue nylon hood away from her face and she tried to fumble for it at the nape of her neck, then gave up. She shouted something, but just at that moment a wave exploded against the shore behind her. She smiled helplessly, waited until the noise had subsided, then cupped her hands and shouted, "What are you doing?"

"Oh, just taking the air."

"No—really."

"I wanted to see where Mike McAra was found."

"Why?"

I shrugged. "Curiosity."

"But you didn't even know him."

"I'm starting to feel as if I did."

"Where's your bike?"

"Just behind the dunes."

"We came to fetch you back before the storm started." She beckoned to the policeman. He was standing about five yards away, watching us—soaked, bored, disgruntled. "Barry," she shouted to him, "bring the car round, will you, and meet us on the road? We'll wheel the bike up and find you." She spoke to him as if he were a servant.

"Can't do that, Mrs. Lang, I'm afraid," he yelled back. "Regulations say I have to stay with you at all times."

"Oh, for God's sake!" she said scornfully. "Do you seriously think there's a terrorist cell at Uncle Seth's Pond? Go and get the car before you catch pneumonia."

I watched in his square, unhappy face, as his sense of duty warred with his desire for dryness. "All right," he said eventually. "I'll meet you in ten minutes. But please don't leave the path or speak to anyone."

"We won't, officer," she said with mock humility. "I promise."

He hesitated, then began jogging back the way he'd come.

"They treat us like children," complained Ruth, as we climbed up the beach. "I sometimes think their orders aren't to protect us so much as to spy on us."

We reached the top of the dune and automatically we both turned round to stare at the sea. After a second or two, I risked a quick glance at her. Her pale skin was shiny with rain, her short dark hair flattened and glistening like a swimmer's cap. Her flesh looked hard, like alabaster in the cold. People used to say they couldn't understand what her husband saw in her, but at that moment I could. There was a tautness about her, a quick, nervous energy: she was a force.

"To be honest, I've come back here a couple of times myself," she said. "Usually I bring a few flowers and wedge them under a stone. Poor Mike. He hated to be away from the city. He hated country walks. He couldn't even swim."

She quickly brushed her cheeks with her hand. Her face was too wet for me to tell whether she was crying or not.

"It's a hell of a place to end up," I said.

"Oh, no. No it's not. When it's sunny, it's rather wonderful. It reminds me of Cornwall."

She scrambled down the little footpath to the bike, and I followed her. To my surprise, she suddenly mounted it and pedaled away, coming to a stop about a hundred yards up the track, at the edge of the wood. When I reached her, she gazed intently at me, her dark brown eyes almost black in the fading afternoon light. "Do you think his death was suspicious?"

The directness of the question took me unawares. "I'm not sure," I said. It was all I could do to stop myself telling her right then what I'd heard from the old man. But I sensed this was neither the time nor the place. I wasn't sufficiently sure of my facts, and it seemed crass, somehow, to pass unverified gossip on to a grieving friend. Besides, I was a little scared of her: I didn't want to be on the receiving end of one of her scathing cross-examinations. So all I said was, "I don't know enough about it, to be honest. Presumably the police have investigated the whole thing pretty thoroughly."

"Yes. Of course."

She got off the bike and handed it to me and we started ascending through the scrub oak toward the road. It was much calmer away from the sea. The downpour had almost stopped and the rain had released rich, cold smells of earth and wood and herbs. I could hear the ticking of the rear wheel as we walked.

"The police were very active at first," she said, "but it's all gone quiet lately. I think the inquest was adjourned. Anyway, they can't be that concerned—they released Mike's body last week and the embassy have flown it back to the UK."

"Oh?" I tried not to sound too surprised. "That seems very quick."

"Not really. It's been three weeks. They did an autopsy. He was drunk and he drowned. End of story."

"But what was he doing on the ferry in the first place?"

She gave me a sharp look. "That I don't know. He was a grown man. He didn't have to account for his every move."

We walked on in silence and the thought occurred to me that McAra could easily have left the island for the weekend to visit Richard Rycart in New York. That would explain why he'd written down Rycart's number and also why he hadn't told the Langs where he was going. How could he? *So long, guys. I'm just off to the United Nations to see your bitterest political enemy . . .*

We passed the house where I'd sought shelter from the downpour. I kept an eye out for the old man, but the white clapboard property appeared as deserted as when I'd first seen it—so freezing, locked, and abandoned, in fact, that I half wondered if I might not have imagined the whole encounter.

Ruth said, "The funeral's in London on Monday. He's being buried in Streatham. His mother's too ill to attend. I've been thinking that perhaps I ought to go. One of us should put in an appearance, and it doesn't seem likely to be my husband."

"I thought you said you didn't want to leave him."

"It rather looks as though he's left me, wouldn't you say?"

She didn't talk anymore after that but started fumbling around for her hood again, even though she didn't really need it. I found it for her with my free hand and she pulled it up roughly, without thanking me, and walked on, slightly ahead, staring at the ground.

Barry was waiting for us at the end of the track in the minivan, reading a Harry Potter novel. The engine was running and the headlights were on. Occasionally, the big windscreen wiper scraped noisily across the glass. He put aside his book with obvious reluctance, got out, opened up the rear door, and pushed the seats forward. Between us we maneuvered the bike into the back of the van, then he returned to his place behind the wheel and I climbed in beside Ruth.

We took a different route from the one I'd cycled, the road twisting up a hill away from the sea. The dusk was damp and gloomy, as if one of the massive storm clouds had failed to rupture but had gradually subsided to earth like a deflated airship and settled over the island. I could understand why Ruth said the landscape reminded her of Cornwall. The minivan's headlights fell on wild, almost moorland country and in the side mirror I could just make out the luminous white horses flecking the waters of Vineyard Sound. The heater was turned up full and I had to keep rubbing a porthole in the condensation to see where we were going. I could feel my clothes drying, sticking to my skin, releasing the same faintly unpleasant odor of sweat and dry cleaning fluid I had smelled in McAra's room.

Ruth didn't speak for the whole of the journey. She kept her back turned slightly toward me and stared out of the window. But just as we passed the lights of the airport, her cold, hard hand moved across the seat and grasped mine. I didn't know what she was thinking, but I could guess, and I returned her pressure: even a ghost can show a little human sympathy from time to time. In the rearview mirror, Barry's eyes stared into mine. As he indicated to turn right into the wood, the images of death and torture, and the words "for as in Adam all die" flickered briefly in the darkness, but as far as I could see the little hut was empty. We rocked down the track toward the house.

ELEVEN

———————— ★ ————————

There may be occasions on which the subject will tell
the ghost something that contradicts something else
they have said, or something that the ghost already
knows about them. If that happens, it is important to
mention it immediately.

Ghostwriting

THE FIRST THING I did when we got back was run a hot bath,
tipping in half a bottle of organic bath oil (pine, cardamom, and
ginger) I found in the bathroom cabinet. While that was filling, I
drew the curtains in the bedroom and peeled off my damp clothes.
Naturally, a house as modern as Rhinehart's didn't have anything
so crudely useful as a radiator, so I left them where they fell, went
into the bathroom, and stepped into the large tub.

Just as it's worth getting really hungry occasionally, simply to
savor the taste of food, so the pleasure of a hot bath can truly be

appreciated only if you've been chilled by the rain for hours. I groaned with relief, let myself slide right down until only my nostrils were above the aromatic surface, and lay there like some basking alligator in its steamy lagoon for several minutes. I suppose that's why I didn't hear anyone knock on my bedroom door and became aware that someone was next door only when I broke the surface and heard a person moving around.

"Hello?" I called.

"Sorry," Ruth called back. "I did knock. It's me. I was just bringing you some dry clothes."

"That's all right," I said. "I can manage."

"You need something that's been properly aired, or you'll catch your death. I'll get Dep to clean the others."

"Really, there's no need."

"Dinner's in an hour. Is that okay?"

"That's fine," I said, surrendering. "Thank you."

I listened for the click of the door as she left. Immediately I rose from the bath and grabbed a towel. On the bed, she had laid out a freshly laundered shirt belonging to her husband (it was handmade, with his monogram, APBL, on the pocket), a sweater, and a pair of jeans. Where my own discarded clothes had been there was only a wet mark on the floor. I lifted the mattress—the package was still there—then let it fall.

There was something disconcerting about Ruth Lang. You never knew where you were with her. Sometimes she could be aggressive for no reason—I hadn't forgotten her behavior during our first conversation, when she virtually accused me of planning to write a kiss-and-tell memoir about her and Lang—and then at others she was bizarrely overfamiliar, holding hands or dictating what you should wear. It was as if some tiny mechanism was missing from her brain, the bit that told you how to behave naturally with other people.

I drew my towel more tightly around me, knotted it at my waist, and sat down at the desk. I'd been struck before by how strangely absent she was from her husband's autobiography. That was one of the reasons I'd wanted to begin the main part of the book with the story of their meeting—until I discovered that Lang had made it up. She was there, naturally enough, on the dedication page—

> *To Ruth,*
> *and my kids,*
> *and the people of Britain*

—but then one had to wait another fifty pages until she actually appeared in person. I leafed through the manuscript until I reached the passage.

> It was at the time of the London elections that I first got to know Ruth Capel, one of the most energetic members of the local association. I would like to be able to say that it was her political commitment that first drew me to her, but the truth is that I found her immensely attractive—small, intense, with very short dark hair and piercing dark eyes. She was a North Londoner, the only child of two university lecturers, and had been passionately interested in politics almost from the time she could speak— unlike me! She was also, as my friends never tired of pointing out, much cleverer than I was! She had

gained a First at Oxford in politics, philosophy, and economics, and then done a year's postgraduate research in postcolonial government as a Fulbright scholar. As if that were not enough to intimidate me, she had also come top in the Foreign Office entrance examinations, although she later left to work for the party's foreign affairs team in parliament.

Nevertheless, the Lang family motto has always been, "Nothing ventured, nothing gained," and I managed to arrange for us to go canvassing together. It was then a relatively easy matter, after a hard evening's knocking on doors and handing out leaflets, to suggest a casual drink in a local pub. At first, other members of the campaign team used to join us on these excursions, but gradually they became aware that Ruth and I wanted to spend time alone together. A year after the elections, we began sharing a flat, and when Ruth became pregnant with our first child, I asked her to marry me. Our wedding took place at Marylebone registry office in June 1979, with Andy Martin, one of my old friends from Footlights, acting as my best man. For our honeymoon, we borrowed Ruth's parents' cottage near Hay-on-Wye. After two blissful weeks, we returned to London, ready for the very different political fray following the election of Margaret Thatcher.

That was the only substantial reference to her.

I slowly worked my way through the succeeding chapters, underlining the places where she was mentioned. Her "lifelong knowledge of the party" was "invaluable" in helping Lang gain his safe parliamentary seat. "Ruth saw the possibility that I might become party leader long before I did" was the promising opening of chapter three, but how or why she reached this prescient conclusion weren't explained. She surfaced to give "characteristically shrewd advice" when he had to sack a colleague. She shared his hotel suites at party conferences. She straightened his tie on the night he became prime minister. She went shopping with the wives of other world leaders on official visits. She even gave birth to his children ("my kids have always kept my feet firmly on the ground"). But for all that hers was a phantom presence in the memoirs, which puzzled me, because she certainly wasn't a phantom presence in his life. Perhaps this was why she had been keen to hire me: she guessed I would want to put in more about her.

When I checked my watch I realized I'd already spent an hour going over the manuscript, and it was time for dinner. I contemplated the clothes she had laid out on the bed. I'm what the English would call "fastidious" and the Americans "tight-assed": I don't like eating food that's been on someone else's plate, or drinking from the same glass, or wearing clothes that aren't my own. But these were cleaner and warmer than anything I possessed, and she had gone to the trouble of fetching them, so I put them on—rolling up the sleeves because I had no cuff links—and went upstairs.

THERE WAS A LOG fire burning in the stone hearth, and someone, presumably Dep, had lit candles all around the room. The security lights in the grounds had also been turned on, illuminating the gaunt white outlines of trees and the greenish-yellow vegetation bending in the wind. As I came up into the room, a gust of rain slashed across the huge picture window. It was like the lounge of some luxurious boutique hotel out of season, which had only two guests.

Ruth was sitting on the same sofa, in the same position she had adopted that morning, with her legs drawn up beneath her, reading the *New York Review of Books*. Arranged in a fan on the low table in front of her was an array of magazines, and beside them—a harbinger of things to come, I hoped—a long-stemmed glass of what looked like white wine. She glanced up approvingly.

"A perfect fit," she said. "And now you need a drink." She leaned her head over the back of the sofa—I could see the cords of muscle standing out in her neck—and called in her mannish voice in the direction of the stairs, "Dep!" And then to me, "What will you have?"

"What are you having?"

"Biodynamic white wine," she said, "from the Rhinehart Vinery in Napa Valley."

"He doesn't own a distillery, I suppose?"

"It's delicious. You must try it. Dep," she said to the housekeeper, who had appeared at the top of the stairs, "bring the bottle, would you, and another glass?"

I sat down opposite her. She was wearing a long red wraparound dress, and on her normally scrubbed-clean face was a trace of makeup. There was something touching about her determination to put on a show, even as the bombs, so to speak, were falling all around her. All we needed was a windup gramophone and we could have played the plucky English couple in a Noël Coward play, keeping up brittle appearances while the world went smash around us. Dep poured me some wine and left the bottle.

"We'll eat in twenty minutes," instructed Ruth, "because first," she said, picking up the remote control and jabbing it fiercely at the television, "we must watch the news. Cheers," she said and raised her glass.

"Cheers," I replied and did the same.

I drained the glass in thirty seconds. White wine. What *is* the point of it? I picked up the bottle and studied the label. Apparently the vines were grown in soil treated in harmony with the lunar cycle, using manure buried in a cow's horn and flower heads of yarrow fermented in a stag's bladder. It sounded like the sort of suspicious activity for which people quite rightly used to be burned as witches.

"You like it?" asked Ruth.

"Subtle and fruity," I said, "with a hint of bladder."

"Pour us some more, then. Here comes Adam. Christ, it's the lead story. I think I may have to get drunk for a change."

The headline behind the announcer's shoulder read "LANG: WAR CRIMES." I didn't like the fact that they weren't bothering to use a question mark anymore. The familiar scenes from the morning unfolded: the press conference at The Hague, Lang leaving the Vineyard house, the statement to reporters on the West Tisbury highway. Then came shots of Lang in Washington, first greeting members of Congress in a warm glow of flashbulbs and mutual admiration, and then, more somberly, Lang with the secretary of state. Amelia Bly was clearly visible in the background: the official wife. I didn't dare look at Ruth.

"Adam Lang," said the secretary of state, "has stood by our side in the war against terror, and I am proud to stand by his side this afternoon and to offer him, on behalf of the American people, the hand of friendship. Adam. Good to see you."

"Don't grin," said Ruth.

"Thank you," said Adam, grinning and shaking the proferred hand. He beamed at the cameras. He looked like an eager student collecting a prize on speech day. "Thank you very much. It's good to see you."

"Oh, for fuck's sake!" shouted Ruth.

She pointed the remote and was about to press it when Richard Rycart appeared, passing through the lobby of the United Nations, surrounded by the usual bureaucratic phalanx. At the last minute he seemed to swerve off his planned course and walked over to the cameras. He was a little older than Lang, just coming up to sixty. He'd been born in Australia, or Rhodesia, or some part of the Commonwealth, before coming to England in his teens. He had a cascade of dark gray hair that flooded dramatically over his collar and was well aware—judging by the way he positioned himself—of which was his better side: his left. His tanned and hook-prowed profile reminded me slightly of a Sioux Indian chief.

"I watched the announcement in The Hague today," he said, "with great shock and sadness." I sat forward. This was definitely the voice I'd heard on the phone earlier in the day: that residual, singsong accent was unmistakable. "Adam Lang was and is an old friend of mine—"

"You hypocritical bastard," said Ruth.

"—and I regret that he's chosen to bring this down to a personal level. This isn't about individuals. This is about justice. This is about whether there's to be one law for the rich, white, Western nations and another for the rest of the world. This is about making sure that every political and military leader, when he makes a decision, knows that he will be held to account by international law. Thank you."

A reporter shouted, "If you're called to testify, sir, will you go?"

"Certainly I'll go."

"I bet you will, you little shit," said Ruth.

The news bulletin moved on to a report about a suicide bombing in the Middle East, and she turned off the television. At once her mobile phone started ringing. She glanced at it.

"It's Adam, calling to ask how I think it went." She turned that off, as well. "Let him sweat."

"Does he always ask your advice?"

"Always. And he always used to take it. Until just lately."

I poured us some more wine. Very slowly, I could feel it starting to have an effect.

"You were right," I said. "He shouldn't have gone to Washington. It did look bad."

"We should never have come *here*," she said, gesturing with her wine to the room. "I mean, look at it. And all for the sake of the Adam Lang Foundation. Which is what, exactly? Just a high-class displacement activity for the recently unemployed." She leaned forward. "Shall I tell you the first rule of politics?"

"Please."

"Never lose touch with your base."

"I'll try not to."

"Shut up. I'm being serious. You can reach beyond it, by all means—you've got to reach beyond it, if you're going to win. But never, ever lose touch with it altogether. Because once you do, you're finished. Imagine if those pictures tonight had been of him arriving in London—flying back to fight these ridiculous people and their absurd allegations. It would've looked magnificent! Instead of which—God!" She shook her head and gave a sigh of anger and frustration. "Come on. Let's eat."

She pushed herself off the sofa, spilling a little wine in the process. It spattered the front of her red woolen dress. She didn't seem to notice, and I had a horrible premonition that she was going to get drunk. (I share the serious drinker's general prejudice that there's nothing more irritating than a man drunk, except a woman drunk: they somehow manage to let everybody down.) But when I offered to top her up, she covered her glass with her hand.

"I've had enough."

The long table by the window had been laid for two, and the sight of Nature raging silently beyond the thick screen heightened the sense of intimacy: the candles, the flowers, the crackling fire. It felt slightly overdone. Dep brought in two bowls of clear soup and for a while we clinked our spoons against Rhinehart's porcelain in self-conscious silence.

"How is it going?" she said eventually.

"The book? It's not, to be honest."

"Why's that—apart from the obvious reason?"

I hesitated.

"Can I talk frankly?"

"Of course."

"I find it difficult to understand him."

"Oh?" She was drinking iced water now. Over the rim of her glass, her dark eyes gave me one of her double-barreled-shotgun looks. "In what way?"

"I can't understand why this good-looking eighteen-year-old lad who goes to Cambridge without the slightest interest in politics, and who spends his time acting and drinking and chasing girls, suddenly ends up—"

"Married to me?"

"No, no, not that. Not that at all." (Yes, is what I meant: yes, yes, that; of course.) "No. I don't understand why, by the time he's twenty-two or twenty-three, he's suddenly a member of a political party. Where's that coming from?"

"Didn't you ask him?"

"He told me he joined because of you. That you came and canvassed him, and that he was attracted to you, and that he followed you into politics out of love, essentially. To see more of you. I mean, *that* I can relate to. It *ought* to be true."

"But it isn't?"

"You know it isn't. He was a party member for at least a year before he even met you."

"Was he?" She wrinkled her forehead and sipped some more water. "But that story he always tells about what drew him into politics—I do have a distinct memory of that episode, because I canvassed in the London elections of seventy-seven, and I definitely knocked on his door, and after that was when he started showing up at party meetings regularly. So there has to be a grain of truth in it."

"A grain," I conceded. "Maybe he'd joined in seventy-five, hardly showed any interest for two years, and then he met you and became more active. It still doesn't answer the basic question of what took him into a political party in the first place."

"Is it really that important?"

Dep arrived to clear away the soup plates, and during the pause in our conversation I considered Ruth's question.

"Yes," I said when we were alone again, "oddly enough I think it is important."

"Why?"

"Because even though it's a tiny detail, it still means he isn't quite who we think he is. I'm not even sure he's quite who *he* thinks he is—and that's really difficult, if you've got to write the guy's memoirs. I just feel I don't know him at all. I can't catch his voice."

Ruth frowned at the table and made minute adjustments to the placing of her knife and fork. She said, without looking up, "How do you know he joined in seventy-five?"

I had a moment's alarm that I'd said too much. But there seemed no reason not to tell her. "Mike McAra found Adam's original party membership card in the Cambridge archives."

"Christ," she said, "those archives! They've got everything, from his infant school reports to our laundry bills. Typical Mike, to ruin a good story by too much research."

"He also dug out some obscure party newsletter that shows Adam canvassing in seventy-seven."

"That must be after he met me."

"Maybe."

I could tell something was troubling her. Another volley of rain burst against the window and she put the tips of her fingers to the heavy glass, as if she wanted to trace the raindrops. The effect of the lighting in the garden made it look like the ocean bed: all waving fronds and thin gray tree trunks, rising like the spars of sunken boats. Dep came in with the main course—steamed fish, noodles, and some kind of obscure pale green vegetable that resembled a weed, probably *was* a weed. I ostentatiously poured the last of the wine into my glass and studied the bottle.

Dep said, "You want another, sir?"

"I don't suppose you have any whiskey, do you?"

The housekeeper looked to Ruth for guidance.

"Oh, bring him some bloody whiskey," said Ruth.

She returned with a bottle of fifty-year-old Chivas Regal Royal Salute and a cut-glass tumbler. Ruth started to eat. I mixed myself a scotch and water.

"This is delicious, Dep!" called Ruth. She dabbed her mouth with the corner of her napkin and then inspected the smear of lipstick on the white linen with surprise, as if she thought she might have started bleeding. "Coming back to your question," she said to me, "I don't think you should try to find mystery where there is none. Adam always had a social conscience—he inherited that from his mother—and I know that after he left Cambridge and moved to London he became very unhappy. I believe he was actually clinically depressed."

"Clinically depressed? He may have had treatment for it? Really?" I tried to keep the excitement out of my voice. If this was true, it was the best piece of news I'd received all day. Nothing sells a memoir quite so well as a good dose of misery. Childhood sexual abuse, grinding poverty, quadriplegia: in the right hands, these are money in the bank. There ought to be a separate section in bookshops labeled "schadenfreude."

"Put yourself in his place." Ruth continued eating, gesturing with her laden fork. "His mother and father were both dead. He'd left university, which he'd loved. Many of his acting friends had agents and were getting offers of work. But he wasn't. I think he was lost, and I think he turned to political activity to compensate. He might not want to put it in those terms—he's not one for self-analysis—but that's my reading of what happened. You'd be surprised how many people end up in politics because they can't succeed in their first choice of a career."

"So meeting you must have been a very important moment for him."

"Why do you say that?"

"Because you had genuine political passion. And knowledge. And contacts in the party. You must have given him the focus to really go forward." I felt as if a mist were clearing. "Do you mind if I make a note of this?"

"Go ahead. If you think it's useful."

"Oh, it is." I put my knife and fork together—I'm not really a fish and weed man—took out my notebook, and opened it to a new page. I was imagining myself in Lang's place again: in my early twenties, orphaned, alone, ambitious, talented but not quite talented enough, looking for a path to follow, taking a few tentative steps into politics, and then meeting a woman who suddenly made the future possible.

"Marrying you was a real turning point."

"I was certainly a bit different from his Cambridge girlfriends, all those Jocastas and Pandoras. Even when I was a girl I was always more interested in politics than ponies."

"Didn't you ever want to be a proper politician in your own right?" I asked.

"Of course. Didn't you ever want to be a proper writer?"

It was like being struck in the face. I'm not sure if I didn't put down my notebook.

"Ouch," I said.

"I'm sorry. I didn't mean to be rude. But you must see that we're in the same boat, you and I. I've always understood more about politics than Adam. And you know more about writing. But in the end, he's the star, isn't he? And we both know our job is to service the star. It's his name on the book that's going to sell it, not yours. It was the same for me. It didn't take me long to realize that he could go all the way in politics. He had the looks and the charm. He was a great speaker. People liked him. Whereas I was always a bit of an ugly duckling, with this brilliant gift for putting my foot in it. As I've just demonstrated." She put her hand on mine again. It was warm now, fleshier. "I'm so sorry. I've hurt your feelings. I suppose even ghosts must have feelings, just like the rest of us?"

"If you prick us," I said, "we bleed."

"You've finished eating? In that case, why don't you show me this research that Mike dug out? It might jog my memory. I'm interested."

I WENT DOWN TO my room and retrieved McAra's package. By the time I returned upstairs, Ruth had moved back to the sofa. Fresh logs had been thrown on the fire and the wind in the chimney was roaring, sucking up orange sparks. Dep was clearing away the dishes. I just managed to rescue my tumbler and the bottle of scotch.

"Would you like dessert?" asked Ruth. "Coffee?"

"I'm fine."

"We're finished, Dep. Thank you." She moved up slightly, to indicate that I should sit next to her, but I pretended not to notice and took my former place opposite her, across the table. I was still smarting from her crack about my not being a proper writer. Perhaps I'm not. I've never composed poetry, it's true. I don't write sensitive explorations of my adolescent angst. I have no opinion on the human condition, except perhaps that it's best not examined too closely. I see myself as the literary equivalent of a skilled lathe operator, or a basket weaver; a potter, maybe: I make mildly diverting objects that people want to buy.

I opened the envelope and took out the photocopies of Lang's membership card and the articles about the London elections. I slid them across to her. She crossed her legs at the ankles, leaned forward to read, and I found myself staring into the surprisingly deep and shadowy valley of her cleavage.

"Well, there's no arguing with that," she said, putting the membership card to one side. "That's his signature, all right." She tapped the report on the canvassers in 1977. "And I recognize some of these faces. I must have been off that night, or campaigning with a different group. Otherwise I would have been in the picture with him." She looked up. "What else have you got there?"

There didn't seem much point in hiding anything, so I passed over the whole package. She inspected the name and address, and then the postmark, and then glanced across at me. "What was Mike up to, then?"

She opened the neck of the envelope and held it apart with her thumb and forefinger, and peered inside cautiously, as if there might be something in the padded interior that could bite her. Then she upended it and tipped the contents out over the table. I watched her intently, as she sorted through the photographs and programs, studied her pale, clever face for any clue as to why this might have been so important to McAra. I saw the hard lines soften as she picked out a photograph of Lang in his striped blazer on a dappled riverbank.

"Oh, look at him," she said. "Isn't he pretty?" She held it up next to her cheek.

"Irresistible," I said.

She inspected the picture more closely. "My God, look at them. Look at his *hair*. It was another world, wasn't it? I mean, what was happening while this was being taken? Vietnam. The cold war. The first miners' strike in Britain since 1926. The military coup in Chile. And what do they do? They get a bottle of champagne and they go punting!"

"I'll drink to that."

She picked up one of the photocopies.

"Listen to this," she said and started to read:

> *"The girls they all will miss us*
> *As the train it pulls away.*
> *They'll blow a kiss and say 'Come back*
> *To Cambridge town someday.'*
> *We'll throw a rose neglectfully and turn and sigh*
>   *farewell*
> *Because we know the chance they've got*
> *Is a snowball's chance in hell.*
> *Cheer oh, Cambridge, suppers, bumps and Mays,*
> *Trinners, Fenners, cricket, tennis*
> *Footlights shows and plays.*
> *We'll take a final, farewell stroll*
> *Along dear old K.P.,*
> *And a final punt up old man Cam*
> *To Grantchester for tea."*

She smiled and shook her head. "I can't even understand half of it. It's in Cambridge code."

"Bumps are college boat races," I said. "Actually, you had those at Oxford as well, but you were probably too busy with the miners' strike to notice. Mays are May balls—they're at the beginning of June, obviously."

"Obviously."

"Trinners is Trinity College. Fenners is the university cricket ground."

"And K.P.?"

"King's Parade."

"They wrote it to send the place up," she said. "But now it sounds nostalgic."

"That's satire for you."

"And what's this telephone number?"

I should have known that nothing would escape her. She showed me the photograph with the number written on the back. I didn't reply. I could feel my face beginning to flush. Of course, I ought to have told her earlier. Now I'd made myself look guilty.

"Well?" she insisted.

I said quietly, "It's Richard Rycart's."

It was almost worth it just for her expression. She looked as though she'd swallowed a hornet. She put her hand to her throat.

"*You've* been calling Richard Rycart?" she gasped.

"*I* haven't. It must have been McAra."

"That's not possible."

"Who else could have written down that number?" I held out my cell phone. "Try it."

She stared at me for a while, as if we were playing a game of Truth or Dare, then she reached over, took my phone, and entered the fourteen digits. She raised it to her ear and stared at me again. About thirty seconds later a flicker of alarm passed across her face. She fumbled to press the disconnect button, and put the phone back on the table.

"Did he answer?" I asked.

She nodded. "It sounded as though he was in a restaurant."

The phone began to ring again, throbbing along the surface of the table as if it had come alive.

"What should I do?" I asked.

"Do what you want. It's your phone."

I turned it off. There was a silence, broken only by the roaring and cracking of the log fire.

She said, "When did you discover this?"

"Earlier today. When I moved into McAra's room."

"And then you went to Lambert's Cove to look at where his body came ashore?"

"That's right."

"And why did you do that?" Her voice was very quiet. "Tell me honestly."

"I'm not sure." I paused. "There was a man there," I blurted out. I couldn't keep it to myself any longer. "An old-timer, who's familiar with the currents in Vineyard Sound. He says there's no way, at this time of year, that a body from the Woods Hole ferry would wash up at Lambert's Cove. And he also said another woman, who has a house just behind the dunes, had seen flashlights on the beach during the night when McAra went missing. But then she fell downstairs and is in a coma. So she can't tell the police anything." I spread my hands. "That's all I know."

She was looking at me with her mouth slightly open.

"That," she said slowly, "is *all* you know. *Jesus.*" She started feeling around on the sofa, patting the leather with her hands, then turned her attention to the table, searching under the photographs. "Jesus. Shit." She flicked her fingers at me. "Give me your phone."

"Why?" I asked, handing it over.

"Isn't it obvious? I need to call Adam." She held it outstretched in her palm, inspected it, and quickly started entering his number with her thumb. She got about halfway through, then stopped.

"What?" I said.

"Nothing." She was looking beyond me, over my shoulder, chewing the inside of her lip. Her thumb was poised over the keypad, and for a long moment it stayed there, until at last she put the phone back down on the table.

"You're not going to call him?"

"Maybe. In a while." She stood. "I'm going for a walk first."

"But it's nine o'clock at night," I protested. "It's pouring rain."

"It'll clear my head."

"I'll come with you."

"No. Thanks, but I need to think things through on my own. You stay here and have another drink. You look as though you need one. Don't wait up."

IT WAS POOR BARRY I felt sorry for. No doubt he'd been downstairs, with his feet up in front of the television, looking forward to a quiet night in. And suddenly here was Lady Macbeth again, off on yet another of her ceaseless walks, this time in the middle of an Atlantic storm. I stood at the window and watched them cross the lawn, toward the silently raging vegetation. She was in the lead, as usual, her head bowed, as if she'd lost something precious and was retracing her steps, searching the ground, trying to find it. The floodlights spread her shadow four ways. The Special Branch man was still pulling on his coat.

I suddenly felt overwhelmingly tired. My legs were stiff from cycling. I felt shivery with an incipient cold. Even Rhinehart's whiskey had lost its allure. She had said not to wait up, and I decided I wouldn't. I put the photographs and photocopies away in the envelope and went downstairs to my room. When I took off my clothes and switched off the light, sleep seemed to swallow me instantly, to suck me down through the mattress and into its dark waters, as if it were a strong current and I an exhausted swimmer.

I surfaced at some point to find myself alongside McAra, his large, clumsy body turning in the water like a dolphin's. He was fully clothed, in a thick black raincoat and heavy, rubber-soled shoes. *I'm not going to make it,* he said to me, *you go on without me.*

I sat up in alarm. I'd no idea how long I'd been asleep. The room was in darkness, apart from a vertical strip of light to my left.

"Are you awake?" said Ruth softly, knocking on the door. She had opened it a few inches and was standing in the corridor.

"I am now."

"I'm sorry."

"It doesn't matter. Hold on."

I went into the bathroom and put on the white terry-cloth robe that was hanging on the back of the door, and when I returned to the bedroom and let her in I saw that she was wearing an identical robe to mine. It was too big for her. She looked unexpectedly small and vulnerable. Her hair was soaking wet. Her bare feet had left a trail of damp prints from her room to mine.

"What time is it?" I said.

"I don't know. I just spoke to Adam." She seemed stunned, trembling. Her eyes were open very wide.

"And?"

She glanced along the corridor. "Can I come in?"

Still groggy from my dream, I turned on the bedside light. I stood aside to let her pass and closed the door after her.

"The day before Mike died, he and Adam had a terrible row," she said, without preliminaries. "I haven't told anyone this before, not even the police."

I massaged my temples and tried to concentrate.

"What was it about?"

"I don't know, but it was furious—terminal—and they never spoke again. When I asked Adam about it, he refused to discuss it. It's been the same every time I've broached it since. In light of what you've found out today, I felt I had to have it out with him once and for all."

"What did he say?"

"He was having dinner with the vice president. At first, that bloody woman wouldn't even go in and give him the phone."

She sat on the edge of the bed and put her face in her hands. I didn't know what to do. It seemed incongruous to remain standing, towering over her, so I sat down next to her. She was shaking from head to toe: it could have been fear, or anger, or maybe it was just the cold.

"He said to begin with he couldn't talk," she went on, "but I said he bloody well had to talk. So he took the phone into the men's room. When I told him Mike had been in touch with Rycart just before he died, he didn't even pretend to be surprised." She turned to me. She looked stricken. "He *knew*."

"He said that?"

"He didn't need to. I could tell by his voice. He said we shouldn't say any more over the telephone. We should talk when he gets back. Dear God, help us—what has he got himself mixed up in?"

Something seemed to give way in her and she sagged toward me, her arms outstretched. Her head came to rest against my chest and I thought for a moment she might have fainted, but then I realized she was clinging to me, holding on so fiercely I could feel her bitten fingertips through the thick material of the robe. My hands hovered an inch or two above her, moving back and forth uncertainly, as if she was giving off some kind of magnetic field. Finally, I stroked her hair and tried to murmur words of reassurance I didn't really believe.

"I'm afraid," she said in a muffled voice. "I've never been frightened in my life before. But I am now."

"Your hair's wet," I said gently. "You're drenched. Let me get you a towel."

I extricated myself and went into the bathroom. I looked at myself in the mirror. I felt like a skier at the top of an unfamiliar black run. When I returned to the bedroom, she'd taken off her robe and had got into bed, pulling up the sheet to cover her breasts.

"Do you mind?" she said.

"Of course not," I said.

I turned off the light and climbed in beside her, and lay on the cold side of the bed. She rolled over and put her hand on my chest and pressed her lips very hard against mine, as if she were trying to give me the kiss of life.

TWELVE

———————— ★ ————————

The book is not a platform for the ghost to air their
own views on anything at all.

Ghostwriting

WHEN I WOKE THE next morning, I expected to find her gone.
That's the usual protocol in these situations, isn't it? The business
of the night transacted, the visiting party retreats to his or her own
quarters, as keen as a vampire to avoid the unforgiving rays of
dawn. Not so Ruth Lang. In the dimness I could see her bare
shoulder and her crop of black hair, and I could tell by her irregular, almost inaudible breathing, that she was as awake as I was and
lying there listening to me.

I reclined on my back, my hands folded across my stomach, as
motionless as the stone effigy of a crusader knight on his tomb,
shutting my eyes periodically as some fresh aspect of the mess occurred to me. On the Richter scale of bad ideas, this surely had

registered a ten. It was a meteor strike of folly. After a while, I let one hand travel crabwise to the bedside table and feel for my watch. I brought it up close to my face. It was seven-fifteen.

Cautiously, still pretending I didn't know that she was pretending, I slipped out of the bed and crept toward the bathroom.

"You're awake," she said, without moving.

"I'm sorry if I disturbed you," I said. "I thought I'd take a shower."

I locked the door behind me, turned the water up as hot and strong as I could bear, and let it pummel me—back, stomach, legs, scalp. The little room quickly filled with steam. Afterward, when I shaved, I had to keep rubbing at my reflection in the mirror to stop myself from disappearing.

By the time I returned to the bedroom, she had put on her robe and was sitting at the desk, leafing through the manuscript. The curtains were still closed.

"You've taken out his family history," she said. "He won't like that. He's very proud of the Langs. And why have you underlined my name every time?"

"I wanted to check how often you were mentioned. I was surprised there wasn't more about you."

"That will be a hangover from the focus groups."

"I'm sorry?"

"When we were in Downing Street, Mike used to say that every time I opened my mouth I cost Adam ten thousand votes."

"I'm sure that's not true."

"Of course it is. People are always looking for someone to resent. I often think my main usefulness, as far as he was concerned, was to serve as a lightning rod. They could take their anger out on me instead of him."

"Even so," I said, "you ought not to be written out of history."

"Why not? Most women usually are. Even the Amelia Blys of this world are written out eventually."

"Well, then, I shall reinstate you." I slid open the door of the closet so hard in my haste it banged. I had to get out of that house. I had to put some distance between myself and their destructive ménage à trois before I ended up as crazed as they were. "I'd like to sit down with you, when you have the time, and do a really long interview. Put in all the important occasions that he's forgotten."

"How very kind of you," she said bitterly. "Like the boss's secretary whose job is to remember his wife's birthdays for him?"

"Something like that. But then, as you say, I can't claim to be a proper writer."

I was conscious of her watching me carefully. I put on a pair of boxer shorts, pulling them up under my robe.

"Ah," she said dryly, "the modesty of the morning after."

"A bit late for that," I said.

I took off the dressing gown and reached for a shirt, and as the hanger rang its hollow chime, I thought that this was exactly the sort of miserable scene that the discreet nocturnal departure was invented to avoid. How typical of her not to sense what the occasion required. Now our former intimacy lay between us like a shadow. The silence lengthened, and hardened, until I could feel her resentment as an almost solid barrier. I could no more have gone across and kissed her now than I could on the day we met.

"What are you going to do?" she said.

"Leave."

"That's not necessary as far as I'm concerned."

"I'm afraid it is, as far as I am."

I pulled on my trousers.

"Are you going to tell Adam about this?" she said.

"Oh, for God's sake!" I cried. "What do you think?"

I laid my suitcase on the bed and unzipped it.

"Where will you go?" She looked as if she might be about to cry again. I hoped not; I couldn't take it.

"Back to the hotel. I can work much better there." I started throwing in my clothes, not bothering to fold them, such was my eagerness to get away. "I'm sorry. I should never have stayed in a client's house. It always ends—" I hesitated.

"With you fucking the client's wife?"

"No, of course not. It just makes it hard to keep a professional distance. Anyway, it wasn't *entirely* my idea, if you recall."

"That's not very gentlemanly of you."

I didn't answer. I carried on packing. Her gaze followed my every move.

"And the things I told you last night?" she said. "What do you propose to do about them?"

"Nothing."

"You can't simply ignore them."

"Ruth," I said, stopping at last, "I'm his ghostwriter, not an investigative reporter. If he wants to tell the truth about what's been going on, I'm here to help him. If he doesn't, fine. I'm morally neutral."

"It isn't morally neutral to conceal the facts if you know something illegal has happened—that's criminal."

"But I don't know that anything illegal *has* happened. All I have is a phone number on the back of a photograph and gossip from some old man who may well be senile. If anyone has any evidence, it's you. That's the real question, actually: what are *you* going to do about it?"

"I don't know," she said. "Perhaps I'll write my own memoirs. 'Ex–Prime Minister's Wife Tells All.' "

I resumed packing.

"Well, if ever you do decide to do that, give me a call."

She emitted one of her trademark full-throated laughs.

"Do you really think I need someone like *you* to enable me to produce a book?"

She stood up then and undid her belt, and for an instant I thought she was about to undress, but she was only loosening it in order to wrap the robe more closely around herself. She drew the belt very tight and knotted it, and the finality of the gesture somehow restored her superiority over me. My rights of access were hereby revoked. Her resolve was so firm I felt almost wistful, and if she had held out her arms it would have been my turn to fall against her, but instead, she turned and, in the practiced manner of a prime minister's wife, pulled the nylon cord to open the curtains.

"I declare this day officially open," she said. "God bless it, and all who have to get through it."

"Well," I said, looking out at the scene, "that really is the morning after the night before."

The rain had turned to sleet and the lawn was covered with debris from the storm—small branches, twigs, a white cane chair thrown on its side. Here and there, around the edges of the door, where it was sheltered the sleet had stuck together and frozen into strips, like bits of polystyrene packaging. The only brightness in the murk was the reflection of our bedroom light. It resembled a flying saucer hovering above the dunes. I could see Ruth's face quite clearly in the glass: watchful, brooding.

"I'm not going to give you an interview," she said. "I don't want to be in his bloody book, being patronized and thanked by him, using your words." She turned and brushed past me. At the bedroom door she paused. "He's on his own now. I'll get a divorce. And then she can do the prison visits."

I listened to the sound of her own door opening and closing, and shortly afterward the barely audible sound of a toilet flushing. I had almost finished packing. I folded the clothes she had lent me the previous evening and laid them on the chair, put my laptop into my shoulder bag, and then the only thing left was the manuscript. It sat in a thick pile on the table where she had left it, three sullen inches of it—my millstone, my albatross, my meal ticket. I couldn't make any progress without it, yet I wasn't supposed to take it from the house. It occurred to me that perhaps I could argue the war crimes investigation had changed the circumstances of Lang's life so completely that the old rules no longer applied. At any rate, I could use that as an excuse. I certainly couldn't face the embarrassment of staying here and running into Ruth every few hours. I put the manuscript into my suitcase, along with the package from the archive, zipped them up, and went out into the corridor.

Barry was sitting with his Harry Potter novel in the chair by the front door. He raised his great slab of a face from the pages and gave me a look of weary disapproval, tinged with a sneer of amused contempt.

"Morning, sir," he said. "Finished for the night, have we?"

I thought, he knows. And then I thought, of course he knows, you bloody fool; it's his job to know. In a flash I saw his sniggering conversations with his colleagues, the log of his official observations passed to London, a discreet entry in a file somewhere, and I felt a thrust of fury and resentment. Perhaps I should have responded with a wink or a colluding quip—"Well, officer, you know what they say: there's many a good tune played on an old fiddle," or something of the sort—but instead I said, coldly, "Why don't you just fuck off?"

It wasn't exactly Oscar Wilde, but it got me out of the house. I walked through the door and set off toward the track, only belatedly registering that, unfortunately, high moral dudgeon offers no protection against stinging squalls of sleet. I trudged on with an effort at dignity for a few more yards, then ducked for cover into the lee of the house. Rainwater was overflowing from the gutter and drilling into the sandy soil. I took off my jacket and held it over my head, and considered how I was going to reach Edgartown. That was when the idea of borrowing the tan-colored Ford Escape SUV popped helpfully into my mind.

How different—how very different—the course of my life would have been if I hadn't immediately gone running toward that garage, dodging the puddles, the tent of my jacket raised over me with one hand, the other dragging my little suitcase. I see myself now as if in a movie, or perhaps, more aptly, in one of those filmed reconstructions on a TV crime show: the victim skipping unknowingly toward his fate, as ominous chords underscore the portentousness of the scene. The door was still unlocked from the previous day and the keys of the Ford were in the ignition—after all, who worries about robbers when you live at the end of a two-mile track protected by six armed bodyguards? I heaved my case into the front passenger seat, put my jacket back on, and slid behind the steering wheel.

It was as cold as a morgue, that Ford, and as dusty as an old attic. I ran my hands over the unfamiliar controls and my fingertips came away gray. I don't own a car—I've never found much need, living alone in London—and on the rare occasions I hire one, it always seems that another layer of gadgets has been added, so that the instrument panel of the average family sedan now looks to me like the cockpit of a jumbo. There was a mystifying screen to the right of the wheel, which came alive when I switched on the engine. Pulsing green arcs were shown radiating upward from Earth to an orbiting space station. As I watched, the pulse switched direction and the arcs beamed down from the heavens. An instant later, the screen showed a large red arrow, a yellow path, and a great patch of blue.

An American woman's voice, soft but commanding, said, from somewhere behind me: *Join the road as soon as possible.*

I would have turned her off, but I couldn't see how, and I was conscious that the noise of the engine might soon bring Barry lumbering out of the house to investigate. The thought of his lubricious gaze was enough to get me moving. I quickly put the Ford into reverse and backed out of the garage. Then I adjusted the mirrors, switched on the headlights and the windscreen wipers, engaged drive, and headed for the gate. As I passed the guard post, the scene on the little satellite navigation monitor swung pleasingly, as if I were playing on an arcade game, and then the red arrow settled over the center of the yellow path. I was away.

There was something oddly soothing about driving along and seeing all the little paths and streams, neatly labeled, appear at the top of the screen and then scroll down before disappearing off the bottom. It made me feel as if the world were a safe and tamed place, its every feature tagged and measured and stored in some celestial control room, where softly spoken angels kept a benign vigil on the travelers below.

In two hundred yards, instructed the woman, *turn right.*

In fifty yards, turn right.

And then, *Turn right.*

The solitary demonstrator was huddled in his hut, reading a newspaper. He stood as he saw me at the junction and came out into the sleet. I noticed he had a car parked nearby, a big old Volkswagen camper van, and I wondered why he didn't shelter in that. As I swung right, I got a good look at his gaunt gray face. He was immobile and expressionless, taking no more notice of the drenching rain than if he had been a carved wooden figure outside a drugstore. I pressed my foot on the accelerator and headed toward Edgartown, enjoying the slight sense of adventure that always comes from driving in a foreign country. My disembodied guide was silent for the next four miles or so, and I had forgotten all about her until, as I reached the outskirts of the town, she started up again.

In two hundred yards, turn left. Her voice made me jump.

In fifty yards, turn left.

Turn left, she repeated, when we reached the junction.

Now she was beginning to get on my nerves.

"I'm sorry," I muttered and took a right toward Main Street.

Turn around when possible.

"This is getting ridiculous," I said out loud and pulled over. I pressed various buttons on the navigator's console, with the aim of shutting it down. The screen changed and offered me a menu. I can't remember all the options. one was ENTER A NEW DESTINATION. I think another was RETURN TO HOME ADDRESS. And a third—the one highlighted—was REMEMBER PREVIOUS DESTINATION.

I stared at it for a while, as the potential implications slowly filtered into my brain. Cautiously, I pressed SELECT.

The screen went blank. The device was obviously malfunctioning.

I turned off the engine and hunted around for the instructions. I even braved the sleet and opened up the back of the Ford to see if they'd been left there. I returned empty-handed and turned on the ignition. Once again the navigation system lit up. As it went through its start-up routine, communicating with its mother ship, I put the car into gear and headed down the hill.

Turn around when possible.

I tapped the steering wheel with my forefingers. For the first time in my life I was confronted with the true meaning of the word "predestination." I had just passed the Victorian whaling church. Before me the hill dipped toward the harbor. A few white masts were faintly visible through the dirty lace curtain of rain. I was not far from my old hotel—from the girl in the white mobcap, and the sailing prints, and old Captain John Coffin staring sternly from the wall. It was eight o'clock. There was no traffic on the road. The sidewalks were deserted. I carried on down the slope, past all the empty shops with their cheery closed-for-the-winter-see-you-next-year!! notices.

Turn around when possible.

Wearily, I surrendered to fate. I flicked the indicator and turned into a little street of houses—Summer Street, I think it was called, inappropriately enough—and braked. The rain pounded on the roof of the Ford; the windscreen wiper thudded back and forth. A small black-and-white terrier was defecating in the gutter, with an expression of intense concentration on its ancient wise face. Its owner, too thickly swaddled against the wet and cold for me to tell either age or sex, turned clumsily to look at me, like a spaceman maneuvering himself on a lunar walk. In one hand was a pooper-scooper, in the other a white plastic scrotum of dog's crap. I quickly reversed back out into Main Street, swinging the wheel so hard I briefly mounted the curb. With a thrilling screech of tire, I set off back up the hill. The arrow swung wildly, before settling content-edly over the yellow route.

Exactly what I thought I was doing I still don't really know. I couldn't even be sure that McAra had been the last driver to enter an address. It might have been some other guest of Rhinehart's; it might have been Dep or Duc; it could even have been the police. Whatever the truth, it was certainly in the back of my mind that if things started to get remotely alarming, I could stop at any point, and I suppose that gave me a false sense of reassurance.

Once I was out of Edgartown and onto Vineyard Haven Road, I heard nothing more from my heavenly guide for several minutes. I passed dark patches of woodland and small white houses. The few approaching cars had their headlights on and were traveling slowly, swishing over the water-slicked road. I sat well forward, peering into the grimy morning. I passed a high school, just start-ing to get busy for the day, and beside it the island's set of traffic lights (they were marked on the map, like a tourist attraction: something to go and look at in the winter). The road bent sharply, the trees seemed to close in; the screen showed a fresh set of evoc-ative names: Deer Hunter's Way, Skiff Avenue.

In two hundred yards, turn right.

In fifty yards, turn right.

Turn right.

I steered down the hill into Vineyard Haven, passing a school bus toiling up it. I had a brief impression of a deserted shopping street away to my left, and then I was into the flat, shabby area around the port. I turned a corner, passed a café, and pulled up in a big car park. About a hundred yards away, across the puddled, rain-swept tarmac, a queue of vehicles was driving up the ramp of a ferry. The red arrow pointed me toward it.

In the warmth of the Ford, as shown on the navigation screen, the proposed route was inviting, like a child's painting of a summer holiday—a yellow jetty extending into the bright blue of Vineyard Haven Harbor. But the reality through the windscreen was distinctly uninviting: the sagging black mouth of the ferry, smeared at the corners with rust, and, beyond it, the heaving gray swell and the flailing hawsers of sleet.

Someone tapped on the glass beside me and I fumbled for the switch to lower the window. He was wearing dark blue oilskins with the hood pulled up, and he had to keep one hand pressed firmly on top of it to prevent it flying off his head. His spectacles were dripping with rain. A badge announced that he worked for the Steamship Authority.

"You'll have to hurry," he shouted, turning his back into the wind. "She leaves at eight-fifteen. The weather's getting bad. There might not be another for a while." He opened the door for me and almost pushed me toward the ticket office. "You go pay. I'll tell them you'll be right there."

I left the engine running and went into the little building. Even as I stood at the counter, I remained of two minds. Through the window I could see the last of the cars boarding the ferry, and the car park attendant standing by the Ford, stamping his feet to ward off the cold. He saw me staring at him and beckoned at me urgently to get a move on.

The elderly woman behind the desk looked as though she, too, could think of better places to be at a quarter past eight on a Friday morning.

"You going or what?" she demanded.

I sighed, took out my wallet, and slapped down seven ten-dollar bills.

ONCE I'D DRIVEN UP the clanking metal gangway into the dark, oily belly of the ship, another man in waterproofs directed me to a parking space, and I inched forward until he held up his hand for me to stop. All around me, drivers were leaving their vehicles and squeezing through the narrow gaps toward the stairwells. I stayed where I was and carried on trying to figure out how the navigation system worked. But after about a minute the crewman tapped on my window and indicated by a mime that I had to switch off the ignition. As I did so, the screen died again. Behind me, the ferry's rear doors closed. The ship's engines started to throb, the hull lurched, and with a discouraging scrape of steel we began to move.

I felt trapped all of a sudden, sitting in the chilly twilight of that hold, with its stink of diesel and exhaust fumes, and it was more than just the claustrophobia of being belowdecks. It was McAra. I could sense his presence next to me. His dogged, leaden obsessions now seemed to have become mine. He was like some heavy, half-witted stranger one makes the mistake of talking to on a journey and who then refuses to leave one alone. I got out of the car and locked it, and went in search of a cup of coffee. At the bar on the upper deck I queued behind a man reading *USA Today*, and over his shoulder I saw a picture of Lang with the secretary of state. "Lang to face war crimes trial" was the headline. "Washington shows support." The camera had caught him grinning.

I took my coffee over to a corner seat and considered where my curiosity had led me. For a start, I was technically guilty of stealing a car. I ought at least to call the house and let them know I'd taken it. But that would probably entail talking to Ruth, who would demand to know where I was, and I didn't want to tell her. Then there was the question of whether or not what I was doing was wise. If this *was* McAra's original route I was following, I had to face the fact that he hadn't returned from the trip alive. How was I to know what lay at the end of the journey? Perhaps I should tell someone what I was contemplating, or better still, take a companion along as a witness? Or perhaps I should simply disembark at Woods Hole, wait in one of the bars, catch the next ferry back to the island, and plan the whole thing properly, rather than launch myself into the unknown so unprepared?

Oddly enough, I didn't feel any particular sense of danger—I suppose because it was all so ordinary. I glanced around at the faces of my fellow passengers: working people mostly, to judge by their denims and boots—weary guys who had just made an early-morning delivery to the island, or people going over to America to pick up supplies. A big wave hit the side of the ship and we all swayed as one, like rippling weed on the seabed. Through the brine-streaked porthole, the low gray line of coast and the restless, freezing sea appeared completely anonymous. We could have been in the Baltic or the Solent or the White Sea—any dreary stretch of flattened shoreline where people have to find a means of turning a living at the very edge of the land.

Someone went out on deck for a cigarette, letting in a gust of cold, wet air. I didn't attempt to follow him. I had another coffee and relaxed in the safety of the warm, damp, yellowish atmosphere of the bar, until, about half an hour later, we passed Nobska Point Lighthouse and a loudspeaker instructed us to return to our vehicles. The deck pitched badly in the swell, hitting the side of the dock with a clang that rang down the length of the hull. I was knocked against the metal doorframe at the foot of the stairs. A couple of car alarms started howling and my feeling of security vanished, replaced by panic that the Ford was being broken into. But as I swayed closer, it looked untouched, and when I opened my case to check, Lang's memoirs were still there.

I switched on the engine, and by the time I emerged into the gray rain and wind of Woods Hole, the satellite screen was offering me its familiar golden path. It would have been a simple matter to have pulled over and gone into one of the nearby bars for breakfast, but instead I stayed in the convoy of traffic and let it carry me on—on into the filthy New England winter, up Woods Hole Road to Locust Street and Main Street, and beyond. I had half a tank of fuel and the whole day stretched ahead of me.

In two hundred yards, at the circle, take the second exit.

I took it, and for the next forty-five minutes I headed north on a couple of big freeways, more or less retracing my route back to Boston. That appeared to answer one question, at any rate: whatever else McAra had been up to just before he died, he hadn't been driving to New York to see Rycart. I wondered what could have tempted him to Boston. The airport, perhaps? I let my mind fill with images of him meeting someone off a plane—from England, maybe—his solemn face turned expectantly toward the sky, a hurried greeting in the arrivals hall, and then off to some clandestine rendezvous. Or perhaps he had planned to fly somewhere by himself? But just as that scenario was taking firm shape in my imagination, I was directed west toward Interstate-95, and even with my feeble grasp of Massachusetts geography I knew I must be heading away from Logan Airport and downtown Boston.

I drove as slowly as I could along the wide road for perhaps fifteen miles. The rain had eased, but it was still dark. The thermometer showed an outside temperature of twenty-five degrees Fahrenheit. I remember great swathes of woodland, interspersed with lakes and office blocks and high-tech factories gleaming brightly amid landscaped grounds, as delicately positioned as country clubs, or cemeteries. Just as I was beginning to think that perhaps McAra had been making a run for the Canadian border, the voice told me to take the next exit from the interstate, and I came down onto another big six-lane freeway which, according to the screen, was the Concord Turnpike.

I could make out very little through the screen of trees, even though their branches were bare. My slow speed was infuriating the drivers behind me. A succession of big trucks came lumbering up behind me and blazed their headlights and blared their horns, before pulling out to overtake in a fountain of dirty spray.

The woman in the back seat spoke up again. *In two hundred yards, take the next exit.*

I moved into the right-hand lane and came down the access road. At the end of the curve I found myself in a sylvan suburbia of big houses, double garages, wide drives, and open lawns—a rich but neighborly kind of a place, the houses screened from one another by trees, almost every mailbox bearing a yellow ribbon in honor of the military. I believe it was actually called Pleasant Street.

A sign pointed to Belmont Center, and that was more or less

the way I went, along roads that gradually became less populated as the price of the real estate rose. I passed a golf course and turned right into some woods. A red squirrel ran across the road in front of me and jumped on top of a sign forbidding the lighting of campfires, and that was when, in the middle of what seemed to be nowhere, my guardian angel at last announced, in a tone of calm finality: *You have reached your destination.*

THIRTEEN

★

Because I am so enthusiastic about the ghostwriting profession, I may have given the impression that it is an easy way to make a living. If so, then I should qualify my words just a little with a warning.

Ghostwriting

I PULLED UP ONTO the verge and turned off the engine. Looking around at the dense and dripping woodland, I felt a profound sense of disappointment. I wasn't sure exactly what I'd been expecting—not Deep Throat in an underground car park, necessarily, but certainly more than this. Yet again, McAra had surprised me. Here was a man reportedly even more hostile to the country than I was, and yet his trail had merely led me to a hiker's paradise.

I got out of the car and locked it. After two hours' driving I needed to fill my lungs with cold, damp New England air. I stretched and started to walk down the wet lane. The squirrel watched me from its perch across the road. I took a couple of paces toward it and clapped my hands at the cute little rodent. It streaked up into a nearby tree, flicking its tail at me like a swollen middle finger. I hunted around for a stick to throw at it, then stopped myself. I was spending far too much time alone in the woods, I decided, as I moved on down the road. I'd be happy not to hear the deep, vegetative silence of ten thousand trees for a very long while to come.

I walked on for about fifty yards until I came to an almost invisible gap in the trees. Demurely set back from the road, a five-barred electric gate blocked access to a private drive, which turned sharply after a few yards and disappeared behind trees. I couldn't see the house. Beside the gate was a gray metal mailbox with no name on it, just a number—3551—and a stone pillar with an intercom and a code pad. A sign said, THESE PREMISES ARE PROTECTED BY CYCLOPS SECURITY; a toll-free number was printed across an eyeball. I hesitated, then pressed the buzzer. While I waited, I glanced around. A small video camera was mounted on a nearby branch. I tried the buzzer again. There was no answer.

I stepped back, uncertain what to do. It briefly crossed my mind to climb the gate and make an unauthorized inspection of the property, but I didn't like the look of the camera, and I didn't like the sound of Cyclops Security. I noticed that the mailbox was crammed too full to close properly, and I saw no harm in at least discovering the name of the house's owner. With another glance over my shoulder, and an apologetic shrug toward the camera, I pulled out a handful of mail. It was variously addressed to Mr. and Mrs. Paul Emmett, Professor and Mrs. Paul Emmett, Professor Emmett, and Nancy Emmett. Judging by the postmarks, it looked as though there was at least two days' worth uncollected. The Emmetts were either away, or—what? Lying inside, dead? I was developing a morbid imagination. Some of the letters had been forwarded, with a sticker covering the original address. I scraped one of the labels back with my thumb. Emmett, I learned, was president emeritus of something called the Arcadia Institution, with an address in Washington, DC.

Emmett . . . Emmett . . . For some reason that name was familiar to me. I stuffed the letters back in the box and returned to my car. I opened my suitcase, took out the package addressed to McAra, and ten minutes later I'd found what I had vaguely remembered: P. Emmett (St. John's) was one of the cast of the Footlights revue, pictured with Lang. He was the oldest of the group, the one who I'd thought was a postgraduate. He had shorter hair than the others, looked more conventional: "square," as the expression went at that time. Was this what had brought McAra all the way up here: yet more research about Cambridge? Emmett was mentioned in the memoirs, too, now I came to think about it. I picked up the manuscript and thumbed my way through the section on Lang's university days, but his name didn't appear there. Instead he was quoted at the start of the very last chapter:

> Professor Paul Emmett of Harvard University has written of the unique importance of the English-speaking peoples in the spread of democracy around the world: "As long as these nations stand together, freedom is safe; whenever they have faltered, tyranny has gathered strength." I profoundly agree with this sentiment.

The squirrel came back and regarded me malevolently from the roadside.

Odd: that was my overwhelming feeling about everything at that moment. *Odd*.

I don't know exactly how long I sat there. I do remember that I was so bemused I forgot to turn on the Ford's heater, and it was only when I heard the sound of another car approaching that I realized how cold and stiff I had become. I looked in the mirror and saw a pair of headlights, and then a small Japanese car drove past me. A middle-aged, dark-haired woman was at the wheel, and next to her was a man of about sixty, wearing glasses and a jacket and tie. He turned to stare at me, and I knew at once it was Emmett, not because I recognized him (I didn't) but because I couldn't imagine who else would be traveling down such a quiet road. The car pulled up outside the entrance to the drive, and I saw Emmett get out to empty his mailbox. Once again, he peered in my direction, and I thought he might be about to come down and challenge me. Instead, he returned to the car, which then moved on, out of my line of sight, presumably up to the house.

I stuffed the photographs and the page from the memoirs into my shoulder bag, gave the Emmetts ten minutes to open the place up and settle themselves in, then turned on the engine and drove up to the gate. This time, when I pressed the buzzer, the answer came immediately.

"Hello?" It was a woman's voice.

"Is that Mrs. Emmett?"

"Who is this?"

"I wondered if I could have a word with Professor Emmett."

"He's very tired." She had a drawling voice, something between an English aristocrat and a southern belle, and the tinny quality of the intercom accentuated it: *"S'vair tahd."*

"I won't keep him long."

"Do you have an appointment?"

"It's about Adam Lang. I'm assisting him with his memoirs."

"Just a moment please."

I knew they'd be studying me on the video camera. I tried to adopt a suitably respectable pose. When the intercom crackled again, it was an American male voice that spoke: resonant, fruity, actorish.

"This is Paul Emmett. I believe you must have made a mistake."

"You were at Cambridge with Mr. Lang, I believe?"

"We were contemporaries, yes, but I can't claim to know him."

"I have a picture of the two of you together in a Footlights revue."

There was a long pause.

"Come on up to the house."

There was a whine of an electric motor, and the gate slowly opened.

As I followed the drive, the big three-story house gradually appeared through the trees: a central section built of gray stone flanked by wings made of wood and painted white. Most of the windows were arched, with small panes of rippled glass and big slatted shutters. It could have been any age, from six months to a century. Several steps led up to a pillared porch, where Emmett himself was waiting. The extent of the land and the encroaching trees provided a deep sense of seclusion. The only sound of civilization was a big jet, invisible in the low cloud, dropping toward the airport. I parked in front of the garage, next to the Emmetts' car, and got out carrying my bag.

"You must forgive me if I seem a little groggy," said Emmett after we'd shaken hands. "We just flew in from Washington and I'm feeling somewhat tired. I normally never see anyone without an appointment. But your mention of a photograph did rather stimulate my curiosity."

He dressed as precisely as he spoke. His spectacles had fashionably modern tortoiseshell frames, his jacket was dark gray, his shirt was duck egg blue, his bright red tie had a motif of pheasants on the wing, there was a matching silk handkerchief in his breast pocket. Now I was closer to him, I could discern the younger man staring out from the older: age had merely blurred him, that was all. He couldn't keep his eyes off my bag. I knew he wanted me to produce the photograph right there on the doorstep. But I was too canny for that. I waited, and kept on waiting, so that eventually he had to say, "Fine. Please, do come in."

The house had polished wood floors and smelled of wax polish and dried flowers. It had an uninhabited chill about it. A grandfather clock ticked very loudly on the landing. I could hear his wife on the telephone in another room. "Yes," she said, "he's here now." Then she must have moved away. Her voice became indistinct and faded altogether.

Emmett closed the front door behind us.

"May I?" he said.

I took out the cast photograph and gave it to him. He pushed his glasses up onto his silvery thatch of hair and wandered over with it to the hall window. He looked fit for his age and I guessed he played some regular sport: squash, probably; golf, definitely.

"Well, well," he said, holding the monochrome image up to the weak winter light, tilting it this way and that, peering at it down his long nose, like an expert checking a painting for authenticity, "I have literally no recollection of this."

"But it *is* you?"

"Oh, yes. I was on the board of the Dramat in the sixties. Which was quite a time, as you can imagine." He shared a complicit chuckle with his youthful image. "Oh, yes."

"The Dramat?"

"I'm sorry." He looked up. "The Yale Dramatic Association. I thought I'd maintain my theatrical interests when I went over to Cambridge for my doctoral research. Alas, I only managed a term in the Footlights before pressure of work put an end to my dramatic career. May I keep this?"

"I'm afraid not. But I'm sure I can get you a copy."

"Would you? That would be very kind." He turned it over and inspected the back. "The *Cambridge Evening News*. You must tell me how you came by it."

"I'd be happy to," I said. And again I waited. It was like playing a hand of cards. He would not yield a trick unless I forced him. The big clock ticked back and forth a few times.

"Come into my study," he said.

He opened a door and I followed him into a room straight out of Rick's London club: dark green wallpaper, floor-to-ceiling books, library steps, overstuffed brown leather furniture, a big brass lectern in the shape of an eagle, a Roman bust, a faint odor of cigars. One wall was devoted to memorabilia: citations, prizes, honorary degrees, and a lot of photographs. I took in Emmett with Bill Clinton and Al Gore, Emmett with Margaret Thatcher and Nelson Mandela. I'd tell you the names of the others if I knew who they were. A German chancellor. A French president. There was also a picture of him with Lang, a grin-and-grip at what seemed to be a cocktail party. He saw me looking.

"The wall of ego," he said. "We all have them. Think of it as the equivalent of the orthodontist's fish tank. Do take a seat. I'm afraid I can only spare a few minutes, unfortunately."

I perched on the unyielding brown sofa while he took the captain's chair behind his desk. It rolled easily back and forth. He swung his feet up onto the desk, giving me a fine view of the slightly scuffed soles of his brogues.

"So," he said. "The picture."

"I'm working with Adam Lang on his memoirs."

"I know. You said. Poor Lang. It's a very bad business, this posturing by The Hague. As for Rycart—the worst foreign secretary since the war, in my view. It was a terrible error to appoint him. But if the ICC continues to behave so foolishly, they will succeed merely in making Lang first a martyr and then a hero, and thus," he added, gesturing graciously toward me, "a bestseller."

"How well do you know him?"

"Lang? Hardly at all. You look surprised."

"Well, for a start, he mentions you in his memoirs."

Emmett appeared genuinely taken aback. "Now it's my turn to be surprised. What does he say?"

"It's a quote, at the start of the final chapter." I pulled the relevant page from my bag. " 'As long as these nations'—that's everyone who speaks English—'stand together,' " I read, " 'freedom is safe; whenever they have faltered, tyranny has gathered strength.' And then Lang says, 'I profoundly agree with this sentiment.' "

"Well, that's decent of him," said Emmett. "And his instincts as prime minister were good, in my judgment. But that doesn't mean I know him."

"And then there's that," I said, pointing to the wall of ego.

"Oh, *that*." Emmett waved his hand dismissively. "That was just taken at a reception at Claridge's, to mark the tenth anniversary of the Arcadia Institution."

"The Arcadia Institution?" I repeated.

"It's a little organization I used to run. It's very select. No reason why you should have heard of it. The prime minister graced us with his presence. It was purely professional."

"But you must have known Adam Lang at Cambridge," I persisted.

"Not really. One summer term, our paths crossed. That was it."

"Can you remember much about him?" I took out my notebook. Emmett eyed it as if I'd just pulled out a revolver. "I'm sorry," I said. "Do you mind?"

"Not at all. Go ahead. I'm just rather bewildered. No one's ever mentioned the Cambridge connection between us in all these years. I've barely thought about it myself until this moment. I don't think I can tell you anything worth writing down."

"But you performed together?"

"In one production. The summer revue. I can't even remember now what it was called. There were a hundred members, you know."

"So he made no impression on you?"

"None."

"Even though he became prime minister?"

"Obviously if I'd known he was going to do that, I'd have taken the trouble to get to know him better. But in my time I've met eight presidents, four popes, and five British prime ministers, and none of them was what I would describe as personally truly outstanding."

Yes, I thought, and has it ever occurred to you they might not have reckoned you were up to much, either? But I didn't say that. Instead I said, "Can I show you something else?"

"If you really think it will be of interest." He ostentatiously checked his watch.

I took out the other photographs. Now that I looked at them again, it was clear that Emmett featured in several. Indeed, he was unmistakably the man on the summer picnic, giving the thumbs-up behind Lang's back, while the future prime minister did a Bogart with his joint and was fed strawberries and champagne.

I reached across and handed them to Emmett, who performed his affected little piece of stage business again, pushing up his glasses so that he could study the pictures with his naked eyes. I can see him now: sleek and pink and imperturbable. His expression didn't flicker, which struck me as peculiar, because mine certainly would have done, in similar circumstances.

"Oh my," he said. "Is that what I think it is? Let's hope he didn't inhale."

"But that is you standing behind him, isn't it?"

"I do believe it is. And I do believe I'm on the point of issuing a stern warning to him on the perils of drug abuse. Can't you just sense it forming on my lips?" He gave the pictures back to me and pulled his spectacles back down onto his nose. Tilting farther back in his chair, he scrutinized me. "Does Mr. Lang really want these published in his memoirs? If so, I would prefer it if I weren't identified. My children would be mortified. They're so much more puritanical than we were."

"Can you tell me the names of any of the others in the picture? The girls, perhaps?"

"I'm sorry. That summer is just a blur, a long and happy blur. The world may have been going to pieces around us, but we were making merry."

His words reminded me of something that Ruth had said, about all the things that were going on at the time the picture was taken.

"You must have been lucky," I said, "given you were at Yale in the late sixties, to avoid being drafted to Vietnam."

"You know the old saying: 'if you had the dough, you didn't have to go.' I got a student deferment. Now," he said, twirling in his chair and lifting his feet off the desk. He was suddenly much more businesslike. He picked up a pen and opened a notebook. "You were going to tell me where you got those pictures."

"Does the name Michael McAra mean anything to you?"

"No. Should it?" He answered just a touch too quickly, I thought.

"McAra was my predecessor on the Lang memoirs," I said. "He was the one who ordered the pictures from England. He drove up here to see you nearly three weeks ago and died a few hours afterward."

"Drove up to see *me*?" Emmett shook his head. "I'm afraid you're mistaken. Where was he driving from?"

"Martha's Vineyard."

"Martha's Vineyard! My dear fellow, *nobody* is on Martha's Vineyard at this time of year."

He was teasing me again: anyone who had watched the news the previous day would have known where Lang had been staying.

I said, "The vehicle McAra was driving had your address programmed into its navigation system."

"Well, I can't think why that should be the case." Emmett stroked his chin and seemed to weigh the matter carefully. "No, I really can't. And even if it's true, it certainly doesn't prove he actually made the journey. How did he die?"

"He drowned."

"I'm very sorry to hear it. I've never believed the myth that death by drowning is painless, have you? I'm sure it must be agonizing."

"The police never said anything to you about this?"

"No. I've had no contact with the police whatsoever."

"Were you here that weekend? This would have been January the eleventh and twelfth."

Emmett sighed. "A less equable man than I would start to find your questions impertinent." He came out from behind his desk and went over to the door. "Nancy!" he called. "Our visitor wishes to know where we were on the weekend of the eleventh and twelfth of January. Do we possess that information?" He stood holding the door open and gave me an unfriendly smile. When Mrs. Emmett appeared, he didn't bother to introduce me. She was carrying a desk diary.

"That was the Colorado weekend," she said and showed the book to her husband.

"Of course it was," he said. "We were at the Aspen Institute." He flourished the page at me. " 'Bipolar Relationships in a Multipolar World.' "

"Sounds fun."

"It was." He closed the diary with a definitive snap. "I was the main speaker."

"You were there the whole weekend?"

"I was," said Mrs. Emmett. "I stayed for the skiing. Emmett flew back on Sunday, didn't you, darling?"

"So you could have seen McAra," I said to him.

"I could have, but I didn't."

"Just to return to Cambridge—" I began.

"No," he said, holding up his hand. "Please. If you don't mind, let's *not* return to Cambridge. I've said all I have to say on the matter. Nancy?"

She must have been twenty years his junior, and she jumped when he addressed her in a way no first wife ever would.

"Emmett?"

"Show our friend here out, would you?"

As we shook hands, he said, "I am an avid reader of political memoirs. I shall be sure to get hold of Mr. Lang's book when it appears."

"Perhaps he'll send you a copy," I said, "for old time's sake."

"I doubt it very much," he replied. "The gate will open automatically. Be sure to make a right at the bottom of the drive. If you turn left, the road will take you deeper into the woods and you'll never be seen again."

MRS. EMMETT CLOSED THE door behind me before I'd even reached the bottom step. I could sense her husband watching me from the window of his study as I walked across the damp grass to the Ford. At the bottom of the drive, while I waited for the gate to open, the wind moved suddenly through the branches of the high trees on either side of me, laying a heavy lash of rainwater across the car. It startled me so much I felt the hairs on the back of my head stand out in tiny spikes.

I pulled out into the empty road and headed back the way I had come. I felt slightly unnerved, as if I'd just descended a staircase in the darkness and missed the bottom few steps. My immediate priority was to get clear of those trees.

Turn around where possible.

I stopped the Ford, grabbed the navigation system in both hands, and twisted and yanked it at the same time. It came away from the front panel with a satisfying twang of breaking cables, and I tossed it into the foot well on the passenger's side. At the same time I became aware of a large black car with bright headlights coming up close behind me. It overtook the Ford too quickly for me to see who was driving, accelerated up to the junction, and disappeared. When I looked back, the country lane was once again deserted.

It's curious how the processes of fear work. If I'd been asked a week earlier to predict what I might do in such a situation, I'd have said that I'd drive straight back to Martha's Vineyard and try to put the whole business out of my mind. In fact, I discovered, Nature mingles an unexpected element of anger in with fear, presumably to encourage the survival of the species. Like a caveman confronted by a tiger, my instinct at that moment was not to run; it was somehow to get back at the supercilious Emmett—the sort of crazy, atavistic response that leads otherwise sane householders to chase armed burglars down the street, usually with disastrous results.

So instead of sensibly trying to find my way back to the interstate, I followed the road signs to Belmont. It's a sprawling, leafy, wealthy town of terrifying cleanliness and orderliness—the sort of place where you need a license just to keep a cat. The neat streets, with their flagpoles and their four-by-fours, slipped by, seemingly identical. I cruised along the wide boulevards, unable to get my bearings, until at last I came to something that seemed to resemble the middle of town. This time, when I parked my car, I took my suitcase with me.

I was on a road called Leonard Street, a curve of pretty shops with colored canopies set against a backdrop of big bare trees. One building was pink. A coating of snow, melted at the edges, covered the gray roofs. It could have been a ski resort. It offered me various things I didn't need—a real estate agent, a jeweler, a hairdresser—and one thing I did: an internet café. I ordered coffee and a bagel and took a seat as far away from the window as I could. I put my case on the chair opposite, to discourage anyone from joining me, sipped my coffee, took a bite out of my bagel, clicked on Google, typed in "Paul Emmett" + "Arcadia Institution," and leaned toward the screen.

ACCORDING TO WWW.ARCADIAINSTITUTION.ORG, the Arcadia Institution was founded in August 1991 on the fiftieth anniversary of the first summit meeting between Prime Minister Winston S. Churchill and President Franklin D. Roosevelt, at Placentia Bay in Newfoundland. There was a photograph of Roosevelt on the deck of a U.S. battleship, wearing a smart gray suit, receiving Churchill, who was about a head shorter and dressed in some peculiar rumpled, dark blue naval outfit, complete with a cap. He looked like a crafty head gardener paying his respects to a local squire.

The aim of the institution, the website said, was "to further Anglo-American relations and foster the timeless ideals of democracy and free speech for which our two nations have always stood in times of peace and war." This was to be achieved "through seminars, policy programs, conferences, and leadership development initiatives," as well as through the publication of a biannual journal, the *Arcadian Review*, and the funding of ten Arcadia Scholarships, awarded annually, for postgraduate research into "cultural, political, and strategic subjects of mutual interest to Great Britain and the United States." The Arcadia Institution had offices in St. James's Square, London, and in Washington, and the names of its board of trustees—ex-ambassadors, corporate CEOs, university professors—read like the guest list for the dullest dinner party you would ever endure in your life.

Paul Emmett was the institution's first president and CEO, and the website usefully offered his life in a paragraph: born Chicago 1949; graduate of Yale University and St. John's College, Cambridge; lecturer in international affairs at Harvard University, 1975–79, and subsequently Howard T. Polk III Professor of Foreign Relations, 1979–91; thereafter the founding head of the Arcadia Institution; president emeritus since 2007; publications: *Whither Thou Goest: The Special Relationship 1940–1956; The Conundrum of Change; Losing Empires, Finding Roles: Some Aspects of US-UK Relations Since 1956; The Chains of Prometheus: Foreign Policy Constraints in the Nuclear Age; The Triumphant Generation: America, Britain, and the New World Order; Why We Are in Iraq.* There was a profile in *Time* magazine, which described his hobbies as squash, golf, and the operas of Gilbert and Sullivan, "which he and his second wife, Nancy Cline, a defense analyst from Houston, Texas, regularly call upon their guests to perform at the end of one of their famous supper parties in the prosperous Harvard bedroom community of Belmont."

I worked my way through the first of what Google promised would eventually prove to be thirty-seven thousand entries about Emmett and Arcadia:

Arcadia Institution - Roundtable on Middle East Policy
The establishment of democracy in Syria and Iran . . .
Paul Emmett in his opening address stated his belief . . .
www.arcadiainstitution.org/site/roundtable/A56fL%2004
.htm - 35k - Cached - Similar pages

Arcadia Institution - Wikipedia, the free encyclopedia
The **Arcadia Institution** is an Anglo-American nonprofit
organization founded in 1991 under the presidency of
Professor **Paul Emmett** . . .
en.wikipedia.org/wiki/**Arcadia Institution** - 35k - Cached
- Similar pages

Arcadia Institution/Arcadia Strategy Group - Source
Watch The **Arcadia Institution** describes itself as dedicated to fostering . . . Professor **Paul Emmett,** an expert
in Anglo-American . . .
www.sourcewatch.org/index.php?title=**Arcadia
Institution** - 39k - Cached - Similar pages

USATODAY.com - 5 Questions for **Paul Emmett**
Paul Emmett, former professor of foreign relations
at Harvard, now heads the influential **Arcadia
Institution** . . .
www.usatoday.com/world/2002-08-07/questions
x.htm?tab1.htm - 35k - Cached - Similar pages

When I got bored with the same old stuff about seminars and summer conferences, I changed my search request to "Arcadia Institution" + "Adam Lang" and got a news story from the *Guardian* website about Arcadia's anniversary reception and the prime minister's attendance. I switched to Google Images and was offered a mosaic of bizarre illustrations: a cat, a couple of acrobats in leotards, a cartoon of Lang blowing into a bag with the caption "soon to be humiliated." This is the trouble with internet research, in my experience. The proportion of what's useful to what's dross dwindles very quickly, and suddenly it's like searching for something dropped down the back of a sofa and coming up with handfuls of old coins, buttons, fluff, and sucked sweets. What's important is to ask the right question, and somehow I sensed I was getting it wrong.

I broke off to rub my aching eyes. I ordered another coffee and another bagel and checked out my fellow diners. It was a light crowd, considering it was lunchtime: an old fellow with his paper, a man and woman in their twenties holding hands, two mothers—or, more likely, nannies—gossiping while their three toddlers played unheeded under the table, and a couple of young guys with short-cropped hair, who could have been in the armed forces or one of the emergency services, perhaps (I'd seen a fire station nearby), sitting on stools at the counter with their backs to me, engaged in earnest conversation.

I returned to the Arcadia Institution website and clicked on the board of trustees. Up they all came, like spirits summoned from the vasty transatlantic deep: Steven D. Engler, former U.S. defense secretary; Lord Leghorn, former British foreign secretary; Sir David Moberly, GCMG, KCVO, the thousand-year-old former British ambassador to Washington; Raymond T. Streicher, former

U.S. ambassador to London; Arthur Prussia, president and CEO of the Hallington Group; Professor Mel Crawford of the John F. Kennedy School of Government; Dame Unity Chambers of the Strategic Studies Foundation; Max Hardaker of Godolphin Securities; Stephanie Cox Morland, senior director of Manhattan Equity Holdings; Sir Milius Rapp of the London School of Economics; Cornelius Iremonger of Cordesman Industrials; and Franklin R. Dollerman, senior partner of McCosh & Partners.

Laboriously, I began entering their names, together with Adam Lang's, into the search engine. Engler had praised Lang's steadfast courage on the op-ed page of the *New York Times*. Leghorn had made a hand-wringing speech in the House of Lords, regretting the situation in the Middle East but calling the prime minister "a man of sincerity." Moberly had suffered a stroke and was saying nothing. Streicher had been vocal in his support at the time Lang flew to Washington to pick up his Presidential Medal of Freedom. I was starting to weary of the whole procedure until I typed in Arthur Prussia. I got a one-year-old press release:

> LONDON—The Hallington Group is pleased to announce that Adam Lang, the former prime minister of Great Britain, will be joining the company as a strategic consultant.
>
> Mr. Lang's position, which will not be full-time, will involve providing counsel and advice to senior Hallington investment professionals worldwide.
>
> Arthur Prussia, Hallington's president and chief executive officer, said: "Adam

Lang is one of the world's most respected and experienced statesmen, and we are honoured to be able to draw on his well of experience."

Adam Lang said: "I welcome the challenge of working with a company of such global reach, commitment to democracy, and renowned integrity as the Hallington Group."

The Hallington Group rang only the faintest of bells, so I looked it up. Six hundred employees; twenty-four worldwide offices; a mere four hundred investors, mainly Saudi; and *thirty-five billion dollars* of funds at its disposal. The portfolio of companies it controlled looked as if it had been drawn up by Darth Vader. Hallington's subsidiaries manufactured cluster bombs, mobile howitzers, interceptor missiles, tank-busting helicopters, swing-wing bombers, tanks, nuclear centrifuges, aircraft carriers. It owned a company that provided security for contractors in the Middle East, another that carried out surveillance operations and data checks within the United States and worldwide, and a construction company that specialized in building military bunkers and airstrips. Two members of its main board had been senior directors of the CIA.

I know the internet is the stuff a paranoiac's dreams are made of. I know it parcels up everything—Lee Harvey Oswald, Princess Diana, Opus Dei, Al Qaeda, Israel, MI6, crop circles—and with pretty blue ribbons of hyperlinks it ties them all into a single grand conspiracy. But I also know the wisdom of the old saying that a paranoiac is simply a person in full possession of the facts, and as I typed in "Arcadia Institution" + "Hallington Group" + "CIA," I sensed that something was starting to emerge, like the lineaments of a ghost ship, out of the fog of data on the screen.

washingtonpost.com: **Hallington** jet linked to **CIA** "torture flights"
The company denied all knowledge of the **CIA** program of "extraordinary rendition" . . . member of the board of the prestigious **Arcadia Institution** has . . .
www.washingtonpost.com/ac2/wp-dyn/A27824-2007Dec26language= - Cached - Similar pages

I clicked on the story and scrolled down to the relevant part:

The Hallington Gulfstream Four was clandestinely photographed—minus its corporate logo—at the Stare Kiejkuty military base in Poland, where the CIA is believed to have maintained a secret detention center, on February 18.

This was two days after four British citizens—Nasir Ashraf, Shakeel Qazi, Salim Khan, and Faruk Ahmed—were allegedly kidnapped by CIA operatives from Peshawar, Pakistan. Mr. Ashraf is reported to have died of heart failure after the interrogation procedure known as "water boarding."

Between February and July of that same year, the jet made 51 visits to Guantánamo and 82 visits to Washington Dulles International Airport as well as landings at Andrews Air Force

Base outside the capital and the U.S. air bases at Ramstein and Rhein-Main in Germany.

The plane's flight log also shows visits to Afghanistan, Morocco, Dubai, Jordan, Italy, Japan, Switzerland, Azerbaijan, and the Czech Republic.

The Hallington logo was visible in photographs taken at an air show in Schenectady, N.Y., on August 23, eight days after the Gulfstream returned to Washington from an around-the-world flight that included Anchorage, Osaka, Dubai, and Shannon.

The logo was not visible when the Gulfstream was photographed during a fuel stop at Shannon on September 27. But when the plane turned up at Denver's Centennial Airport in February of this year, a photo showed it was sporting not only the Hallington logo but also a new registration number.

A spokesman for Hallington confirmed that the Gulfstream had been frequently leased to other operators but insisted the company had no knowledge of the uses to which it might have been put.

Water boarding? I had never heard of it. It sounded harmless enough, a kind of healthy outdoor sport, a cross between windsurfing and white-water rafting. I looked it up on a website.

Water boarding consists of tightly binding a prisoner to an inclined board in such a manner that the victim's feet are higher than the head and all movement is impossible. Cloth or cellophane is then used to cover the prisoner's face, onto which the interrogator pours a continuous stream of water. Although some of the liquid may enter the victim's lungs, it is the psychological sensation of being under water that makes water boarding so effective. A gag reflex is triggered, the prisoner literally feels himself to be drowning, and almost instantly begs to be released. CIA officers who have been subjected to water boarding as part of their training have lasted an average of fourteen seconds before caving in. Al Qaeda's toughest prisoner, and alleged mastermind of the 9/11 bombings, Khalid Sheik Mohammed, won the admiration of his CIA interrogators when he was able to last two and a half minutes before begging to confess.

Water boarding can cause severe pain and damage to the lungs, brain damage due to oxygen deprivation, limb breakage and dislocation due to struggling against restraints, and long-term psychological trauma. In 1947, a Japanese officer was convicted of using water boarding on a US citizen and sentenced to fifteen years hard labor for a war crime. According to an investigation by ABC News, the CIA was authorized to begin using water boarding in mid-March 2002, and recruited a cadre of fourteen interrogators trained in the technique.

There was an illustration, from Pol Pot's Cambodia, of a man bound by his wrists and ankles to a sloping table, lying on his back, upside down. His head was in a sack. His face was being saturated by a man holding a watering can. In another photograph, a Vietcong suspect, pinioned to the ground, was being given similar treatment by three GIs using water from a drinking bottle. The soldier pouring the water was grinning. The man sitting on the prisoner's chest had a cigarette held casually between the second and third fingers of his right hand.

I sat back in my chair and thought of various things. I thought, especially, of Emmett's comment about McAra's death—that drowning wasn't painless but agonizing. It had struck me at the time as an odd thing for a professor to say. Flexing my fingers, like a concert pianist preparing to play a challenging final movement, I typed a fresh request into the search engine: "Paul Emmett" + "CIA."

Immediately, the screen filled with results, all of them, at first sight, dross: articles and book reviews by Emmett that happened to mention the CIA; articles by others about the CIA that also contained references to Emmett; articles about the Arcadia Institution in which the words "CIA" and "Emmett" had featured. I must have gone through thirty or forty in all, until I came to one which sounded promising.

<u>The **CIA** in Academia</u>
The Central Intelligence Agency is now using several
hundred American academics . . . **Paul Emmett** . . .
www.spooks-on-campus.org/Church/listK1897a/html -
11k

The web page was headed "Who Did Frank Have in Mind???"
and started with a quote from Senator Frank Church's Select
Committee report on the CIA, published in 1976:

> The Central Intelligence Agency is now us-
> ing several hundred American academics
> ("academics" includes administrators, faculty
> members, and graduate students engaged in
> teaching), who in addition to providing leads
> and, on occasion, making introductions for
> intelligence purposes, occasionally write
> books and other material to be used for pro-
> paganda purposes abroad. Beyond these, an
> additional few score are used in an unwitting
> manner for minor activities.

Beneath it, in alphabetical order, was a hyperlinked list of
about twenty names, among them Emmett's, and when I clicked
on it, I felt as though I had fallen through a trapdoor.

> Yale graduate Paul Emmett was reported by
> CIA whistleblower Frank Molinari to have
> joined the Agency as an officer in either 1969
> or 1970, where he was assigned to the For-

eign Resources Division of the Directorate of
Operations. (Source: *Inside the Agency*, Am-
sterdam, 1977)

"Oh no," I said quietly. "No, no. That can't be right."

I must have stared at the screen for a full minute, until a sudden crash of breaking crockery snapped me out of my reverie and
I looked round to see that one of the kids playing under the nearby
table had tipped the whole thing over. As a waitress hurried across
with a dustpan and brush, and as the nannies (or mothers) scolded
the children, I noticed that the two short-haired men at the counter weren't taking any notice of this little drama: they were staring
hard at me. One had a cell phone to his ear.

Fairly calmly—more calmly, I hoped, than I felt—I turned off
the computer and pretended to take a final sip of coffee. The liquid had gone cold while I'd been working and was freezing and
bitter on my lips. Then I picked up my suitcase and put a twenty-
dollar bill on the table. Already I was thinking that if something
happened to me, the harassed waitress would surely remember the
solitary Englishman who took the table farthest from the window
and absurdly overtipped. What good this would have done me, I
have no idea, but it seemed clever at the time. I made sure I didn't
look at the short-haired pair as I passed them.

Out on the street, in the cold gray light, with the green-
canopied Starbucks a few doors down and the slowly passing traffic ("Baby on Board: Please Drive Carefully") and the elderly
pedestrians in their fur hats and gloves, it was briefly possible to
imagine that I'd spent the past hour playing some homemade vir-
tual reality game. But then the door of the café opened behind me
and the two men came out. I walked briskly up the street toward

the Ford, and once I was behind the wheel I locked myself in. When I checked the mirrors I couldn't see either of my fellow diners.

I didn't move for a while. It felt safer simply sitting there. I fantasized that perhaps if I stayed put long enough, I could somehow be absorbed by osmosis into the peaceful, prosperous life of Belmont. I could go and do what all these retired folk were bent on doing—playing a hand of bridge, maybe, or watching an afternoon movie, or wandering along to the local library to read the papers and shake their heads at the way the world was all going to hell now that my callow and cosseted generation was in charge of it. I watched the newly coiffed ladies emerge from the salon and lightly pat their hair. The young couple who had been holding hands in the café were inspecting rings in the window of the jeweler.

And I? I experienced a twinge of self-pity. I was as separate from all this normality as if I were in a bubble of glass.

I took out the photographs again and flicked through them until I came to the one of Lang and Emmett onstage together. A future prime minister and an alleged CIA officer, prancing around wearing gloves and hats in a comic revue? It seemed not so much improbable as grotesque, but here was the evidence in my hand. I turned the picture over and considered the number scrawled on the back, and the more I considered it, the more obvious it seemed that there was only one course of action open to me. The fact that I would, once again, be trailing along in the footsteps of McAra could not be helped.

I waited until the young lovers had gone into the jewelry store and then took out my mobile phone. I scrolled down to where the number was stored and called Richard Rycart.

FOURTEEN

★

Half the job of ghosting is about finding out about
other people.

Ghostwriting

THIS TIME, HE ANSWERED within a few seconds.

"So you rang back," he said quietly, in that nasal, singsong
voice of his. "Somehow I had a feeling you would, whoever you
are. Not many people have this number." He waited for me to
reply. I could hear a man talking in the background—delivering a
speech, it sounded like. "Well, my friend, are you going to stay on
the line this time?"

"Yes," I said.

He waited again, but I didn't know how to begin. I kept
thinking of Lang, of what he would think if he could see me
talking to his would-be nemesis. I was breaking every rule in
the ghosting guidebook. I was in breach of the confiden-

tiality agreement I'd signed with Rhinehart. It was professional suicide.

"I tried to call you back a couple of times," he continued. I detected a hint of reproach.

Across the street, the young lovers had come out of the jewelry store and were strolling toward me.

"I know," I said, finding my voice at last. "I'm sorry. I found your number written down somewhere. I didn't know whose it was. I called it on the off chance. It didn't seem right to be talking to you."

"Why not?"

The couple passed by. I followed their progress in the mirror. They had their hands in one another's back pockets, like pickpockets on a blind date.

I took the plunge. "I'm working for Adam Lang. I—"

"Don't tell me your name," he said quickly. "Don't use any names. Keep everything nonspecific. Where exactly did you find my number?"

His urgency unnerved me.

"On the back of a photograph."

"What sort of photograph?"

"Of my client's days at university. My predecessor had it."

"Did he, by God?" Now it was Rycart's turn to pause. I could hear people clapping at the other end of the line.

"You sound shocked," I said.

"Yes, well, it ties in with something he said to me."

"I've been to see one of the people in the photograph. I thought you might be able to help me."

"Why don't you talk to your employer?"

"He's away."

"Of course he is." He had a satisfied smile in his voice. "And where are you? Without being too specific?"

"In New England."

"Can you get to the city where I am, right away? You know where I am, I take it? Where I work?"

"I suppose so," I said doubtfully. "I have a car. I could drive."

"No, don't drive. Flying's safer than the roads."

"That's what the airlines say."

"Listen, my friend," whispered Rycart fiercely, "if I was in your position, I wouldn't joke. Go to the nearest airport. Catch the first available plane. Text me the flight number, nothing else. I'll arrange for someone to collect you when you land."

"But how will they know what I look like?"

"They won't. You'll have to look out for them."

There was a renewed burst of applause in the background. I started to raise a fresh objection, but it was too late. He had hung up.

I DROVE OUT OF Belmont without any clear idea of the route I was supposed to take. I checked the rearview mirror neurotically every few seconds, but if I was being followed, I couldn't tell. Different cars appeared behind me, and none seemed to stay for longer than a couple of minutes. I kept my eyes open for signs to Boston and eventually crossed a big river and joined the interstate, heading east.

It was not yet three in the afternoon, but already the day was starting to darken. Away to my right, the downtown office blocks gleamed gold against a swollen Atlantic sky, while up ahead the lights of the big jets fell toward Logan like shooting stars. I maintained my usual cautious pace over the next couple of miles. Logan Airport, for those who have never had the pleasure, sits in the middle of Boston Harbor, approached from the south by a long tunnel. As the road descended underground, I asked myself whether I was really going to go through with this, and it was a good measure of my uncertainty that when—a mile later—I rose again into the deeper gloom of the afternoon, I still hadn't decided.

I followed the signs to the long-term car park and was just reversing into a bay when my telephone rang. The incoming number was unfamiliar. I almost didn't answer. When I did, a peremptory voice said, "What on earth are you doing?"

It was Ruth Lang. She had that presumption of beginning a conversation without first announcing who was calling, a lapse in manners I was sure her husband would never have been guilty of, even when he was prime minister.

"Working," I said.

"Really? You're not at your hotel."

"Aren't I?"

"Well, are you? They told me you hadn't even checked in."

I flailed around for an adequate lie and hit on a partial truth. "I decided to go to New York."

"Why?"

"I wanted to see John Maddox, to talk about the structure of the book, in view of the"—a tactful euphemism was needed, I decided—"the changed circumstances."

"I was worried about you," she said. "All day I've been walking up and down this fucking beach thinking about what we discussed last night—"

I interrupted. "I wouldn't say anything about that on the phone."

"Don't worry, I won't. I'm not a total fool. It's just that the more I go over things, the more worried I get."

"Where's Adam?"

"Still in Washington, as far as I know. He keeps trying to call and I keep not answering. When will you be back?"

"I'm not sure."

"Tonight?"

"I'll try."

"Do, if you can." She lowered her voice; I imagined the body-guard standing nearby. "It's Dep's night off. I'll cook."

"Is that supposed to be an incentive?"

"You rude man," she said and laughed. She rang off as abruptly as she had called, without saying good-bye.

I tapped my phone against my teeth. The prospect of a confid-ing fireside talk with Ruth, perhaps to be followed by a second round in her vigorous embrace, was not without its attractions. I could call Rycart and tell him I'd changed my mind. Undecided, I took my case out of the car and wheeled it through the puddles toward the waiting bus. Once I was aboard, I cradled it next to me and studied the airport map. At that point yet another choice pre-sented itself. Terminal B—the shuttle to New York and Rycart—or terminal E—international departures and an evening flight back to London? I hadn't considered that before. I had my passport, ev-erything. I could simply walk away.

B or E? I seriously weighed them. I was like an unusually dim lab rat in a maze, endlessly confronted with alternatives, endlessly picking the wrong one.

The bus doors opened with a heavy sigh.

I got off at B, bought my ticket, sent a text message to Rycart, and caught the US Airways Shuttle to LaGuardia.

FOR SOME REASON OUR plane was delayed on the tarmac. We taxied out on schedule but then stopped just short of the runway, pulling aside in a gentlemanly fashion to let the queue of jets behind us go ahead. It began to rain. I looked out of the porthole at the flattened grass and the welded sheets of sea and sky. Clear veins of water pulsed across the glass. Every time a plane took off, the thin skin of the cabin shook and the veins broke and reformed. The pilot came over the intercom and apologized: there was some problem with our security clearance, he said. The Department of Homeland Security had just raised its threat assessment from yellow (elevated) to orange (high) and our patience was appreciated. Among the businesspeople around me, agitation grew. The man sitting next to me caught my eye above the edge of his pink paper and shook his head.

"It just gets worse," he said.

He folded his *Financial Times*, placed it on his lap, and closed his eyes. The headline was "Lang wins US support," and there was that grin again. Ruth had been right. He shouldn't have smiled. It had gone round the world.

My small suitcase was in the luggage compartment above my head; my feet were resting on the shoulder bag beneath the seat in front of me. All was in order. But I couldn't relax. I felt guilty, even though I had done nothing wrong. I half expected the FBI to storm the plane and drag me away. After about forty-five minutes, the engines suddenly started to roar again and the pilot broke radio silence to announce that we had finally been given permission to take off, and thank you again for your understanding.

We labored along the runway and up into the clouds, and such was my exhaustion that, despite my anxiety—or perhaps because of it—I actually drifted into sleep. I came awake with a jerk when I felt someone leaning across me, but it was only the cabin attendant, checking that my seat belt was fastened. It seemed to me that I had been unconscious no more than a few seconds, but the pressure in my ears told me that already we were coming in to land at LaGuardia. We touched down at six minutes past six—I remember the time exactly: I checked my watch—and by twenty past I was avoiding the impatient crowds around the baggage carousel and heading out of the gate into the arrivals hall.

It was busy, early evening, and people were in a hurry to get downtown or home for dinner. I scanned the bewildering array of faces, wondering if Rycart himself had turned out to greet me, but there was no one I recognized. The usual lugubrious drivers were waiting, holding the names of their passengers against their chests. They stared straight ahead, avoiding eye contact, like suspects in a police lineup, while I, in the manner of a nervous witness, walked along in front of them, checking each carefully, not wanting to make a mistake. Rycart had implied I'd recognize the right person when I saw him, and I did, and my heart almost stopped. He was standing apart from the others, in his own patch of space—wan faced, dark haired, tall, heavyset, early fifties, in a badly fitting chain-store suit—and he was holding a small blackboard on which was chalked "Mike McAra." Even his eyes were as I had imagined McAra's to be: crafty and colorless.

He was chewing gum. He nodded to my suitcase. "You okay

with that." It was a statement, not a question, but I didn't care. I'd never been more pleased to hear a New York accent in my life. He turned on his heel and I followed him across the hall and out into the pandemonium of the night: shrieks, whistles, slamming doors, the fight to grab a cab, sirens in the distance.

He brought round his car, wound down his window, and beckoned to me to get in quickly. As I struggled to get my case into the backseat, he stared straight ahead, his hands on the wheel, discouraging conversation. Not that there was much time to talk. Barely had we left the perimeter of the airport than we were pulling up in front of a big, glass-fronted hotel and conference center overlooking Grand Central Parkway. He grunted as he shifted his heavy body round in his seat to address me. The car stank of his sweat and I had a moment of pure existential horror, staring beyond him, through the drizzle, to that bleak and anonymous building: what, in the name of God, was I doing?

"If you need to make contact, use this," he said, giving me a brand-new cell phone, still in its plastic wrapper. "There's a chip inside with twenty dollars' worth of calls on it. Don't use your old phone. The safest thing is to turn it off. You pay for your room in advance, with cash. Have you got enough? It'll be about three hundred bucks."

I nodded.

"You're staying one night. You have a reservation." He wriggled his fat wallet out from his back pocket. "This is the card you use to guarantee the extras. The name on the card is the name you register under. Use an address in the United Kingdom that isn't your own. If there *are* any extras, make sure you pay for them in cash. This is the telephone number you use to make contact in future."

"You used to be a cop," I said. I took the credit card and a torn-out strip of paper with a number written on it in a childish hand. The paper and plastic were warm from the heat of his body.

"Don't use the internet. Don't speak to strangers. And especially avoid any women who might try to come on to you."

"You sound like my mother."

His face didn't flicker. We sat there for a few seconds. "Well," he said impatiently. He waved a meaty hand at me. "That's it."

Once I was through the revolving glass door and inside the lobby, I checked the name on the card. Clive Dixon. A big conference had just ended. Scores of delegates wearing black suits with bright yellow lapel badges were pouring across the wide expanse of white marble, chattering to one another like a flight of crows. They looked eager, purposeful, motivated, newly fired up to meet their corporate targets and personal goals. I saw from their badges they belonged to a church. Above our heads, great glass globes of light hung from a ceiling a hundred feet high and shimmered on walls of chrome. I wasn't just out of my depth anymore; I was out of sight of land.

"I have a reservation, I believe," I said to the clerk at the desk, "in the name of Dixon."

It's not an alias I'd have chosen. I don't think of myself as a Dixon, whatever a Dixon is. But the receptionist was untroubled by my embarrassment. I was on his computer, that was all that mattered to him, and my card was good. The room rate was two hundred and seventy-five dollars. I filled out the reservation form and gave as my false address the number of Kate's small terraced house in Shepherd's Bush and the street of Rick's London club. When I said I wanted to pay in cash, he took the notes between his finger and thumb as if they were the strangest things he had ever seen. *Cash?* If I'd tied a mule to his desk and offered to pay him in animal skins and sticks that I'd spent the winter carving, he couldn't have looked more nonplussed.

I declined to be assisted with my bags, took the elevator to the sixth floor, and stuck the electronic key card into the door. My room was beige and softly lit by table lamps, with a view across Grand Central Parkway to LaGuardia and the unfathomable blackness of the East River. The TV was playing "I'll Take Manhattan" over a caption that read "Welcome to New York Mr. Nixon." I turned it off and opened the minibar. I didn't even bother to find a glass. I unscrewed the cap and drank straight from the miniature bottle.

It must have been about twenty minutes and a second miniature later that my new telephone suddenly glowed blue and began to emit a faintly ominous electronic purr. I left my post at the window to answer it.

"It's me," said Rycart. "Have you settled in?"

"Yes," I said.

"Are you alone?"

"Yes."

"Open the door, then."

He was standing in the corridor, his phone to his ear. Beside him was the driver who had met me at LaGuardia.

"All right, Frank," said Rycart to his minder. "I'll take it from here. You keep an eye out in the lobby."

Rycart slipped his phone into the pocket of his overcoat as Frank plodded back toward the elevators. He was what my mother would have called "handsome, and knows it": a striking profile, narrowly set bright blue eyes accentuated by an orangey tan, and that swept-back waterfall of hair the cartoonists loved so much. He looked a lot younger than sixty. He nodded at the empty bottle in my hand. "Tough day?"

"You could say that."

He came into the room without waiting for an invitation and went straight over to the window and drew the curtains. I closed the door.

"My apologies for the location," he said, "but I tend to be recognized in Manhattan. Especially after yesterday. Did Frank look after you all right?"

"I've rarely had a warmer welcome."

"I know what you mean, but he's a useful guy. Ex-NYPD. He handles logistics and security for me. I'm not the most popular kid on the block right now, as you can imagine."

"Can I get you something to drink?"

"Water would be fine."

He prowled around the room while I poured him a glass. He checked the bathroom, even the closet.

"What is it?" I said. "Do you think this is a trap?"

"It crossed my mind." He unbuttoned his coat and laid it carefully on the bed. I guessed his Armani suit cost about twice the annual income of a small African village. "Let's face it, you do work for Lang."

"I met him for the first time on Monday," I said. "I don't even know him."

Rycart laughed. "Who does? If you met him on Monday you probably know him as well as anyone. I worked with him for fifteen years, and I certainly don't have a clue where he's coming from. Mike McAra didn't, either, and he was with him from the beginning."

"His wife said more or less the same thing to me."

"Well, there you go. If someone as sharp as Ruth doesn't get him—and she's married to him, for God's sake—what hope do the rest of us have? The man's a mystery. Thanks." Rycart took the water. He sipped it thoughtfully, studying me. "But you sound as though you're starting to unravel him."

"I feel as though I'm the one who's unraveling, quite frankly."

"Let's sit down," said Rycart, patting my shoulder, "and you can tell me all about it."

The gesture reminded me of Lang. A great man's charm. They made me feel like a minnow swimming between sharks. I would need to be on my guard. I sat down carefully in one of the two small armchairs—it was beige, like the walls. Rycart sat opposite me.

"So," he said. "How do we begin? You know who I am. Who are you?"

"I'm a professional ghostwriter," I said. "I was brought in to rewrite Adam Lang's memoirs after Mike McAra died. I know nothing about politics. It's as if I've stepped through the looking glass."

"Tell me what you've found out."

Even I was too canny for that. I hemmed and hawed.

"Perhaps you could tell me about McAra first," I said.

"If you like." Rycart shrugged. "What can I say? Mike was the consummate professional. If you'd pinned a rosette to that suitcase over there and told him it was the party leader, he'd have followed it. Everyone expected Lang would fire him when he became leader and bring in his own man. But Mike was too useful. He knew the party inside out. What else do you want to know?"

"What was he like, as a person?"

"What was he like *as a person?*" Rycart gave me a strange look, as if it were the oddest question he'd ever heard. "Well, he had no life outside politics, if that's what you mean, so you could say that Lang was everything to him—wife, kids, friends. What else? He was obsessive, a detail man. Almost everything Adam wasn't, Mike was. Maybe that was why he stayed on, right through Downing Street and all the way out again, long after the others had all cashed in and gone to make some money. No fancy corporate jobs for our Mike. He was very loyal to Adam."

"Not that loyal," I said. "Not if he was in touch with you."

"Ah, but that was only right at the very end. You mentioned a photograph. Can I see it?"

When I fetched the envelope, his face had the same greedy expression as Emmett's, but when he saw the picture, he couldn't hide his disappointment.

"Is this it?" he said. "Just a bunch of privileged white kids doing a song-and-dance act?"

"It's a bit more interesting than that," I said. "For a start, why's your number on the back of it?"

Rycart gave me a sly look. "Why exactly should I help you?"

"Why exactly should *I* help *you?*"

We stared at one another. Eventually he grinned, showing large, polished white teeth.

"You should have been a politician," he said.

"I'm learning from the best."

He bowed modestly, thinking I meant him, but actually it was Lang I had in mind. Vanity, that was his weakness, I realized. I could imagine how deftly Lang would have flattered him, and what a blow his sacking must have been to his ego. And now, with his lean face and his prow of a nose and those piercing eyes, he was as hell-bent on revenge as any discarded lover. He got to his feet and went over to the door. He checked the corridor up and down. When he returned he loomed over me, pointing a tanned finger directly at my face.

"If you double-cross me," he said, "you'll pay for it. And if you doubt my willingness to hold a grudge and eventually settle the score, ask Adam Lang."

"Fine," I said.

He was too agitated now to sit still, and that was something else I only realized at that moment: the pressure he was under. You had to hand it to Rycart. It did take a certain nerve to drag your former party leader and prime minister in front of a war crimes tribunal.

"This ICC business," he said, patrolling up and down in front of the bed, "it's only hit the headlines in the past week, but let me tell you I've been pursuing this thing behind the scenes for *years*. Iraq, rendition, torture, Guantánamo—what's been done in this so-called war on terror is illegal under international law, just as much as anything that happened in Kosovo or Liberia. The only difference is we're the ones doing it. The hypocrisy is nauseating."

He seemed to realize he was starting on a speech he'd already made too many times before and checked himself. He took a sip of water. "Anyway, rhetoric is one thing and evidence is another thing entirely. I could sense the political climate changing; that was helpful. Every time a bomb went off, every time another soldier was killed, every time it became a little bit clearer we'd started another Hundred Years' War without a clue how to end it, things shifted farther my way. It was no longer inconceivable that a Western leader could wind up in the dock. The worse the mess he'd left behind him got, the more people were willing to see it, wanted to see it. What I needed was just one piece of evidence that would meet the legal standard of proof—a single document with his name on it would have been enough—and I didn't have it.

"And then suddenly, just before Christmas, there it was. I had it in my hands. It just came through the post. Not even a covering letter. 'Top Secret: Memorandum from the Prime Minister to the Secretary of State for Defence.' It was five years old, written back in the days when I was still foreign secretary, but I'd no idea it even existed. A smoking gun if ever there was one—Christ, the barrel was still hot! A directive from the British prime minister that these four poor bastards should be snatched off the streets in Pakistan by the SAS and handed over to the CIA."

"A war crime," I said.

"A war crime," he agreed. "A minor one, okay. But so what? In the end, they could only get Al Capone for tax evasion. It didn't mean Capone wasn't a gangster. I carried out a few discreet checks to make sure the memo was authentic, then I took it to The Hague in person."

"You'd no idea who it came from?"

"No. Not until my anonymous source called and told me. And just you wait till Lang hears who it was. This is going to be the worst thing of all." He leaned in close to me. "Mike McAra!"

Looking back, I suppose I already knew it. But suspicion is one thing, confirmation another, and to see Rycart's exultation at that moment was to appreciate the scale of McAra's treachery.

"*He* called *me*! Can you believe that? If anyone had predicted I'd ever be given help by Mike McAra, of all people, I'd have laughed at him."

"When did he call?"

"About three weeks after I first got the document. The eighth of January? The ninth? Something like that. 'Hello, Richard. Did you get the present I sent you?' I almost had a heart attack. Then I had to shut him up quickly. Because of course you know that the phone lines at the UN are all bugged?"

"Are they?" I was still trying to absorb everything.

"Oh, completely. The National Security Agency monitors every word that's transmitted in the western hemisphere. Every syllable you ever utter on a phone, every email you ever send, every credit card transaction you ever make—it's all recorded and stored. The only problem is sorting through it. At the UN, we're briefed that the easiest way to get round the eavesdropping is to use disposable mobile phones, try to avoid mentioning specifics, and change our numbers as often as possible—that way we can at least keep a bit ahead of them. So I told Mike to stop right there. Then I gave him a brand-new number I'd never used before and asked him to call me straight back."

"Ah," I said. "I see." And I could. I could visualize it perfectly. McAra with his phone wedged between shoulder and ear, grabbing his cheap blue Bic. "He must have scribbled the number on the back of the photograph he was holding at the time."

"And then he called me," said Rycart. He had stopped pacing and was looking at himself in the mirror above the chest of drawers. He put both hands to his forehead and smoothed his hair back over his ears. "Christ, I'm shattered," he said. "Look at me. I was never like this when I was in government, even when I was working eighteen hours a day. You know, people get it all wrong. It isn't having power that's exhausting—it's *not* having it that wears you out."

"What did he say when he called? McAra?"

"The first thing that struck me was that he didn't sound his usual self at all. You were asking me what he was like. Well, he was a pretty tough operator, which of course is what Adam liked about him: he knew he could always rely on Mike to do the dirty work. He was sharp, businesslike. You could almost say he was brutal, especially on the phone. My private office used to call him McHorror: 'The McHorror just rang for you, Foreign Secretary . . .' But that day, I remember, his voice was completely flat. He sounded broken, actually. He said he'd just spent the past year in the archives in Cambridge, working on Adam's memoirs, going over our whole time in government, and just getting more and more disillusioned with it all. He said that that was where he'd found the memorandum about Operation Tempest. But the real reason he was calling, he said, was that that was just the tip of the iceberg. He said he'd just discovered something much more important, something that made sense of everything that had gone wrong while we were in power."

I could hardly breathe. "What was it?"

Rycart laughed. "Well, oddly enough, I did ask him that, but he wouldn't tell me over the phone. He said he wanted to meet me to discuss it face-to-face: it was that big. The only thing he would say was that the key to it could be found in Lang's autobiography, if anyone bothered to check, that it was all there in the beginning."

"Those were his exact words?"

"Pretty much. I made a note as he was talking. And that was it. He said he'd call me in a day or two to fix a meeting. But I heard nothing, and then about a week later it was in the press that he was dead. And nobody else ever called me on that phone, because nobody else had that number. So you can imagine why I was so excited when it suddenly started ringing again. And so here we are," he said, gesturing to the room, "the perfect place to spend a

Thursday night. And now I think you should tell me exactly what the hell is going on."

"I will. Just one more thing, though. Why didn't you tell the police?"

"You are joking, are you? Discussions at The Hague were at a very delicate stage. If I'd told the police that McAra had been in contact with me, naturally they'd have wanted to know why. Then it would have been bound to get back to Lang, and he would have been able to make some kind of preemptive move against the war crimes court. He's still a hell of an operator, you know. That statement he put out against me the day before yesterday—'The international struggle against terror is too important to be used for the purposes of domestic political revenge.' Wow." He shuddered admiringly. "Vicious."

I squirmed slightly in my chair, but Rycart didn't notice. He'd gone back to inspecting himself in the mirror. "Besides," he said, sticking out his chin, "I thought it was accepted that Mike had killed himself, either because he was depressed, or drunk, or both. I'd only have confirmed what they already knew. He was certainly in a poor state when he rang me."

"And I can tell you why," I said. "What he'd just found out was that one of the men in that picture with Lang at Cambridge— the picture McAra had in his hand when he spoke to you—was an officer in the CIA."

Rycart had been checking his profile. He stopped. His brow corrugated. And then, with great slowness, he turned his face toward me.

"He was *what*?"

"His name is Paul Emmett." Suddenly I couldn't get the words out fast enough. I was desperate to unburden myself—to share it—to let someone else try to make sense of it. "He later became a professor at Harvard. Then he went on to run something called the Arcadia Institution. Have you heard of it?"

"I've heard of it—of course I've heard of it, and I've always steered well clear of it, precisely because I've always thought it had CIA written all over it." Rycart sat down. He seemed stunned.

"But is that really plausible?" I asked. "I don't know how these things work. Would someone join the CIA and then immediately be sent off to do postgraduate research in another country?"

"I'd say that's highly plausible. What better cover could you want? And where better than a university to spot the future best and the brightest?" He held out his hand. "Show me the photograph again. Which one is Emmett?"

"It may all be balls," I warned, pointing Emmett out. "I've no proof. I just found his name on one of those paranoid websites. They said he joined the CIA after he left Yale, which must have been about three years before this was taken."

"Oh, I can believe it," said Rycart, studying him intently. "In fact, now you mention it, I think I did hear some gossip once. But then that whole international conference circuit world is crawling with them. I call them the military-industrial-academic complex." He smiled at his own wit, then looked serious again. "What's really suspicious is that he should have known Lang."

"No," I said, "what's *really* suspicious is that a matter of hours after McAra tracked down Emmett to his house near Boston, he was found washed up dead on a beach in Martha's Vineyard."

AFTER THAT I TOLD him everything I'd discovered. I told him the story about the tides and the flashlights on the beach at

Lambert's Cove, and the curious way the police investigation had been handled. I told him about Ruth's description of McAra's argument with Lang on the eve of his death, and about Lang's reluctance to discuss his Cambridge years, and the way he'd tried to conceal the fact that he'd become politically active immediately after leaving university rather than two years later. I described how McAra, with his typical dogged thoroughness, had discovered all this, turning up detail after detail that gradually destroyed Lang's account of his early years. That was presumably what he meant when he said that the key to everything was in the beginning of Lang's autobiography. I told him about the satellite navigation system in the Ford and how it had taken me to Emmett's doorstep, and how strangely Emmett had behaved.

And, of course, the more I talked, the more excited Rycart became. I guess it must have been like Christmas for him.

"Just suppose," he said, pacing up and down again, "that it was Emmett who originally suggested to Lang that he should think about a career in politics. Let's face it, someone must have put the idea into his pretty little head. I'd been a junior member of the party since I was fourteen. What year did Lang join?"

"Nineteen seventy-five."

"Seventy-five! You see, that would make perfect sense. Do you remember what Britain was like in seventy-five? The security services were out of control, spying on the prime minister. Retired generals were forming private armies. The economy was collapsing. There were strikes, riots. It wouldn't exactly be a surprise if the CIA had decided to recruit a few bright young things and had encouraged them to make their careers in useful places—the civil service, the media, politics. It's what they do everywhere else, after all."

"But not in Britain, surely," I said. "We're an ally."

Rycart looked at me with contempt. "The CIA was spying on *American* students back then. Do you really think they'd have been squeamish about spying on ours? Of course they were active in Britain! They still are. They have a head of station in London and a huge staff. I could name you half a dozen MPs right now who are in regular contact with the CIA. In fact—" He stopped pacing and clicked his fingers. "That's a thought!" He whirled round to look at me. "Does the name Reg Giffen mean anything to you?"

"Vaguely."

"Reg Giffen—Sir Reginald Giffen, later Lord Giffen, now dead Giffen, thank God—spent so long making speeches in the House of Commons on behalf of the Americans, we used to call him the member for Michigan. He announced his resignation as an MP in the first week of the nineteen eighty-three election general campaign, and it caught everyone by surprise, apart from one very enterprising and photogenic young party member, who just happened to have moved into his constituency six months earlier."

"And who then got the nomination to become the party's candidate, with Giffen's support," I said, "and who then won one of the safest seats in the country when he was still only thirty." The story was legendary. It was the start of Lang's rise to national prominence. "But you can't really think that the CIA asked Giffen to help fix it so that Lang could get into parliament? That sounds very far-fetched."

"Oh, come on! Use your imagination! Imagine you're Professor Emmett, now back in Harvard, writing unreadable bilge about the alliance of the English-speaking peoples and the need to combat the Communist menace. Haven't you got potentially the most amazing agent in history on your hands? A man who's already starting to be talked about as a future party leader? A possible prime minister? Aren't you going to persuade the powers that be at the Agency to do everything they can to further this man's career? I was already in parliament myself when Lang arrived. I watched him come from nowhere and streak past all of us." He scowled at the memory. "Of course he had *help*. He had no real connection with the party at all. We couldn't begin to understand what made him tick."

"Surely that's the point of him," I said. "He didn't have an ideology."

"He may not have had an ideology, but he sure as hell had an agenda." Rycart sat down again. He leaned toward me. "Okay. Here's a quiz for you. Name me one decision that Adam Lang took as prime minister that wasn't in the interests of the United States of America."

I was silent.

"Come on," he said. "It's not a trick question. Just name me one thing he did that Washington wouldn't have approved of. Let's think." He held up his thumb. "One: deployment of British troops to the Middle East, against the advice of just about every senior commander in our armed forces and all of our ambassadors who know the region. Two"—up went his right index finger—"complete failure to demand any kind of quid pro quo from the White House in terms of reconstruction contracts for British firms, or anything else. Three: unwavering support for U.S. foreign policy in the Middle East, even when it's patently crazy for us to set ourselves against the entire Arab world. Four: the stationing of an

American missile defense system on British soil that does absolutely nothing for our security—in fact, the complete opposite: it makes us a more obvious target for a first strike and can provide protection only for the U.S. Five: the purchase, for fifty billion dollars, of an American nuclear missile system that we call 'independent' but that we wouldn't be able to fire without U.S. approval, thus binding his successors to another twenty years of subservience to Washington over defense policy. Six: a treaty that allows the U.S. to extradite our citizens to stand trial in America but doesn't allow us to do the same to theirs. Seven: collusion in the illegal kidnapping, torture, imprisonment, and even murder of our own citizens. Eight: a consistent record of sacking of any minister—I speak with experience here—who is less than one hundred percent supportive of the alliance with the United States. Nine—"

"All right," I said, holding up my hand. "I get the message."

"I have friends in Washington who just can't believe the way that Lang ran British foreign policy. I mean, they were *embarrassed* by how much support he gave and how little he got in return. And where has it got us? Stuck fighting a so-called war we can't possibly win, colluding in methods we didn't use even when we were up against the Nazis!" Rycart laughed ruefully and shook his head. "You know, in a way, I'm almost relieved to discover there might be a rational explanation for what we got up to in government while he was prime minister. If you think about it, the alternative's actually worse. At least if he was working for the CIA it makes sense. So now," he said, patting my knee, "the question is: what are we going to do about it?"

I didn't like the sound of that first person plural.

"Well," I said, wincing slightly, "I'm in a tricky position. I'm supposed to be helping him with his memoirs. I have a legal obligation not to divulge anything I hear in the course of my work to a third party."

"It's too late to stop now."

I didn't like the sound of that, either.

"We don't actually have any *proof*," I pointed out. "We don't even know for sure that *Emmett* was in the CIA, let alone that he recruited Lang. I mean, how is this relationship supposed to have worked after Lang got into Number Ten? Did he have a secret radio transmitter hidden in the attic, or what?"

"This isn't a joke, my friend," said Rycart. "I know something of how these things are done from when I was at the Foreign Office. Contact can be managed easily enough. For a start, Emmett was always coming to London, because of Arcadia. It was the perfect front. In fact, I wouldn't be surprised if the whole institution wasn't set up as part of the covert operation to run Lang. The timing would fit. They could have used intermediaries."

"But there's still no *proof*," I repeated, "and short of Lang confessing, or Emmett confessing, or the CIA opening their files, there never will be."

"Then you'll just have to get some proof," said Rycart flatly.

"What?" My mouth sagged; my everything sagged.

"You're in the perfect position," Rycart went on. "He trusts you. He lets you ask him whatever you like. He even allows you to tape his answers. You can put words in his mouth. We'll have to devise a series of questions that gradually entrap him, and then finally you can confront him with the allegation, and let's see how he reacts. He'll deny it, but that won't matter. The mere fact you're laying the evidence in front of him will put the story on the record."

"No it won't. The tapes are his property."

"Yes it will. The tapes can be subpoenaed by the war crimes court, as evidence of his direct complicity with the CIA rendition program."

"What if I don't make any tapes?"

"In that case, I'll suggest to the prosecutor that she subpoenas *you*."

"Ah," I said craftily, "but what if I deny the whole story?"

"Then I'll give her this," said Rycart, and opened his jacket to show a small microphone clipped to the front of his shirt, with a wire trailing into his inside pocket. "Frank is recording every word down in the lobby, aren't you, Frank? Oh, come on! Don't look so shocked. What did you expect? That I'd come to a meeting with a complete stranger, who's working for Lang, without taking any precautions? Except that you're not working for Lang anymore." He smiled, showing again that row of teeth, more brilliantly white than anything in nature. "You're working for me."

FIFTEEN

★

Authors need ghosts who will not challenge them, but
will simply listen to what they have to say and understand why they did what they did.

Ghostwriting

AFTER A FEW SECONDS I started to swear, fluently and indis-
criminately. I was swearing at Rycart and at my own stupidity, at
Frank and at whoever would one day transcribe the tape. I was
swearing at the war crimes prosecutor, at the court, the judges, the
media. And I would have gone on for a lot longer if my telephone
hadn't started to ring—not the one I'd been given to contact Rycart but the one I'd brought from London. Needless to say, I'd
forgotten to switch it off.

"Don't answer it," warned Rycart. "It'll lead them straight to us."

I looked at the incoming number. "It's Amelia Bly," I said. "It
could be important."

"Amelia Bly," repeated Rycart, his voice a blend of awe and lust. "I haven't seen her for a while." He hesitated; it was obvious he was desperate to know what she wanted. "If they're monitoring you, they'll be able to fix your location to within a hundred yards, and this hotel is the only building where you're likely to be."

The phone continued to throb in my outstretched palm. "Well, to hell with you," I said. "I'm not taking my orders from you."

I pressed the green button. "Hi," I said. "Amelia."

"Good evening," she said, her voice as crisp as a matron's uniform. "I have Adam for you."

I mouthed, "It's Adam Lang," at Rycart and waved my hand at him to warn him against saying anything. An instant later the familiar, classless voice filled my ear.

"I was just speaking to Ruth," he said. "She tells me you're in New York."

"That's right."

"So am I. Whereabouts are you?"

"I'm not sure exactly where I am, Adam." I made a helpless gesture at Rycart. "I haven't checked in anywhere yet."

"We're at the Waldorf," said Lang. "Why don't you come over?"

"Hold on a second, Adam." I pressed Mute.

"You," said Rycart, "are a fucking idiot."

"He wants me to go over and see him at the Waldorf."

Rycart sucked in his cheeks, appraising the options. "You should go," he said.

"What if it's a trap?"

"It's a risk, but it'll look odd if you don't go. He'll get suspicious. Tell him yes, quickly, and then hang up."

I pressed Mute again.

"Hi, Adam," I said, trying to keep the tension out of my voice. "That's great. I'll be right over."

Rycart passed his finger across his throat.

"What brings you to New York, in any case?" asked Lang. "I thought you had plenty to occupy you at the house."

"I wanted to see John Maddox."

"Right. And how was he?"

"Fine. Listen, I've got to go now."

Rycart's throat slashing was becoming ever more urgent.

"We've had a great couple of days," continued Lang, as if he hadn't heard me. "The Americans have been fantastic. You know, it's in the tough times that you find out who your real friends are."

Was it my imagination, or did he freight those words with extra emphasis for my benefit?

"Great. I'll be with you as fast as I can, Adam."

I ended the call. My hand was shaking.

"Well done," said Rycart. He was on his feet, retrieving his coat from the bed. "We have about ten minutes to get out of here. Get your stuff together."

Mechanically, I began gathering up the photographs. I put them back in the case and fastened it while Rycart went into the bathroom and peed noisily.

"How did he sound?" called Rycart.

"Cheerful."

He flushed the lavatory and emerged buttoning his fly. "Well, we'll just have to do something about that, won't we?"

The elevator down to the lobby was crammed with members of the Church of Latter-Day Online Traders, or whoever the hell they were. It stopped at every floor. Rycart grew more and more nervous.

"We mustn't be seen together," he muttered as we stepped out at the ground floor. "You hang back. We'll meet you in the car park."

He quickened his pace, drawing ahead of me. Frank was already on his feet—presumably he had been listening and knew of our intentions—and the two of them set off without a word: the dapper, silver Rycart and his taciturn and swarthy sidekick. What a double act, I thought. I bent and pretended to tie my shoelace, then took my time crossing the lobby, deliberately circling the groups of chattering guests, keeping my head down. There was something now so ludicrous about this whole situation that, as I joined the crush at the door waiting to get out, I actually found myself smiling. It was like a Feydeau farce: each new scene more far-fetched than the last, yet each, when you examined it, a logical development of its predecessor. Yes, that was what this was: a farce! I stood in line until my turn came, and that was when I saw Emmett, or at least that's when I thought I saw Emmett, and suddenly I wasn't smiling anymore.

The hotel had one of these big revolving doors, with compartments that hold five or six people at a time, all of whom are obliged to lunge into it and shuffle forward to avoid knocking into one another, like convicts on a chain gang. Luckily for me, I was in the middle of the outgoing group, which is probably the reason Emmett didn't see me. He had a man on either side of him, and they were in the compartment that was swinging into the hotel, all three pushing at the glass in front of them, as if they were in a violent hurry.

We came out into the night and I stumbled, almost falling over, in my anxiety to get away. My suitcase toppled onto its side and I dragged it along after me, as if it were a stubborn dog. The car park was separated from the hotel forecourt by a flower bed, but instead of going round it I walked straight through it. Across the parking lot, a pair of headlights came on and then drove straight at me. The car swerved at the last moment and the rear passenger door flew open.

"Get in," said Rycart.

The speed with which Frank accelerated away served to slam the door shut after me and threw me back in my seat.

"I just saw Emmett," I said.

Rycart exchanged looks in the mirror with his driver.

"Are you sure?"

"No."

"Did he see you?"

"No."

"Are you sure?"

"Yes."

I was holding onto my suitcase. It had become my security blanket. We sped down the access road and pulled into the heavy traffic heading toward Manhattan.

"They could have followed us from LaGuardia," said Frank.

"Why did they hold back?" asked Rycart.

"Could be they were waiting for Emmett to arrive from Boston, to make a positive ID."

Up to that point, I hadn't taken Rycart's amateur tradecraft too seriously, but now I felt a fresh surge of panic.

"Listen," I said, "I don't think it's a good idea for me to go and see Lang right now. Assuming that was Emmett, Lang must surely have been alerted to what I've been doing. He'll know that I've driven up to Boston and shown Emmett the photographs."

"So? What do you think he's going to do about it?" asked Rycart. "Drown you in his bathtub at the Waldorf-Astoria?"

"Yeah, right," said Frank. His shoulders shook slightly with amusement. "As if."

I felt sick, and despite the freezing night, I lowered the window. The wind was blowing from the east, gusting off the river, carrying on its cold, industrial edge the sickly tang of aviation fuel. I can still taste it at the back of my throat whenever I think of it, and that, for me, will always be the taste of fear.

"Don't I need to have a cover story?" I said. "What am I supposed to tell Lang?"

"You've done nothing wrong," said Rycart. "You're just following up your predecessor's work. You're trying to research his Cambridge years. Don't act so guilty. Lang can't know for sure that you're on to him."

"It's not Lang I'm worried about."

We both lapsed into silence. After a few minutes the nighttime Manhattan skyline came into view, and my eyes automatically sought out the gap in the glittering façade, even though we were at the wrong angle to see it. Strange how an absence can be a landmark. It was like a black hole, I thought: a tear in the cosmos. It could suck in anything—cities, countries, laws; it could certainly swallow me. Rycart seemed equally oppressed by the journey.

"Close the window, would you?" he said. "I'm freezing to death."

I did as he asked. Frank had turned the radio on, a jazz station, playing softly.

"What about the car?" I said. "It's still at Logan Airport."

"You can pick it up in the morning."

The station switched to playing the blues. I asked Frank to turn it off. He ignored me.

"I know Lang thinks it's personal," Rycart said, "but it's not.

All right, there's an element of getting my own back, I'll admit—
who likes to be humiliated? But if we carry on licensing torture,
and if we judge victory simply by the number of the enemy's skulls
we can carry back to decorate our caves—well, what will become
of us?"

"I'll tell you what will become of us," I said savagely. "We'll
get ten million dollars for our memoirs and live happily ever after."
Once again, I found that my nervousness was making me angry.
"You do know this is pointless, don't you? In the end he'll just
retire over here on his CIA pension and tell you and your bloody
war crimes court to go screw yourselves."

"Maybe he will. But the ancients thought exile a worse punishment than death—and boy, will Lang be an exile. He won't be
able to travel anywhere in the world, not even the handful of shitty
little countries that don't recognize the ICC, because there'll always be a danger that his plane may have to put in somewhere with
engine trouble or to refuel. And we'll be waiting for him. And
that's when we'll get him."

I glanced at Rycart. He was staring straight ahead, nodding
slightly.

"Or the political climate may change here one day," he went
on, "and there'll be a public campaign to hand him over to justice.
I wonder if he's thought of that. His life is going to be hell."

"You almost make me feel sorry for him."

Rycart gave me a sharp look. "He's charmed you, hasn't he?
Charm! The English disease."

"There are worse afflictions."

We crossed the Triborough Bridge, the tires thumping on the
joints in the road like a fast pulse.

"I feel as though I'm in a tumbril," I said.

It took us a while to make the journey downtown. Each time the traffic came to a stop, I thought of opening the door and making a run for it. The trouble was, I could imagine the first part well enough—darting through the stationary cars and disappearing down one of the cross streets—but then it all became a blank. Where would I go? How would I pay for a hotel room if my own credit card, and presumably the false one I'd used earlier, were known to my pursuers? My reluctant conclusion, from whichever angle I examined my predicament, was that I was safer with Rycart. At least he knew how to survive in this alien world into which I had blundered.

"If you're that worried, we can arrange to have a fail-safe signal," said Rycart. "You can call me using the phone Frank gave you, let's say at ten past every hour. We don't have to speak. Just let it ring a couple of times."

"What happens if I don't make the call?"

"I won't do anything if you miss the first time. If you miss a second, I'll call Lang and tell him I hold him personally responsible for your safety."

"Why is it that I don't find that very reassuring?"

We were almost there. I could see ahead, on the opposite side of Park Avenue, a great, floodlit Stars and Stripes, and beside it, flanking the Waldorf's entrance, a Union Jack. The area in front of the hotel was cordoned off by concrete blocks. I counted half a dozen police motorcycles waiting, four patrol cars, two large black limousines, a small crowd of cameramen, and a slightly larger one of curious onlookers. As I eyed it, my heart began to accelerate. I felt breathless.

Rycart squeezed my arm. "Courage, my friend. He's already

lost one ghost in suspicious circumstances. He can hardly afford to lose another."

"This can't *all* be for him, surely?" I said in amazement. "Anyone would think he was still prime minister."

"It seems I've only made him even more of a celebrity," said Rycart. "You people should be grateful to me. Okay, good luck. We'll talk later. Pull over here, Frank."

He turned up his collar and sank down in his seat, and there was pathos as well as absurdity in the precaution. Poor Rycart: I doubt if one person in ten thousand in New York would have known who he was. Frank pulled up briefly on the corner of East Fiftieth Street to let me out and then eased deftly back into the traffic, so that the last view I ever had of Rycart was of the back of his silvery head dwindling into the Manhattan evening.

I was on my own.

I crossed the great expanse of road, yellow with taxis, and made my way past the crowds and the police. None of the cops standing around challenged me; seeing my suitcase, they must have assumed I was just a guest checking in. I went through the art deco doors, up the grand marble staircase, and into the Babylonian splendor of the Waldorf's lobby. Normally I would have used my mobile to contact Amelia, but even I had learned my lesson there. I went over to one of the concierges at the front desk and asked him to call her room.

There was no reply.

Frowning, he hung up. He was just starting to check his computer when a loud detonation sounded on Park Avenue. Several guests who were checking in ducked, only to straighten ruefully when the explosion turned into a cannonade of gunning motorcycle engines. From the interior of the hotel, across the immense expanse of the golden lobby, came a wedge of security men, Special Branch and Secret Service, with Lang enclosed among them, marching purposefully in his usual rolling, muscular way. Behind him walked Amelia and the two secretaries. Amelia was on the phone. I moved toward the group. Lang swept by me, his eyes fixed straight ahead, which was unlike him. Usually he liked to connect with people when he passed them: flash them a smile they'd remember always. As he began descending the staircase, Amelia saw me. She appeared flustered for once, a few blonde hairs actually out of place.

"I was just trying to call you," she said as she went by. She didn't break step. "There's been a change of plan," she said over her shoulder. "We're flying back to Martha's Vineyard now."

"Now?" I hurried after her. "It's rather late, isn't it?"

We started descending the stairs.

"Adam's insisting. I've managed to find us a plane."

"But why now?"

"I've no idea. Something's come up. You'll have to ask him."

Lang was below and ahead of us. He'd already reached the grand entrance. The bodyguards opened the doors and his broad shoulders were suddenly framed by a halogen glow of light. The shouts of the reporters, the fusillade of camera shutters, the rumble of the Harley-Davidsons—it was as if someone had rolled back the doors to hell.

"What am I supposed to do?" I asked.

"Get into the backup car. I expect Adam will want to talk to you on the plane." She saw my look of panic. "You're very odd. Is there something the matter?"

Now what am I supposed to do? I wondered. Faint? Plead a

prior engagement? I seemed to be trapped on a moving walkway with no means of escape.

"Everything seems to be happening in a rush," I said weakly.

"This is nothing. You should have been with us when he was prime minister."

We emerged into the tumult of noise and light, and it was as if all the controversy generated by the war on terror, year after year of it, had briefly converged on one man and rendered him incandescent. The door to Lang's stretch limousine was open. He paused to wave briefly at the crowd beyond the security cordon, then ducked inside. Amelia took my arm and propelled me toward the second car. "Go on!" she shouted. The motorbikes were already pulling away. "Don't forget, we can't stop if you're left behind."

She slipped in beside Lang, and I found myself stepping into the second limo, next to the secretaries. They shifted cheerfully along the bench seat to make room for me. A Special Branch man climbed in the front, next to the driver, and then we were away, with an accompanying *whoop whoop* from one of the motorbikes, ringing out like the cheerful whistle of a little tugboat escorting a big liner out to sea.

IN DIFFERENT CIRCUMSTANCES, I would have relished that journey: my legs stretched out before me; the Harley-Davidsons gliding past us to hold back the traffic; the pale faces of the pedestrians, glimpsed through the smoked glass, turning to watch us as we hurtled by; the noise of the sirens; the vividness of the flashing lights; the speed; the *force*. I can think of only two categories of human being who are transported with such pomp and drama: world leaders and captured terrorists.

In my pocket, I surreptitiously fingered my new mobile phone. Ought I to alert Rycart to what was happening? I decided not. I didn't want to call him in front of witnesses. I would have felt too uncomfortable, my guilt too obvious. Treachery needs privacy. I surrendered myself to events.

We flew over the Fifty-ninth Street Bridge like gods, Alice and Lucy giggling with excitement, and when we reached LaGuardia a few minutes later we drove past the terminal building, through an open metal gate, and directly onto the tarmac, where a big private jet was being fueled. It was a Hallington plane, in its dark blue livery, with the corporate logo painted on its high tail: Earth with a circle girdling it, like the Colgate ring of confidence. Lang's limousine swerved to a halt and he was the first to emerge. He dived through the doorway of the mobile body scanner and up the steps into the Gulfstream without a backward glance. A bodyguard hurried after him.

As I clambered out of the car I felt almost arthritic with anxiety. It took an effort simply to walk over to the steps where Amelia was standing. The night air was shaking with the noise of jets coming in to land. I could see them stacked five or six deep above the water, steps of light ascending through the darkness.

"Now that's the way to travel," I said, trying to sound relaxed. "Is it always like that?"

"They want to show him they love him," said Amelia. "And no doubt it helps to show everyone else how they treat their friends. *Pour encourager les autres.*"

Security men with metal wands were inspecting all the luggage. I added my suitcase to the pile.

"He says he has to get back to Ruth," she continued, gazing up at the plane. The windows were bigger than on a normal aircraft. Lang's profile was plainly visible toward the rear. "There's something he needs to talk over with her." Her voice was puzzled. She was almost talking to herself, as if I weren't there. I wondered if they'd had a row during the drive to the airport.

One of the security men told me to open my suitcase. I unzipped it and held it up to him. He lifted out the manuscript to search underneath it. Amelia was so preoccupied, she didn't even notice.

"It's odd," she said, "because Washington went so well." She stared vacantly toward the lights of the runway.

"Your shoulder bag," said the security man.

I handed it to him. He took out the package of photographs, and for a moment I thought he was going to open it, but he was more interested in my laptop. I felt the need to keep talking.

"Perhaps he's heard something from The Hague," I suggested.

"No. It's nothing to do with that. He would have told me."

"Okay, you're clear to board," said the guard.

"Don't go near him just yet," she warned, as I moved to pass through the scanner. "Not in his present mood. I'll take you back to him if he wants to talk."

I climbed the steps.

Lang was seated in the very end seat, nearest to the tail, his chin in his hand, gazing out of the window. (The security people always liked him to sit in the last row, I discovered later; it meant no one could get behind him.) The cabin was configured to take ten passengers, two each on a couple of sofas that ran along the side of the fuselage, and the rest in six big armchairs. The armchairs faced one another in pairs, with a stowaway table between them. It looked like an extension of the Waldorf's lobby: gold fittings, polished walnut, and padded, creamy leather. Lang was in one of the armchairs. The Special Branch man sat on a nearby sofa. A steward in a white jacket was bending over the former prime minister. I couldn't see what drink he was being served, but I could hear it. Your favorite sound might be a pair of nightingales in a summer dusk, or a peal of village church bells. Mine is the clink of ice against cut glass. Of this I am a connoisseur. And it sounded distinctly to me as if Lang had given up tea in favor of a stiff whiskey.

The steward saw me staring and came down the gangway toward me. "Can I get you something, sir?"

"Thanks. Yes. I'll have whatever Mr. Lang is having."

I was wrong: it was brandy.

By the time the door was closed, there were twelve of us on board: three crew (the pilot, copilot, and steward), and nine passengers—two secretaries, four bodyguards, Amelia, Adam Lang, and me. I sat with my back to the cockpit so that I could keep an eye on my client. Amelia was directly opposite him, and as the engines started to whine it was all I could do not to hurl myself at the door and wrench it open. That flight felt doomed to me from the start. The Gulfstream shuddered slightly, and slowly the terminal building seemed to drift away. I could see Amelia's hand making emphatic gestures, as if she were explaining something, but Lang just continued to stare out at the airfield.

Someone touched my arm. "Do you know how much one of these things costs?"

It was the policeman who'd been in my car on the drive from the Waldorf. He was in the seat across the aisle.

"I don't, no."

"Have a guess."

"I genuinely have no idea."

"Go on. Try."

I shrugged. "Ten million dollars?"

"*Forty* million dollars." He was triumphant, as if knowing the price somehow implied he was involved in the ownership. "Hollington has *five*."

"Makes you wonder what they can possibly use them all for."

"They lease them out when they don't need them."

"Oh, yes, that's right," I said. "I'd heard that."

The noise of the engines increased and we began our charge down the runway. I imagined the terrorist suspects, handcuffed and hooded, strapped into their luxurious leather armchairs as they lifted off from some red-dusted military airstrip near the Afghan border, bound for the pine forests of eastern Poland. The plane seemed to spring into the air, and I watched over the edge of my glass as the lights of Manhattan spread to fill the window, then slid and tilted, and finally flickered into darkness as we rose into the low cloud. It felt as though we were climbing blindly for a long time in our vulnerable metal tube, but then the gauze fell away and we came up into a bright night. The clouds were as massive and solid as alps, and the moon appeared occasionally from behind the peaks, lighting valleys and glaciers and ravines.

Some time after the plane leveled off, Amelia rose and came down the aisle toward me. Her hips swayed, involuntarily seductive, with the motion of the cabin.

"All right," she said, "he's ready to have a word. But go easy on him, okay? He's had a hell of a couple of days."

He and I both, I thought.

"Will do," I said.

I fished out my shoulder bag from beside my seat and began to squeeze past her. She caught my arm.

"You haven't got long," she warned. "This flight's only a hop. We'll be starting to descend any minute."

IT CERTAINLY WAS A hop. I checked afterward. Only two hundred and sixty miles separate New York City and Martha's Vineyard, and the cruising speed of a Gulfstream G450 is five hundred and twenty-eight miles per hour. The conjunction of these two facts explains why the tape of my conversation with Lang lasts a mere eleven minutes. We were probably already losing altitude even as I approached him.

His eyes were closed, his glass still held in his outstretched hand. He had removed his jacket and tie and eased off his shoes, and was sprawled back in his seat like a starfish, as if someone had pushed him into it. At first I thought he'd fallen asleep, but then I realized his eyes were narrowed to slits and he was watching me closely. He gestured vaguely with his drink toward the seat opposite him.

"Hi, man," he said. "Join me." He opened his eyes fully, yawned, and put the back of his hand to his mouth. "Sorry."

"Hello, Adam."

I sat down. I had my bag in my lap. I fumbled to pull out my notebook, the minirecorder, and a spare disk. Wasn't this what Rycart wanted? Tapes? Nervousness made me clumsy, and if Lang had so much as raised an eyebrow, I would have put the recorder away again. But he didn't appear to notice. He must have gone through this ritual so many times at the end of some official visit—

the journalist conducted into his presence for a few minutes' exclusive access, the tape machine nervously examined to make sure it works, the illusion of informality over the relaxing prime ministerial drink. In the recording you can hear the exhaustion in his voice.

"So," he said, "how's it going?"

"It's going," I said. "It's certainly going."

When I listen to the disk, my register's so high from the anxiety, it sounds as I've been sucking helium.

"Found out anything interesting?"

There was a gleam of something in his eyes. Contempt? Amusement? I sensed he was playing with me.

"This and that. How was Washington?"

"Washington was great, actually." There's a rustling noise as he straightens slightly in his chair, drawing himself up to give one last performance before the theater closes for the night. "I got the most terrific support everywhere—on the Hill, of course, as you probably saw, but also the vice president and the secretary of state. They're going to help me in every way they can."

"And is the bottom line that you'll be able to settle in America?"

"Oh, yes. If worst comes to worst, they'll offer me asylum, certainly. Maybe even a job of some kind, as long as it doesn't involve overseas travel. But it won't get that far. They're going to supply something much more valuable."

"Really?"

Lang nodded. "Evidence."

"Right." I hadn't a clue what he was talking about.

"Is that thing working?" he asked.

There is a deafening clunk as I pick up the recorder.

"Yes, I think so. Is that okay?"

With a thump, I replace it.

"Sure," said Lang. "I just want to make sure you get this down, because I definitely think we can use this. This is important. We should keep it as an exclusive for the memoirs. It will do wonders for the serialization deal." He leaned forward to emphasize his words. "Washington is prepared to provide sworn testimony that no United Kingdom personnel were directly involved in the capture of those four men in Pakistan."

"Really?" *Really? Really?* I keep on parroting it, and I wince every time I hear the sycophancy in my voice. The fawning courtier. The self-effacing ghost.

"You bet. The director of the CIA himself will provide a deposition to the court in The Hague, saying that this was an entirely American covert operation, and if that doesn't do the trick he's prepared to let the actual officers who were running the mission provide evidence in camera." Lang sat back and sipped his brandy. "That should give Rycart something to think about. How's he going to make a charge of war crimes stick now?"

"But your memorandum to the Ministry of Defence—"

"That's genuine," he conceded with a shrug. "It's true, I can't deny that I urged the use of the SAS. And it's true the British government can't deny that our special forces were in Peshawar at the time of Operation Tempest. And we also can't deny that it was our intelligence services that tracked down those men to the particular location where they were arrested. But there's no proof that we passed that intelligence on to the CIA."

Lang smiled at me.

"But we did?"

"There's no proof that we passed that intelligence on to the CIA."

"But if we did, surely that would be aiding and abetting—"

"There's no proof that we passed that intelligence on to the CIA."

He was still holding his smile, albeit now with just a crease of concentration in his brow, as a tenor might hold a note at the end of a difficult aria.

"Then how did it get to them?"

"That's a difficult question. Not through any official channel, that's for sure. And certainly it was nothing to do with me." There was a long pause. His smile died. "Well," he said. "What do you think?"

"It sounds a bit"—I tried to find some diplomatic way of saying it—"technical."

"Meaning?"

My reply on the tape is so slippery, so sweaty with nervous circumlocutions, it's enough to make one laugh out loud.

"Well . . . you know . . . you admit yourself you wanted the SAS to pick them up—no doubt for, you know, understandable reasons—and even if they didn't actually do the job themselves, the Ministry of Defence—as I understand it—hasn't really been able to *deny* they were involved, presumably because they were, in a way, even if . . . even if . . . they were only parked in a car around the corner. And apparently British, you know, intelligence gave the CIA the location where they could be picked up. And when they were tortured, you didn't condemn it."

The last line was delivered in a rush. Lang said coldly, "Sid Kroll was very pleased with the commitment he was given by the

CIA. He believes the prosecutor may even have to drop the case."

"Well, if Sid says that—"

"But *fuck it*," said Lang suddenly. He banged his hand on the edge of the table. On the tape it sounds like an explosion. The dozing Special Branch man on the nearby sofa looked up sharply. "I don't regret what happened to those four men. If we'd relied on the Pakistanis we'd never have got them. We had to grab them while we had the chance, and if we'd missed them, they'd have gone underground and the next time we'd have known anything about them would've been when they were killing our people."

"You really don't regret it?"

"No."

"Not even the one who died under interrogation?"

"Oh, him," said Lang dismissively. "He had a heart problem, an undiagnosed heart problem. He could have died anytime. He could have died getting out of bed one morning."

I said nothing. I pretended to make a note.

"Look," said Lang, "I don't condone torture, but let me just say this to you. First, it does actually produce results—I've seen the intelligence. Second, having power, in the end, is all about balancing evils, and when you think about it, what are a couple of minutes of suffering for a few individuals compared to the deaths— the *deaths*, mark you—of thousands. Third, don't try telling me this is something unique to the war on terror. Torture's always been part of warfare. The only difference is that in the past there were no fucking media around to report it."

"The men arrested in Pakistan claim they were innocent," I pointed out.

"Of course they claim they were innocent! What else are they going to say?" Lang studied me closely, as if seeing me properly for the first time. "I'm beginning to think you're too naïve for this job."

I couldn't resist it. "Unlike Mike McAra?"

"Mike!" Lang laughed and shook his head. "Mike was naïve in a different way."

The plane was beginning to descend quite rapidly now. The moon and stars had gone. We were dropping through cloud. I could feel the pressure change in my ears, and I had to pinch my nose and swallow hard.

Amelia made her way down the aisle.

"Is everything all right?" she asked. She looked concerned. She must have heard Lang's outburst of temper; everyone must have.

"We're just doing some work on my memoirs," said Lang. "I'm telling him what happened over Operation Tempest."

"You're taping it?" said Amelia.

"If that's all right," I said.

"You need to be careful," she told Lang. "Remember what Sid Kroll said—"

"The tapes will be yours," I interrupted, "not mine."

"They could still be subpoenaed."

"Stop treating me as though I'm a child," said Lang abruptly. "I know what I want to say. Let's deal with it once and for all."

Amelia permitted herself a slight widening of her eyes and withdrew.

"Women!" muttered Lang. He took another gulp of brandy. The ice had melted, but the color of the liquid remained dark. It must have been a very full measure, and it occurred to me that our former prime minister was slightly drunk. I sensed this was my moment.

"In what way," I asked, "was Mike McAra naïve?"

"Never mind," muttered Lang. He nursed his drink, his chin on his chest, brooding. He suddenly jerked up again. "I mean, take for instance all this civil liberties crap. You know what I'd do if I were in power again? I'd say, okay then, we'll have two queues at the airports. On the left, we'll have queues to flights on which we've done no background checks on the passengers, no profiling, no biometric data, nothing that infringed anyone's precious civil liberties, used no intelligence obtained under torture—nothing. On the right, we'll have queues to the flights where we've done everything possible to make them safe for passengers. Then people can make their own minds up which plane they want to catch. Wouldn't that be great? To sit back and watch which queue the Rycarts of this world would *really* choose to put their kids on, if the chips were down?"

"And Mike was like that?"

"Not at the beginning. But Mike, unfortunately, discovered idealism in his old age. I said to him—it was our last conversation, actually—I said, if our Lord Jesus Christ was unable to solve all the problems of the world when he came down to live among us—and he was the son of God!—wasn't it a bit unreasonable of Mike to expect me to have sorted out everything in ten years?"

"Is it true you had a serious row with him? Just before he died?"

"Mike made certain wild accusations. I could hardly ignore them."

"May I ask what kind of accusations?"

I could imagine Rycart and the special prosecutor sitting listening to the tape, straightening in their chairs at that. I had to swallow again. My voice sounded muffled in my ears, as if I was talking in a dream, or hailing myself from a great distance. On the tape, the pause that followed is quite short, but at the time it seemed endless, and Lang's voice when it came was deadly quiet.

"I'd prefer not to repeat them."

"Were they to do with the CIA?"

"But surely you already know," said Lang bitterly, "if you've been to see Paul Emmett?"

And this time the pause is as long on the recording as it is in my memory.

Delivered of his bombshell, Lang gazed out of the window and sipped his drink. A few isolated lights had begun to appear beneath us. I think they must have been ships. I looked at him and I saw that the years had caught up even with him at last. It was in the droop of the flesh around his eyes and in the loose skin beneath his jaw. Or perhaps it wasn't age. Perhaps he was simply exhausted. I doubt he could have had much sleep for weeks, probably not since McAra had confronted him. Certainly, when at last he turned back to me, there wasn't anger in his expression, merely a great weariness.

"I want you to understand," he said with heavy emphasis, "that everything I did, both as party leader and as prime minister—everything—I did out of conviction, because I believed it was right."

I mumbled a reply. I was in a state of shock.

"Emmett claims you showed him some photographs. Is that true? May I see?"

My hands shook slightly as I removed them from the envelope and pushed them across the table toward him. He flicked through the first four very quickly, paused over the fifth—the one that showed him and Emmett onstage—then went back to the beginning and started looking at them again, lingering over each image.

He said, without raising his eyes from the pictures, "Where did you get them?"

"McAra ordered them up from the archive. I found them in his room."

Over the intercom, the copilot asked us to fasten our seat belts.

"Odd," murmured Lang. "Odd the way we've all changed so much and yet also stayed exactly the same. Mike never mentioned anything to me about photographs. Oh, that bloody archive!" He squinted closely at one of the riverbank pictures. It was the girls, I noticed, rather than himself or Emmett, who seemed to fascinate him the most. "I remember her," he said, tapping the picture. "And her. She wrote to me once, when I was prime minister. Ruth was not pleased. Oh, God," he said, and passed his hand across his face. "Ruth." For a moment, I thought he was about to break down, but when he looked at me his eyes were dry. "What happens next? Is there a procedure in your line of work to deal with this sort of situation?"

Patterns of light were very clear in the window now. I could see the headlamps of a car on a road.

"The client always has the last word about what goes in a book," I said. "Always. But, obviously, in this case, given what happened—"

On the tape, my voice trails away, and then there is a loud clunk, as Lang leans forward and grabs my forearm.

"If you mean what happened to Mike, then let me tell you I was absolutely appalled by that." His gaze was fixed unwaveringly on me; he was putting everything he had left within him into the task of convincing me, and I'll freely confess, despite everything I'd discovered, he succeeded: to this day, I'm sure he was telling the truth. "If you believe nothing else, you must please believe that his death had nothing to do with me, and I shall carry that image of Mike in the morgue until my own dying day. I'm sure it was an accident. But okay, let's say, for the sake of argument, it wasn't." He tightened his grip on my arm. "What was he thinking of, driving up to Boston to confront Emmett? He'd been around politics long enough to know that you don't do something like that, not when the stakes are this high. You know, in a way, he did kill himself. It was a suicidal act."

"That's what worries me," I said.

"You can't seriously think," said Lang, "that the same thing could happen to you?"

"It has crossed my mind."

"You need have no fears on that score. I can guarantee it." I guess my disbelief must have been obvious. "Oh, come on, man!" he said urgently. Again, the fingers clenched on my flesh. "There are four policemen traveling on this plane with us right now! What kind of people do you think we are?"

"Well, that's just it," I said. "What kind of people *are* you?"

We were coming in low over the treetops. The lights of the Gulfstream gleamed across dark waves of foliage.

I tried to pull my arm away. "Excuse me," I said.

Lang reluctantly let go of me and I fastened my seat belt. He did the same. He glanced out of the window at the terminal, then back at me, appalled, as we dipped gracefully onto the runway.

"My God, you've already told someone, haven't you?"

I could feel myself turning scarlet. "No," I said.

"You have."

"I haven't." On the tape I sound as feeble as a child caught red-handed.

He leaned forward again. "Who have you told?"

Looking out at the dark forest beyond the perimeter of the airport, where anything could be lurking, it seemed like the only insurance policy I had.

"Richard Rycart," I said.

That must have been a devastating blow to him. He must have known then that it was the end of everything. In my mind's eye I see him still, like one those once grand but now condemned apartment blocks, moments after the demolition charges have been exploded: for a few seconds, the façade remains bizarrely intact, before slowly beginning to slide. That was Lang. He gave me a long blank look and then subsided back into his seat.

The plane came to a halt in front of the terminal building. The engines died.

AT THIS POINT, AT long last, I did something smart.

As Lang sat contemplating his ruin, and as Amelia came hurrying down the aisle to discover what I'd said, I had the presence of mind to eject the disk from the minirecorder and slip it into my pocket. In its place I inserted the blank. Lang was too stunned to care and Amelia too fixated on him to notice.

"All right," she said firmly, "that's enough for tonight." She lifted the empty glass from his unresisting hand and gave it to the steward. "We need to get you home, Adam. Ruth's waiting at the gate." She reached over and unfastened his seat belt and then removed his suit jacket from the back of his seat. She held it out ready for him to slip into, and shook it slightly, like a matador with a cloak, but her voice was very tender. "Adam?"

He rose, trancelike, to obey, gazing vacantly toward the cockpit as she guided his arms into the sleeves. She glared at me over his shoulder, and mouthed, furiously and very distinctly, and with her customarily precise diction, "What the fuck are you doing?"

It was a good question. What the fuck *was* I doing? At the front of the plane, the door had opened and three of the Special Branch men were disembarking. A blast of cold air ran down the cabin. Lang began to walk toward the exit, preceded by his fourth bodyguard, Amelia at his back. I quickly stuffed my recorder and the photographs into my shoulder bag and followed them. The pilot had come out of the cockpit to say good-bye and I saw Lang square his shoulders and advance to meet him, his hand outstretched.

"That was great," said Lang vaguely, "as usual. My favorite airline." He shook the pilot's hand, then leaned past him to greet the copilot and the waiting steward. "Thanks. Thanks so much." He turned to us, still smiling his professional smile, but it faded fast; he looked stricken. The last bodyguard was already halfway down the steps. There was just Amelia, me, and the two secretaries waiting to follow him off the plane. Standing in the lighted glass window of the terminal I could just make out the figure of Ruth. She was too far away for me to judge her expression. "Would you mind just hanging back a minute?" he said to Amelia. "And you, too?" he added to me. "I need to have a private word with my wife."

"Is everything all right, Adam?" asked Amelia. She had been with him too long, and I suppose she loved him too much, not to know that something was terribly wrong.

"It'll be fine," said Lang. He touched her elbow lightly, then gave us all, including me and the plane crew, a slight bow. "Thank you, ladies and gentlemen, and good night."

He ducked through the door and paused at the top of the steps, glancing around, smoothing down his hair. Amelia and I watched him from the interior of the plane. He was just as he was when I first saw him—still, out of habit, searching for an audience with whom he could connect, even though the windy, floodlit concourse was deserted, apart from the waiting bodyguards, and a ground technician in overalls, working late, no doubt eager to get home.

Lang must also have seen Ruth waiting at the window, because he suddenly raised his hand in acknowledgment, then set off down the steps, gracefully, like a dancer. He reached the tarmac and had gone about ten yards toward the terminal when the technician shouted out, "Adam!" and waved. The voice was English, and Lang must have recognized the accent of a fellow countryman because he suddenly broke away from his bodyguards and strode toward the man, his hand held out. And that is my final image of Lang: a man always with his hand held out. It is burned into my retinas—his yearning shadow against the expanding ball of bright white fire that suddenly engulfed him, and then there was only the flying debris, the stinging grit, the glass, the furnace heat, and the underwater silence of the explosion.

SIXTEEN

————————— ★ —————————

> If you are going to be the least bit upset not to see
> your name credited or not to be invited to the launch
> party then you are going to have a miserable time
> ghosting altogether.
>
> *Ghostwriting*

I SAW NOTHING MORE after that initial flash of brilliant light;
there was too much glass and blood in my eyes. The force of the
blast flung us all backward. Amelia, I learned later, hit her head on
the side of a seat and was knocked unconscious, while I lay across
the aisle in darkness and silence for what could have been minutes
or hours. I felt no pain, except when one of the terrified secretaries
trod on my hand with her high heel in her desperation to get out
of the plane. But I couldn't see, and it was also to be several hours
before I could hear properly. Even today I get an occasional buzzing in my ears. It cuts me off from the world, like radio interfer-

ence. Eventually, I was lifted away and given a wonderful shot of morphine that burst like warm fireworks in my brain. Then I was airlifted by helicopter with all the other survivors to a hospital near Boston—an institution very close, it turned out, to the place where Emmett lived.

Did you ever do something secretly as a child that seemed really bad at the time, and for which you were sure you were going to be punished? I remember breaking a precious old long-playing gramophone record of my father's and putting it away in its sleeve again and saying nothing about it. For days, I lived in a sweat of terror, convinced that retribution would arrive at any moment. But nothing was ever said. The next time I dared to look, the record had disappeared. He must have found it and thrown it away.

I had similar feelings following the assassination of Adam Lang. Throughout the next day or two, as I lay in my hospital room, my face bandaged, and with a policeman on guard in the corridor outside, I repeatedly ran over in my mind the events of the previous week, and it always seemed to me a certainty that I would never leave that place alive. If you stop to think of it, there's nowhere easier to dispose of someone than in a hospital; I should imagine it's almost routine. And who makes a better killer than a doctor?

But it turned out to be like the incident of my father's broken record. Nothing happened. While I was still blinded, I was gently questioned by a Special Agent Murphy from the Boston office of the FBI about what I could remember. The next afternoon, when the bandages were removed from my eyes, Murphy returned. He looked like a muscular young priest in a fifties movie, and this time he was accompanied by a saturnine Englishman from the British

Security Service, MI5, whose name I never quite caught—because, I assume, I was never quite meant to catch it.

They showed me a photograph. My vision was still bleary, but I was nevertheless able to identify the crazy man I had met in the bar of my hotel and who had staged that lonely vigil, with the biblical slogan, at the end of the track from the Rhinehart compound. His name, they said, was George Arthur Boxer, a former major in the British army, whose son had been killed in Iraq and whose wife had died six months later in a London suicide bombing. In his unhinged state, Major Boxer had held Adam Lang personally responsible, and had stalked him to Martha's Vineyard just after McAra's death had been reported in the papers. He had plenty of expertise in munitions and intelligence. He had studied tactics for suicide bombing on jihadist websites. He had rented a cottage in Oak Bluffs, brought in supplies of peroxide and weed killer, and turned it into a minor factory for the production of homemade explosives. And it would have been easy for him to know when Lang was returning from New York, because he would have seen the bombproof car heading to the airport to meet him. How he had got onto the airfield nobody was quite sure, but it was dark, there was a four-mile perimeter fence, and the experts had always assumed that four Special Branch men and an armored car were sufficient protection.

But one had to be realistic, said the man from MI5. There was a limit to what security could do, especially against a determined suicide bomber. He quoted Seneca, in the original Latin, and then helpfully translated: "Who scorns his own life is lord of yours." I got the impression everyone was slightly relieved by the way things had worked out: the British, because Lang had been killed on American soil; the Americans, because he'd been blown up by a Brit; and both because there would now be no war crimes trial, no

unseemly revelations, and no guest who has overstayed his welcome, drifting around the dinner tables of Georgetown for the
next twenty years. You could almost say it was the special relationship in action.

Agent Murphy asked me about the flight from New York and
whether Lang had expressed any worries about his personal security. I said truthfully that he hadn't.

"Mrs. Bly," said the MI5 man, "tells us you recorded an interview with him during the final part of the flight."

"No, she's wrong about that," I said. "I had the machine in
front of me, but I never actually switched it on. It wasn't really an
interview, in any case. It was more of a chat."

"Do you mind if I take a look?"

"Go ahead."

My shoulder bag was on the nightstand next to my bed. The
MI5 man took out the minirecorder and ejected the disk. I watched
him, dry-mouthed.

"Can I borrow this?"

"You can keep it," I said. He started poking through the rest
of my belongings. "How is Amelia, by the way?"

"She's fine." He put the disk into his briefcase. "Thanks."

"Can I see her?"

"She flew back to London last night." I guess my disappointment must have been evident, because the MI5 man added, with
chilly pleasure, "It's not surprising. She hasn't seen her husband
since before Christmas."

"And what about Ruth?" I asked.

"She's accompanying Mr. Lang's body home right now," said
Murphy. "Your government sent a plane to fetch them."

"He'll get full military honors," added the MI5 man. "A statue in the Palace of Westminster, and a funeral in the Abbey if she wants it. He's never been more popular than since he died."

"He should have done it years ago," I said. They didn't smile. "And is it really true that nobody else was killed?"

"Nobody," said Murphy, "which was a miracle, believe me."

"In fact," said the man from MI5, "Mrs. Bly wonders if Mr. Lang didn't actually recognize his assassin and deliberately head toward him, knowing that something like this might happen. Can you shed any light on that?"

"It sounds far-fetched," I said. "I thought a fuel truck had exploded."

"It was certainly quite a bang," said Murphy, clicking his pen and slipping it into his inside pocket. "We eventually found the killer's head on the terminal roof."

I WATCHED LANG'S FUNERAL on CNN two days later. My eyesight was more or less restored. I could see it was tastefully done: the queen, the prime minister, the U.S. vice president and half the leaders of Europe; the coffin draped in the Union Jack; the guard of honor; the solitary piper playing a lament. Ruth looked very good in black, I thought; it was definitely her color. I kept a lookout for Amelia, but I didn't see her. During a lull in proceedings, there was even an interview with Richard Rycart. Naturally, he hadn't been invited to the service, but he'd gone to the trouble of putting on a black tie and paid a very moving tribute from his office in the United Nations: a great colleague . . . a true patriot . . . we had our disagreements . . . remained friends . . . my heart goes out to Ruth and the family . . . as far as I'm concerned the whole chapter is closed.

I found the mobile phone he had given me and threw it out the window.

The next day, when I was due to be discharged from hospital, Rick came up from New York to say good-bye and take me to the airport.

"Do you want the good news or the good news?" he said.

"I'm not sure your idea of good news is the same as mine."

"Sid Kroll just called. Ruth Lang still wants you to finish the memoirs, and Maddox will give you an extra month to work on the manuscript."

"And the good news is?"

"Very cute. Listen, don't be so goddamned snooty about it. This is a really hot book now. This is Adam Lang's voice from the grave. You don't have to work on it here anymore; you can finish it in London. You look terrible, by the way."

"His 'voice from the grave'?" I repeated incredulously. "So now I'm to be the ghost of a ghost?"

"Come on, the whole situation is rich with possibilities. Think about it. You can write what you like, within reason. Nobody's going to stop you. And you liked him, didn't you?"

I thought about that. In fact, I had been thinking about it ever since I came round from the sedative. Worse than the pain in my eyes and the buzzing in my ears, worse even than my fear that I would never emerge from the hospital, was my sense of guilt. That may seem odd, given what I'd learned, but I couldn't work up any sense of self-justification or resentment against Lang. I was the one at fault. It wasn't just that I'd betrayed my client, personally and professionally; it was the sequence of events my actions had set in motion. If I hadn't gone to see Emmett, Emmett wouldn't have contacted Lang to warn him about the photograph. Then maybe

Lang wouldn't have insisted on flying back to Martha's Vineyard that night to see Ruth. Then I wouldn't have had to tell him about Rycart. And then, and then . . . ? It nagged away at me as I lay in the darkness. I just couldn't erase the memory of how bleak he had looked on the plane at the very end.

"Mrs. Bly wonders if Mr. Lang didn't actually recognize his assassin and deliberately head toward him, knowing that something like this might happen . . ."

"Yes," I said to Rick. "Yes, I did like him."

"Well, there you go. You owe it to him. And besides, there's another consideration."

"Which is what?"

"Sid Kroll says that if you don't fulfill your contractual obligations and finish the book, they'll sue your ass off."

AND SO I RETURNED to London, and for the next six weeks I barely emerged from my flat, except once, early on, to go out for dinner with Kate. We met in a restaurant in Notting Hill Gate, midway between our homes—territory as neutral as Switzerland and about as expensive. The manner of Adam Lang's death seemed to have silenced even her hostility, and I suppose a kind of glamour attached to me as an eyewitness. I had turned down a score of requests to give interviews, so that she was the first person, apart from the FBI and MI5, to whom I described what had happened. I desperately wanted to tell her about my final conversation with Lang. I would have done, too. But in the way of these things, just as I was about to broach it, the waiter came over to discuss dessert, and when he left she announced she had something she wanted to tell me, first.

She was engaged to be married.

I confess it was a shock. I didn't like the other man. You'd know him if I mentioned his name: craggy, handsome, soulful. He specializes in flying briefly into the world's worst trouble spots and flying out again with moving descriptions of human suffering, usually his own.

"Congratulations," I said.

We skipped dessert. Our affair, our relationship—our *thing*—whatever it was—ended ten minutes later with a peck on the cheek on the pavement outside the restaurant.

"You were going to tell me something," she said, just before she got into her taxi. "I'm sorry I cut you off. I only didn't want you to say anything, you know . . . too personal . . . without telling you first about how things were with me and—"

"It doesn't matter," I said.

"Are you sure you're all right? You seem . . . different."

"I'm fine."

"If you ever need me, I'll always be there for you."

"There?" I said. "I don't know about you, but I'm here. Where's there?"

I held open the door of her cab for her. I couldn't help overhearing that the address she gave the driver wasn't hers.

After that, I withdrew from the world. I spent my every waking hour with Lang, and now that he was dead, I found I suddenly had his voice. It was more a Ouija board than a keyboard that I sat down to every morning. If my fingers typed out a sentence that sounded wrong, I could almost physically feel them being drawn to the Delete key. I was like a screenwriter producing lines with a particularly demanding star in mind: I knew he might say this, but not that; might do this scene, never that.

The basic structure of the story remained McAra's sixteen chapters. My method was to work always with his manuscript on my left, to retype it completely, and in the process of passing it through my brain and fingers and on to my computer, to strain it of my predecessor's lumpy clichés. I made no mention of Emmett, of course, cutting even the anodyne quote of his that had opened the final chapter. The image of Adam Lang that I presented to the world was very much the character he'd always chosen to play: the regular guy who fell into politics almost by accident and who rose to power because he was neither tribal nor ideological. I reconciled this with the chronology by taking up Ruth's suggestion that Lang had turned to politics as solace for his depression when he first arrived in London. I didn't really need to play up the misery here. Lang was dead, after all, his whole memoir suffused by the reader's knowledge of what was to come. That ought to be sufficient, I reckoned, to keep the ghouls happy. But it was still useful to have a page or two of heroic struggle against inner demons, etc., etc.

> In the superficially tedious business of politics I found solace for my hurt. I found activity, companionship, an outlet for my love of meeting new people. I found a cause that was bigger than myself. Most of all, I found Ruth . . .

In my telling of his story, Lang's political involvement really got going only when Ruth came knocking at his door two years later. It sounded plausible. Who knows? It might even have been true.

I started writing *Memoirs by Adam Lang* on February the tenth and promised Maddox I'd have the whole thing done, all one hundred and sixty thousand words, by the end of March. That meant I had to produce thirty-four hundred words a day, every day. I had a chart on the wall and marked it up each morning. I was like Captain Scott returning from the South Pole: I had to make those daily distances, or I'd fall irrevocably behind and perish in a white wilderness of blank pages. It was a hard slog, especially as almost no lines of McAra's were salvageable, except, curiously, the very last one in the manuscript, which had made me groan aloud when I read it on Martha's Vineyard: *"Ruth and I look forward to the future, whatever it may hold."* Read that, you bastards, I thought, as I typed it in on the evening of the thirtieth of March: read that, and close this book without a catch in your throat.

I added "The End" and then, I guess, I had a kind of nervous breakdown.

I DISPATCHED ONE COPY of the manuscript to New York and another to the office of the Adam Lang Foundation in London, for the personal attention of Mrs. Ruth Lang—or, as I should more properly have styled her by then, Baroness Lang of Calderthorpe, the government having just given her a seat in the House of Lords as a mark of the nation's respect.

I hadn't heard anything from Ruth since the assassination. I'd written to her while I was still in hospital, one of more than a hundred thousand correspondents who were reported to have sent their condolences, so I wasn't surprised that all I got back was a standard printed reply. But a week after she received the manuscript, a handwritten message arrived on the red-embossed notepaper of the House of Lords:

You have done all that I ever hoped you wd do—
and more! You have caught his tone beautifully &
brought him back to life—all his wonderful humor
& compassion & energy. Pls. come & see me here in
the HoL when you have a spare moment. It wd be
great to catch up. Martha's V. seems a v long time
ago, & a long way away! Bless you again for yr
talent. And it is a <u>proper book</u>!!

                                          Much love,
                                          R.

Maddox was equally effusive, but without the love. The first printing was to be four hundred thousand copies. The publication date was the end of May.

So that was that. The job was done.

It didn't take me long to realize I was in a bad state. I'd been kept going, I suppose, by Lang's "wonderful humor & compassion & energy," but once he was written out of me, I collapsed like an empty suit of clothes. For years I had survived by inhabiting one life after another. But Rick had insisted we wait until the Lang memoirs were published—my "breakthrough book," he called it—before negotiating new and better contracts, with the result that, for the first time I could remember, I had no work to go to. I was afflicted by a horrible combination of lethargy and panic. I could barely summon the energy to get out of bed before noon, and when I did I moped on the sofa in my dressing gown, watching daytime television. I didn't eat much. I stopped opening my letters or answering the phone. I didn't shave. I left the flat for any length of time only on Mondays and Thursdays, to avoid seeing my cleaner—I wanted to fire her, but I didn't have the nerve—and then I either sat in a park, if it was fine, or in a nearby greasy café, if it wasn't; and this being England, it mostly wasn't.

And yet, paradoxically, at the same time as being sunk in a stupor I was also permanently agitated. Nothing was in proportion. I fretted absurdly about trivialities—where I'd put a pair of shoes, or if it was wise to keep all my money with the same bank. This nerviness made me feel physically shaky, often breathless, and it was in this spirit, late one night, about two months after I finished the book, that I made what to me, in my condition, was a calamitous discovery.

I'd run out of whiskey and knew I had about ten minutes to get to the little supermarket on Ladbroke Grove before it closed. It was toward the end of May, dark and raining. I grabbed the nearest jacket and was halfway down the stairs when I realized it was the one I'd been wearing when Lang was killed. It was torn at the front and stained with blood. In one pocket was the recording of my final interview with Adam, and in the other the keys to the Ford Escape SUV.

The car! I had forgotten all about it. It was still parked at Logan Airport! It was costing eighteen dollars a day! I must owe *thousands*!

To you, no doubt—and indeed to me, now—my panic seems ridiculous. But I raced back up those stairs with my pulse drumming. It was after six in New York and Rhinehart Inc. had closed for the day. There was no reply from the Martha's Vineyard house, either. In despair, I called Rick at home and, without preliminaries, began gabbling out the details of the crisis. He listened for about thirty seconds, then told me roughly to shut up.

"This was all sorted out weeks ago. The guys at the car park got suspicious and called the cops, and they called Rhinehart's office. Maddox paid the bill. I didn't bother you with it because I knew you were busy. Now listen to me, my friend. It seems to me you've got a nasty case of delayed shock. You need help. I know a shrink—"

I hung up.

When I finally fell asleep on the sofa, I had my usual recurrent dream about McAra, the one in which he floated fully clothed in the sea beside me and told me he wasn't going to make it: *You go on without me.* But this time, instead of ending with my waking up, the dream lasted longer. A wave took McAra away, in his heavy raincoat and rubber-soled boots, until he became only a dark shape in the distance, facedown in the shallow foam, sliding back and forth at the edge of the beach. I waded toward him and managed to get my hands around his bulky body and, with a supreme effort, to roll him over, and then suddenly he was staring up naked from a white slab, with Adam Lang bending over him.

The next morning I left the flat early and walked down the hill to the tube station. It really wouldn't take much to kill myself, I thought. One swift leap out in front of the approaching train, and then oblivion. Much better than drowning. But it was only the briefest of impulses, not least because I couldn't bear the idea of someone having to clean up afterward. (*"We eventually found the killer's head on the terminal roof."*) Instead I boarded the train and traveled to the end of the line at Hammersmith, then crossed the road to the other platform. Motion, that's the cure for depression, I decided. You have to keep moving. At Embankment I changed again for Morden, which always sounds to me like the end of the world. We passed through Balham and I got off two stops later.

It didn't take me long to find the grave. I remembered Ruth

had said the funeral was at Streatham Cemetery. I looked up his name and a groundsman pointed the way toward the plot. I passed stone angels with vultures' wings, and mossy cherubs with lichened curls, Victorian sarcophagi the size of garden sheds, and crosses garlanded with marble roses. But McAra's contribution to the necropolis was characteristically plain. No flowery mottoes, no "Say not the struggle naught availeth" or "Well done, thou good and faithful servant" for our Mike. Merely a slab of limestone with his name and dates.

It was a late spring morning, drowsy with pollen and petrol fumes. In the distance, the traffic rolled up Garratt Lane toward central London. I squatted on my haunches and pressed my palms to the dewy grass. As I've said before, I'm not the superstitious type, but at that moment I did feel a current of relief pass through me, as if I'd closed a circle, or fulfilled a task. I sensed he had wanted me to come here.

That was when I noticed, resting against the stone, half obscured by the overgrown grass, a small bunch of shriveled flowers. There was a card attached, written in an elegant hand, just legible after successive London downpours: "In memory of a good friend and loyal colleague. Rest in peace, dear Mike. Amelia."

WHEN I GOT BACK to my flat, I called her on her mobile number. She didn't seem surprised to hear from me.

"Hello," she said. "I was just thinking about you."

"Why's that?"

"I'm reading your book—Adam's book."

"And?"

"It's good. No, actually, it's better than good. It's like having him back. There's only one element missing, I think."

"And what's that?"

"Oh, it doesn't matter. I'll tell you if I see you. Perhaps we'll get the opportunity to talk at the reception tonight."

"What reception?"

She laughed. "*Your* reception, you idiot. The launch of your book. Don't tell me you haven't been invited."

I hadn't spoken to anyone in a long while. It took me a second or two to reply.

"I don't know whether I have or not. To be honest, I haven't checked my post in a while."

"You must have been invited."

"Don't you believe it. Authors tend to be funny about having their ghosts staring at them over the canapés."

"Well, the author isn't going to be there, is he?" she said. She wanted to sound brisk, but she came across as desperately hollow and strained. "You should go, whether you've been invited or not. In fact, if you really haven't been invited, you can come as my guest. My invitation has 'Amelia Bly plus one' written on it."

The prospect of returning to society made my heartbeat start to race again.

"But don't you want to take someone else? What about your husband?"

"Oh, him. That didn't work out, I'm afraid. I hadn't realized quite how bored he was with being my 'plus one.' "

"I'm sorry to hear that."

"Liar," she said. "I'll meet you at the end of Downing Street at seven o'clock. The party's just across Whitehall. I'll only wait five minutes, so if you decide you do want to come, don't be late."

AFTER I FINISHED SPEAKING to Amelia, I went through my weeks of accumulated mail carefully. There was no invitation to the party. Bearing in mind the circumstances of my last encounter with Ruth, I wasn't too surprised. There was, however, a copy of the finished book. It was nicely produced. The cover, with an eye to the American market, was a photograph of Lang, looking debonair, addressing a joint session of the U.S. Congress. The photographs inside did not include any of the ones from Cambridge that McAra had discovered; I hadn't passed them on to the picture researcher. I flicked through to the acknowledgments, which I had written in Lang's voice:

> This book would not exist without the dedication, support, wisdom, and friendship of the late Michael McAra, who collaborated with me on its composition from the first page to the last. Thank you, Mike—for everything.

My name wasn't mentioned. Much to Rick's annoyance, I'd forgone my collaborator credit. I didn't tell him why, which was that I thought it was safer that way. The expurgated contents and my anonymity would, I hoped, serve as a message to whoever out there might be paying attention that there would be no further trouble from me.

I soaked in the bath for an hour that afternoon and contemplated whether or not to go to the reception. As usual, I was able to spin out my procrastination for hours. I told myself I still hadn't necessarily made up my mind as I shaved off my beard, and as I dressed in a decent dark suit and white shirt, and as I went out into the street and hailed a taxi, and even as I stood on the corner of Downing Street at five minutes to seven; it still wasn't too late to turn back. Across the broad, ceremonial boulevard of Whitehall, I could see the cars and taxis pulling up outside the Banqueting House, where I guessed the party must be taking place. Photographers' flashbulbs winked in the evening sunshine, a pale reminder of Lang's old glory days.

I kept looking for Amelia, up the street toward the mounted sentry outside Horse Guards, and down it again, past the Foreign Office, to the Victorian Gothic madhouse of the Palace of Westminster. A sign on the opposite side of the entrance to Downing Street pointed to the Cabinet War Rooms, with a drawing of Churchill, complete with V sign and cigar. Whitehall always reminds me of the Blitz. I can picture it from the images I was brought up on as a child: the sandbags, the white tape across the windows, the searchlights blindly fingering the darkness, the drone of the bombers, the crump of high explosive, the red glow from the fires in the East End. Thirty thousand dead in London alone. Now *that*, as my father would have said, is what you call a *war*— not this drip, drip, drip of inconvenience and anxiety and folly. Yet Churchill used to stroll to parliament through St. James's Park, raising his hat to passersby, with just a solitary detective walking ten feet behind him.

I was still thinking about it when Big Ben finished chiming the hour. I peered left and right again, but there was still no sign of Amelia, which surprised me, as I had her down as the punctual type. But then I felt a touch on my sleeve and turned to find her standing behind me. She had emerged from the sunless canyon of Downing Street in her dark blue suit, carrying a briefcase. She looked older, faded, and just for an instant I glimpsed her future: a tiny flat, a smart address, a cat. We exchanged polite hellos.

"Well," she said, "here we are."

"Here we are." We stood awkwardly, a few feet apart. "I didn't realize you were back working in Number Ten," I said.

"I was only on attachment to Adam. The king is dead," she said, and suddenly her voice cracked. I put my arms around her and patted her back, as if she were a child who had fallen over. I felt the wetness of her cheek against mine. When she pulled back, she opened her briefcase and took out a handkerchief. "Sorry," she said. She blew her nose and stamped her high-heeled foot in self-reproach. "I keep thinking I'm over it, and then I realize I'm not. You look terrible," she added. "In fact, you look—"

"Like a ghost?" I said. "Thanks. I've heard it before."

She checked herself in the mirror of her powder compact and carried out some swift repairs. She was apprehensive, I realized. She needed someone to accompany her; even I would do.

"Right," she said, shutting it with a click. "Let's go."

We walked up Whitehall, through the crowds of spring tourists.

"So, were you invited in the end?" she asked.

"No, I wasn't. Actually, I'm rather surprised that you were."

"Oh, that's not so odd," she said, with an attempt at careless-ness. "She's won, hasn't she? She's the national icon. The grieving widow. Our very own Jackie Kennedy. She won't mind having me around. I'm hardly a threat, just a trophy in the victory parade." We crossed the road. "Charles the First stepped out of that window to be executed," she said, pointing. "You'd have thought someone would have realized the association, wouldn't you?"

"Poor staff work," I said. "It wouldn't have happened when you were in charge."

I knew it was a mistake to have come the moment we stepped inside. Amelia had to open her briefcase for the security men. My keys set off the metal detector and I had to be searched. It's come to something, I thought, standing with my hands up, having my groin felt, when you can't even go to a drinks party without being frisked. In the great open space of the Banqueting House, we were confronted by a roar of conversation and a wall of turned backs. I'd made it a rule never to attend the launch parties of my own books, and now I remembered why. A ghostwriter is about as welcome as the groom's unacknowledged love child at a society wedding. I didn't know a soul.

Deftly, I seized a couple of flutes of champagne from a passing waiter and presented one to Amelia.

"I can't see Ruth," I said.

"She'll be in the thick of it, I expect. Your health," she said.

We clicked glasses. Champagne: even more pointless than white wine, in my opinion. But there didn't seem to be anything else.

"It's Ruth, actually, who is the one element missing from your book, if I had to make a criticism."

"I know," I said. "I wanted to put in more about her, but she wouldn't have it."

"Well, it's a pity." Drink seemed to embolden the normally cautious Mrs. Bly. Or perhaps it was just that we had a bond now. After all, we were survivors—survivors of the Langs. At any rate, she leaned in close to me, giving me a familiar lungful of her scent. "I adored Adam, and I think he had similar feelings for me. But I wasn't under any illusions: he'd never have left her. He told me that during that last drive to the airport. They were a complete team. He knew perfectly well he'd have been nothing without her. He made that absolutely clear to me. He owed her. She was the one who really understood power. She was the one who originally had the contacts in the party. In fact, *she* was the one who was supposed to go into parliament, did you know that? Not him at all. That isn't in your book."

"I didn't know."

"Adam told me about it once. It isn't widely known—at least I've never seen it written up anywhere. But apparently his seat was originally all lined up for her, only at the last minute she stood aside and let him have it."

I thought of my conversation with Rycart.

"The member for Michigan," I murmured.

"Who?"

"The sitting MP was a man called Giffen. He was so pro-American he was known as the member for Michigan." Something moved uneasily inside my mind. "Can I ask you a question? Before Adam was killed, why were you so determined to keep that manuscript under lock and key?"

"I told you: security."

"But there was nothing in it. I know that better than anyone. I've read every tedious word a dozen times."

Amelia glanced around. We were still on the fringe of the party. Nobody was paying us any attention.

"Between you and me," she said quietly, "*we* weren't the ones who were concerned. Apparently, it was the Americans. I was told they passed the word to MI5 that there might be something early on in the manuscript that was a potential threat to national security."

"How did they know that?"

"Who's to say? All I can tell you is that immediately after Mike died, they requested we take special care to ensure the book wasn't circulated until they'd had a chance to clear it."

"And did they?"

"I've no idea."

I thought again of my meeting with Rycart. What was it he claimed McAra had said to him on the telephone, just before he died? *"The key to everything is in Lang's autobiography—it's all there at the beginning."*

Did that mean their conversation had been bugged?

I sensed that something important had just changed—that some part of my solar system had tilted in its orbit—but I couldn't quite grasp what it was. I needed to get away to somewhere quiet, to take my time and think things through. But already I was aware that the acoustics of the party had changed. The roar of talk was dwindling. People were shushing one another. A man bellowed pompously, "Be quiet!" and I turned around. At the side of the room, opposite the big windows, not very far from where we were standing, Ruth Lang was waiting patiently on a platform, holding a microphone.

"Thank you," she said. "Thank you very much. And good evening." She paused, and a great stillness spread across three hundred people. She took a breath. There was a catch in her throat. "I miss Adam all the time. But never more than tonight. Not just because we're meeting to launch his wonderful book, and he should be here to share the joy of his life story with us, but because he was so brilliant at making speeches, and I'm so terrible."

I was surprised at how professionally she delivered the last line, how she built the emotional tension and then punctured it. There was a release of laughter. She seemed much more confident in public than I remembered her, as if Lang's absence had given her room to grow.

"Therefore," she continued, "you'll be relieved to hear I'm not going to make a speech. I'd just like to thank a few people. I'd like to thank Marty Rhinehart and John Maddox for not only being marvelous publishers, but also being great friends. I'd like to thank Sidney Kroll for his wit and his wise counsel. And in case this sounds as though the only people involved in the memoirs of a British prime minister are Americans, I'd also like to thank in particular, and especially, Mike McAra, who tragically also can't be with us. Mike, you are in our thoughts."

The great hall rang with a rumble of "hear hear."

"And now," said Ruth, "may I propose a toast to the one we really need to thank?" She raised her glass of macrobiotic orange juice, or whatever it was. "To the memory of a great man and a great patriot, a great father and a wonderful husband—to Adam Lang!"

"To Adam Lang!" we all boomed in unison, and then we clapped, and went on clapping, redoubling the volume, while Ruth nodded graciously to all corners of the hall, including ours, at which point she saw me and blinked, then recovered, smiled, and hoisted her glass to me in salute.

She left the platform quickly.

"The merry widow," hissed Amelia. "Death becomes her, don't you think? She's blossoming by the day."

"I have a feeling she's coming over," I said.

"Shit," said Amelia, draining her glass, "in that case I'm getting out of here. Would you like me to take you to dinner?"

"Amelia Bly, are you asking me on a *date*?"

"I'll meet you outside in ten minutes. Freddy!" she called. "Nice to see you."

Even as she moved away to talk to someone else, the crowd before me seemed to part, and Ruth emerged, looking very different from the last time I had seen her: glossy haired, smooth skinned, slimmed by grief, and designer clad in something black and silky. Sid Kroll was just behind her.

"Hello, you," she said.

She took my hands in hers and mwah-mwahed me, not kissing me but brushing her thick helmet of hair briefly against each of my cheeks.

"Hello, Ruth. Hello, Sid."

I nodded to him. He winked.

"I was told you couldn't stand these kinds of parties," she said, still holding my hands and fixing me with her glittering dark eyes, "or else I would have invited you. Did you get my note?"

"I did. Thanks."

"But you didn't call me!"

"I didn't know if you were just being polite."

"Being polite!" She briefly shook my hands in reproach. "Since when was I ever polite? You must come and see me."

And then she did that thing that important people always do to me at parties: she glanced over my shoulder. And I saw, almost immediately and quite unmistakably in her gaze, a flash of alarm, which was followed at once by a barely perceptible shake of her head. I detached my hands and turned around and saw Paul Emmett. He was no more than five feet away.

"Hello," he said. "I believe we've met."

I swung back to Ruth. I tried to speak, but no words would come.

"Ah," I said. "Ah—"

"Paul was my tutor," she said calmly, "when I was a Fulbright scholar at Harvard. You and I must talk."

"Ah—"

I backed away from them all. I knocked into a man who shielded his drink and told me cheerfully to watch out. Ruth was saying something earnestly, and so was Kroll, but there was a buzzing in my ears and I couldn't hear them. I saw Amelia staring at me and I waved my hands feebly, and then I fled from the hall, across the lobby and out into the hollow, imperial grandeur of Whitehall.

IT WAS OBVIOUS THE moment I got outside that another bomb had gone off. I could hear the sirens in the distance, and a pillar of smoke was already dwarfing Nelson's Column, rising from somewhere behind the National Gallery. I set off at a loping run toward Trafalgar Square and barged in front of an outraged couple to seize their taxi. Avenues of escape were being closed off all over central London, as if by a spreading forest fire. We turned into a one-way street, only to find the police sealing the far end with yellow tape. The driver flung the cab into reverse, jerking me forward and onto the edge of my seat, and that was how I stayed throughout the rest of the journey, clinging to the handle beside the door, as we twisted and dodged through the back routes north. When we reached my flat I paid him double the fare.

"The key to everything is in Lang's autobiography—it's all there at the beginning."

I grabbed my copy of the finished book, took it over to my desk, and started flicking through the opening chapters. I ran my finger swiftly down the center of the pages, sweeping my eyes over all the made-up feelings and half-true memories. My professional prose, typeset and bound, had rendered the roughness of a human life as smooth as a plastered wall.

Nothing.

I threw it away in disgust. What a worthless piece of junk it was, what a soulless commercial exercise. I was glad Lang wasn't around to read it. I actually preferred the original; for the first time I recognized something honest at least in its plodding earnestness. I opened a drawer and grabbed McAra's original manuscript, tattered from use and in places barely legible beneath my crossings-out and overwritings. *"Chapter One. Langs are Scottish folk originally, and proud of it . . ."* I remembered the deathless beginning I had cut so ruthlessly in Martha's Vineyard. But then, come to think of it, every single one of McAra's chapter beginnings had been particularly dreadful. I hadn't left one unaltered. I searched through the loose pages, the bulky manuscript fanning open and twisting in my clumsy hands like a living thing.

"Chapter Two. Wife and child in tow, I decided to settle in a small town where we could live away from the hurly-burly of London life . . . Chapter Three. Ruth saw the possibility that I might become party leader long before I did . . . Chapter Four. Studying the failures of my predecessors, I resolved to be different . . . Chapter Five. In retrospect, our general election victory seems inevitable, but at the time . . . Chapter Six. Seventy-six separate agencies oversaw social security . . . Chapter Seven. Was ever a land so haunted by history as Northern Ireland . . . Chapter Eight. Recruited from all walks of life, I was proud of our candidates in the European elections . . . Chapter Nine. As a rule, nations pursue self-interest in their foreign policy . . . Chapter Ten. A major problem facing the new govern-

ment . . . Chapter Eleven. CIA assessments of the terrorist threat . . . Chapter Twelve. Agent reports from Afghanistan . . . Chapter Thirteen. In deciding to launch an attack on civilian areas, I knew . . . Chapter Fourteen. America needs allies who are prepared . . . Chapter Fifteen. By the time of the annual party conference, demands for my resignation . . . Chapter Sixteen. Professor Paul Emmett of Harvard University has written of the importance . . ."

I took all sixteen chapter openings and laid them out across the desk in sequence.

"The key to everything is in Lang's autobiography—it's all there at the beginning."

The *beginning* or the *beginnings*?

I was never any good at puzzles. But when I went through the pages and circled the first word of each chapter, even I couldn't help but see it—the sentence that McAra, fearful for his safety, had embedded in the manuscript, like a message from the grave: "Langs Wife Ruth Studying In Seventy-six Was Recruited As A CIA Agent In America By Professor Paul Emmett of Harvard University."

SEVENTEEN

———————— ★ ————————

A ghost must expect no glory.

Ghostwriting

I LEFT MY FLAT that night, never to return. Since then a month has passed. As far as know, I haven't been missed. There were times, especially in the first week, sitting alone in my scruffy hotel room—I've stayed in four by now—when I was sure I had gone mad. I ought to ring Rick, I told myself, and get the name of his shrink. I was suffering from delusions. But then, about three weeks ago, after a hard day's writing, just as I was falling asleep, I heard on the midnight news that the former foreign secretary Richard Rycart had been killed in a car accident in New York City, along with his driver. It was the fourth headline, I'm afraid. There's nothing more ex than an ex-politician. Rycart would not have been pleased.

I knew after that there was no going back.

Although I've done nothing but write and think about what happened, I still can't tell you precisely how McAra uncovered the truth. I presume it must have started back in the archives, when he came across Operation Tempest. He was already disillusioned with Lang's years in power, unable to understand why something that had started with such high promise had ended in such a bloody mess. When, in his dogged way, researching the Cambridge years, he stumbled on those photographs, it must have seemed like the key to the mystery. Certainly, if Rycart had heard rumors of Emmett's CIA links, it's reasonable to assume that McAra must have done so, too.

But McAra knew other things as well. He would have known that Ruth was a Fulbright scholar at Harvard, and it wouldn't have taken him more than ten minutes on the internet to discover that Emmett was teaching her specialist subject on the campus in the midseventies. He also knew better than anyone that Lang rarely made a decision without consulting his wife. Adam was the brilliant political salesman, Ruth the strategist. If you had to pick which of them would have had the brains, the nerve, and the ruthlessness to be an ideological recruit, there could only be one choice. McAra can't have known for sure, but I believe he'd put together enough of the picture to blurt out his suspicions to Lang during that heated argument on the night before he went off to confront Emmett.

I try to imagine what Lang must have felt when he heard the accusation. Dismissive, I'm sure; furious also. But a day or two afterward, when a body was washed up, and he went to the morgue to identify McAra—what did he think then?

Most days I have listened to the tape of my final conversation with Lang. The key to everything is there, I'm sure, but always the whole story remains just tantalizingly out of reach. Our voices are thin but recognizable. In the background is the rumble of the jet's engines.

ME: Is it true you had a serious row with him? Just before he died?

LANG: Mike made certain wild accusations. I could hardly ignore them.

ME: May I ask what kind of accusations?

LANG: I'd prefer not to repeat them.

ME: Were they to do with the CIA?

LANG: But surely you already know, if you've been to see Paul Emmett?

[A pause, lasting seventy-five seconds]

LANG: I want you to understand that everything I did, both as party leader and as prime minister—everything—I did out of conviction, because I believed it was right.

ME: [Inaudible]

LANG: Emmett claims you showed him some photographs. Is that true? May I see?

And then there is nothing for a while but engine sound, as he studies them, and I spool forward to the part where he lingers over the girls at the picnic on the riverbank. He sounds inexpressibly sad.

"I remember her. And her. She wrote to me once, when I was prime minister. Ruth was not pleased. Oh, God, Ruth—"

"Oh, God, Ruth—"

"Oh, God, Ruth—"

I play it over and over again. It's obvious from his voice, now that I've listened to it often enough, that at that moment, when he remembers his wife, his concern is entirely for her. I guess she must have called him late that afternoon in a panic to report I'd been to see Emmett and shown him some photographs. She would have needed to talk to him face-to-face as soon as possible—the whole story was threatening to unravel—hence the scramble to find a plane. God knows if she was aware of what might be waiting for her husband on the tarmac. Surely not, is my opinion, although the questions about the lapses in security that allowed it to happen have never been fully answered. But it's Lang's failure to complete the sentence that I find moving. *What have you done?* is surely what he means to add. *"Oh, God, Ruth—what have you done?"* This, I think, is the instant when the days of suspicion abruptly crystallize in his mind, when he realizes that McAra's "wild accusations" must have been true after all, and his wife of thirty years is not the woman he thought she was.

No wonder I was the one she suggested should complete the book. She had plenty to hide, and she must have been confident that the author of Christy Costello's hazy memoir would be just about the least likely person on the planet to discover it.

I would like to write more, but, looking at the clock, I fear that this will have to do, at least for the present. As you can appreciate, I don't care to linger in one place too long. Already I sense that strangers are starting to take too close an interest in me. My plan is to parcel up a copy of this manuscript and give it to

Kate. I shall put it through her door in about an hour's time, before anyone is awake, with a letter asking her not to open it but to look after it. Only if she doesn't hear from me within a month, or if she discovers that something has happened to me, is she to read it and decide how best to get it published. She will think I'm being melodramatic, which I am. But I trust her. She will do it. If anyone is stubborn enough and bloody-minded enough to get this thing into print, it is Kate.

I wonder where I'll go next? I can't decide. I certainly know what I'd like to do. It may surprise you. I'd like to go back to Martha's Vineyard. It's summer there now, and I have a peculiar desire to see those wretched scrub oaks actually in leaf and to watch the yachts go skimming out full-sailed from Edgartown across Nantucket Sound. I'd like to return to that beach at Lambert's Cove and feel the hot sand beneath my bare feet, and watch the families playing in the surf, and stretch my limbs in the warmth of the clear New England sun.

This puts me in something of a dilemma, as you may appreciate, now that we reach the final paragraph. Am I supposed to be pleased that you are reading this, or not? Pleased, of course, to speak at last in my own voice. Disappointed, obviously, that it probably means I'm dead. But then, as my mother used to say, I'm afraid in this life you just can't have everything.

ROBERT HARRIS is the author of *Imperium, Pompeii, Archangel, Enigma, Fatherland*, and *Selling Hitler*. He has been a television correspondent with the BBC and a newspaper columnist for the London *Sunday Times* and the *Daily Telegraph*. His novels have sold more than ten million copies and been translated into thirty-seven languages. He lives in Berkshire, England, with his wife and four children.

CHRISTOPHER BROOKE is Professor of History at Westfield College, University of London. He is a Major Scholar of Gonville and Caius College, Cambridge, and was a Fellow of this college from 1949 to 1956. He has published extensively in scholarly journals and is the General Editor of The Norton Library History of England and Nelson's Medieval Texts. His own books include: *The Dullness of the Past* (1957), *From Alfred to Henry III* (1961), and *The Saxon and Norman Kings* (1963).

THE NORTON LIBRARY HISTORY OF ENGLAND

General Editors

CHRISTOPHER BROOKE
Professor of History, Westfield College,
University of London

and

DENIS MACK SMITH
Fellow of All Souls College, Oxford

Already published:

ROMAN BRITAIN AND EARLY ENGLAND, 55 B.C.–A.D. 871
Peter Hunter Blair

FROM ALFRED TO HENRY III, 871–1272
Christopher Brooke

THE LATER MIDDLE AGES, 1272–1485
George Holmes

THE CENTURY OF REVOLUTION, 1603–1714
Christopher Hill

THE EIGHTEENTH CENTURY, 1714–1815
John B. Owen

FROM CASTLEREAGH TO GLADSTONE, 1815–1885
Derek Beales

MODERN BRITAIN, 1885–1955
Henry Pelling

Forthcoming:

THE TUDOR AGE, 1485–1603
M. E. James

From Alfred
to Henry III

871-1272

CHRISTOPHER BROOKE

W · W · NORTON & COMPANY

New York · London

Published simultaneously in Canada by
Penguin Books Canada Ltd,
2801 John Street, Markham, Ontario L3R 1B4.

W. W. Norton & Company, Inc., 500 Fifth Avenue, New York, N.Y. 10110
W. W. Norton & Company Ltd., 37 Great Russell Street, London WC1B 3NU

First published in the Norton Library 1966 by
arrangement with Thomas Nelson and Sons Ltd.

First edition 1961

Second printing 1968

Third printing with corrections 1969

BOOKS THAT LIVE

The Norton imprint on a book means that in the publisher's
estimation it is a book not for a single season but for the years.

ISBN 0-393-00362-0

Printed in the United States of America

8 9 0

General Editors' Preface

KNOWLEDGE and understanding of English history change and develop so rapidly that a new series needs little apology. The present series was planned in the conviction that a fresh survey of English history was needed, and that the time was ripe for it. It will cover the whole span from Caesar's first invasion in 55 B.C. to 1955, and be completed in eight volumes. The precise scope and scale of each book will inevitably vary according to the special circumstances of its period ; but each will combine a clear narrative with an analysis of many aspects of history —social, economic, religious, cultural and so forth—such as is essential in any approach to English history today.

The special aim of this series is to provide serious and yet challenging books, not buried under a mountain of detail. Each volume is intended to provide a picture and an appreciation of its age, as well as a lucid outline, written by an expert who is keen to make available and alive the findings of modern research. They are intended to be reasonably short—long enough that the reader may feel he has really been shown the ingredients of a period, not so long that he loses appetite for anything further. The series is intended to be a stimulus to wider reading rather than a substitute for it ; and yet to comprise a set of volumes, each, within its limits, complete in itself. Our hope is to provide an introduction to English history which is lively and illuminating, and which makes it at once exciting and more intelligible.

C. N. L. B.
D. M. S.

TO MY WIFE

Author's Preface

My first aim in this book has been to make a remote period intelligible. In the Introduction I have tried to give a brief sketch of the materials with which our knowledge of these centuries is built, and a brief outline of what happened in them ; and, above all, to describe some of the fundamental differences between the medieval and the modern world. Some of the chapters which follow are narrative ; some describe and analyse social life, institutions, the Church, farming, trade and so forth. Planning the layout of these topics was no easy task ; they could not be divided in a simple and logical way, as is possible in dealing with shorter, or later, periods. The history of the Church, for instance, falls naturally into three : the tenth-century reform (pp. 55–8), the century after the Conquest (chapter 8), and the thirteenth century (pp. 246–251). If the history of farming were divided in the same way, the first section would be a catalogue of insoluble problems, and the partitions would have hindered any rational explanation of the subject. It is much more satisfactory to treat it as a whole (chapter 7), and in close connection with the history of markets, trade and industry (pp. 125–33) —only so can one expound coherently these various aspects of economic life. Thus the plan of the analytical chapters is deliberately untidy ; it has been devised for use, not for show. If anyone should get lost in the more devious passages, he should find help in the appendices and the index. The illustrations have been chosen to provide a concrete setting for an imaginative rebuilding of the medieval world, and to support the text ; a few introduce artistic themes which I could not describe in cold print. If my efforts have any success, most readers will feel that the building is incomplete ; for them I have provided a list of ' Books for Further Reading '.

The errors in this book are my own ; for the rest it is the

fruit of a combined operation over many years by my father and my other teachers, my colleagues and my pupils, to give me some understanding of medieval England. I have also been much influenced by many of the books which I have listed, and by many books and articles which could not be included in the list. Such debts cannot be properly specified in a book of this character ; but I am very much aware of them. In the preparation of the book, I am indebted to Mr Denis Mack Smith for his penetrating criticism and for translating many passages into English ; to Mr Peter Hunter Blair and Dr George Holmes, who read the book at various times and gave me valuable corrections ; to Mr C. A. F. Meekings, who interpreted Plate 7*b* for me ; to my eldest son, Francis, who helped with the maps ; to Miss H. Otto for typing my manuscript; to my colleagues in the Department of Mediaeval History at Liverpool for discussing some of the book's problems with me, and above all to Dr Alec Myers, who read the whole book in typescript and in proof, saved me from many errors, and gave me much generous help.

The dedication is a token of the many debts I owe to a fellow historian—and a colleague in countless other ways.

C. N. L. B.

PREFACE TO THIRD IMPRESSION

The opportunity has now been taken to make such corrections as a reprint permits. I am indebted to several friends, colleagues and reviewers for corrections and criticisms, and in particular to Professor Dorothy Whitelock and Miss Margaret Gibson.

C. N. L. B.

Contents

Grateful acknowledgement is due to the following for granting permission to quote : to Miss Margaret Ashdown and the Syndics of the Cambridge University Press for extracts from ' The Song of Maldon ' (*English and Norse Documents*, 1930) ; to Professor G. N. Garmonsway, Messrs J. M. Dent & Sons Ltd, and Messrs E. P. Dutton & Co. Inc., New York, for extracts from the *Anglo-Saxon Chronicle* (Everyman's Library) ; to Professor Sir Maurice Powicke and the Delegates of the Clarendon Press for an extract from *King Henry III and the Lord Edward* ; to Professor Sir Frank Stenton and the Delegates of the Clarendon Press for extracts from *Anglo-Saxon England* (1943) ; and to Professor Dorothy Whitelock, Professor D. C. Douglas, Messrs Eyre & Spottiswoode Ltd, and Oxford University Press, Inc., New York, for extracts from *English Historical Documents*, vols. I and II (1955, 1953) (from vol. I, below, pp. 37, 40, 45–8, 58, 62–3, 70, 77 ; from vol. II, p. 77).

List of Plates

Maps and Plans

Acknowledgment is made to the Air Ministry and the Cambridge University Committee for Aerial Photography (photographs by Dr J. K. S. St Joseph, Cambridge University Curator of Aerial Photography; Crown copyright reserved); the Bodleian Library, Oxford; the British Museum; the Controller of H.M. Stationery Office (Public Record Office; Crown copyright reserved); Mrs M. Crossley and the Courtauld Institute of Art; Mr A. F. Kersting; the Ministry of Works (Crown copyright reserved); Phaidon Press Ltd.; and the Pierpont Morgan Library, New York, for permission to use photographs reproduced in this book.

The plan of Rievaulx Abbey is reproduced by permission of the Controller of H.M. Stationery Office (Ministry of Works).

1 Introduction

A DESCRIPTION of the materials from which the story is compiled may seem out of place in a book of this character. But it is one of its chief aims to act as an introduction and guide to more advanced reading. This should always include some reading of sources, however swift our study may be ; and in this period many of the chief sources are literary histories and chronicles—vivid and readable narratives which tell the story better than it can be re-told. At the same time the sources are far from copious ; they grow fuller as the centuries pass, but are still by modern standards exceedingly fragmentary. There is more material for a single week in the twentieth century than for several centuries in the Middle Ages. History, furthermore, is a peculiar science in that its materials are open to inspection by all : anyone can read a chronicle or a charter and understand something of its message. There is a great deal in historical reconstruction which requires expert treatment—learning, technical skill, experience, above all, knowledge of what other historians have done. But the materials are open to inspection ; and in a period when they are both vivid and scanty they form the ideal mode of entry to the history of an age.

The great age of the ' literary ' source—the chronicle and the history—was the twelfth century ; this was the case all over Europe, and nowhere more than in England. Among the most distinguished authors was William of Malmesbury, who wrote a number of books which reflect the various interests of medieval historians very well. He wrote saints' lives and the histories of individual monasteries ; he wrote a history of the English Church (*Acts of the Bishops*) and a history of the English kings (*Acts of the Kings*). Like all English historians of his day, he was aware of working in a great tradition. The

Venerable Bede, most distinguished of all his predecessors, had been an Englishman.

'Bede, that man of great learning and deep humility,' wrote William in the preface to his *Acts of the Kings* (*c.* 1125), 'wrote a full account of the history of the English from their coming into Britain down to his own day, in a clear and graceful style. But I do not think you will easily find anyone after him who has given his mind to weaving the threads of English history in Latin. . . . There are indeed some fragments of antiquity laid out in annal form [with an entry for each year of grace], written like chronicles and in the vernacular. By their means the periods following Bede's death are saved from total oblivion.' In this patronising way William dismisses the *Anglo-Saxon Chronicle*. 'Concerning Aethelweard, a noble and generous man, who strove to render the Chronicle in Latin, silence is best'—a sarcastic reference to the extreme clumsiness of Aethelweard's Latin. 'Nor have I forgotten Eadmer's work, written in a quiet, pleasurable style ; in which he dealt swiftly with the time from King Edgar to William I, then spread himself more freely down to the death of Archbishop Anselm [1109]. . . .' Even so, William claims, there is no proper account of the period between Bede and Edgar, and this gap he sets out to fill, carrying his history on down to the time at which he was writing.

William was less than fair to his predecessors, and he ignores less formal kinds of historical writing. Thus we have a number of biographies : Asser's life of Alfred, numerous saints' lives and even occasional fragments of autobiography ; above all, the unique description of the events leading up to the battle of Hastings, in the Bayeux Tapestry. This splendid piece of embroidery was probably made by English needle-women at the orders of Odo, Bishop of Bayeux. It was made to be hung in Bayeux Cathedral on the feast of the relics. It tells the story, not of the Norman Conquest, but of the decline and fall of King Harold. It ends with Harold's death and the English flight from the battle. Its central scene shows Harold swearing on the relics of Bayeux a solemn oath that he will not take the English crown. He takes it and the moral unfolds : swift retribution on the man who despised the Bayeux relics. But to us its great interest lies in the vivid portrayal of the central event of English history in this period, and of all the incidentals—armour, castles, ships, food, furniture —normally omitted from literary texts.

In spite of these qualifications, it remains true that there is little in the way of narrative history between Bede and the Conquest apart from the *Anglo-Saxon Chronicle*. From then on we have the help of numerous writers from both sides of the Channel : men like the English Eadmer who wrote especially on St Anselm, and the Anglo-Norman Orderic, who was born in Shropshire, but spent his life in a Norman monastery, and wrote an immense history, covering Norman and English affairs and much of wider interest too. Eadmer is notable for his vivid account of Anselm in his *History of Modern Times* and in his life of the saint ; and the *History* also contains striking descriptions of Anselm's relations with the English kings. Orderic's history is full of lively descriptions of persons and events ; he was prolix and formless as a writer, but full of interest ; it makes a good bedside book.

Histories and chronicles grew in quantity and fullness as the twelfth century went on, culminating in the immense semi-official chronicles of Roger of Howden, royal clerk under Henry II (died 1189) and Richard I (1189–99), which finally stopped in 1201. Literary sources of other kinds are also common, and unusually valuable to the historian in this century. The long quarrel between Thomas Becket and Henry II produced a massive body of literature. It was an age when men, following a classical model, collected their letters ; and partly owing to literary vanity, partly to the desire of one or two of the participants to justify their cause or commemorate the martyr, large collections of the day-to-day correspondence of the crisis were preserved. Becket's murder and canonisation led to a flood of biography (some of it good, much indifferent) and of miracle stories. It is characteristic of this century that the life and death of Becket should be its best-documented event.

At the turn of the twelfth and thirteenth centuries lived and wrote one of the most popular of all medieval chroniclers, Jocelin of Brakelond, monk of Bury St Edmunds. His little book has been famous ever since Thomas Carlyle took Jocelin's hero, Abbot Samson (who died in 1211), as one of the central characters in his *Past and Present*. There are few more vivid and lively pictures of medieval life, and the account of Samson's election, with all the gossip and lobbying which preceded it, and of the abbot's personality, are particularly telling. As a picture of monastic life it is one-sided : Jocelin was the abbey cellarer, concerned with food supply and administration, and he has much to say of worldly concerns, little of the spiritual or intellectual life of the abbey ; and Samson, splendid man of business that he was, represents the shrewd, hard-headed merchants and estate-agents who made England prosperous in the thirteenth century, rather than the monastic tradition of St Dunstan or St Ailred of Rievaulx,

In the course of the thirteenth century literary histories declined both in quality and quantity. The most famous chronicler of the reign of Henry III was Matthew Paris, monk of St Albans, who died about 1259. Matthew was a character ; a vivid and facile writer with a strong urge to write and no sense of discipline ; a man of violent but very human prejudices ; more of a journalist, perhaps, than a historian. Matthew was known in his own day as a writer of distinction. In marked contrast to him was the humble friar, Brother Thomas of Eccleston, who wrote about the coming of the Franciscan Order to England. Eccleston's chronicle is a collection of brief notes and stories. He differed from Matthew Paris in having no pretension to literary airs and graces ; also in being remarkably accurate. His simple vignettes of Franciscan life make his chronicle a splendid source for the religious life of the time.

The great days of the literary source were departing. Neither Matthew Paris nor Thomas of Eccleston had successors of comparable interest. None the less the materials for thirteenth-century history are abundant. This is mainly due to a rapid growth in official documents starting at the turn of the twelfth and thirteenth centuries. Documents of some sort there had been throughout the period covered by this book, charters, for instance, official letters, and wills. Of one type of document, the royal writ, we shall have more to say when we study Anglo-Saxon and Norman government. In early days they were rare. One hundred and twenty royal writs (some spurious) survive from before 1066 ; about 500 between 1066 and 1100. Then the number grows : 1,500 for Henry I, and probably several thousand from the reigns of Henry II and Richard I. In 1199 the clerks of the royal Chancery began to make copies, kept on rolls of parchment, of writs sent out under the Great Seal of England. Before 1199 it is a matter very largely of chance whether a writ survives ; after 1199, even if it does not, we can study its contents from the Chancery rolls. One of these sets of rolls, the rolls of letters patent, has been preserved ever since 1201. The proliferation of official records means that we can trace the details of events far more fully than before ; what we lack in comment and vivid narrative we make up in formal, precise record of events.

Writs were not the only thing enrolled by the royal clerks in the thirteenth century, nor was the Chancery the only office in which rolls were kept. In fact, the other great organ of government, the Treasury, which from the early twelfth century had been controlled by its office of audit, the Exchequer, as we still call it, kept rolls of accounts, of which the earliest survivor dates from 1130. These rolls tell us much about royal finance ; and their character is made intelligible to us by an elaborate account of the workings of the Exchequer, the *Dialogue on the Exchequer* (begun in 1177), written by no less a person than the royal Treasurer himself, the head of the office, Richard FitzNeal.

Records of law-courts always give us a somewhat raw picture of society ; and the records of medieval cases are so prolific that medieval man has acquired the undeserved reputation of being incorrigibly litigious. But these legal records are not just a chronicle of the crimes and follies of mankind. They reveal something incidentally of the rich variety of everyday life ; they can be made to illuminate a thousand dark corners of medieval society. They need patience in the unravelling. Their sheer bulk from John's reign on surpasses all other official records. But we are beginning to learn their value, and although only a small proportion have yet been excerpted, many tales from them have found their way into recent books.

Chronicles and official records, and documents of every kind, are the historian's traditional tools. But he has come in recent years to look for evidence wherever he can find it ; and also to take an interest in every aspect of the life of the past. Survivals of every kind are useful to him : physical survivals, like fields and boundary walls, and the countryside at large ; material survivals, churches, castles, and houses—the remains of town and village and monastery as they can be revealed by aerial photography or archaeology. We shall see when we talk of the Danish invasions how valuable is the evidence of place-names—the meaning and more particularly the language of the original name—in showing how the peoples who settled in this country were distributed. When we talk of Old English society, of the work of King Alfred, or the court of Henry II, we shall see how much of the life of the time is reflected in its literature. When we discuss the impact of the Norman Conquest on English life, we shall see how much essential evidence must be gathered from the fascinating history of the English language—of how it became Frenchified without becoming French ; and also of how English skills in painting and design and English traditions survived, modified and moulded by Norman ideas and Norman energy. Finally, not least important, history is mainly the study of men and women ; and at every turn the historian, attempting to describe and explain their actions, is compelled to use his knowledge of human nature. This has its dangers, since human nature is liable to change. Into this as into every type of evidence historians are tempted to read too much. But it is a vital basis for our reconstruction of the past.

This catalogue is not intended to bewilder or discourage. On the contrary, it shows the rich profusion of material from which the student of history can select. There is something here to suit every taste. That is the special value of history. It gives its students great freedom of choice. But for those who want to study history as it should be studied, imaginatively and for pleasure, three things are necessary : a well-stocked library, a readiness to explore, and eyes open to observe whatever they find, in or out of books.

(2) 871–1272

This volume covers just over 400 years, from the accession of Alfred to the death of Henry III ; 400 years of great interest and importance in English history, and full of change. They saw the last three waves of successful conquest and extensive settlement : the two Danish invasions of the ninth and early eleventh centuries, and the Norman Conquest. Each conquest carried with it extensive political and social changes : profound alterations in the structure of English life and government. The Norman Conquest gave England an entirely new ruling class, and with it new social arrangements and customs. From any viewpoint, the Norman Conquest is the watershed in the history of these centuries. But there is another story unfolding behind these dramatic events. The main theme in ninth- and tenth-century history is the creation of an English monarchy out of the smaller units which had hitherto dominated the country. With the English kingdom grew up the first semblance of national institutions—institutions of central and local government which made the English monarchy among the most mature in the Europe of its time. It was not until the eleventh century that a united England really emerged, under the aegis of the Danish King Cnut ; but its foundations had been laid in the hundred years after 871 by the dynasty of Alfred. These established institutions were not destroyed by the Normans ; they adapted and developed them. There was a certain continuity of institutional life even through the Conquest. This, then, is the theme of the first four chapters of the book : the emergence of a united English monarchy.

In every sphere of life eleventh- and twelfth-century Europe was changing rapidly. The Church was finding new inspiration in monastic reforms and in the reform of the papacy. With these came new methods of Church government ; and at the same time a great intellectual revival, which culminated, in the late twelfth and thirteenth centuries, in the creation of universities. But it was not only the Church which was changing. Economic life was reawakening ; the Mediterranean was once more freely used by western merchants, and in the twelfth century, by western soldiers on their way to the Crusades. Social codes, systems of government were changing ; the code of chivalry was being devised. All these changes tended to enhance the impact of the Norman Conquest, which brought England into closer touch with European life, and made it politically very close to France, the centre of new fashions in thought and literature and art and war and, even then, in dress. Politically, the Norman Conquest made England the partner in an Anglo-French state ; culturally, it speeded the process by which she became a partner in the new Europe. One of the most striking developments of the twelfth century was the emergence of a new kind of statecraft, of a government organised more elaborately and effectively than anything Europe had known for centuries. The two outstanding examples were both Norman creations : the Norman kingdom of Sicily and the Norman kingdom of England. These are the themes of chapters 5–11.

The Norman and early Angevin kings were in many ways remarkably despotic ; they ruled by personal strength and through fear, and kept a close hold on the institutions of government. But they also ruled to some extent by consent ; and the more they developed their judicial, administrative, and fiscal powers, the more some form of consent was necessary. It was in the reigns of John (1199–1216) and Henry III (1216–72) that these tensions came into the open. Neither man was successful enough as a king to maintain the machinery of government without concessions to the magnates. At first, the concession took the form of the issue and frequent re-issue of Magna Carta. As time went on government by consent began to take more self-conscious and elaborate shape in more formal arrangements for meetings of the King's Council, and in formal talks, ' parleyings ', parliaments between kings and lords, and sometimes between king, lords, and representatives of the commons as well. Parliament as an institution was still remote enough when Henry III died ; but new principles of government were astir. Henry III's court was a very active place. His civil service and his judicial system were growing ; and the palace and abbey of Westminster reflected the taste of an artistic king in a great age of art and architecture. The new attitude to government is the theme of chapters 12–14.

(3) FUNDAMENTALS

It is my aim in this book to help anyone who reads it to understand a period of this country's distant past ; to make it more real and less remote. England was a very different place in 1272, still more in 1066 or in 871, from what it is today ; the understanding of these differences is the key to an understanding of its history. Not everything has changed. The geography, the climate are with us still ; the barons and villeins of Domesday Book and Magna Carta were our ancestors. But in different conditions geography may have different effects ; human nature may, and does, change; chance similarities may be most misleading. Medieval history demands imagination from its student ; he must live himself into the past in order to appreciate a world of ideas, activities, and aspirations very different from his own. But the rewards are great. If we make the effort, we can meet our own ancestors working out their lives against the same physical background which we know ; but on utterly different lines. Our first business as historians is to mark the contrasts ; to make sure that we are not reading the present into the past, making our forbears in our own image. Once we have done that, the element of continuity, the links between past and present, will return in truer colours ; we shall find that for all the changes the links are real ; and both contrast and continuity are profoundly interesting and profoundly instructive—especially to anyone curious to know, as was King William in 1086, ' about this land and how it was peopled, and with what sort of men '.

There is an astonishing continuity in English institutions, which makes it possible for us in a way more immediately than any other European people to feel contact with our medieval past ; and yet this continuity can be very deceptive. We have an institution which we call Parliament ; its name has not altered since the thirteenth century. But the ' mother of Parliaments ' today bears little resemblance to the confabulations between Edward I and his peers and councillors, to which it owes its name. If we listed the really significant things about our present Parliament—the things which give it meaning to us—it is highly unlikely that many or any of the points we should make would also have been true of its medieval ancestor.

We cannot study the Middle Ages without being constantly reminded of the elements of continuity and the profundity of the changes which have taken place. The continuity gives us contact, helps us to get in touch with our medieval ancestors. If we wish to study medieval life, we can learn a great deal by living in the present. The earth and stone walls which surround

so many fields in Wales and south-western England are often
of great antiquity ; and sometimes the deep meandering lanes
represent pre-Conquest boundaries of farms and estates, sometimes boundaries still. These walls and boundaries are the
product of social conditions ; they are also related to farming
needs which have not entirely disappeared, even in these days
of tractors and combines and marketing boards. In a different
way the enthusiasm with which medieval thought and medieval
art are now studied reveals that the tastes and values which
gave them birth are not in every particular foreign to us.
If we are alive to it, our medieval past is always at our elbow ;
and its study is no remote esoteric adventure for the expert
alone.

From time to time in this book we shall notice these contacts
between present and past. For the moment we must concentrate
on the differences : on those attitudes which differentiate
medieval from modern England, and make it a world apart.
One cannot cover every difference in a brief introduction ;
what I plan to do is to select from various aspects of medieval
life, and to give a few examples. If we could visit a medieval
village or a medieval town we should be struck immediately
by the difference in physical environment. As we lived with the
people, we should perhaps in course of time be even more struck
by the difference in their unspoken assumptions, their attitudes,
and beliefs. We shall start, then, with a look at their houses
and furniture and ideas of physical comfort. Since this is a
book on English history, we shall next inquire, was there such
a thing as England ? How was it viewed by Englishmen and
foreigners ? Since this is a book about the Middle Ages, the
ages of faith, we shall go on to inquire about the Church and
its place in men's lives ; and finally, about how men's attitude
to God affected their attitude to the material world—about
their notions of science.

In the Middle Ages men built in mud and wood and stone.
Since stone is durable, and stone buildings more easily adapted
to changing fashions of internal furnishing and decoration than
removed altogether, it is the stone buildings which survive.
To us medieval building means stone churches, cathedrals, and
castles, although we may have seen the impressive wooden nave
in the church at Greenstead in Essex, or the timber structures

of a few old barns and houses. Today the great English cathedrals are surrounded by modern cities. There is still a notable contrast between the architecture of the cathedral and of the modern secular buildings close at hand. But the contrast must often have been sharper when the cathedral was first built. Here and there in the city might be the stone house of a lord or a prominent citizen, like the ancient stone houses still to be seen on the hill leading up to Lincoln Cathedral. But the majority of the houses would be small structures of wood and wattle and daub, clustering along narrow streets and around courtyards. In the villages the houses would not be so tightly packed, but their structure might be even more primitive. The peasant commonly lived in a mud hovel with one room, or at best two ; and these apartments would house his whole family and some livestock besides. We know very little about them ; hardly any survive before the very end of the Middle Ages. But we do occasionally find inventories of their contents. If they were crowded with living things, not much space needed to be reserved for furniture. This was of the barest and simplest, and the personal possessions of a peasant rarely went much beyond the pots and pans with which his wife did her cooking, a rough bench and table, and the essential tools of a small farmer.

What we miss immediately in any description of a peasant's house is any sign of privacy and comfort. Before the twelfth and thirteenth centuries the same is as true, by and large, in the houses of the wealthy. Indeed, it is not before the sixteenth century that the English gentry began to turn the hens out of doors and build private rooms for the various members of their family ; and it was the Industrial Revolution which first brought notable improvement in the houses of the labouring poor.

The houses of the English kings and nobles in the early Middle Ages were substantial enough, but almost as innocent of comfort as were the cottages. The great halls described in Anglo-Saxon poetry, like the halls of the Northumbrian kings excavated at Yeavering, were large open structures with a single room in which the whole court ate and slept. The Norman Conquest saw the introduction of the characteristic symbol of feudal lordship, the castle, built both for defence and as a home, but more suited to the necessities of war than to the comforts of peace. At first the castle keep was usually of timber, on the summit of a mound ; the Norman kings set the fashion for building more permanent keeps of stone on solid foundations. From the first some buildings lay in an outer court, and in the late twelfth and thirteenth centuries the great rooms of the keep were less and less used. But even the royal court in Henry II's day (1154–89) might meet in the hall and chamber of the Tower of London or Dover Castle ; and the dramatic encounter of Henry and Archbishop Thomas Becket in October 1164 took place in the great keep at Northampton (now the site of a railway station). Hall and chamber : these were the two essential living rooms of a great house. In the hall the whole household ate and slept ; the chamber was at first the more private apartment of the lord or king and his immediate household. The riff-raff was excluded ; but even so there was little privacy. Gradually the castles and palaces grew, and more private chambers were provided. This had happened earlier in the great royal palaces at Winchester and Westminster, and in the late twelfth and thirteenth centuries it became the case in many large houses up and down England. The early Norman castle, as portrayed in the Bayeux Tapestry, had an outer court, or bailey, and an inner keep, the mound or ' motte '. The motte grew into the great stone keep ; the bailey acquired more and more buildings to be used in times of peace. And as peace became more normal and more generally expected, the buildings of the bailey came to replace those of the keep in importance. The palace of Westminster sprawled over an even wider area ; and the castles of king and nobles up and down the country grew in proportion. The great stone keep of the Tower of London or Dover Castle gave way to the more elaborate castles of Edward I, which can still be seen in many corners of Wales : the fortifications are more elaborate and more sophisticated, and consist of a series of curtain walls with towers and turrets and battlements and barbicans. The chambers of the keep have given way to more convenient apartments ; these are scattered over the larger space enclosed within the walls of the inner and outer courtyards.

Beside the changing fashions of architecture there took

place a corresponding change in furnishing and decoration. As in so many things, the Church led the way. First, sumptuous hangings were provided for the altar, for shrines, and for the walls of the greater churches. Then the windows (hitherto frequently open to wind and rain) began to be filled with glass, often exquisitely painted ; then the more important inmates—bishops, monks, canons, and leading laymen—were provided with seats ; and even, as the centuries passed, with cushions and carpets on which to kneel. All these things gradually made their way into palaces and great houses. Often they were provided more for magnificence than for comfort. In this period there were benches and tables for meals, thrones for kings, and a few stools ; but chairs were rare, and chairs and beds, by our standards, exceedingly hard and uncomfortable.

In dress, especially ladies' dress, the Church strove to avoid setting the fashion, but it was not entirely successful. The twelfth century saw new standards of comfort and luxury in many things ; notably in the use of furs by great ladies. An English Church council in 1138 had to forbid nuns the use of vair, gris (probably miniver), sable, marten, ermine, and beaver—and this is the first known mention of some of these articles in an English document. Fashions were shifting ; standards of living were rising, and affecting even the religious Orders. Monastic reformers of this age laid a quite new stress on simplicity and austerity in clothing and food and comfort, and this was in part because these things were improving in the secular world. In earlier ages there had been little of comfort and luxury in the lay world for the monk to avoid.

Fashions of every kind often had their origin in France. They remind us that from 1066 England was ruled by a dynasty of Norman origin, that the English kings were usually lords of large dominions in France ; that French was the language most commonly heard in castle and palace ; and that England and the Continent were closely bound together.

The ideas of nationality and nationalism are linked in our minds today with our sense of loyalty. We all have many loyalties—to our family, to our friends, our town, to a host of other groups with which we may be connected in one way or another, and finally, to our country. This last loyalty is connected with the idea that there is something which sets all folk of British nationality apart, or rather ties them together ; most of us assume the existence of this, even if we cannot analyse its nature. National frontiers are sometimes identical with natural geographical frontiers, like the shores of this island ; sometimes with linguistic frontiers, like the Pyrenees or the boundaries of France and Germany. But it is very rare for all the possible factors which can contribute to a sense of nationality—geography, race, language, politics, religion and, above all, the sense of a common history—to meet together in any single nation. All these ingredients play their part ; but the modern idea of nationalism is something which exists apart from these and in some ways overrides them. Nationalism of such an overpowering kind is a very recent thing ; and with its rise in the last 150 years loyalty to state and nation has assumed a place in the hierarchy of our loyalties that it never claimed before. That is not to say that there was no sense of nationhood or Englishness in medieval England ; but it was something quite different from what we mean by the word. Let us take a look at some of the elements—geography, language, and politics—and see where the difference lay.

Frontiers are troublesome things ; they are always shifting, and sometimes an obvious ' natural frontier ' is translated into a highway overnight. ' Natural frontiers ' are of two kinds. First, there are barriers, boundaries either difficult to cross, like the Pyrenees or the Himalayas, or so obvious as to be a convenient line of demarcation to successive negotiators, like the great rivers of Europe or North America. The second kind of ' natural frontier ' may include no barrier of any kind, but may represent the shift from one kind of country to another ; say, from hill to valley or from chalk to clay. In the history of Europe the second kind has been of greater importance than the first. To a maritime people a sea or a river is a highway, not a frontier. Mountains have passes, and even elephants can be transported across the Alps. But for a people used to living in the hills to take to the plain, or a people used to cultivating light soil to take to heavy clay, is to change a whole way of life. The most stable frontier in the history of this island has been that between the lowland and the highland zone ; very roughly, between land below and land above 600 feet. The lower land is usually suitable for large-scale intensive arable farming, especially in the heavy clay lands of the Midlands ; the higher land only for dairy farming, sheep grazing and lighter, scattered arable farming. The boundary between the two is nowhere very precise, and has never very precisely conformed to the political frontiers of the country ; but it is none the less important for that. The Romans divided their British provinces into two sections, the civil and the military ; and the civil, with its centre in London, conformed pretty much to the lowland zone of the south-east. The Anglo-Saxon invaders were arable farmers, and liked heavy soils. They occupied the lowland zone more thoroughly than it had been occupied before, reclaiming large areas of land from the forest. The old British populations, in great measure excluded from the lowland zone, were happy to cultivate areas of the country with lighter soils ; they had always avoided the heavy clay. The Celtic lands—Wales, Cumberland, and Scotland—lie wholly in the highland zone ; the main core of England lies in the lowland zone. The frontiers between England and Wales and between England and Scotland were never settled in the period covered by this book ; but this basic distinction between England and non-English Britain is fundamental to an understanding of the island's history. Compared with the distinction of lowland and highland, the English Channel was less a barrier than a highway. A barrier to some the Channel has always been ; but in an age which knew no railways and when most roads were worse than anything we can readily imagine, water provided the main means of transport ; and water transport, for an island, very largely meant sea and coastal transport. The Channel was never in the Middle Ages, in any profound sense, either a political or a cultural frontier. Our twelfth- and thirteenth-century kings held sway over large tracts of France and spent much of their time trying to govern and to extend them. Much was lost to the English kings in the thirteenth century ; but they were never entirely excluded from French territory until the sixteenth century. From 1340 until 1802,[1] indeed, the official title of our monarchs, which appeared on every formal document issued in their name, was ' King of England and France '. They knew the difference

[1] Except between 1360 and 1369

between England and France, but at least until the late fifteenth century an English king crossing the Channel thought of himself as passing from one part of his dominions to another ; and over much of the period between 1066 and 1272 a number of his leading subjects also held extensive properties on both sides of the water.

In some ways the role of the Irish Sea, and the long stretches of water which lie to the south and south-west of it right down to the Bay of Biscay, was more striking still. Throughout the Middle Ages this was the highway of a group of peoples with common traditions and a language basically one, yet never politically united. The shores of this great highway were peopled with all the Celtic peoples, the Irish, Scots, Welsh, and Bretons, who had a sense of unity among themselves based on common language, common traditions, and trade, which was very persistent in spite of the very different political allegiances which they owed.

Before 1272 England was invaded so many times that we have no possible means of counting the number of the invasions. It was invaded by a variety of prehistoric tribes and armies, by the Romans, by countless bands of Angles, Saxons, ' Jutes ', Irish, Norse, Danes ; and by the Normans and their confederates. Even 1066 is not the end of the story. The Norwegians came again, Henry II had invaded the country three times before he was recognised as king in 1154 ; when King John died in 1216 a French army was at large in the kingdom, and it was by no means clear whether the infant King Henry III or the Dauphin would succeed ; quite possible that the French kings, who had already swallowed most of the Angevin [1] inheritance in France, would swallow England too.

The Roman invaders, the Norman Conquest, and the Angevin Empire remind us how often England was a part of a continental empire : a distant province of Rome ; the most stable element in the diffuse empire of the Danish Cnut ; the glittering prize of the Norman expansion of the late eleventh century ; less than half of the great expanse of the Angevin Empire in the twelfth. These facts were the play of political circumstance ; of deeper significance perhaps was the close

[1] See pp. 185-6n

relation between England and Europe in religion and civilisation. A history of English art or religion from the seventh to the twelfth century which ignored Europe would be meaningless ; and a history of the western, Catholic Church in the same period would be meaningless if it ignored England. Why did Henry III succeed and not the future Louis VIII ? There were many reasons ; one was that Henry was supported by an Italian cleric called Guala, who was without roots or connections or intimate friends in the country. But his word was none the less effective, because he was the pope's legate. England at this date was a papal fief.

The Channel was no frontier, but its influence was none the less crucial. It was between the accession of Alfred in 871 and the twelfth century that England achieved political unity and something like its present frontiers with Wales and Scotland. The foundations of this unity had been laid long before. The unity was based, as we have seen, on the geography and the soil of the lowland zone ; ' England ' conformed in great part to the civil provinces of the Romans ; it represented the area over which the Anglo-Saxons found it congenial or possible to settle—hence its name, Angel-land. But if we look at the English kingdom at the height of its greatness under Henry II, we find a kingdom with its capital in London and a Church with its headquarters in Canterbury, both in the extreme south-east of the country. These things owe something to the Romans, who established the capital in London and built a network of great roads from London to the main cities of the kingdom—roads which were never effectively replaced until the eighteenth century. They owe something to the accidents of politics of the sixth century, which established St Augustine and the Roman mission in the kingdom of Kent. But Rome and the kingdom of Kent were very distant memories long before the Norman Conquest. The survival of the road system and the main network of towns on Roman lines—or rather their revival, because many had almost disappeared in the interval—was due in great measure to the recurrence of a situation similar to that which had given them birth. Norman England was not an outpost of a great empire ; but it was ruled by a king as much at home in France as in England. The lowland zone in England lay opposite a lowland zone in northern France, and the exigencies of government and commerce made a system of towns and communications radiating from London once again natural and convenient.

The Channel was a key factor in English history as a centre of communications. That it was far less of a barrier then than now will be apparent in many chapters of this book. Feudal institutions and social organisation of every kind, especially the ' manor ', were the local expression of forms of organisation common to much of northern Europe. The castle was imported from the Continent, and so were many themes of our art and architecture. This does not mean that English art was purely derivative ; in some ways the use the English made of their continental models, especially in Norman and Gothic architecture, was of crucial importance for continental development, and in the art of illuminating manuscripts the balance of trade was very often in England's favour. The Channel was one of the main arteries of Europe.

And yet there is a paradox in what has just been said. Can it really be true that the triumphs of modern science have done nothing to bring the Continent nearer to us ? Speed and ease of communication have increased enormously, and it is now possible for a far higher proportion of the English population to visit the Continent than ever before. But there is something in the paradox none the less. It was partly that to a small proportion of the population England and the Continent really seemed to be less apart than they do today ; and partly that for most of the population even England was a concept too vast to be grappled with. The man from the next village or the next shire was as foreign as a visitor from abroad. By such folk the existence of ' England ' as a country or a nation was scarcely felt at all.

Medieval England was a country of villages, towns (most of them, by our standards, slightly swollen villages), castles, and monasteries—small communities living very much isolated from one another. Such communities entirely lacked modern means of communication. There was a certain compensation : news could travel remarkably fast and often quite accurately, as is observed today in backward countries. But this is only a slight qualification to the fact that most men's horizons would be bounded by the small group of villages which they knew personally. And if they did move, it was as easy to move by water as by land—if you were carrying heavy goods, far easier.

I have often tried to visualise what picture of England a man would have who had never seen a map. Maps, in the modern sense, were extremely rare and usually most inaccurate. They certainly formed no part of the mental equipment of most men before the sixteenth and seventeenth centuries. It is hard to believe in something of which one can form no mental picture. One might acknowledge loyalty to distant potentates whom one had never seen—to king and pope ; but the man living in Westminster or Rome meant little. In the later Middle Ages there were beginning to be some of those instruments of government which make us aware of government as an abstract thing, to be disliked, perhaps, but obeyed—organs of jurisdiction, taxation, and so forth of a permanent kind, the beginnings of bureaucracy. It is this abstract conception of government to which we give the label ' the state ' ; and in this sense the state scarcely existed in England before the fourteenth century. Loyalty remained still at heart a personal matter, and few medieval monarchs really stirred the sense of loyalty of the majority of their subjects unless they were constantly travelling. Pageantry was tremendously important to the medieval king. It was the means by which he showed himself to his people ; by which they became aware of him as a person to whom one could feel loyalty and allegiance. The pageantry itself expressed in symbolic language the power of the king and his relation to the people.

It is interesting to compare a medieval and a modern coronation. In ceremonial, in their symbolic significance, they are much alike. In recent years the similarities have been self-consciously fostered. But there are two profound differences. On the one hand, the medieval coronation was a symbol of actual power—of the divine blessing on a man who was himself going to exercise authority. On the other hand, the medieval audience was infinitely smaller. The second difference is really the less profound. Medieval England was not a democracy. The king had to reckon on the consent and co-operation of a large number of people—large, but not beyond counting ; less, for example, than the number of voters in a modern constituency. A significant proportion of them could actually witness his coronation.

By constant pageantry an able monarch could become personally known to a fair proportion of his subjects, to a large proportion of those who counted. But he never became the focus of loyalty which the monarch is today. Horizons were far narrower, local patriotisms more local, and sheer lack of communications made government, state, and nation far remoter things. That is the negative side of the picture. To differentiate England from Europe presupposes a fairly sharp image of what England is and what Europe is. Neither existed in the minds of most medieval Englishmen.

Nor did a common language separate Englishmen from their neighbours on the Continent. The English language of today is a hybrid with many ancestors. Chiefly it is a mingling of one Germanic and one Romance language, of Old English or Anglo-Saxon and Norman French (or ' Anglo-Norman '). The arrival of Anglo-Norman was one of the many consequences of the Norman Conquest ; but in the two centuries which followed, the languages were still distinct. Indeed, there were at least three languages currently spoken in England after the Conquest, excluding the Celtic tongues of Cornwall, Wales, and Scotland : English, Anglo-Norman, and Latin, the international language of the Church—at least three, because doubtless in the north and east the Scandinavian dialects of the Danes and Norse settlers still survived, though decreasingly. In 1100 a common tongue united the upper clergy of England and western Europe at large ; a common tongue united the lay aristocracy of England and north-western France. These languages divided the upper classes from the great mass of the English people, who spoke their various dialects of English. Doubtless by this time many of the laity were bi-lingual and many of the clergy tri-lingual. But it is evident that language could not be a coherent factor in English nationalism. Between 1066 and 1272 Latin and French were the languages of the court, and the English kings could talk more easily with their French than with their English peasantry.

One possible ground of nationhood, and that a very powerful one, did exist, and was recognised by men of learning and reflection. Long before the birth of Alfred, Bede had written

ENGLAND
871 ~ 1066
Newcastle and Battle were founded
soon after 1066

Frontier unsettled

• (Newcastle)
• Durham

NORTHUMBRIA

• Stamford Bridge
• York
• Fulford

Humber

Wirral

Doncaster •

Eddisbury •   Lincoln
• Chester   • Bakewell
         Derby •   Nottingham

Offa's Dyke

M E R C I A
Tettenhall   Leicester •   • Stamford

Warwick •   • Northampton
                • Bedford

St. Albans •   Hertford
               • Maldon
         LONDON ▪
• Chippenham   Isle of Sheppey
• Edington   • Canterbury
Carhampton W E S S E X   The Weald   • Dover
   • Athelney   (Battle)
              • Porchester   • Hastings

his *Ecclesiastical History of the English People*, one of the finest
and most widely read of medieval histories. In Alfred's time
the more modest, but equally significant *Anglo-Saxon Chronicle*
was begun ; copies were circulated, and these copies added
to in various monasteries until after the Conquest. The
eleventh and twelfth centuries saw a host of historical writers
at work, some on national histories, some on world histories ;
but many of them revealing an intense patriotism. Most
popular of these was the *History of the Kings of Britain* by

Geoffrey of Monmouth (*c.* 1138). There is a nice ambiguity about this book, since Britain and England are not, and were not, interchangeable terms. It deals with a long line of kings starting many centuries B.C., passing via King Lear and King Arthur to the seventh century A.D. Then it ceases. Were these British kings meant to be the predecessors or the rivals of the kings of the English ? The problem is not made easier by the character of the book. It was cleverly written, and almost everyone took it seriously at the time ; but in fact it was almost entirely fictitious.

The legend of King Arthur, which had formed the centre of Geoffrey's book, became the common possession of western European literature, much as the siege of Troy had been the common possession of the Greeks. In so far as it served a political end, it enhanced the prestige of the Anglo-Norman kings, Arthur's ultimate successors. It did little to draw together the English and the Welsh ; but its fictions puffed up the English with a sense of the greatness of their past. Above all, its legends were used by the reigning dynasty to make itself a glittering reflection of Arthurian glory. This was done self-consciously by Edward I and Edward III, and again by the Tudors ; and when an intelligent Italian historian in the reign of Henry VIII coolly observed that the whole story was nonsense, something very like national resentment was aroused.

There have been men in every age who understood something of the elements of nationality and their significance. Among other signs of this, the game of describing national characteristics was already well established. Then as now, much of it was crude. To English and Norman alike the Welsh and Scots were *barbari*, partly because they spoke a foreign language. An Englishman writing to a French friend said in fun, ' you know that their assiduity in drinking has made the English famous among the foreign nations '. And he goes on to state the age-long contrast between the French who drink wine and the English who drink beer. ' I however am fond of both wine and beer, and do not abhor any liquor that can make me drunk.' The friend to whom he wrote, a French monk with many English friends, felt moved on another occasion to draw a more sophisticated distinction between the races. In the eleven-seventies he became involved in a theological controversy on the Immaculate Conception of the Blessed Virgin, then a novel idea in the West, which was being strongly supported by a group of English monks. ' And so I come to your fantasies, alluring and attractive in their way, but quivering on a tenuous foundation ; for whatever is not supported by the authority of Scripture is not soundly based. Do not be put off if Gallic maturity prove more soundly based than English levity. Your island is surrounded by water, and the inhabitants are not unnaturally affected by the qualities of that element, and by its constant movement drawn to the most slender and subtle fantasies, comparing, not to say preferring, their dreams to genuine visions. Can we blame their nature, the country being what it is ? Certainly I know from experience that the English are more often dreamers than the French. In a damp climate the brain is swiftly caught up in vapours from the stomach—to be attributed to physical as much as spiritual causes . . . ; and what is so produced, and falls short of sound conviction, is properly called a fantasy or dream. My France is neither hollow nor watery after this fashion : there the mountains are made of stone, there iron is found, there the land is *terra firma*.' [1]

The word ' Europe ', though it was known, was very little used in the Middle Ages. The nearest equivalent was ' Christendom ', *Christianitas*. This expressed a sense of unity, even of community, based on religious and cultural bonds. It gave expression to the most potent factor in medieval unity and modern disunity, the religious factor. There is a sense in which all the English monarchs and many English nobles felt themselves to be members of a European rather than just of an English ruling class. In this they differed little, perhaps, from their descendants in more recent times, in the eighteenth and early nineteenth centuries. But far more powerful was the sense of common values, interests, language, and education which bound together the higher clergy of England and Europe.

Medieval society was fundamentally and ineradicably hierarchical, though the class structure was never rigid. One

[1] Cf. R. W. Southern in *Mediaeval and Renaissance Studies*, iv (1958), pp. 204–5

of its most fundamental divisions, indeed, was not horizontal at all, but vertical—the division between cleric and layman. We may simplify a complex picture by saying that there were four principal classes in medieval England : the upper clergy, the lower clergy, and the two classes of lay-folk, knights and nobles on the one hand, and yeomen and peasants on the other—those who fought and those who worked. The upper clergy were bishops, archdeacons, canons, and monks—and also the high civil servants. We might define them as the educated clergy. From the twelfth century on, the leading schools, later to become universities, were manned by and primarily designed for the upper clergy, and an increasing share of the Church's wealth was organised so as to be at their disposal. It was they who spoke and wrote the language of learning, Latin ; and in whatever country they lived they represented the standards and values of the Catholic Church— or, as they themselves often called it, the Holy Roman Church —of western Christendom. The schools and universities were open to men of every nation, and scholars came and went freely between them. The English (or Anglo-Norman) Thomas Becket began his education at a grammar school in London, then studied at Auxerre, Paris, and Bologna ; and he visited Rome. In these centres he learned the theological doctrines of the time ; and also something at least of canon law, the law of the Church. This revealed to him, as to countless thousands of other scholars of his day, the great structure of Church government, and the doctrines which both supported and depended on the primacy of the Roman see. He rose to prominence after his return to England in the service of Theobald, Archbishop of Canterbury, and then of the King, Henry II. For eight years he was a very faithful henchman and minister of Henry II ; one of the architects of royal power. But after his elevation to the archbishopric of Canterbury in 1162, his early training and the clerical principles absorbed in his earlier career reasserted themselves. If it came to the point where he had to choose between his allegiance to the pope and his allegiance to the King, the strength of his clerical education, his vision of the churchman's first duty and first loyalty, overcame his loyalty to the King and his personal friendship with him. His murder in Canterbury Cathedral in 1170 summed up in extreme form all the various tensions which could exist between layman and cleric. Most people agreed in principle that it was the duty of the twin authorities of Church and state to co-operate in doing God's work on earth ; but on the precise limits of the two authorities there was a good deal of disagreement. And when difficulties arose they were made worse by the social cleavage of clerical and lay, between the upper clergy with their very elaborate education and sophisticated theological and legal learning, and the lay aristocracy, uneducated or half-educated at best in the sense in which we use the term, bred for the arts of war and (in a rudimentary way) of government. To them allegiance to the king had a religious aura all the more deeply felt for being allegiance to a man they all knew and could see. The authority of the pope they acknowledged ; but it was a remote loyalty for most of them, and it seemed like treachery if it were invoked as an excuse for not obeying the king. Under certain circumstances the nobles were themselves prepared to break their fealty to the king—it was part of the feudal code that under certain circumstances they might—but they were not prepared for anyone else to disobey him. On occasion the tension between clerical and lay assumed something of the problem of a colour bar, of two races within one kingdom ; but with this difference, that layman and cleric came from the same homes, that each had brothers and cousins in the other camp ; that social disputes, when they arose, were fought out against a background of personal intimacy between many individuals of the two groups. In the end we must not overstress the conflicts between clergy and laity or between royal and papal authority. The conflicts are famous and fill a large place in our history books ; but they were always the exception, and most of the time kings, popes, and bishops agreed to co-operate or agreed to differ.

These divergences of interest and background between laymen and churchmen provided perhaps the most striking qualification to local separatism or nascent nationalism in medieval Europe. They are, in a sense, the keynote of the Middle Ages. When they cease to be more fundamental than the difference between Englishman, Frenchman, and German, when government and literature come to be conducted in the vernacular, then we know that the Middle Ages are on the way out. This characteristic of medieval society arose out of the way in which the Middle Ages came to birth. In the break-up of the Roman Empire the tenets and standards of the Christian faith, and with them something of the learning of the ancient world, were preserved by churchmen in an increasingly barbarian and barbarised Europe ; and in such a world it was inevitable that education and the standards of Christian life and thought should become a specialised possession. The great achievement of the Church in the early Middle Ages was to preserve the faith and something of the civilisation of the Christian Roman Empire, and to convert the barbarian peoples to Christianity. In the ninth and tenth centuries this work was still very actively in progress. The cultural inheritance was still precarious ; with the Danes in occupation of large areas of the country, the English Church became once again a missionary church. By the twelfth and thirteenth centuries all this was over. Medieval civilisation had staked its claim to what it could absorb of ancient culture ; a great revival of learning had taken place. The Danes, too, had been converted, both in England and in Denmark. Almost every corner of Europe was nominally Christian. To the east lay the world of the Byzantine (Eastern Orthodox) Churches, now usually out of communion with Rome, and the great expanse of Islam. But in western Europe, however kings and popes might dispute, the Catholic faith was a secure possession ; and in England, before the fourteenth century, the outbreaks of heresy were no great matter.

This background of assured faith is commonly taken to be the supreme characteristic of England and Europe in the Middle Ages. Faith, indeed, did not preclude inquiry. The most characteristic activity of the educated clergy of the later Middle Ages was the application of reason and logic to the investigation of the faith. The logical and metaphysical systems which they produced were among the maturest fruits of medieval culture ; and however we regard them, we cannot but admire the toughness and subtlety of mind of these great technicians who taught Europe how to think, or rather, re-taught her, because their work was made possible by the rediscovery of ancient Greek thought, enriched by the systematic efforts of the leading Arab (and Jewish) thinkers of the preceding centuries to adapt Aristotle to the special needs of a religion of Semitic origin. But our present concern is with the world of ordinary attitudes and assumptions, rather than with the more rarefied speculations of the schools. The scholastic systems were *tours de force* of abstract thinking. Abstract thought was alien to most men : they expressed their thoughts in concrete symbols.

In a modern Roman Catholic church the most important and the most sacred object present is the tabernacle and its contents, the Reserved Sacrament. In the period covered by this book the sacrament was sometimes reserved ; God was always supreme among the inmates of his churches ; the celebration of the Eucharist, the Mass—the re-creation, by symbolic act, of his Body and Blood—was always the central event of the church's day. But the most conspicuous objects in the church were more commonly connected with its other most distinguished occupant, the saint to whom it was dedicated. This is especially true of the eleventh, twelfth, and thirteenth centuries. In a church of any size a shrine would be built to house the relics of the saint behind the high altar. In number-less churches a solemn ' translation ' of the relics to a new shrine took place in this period. If the relics were substantial, the shrine might well become a centre of pilgrimage—and a source of great prestige and prosperity to its possessors, as was the shrine of St Thomas Becket at Canterbury.

The Eucharist itself was the supreme symbol ; the symbol of God himself, and of the whole drama of the Passion. The cult of relics reflected the belief that spiritual power was symbolised, mediated on earth in concrete physical objects. There were numerous cases in which one of the great saints of the Church was eclipsed as patron of a particular cathedral, abbey, or parish church by a lesser man, simply because the church was more amply provided with the supplanter's remains. The saint whose presence the relics symbolised was very much alive. He owned the church ; its head—be he bishop, abbot, or rector—acted as his representative. On occasion the saint found it necessary to intervene, to help the pilgrims who came to his shrine, to heal the sick, to comfort the oppressed, to destroy the oppressor. In a parish, the patron saint was the most important person in the village ; a sort of super-squire. His house, and the house which God himself was to visit, was not unnaturally the most magnificent building in the village. But the saint was not the only super-natural resident ; the devil had his representatives too. The supernatural was close at hand in countless forms, not all of them pleasant.

There was very little science in the Middle Ages, in our sense of the word. The later scholastics provided the necessary intellectual apparatus for the beginnings of empirical inquiry ; some quite elaborate machines (like clockwork) were brought in from the East in the later Middle Ages ; some new ones were developed. But the world of ideas was radically unsuited to scientific inquiry as we understand it. Science proceeds by the application of scepticism—of disbelief in the accepted explanation of some natural phenomenon. To the man of science and to modern man in general, an event, however odd, is presumed to have a natural or scientific explanation until proved otherwise. This does not necessarily involve a total disbelief in miracles ; but most of us agree not to call a thing a miracle until we have exhausted the possibilities of giving it a ' natural ' explanation. The medieval attitude was quite opposed to this. There were not lacking those who applied critical principles to the investigation of miracles. In 1100 William Rufus was buried under the tower of Winchester Cathedral ; in 1101 the tower collapsed. ' I forbear to tell the opinions which were held on this event,' said William of Malmesbury, ' lest I seem to believe in trifles—especially since it could have collapsed in any case, even if he had not been buried there, because it was badly built.' But on the whole, medieval man preferred to give an event a supernatural explana-tion if he possibly could. He went about looking for events to which a supernatural explanation could be given. We may think this excessively credulous, and no doubt there was much credulity and superstition in the Middle Ages. But he was encumbered with a view of the ' natural ' world so absurd and improbable that his pursuit of the marvellous was not so irrational as it may sound. Whatever the explanation, medieval books of miracles are full of stories which we should never think of calling miraculous—strange coincidences, striking dreams, and so forth—as well as stories which we cannot pretend to understand or explain.

' In the region of Chiusa [in Italy] there is a kind of wine which is particularly red, like blood ; and this wine is used for mass in preference to white, lest white wine be confused with water, which is easily done, and water offered instead. This red wine has the property of staining linen so that it can in no wise be washed out '. Thus opens the pathetic story of the young clerk who spilled wine on the corporal and was filled with panic ; then, seeing no way to clean the cloth or undo the damage, he prayed with special fervour to the Blessed Virgin, and the stain disappeared.[1] It is a trivial story, as many miracle stories were not ; but otherwise wholly characteristic.

What had Chiusa to do with England ? The author of this story, the young clerk himself, was called Anselm ; he was a nephew of St Anselm of Aosta and Bec, the second Archbishop of Canterbury after the Norman Conquest (1093–1109). The younger Anselm followed his uncle to England, and became abbot of Bury St Edmunds. The uncle was one of the great figures of the medieval church : monk and scholastic, a profound theologian and devotional writer, before circumstances made him an ecclesiastical statesman. In a more humble way the nephew was a more typical product of his age. Though an Italian and a cosmopolitan churchman, he quickly absorbed many English traditions. In writing down the *Miracles of the Virgin*, he was engaged in an activity especially characteristic of English churchmen at this time. In championing, as he did in later life, the Immaculate Conception, he was engaged in an activity which our French monk regarded as a natural aberration of the foggy-minded English.

Many morals can be drawn from the study of the two Anselms. He who wishes to emphasise the lofty nature of Christian theology and devotion in this period can find much comfort in the uncle. He who wishes to emphasise the growth of ' Mariolatry ' can find many texts in the writings of the nephew. The Immaculate Conception was at this date a local

[1] See R. W. Southern in *Mediaeval and Renaissance Studies*, IV (1958), pp. 190–1

English devotion. No-one could find nascent Protestantism in that. But the way in which it was fostered in spite of the Norman Conquest and then spread abroad by cosmopolitan churchmen shows that local traditions could prosper ; it also shows, as does every detail of the career of both nephew and uncle, how cosmopolitan the Church was becoming in the late eleventh and twelfth centuries.

2   The Reign of Alfred

(1) ENGLAND IN THE NINTH CENTURY

ALFRED is commonly thought of today as a great pioneer :
a man who planned many aspects of a united English kingdom,
although he did not live to see his plans completed. But to
contemporaries he must often have appeared more like the
last heir of a doomed kingdom, a man struggling to save
something from the kingdom of Egbert and the inheritance
of the Anglo-Saxon monarchs of the eighth century.

By 871 most of the old-established English kingdoms had
collapsed. Hitherto England had been divided into a number
of kingdoms—tradition says seven, that England had been a
' heptarchy ' ; but it is impossible to point to any period in
which there were precisely seven kingdoms in the land ; and the
word ' heptarchy ' suggests a division of the country far tidier
than ever existed in the centuries following the departure of
the Romans and the Anglo-Saxon conquest.   Over the three
and a half centuries preceding 871 the fortunes of the country
had mainly depended on the heads of three confederations, of
the Northumbrians, the Mercians, and the West Saxons. Each
in turn had held hegemony in England—Northumbria in the
seventh century, Mercia in the eighth ; last of all Wessex, for a
short space under King Egbert, had been recognised as the
first kingdom in the country.   But within thirty years of
Egbert's death the other kingdoms had been overwhelmed
by Viking hosts : Kent and East Anglia were Danish bases,
Northumbria on the verge of becoming a Norse kingdom,
Mercia divided between the Danes and English, with the
English kingdom reduced to a mere satellite.

The first mention of Viking raids on this country is in 789 ;
but it was not until the later years of Egbert, King of Wessex,
who died in 839, that they became frequent. From then on
the tale of attack and disaster is continuous. The movements

of heathen hosts—of Danes and Norsemen—is the constant theme of the *Anglo-Saxon Chronicle*. In 843 'King Aethelwulf [Egbert's son] fought at Carhampton against thirty-five ships' companies, and the Danes had possession of the place of slaughter'; in 855 'the heathen for the first time wintered in Sheppey'; in 865 'Ethelred [Aethelwulf's third son] succeeded to the kingdom of Wessex. And this same year came a great host to England and took winter-quarters in East Anglia.' In 866 the host moved into Northumbria, in 867 into Mercia; 'and Burhred, king of Mercia, and his councillors begged Ethelred, king of Wessex, and his brother Alfred to help them fight against the host.' The two brothers came into Mercia the next year, but without decisive result, and 870 saw desperate fighting in Wessex itself. Three major engagements failed to give the West Saxon leaders an advantage, and after a series of minor conflicts they were compelled to make their peace with the host. It was in these circumstances that King Ethelred died, and his brother, Alfred, succeeded to the throne (871).

In spite of the great energy with which Wessex was being defended in this year, it might have seemed only a matter of time before this kingdom, too, succumbed. The events of the following years could only confirm this impression; and in 878 'the [Danish] host went secretly in midwinter [when Alfred and his followers felt secure from attack] after Twelfth Night to Chippenham, and rode over Wessex and occupied it, and drove a great part of the inhabitants oversea, and reduced the greater part of the rest, except Alfred the king; and he with a small company moved under difficulties through woods and into inaccessible places in marshes.' [1]

878 proved not to be the end of English history, but, in a way, its beginning; and it is our business in this chapter to understand how this could be. When Alfred died twenty-one years later, his kingdom was still precarious; the Danes far

[1] To this period of Alfred's career tradition has attached the famous story of how he was sitting in a cowherd's cottage, preparing his bow and arrows and other weapons, when the cowherd's wife saw her cakes burning in the hearth, and scolded the luckless king for not paying attention to them. The story first appears in a saint's life written a generation or two after the Norman Conquest; it may be based on ancient tradition, but it may equally well be the author's invention, like many other things in the book. (See W. H. Stevenson, *Asser's Life of King Alfred* (Oxford, 1904), pp. 136, 256ff.)

from subdued. But Wessex was more settled, more powerful than when Alfred succeeded to the throne ; he was the acknowledged leader of the English survivors throughout the south and west of the country ; he had shown that Vikings could be defeated, and even baptised. The creation of a united kingdom of England was begun by Alfred's successors, and not fully achieved before the eleventh century ; but many essential foundations had been laid. Much of this was due to the unique personality of Alfred. But he was helped by some of the tendencies of the situation ; and also, paradoxically, by the Danes themselves.

The Danes were farmers and pirates. Like many pirates, they became in course of time great traders. But it is a mistake to think of Alfred's opponents as traders in any orthodox sense. They valued the things which merchants valued—money, gold (which was very scarce at this time), silver in any form, and all the materials which went to make a man wealthy and proved him to be so. It is clear that the population of the Scandinavian countries was growing in these years ; and that their own lands were becoming insufficient to support these peoples by the elementary agriculture and fishing on which they had hitherto depended. But ' land-hunger ' can be only a part of the explanation of the rapidity with which they spread all over northern and western Europe, raiding, settling, forming principalities in Russia, northern France, the British islands, and ultimately in Iceland and Greenland ; even (in all probability) visiting North America. The deeper explanation of these extraordinary movements lies in the social organisation and the social ideals and aspirations of the Viking peoples. By custom and training they enjoyed adventure, travel, and war ; and their upper classes had learned to live by plunder. When on the move they were organised by war bands, with the ship's company as the basic unit. The leaders of companies and hosts had to reward their followers with lavish gifts ; and yet to retain still greater wealth in their own hands. The splendour of their armour and their halls, and the ornaments and jewellery with which they could adorn their wives and daughters, were the symbols of their greatness. A man who failed in generosity or became impoverished was lost. Small wonder that it is in the Scandinavian homeland and the

Baltic islands that the most wonderful finds of silver coins and silver ornaments of this period have been discovered. They come from the Arab world, from Byzantium, from many parts of Europe, and from England.

The bulk of this wealth was acquired by tribute and by loot. The Viking leaders valued above all a rich country which could be plundered year after year ; the raids gave their men exercise, occupied them in their proper and favourite pursuits, and provided for both men and leaders generous pay at no cost to either. A really sophisticated pirate is deeply concerned for the welfare of the trade on which he preys. But pirates are rarely sophisticated, and loot and plunder seem to have been the only concern of the Danes at this time. None the less, they were not out for a speedy conquest of the whole country. For decades they came as raiders and plunderers, and it was only slowly that they conceived the idea of settling. When the host first wintered in Kent and East Anglia, it settled in old fortified places, which it used merely as bases for long-distance plundering in the winter. It was natural that prolonged acquaintance with the country should suggest to the Danes other ways of exploiting it ; the decline of its wealth was bound sooner or later to force them to more creative activities, or to abandon the country altogether ; and the breakdown of authority tempted the Danish leaders to replace the old monarchs with themselves. The Danish invasions of the ninth century thus passed through many phases. They started as occasional plundering raids. Then large hosts established themselves under kings and jarls (earls) on a more permanent footing. Finally these hosts began to settle in various parts of the country, and the leaders took to rewarding their followers with land as well as with loot. In Yorkshire, Lincolnshire, and the north-east Midlands hundreds of place-names deriving from Old Danish roots show us where the Danish peasantry settled thickly at this time ; the English had lived in hams and tuns (our ' homes ' and ' towns '), the Danes colonised bys and thorpes. Among the Vikings in England Danes were in the majority ; in Ireland, Scotland, and the Western Isles, Norwegians. But in the north of England the two met and mingled. The north-west is thickly studded with Norse place-names, from Irby, Thingwall, and others in the Wirral peninsula up to the gills, fells, and thwaites of Cumberland.[1] East Lancashire and Yorkshire were more Danish than Norse, though the kings of York were sometimes Norwegian (i.e. Norse from Ireland), and the links between the two peoples were close.

It was only slowly, then, that the Vikings conceived the idea of replacing the native dynasties with their own kings ; and only sporadically that they tried to replace existing systems of government with their own institutions. The slow transition gave the kingdom of Wessex a breathing-space ; it also gave the leaders of Wessex time to prepare against the challenge of the Danish attack. In these two ways Alfred was helped by the habits of the Vikings to take advantage of what survived of his inheritance in Wessex.

His inheritance consisted, first of all, of a society, of human material moulded by the ancient custom of the English. There were many signs of what we should call civilisation in English life in the eighth and early ninth centuries. The Christian conversion had struck deep roots ; with it had come a renaissance of art ; literature and learning (after the fashion of the Dark Ages) had flourished in Northumbria in the days of Bede and in the country at large in the mid and late eighth century. More superficial were the traces of a money economy, of permanent markets, of literate government. All these things were to recover and develop during the period covered by this book beyond what anyone could have imagined in the ninth century. Nor were the Anglo-Saxons or Vikings savages : both had lived for centuries in some kind of contact with civilised peoples and civilised standards, and were not unaffected by them. But all this does not alter the fact that English society in the eighth and ninth centuries knew little of what we should call civilisation ; that the lay aristocracy consisted of fundamentally barbarian warriors who did not differ greatly from their Viking enemies in aspirations, in methods of war, and way of life.

[1] Irby is ' the *by* (village) of the Irish ', reminding us that the Norse came by way of Ireland ; Thingwall, ' the field of assembly ', the place where the local court or assembly of Wirral (forerunner of the ' hundred ' court), the ' thing ' familiar to readers of Icelandic sagas, met. *Gill* (ravine with a stream) and *fell* are Norse words ; *thwaite* (clearing in woodland) was used both by Norwegians and by Danes.

The qualities of Anglo-Saxon lay society are revealed to us more clearly than those of any other Teutonic people of the period, owing to the survival of a quite large quantity of Old English literature—of poems written to be sung to the harp in the great halls of the English warriors ; the staple of entertainment in the early Middle Ages, and, more than that, a vital form of education, moulding the tastes and ideals of generations of warriors. The lay upper classes were illiterate ; that is to say, they had no education as we understand the term. But they were brought up to a knowledge of the traditional crafts of their class—the arts of war, justice, and government, hunting and hawking ; and their outlook was moulded by the heroic lays of the minstrels. The best known of these poems is an epic, *Beowulf*, probably of the eighth century. *Beowulf* must be read and re-read by anyone who wishes to understand Old English society : it is full of insights into the minds of our ancestors, insights of a kind normally very difficult to obtain. In one way it is probably untypical. Most of the early lays and epics were tales of blood feud and human glory ; blood and thunder stories of war and plunder and revenge. *Beowulf* is the work of a Christian cleric determined to point a moral : blood feuds are kept well in the background, and Beowulf slaughters dragons and not men—indeed, it is specifically noted that Beowulf's own people were astonished at his prowess, because he had none of the previous record of slaughter which usually preluded a glorious career.

But if the author of *Beowulf* has attempted to suppress the more barbarous elements in such stories, he none the less makes Beowulf display very clearly the proper heroic qualities : courage and prowess in war, and loyalty—loyalty to his kin, loyalty to his chief, and loyalty and generosity to his followers ; and after Beowulf has become king he maintains justice and the rights and privileges of his people. Here we are shown the characteristics of Anglo-Saxon society at its best. It is a society in which kinship and personal loyalty are the principal bonds. It is an aristocratic society : above the clans of kindred are the tribal chiefs and the kings ; and every chief and every king is surrounded by a company of followers, the ' following ' or *comitatus*. This crucial institution in all Germanic peoples meets us in the first century A.D. in the *Germania* of Tacitus, meets us in the military following of barbarian leaders in the fifth and sixth centuries, in royal and princely courts of the seventh, eighth, and ninth ; meets us again in the knights of a feudal lord in the tenth and eleventh centuries, and in the knights of the Round Table as they were described in the twelfth. Followers were drawn from a number of sources, from the chief's own kin, from the leading warriors of his land, and from other tribes or kingdoms : it was a common practice for kings and nobles to send their younger sons to the courts of neighbouring princes to be brought up and to learn the art of war and the skills of a warrior. These followers gave their chief unstinted support in his enterprises, and in return he asked their advice, protected them and kept them. It was a similar relationship which compelled the Viking leader to shower gifts upon his followers ; and even in the more settled Anglo-Saxon courts gifts were still vitally important, although the followers of an Anglo-Saxon lord expected first and foremost a landed estate.

There are in *Beowulf* two common synonyms for a king— ' the giver of treasure ' or ' the lord of rings '. In the poem, the treasure consists of gold cups and gold ornaments ; the rings are golden rings. But there was very little gold in eighth-century England. In this as in other respects there is an archaic flavour about the poem : it holds up the past as a mirror to the present. And since it was already about a century old before Alfred was born, it may seem to have little bearing on the relations of Alfred and his followers. But for two reasons this is not so. First of all, it is the representative of an oral literature which changed comparatively little over the generations. Alfred was apparently brought up on just such heroic stories, although we cannot tell if he knew *Beowulf* itself. ' He listened attentively to Saxon poems day and night,' writes his biographer, ' and hearing them often recited by others committed them to his retentive memory.' Although his taste in literature developed and matured, he never lost his fondness for the heroic lays of his own people. Furthermore, the minstrels were still busy composing their own versions of this kind of poem, and some of the meagre survivors from the ninth and tenth centuries reveal that the same emotions and qualities were preserved in them as appear in *Beowulf*. Finest of all is the poem on the battle of Maldon, which describes very movingly the last stand of an English leader against the Danes. The incident took place much later than Alfred's time, in the second wave of Danish invasions at the end of the tenth century ; ealdorman (or earl) Brihtnoth fell in 991. Thus the poem serves to show the continuity in the ideals of English warriors. It is very short. It opens with an account of the preparation for the fight ; it tells how Brihtnoth deployed his men : ' he rode and gave counsel and taught his warriors how they should stand and keep their ground, bade them hold their shields aright, firm with their hands and fear not at all. When he had meetly arrayed his host, he alighted among the people where it pleased him best, where he knew his bodyguard to be most loyal.

' Then the messenger of the Vikings stood on the bank, he called sternly, uttered words, boastfully speaking the seafarers' message to the earl, as he stood on the shore. " Bold seamen have sent me to you, and bade me say, that it is for you to send treasure quickly in return for peace, and it will be better for you all that you buy off an attack with tribute, rather than that men so fierce as we should give you battle. There is no need that we destroy each other, if you are rich enough for this. In return for the gold we are ready to make a truce with you. If you who are richest determine to redeem your people, and to give to the seamen on their own terms wealth to win their friendship and make peace with us, we will betake us to our ships with the treasure, put to sea and keep faith with you."

' Brihtnoth lifted up his voice, grasped his shield and shook his supple spear, gave forth words, angry and resolute, and made him answer : " Hear you, searover, what this folk says ? For tribute they will give you spears, poisoned point and ancient sword, such war gear as will profit you little in the battle. Messenger of the seamen, take back a message, say to your people a far less pleasing tale, how that there stands here with his troop an earl of unstained renown, who is ready to guard this realm, the home of Ethelred my lord [the King], people and land ; it is the heathen that shall fall in the battle. It seems to me too poor a thing that you should go with our treasure unfought to your ships, now that you have made your way thus far into our land. Not so easily shall you win tribute ; peace must be made with point and edge, with grim battle-play, before we give tribute.''

' Then he bade the warriors advance, bearing their shields, until they all stood on the river bank.' There the two armies waited as the tide went out and left them dry land on which to fight. For all their heroism, the English company was defeated, and their leader killed.

' Brihtwold spoke and grasped his shield (he was an old companion [follower]) ; he shook his ash-wood spear and exhorted the men right boldly : '' Thoughts must be the braver, heart more valiant, courage the greater as our strength grows less. Here lies our lord, all cut down, the hero in the dust. Long may he mourn who thinks now to turn from the battle-play. I am old in years ; I will not leave the field, but think to lie by my lord's side, by the man I held so dear.'' ' Another member of the following also encourages them to battle, leads his men against the Vikings, falls in the strife ; and there, as suddenly as it began, the poem ends.

The old follower's speech is one of the most moving things in Anglo-Saxon literature ; it also catches to perfection the finest spirit of the German heroic lay—courage in defeat. This was no doubt the theme of many of the Saxon songs which King Alfred learned by heart ; and it was this element in the tradition of the English warrior families which enabled them in the end to react so powerfully to the Danish challenge.

But the warrior aristocracy was itself only one element in English society, and not the only one which played its part in King Alfred's success. His armies were partly manned by peasants ; and in any case, as Alfred himself said, a king needed ' men who pray, and soldiers and workmen '. It is time to look at those who prayed and those who worked.

The conversion of the English had been accomplished in the seventh and early eighth centuries ; from then on, England was a nominally Christian country, even if some of the missionary work had to be done again after the coming of the Danes. With Christianity came literacy, at least for the small band of educated clergy. In the Byzantine Empire in this period, and especially in the capital, Constantinople—incomparably the greatest centre of culture and learning in the Christian world before the twelfth century—literacy was widespread among laymen as well as among the clergy. In contrast, there existed throughout western Christendom a sharp distinction between the literate, educated, Latin-speaking clergy and the lay aristocracy, illiterate, bred for war. The upper clergy were at once the mediators of the Christian tradition and of the learning and civilised standards of the ancient world. They were usually very few in number, and partly for that reason their standards of learning were precarious. Learning and the knowledge of Latin literature rose and fell in the early Middle Ages with astonishing rapidity, largely because they depended on a small number of good teachers and their pupils. In the days of Bede and Alcuin, in the eighth century, England was famous for its learned men. But there is no reason to think that Alfred was exaggerating much when he said of his own youth : ' So completely had learning decayed in England that there were very few men on this side the Humber who could apprehend their [Latin] services in English or even translate a letter from Latin into English, and I think that there were not many beyond the Humber. There were so few of them that I cannot even recollect a single one south of the Thames when I succeeded to the kingdom.' The upper clergy were few, and the educated clergy almost non-existent.

Who were the upper clergy ? In the last chapter I defined them as bishops, archdeacons, canons, and monks ; and distinguished them from the lower clergy, the parish priests, most of whom were socially and economically much less privileged, often of peasant stock and semi-literate at best. This general picture is true of the period after the Conquest ; for the ninth century it needs two major qualifications. Before the Conquest the upper clergy were small in numbers. The staffs of bishops and cathedrals were usually modest compared with what they later became ; no hierarchy of officials separated the bishop from the parish clergy—there was no-one comparable to the later archdeacon or rural dean. In 1066 there were well under 1,000 monks. In Alfred's time the figures must be scaled down still further. Outside the small and struggling community he himself established at Athelney, there were no monks at all—no monks, that is, in the formal sense of men living in community according to a monastic rule. On paper there were about sixteen bishoprics. Of these, at the time of Alfred's death, four or five were in places occupied by the Danes and had long been vacant ; two (Dunwich in Suffolk, later surrendered to the sea, and Leicester, revived only in very modern times) were allowed to lapse. The rest reappeared in the course of the tenth century. How active the remaining cathedrals were we have little means of knowing ; but they were certainly not centres of vigorous intellectual or religious life. The disappearance of most of the old monasteries meant that the libraries, on whose shelves books might survive for centuries, even if no-one read them, were tending to be lost. The future of learning in England depended on a thin trickle of tradition, or on the chance of a great patron appearing who could restore links with the scholars and the libraries of Europe. The only gleams of light in the island at the beginning of Alfred's reign were the frequent visits of Irish scholars to the court of Gwynedd in North Wales, and their journeys through England on their way to the Continent ; and it was to Wales and Ireland—whose schools still retained much of their ancient tradition of learning—as well as to the Continent that Alfred looked when he tried to revive English schools and libraries.

Compared with later times, the lower clergy were also few. The parish system was only beginning to be formed. Christianity had originally been a religion of the town, based on the cities of the Roman Empire ; and it was slow to accommodate itself to the needs of the village-dwelling peoples. At first the cathedral clergy were the clergy of the diocese ; then other large churches, ' minsters ', were built, where small communities of clerks could live and serve the needs of a large area. This might suit a missionary church, but was a makeshift in a settled Christian country. And so local lords and the leading men of the villages laid out the money to build churches, and paid their tithes for the support of priests. Gradually the parish system spread about the country. Even by the Norman Conquest it was far from complete, especially in the north and west. In Alfred's day the parish church was far from being the common sight it later became ; and in the areas occupied by the Danes, it must have been virtually unknown. Paradoxically, it is precisely in the Danelaw that churches were built most rapidly in the tenth century ; and partly for this reason, partly on account of the availability of stone for build-ing, Lincolnshire and Northamptonshire have more visible traces of Saxon architecture than any other counties. The English Church was weak ; the English monarchs therefore possessed very few tools for creating even the first beginnings of literate government.

About the great mass of the English peasantry, ' those who work ', we are singularly ill-informed. A few glimpses reveal to us a peasantry divided into *geneatas*, *cotsetlan*, and *geburas* ; and in Domesday Book (1086) we are given a rich vocabulary of peasant groups. The *gebur* was the normal peasant of early medieval society, much like the Roman *colonus* or the later villein in status ; provided with a plot of land on which he and his family could maintain a living, though sometimes a meagre one, in return for services often very burdensome ; personally free, but often tied to the land he held. The *cotsetla* was a cottager, with or without a small holding of land ; a man whose livelihood could not entirely depend on what he grew, but must expect some supplement from wages earned by occasional or regular labour on other men's estates. The *geneat* was the aristocrat of the Anglo-Saxon peasantry ; the ' free man ' or ' sokeman ' of Domesday Book or even something more. He was sometimes a substantial small farmer. The boundary between him and the *gesith* or *thegn*, the lord or the lord's companion, was not always very great or impassable.

The *gebur* was personally free : he could not be bought and sold ; he lived on his own plot of land. But there were also in eleventh-century England large numbers of slaves— 25,000 of them are recorded in Domesday Book. The number was declining : the freeing of slaves was a work of mercy, and the *gebur* or villein suited the farming ideas of the Norman lords better than did the slave. The slaves performed the function later carried out by the wage-labourer, and one reason for their disappearance was that the increasing use of money in late Saxon and early Norman times meant that it was easier for a lord to pay for labour when he wanted it than to feed and care for a team of slaves in and out of season. But throughout Saxon times the slaves must have been a familiar sight in many English villages ; and even in the late eleventh century it required a special mission to Bristol by the Bishop of Worcester, St Wulfstan, to suppress the trading of English slaves to Ireland.

(2) 878–99

At the end of March 878 Alfred and his following established themselves in a secret base among the marshes of Somerset, at Athelney ; and from there resistance was planned. Alfred summoned the 'fyrd' or militia of Somerset, Wiltshire, and western Hampshire—that part of Wessex with which he could still keep in touch—to be ready for a rapid attack on the Danes early in May. And with these forces he fell on the Danes at Edington, pursued them to their camp, and after a fortnight's siege compelled them to surrender. Three weeks later the Danish king, Guthrum, and thirty of his leading followers were baptised in Alfred's presence.

Decisive as was the battle of Edington in saving Wessex from total destruction, it did not lead to any lasting peace. In the mid eight-eighties war was renewed, and this time Alfred had the opportunity to take the initiative. In 886 he captured London, and put it in charge of his close ally, Ethelred, Ealdorman of the Mercians, who shortly after married Alfred's daughter, Aethelflaed. Soon after 886 another truce was made between Alfred and Guthrum, which established a temporary frontier between English and Danish England. It divided the lowland zone into two, by drawing a line along the Thames from its mouth, skirting north of London, then running north-west to Bedford, and so along Watling Street (now the A5) to the Welsh border. But it did not lead to peace. From 892 to 896 a new Danish army was at large in England ; and throughout the last decade of Alfred's reign there was the threat of raids from the Danish kingdom of York.

Alfred was never free from wars or rumours of wars. But in the last ten years of his life he was able to reorganise the English defences and establish a military organisation which saved the country from a repetition of the disastrous winter of 877–8, prepared the way for the successes of Edward the Elder and Athelstan, Alfred's son and grandson, and in some respects provided the model on which another distinguished Saxon, Henry the Fowler, repaired the defences of German Saxony against the Magyars a generation later.

The Danes had the great advantage that they were highly mobile, could move great distances by sea, and very frequently achieved surprise. Alfred was concerned to meet them on their own terms. First of all, he built ships, large and swift, ' neither after the Frisian design nor after the Danish, but as it seemed to himself that they could be most serviceable '. The interest Alfred took in designing the ships is characteristic of his restless inquiring mind and searching imagination, and also reveals the attention to detail of the fine administrator. But the Danes were not only mobile by sea. Their armies were always in being, and could be swiftly mobilised. The disaster in 877–8 had occurred because the English militia took so long to mobilise. Alfred simplified its organisation and divided it, so that manpower was available to supply the militia, man the fortresses, and till the soil at the same time. Hitherto the militia, the ' fyrd ', had been exceedingly reluctant to remain under arms for more than a short campaign, or to move any distance. This division meant that their work at home was not totally neglected, although we do not know how the arrangement worked in detail. A large, and perhaps increasing, part of the English army consisted of nobles and their retinues, the more permanent military class, the thegns and their followers. A division of the thegns similar to that of the fyrd made longer campaigns possible for them too.

The militia was not a new instrument, but an old royal right reorganised. Another public obligation developed by Alfred was that of building and repairing fortresses—a duty incumbent on almost all holders of land. Alfred in fact began, and Edward the Elder completed, the construction of a national network of fortifications. By the early tenth century no village in Sussex, Surrey, or Wessex was more than twenty miles from one of these fortresses. They provided defence in depth against an enemy who might come from any direction—from land or sea ; and they provided refuge for men and cattle against an enemy whose chief motive was plunder. The fortresses were normally large enclosures, walled towns rather than castles ; and many of them were sited in, or later became, towns. Indeed, the building of the *burhs* (our ' boroughs ') by Alfred and his son marked an important stage in the recovery of English towns and so in the long run of trade and economic life generally.

Alfred's achievement in saving Wessex from the Danes and laying its defences on a more stable base was remarkable enough. What is even more remarkable is that in the brief intervals of war and defence he showed so much concern for the general welfare and for every aspect of the life of the kingdom whose very existence still lay in the balance. He had a vision of a kingdom more stable, more peaceful, and more civilised than anything he could hope to live to see. These points are remarkably illustrated by his *Laws* and his translations.

The written laws of Anglo-Saxon kings were not comprehensive codes. The main body of the law was customary and unwritten. When custom had to be altered, or clarified, or emphasised, it might be put in writing. The result is that the law-books from the time of King Ethelbert of Kent to King Cnut are at once very particular and precise and very fragmentary. It appears that Alfred, in issuing his code, was reviving a custom which had not been exercised for a century. During this period law-making as a royal right disappeared in the French kingdom ; the revival in England under Alfred may have saved it from a similar oblivion.

Human law was felt to be a reflection of divine law. Alfred had the conviction that the divine law was the source of first principles ; and that the Bible, which contained the divine law, might provide texts of more particular application too. Alfred's laws have a long introduction attempting to tie English law on to Biblical (Mosaic) law and the law of the early Church, as deduced from the Acts of the Apostles. The rest of the book is an attempt to select and record what was valuable and necessary from earlier collections. ' Then I, King Alfred, collected these together and ordered to be written many of them which our forefathers observed, those which I liked ; and many of those which I did not like, I rejected with the advice of my councillors, and ordered them to be differently observed. For I dared not presume to set in writing at all many of my own, because it was unknown to me what should please those who should come after us. But those which I found anywhere, which seemed to me most just, either of the time of my kinsman, King Ine [688–726], or of Offa, King of the Mercians [757–96], or of Ethelbert [King of Kent, 560–616], who first among the English received baptism, I collected herein, and omitted the others. Then I, Alfred, King of the West Saxons, showed these to all my councillors, and they then said that they were all pleased to observe them.'

This is the first description of English law-making, and it is altogether more informal than later processes. The custom of his predecessors, for the most part, was treated with great respect ; nothing was done without the advice of his councillors. Yet Alfred knew his own mind. ' I, King Alfred, collected these together and ordered to be written . . . those which I liked.' Especially significant is his use of the Mercian laws. He was King of the West Saxons ; but he felt a responsibility to all the English—even to the English subjects of King Guthrum, whose interests he protected in the peace treaty.

' Judge thou very fairly. Do not judge one judgment for the rich and another for the poor ; nor one for the one more dear and another for the one more hateful.' This sentiment was introduced by Alfred into the introduction to his *Laws* from the Book of Exodus ; but the sentence has been a good deal elaborated in the course of translation, and has become a full expression of one of Alfred's basic beliefs. In a similar way in his translations Alfred interprets the thought of his source, expands, annotates, and illustrates it ; makes it his own.

' His unique importance in the history of English letters,' writes Sir Frank Stenton, ' comes from his conviction that a life without knowledge or reflection was unworthy of respect, and his determination to bring the thought of the past within the range of his subjects' understanding.' Here is Alfred's own account of the genesis of his translation of Gregory the Great's *Pastoral Care*, a manual on the office of a bishop. ' When I remembered how the knowledge of the Latin language had previously decayed throughout England, and yet many could read things written in English, I began in the midst of the other various and manifold cares of this kingdom to turn into English the book which is called in Latin *Pastoralis* and in English *Shepherd-book*, sometimes word for word, sometimes by a paraphrase ; as I had learned it from my Archbishop

Plegmund, and my Bishop Asser, and my priest Grimbald and my priest John. When I had learned it, I turned it into English according as I understood it and as I could render it most intelligibly ; and I will send one to every see in my kingdom.'

This describes, in a nutshell, Alfred's concern and his method. His subjects were ignorant of Latin. The treasures of ancient literature must be translated. He himself had neither time nor the fluency in Latin to translate alone ; so he presided over a seminar of learned men who assisted and advised him. It is an astonishing story. A warrior king on his own initiative feels the lack of learning in himself and his people ; struggles to learn to read and write ; collects scholars ; presides over their work and as time passes himself takes a hand in it ; founds schools in which not only churchmen but laymen, too, may learn. His immediate success was slight—there was too much ground to be covered ; his lay followers were not accustomed to learning and not seriously amenable to it. But on a longer view the achievement was extremely impressive.

Alfred's own childhood had accustomed him to the existence of a great European heritage : as a small boy he had twice been on a pilgrimage to Rome. But it was only gradually that he worked out his programme and collected his band of scholars. He had to search widely for them. Plegmund and Werferth (not included in the list in the *Pastoral Care*), were native Englishmen. Grimbald came from the north of France, John from the north of Germany, Asser from Wales. All took a hand in the work of translation.

Gregory's *Pastoral Care* was throughout the Middle Ages the fundamental book on the duty of a bishop—and of special interest to Alfred in stressing the responsibility of a bishop for educating laymen. Gregory's *Dialogues*, translated by Werferth, contained miracle stories, especially the miracles of St Benedict, author of the famous monastic rule. Its choice reflected Alfred's desire to see monasticism re-established. The library of translations also included two distinguished works of history, the English history of Bede, and the world history of Orosius. To Orosius Alfred added his own reflections on the countries and peoples of Europe, especially on the Scandinavian and Baltic countries unknown to Orosius (who had lived in Spain), but of special interest to Alfred, whose whole life was spent fighting the Vikings. This geographical lore shows again the width of his interests, his passion for inquiry. Finally he turned his hand to two books of more personal interest to him. Boethius had written his *Consolations of Philosophy* while awaiting execution at the hands of the Goths. Its comforts seemed specially appropriate to Alfred's own circumstances. And in his rendering of St Augustine's soliloquies, the book in which he departed most freely from his original, Alfred expounded his philosophy of learning. It marks the end of the road whose beginning he had described in the *Pastoral Care*. He tells how he had been, as it were, a forester cutting timber in the wood of ancient knowledge.

' Then I gathered for myself staves and props and bars, and handles for all the tools I knew how to use, and cross-bars and beams for all the structures which I knew how to build, the fairest pieces of timber, as many as I could carry. I neither came home with a single load, nor did it suit me to bring home all the wood, even if I could have carried it. In each tree I saw something that I required at home. For I advise each of those who is strong and has many wagons, to plan to go to the same wood where I cut these props, and fetch for himself more there, and load his wagons with fair rods, so that he can plait many a fine wall, and put up many a peerless building, and build a fair enclosure with them ; and may dwell therein pleasantly and at his ease winter and summer, *as I have not yet done*. But he who advised me, to whom the wood was pleasing, may bring it to pass that I shall dwell at greater ease both in this transitory habitation by this road while I am in this world, and also in the eternal home which he has promised us through St Augustine and St Gregory and St Jerome and through many other holy fathers ; as also I believe he will, for the merits of them all, both make this road more convenient than it has hitherto been, and also enlighten the eyes of my mind so that I can find out the straight road to the eternal home, and to the eternal mercy, and to the eternal rest which is promised to us by the holy fathers. So be it.'

3 The Making of the English Kingdom, 899–1035

(1) 899–959

THOUGH Alfred was never free to dwell in his enclosure at ease winter and summer, and though Danish raids continued right to the eve of his death, the most serious threat to the survival of Wessex had passed. His practical measures and his great prestige had strengthened the material and psychological defences of his kingdom. The impetus of the Viking attacks, meanwhile, had weakened. In Ireland, Scotland, England, and northern France, as the ninth century turned into the tenth, the Viking bands were turning from pillage to settlement ; they had reached the limits of their expansion.

The end of the great Viking offensive did not mean an end to the problems of English defence. Alfred's son and successor, Edward the Elder (899–924), was as frequently engaged in war as his father ; and, in his way, as notable a warrior. Kingship was a very personal thing in the Middle Ages. However strongly one king might build up the bases of his power, his successor's position always depended to a great extent on his own achievements. Alfred's positive achievements, however sensational, did not give Wessex stability or permanent security. His work would have foundered if he had not been succeeded by a line of able kings. It was carried on, and in certain respects completed, by his remarkably able descendants, notably by his son Edward, his grandson Athelstan (King, 924–39) and his great-grandson, Athelstan's nephew, Edgar (959–75). After Edgar's death the throne passed to lesser men, and the long rule of Ethelred II (978–1016) coincided with the renewal of Danish attacks. With Ethelred the dynasty collapsed, though not, as we shall see, the kingdom.

For the first ten years of Edward's reign no further progress is recorded in the recovery of English territory from the Danes. Danish armies indeed supported a cousin of Edward in rebellion against him. Apart from this there were signs that relations between English and Danes were becoming more peaceable, that Edward and his thegns were finding opportunities for peaceful infiltration. In 909 the armies of Wessex and Mercia attacked the Northumbrian Danes and dictated terms of peace to them. In the following year the Danes retaliated by raiding English Mercia, but their army was caught on its way home near Tettenhall in Staffordshire, and annihilated. From then on the leaders of Wessex and Mercia were free to reconquer the southern Danish kingdoms without serious interruption from the north. Ethelred, Ealdorman of Mercia, died in 911, but co-operation did not cease with his death. His place was filled by his wife, Edward's sister, Aethelflaed, 'Lady of the Mercians', who continued her husband's work in close association with her brother until her own death in 918 ; from then on Wessex and Mercia were united.

The *Anglo-Saxon Chronicle* had hitherto devoted most space to the doings of the ' heathen ', the ' host '—that is, the Danes. First compiled in the reign of Alfred, not perhaps under his direct inspiration, but clearly reflecting the literary revival of his time, its main entries for the mid and late ninth century tell the tale of attack and disaster in plain, unemotional, but effective prose. In Alfred's later years more is said of the King's activities ; one senses the feeling that at last the initiative is shifting. But the hosts are frequently the subject of annals still. In 914 a great pirate host of Danes came from Brittany and attacked south and central Wales, but it was turned back on the English border. This apart, the main burden of the annals from 911 to 925 is the steady progress of Edward's reconquest.

After the Ealdorman Ethelred's death in 911, Edward took over London and the south-east Midlands, leaving the rest of English Mercia to Aethelflaed. The building of fortresses and the advance east and north went on steadily through the following years. In 914 Aethelflaed built a fortress at Eddisbury (Cheshire) and at Warwick ; in 917 she captured Derby ; in 918 Leicester, and but for her death that year she might have received the submission of York. In 912 Edward built a *burh* at Hertford, and prepared for campaigns to east and north. In 914 and 915 he received the submission of Bedford and Northampton ; in 916 he built a *burh* at Maldon in Essex ; in 917 he and his followers defeated a great counter-offensive mounted by the Danes, and occupied Essex and East Anglia, restoring the *burh* at Colchester. In 918 he was at Stamford and Nottingham. These places had been two of the crucial Danish centres of power south of the Humber ; it is likely that a third, Lincoln, also submitted to Edward in this year. By these surrenders he became lord of the Danelaw up to the line of the Humber ; by his sister's death he was lord of Mercia ; and in the same year the kings of several leading Welsh kingdoms accepted his overlordship.

The offer by the Danes of York to submit to Aethelflaed— an offer not repeated to Edward after her death—and the rapid submission of the Danish armies of the north Midlands and of Lincolnshire was partly inspired by the progress of another Viking power, this time of Norse origin and leadership. Many of the place-names in the Wirral peninsula in north-west Cheshire, in the angle between Wales and the Mersey, are of Norse origin ; and the Norse settlements in this area date from the first decade of the tenth century. The Norsemen came, immediately, from Ireland. If the Wirral was their chief point of entry, their settlements must have spread all along the coast of Lancashire and Cumberland and south-western Scotland. In 919 the most powerful of the Irish-Norse leaders, Raegnald, established himself as King of York.

The Norse kingdom of York acted as a check on the English advance for a number of years, but it forms only a slight qualification to Edward's remarkable tale of success. His last years saw the rebuilding of more *burhs*, and as a final coping-stone to his prestige, after the building of the *burh* at Bakewell in the Peak of Derbyshire in 920, ' the king of Scots and the whole Scottish nation accepted him as " father and lord " : so also did Raegnald [King of York] and the sons of Eadwulf and all the inhabitants of Northumbria, both English and Danish, Norwegians and others ; together with the king of the Strathclyde Welsh and all his subjects.'

In 924 Edward died, and was succeeded by his eldest son, Athelstan. Athelstan had been brought up in the household of the Lord and Lady of the Mercians, and was as readily accepted as king in Mercia as in Wessex. In his time the local particularisms of these two countries were rapidly breaking down. But it is still too early to talk of a united English kingdom. The north of the country was only slowly conquered ; and Athelstan was lord over an assemblage of peoples, English, Danes, and Norse, with diverse traditions and diverse motives for allegiance and disaffection. The royal scribes pronounced the unity of his kingdom in Latin of immense portentousness and obscurity. They protested too much ; though the words of one of the charters, 'most glorious king of the Anglo-Saxons and the Danes' came near the truth. But true unity was not to come to the English peoples until a Dane sat on Alfred's throne, in 1016.

The first years of Athelstan's reign saw him established as king in almost every part of England, and received as overlord by the border kingdoms in Wales and southern Scotland. His relations with the Welsh princes were closer and more effective than had been established by any of his predecessors. The methods of his government, his coinage, and his laws all seem to have influenced the most distinguished of these princes, Hywel Dda of Dyfed, whose name became traditionally attached to later editions of Welsh law-books. Of more immediate importance to the English kingdom was Athelstan's conquest of the Norse kingdom of York.

His relations with the Scottish kings soon broke down. In 934 he paraded a large army through Scotland as a demonstration of power, but the Scots avoided battle. In 937 an Irish king, son of the last king of York, joined the kings of Scotland and Strathclyde in a combined invasion of England. Their army was met by a large English force led by Athelstan and Edmund, his brother ; and the decisive English victory at Brunanburh (the site has not been identified) is recorded in the *Chronicle* in stirring verse. 'With their hammered blades, the sons of Edward clove the shield-wall and hacked the linden bucklers. . . . There the prince of Norsemen . . . was forced to flee to the·prow of his ship with a handful of men. . . . There, likewise, the aged Constantine [King of the Scots], the grey-haired warrior, set off in flight, north to his native land. No cause had he to exult in that clash of swords,

Plate 1 AN EARLY CASTLE. The Bayeux Tapestry was probably embroidered in England in the second half of the eleventh century had fortress and living quarters combined. This picture shows three stages : the Norman assault on the left ; Norman soldiers setting fire to the fort in the middle ; and Count Conan surrendering the keys of the castle on the right. The inscription reads : (HIC MILITES VVILLELMI DUCIS PUGNANT CONTRA DINANTES : ET CUNAN CLA(VES PORREXIT). 'Here the soldiers of Duke William fight against the men of Dinan ; and Conan offered up the keys' (Phaidon Press ed., pls. 25–6).

Plate 1 AN EARLY CASTLE. The Bayeux Tapestry was probably embroidered in England for Odo, Bishop of Bayeux, between 1066 and 1077. The early part shows Harold's visit to Normandy in 1064, in the course of which he joined Duke William in an attack on Count Conan of Brittany. This attack ended with the siege and capture of the castle of Dinan. The picture is stylised, but it shows the basic defence of a castle of the period : a motte, or mound, with a wooden fort on top, which was fortress and lookout tower, and adjacent buildings would lie in an adjacent court-yard, or bailey. But the great stone keeps like the Tower of London

Plate 2 ONE OF THE EARLIEST MAPS OF BRITAIN. No detailed maps of Britain survive before the mid-thirteenth century : the earliest are those of Matthew Paris, monk of St Albans, the famous historian and artist. This plate shows the best-preserved of his English maps (British Museum, Cotton MS. Claudius D.vi, f.8v ; a list of all his maps is given in R. Vaughan, *Matthew Paris* (1958), pp. 241-2). At the centre, from bottom to top, is an itinerary from Dover to Newcastle, via Canterbury, London, St Albans, Northampton, Leicester, Doncaster and Durham ; all these places are set in a straight line, and this has led to some serious dislocation of the map. Norfolk and Suffolk lie in the south-east, and the east and west coasts are out of scale, so that Cheshire, Lancashire and Cumberland have coalesced.

bereaved of his kinsmen, robbed of his friends on the field of battle.'

When he died in 939, Athelstan was recognised as one of the leading princes of western Europe. The composition of his court from time to time reflected his sway over the princes of Wales, the Scottish border, and Scotland. The solemn language of his charters evidently reflects a court conscious of its distinction, concerned to cut a figure in the world. In 926 one of his sisters married the Duke of the Franks. This was the response to an embassy carrying rich gifts to the King, including jewels, perfumes, and relics—of which Athelstan was a princely collector. In 928 another sister married the heir of Germany, the future Otto the Great, reopening traditional links between old and new Saxony, between the English and their Saxon homeland. These were the most impressive symbols of the European reputation of Athelstan, which involved him in the affairs of Brittany and Lotharingia (Lorraine), and brought him also friendship with the King of Norway. We should like to know more about him as a man : what we do know suggests some likeness to his grandfather.

With Athelstan's death in 939 English rule over the Norse kingdom of York became extremely precarious ; and a great part of the reigns of his brothers Edmund (939–46) and Eadred (946–55) was spent in the attempt to re-establish Athelstan's supremacy in the north. The key to much of the fighting of this period is the growing antagonism between Norse and Dane in the kingdom of York, and the close links between the Vikings and their Scandinavian homeland. Norse war-lords were established between the Humber and the Tees, and Norse settlers in the north-west. But in the Danish areas south of the Humber the Norse kings of York were never popular, and never won more than a temporary supremacy. Late in Edmund's reign and early in Eadred's, the English kings were successful for brief periods in mastering the north. But in the middle years of Eadred's reign two distinguished Vikings, one from Ireland and one from Norway, held sway at York. Eric Bloodaxe indeed had been King of Norway for a time, and had made a considerable name for himself for violence and adventure. After his expulsion he twice succeeded in winning the kingdom of York (948–9, 952–4). But it was difficult even for a great Viking leader like Eric to establish himself on English soil for any length of time. In 954 the Northumbrians expelled him, and Eadred ruled over the whole of England. In the following year he died.

Thus, after some vicissitudes, the inheritance of Edward the Elder and Athelstan passed into the next generation intact and well established. It was well that it did so, because the next generation was represented by Edmund's sons, of whom the elder, Eadwig, cannot have been more than fifteen and the younger, Edgar, was twelve. Eadwig lived only four years after his accession ; long enough to acquire an evil reputation in those circles to which we owe record of his reign, not long enough to redeem it by any notable act. It is noteworthy that several of the leading associates of his brother, Edgar, had already been promoted under Eadwig ; but that Eadwig quarrelled with the greatest of Edgar's colleagues, St Dunstan. It was probably to this quarrel, whose true origin is quite obscure, that Eadwig owed his bad reputation.

(2) 959–75 : EDGAR AND THE MONASTIC REVIVAL

Edgar began his reign while still a boy and died in his early thirties ; the prestige he acquired is all the more remarkable. As a soldier, Edgar acquired little glory, because, as one version of the *Chronicle* has it, ' God granted him to live his days in peace '. But his reign was not weak, and his prestige stood very high. In 973, at the age of thirty—the age when a man might be ordained priest—Edgar was solemnly anointed and crowned king by Archbishop Dunstan, in a ceremony which laid special emphasis on the analogies of kingship and priesthood, and provided for the first time in England a fully elaborated coronation service on the Frankish model. The coronation emphasised the divine source of royal authority, and the close bonds between king and Church. Later in the same year, in an equally famous scene at Chester, Edgar received the submission of seven Welsh and Scottish kings—who rowed him, as legend has it, on the Dee, between his palace and the church of St John. This show of power was accompanied by an act of policy which was probably characteristic of Edgar. The King of Scots became Edgar's man ; in return Edgar granted him Lothian, the land between the Tweed and the Forth, a country always remote from English authority and difficult to control. The grant was the first step towards establishing the present frontier of England and Scotland. Within England itself, Edgar recognised that English and Danes lived by different customs, and he allowed the Danes to regulate their own customs ; thus recognising the existence and native rights of a vital minority in his kingdom.

The coronation ceremony in 973 was the climax of the collaboration between the King and his chief councillor, Dunstan, Archbishop of Canterbury. Like Lanfranc and Stephen Langton in later days, Dunstan combined the fullest appreciation of the spiritual aspect of his office with political statesmanship of a high order. The dual capacity of a bishop's office, on the one hand, that of royal councillor and leading subject, on the other, that of spiritual leader, was often an embarrassment to a conscientious medieval bishop. Dunstan, like Lanfranc, lived both lives to the full. In Dunstan's case the difference was hidden by his strong conviction that Church and state were one ; that the king was natural ruler of the Church, ' king and priest '. This union of offices did not give the king the specifically clerical function of performing the rites and administering the sacraments of the Church ; but it meant that in return for protection and patronage the Church recognised in him God's instrument for controlling its government. The close liaison of king and Church gave a special character to the English Church ; and the Church's support made possible the dramatic developments in English government in the tenth and early eleventh centuries.

In 940 King Edmund had nearly perished while hunting the stag in the Cheddar Gorge in Somerset. Saved, as it seemed, by a miracle, he at once set about re-establishing the church at Glastonbury, not far away, as a regular monastery, and put Dunstan at its head. Circumstances were different from the days when Alfred had to fetch monks from abroad to furnish a community. Foreign influence was strong in the monastic reform inaugurated by Dunstan ; but its personnel was almost entirely English, and its leaders were quickly supplied from Dunstan's early disciples at Glastonbury. In spreading his movement in the early years Dunstan met difficulties; though highly born and exceedingly well connected, he had enemies at court. But after Edgar's accession in 959 events moved swiftly. Dunstan himself became archbishop in 960, and the diocese of Worcester, which he had held for a brief space, was given to his disciple, Oswald, who from 972 to his death in 992 combined Worcester with the archbishopric of York (an act of pluralism made necessary by the poverty of York). In 963 Dunstan's other leading disciple, Ethelwold, became Bishop of Winchester. From these key positions the three colleagues directed a great revival and reformation of the monastic order in England. Between 940 and the Norman Conquest some sixty houses of monks and nuns were founded or revived. Compared with later figures the number of houses and the number of religious in them (about 1,000 in 1066) were not sensational; but the influence of the monks on English life was out of all proportion to their numbers.

Behind the English reform lay two active movements on the Continent, one centred in Lorraine, the other in the celebrated Burgundian monastic house of Cluny. Cluny was founded in 910; Brogne and Gorze, most important of the houses of Lorraine, were refounded about 920 and 933. These foundations lay between the age of Alfred and the age of Dunstan; they provided Dunstan with a background that had been lacking in Alfred's day. Alfred's attempts at cultural revival and his successors' steady patronage of the Church and learning had slowly taken effect. And Dunstan himself was peculiarly well qualified to found a monastic revival. Brought up near Glastonbury, he was in contact with such elements of monastic tradition as still lingered in the area, and also in touch with the dual tradition of Celtic and Saxon monasticism which gives Glastonbury its special interest and partly explains why it became so powerful a centre of legend. Dunstan and Oswald both spent a few years in continental houses, Dunstan at Ghent and Oswald at Fleury on the Loire. Ghent had recently been reformed from Brogne and Gorze, Fleury from Cluny; so that the English movement came early into contact with both streams of continental tradition.

Gorze and Cluny differed in a number of respects; most obviously in that houses reformed from Gorze retained close bonds with the lay patron who had organised the reform, while Cluny favoured at least a legal independence of secular control. In part this reflected the divergence between the settled monarchy of tenth-century Germany, where the ' connection ' of Gorze flourished, and the feudal anarchy of France. In England we have a situation more similar to Germany's than to France's, and close alliance with the king and other lay patrons became the English tradition.

In other respects Gorze and Cluny were much alike ; especially in owing a profound debt to the constitutions which St Benedict of Aniane had promulgated for all the monasteries of the Frankish dominions at Aachen in 817, under the patronage of the Emperor Louis the Pious, Charlemagne's successor. This piece of history was well known to Dunstan and his colleagues. In or about the year 970, at a great gathering modelled on that at Aachen, Edgar and the bishops and the whole synod promulgated a set of constitutions for the English monasteries, the *Regularis Concordia*, a ' monastic agreement ' or agreed norm for the religious life, to be the basis for the practice in all the English monasteries. It is a nice mingling of influences from Lorraine and Burgundy with native traditions. Its final form probably owed more to Ethelwold than to Dunstan. In the later stages of the revival the details of reform were more in the hands of Ethelwold and Oswald, who were very active in and out of their dioceses—and especially in the east Midlands and East Anglia, which the Church was quickly recovering from Danish paganism, in close alliance with the local ealdormen.

The English Church was becoming thoroughly monastic. Between the accession of Edgar and the Conquest a high proportion of the bishops were monks ; under Edgar and Ethelred II (died 1016) almost all. Fundamentally a monastery is an inward-looking community, a haven apart from the world. But the monasticising of the English Church did not mean a separation of Church and state ; quite the contrary. The English monasteries retained a tradition of more normal contact with the life of the world than was usually favoured by monastic reformers. In the reign of Alfred the higher clergy had been few in number. They were more prolific by Edgar's time ; but very largely because of the increase in the number of monks. A secular [1] higher clergy of any proportions was still lacking. The broad character of the English monastic order, and with it of the English Church in general, reflected the wide interests of St Dunstan. He had been a statesman, a monk, a man of great learning by the standards of the day ; and, curiously enough, an artist as well. In art and sacred literature the monastic reformation was tremendously fruitful ; some impression of its splendour can be gained from Plate 10. Close links between lay patrons [2] and the monasteries ; a powerful monastic influence at court, and every kind of link between Church and king ; and a monastic tradition especially notable for its artistic creativity ; these were the marks of the English Church in the time of St Dunstan.

(3) 975-1016 : ETHELRED II AND THE DANES

Edgar died suddenly, while still a young man, in 975, and was succeeded in turn by his two sons, Edward (975-8) and Ethelred (978-1016). Edward was very young, yet he managed in his brief rule to alienate a number of his subjects by his insufferable manners and bad temper. In 978 he was treacherously murdered, and replaced by Ethelred, who was then still a boy.

The crime which brought him to the throne cast a shadow over the reign of Ethelred and may partly explain the stunted weakness of his character throughout life. It was not the violence of the murder but the treachery of it—betrayal of a lord by his subjects—which shocked contemporaries. In 1008 Ethelred issued a code including this clause : ' The councillors have decreed that St Edward's festival is to be celebrated over all England on 18 March.' In this ironical fashion Ethelred was compelled to celebrate the event which had made him king. The name Ethelred means literally ' noble-

---

[1] The word ' secular ', when used of clergy, distinguishes those who were not committed to a specific rule, i.e. the majority of the cathedral and parish clergy, from monks (and later, friars) and ' canons regular ' ; the ' secular ' clergy were those who lived in the ' world ' (*in saeculo*).

[2] The founder of a monastery became its patron : he protected it and supported it, in return for prayers and for certain rights and privileges. The office of patron was hereditary ; and in early days the patron had great influence in the affairs of a monastery.

counsel'. We do not know whose wit first devised the pun 'no-counsel', 'unræd', for the unfortunate king; the nickname is first recorded in the thirteenth century. But the word had other meanings too, including 'evil counsel', 'a treacherous plot'. If it was devised in his lifetime, it would certainly have got home. The subtlety of the nickname has been lost in the modern corruption 'Ethelred the Unready', though that too is not inappropriate.

The death of a king of high prestige was commonly followed by disorder among leading nobles hitherto held in check by fear or respect for the dead man. To the disorder following Edgar's death was added the horror of Edward's 'martyrdom'. But greater misfortune than these was in store for the unfortunate Ethelred. The mainland of Scandinavia, remarkably quiescent since the fall of Eric Bloodaxe, was ready for another wave of expansion; Viking attacks began again; and the unsettled politics of England combined with England's growing wealth to make it a favoured target.

The second wave of Danish attacks began, like the first, with plundering raids. But the attacks of the period 980-1016 differed fundamentally from those of the ninth century. From the early nine-nineties they became large-scale, highly organised raids, planned by the leading figures of the Scandinavian world, conducted by highly professional armies. This phase lasted until 1013, when Swein, the Danish King, decided to take over the government of his prey, and came in person.

The first of the great leaders of the Vikings in the nine-nineties was Olaf Tryggvason, who came in the raid of 991 which led to the battle of Maldon, celebrated in the poem quoted in an earlier chapter. Olaf shortly after became the first Christian King of Norway; but he never ceased to be a Viking adventurer. In 994 he came accompanied by Swein, heir to the throne of Denmark, at the head of a formidable host. There was talk of making Swein King of England; but his alliance with Olaf was precarious and his campaign not wholly successful, so he agreed to peace for a payment of £16,000. In most years after this, down to 1006, a Danish host attacked England and levied plunder or tribute—the 'Dane-geld'—or both. Then came a gap of two years, when Ethelred and his councillors made feverish attempts to prepare the country's defences against further attacks. From 1009 the attacks were continuous, and aimed for the first time at the conquest of the kingdom.

More than one of the Icelandic sagas describes the legend of how Harold Bluetooth, Swein's father, had built a great fortress at Jomsborg, near the mouth of the Oder, on the German mainland. It consisted, so they tell us, of a fort and fortified harbour ; a large military base, accommodating several thousand professional soldiers, on a permanent war footing. The leaders of these troops in the fortress included Thorkell the Tall, and Swein himself. It has long been disputed how much truth there is in the legend, and the existence of Jomsborg is still in doubt. But the part of the story which was at one time most generally doubted was the size and nature of the camp. In recent years the general truth of this picture has been dramatically confirmed by archaeology. Four forts similar in character to that described in the sagas have been discovered in Scandinavia itself. Three of them, capable of holding about 3,000 men each, probably belong to Swein's own time ; the fourth and largest was constructed somewhat later. Clearly a large professional army existed in the time of Swein ; and this formidable force would have daunted a more capable warrior than Ethelred.

Swein's armies in 1009 were led by three experienced Vikings, including Thorkell the Tall and one of his brothers. From 1009 to 1012 they raided many English shires systematically. In 1012 they made peace with the English in exchange for an immense ransom, assessed in the *Chronicle* at £48,000. But before the Danes would disperse, they demanded an extra ransom from their most illustrious prisoner, Aelfheah, Archbishop of Canterbury. Aelfheah first agreed, then felt this concession to be wrong and withdrew it. Thorkell struggled to control his men ; but they were in ugly mood and murdered the Archbishop in barbarous fashion. Before the end of the year Thorkell and forty-five ships from the Danish fleet went over to Ethelred. It is likely that the two incidents were connected.

In 1013 Swein himself came to England for the third and last time—he had raided in the country in 994 and 1003. This time he was determined on conquest, and after a rapid campaign described in brief but vivid phrases by the chronicler he was accepted as king over most of the country. Then in February 1014 he suddenly died. The period between the death of Swein and the final acknowledgment of his son, Cnut, as king, at the end of 1016 is exceedingly confusing. At the time of his father's death Cnut was about eighteen, and the sudden access of responsibility was evidently too much for him. He withdrew hastily from England ; and when he returned, he was supported by three great Viking leaders, his elder brother, Harold, King of Denmark, Eric, the Regent of Norway, and Thorkell the Tall, who had returned to his old allegiance. At one point Cnut held Wessex and Mercia, while Edmund ' Ironside ', Ethelred's son, held the northern Danelaw—both in defiance of King Ethelred, who was still holding out in the south-east. It was Cnut's unheralded withdrawal which had alienated the Danelaw and made Edmund's intrusion there possible ; while in spite of the momentary recovery of Ethelred in 1014 and 1015, there was treachery in the English court, which aided Cnut to overrun Wessex and Mercia. Ethelred died in April 1016 ; a few months later Edmund was decisively beaten by Cnut, and the uneasy truce which followed was quickly ended by Edmund's sudden death. The events of the civil war had shown that there was no simple division of loyalty between English and Danes, and that a number of leading thegns and jarls were prepared to support a monarch from either side, if he proved more competent than Ethelred, and capable of holding the allegiance of his subjects. It was this circumstance which made possible the notable success of the young Cnut.

(4) 1016-35 : THE REIGN OF CNUT

King Edgar had recognised that his subjects lived by two divergent sets of customs, English and Danish. The events which followed his death had shown that Viking leaders from Scandinavia could still find allies in the Danelaw ; and that under exceptional pressure, both English and Danes were prepared to submit to a Viking lord. At first sight it seems surprising that the first ruler of a really united England should have been a Dane ; but on closer inspection the paradox is easy to understand. Divergent customs and language, links with the north and memories of past glory would tend to make the Danes and Norwegians uneasy subjects of a native English king. The Danes in England, however, had had some generations' experience of English rule—of the rule, that is, of the most considerable monarchy, apart from the German, in northern Europe. They had experienced some of the benefits of a régime more stable than those to which they had been accustomed in Scandinavia, while suffering as much as the native English from the constant passage of armies and levying of tribute in Ethelred's later years. Cnut was thus doubly attractive to them : as a Danish overlord and as a man who could restore peace and stable government. In other ways too Cnut was ideally placed for binding both peoples together in allegiance to himself. Swein had been accepted by a large proportion of the thegns as king ; and, as Swein's son, Cnut had some show of legitimacy. This he confirmed by marrying the young widow of King Ethelred, Emma, a Norman princess, whose advent foreshadows the events of fifty years later. In 1019 he became King of Denmark on his brother's death, and to this he added Norway for a time, and even claimed some part of Sweden. He was for most of his reign in England far and away the greatest lord of the Viking world, and so a natural centre of loyalty for English Scandinavians, and a guarantee of peace to his English subjects.

In the north he reigned as a Viking king ; in England as the successor to King Edgar. In England he was a model of piety and good government ; in Denmark the regency of his English concubine, Aelfgifu of Northampton, and her son, symbolised an irregularity of life not uncharacteristic of the Viking world shortly after its conversion to Christianity. At Oxford in 1018, ' King Cnut with the advice of his councillors completely established peace and friendship between the Danes and the English and put an end to all their former strife,' as the official record describes it. The councillors ' determined that above all things they would ever honour one God and steadfastly hold one Christian faith, and would love King Cnut with due loyalty and zealously observe Edgar's laws.' As well as needing exhortation to piety the Danes needed to be paid off, and a levy of Dane-geld which the *Chronicle* assesses at the enormous figure of £82,500 was necessary for this. Forty ships and a number of Viking leaders remained with Cnut ; the rest sailed for Denmark. From then on Cnut's reign in England saw remarkably little incident. He was very well served, both in defence and lay administration by his Danish earls, led by Thorkell and Eric, and in all the aspects of government requiring literacy by his bishops and the clerks of his chapel, led by Wulfstan II, Archbishop of York (1002-23). Through the influence and writings of this distinguished preacher and statesman the character of the English Church and of English government as laid down by Edgar and Dunstan was preserved. Wulfstan first made his mark in the reign of Ethelred, whose laws he framed, denouncing the while the chaos and wickedness of Ethelred's England. Under Cnut he continued to be a leading councillor, to draft laws and to represent in other ways the continuity of English government. Monastic influence in Church and government was still strong ; but there were beginning to be signs of an influential secular (i.e. non-monastic) element in the upper clergy. The clerks of the royal chapel, the men who sang daily mass before the king and maintained all the services of the royal court, and also wrote his letters and charters and carried out any business demanding a literate or an educated hand, were beginning once again in Cnut's later years to find their way to bishoprics. But in most respects the English Church maintained the traditions of Edgar's day ; including the tradition of royal patronage and royal authority. In other respects, too, Edgar was regarded as the model of English kingship. The councillors at Oxford in 1018 ' determined that . . . they would . . . zealously observe Edgar's laws ', thus ignoring Ethelred and the period of anarchy and misgovernment which had intervened since Edgar's death.

In some respects English traditions of government were developed ; in one respect considerably modified. In Denmark and Norway the authority of the kings had always been qualified by the considerable measure of freedom which they were compelled to allow to their leading jarls or earls. A strong king kept his earls in check, won their steady support. A weak king was ruled by them, or ignored or deposed by them. In conquering England, Cnut owed a great deal to his leading supporters. They naturally expected a corresponding reward. A number of them attained high positions in Cnut's court, and he was regularly attended by his Danish bodyguard, his housecarles, who from this time formed the permanent nucleus of the English army. It is a symptom of the change in personnel that the title of the Old English ealdorman came to be replaced by the Scandinavian jarl, or earl. Six of the sixteen earls of this time whose names are known were English, but only one family maintained through Cnut's reign the power it had had under Ethelred. Leofwine, Ealdorman of the Hwicce (Gloucestershire and Worcestershire), was succeeded by his son Leofric, Earl of Mercia, and Leofric's grandsons survived into the reign of William the Conqueror. Another Englishman, Godwin, who became Earl of Wessex, owed his position to his loyal service to Cnut. (Godwin's sons in due course became earls also of Northumbria, East Anglia, and the home counties, and the most famous of them, Harold, was to be the last of the Old English kings.) In Cnut's time the other great earldoms, Northumbria and East Anglia especially, were in Danish hands. Northumbria went first to Eric of Norway, later to Siward, ' old Siward ' of *Macbeth*, whose long reign on the northern border ended only in 1055, and whose son survived the Norman Conquest. Thus the great earls, at first primarily the pillars of Cnut's court and leaders of his army, gradually acquired immense possessions and a territorial power comparable to that which they might have held in Denmark or Norway. In every way but this, Cnut's reign was a constructive period in the history of the English monarchy. When his strong hand was removed by his early death in 1035, the earls came near to dismembering the state.

In 1027, like several of his predecessors, Cnut went on pilgrimage to Rome, to visit the tombs of the apostles and all its many other sanctuaries and holy places. He chose his time well. His visit coincided with the coronation of the Emperor Conrad II by the Pope, and all the princes of the Empire were there ; ' and they all received me with honour, and honoured me with lavish gifts ' as Cnut himself proudly said in a letter which was sent on his behalf to England to describe the scene. At the same time he won privileges for English pilgrims to Rome, and no doubt took the chance to hold conversations with the Emperor, since the frontier between Denmark and Germany was uneasy. The pilgrimage was the characteristic act of a man of conventional piety, and a distinguished patron of the Church ; it also underlined Cnut's determination to act in the tradition of the English kings—and to cut a figure in European society. He was the greatest monarch in northern Europe in his day, and was evidently much flattered to be well received by Pope and Emperor.

4   Anglo-Saxon Institutions

IN ONE of his most brilliant studies, *Domesday Book and Beyond* (1897), F. W. Maitland tried to penetrate behind the description of England made in 1086 and to discover the structure of English society and English law before the Norman Conquest. ' Unless we have mistaken the general drift of legal history,' he wrote, ' the law implied in Domesday Book ought to be for us very difficult law, far more difficult than the law of the thirteenth century, for the thirteenth century is nearer to us than is the eleventh. The grown man will find it easier to think the thoughts of the schoolboy than to think the thoughts of the baby. And yet the doctrine that our remote forefathers being simple folk had simple law dies hard. Too often we allow ourselves to suppose that, could we but get back to the beginning, we should find that all was intelligible and should then be able to watch the process whereby simple ideas were smothered under subtleties and technicalities. But it is not so. Simplicity is the outcome of technical subtlety ; it is the goal not the starting point. As we go backwards the familiar out-lines become blurred ; the ideas become fluid, and instead of the simple we find the indefinite.' [1]

Anglo-Saxon law is difficult and obscure ; but none the less worth study for that. There is no better way of penetrating the minds of our remote forefathers than by trying to imagine what was their attitude to law. Partly this is because they viewed law quite differently from us ; partly because it played a bigger conscious part in their lives than it does in ours.

Modern society is so settled that it takes law for granted most of the time. We assume a community normally peaceable and obedient, directed, but not (in the main) forcibly controlled

---

[1] *Domesday Book and Beyond*, p. 9

by a corps of policemen. We assume that the law on any topic, however absurd or obscure it may be, is reasonably fixed ; that it can be known ; that much of it can be read. Even if we ourselves do not know it, there are solicitors to consult, policemen to obey, barristers to convince the world of our innocence, judges to sum up the results of all this learning —a large professional body, in fact, dedicated to administering the law.

None of these things existed in England before the Conquest —no habit of obedience comparable to ours, no comprehensive code of laws, no class of professional lawyers whose sole business it was to know the law and enforce it. Society was ' lawless ', not in the sense that it had no law—very far from it—but because crime and violence were regarded as normal excesses, not as occasional signs of ill-health in the society. The surviving law-books frequently recur to the problem of how to enforce law—how to detect criminals, how to compel powerful offenders to come to court, how to enforce the judgments of the court. By our standards, government was exceedingly weak, and throughout the Middle Ages the enforcement of law was a haphazard business. This had been particularly true during the Danish invasions, when the cumbersome machinery had almost broken down. It was one of the chief tasks of Alfred and his successors to revive it ; and they faced the challenge so squarely that royal justice emerged stronger than ever before. The royal rights, especially in controlling the courts of shire and hundred, were sufficiently established to survive the second Danish onslaught unscathed.

Such codes as there were dealt with what was exceptional, or odd, or specially needing to be written down ; or else they stated large legal principles in the hope (often vain) that they would become established. One of the reasons why Anglo-Saxon law was excessively complex is that it came from many different sources. It arose out of attempts to codify and rationalise numerous laws of clans, peoples, and kingdoms. We have seen how Alfred used old codes from Kent, Wessex, and Mercia and tried to put together ' those which I liked '. Soon after the Norman Conquest it was said that there were three laws in England : the Danelaw, the law of Mercia, the law of Wessex. This was a desperate generalisation. The old codes attempted to canalise, to direct the progress of legal ideas ; they attempted to stamp a certain measure of uniformity on the diversities of English law. But they were not codes in the modern sense. They were not in the least comprehensive. Indeed, they fail to answer most of the questions we should like to ask about English law before the Norman Conquest.

There was no comprehensive code ; equally, there were no professional lawyers. Some men knew the law better than others ; there have been ' barrack-room ' lawyers in every age. But no-one was a lawyer and nothing else. There were judges, but the judges were kings, ealdormen, bishops, lesser officials, and the lords or their representatives in private courts.

The Anglo-Saxon court had no jury, in anything like the modern sense. None the less, the jury is the one survivor of early methods of legal procedure ; it is the one survivor from the days when the law was essentially unprofessional. Some of the books tell us that the jury system came over with the Conqueror, and is descended from late Carolingian sworn inquests—from those small groups of local worthies who gave information on oath to royal officials in the Frankish kingdoms. Others tell us that it originated in the Danelaw, in the twelve senior thegns of the wapentake (the Danish ' hundred '), who produced a list of the notorious scoundrels in the neigh-bourhood to provide a basis for criminal proceedings. This has a Scandinavian background, and is very close in principle to the later ' jury of presentment ', which performed the same office in the courts of Henry II. But the vital point about the origin of the jury is that it represented a compromise between the way in which courts were generally conducted in early times, and the convenience which all societies have discovered in delegating essential business to small committees. There are plenty of cases in the years immediately after the Norman Conquest of folk being collected in little groups of four or seven or twelve to give specific information. The Danelaw thegns are the only case known before the Conquest ; but there is no reason to suppose that they were unique. Later on we shall see these committees at work, and study the growth of the jury more closely. Our present interest is in the popular courts from whose practice it originally grew.

The essence of early English law is that it was ' popular '

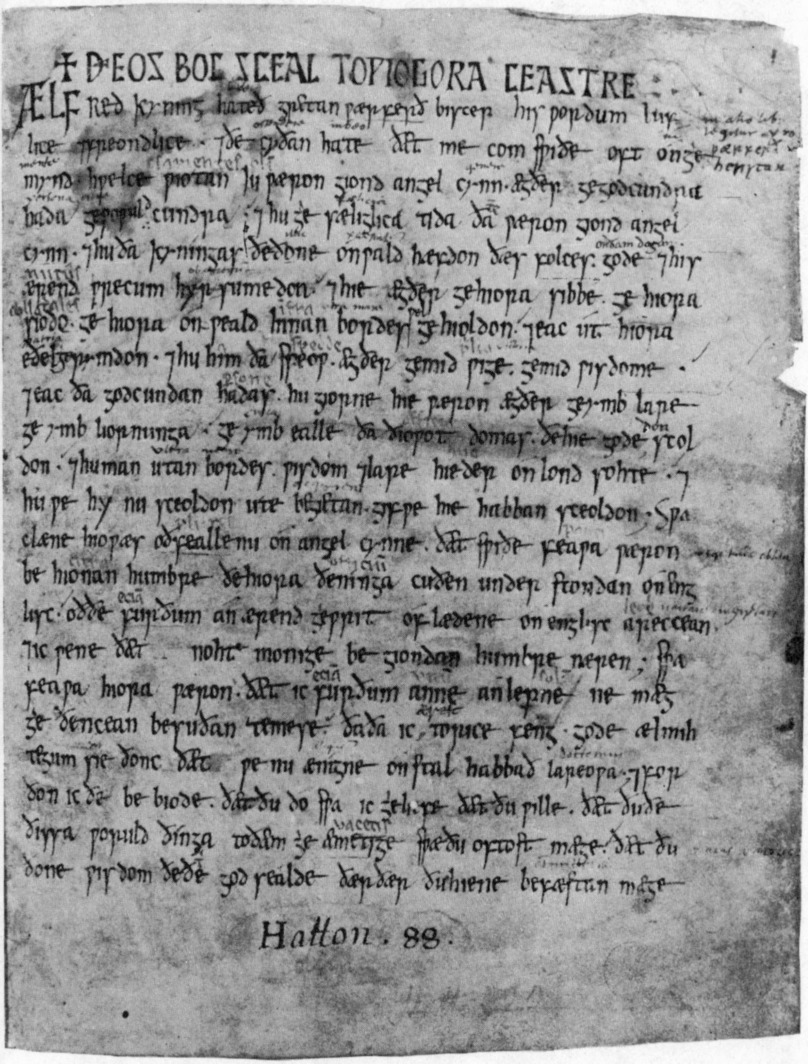

+ ÐEOS BOC SCEAL TO WIOGORA CEASTRE :
Hatton . 88.

Plate 3 KING ALFRED'S TRANSLATION OF THE 'PASTORAL CARE'. Alfred himself arranged for copies of the translation made under his direction of the *Pastoral Care* of Pope Gregory the Great (see pp. 46–7) to be circulated. This shows the first page of the original manuscript sent to Bishop Werferth of Worcester. The top lines read + ÐEOS BOC SCEAL TO WIOGORA CEASTRE ('This book is for Worcester'). 'Aelfred kyning hateth gretan Wærferth biscep his wordum luflice & freondlice ("King Alfred sends greeting to Bishop Werferth in loving and friendly words").' The passage quoted on p. 40 starts on l. 13 (last word: 'Swæ / clæne . . .'). The glosses have been added by several hands; one (e.g. between ll. 5 and 6, at the end) may be the hand of Archbishop Wulfstan (see p. 63). The manuscript is now Oxford, Bodleian Library, Hatton MS.20 (full text and translation by H. Sweet, *Early English Text Society*, 1871).

Plate 4 PORCHESTER CASTLE. Porchester, the 'Roman fort by the port', lies at the head of Portsmouth harbour. The site of the Roman fort was reoccupied in the reign of Edward the Elder (soon after 904), and the outer walls, though they have been largely rebuilt, represent the area of the Edwardian *burh*. In early Norman times, as so often, almost half the space came to be occupied by a castle and a church. The top of the picture shows the castle, with the mid-twelfth-century keep rising above it ; at the foot is the church, also mainly of the twelfth century, and originally the church of a priory of Augustinian canons (founded 1133). Very soon the little town proved too noisy for the canons, who moved inland to Southwick. But not long after, Porchester itself decayed, finally gave place to Richard I's new town of Portsmouth and became merely a fortress.

law. The people at large were the repositories of law ; they were the judges in the public courts. Law represented custom, of which any man with a good memory might be the repository, and local opinion ; it was the one quasi-democratic thing about our early society. The judgments of the 'hundred' court, says Sir Frank Stenton, 'represented the deliberations of peasants learned in the law, who might be guided but could never be controlled by the intervention of the king's reeve, their president.' [1] Guidance was often very important in medieval deliberations. But it was never forgotten that these courts were popular courts.

What was the function of these 'peasants learned in the law'? If we look closer, we find they did almost everything except what a modern jury does. They provided local knowledge. They answered such questions as : Who has held this land in living memory ? Is this man a notorious criminal ? They were witnesses and counsel, so to speak. They also, in theory, stated the law, although they must normally have had to submit to guidance on this point. But they did not normally say whether the party in a criminal suit was innocent or guilty. With a becoming humility they confessed they did not know. Indeed, in many cases it must have been extremely difficult to discover. (Even in the more settled conditions of the thirteenth century hundreds of unsolved crimes might be committed in a single year.) The pre-Conquest court had solid grounds for leaving this question to higher authority. A solemn oath, often on sacred relics, in which the accused man would normally be supported by a team of 'oath-helpers', cleared him of the deed ; or rather, exposed him to the judgment of God, which would be kindly to the innocent, but might later undo the guilty. In early days the oath-helpers came from the kindred of the accused ; in later times from his neighbours and friends, and so constituted a less partial panel of witnesses. The other method of proof was a more direct appeal to divine judgment. 'Among our own forefathers,' wrote Maitland, 'the two most fashionable methods of obtaining a *iudicium Dei* were that which adjured a pool of water to receive the innocent and that which regarded a burnt hand as a proof of guilt.' [2] In the former case the accused

---

[1] *Anglo-Saxon England*, p. 296 : ' never ' is perhaps an overstatement.
[2] Pollock and Maitland, *History of English Law*, II, pp. 598–9

was thrown into the pool : if he floated, he was guilty, if he sank, he was innocent. In the latter case, he was given a red-hot iron to hold ; if he came away unmarked, he was innocent. How these ordeals were conducted, we do not precisely know ; but contrary to what one might expect, it appears that in both cases a suspect had an even chance of escape. Both, no doubt, were open to human intervention as well as to divine.

' The iron which belongs to the three-fold ordeal is to weigh three pounds.' So runs one of the jottings attached to an ordinance of the mid-tenth century ; and its fellow reads : ' A cow's bell, a dog's collar, a blast-horn ; each of these three is worth a shilling, and each is reckoned an informer.' [1] The commonest kind of theft was cattle stealing, and a bell attached to the cow helped the pursuers. So did a good dog. Since there was no police force, the whole neighbourhood had to be roused to the ' hue and cry ' when a thief was to be pursued ; and it was roused by a bugle or ' blast-horn '. The cow's bell, the dog's collar and the blast-horn were symbols of justice as natural and familiar as the policeman's helmet is to us today.

(2) LOCAL GOVERNMENT

Medieval government knew no clear distinction between justice and administration—beween the judicature and the executive, as the eighteenth-century theorists had it. The independence of the English judges is the result of a long and tortuous development. They began as the king's representatives ; and in early days the king himself often presided in his own court. Equally, the presidents of local courts were royal officials, as much concerned with enforcing royal rights, levying taxes, and the other paraphernalia of administration, as with justice. It is for this reason that one cannot discuss the courts and the lawsuits in which they engaged without first surveying the general structure of English local government.

Nothing reveals the continuity of English life and institutional development more clearly than the history of the English shires. With the exception of Lancashire and the four

[1] *English Historical Documents*, i (ed. D. Whitelock), p. 394

counties to its north and the pocket shire of Rutland, all the English shires or counties were established in or before the tenth century. Some represented older units—the kingdoms of Kent, Sussex, Surrey, Essex, Middlesex ; some were of great antiquity as units of local government, like the shires of Wessex. Some grew up round the headquarters of Danish armies— notably round Lincoln, Derby, Nottingham, and Leicester. These were four of the ' five boroughs ' used by the Danes as military centres. Some, including most of the shires of the west Midlands, were artificially created as the power of the kings of Wessex spread north in the tenth century. Recent local government Acts have broken some ' counties' into smaller units ; but this apart, the boundaries of the major areas of local jurisdiction are still today much as they were in the days of Athelstan, Edgar, and Ethelred.

At the same time the smaller unit of jurisdiction, the hundred, was also becoming fixed. The hundreds had grown up in early days in Wessex, haphazardly, and there they were of many different shapes and sizes. In Kent and Sussex they never ousted the older regions, called lathes and rapes, which were of rather larger size than a normal hundred. In the west Midlands they were created at much the same time as the shires ; and here and in other parts of England one finds hundreds of a more uniform size, revealing the origin of the name. There was a much smaller, more ancient unit of land called a hide, traditionally supposed to be land sufficient to support a family. In the course of time it had become the basis of assessments for taxation, and like all assessments for taxation in medieval times it tended to become fossilised. More land might come under cultivation, prosperity might fluctuate ; but the taxpayer found ancient assessments less burdensome than up-to-date ones, and the tax-gatherer found the labour of trying to enforce a new assessment not worth the effort and danger involved. Anglo-Saxon tax-collectors seem to have imagined that they knew what a hide meant in terms of land ; but all we know is what it meant in terms of tax. Since the ' hundred ' court was the place where royal officials and local worthies met to decide how the burden of taxes was to be distributed, there was great administrative convenience in arranging for a ' hundred ' to contain roughly or exactly

100 hides. And so hundreds containing 100 hides—or 200 or 300—were common in the west Midlands.

To us the hundred is an antiquarian memory. The hundred courts have long ceased to meet, though it is not so long since all trace of them died away. The shires are very far from being a memory. These two facts reflect two basic tendencies of late Anglo-Saxon history, which become clearer to us if we contrast what was happening in the Frankish kingdom at this time. In the early ninth century, in the days of Charlemagne, the whole empire was divided into a number of comparatively small local units, called counties. They were units of local jurisdiction ; they were governed by royal officers called counts whose rights and duties resembled those of the later English ealdorman and sheriff. Within the county was a smaller unit, called the *centena*, a word very close to our hundred, though it is doubtful if they were directly connected. When Charlemagne's empire broke up, and the strong controlling hand was relaxed, the counts became hereditary, independent nobles, and often ceased to be royal officials in anything but name. They absorbed into their own body of private rights most of the royal rights they had been set up to administer ; and they and other local notables swallowed the rights and perquisites of the *centena* so that all trace of it disappeared. Many of the counties survived, but as the names of independent principalities, not as units of royal jurisdiction. Private enterprise took over from royal control, and the old organisation was rapidly forgotten.

In England this never happened. Many shires owed their shape to ancient tradition or to the activities of Danish armies But once the pattern of administration had been established in the tenth century, the main lines of local geography remained without alteration for hundreds of years. There were some signs in the eleventh century that the creation of the great earldoms by Cnut might start a movement which would lead to the disappearance of the shires. But this was prevented by the Norman Conquest. The English monarchy was sufficiently strong to prevent the local courts from being swamped by a territorially based nobility. Moreover, the growth in dignity of the ealdorman or earl meant that he became too busy to preside at the court of every shire in his earldom, and in the eleventh century more and more of his duties were delegated to a new official, the shire-reeve or sheriff. At first commonly a protégé of the earl, the sheriff was brought by strong monarchs wholly under the king's direct control ; in his turn the sheriff threatened to become over-powerful, but the Norman kings were able to dominate him, and so make him the pivotal official of English local government.

The story of the hundred courts is not quite so free from ambiguity as that of the shires. The hundred courts began by being, like the shire courts, both royal and popular ; the king had the power of appointing their president, the people were suitors and judges. But in two ways great lords of the neighbourhood might absorb or compete with the king's rights in the hundred. Apart from the royal, shire, and hundred courts there was an ancient body of private courts, ' seignorial ' courts, controlled by lords other than the king. From the tenth century onwards the kings were strong enough to limit and define the jurisdiction of these courts. The courts had very various kinds of jurisdiction—described in the famous jingle ' sac and soc, toll and team and infangenetheof '. ' Sac and soc' referred to the basic jurisdiction of a seignorial court, especially the right to deal with land disputes ; ' toll and team ' granted jurisdiction over cattle as well as over men—the right to levy tolls on cattle sales and the right to give men accused of stealing cattle a hearing. ' Infangenetheof' gave power to do justice on a thief caught red-handed on the estate. They were elements of a crude judicial system, perhaps ; but essential to a lord for two good reasons. They gave him the power to keep elementary order and do elementary justice among his tenants, which was an essential part of any medieval conception of ' lordship ' ; and they provided him with money. Justice, as the medieval proverb had it, was a great source of revenue : *magnum emolumentum iustitia*.

Such was the private court ; and the private court of a great estate could compete with the official hundred court, could even swallow it. Sometimes this was done by open means, and from the tenth century on a great number of hundred courts were granted away, or their usurpation confirmed, by the king. This happened more often after the Conquest than before ; feudal justice in early Norman times was very greedy.

But in most shires in the last century of Anglo-Saxon history the hundred organisation flourished as the meeting-place of local worthies and royal officials—the first breeding ground of the English tradition of administration by discussion and consent.

The special character of English government in the Middle Ages has been called ' self-government at the king's command '. This meant that the king had to listen to what his subjects said ; but it gave him an unusually good opportunity to tell them what to do with some shadow of confidence that they would do it. Only the great met the king in person, in the great council, ' the moot of the wise men ' as it was euphemistically called, the Witenagemot or Witan. But every thegn and many freemen had a chance to meet the royal representative in shire and hundred. Before the Conquest this meant much to the king ; little to the subject. Later on it came to mean more to both.

(3) CENTRAL GOVERNMENT AND THE MONARCHY

In the museums of Scandinavia may be seen great quantities of English coins of the late tenth and early eleventh centuries, all that remains of the immense tributes levied by the Danes from Ethelred and his government. The sums raised in any particular year, varying from £10,000 to £80,000, may not seem startling in modern terms. But the pound now has a tiny fraction of its tenth-century value ; and in the tenth and eleventh centuries, in every European country, the scale of operations was infinitely less than it is today ; even in the twelfth century an English king had normally to be content with an annual revenue of less than £30,000. Towns and markets were small and only slow in growth. A part of the royal revenues was still levied in kind. The first regular silver currency since Roman times had been struck in the eighth century, and its use in everyday life, for buying and selling, for paying rents and for paying taxes, was only slowly spreading. The Dane-geld was paid in what was virtually the only English coin of the day : the silver penny.[1] If we try to imagine

---

[1] Apparently coins of the value of one-third of a penny were struck in Alfred's time ; and throughout the early Middle Ages halfpennies and farthings might be made by cutting a penny into halves or quarters. Apart

Ethelred's subjects going through the process of coining and distributing these pennies, then assessing each hide and hundred for its contribution and collecting these barrowloads of pennies with considerable speed when the Danes demanded payment, we come to appreciate that English government, for its day, had some remarkably sophisticated tools at its command. The mints which struck the coins were subject to an elaborate organisation—perhaps the most elaborate in western Europe. The whole process of taxation, down to the moment when the coins entered the treasury at Winchester in the form of taxes, required large-scale organisation and co-operation between royal officials and the leading thegns of hundreds and wapentakes. All this we may take for granted. But in the early Middle Ages it could not be taken for granted ; that a king could tax directly with a reasonable expectation that most of his subjects would pay up and be fairly treated was a portent.

The Dane-geld was the most direct tax and illustrates the system most clearly. But it was not at this time the most regular or normal source of royal revenue. The Dane-geld was an occasional tax to meet a crisis ; though once the Danish menace was removed, the king levied it for other crises, or imagined a crisis to excuse him for levying so admirable a form of revenue. In principle, as in the sixteenth century, the king lived ' of his own ', that is, out of his private income. As king he was the greatest landowner in the country, and the normal expense of maintaining the royal household was met out of the ancient system of food-farms. Each royal manor or group of manors was responsible for feeding the king's household for one or more days and nights a year—the unit of payment was quaintly called ' the farm of one night '. In early days this is quite literally what happened : a law of King Ine (late seventh century) says precisely how many cheeses and how many pounds of butter and how many eels a lord can demand from ten hides. In practice such highly detailed lists must have been a rough guide rather than a precise tally. Sometimes the food was

---

from coins, payment could be made by weight of silver (or of gold, when gold was available). This explains the pound, the shilling, and the mark, which were in origin weights, and so came to be used very commonly as coins ' of account ' (i.e. in accounting). The mark was two-thirds of a pound, i.e. 13s 4d.

consumed on the manor, if the king happened to be visiting that part of the country ; more often it would have to be carted to wherever the court was staying. When the King of Wessex became King of England, and his court travelled all over the kingdom, the system must have been hard to maintain ; more and more often a part or the whole of these farms came to be commuted for money. This money was collected by the local sheriff, who also collected other items of royal revenue, including profits of justice in royal courts, and brought them to the treasury.

There is no reason to suppose that sheriffs or treasurers were literate : so far as we know, accounting and auditing at Winchester was done without written record, by means of the tally. The tally was simply a notched stick ; the notches registered sums of money. When a sum had changed hands a tally was cut, then split down the middle so that each half showed the identical notches ; one half was given to the man paying in as his receipt, the other stayed in the treasury as its record. Further progress in financial arithmetic, so far as we know, did not come until after the Norman Conquest.

None the less, the sheriff had to have men about him who could read, because he and the other great men of the shire were liable to receive letters from the king containing essential instructions. Before the tenth century messages were mostly sent by word of mouth ; a message or a letter was authenticated by a ring or some other token of the sender. The only formal written instruments of government were charters establishing land ownership, the ' land-books ' as they are called. Most land grants took place without charters ; but under special circumstances, even before the Conquest, written evidence was needed, and institutions whose inmates were literate, like monasteries, were specially keen to possess and preserve written evidence of their most valuable properties and privileges. The charters were usually in Latin, and as time passed their language became increasingly elaborate and increasingly obscure. They reached the height of elaboration in the time of King Athelstan, whose charters describe at length the vileness of the world, and the fearful disasters in this world and the next that will overtake anyone who tampers with the grants described. Formidable documents were produced in many parts of Europe at this time ; but none can compare for pretentiousness and absurdity with Athelstan's. ' If . . . anyone puffed up with the pride of arrogance shall try to destroy or infringe this little document of my agreement and confirmation,' runs one clause from an immense charter, ' let him know that on the last and fearful day of assembly, when the trumpet of the archangel is clanging the call and bodies are leaving the foul graveyards, he will burn with Judas the committor of impious treachery and also with the miserable Jews, blaspheming with sacrilegious mouth Christ on the altar of the Cross, in eternal confusion in the devouring flames of blazing torments in punishment without end.'

When Athelstan granted a large area, Amounderness, in what is now Lancashire, to the Archbishop of York, extreme statements were needed if the grant was to take effect. But the same type of language was also used for quite small grants of land—for anything indeed for which a ' book ' was deemed necessary. It may well be that it was the exceptional contrast between the terms of these fantastic charters and the workaday character of normal business which suggested the use of a simpler document. Whatever the reason, there is no doubt that it was in the English court that the idea was devised of using the simplest kind of document—a mere letter written in English—for grants and instructions to which special thunders did not need to be attached. There could be no greater contrast than that between the old land-book and the new ' writ ', as we call a charter in this simple form. Here is one in which Edward the Confessor greets his successor-to-be : ' Edward the king greets Harold the earl and Tofi his sheriff and all his thegns in Somerset in friendly fashion. And I make known that Alfred has sold to Giso the bishop [of Wells] the land of Litton peacefully and quietly : he did this in my presence at Perrott, and in the presence of Edith, my wife, Harold the earl and many others who were there present with us. We also wish that the same bishop shall hold that land with all its appurtenances which the bishop possesses with sac and soc as freely as any of his predecessors as bishops ever held anything. And if anything be taken away from it unjustly we ask that it may be restored. Nor shall it be done otherwise.'

The writ was a remarkable instrument in its day. It was

a real exercise in literate government in an illiterate age. Being in English, it could be read out to Tofi the sheriff and all the thegns assembled in the shire court of Somerset without any translation or interpretation. It carried, furthermore, large and imposing evidence of its authenticity. The land-book had carried ' signatures ', which were merely crosses supposed to be added by the witnesses of the charter. But the crosses could easily be forged, and a scribe's copy—in which he himself made all the crosses—carried as much weight as an autograph. By the eleventh century the writ carried a seal : a large lump of wax with the impress of the Great Seal of England, which could be shown to an audience to whom a signature would have meant nothing.

Even so, surviving eleventh-century writs are rare, and they were probably never very extensively used before the Conquest. When the custom began we do not know. When we first meet the writ in the late tenth century it has become a bureaucratic instrument of a primitive kind. It was written by one of the clerks of the royal chapel, who were building up what was later to become the royal chancery—the royal writing office, from which came all documents issued under the Great Seal.

It may seem strange to us, who assume the letter as the basis for literate government, that medieval man was so slow to use it. But his assumptions were different ; and the entry of literacy into government was a more difficult and a more fundamental process than is often realised. The writ may have been comparatively little used before the Conquest. But it had a tremendous future before it, and not only in England. Even before the Conquest it symbolised the first real beginnings of literate government, made possible by the specially close alliance of king and Church.

There were in the tenth century only two monarchs in western Europe who possessed power comparable to that of the English kings. Both called themselves kings of the Franks. One of them was king of the area which broadly coincided with what we call France ; king in name that is, because over most of France he had no more stable sway than the English kings in Wales and Scotland. Outside the narrow extent of the royal domain, the ' Île de France ', his influence was slight and fluctuating ; there was certainly no effective structure of royal officials and royal courts. The other Frankish king, the king of what we call Germany, was a far more powerful monarch, the most powerful in Europe. His influence was felt in every corner of Germany ; he ruled through an elaborate hierarchy of royal officials ; his links with the Church were almost as close as Edgar's. There are many interesting parallels between the German and the English monarchies. Both were trying to break down local particularism and the diversity of tradition of the different parts of their kingdom ; both had to struggle against a few great subjects who were determined to carve the kingdom up into duchies or earldoms. In the long run England emerged the more closely knit, the more durable kingdom ; in particular, the structure of royal courts and royal officials was never destroyed, or seriously weakened.

The power of the English monarchy, like that of all medieval monarchies, depended to a great extent on the personality of the king. One can analyse many deep foundations of power —divine right, the force of custom, the idea that the king was in a special sense the people's representative in all his dealings, and the actual instruments of government which we have been describing. It is true that a succession of weak kings between 975 and 1016, and again between 1035 and 1066, failed to undermine these foundations ; that in certain respects the power of the monarchy was even increasing. But it is most unlikely that this could have happened without the strong rule of Cnut from 1016 to 1035 ; and it is probable that some aspects of royal strength would have disappeared had a weak king succeeded in 1066. Every monarchy had to face the problem : either it must ensure a succession of able kings, or face the possibility of collapse.

All medieval kings, in some sense or another, were ' elected '. But when we have said that we have said very little, because no historical label has been susceptible to more different inter- pretations than the word ' election '. To us it means free choice of a representative by a specified body of electors, a choice determined by some kind of majority principle. All these ideas were foreign to the world of thought of the early Middle Ages. Election did not mean free choice, for two good reasons. First of all, the choice lay with God ; the king, once chosen, was king by God's grace. God worked through human agents and above all through the custom of the land. It was custom which dictated how a man became king and who should be chosen. Once again we come up against the maddening indefiniteness of primitive law. When a king died it was usually obvious to the Witenagemot who should succeed him. The leading councillor presented the king-to-be to the Witan, the wise men, who nodded their assent. All early medieval elections seem to have consisted in some form of ' designation ' and acclamation. Who made the designation is another matter. All the documents will tell us is that this or that king was ' elected by the magnates '. How they did it we can only deduce from later cases or continental analogies—or from the result. In 1087, when William the Conqueror lay dying in Rouen, he designated William, his second son, as King of England, and sent instructions to Lanfranc to see to the succession. Lanfranc, as Archbishop of Canterbury, the King's first councillor, and Regent in William's absence, received the instructions from the younger William shortly after the father's death. He summoned the magnates in great haste. In a formal assembly—no doubt preceded by a certain amount of lobbying such as we know to have taken place when Henry I became king —Lanfranc presented William to the magnates. They duly elected him, or, as we should say, acclaimed him ; whereupon Lanfranc set the seal of divine sanction on the new king by anointing and crowning him according to the traditional English rites.

Continental analogies suggest that this would be the normal process. There was no election in our sense. The new king was expected to be next in succession to his predecessor, unless there was some special reason for avoiding the principle of primogeniture. But in practice it was very frequently avoided, and a whole series of somewhat indeterminate notions governed the reasons for overriding it. This meant that there was an element of choice, on somebody's part. But there was no question of a determinate body of electors choosing on a majority principle. Often the choice must effectively have been made in the old king's lifetime. We may be sure that tenth-century kings sometimes designated their successors, as did many of the German kings of this period, and as the Norman kings usually tried to do. When the old king died, a formal election would still be necessary : some leading magnate would doubtless propose and the Witan accept, as they accepted William Rufus ; and then the archbishop would crown, unless as in Edgar's case, there were special reasons for delaying the coronation. When there was serious doubt—as in the anarchy before Cnut's accession—the magnates had to exercise a certain freedom of choice, though doubtless the formal process would be the same. This freedom of choice might or might not have a profound influence on the future of the monarchy. In Germany similar conditions led in the end to the formation of a real body of electors, who chose freely. But in England in the early eleventh century freedom of choice seems to have been an embarrassment, from which one escaped as soon as convenient. There was an element of ' election ' in many king-makings in later medieval England. Sometimes the magnates used these occasions as opportunities to exact special promises from the king. But the English monarchy was never elective in the modern sense of the word.

Nor was it, strictly, a limited monarchy. The king consulted his Witan, and as the monarchy became more civilised and its institutions more complex, effective rule came to depend on the co-operation of more and more people. The more they co-operated, the more the king could govern, the more powerful he was. This formed in a sense a limitation on his autocratic powers. Nevertheless, the Anglo-Saxon king could be a very powerful man. Custom limited his autocracy, but in the vaguest of terms. Churchmen might treat Cnut as a pious protector, a paternal monarch. But to the men who remembered him as the savage young Viking who slaughtered his enemies, his power rested on a different set of qualities. No medieval monarch was wholly successful who could not inspire fear as well as respect in his subjects ; a monarch whom everyone feared could become almost unassailable.

5 The Norman Conquest, 1035–87

ACROSS the English Channel, at its narrowest point, lay another great Viking state, the duchy of Normandy. A Norman princess, Emma, had successively married both Ethelred and Cnut. A Norman duke, Robert I, amiably known to later tradition as Robert the Devil, had gone through a form of marriage with a sister of Cnut. Duke Robert was naturally interested in English politics, all the more because the young sons of Ethelred, Alfred and Edward, were exiles living in his duchy. Had Robert not died on his way back from a pilgrimage to Jerusalem in 1035, it is highly probable that he would have staged an invasion of England on these young men's behalf.

In 1035 Duke Robert died, and his illegitimate son, William, succeeded at the age of seven. His chances of survival seemed slender. His early years were spent in dealing with troubles at home : first with rebellious subjects and then with a dangerous overlord. His duchy was not free from internal and external dangers until 1060, and even then his attention was concentrated on the conquest of Maine until at least 1063. In that year he began to look seriously at his chances of the English throne. He had been in touch with England since his childhood friend, Edward the Aetheling, had become king in 1042 ; he may have visited it in 1051 or 1052, but before 1063 he was too closely engaged in the affairs of his own duchy to think much of foreign adventure. Nature and his fearful upbringing had made William a stern practical man, who ruled by force and not by dreams. But he was also provided with imagination—the imagination needed by a great constructive ruler.

England had been conquered by a Viking leader in 1016, and Cnut's success, and his care to rule in the tradition of his English predecessors, might seem to have left his kingdom secure against another similar conquest. But there were potential weaknesses in Cnut's England which might, if occasion offered, have given a foreign pretender a chance to succeed.

In the first place Cnut died young (1035), and left an uncertain succession. His throne was disputed between his two sons : Harold, his son by his concubine, Aelfgifu, and Harthacnut, his son by his queen, Emma. Each was strongly supported by his mother. In addition, Ethelred's sons, Alfred and Edward, were awaiting their chance. In the event, Harold and Harthacnut succeeded in turn, and Alfred, attempting to intervene, was arrested and cruelly maltreated, and shortly afterwards died. Cnut's two sons each died very young after a short and violent reign, and the way was clear for Edward, later known as Edward the Confessor (1042–66).

Edward the Confessor stepped into an exceedingly difficult inheritance. He had spent most of his life in Normandy and elsewhere on the Continent, and was not personally known to the English leaders. This meant that he could not hope, in his early years at least, to outshine in personal prestige the great earls whom he had inherited from Cnut. In fact they were bound to dominate him until he had proved himself. Edward had some ability, but lacked perhaps the energy and ruthless determination of a successful king. He was not a great warrior, and he never succeeded in mastering the earls. This did not mean that his throne was insecure. He never consummated his marriage, and had no close heirs or rivals—his one nephew died well before him, and his great-nephew was never seriously considered for the throne. There were in fact only two possible alternatives to Edward seriously canvassed before the last years of his reign, the Duke of Normandy and the King of Norway. Duke William was Edward's own choice for his successor, and there was no question of William's trying to usurp Edward's throne. So far as we know, the King of Norway, Harold Hardrada, was not favoured by any of the earls before 1065. It may even be true that it was the threat of foreign invasion which kept them loyal to Edward.

But their loyalty did not make his government easy. In his early years the most powerful of the earls was Godwin of Wessex, the king-maker : the man who had secured the succession of Harold I to Cnut, and probably played a leading part in Edward's own succession. He and his family dominated the south of England and ruled the King ; Godwin's daughter, Edith, was married to Edward. It is clear, nevertheless, that Edward was eager to throw off the tutelage. In itself it was doubtless irksome ; and he knew Godwin to have been responsible for the death of his elder brother, Alfred. Edward waited, gathering round him a group of followers, both lay and clerical, from all over north-western Europe, especially from Lorraine, Brittany, and Normandy. The English court was cosmopolitan as never before. Half the clergy of the royal chapel were recruited from abroad, and it was recognised over a wide area as a place in which an ambitious man might seek wealth and promotion.

In 1051 a Norman, Robert of Jumièges, Bishop of London, was promoted to the see of Canterbury, and Edward received a visit from a leading Norman count, Eustace of Boulogne. These events did not rouse a feeling of national distrust, as some historians have thought ; but they made clear to Godwin and his family that Edward was deliberately surrounding himself with influences more congenial than themselves. Trouble arose between Godwin and the King ; Godwin raised an army and tried to force Edward's hand. But Edward was supported by the earls of Mercia and Northumbria in this crisis, and by skilful manoeuvring he forced the family of Godwin into exile—all save Queen Edith, who was sent into enforced retreat among the nuns of Wherwell. Within a few months Edward had promised Duke William the crown.

Before 1052 was over, Earl Godwin had managed to return and dictate his terms to the King. These included the restoration to the family of their earldoms and to the Queen of her place at court. The brief spell of personal government was over. Godwin himself died in 1053, but his earldom and his standing passed to his eldest surviving son, Harold. The King was no mere cypher in his last years, as he has sometimes been pictured. It is true that he appeared less prone to intrigue, and even less active than before ; that his central interest was the re-founding and rebuilding of Westminster Abbey. He was also compelled in 1052 to dismiss some of his Frenchmen from court, including the Archbishop of Canterbury. But other events seem to show Edward still in control, and a part of

Godwin's earldom went to Edward's Norman nephew, Ralph, who organised Herefordshire on the model of a Norman frontier province. Harold, however, was undoubtedly the first man in the kingdom, the ' under-king ' as one writer calls him, the leader of the English army. Necessity or circumstances had led to something like a true reconciliation between Edward and his wife's family. It may even be that Edward had partly reconciled Harold to Duke William's succession. For some reason now past explaining Harold crossed the Channel in 1064, was captured by the Count of Ponthieu, and rescued by William. Then followed the mysterious arrangement so graphically portrayed in the Bayeux Tapestry. Duke William somehow found the opportunity to cajole or compel Harold into an oath, sworn on the relics of Bayeux Cathedral, to support William's claim to the throne.

The crisis of 1066 came swiftly and with only the slightest of warnings. Tostig, Harold's brother, had been Earl of Northumbria since old Siward's death in 1055. But the Northumbrians owed no natural allegiance to a son of Godwin, and they proved intractable subjects. In 1065 they rebelled and forced the King to appoint Morcar, brother of Edwin, Earl of Mercia, and grandson of Cnut's earl, Leofric, in Tostig's place. At the end of the year the King was known to be dying, and the vultures began to collect. Three men were known to have the ambition to be king : Harold Hardrada of Norway, William of Normandy, and Harold of Wessex. What happened in the King's court at Christmas we shall never know. But in the end he designated Harold of Wessex as his successor ; and on the day after the King's death (6th January 1066) Harold was duly accepted by the magnates and crowned. We do not know what caused the King to change his mind. Either he or those about him must have reckoned that the confusion of the country, the uncertain state of Northumbria, and the threatened invasion of Harold Hardrada, demanded a king who could instantly command the allegiance of a great part of England.

Their calculations were very nearly justified. In his brief reign Harold revealed his skill, determination, and generalship to the full. He is first recorded at York in the early months of the year. Then in May he dealt with an attack by his brother, Tostig, on the south-east coast. This raid was presumed by Harold to be the precursor of an invasion from Normandy, and he mobilised all the military and naval resources at his disposal to meet an attack by William. But these forces could not be held in readiness indefinitely. Early in September the militia was disbanded, and the ships were moved towards London—many of them being lost on the way. Before the end of the month both Harold Hardrada (now in alliance with Tostig) and William of Normandy had landed in England.

The Norwegian came first, and somehow achieved surprise. Earl Edwin and Earl Morcar gathered an army against him, but were checked in a violent battle at Fulford. From now on Harold of England had to rely on his own resources. He was in the south, organising the dispersal of the militia, when the news was brought to him of the Norwegian landing. He marched north with great rapidity, and fell on the enemy before they could have expected him at Stamford Bridge, near York. Three hundred ships or more brought the Norwegian host to England ; twenty-five sufficed to take away the survivors of Fulford and Stamford Bridge. Both Tostig and Harold of Norway were among the slain. Harold of England had won a great and decisive victory. The threat which had hung over the country for twenty years was removed, and rebellion from within his family had been scotched. Harold might well look forward to the fruit of so great a victory : to the prestige of a great warrior and the unquestioned obedience which had been the lot of Athelstan and Cnut after their victories. A few days later he learned of the landing of William of Normandy.

William's preparations had been very swiftly made. He needed ships and supplies, an army more considerable than could be levied in Normandy alone, and he needed moral and spiritual support. To many his scheme must have seemed a desperate adventure. With the resources of a single duchy William was planning to attack one of the richest and most powerful kingdoms in northern Europe, controlled by a soldier as experienced and competent as himself. The odds were heavily against him, and clearly some of his followers told him as much. His critics were what we should call realists, but the destinies of Europe have rarely been decided by *Realpolitik*. William was allowed to go ahead with his plans, and set about gathering support from outside the duchy. The army which assembled on the Norman coast in the summer had been recruited from Normandy, Brittany, Maine (recently made a subject principality), and Flanders, the county of his father-in-law ; with a sprinkling from all over northern France and even from the recently formed Norman states in southern Italy. It was the greatest adventure of the day, and William had given it a coat of respectability by winning papal support. He had claimed at Rome that England was rightly his, that Harold was a perjurer and usurper. The nominal leader of the English Church, Archbishop Stigand, had acquired his see irregularly on the removal of his predecessor in 1052 and held it in plurality with that of Winchester and in defiance of a papal sentence of deposition.[1] William had already won the reputation of being friendly to reform in the Church ; he was in a position to tempt the papacy. The idea was gaining ground in papal circles that even apparently aggressive wars, if fought in a just and holy cause, could be blessed ; the Pope, urged on by Hildebrand, the future Pope Gregory VII, gave William his blessing, and so made the campaign of Hastings something very like a Crusade. The Duke's material preparations—the felling of trees, the building of ships, and gathering of arms and other stores—are very vividly shown in the Bayeux Tapestry. For a number of weeks in August and September the army was held up on the Norman coast by contrary winds. At last, on 27th September, two days after the battle of Stamford Bridge, the wind changed, and William was able to slip across the Channel. He landed at Pevensey, but rapidly established his base at Hastings.

The battle of Hastings was fought on Saturday, 14th October, sixteen days after William's landing, nineteen days

---

[1] There was precedent for holding two sees at the same time in the career of St Oswald in the tenth century (and of more than one of his successors), who combined the bishopric of Worcester with the archbishopric of York. But the circumstances were entirely different. York in the tenth century was a very poor diocese, with a strong Danish element in its population, still in process of conversion to Christianity. Worcester gave Oswald a secure base in the Christian West Country and an income suited to his standing in the kingdom. Stigand had no such excuse: the see of Canterbury had an income sufficient for its needs, and Winchester was probably the richest in the land.

after the battle of Stamford Bridge. The campaign was extraordinarily rapid. After the briefest of pauses Harold hurried south. He left himself no time to collect a substantial army ; but apparently marched into Sussex with his own and his brothers' housecarles, such thegns as had been able to answer his hasty summons and the local levies of the immediate neighbourhood. Nobody has ever explained his haste ; had he waited, he could have collected a far larger army. He may have doubted the loyalty of the southern counties ; he may have wished to protect his own estates, so many of which lay near Pevensey and Hastings. We do not know what intelligence he had ; nor do we know how large a force William had landed. William was reinforced very soon after the battle ; it may be that he had landed only a part of his army, and that Harold calculated on pushing it into the sea before reinforcements came. It is probable in any case that Harold underestimated the Norman strength, and that his great victory in the north had made him over-confident.

The decisive battle was fought between very small forces. Harold had camped his army for the night in a natural defensive position on the edge of the Weald, the great forest of Kent and Sussex and Surrey, nine miles from Hastings, where the town of Battle now lies. It was camped on a promontory of hill, with the forest behind it, and a front of only 500 or 600 yards. Beyond this front lay slopes of varying steepness, up which an advancing enemy must come. It was a strong position, but a very narrow one. Its size suggests that the English army was not much more than 3,000 strong ; and it is unlikely that the effective Norman strength was very much greater. The battle of Hastings was an altogether slighter affair than Stamford Bridge.

Early in the morning of 14th October the Normans began the attack. It seems that they had achieved tactical surprise. Harold hastily organised his camp as a defensive position, placing his best troops, dismounted, shoulder to shoulder along the crest of the hill. Their shields formed a solid and impenetrable wall, and the axes of the housecarles were formidable weapons against the chain mail of the Norman knights.

The battle continued from early morning until dusk. The Norman attacks were beaten off as steadily as the French

charges at Waterloo. At one moment the Normans retreated
in some confusion, and were only rallied by Duke William's
prompt intervention. This retreat proved the undoing of the
English army. A number of the English broke ranks and
pursued the Normans, who, when they had recovered, turned
and cut them down. Later in the day, we are told, the Normans
twice repeated the manoeuvre : they feigned retreat, and then
turned on their pursuers. By such means the English ' shield-
wall ' was gradually whittled away ; and its morale was
constantly impaired by showers of arrows from the Norman
archers. As dusk was falling King Harold himself was killed.
This was decisive. The English resisted some time longer,
and even in their retreat did much damage to the Norman
attackers. But in the end ' the French had possession of the
place of slaughter '.

The death of Harold and his two brothers in the battle
was a vital stroke of fortune for William. If Harold had still
been at large after the battle, William would have had many
difficulties to face. Even so, the English Witan did not
immediately take William as seriously as he had hoped. The
legitimate adults of the large house of Godwin were now
virtually extinct, and the only native heir was Edward the
Confessor's great-nephew, Edgar the Aetheling, whom no-one
had seriously considered hitherto. The Archbishop of York,
the Archbishop of Canterbury, the Earls of Mercia and
Northumbria, and the citizens of London all declared for Edgar.
At this stage they seem to have regarded William as little more
than a lucky adventurer.

William meanwhile returned to Hastings, ' and waited
there to see if there would be any surrender ', and also to
collect his reinforcements. He then began a long roundabout
march on London, via Dover and Southwark, the middle
Thames, and Berkhamstead. This gave him time to subdue the
land between his coastal bases and the city, and to give England
due notice of his methods. William was a pious man ; but
he was also utterly ruthless. He knew from experience that a
successful ruler had to be feared, and he reckoned that this was
even more true of a successful usurper. He harried the countryside as he went, and twenty years later in the signs of declining
value and devastation recorded in the description of the manors

in Domesday Book, the route of his march can still be traced. By the time William reached Berkhamstead most of the English leaders had decided to submit, and on Christmas Day he was anointed and crowned in Westminster Abbey. The ceremony was performed by the Archbishop of York. Stigand of Canterbury had submitted to William, and was left in possession of his see until 1070 ; but as his irregularities had been one of the grounds of papal support for William, the new King could hardly accept anointing from him.

William claimed to have stepped into his rightful inheritance, and at first he took some steps to maintain continuity of rule, as Cnut had done. The main points in the old system of local and central government were continued, but rapidly adapted and developed. For a time the native English earls and thegns mostly remained in possession of their properties. A sufficient number of them had fallen at Hastings to provide the King with land to reward the most outstanding or grasping of his followers. He and his lieutenants began at once to build castles at key places and in many of the larger towns ; symbols to the Normans of normal military organisation, to the English of the beginnings of foreign domination.

William's hopes of succeeding as an English king accepted by the English leaders rapidly disappeared. From 1068 to 1070 he had to deal with almost continuous rebellion in Northumbria and sporadic outbreaks in Wessex and Mercia. The revolt in the north in 1069–70 was made all the more serious by Danish intervention. It was joined by Waltheof, old Siward's son, now the chief power in Northumbria, and royal suspicion drove Edwin and Morcar into the alliance. In the end Waltheof and most of his associates submitted, Edwin was killed by his own men, and Morcar became a fugitive. After 1070 resistance was reduced to guerrilla warfare under such leaders as the celebrated Hereward the Wake, who held out for a time in the Isle of Ely. William's subjection of Mercia and the north was sealed in the same fashion as his original conquest of the south-east, by devastation. His army harried extensive areas in the west Midlands, and he laid waste the vale of York so effectively that large areas of it had to be re-colonised in the twelfth century.

By 1070 England had been conquered and had learned to

fear its conqueror. This did not mean that William was free from wars and rebellions. In France, his position in 1066 had been made secure by the minority of King Philip I, the alliance of Flanders, the submission of Brittany and Maine, and anarchy in Anjou. None of these circumstances was lasting, and in his later years war with Anjou, difficulties in Maine, and the rebellion of his eldest son, Robert, often supported by King Philip, kept him occupied in indecisive campaigns. In England the northern frontier was never entirely quiescent until Robert (in an interval between rebellions), led a punitive expedition in 1080 into Scotland, and strengthened the defences of Northumbria by building a fortress on the north bank of the Tyne at the place still called Newcastle. In England as a whole, the only serious rebellion after 1070 came in 1075. In that year Earl Waltheof allied with the Earl of East Anglia, a Breton whose family had been settled in England by Edward the Confessor, and the Earl of Hereford, son of William's leading viceroy on the Welsh marches, William FitzOsbern ; and the three earls expected support from the Danes, which came too late to help them. Their rebellion was swiftly suppressed. The Breton fled to Brittany ; the Norman, according to Norman custom, was imprisoned and lost his lands ; Earl Waltheof, according to English custom, was beheaded. With him the last of the native earls disappeared from the scene, and although the title of earl has survived from that day to this, the power of Cnut's earldoms was never revived outside the frontier marches of Wales and Scotland.

In 1085 the Conqueror prepared to face the last serious threat to his authority in England, a final attempt at invasion from Scandinavia. Internal troubles in Denmark prevented the attack from developing. But it may well have been this crisis which led William to the great stock-taking which formed the climax of his reign, and underlined the strength of his control over England and the magnitude of the changes he and his followers had made.

In this year the King spent Christmas at Gloucester, and there ' had important deliberations and exhaustive discussions with his council about this land, how it was peopled, and with what sort of men.' Then he sent groups of commissioners to every part of England to collect details of each village from sworn inquests of local men—details which included not only who held what land, but much information about the value of each holding and its stock. These details were collected county by county and then digested in local centres ; and the digests were sent to Winchester for the final version to be made. One of the digests, that for East Anglia, apparently came too late to be included. And so the great survey— ' called by the natives " Domesday " ', as a twelfth-century writer tells us, because it was reckoned to be the final court of appeal in questions of tenure—has been preserved ever since in the national archives in two volumes. Volume I contains the final version of most English counties, volume II is the local digest of East Anglia, never finally revised. There are errors, inequalities, omissions, and incoherences in Domesday Book. But it remains the most impressive record of royal administration in the Europe of its day. It makes modern English historians of the period the envy of continental colleagues. It reminds us that in every sphere of government the elaborate foundations of the Anglo-Saxon monarchy were retained and expanded by the vivid energy of the Normans. Last and not least it is a monument to the imaginative vision and energy of the Conqueror. He may not have conceived the idea, or worked out all its details himself. But only he could have had the energy and confidence to organise so vast an inquiry so swiftly. It is likely that Domesday Book was completed in substantially its present form in little more than a year. While it was being compiled, William confirmed his authority in another way, by a great gathering of landowners at Salisbury, who did homage and renewed their fealty to him. At the end of the year 1086 he left England for his last war in Normandy ; on 9th September 1087 he died.

William was more feared than loved in his lifetime, and his English subjects remembered his oppression, his castle-building, his exactions, his avarice. They remembered, too, some more human qualities : his love of the chase—' he loved the stags as dearly as though he had been their father '— and his love of justice, his piety, and rectitude. ' Though stern beyond measure to those who opposed his will, he was kind to those good men who loved God '—and the chronicler goes on to describe William's benefactions to monasteries, in particular his foundation of Battle Abbey on the site of his victory over Harold. The chronicler might have added that William was the only one of his line who was faithful to his wife. To his enemies he was utterly relentless ; but the final impression is not one of unrelieved oppression. Successful kings in the eleventh century were rarely admirable in their public dealings. But in government William showed the imagination of a creative statesman—crude perhaps, but none the less remarkable for that. Only a fuller analysis of the effects of the Norman Conquest can reveal his essential achievement.

6 Feudalism and the Norman Settlement

(1) ANGLO-NORMAN FEUDALISM

IN THE next three chapters we turn aside from our narrative to analyse English society and the effect on it of the Norman Conquest—concentrating first on the ruling class, from knight to king, then on the life of village and town, and thirdly on the life of the Church. To make the analysis clear we shall cast our eyes back before the Conquest, and forward over at least the first three generations of Norman rule. The life of the village is viewed over the period of the book as a whole. After these chapters we resume the narrative in 1087, and only after we have reached the reign of Henry II shall we try to sum up the whole effect of the Norman Conquest.

Normandy was, so to say, the French Danelaw, the one great French principality which owed its origin to Viking leaders alone. In the days of Alfred and Edward the Elder, Danish and Norse settlers had tried to establish themselves at many points along the French and Flemish coast. But profoundly as they affected the whole of this coastline, the only place where the settlers were powerful enough to oust the local hierarchy for more than a short time was Normandy. In 911 the most considerable Viking chief in Normandy, Rollo, was given some measure of recognition as a subject count by the Frankish king. At first, however, it was easier for the counts of Rollo's dynasty to obtain recognition from their overlord than from their subjects. Rollo was the most powerful of a number of semi-independent Viking leaders, and it was only gradually that his successors enforced their rule in Normandy as a whole. The dukes (or counts, as they were usually called) of the turn of the tenth and eleventh centuries were men of piety, after the rough conventions of their race. They were patrons of monasteries and set their followers an example of lavish generosity. But it is a measure of the uncertainty of their authority, even then, that western Normandy was still largely pagan, and that the bishops of Coutances made no serious attempt to occupy their see before the middle of the eleventh century.

By 1066 Normandy was one of the most highly organised feudal states in northern France. The Norman leaders had accepted the fashions of the day in war, administration, and society as well as in the affairs of the Church. But the duchy had very recently achieved this standing, and accepted these standards. When the Conqueror succeeded to the duchy, there was a tradition of strong ducal rule already established, and a tradition of close liaison between duke and Church. But the immediate situation was anarchic. In the lengthy process of subduing his enemies and establishing himself as effective ruler of the duchy, Duke William was able in many ways to convert his Viking principality into a Norman state ; to bring it into line with French feudal fashions. The Normans were to prove themselves at this period the most adaptable people in Europe, as well as the most energetic. But the rapidity of their expansion and adaptation was partly made necessary by the social changes taking place in Normandy itself.

Already before the Conqueror's accession, Norman bands had begun to seek land and adventure in southern Italy. Many of the great states of northern France were expanding and developing at this time—Flanders, Blois, Champagne, and Normandy's great rival, Anjou. But in the late eleventh century the Normans outstripped them all and founded great states in England and the south of Italy, and also wandered far and wide in the Mediterranean world and the Near East. Norman population was growing fast, and the Normans had somehow acquired or inherited a vigour which made these immense enterprises possible. But there must have been special reasons why they were, notoriously, the most land-hungry people in Europe.

One at least of these reasons is the development of an orderly feudal hierarchy in the Conqueror's early years. This is of special interest to us, because the same men proceeded later to plant feudal institutions in England. This was their dress rehearsal ; and it gives us an opportunity to inquire into the nature of feudalism.

If we wish to understand what Anglo-Norman feudalism was and how it worked, we must first have a clear understanding of two notions which are foreign to us : the attitude of our medieval ancestors to property and their attitude to inheritance. They are the threads by which one may find one's way about what is so unhappily called the feudal system, which I prefer to think of as the feudal labyrinth. Property is a simple idea until one comes to analyse it. A piece of land either is mine or it is not ; it may be let to a tenant ; it may be requisitioned ; but it is mine. Our feudal ancestors had no such simple conception. Property they had—clothes and weapons and jewellery and pots and pans and, sometimes, slaves—but not property in land. In land everyone was a tenant save the king. That did not make even the king owner of the land in our sense of the word ; and there was land here and there which did not belong even in theory to the king.

Indeed, it is best to avoid using the word ' ownership ' in connection with land at all. Land could be held or possessed ; the key words are tenure and possession. The difference between them is quite simple. Possession is a matter of fact ; whoever has hold on the land and is actually exploiting it is in possession of it. Tenure is a matter of right ; the holder of a piece of land must have acquired a right to it from someone else, must hold it *of* someone. The possessor may simply have moved in.

Tenure is the distinctive feature of feudalism. A feudal society was a military society in which land was the basis of the military organisation : by granting out plots of land in exchange for service the king ensured an adequate supply of heavily armed cavalry troopers ; and these knights, as we call them, were the backbone of his army. It was the specific and permanent association of the knights with plots of land which made feudal tenure different from the less organised military society which preceded it ; and it was the close association of land with military service which distinguished feudal tenancies from tenancies such as we are used to. In every plot of land a number of people had an interest, and its produce was divided between them. The share of the peasant, such as it was, and the services he performed, will concern us in the next chapter. The peasant served his lord by working and not by fighting, and so we draw a distinction between the feudal labyrinth which involved the upper classes, ' those who fought ', and, in a slightly odd way, those who prayed, and the manorial labyrinth, which involved ' those who worked ' and subjected them to the needs of the ruling *élite.*

Feudal society was a hierarchy, with the king at the summit and the humble knights, the lowest class of the truly professional soldiers, at its foot. At the time of Domesday Book, most of the land in England was held by the king, by ecclesiastical landlords—bishops, cathedrals, abbeys, minsters—and by about 180 barons. These men, barons and ecclesiastics, were called tenants-in-chief, because they held their land directly of the king. William himself seems to have advanced the theory, early in his reign, that England ought to be able to provide him with about 6,000 knights, and he distributed the land on condition that each baron provided him with what was reckoned a reasonable share of this number ; the greater churches and monasteries were also required to produce their share. Barons and churches were expected to sub-let portions of their estate in return for the service of these knights. Each knight's estate was called a knight's fee. The king had the right, if he wished, to call out the whole feudal host for sixty (later forty) days a year.

So far, the picture is tidy enough ; tidier far than in any other European country. But even in England it was never so simple as this. There never were anything like 6,000 plots of land held by 6,000 knights ; and the ladder of tenure always contained more than three rungs.

Before 1290 the law normally expected a man who held a piece of land to hold it, ' for himself and his heirs ', for ever. Thus if the king granted a piece of land to A, and A re-granted it to B, and B to C, C would continue to hold of B who would hold it of A who would hold it of the king. It was possible for B to contract out of the hierarchy, but it very frequently happened that he stayed in. In time B might grant another manor to A, so that each was tenant (or ' vassal ') of the other. By the late twelfth century the lawyers had discovered that every possible complication could arise.

Land-tenure, moreover, was only one aspect of a complex relationship. The baron did homage and swore fealty to the king for the land he held, for his ' fee ' or ' fief ' or (if it was especially large) his ' honour '. In a ceremony of the greatest solemnity, he knelt before the king, placed his hands between the king's and said, ' I become your man ', promising good faith in all his dealings. This constituted homage ; the vassal then rose, laid his hands on a copy of the Gospels, and swore fealty, faithfulness. The baron's own vassals did homage and swore fealty to him in the same way—and so on, to the foot of the ladder. Homage and fealty were expressions of a very tight, very personal bond ; the bond which held the feudal hierarchy together. It was very difficult for B to be A's vassal for one manor and A to be the vassal of B for another ; at least they had to sort out the relationship in some way, and this was usually done by taking the major tenancy as the key to the situation. A man did liege homage, as it was sometimes called, to the lord from whom he held most of his land, or to the lord who had first given him a fief. But this was never a full answer to the problem, which arose at every level of the feudal hierarchy, even at the summit, where the King of England, as Duke of Normandy, had to do homage to the King of France.

The king's oath to the King of France occasionally influenced his actions. On the whole, most English kings were at enmity with the French king, and paid little heed to their act of homage. But this does not mean that we can take it lightly. It was a solemn matter, and on occasion could be taken very seriously indeed. King John forfeited a great part of his domains in France for taking his oath lightly. The feudal bond, however, was more powerful and more significant when combined with more intimacy than could possibly exist between two rival kings. The structure of law surrounding land-tenure derived mainly from the law of the late Roman Empire, as adapted and modified in the Frankish kingdoms in the eighth and ninth centuries. The origin and atmosphere of the feudal oath is to be sought in the *comitatus*, the following, which we met in the England of King Alfred and, very vividly expressed, in the poem on the battle of Maldon. Loyalty between leader and follower, confirmed by oath, was the deepest obligation a man could have in a feudal society ; just as treachery was its greatest crime. Robbery and murder could be more lightly treated, and they were certainly common ; but no-one took treachery lightly. The vassal swore fealty, faithfulness, obedience, good service, to his lord ; the lord in return undertook protection, justice, and good lordship.

The feudal bond was sacred, but not indissoluble. As we should say, it was a contract ; and if either party broke the contract, the other was freed from normal obligations—was obliged, indeed, to try to restore the contract by force. This game, like all medieval games, had its rules. The vassals of an unfaithful lord were expected to pronounce the breach of faith—the *diffidatio*—in solemn form, as did the barons before Magna Carta. The feudal bond provided a loose cement in a lawless society. Feudal society was in its essence military and violent ; the bond was often broken on a slight excuse, and the complexities of feudal tenure gave plenty of occasion for perplexity, and also for fraud.

The feudal bond, however, was never the only bond in society, the only basis for law and order, least of all in England. It is for this reason that I have insisted on the narrow, legal, tenurial definition of feudalism. The word, indeed, has been very variously used. ' Feudal society ' can be taken to cover all the social arrangements of a society in which feudalism flourished ; that is reasonable enough. It has sometimes been taken by economic historians as a synonym for manorialism, the structure of peasant society, which is merely confusing. It has commonly in modern times been a term of nostalgia or a term of abuse.

Of all the other definitions of feudalism, the most interesting is the military definition. Whatever feudalism was, it was inseparable from a military upper class. It was always looked on as a means of providing a lord with a troop of well-armed, well-trained cavalry. But closer inspection reveals that feudalism did not inevitably accompany a particular type of military tactics. The core of any feudal army was the company of heavily armed knights ; and in a feudal society the majority of these knights were normally provided by feudal military service. But no great military leader of the eleventh, twelfth, or thirteenth centuries reckoned to recruit an army entirely in this way ; all leaders used mercenaries, even among the cavalry. Most of the archers and foot-soldiers in the English army, at least in the twelfth and thirteenth centuries, were paid men.

We still know far too little about military tactics in this period. The English fought on foot at Hastings, and so have usually been supposed to have had no cavalry. They fought with axes, like the Danes. But the Normans could also fight on foot when circumstances dictated, as many did in the battle of Tinchebrai in 1106, when Henry I of England won the duchy of Normandy. Furthermore, the basic equipment of both armies was the same : chain mail, helmet, shield—and the English used sword and spear as well as axe. It has recently been suggested, indeed, that the English housecarles and thegns normally fought on horseback. The question whether English society was profoundly different from Norman is one to which we must shortly turn ; we can say at once that it is doubtful how different they were in military tactics. More certain was the difference in fortification, and this was fundamental, since the defences of a strong castle were the most formidable weapon in eleventh- and twelfth-century warfare. There were few castles in England before the Conquest, and the English fortresses were usually *burhs*, i.e. walled towns. Even so, we know too little about the English methods of defence to be sure that this simple distinction is wholly true ; the early Norman castles were mostly very primitive ; and the significant development was the stone keep—an extreme rarity even in Normandy before 1066.

The heavily armed knight had formed the core of Frankish armies before there was any trace of feudal institutions in the sense in which I have defined them. Feudal institutions in some form survived the great changes in tactics which took place in the twelfth and thirteenth centuries. Vital as were the archers at Hastings, the Norman army more commonly depended for its success on the charge of the heavy phalanx of knights, who might hope to carry all before them by the weight of horse, armour, knight, lance, and shield. In the twelfth century more complex tactics came to be adopted. The knight remained a heavy-weight ; in fact, he became heavier and more expensive. Henry II in the late twelfth century hired him for eightpence a day ; he cost King John early in the thirteenth century two or three shillings. The

Plate 5 PREPARING FOR WAR (1). From the Bayeux Tapestry: preparations for the invasion of England. In this picture we see men felling trees with axes, and shaping planks with an adze; then in the later stages of boat-building (the boats, of course, are out of scale with the men), they work with adze and drill (?) above, and with small axes below (Phaidon Press ed., pl. 38).

Plate 6 PREPARING FOR WAR (2). In this picture swords, helmets, shirts of chain-mail and lances are being carried down to the ships; also other supplies, most notably a vast barrel of wine.

ISTI PORTANT ARMAS AD NAVES : ET HIC TRAHUNT CARRUM CUM VINO ET ARMIS. 'These are carrying arms to the ships ; and here they are pulling a cart laden with wine and arms' (Phaidon Press ed., pls. 40–1).

number of knights expected from each tenant-in-chief had to
be scaled down. From being a heavy cavalry trooper, the
knight was becoming a kind of primitive tank, a change consummated by the arrival of the far heavier plate armour in
the fourteenth century. In the end this development, allied
to a social change which subdivided knights' fees and made
knights more difficult to mobilise, heralded a major alteration
in feudal structure. But it is clear that the history of military
tactics is too loosely connected with feudal history for the
military definition to be helpful.

Feudalism, then, meant the holding of land in exchange
for military service ; respect, obedience, in return for protection. It seems a settled arrangement, if we compare it with
the circumstances under which barbaric warriors had lived
in earlier centuries. But we shall see how artificial and
uncivilised it was when we look at the impact of growing
civilisation on it in the twelfth and thirteenth centuries.

One aspect of its artificiality strikes us at once, for it was
a grave restriction on changes in land-ownership. The plot of
land which was intended to support a particular knight had
been granted by the king to a baron and by the baron to his
knight for the specific purpose of providing baron and king with
a military retainer. King and baron would do everything they
could to ensure that this plot of land continued to provide
them with a knight, and this made them very resistant to any
suggestion that the land should be divided or any part of it
sold. If the knight held it, he could be expected to be reasonably efficient in performance of his service. If it became
divided, endless trouble might be involved in deciding who
should do the service, or how the various tenants should
divide it between them. Many people in twelfth- and thirteenth-
century England had possession of one-half, one quarter, or
one-tenth of a knight's fee ; and these fractions can hardly
have been convenient to the lord.

In strict theory a feudal holding, a fee or fief as it was
called, was not hereditary. When a baron or a knight died,
his heir had to pay a large fine, or ' relief ', to have possession
of his predecessor's land—a relic of the theory that an entirely
new contract was being made. But in course of time a fairly
strict custom of inheritance by primogeniture—by the eldest

son or the nearest blood relation—was established in the upper strata of English feudal society. This partly reflected ancient social traditions ; partly, too, a simple compromise between lord and tenant. The lord wanted his vassal to be succeeded by another able-bodied warrior, and he could reasonably expect his vassal's eldest son to have been trained for the job— the eldest, in addition, was the most likely to be of full age and ready for action when his father died. The vassal would naturally wish to pass on his holding to his family. The normal play of human affection might make him wish to divide it among all his children, or at least to provide portions for his daughters and some kind of support for his younger sons out of the inheritance. From the tenant's point of view a strict rule of primogeniture for the whole holding was better than nothing ; but such a rule was rigid and artificial ; he would undermine it if he could. The efforts of tenants to undermine the unity of holdings in favour of family provision —and the partition of some estates between heiresses—is the explanation of the fractions of knights' fees which one encounters in the late twelfth century and later ; and this partitioning made it more difficult to fasten the duty of knight service on any single tenant.

The history of inheritance was somewhat different on the Continent. No continental monarchy was powerful enough to prevent the partition of many feudal inheritances. The law of Normandy was stricter than most continental laws : it forbade the division of a military holding, while allowing that the elder brother had the moral obligation to provide for his kin as best he might. ' Not upon the Normans as Normans,' wrote Maitland, ' can we throw the burden of our amazing law of inheritance.' [1]

Primogeniture was artificial because it disinherited all a man's heirs save one. From this fact stems a great deal of English social history. In particular, it set the problem of how younger sons were to be employed. There is a story of how an impoverished Norman knight had twelve sons, and scarcely anything with which to endow even the eldest of them ; and of how he sent them to a distant land to earn their bread.

---

[1] *History of English Law*, ii, p. 266

The story is pathetic ; but its consequences were far from trivial. One of the younger sons of Tancred de Hauteville was Robert Guiscard, founder of the Norman principalities of south Italy ; another was Roger, the first Norman lord of Sicily. His grandchildren included Roger the Great, the first King of Norman Sicily, and Bohemund, the most accomplished leader of the first Crusade, the admiration and terror of the Byzantine Empire. In this tale the fearful problem of younger sons in a feudal society and Norman resourcefulness in facing it are both remarkably illustrated.

The barons and knights who came from Normandy with the Conqueror came from a country in which many elements of feudalism had recently become established. In certain respects the feudalism of the Norman settlement in England was more highly organised than the feudalism of Normandy. When William enfeoffed one of his barons with lands in England, he specified the service due from that fee : the number of knights which the baron was expected to settle on his land, the number of ' knights' fees ' he was expected to establish. It might take a number of years for the new tenant-in-chief to distribute the land among so many knights. For the time being he would have to lodge them in his household, as did the first Norman abbot of Peterborough, to the consternation of his monks ; and the word 'knight', *cniht*, originally a servant or household retainer, is an interesting reminder of this stage in the Norman settlement. But once he had placed his knights on the land he was expected to find no less and no more than the number of knights' fees on which the king had decided. If he enfeoffed more knights than the ' service due ', his service was increased ; and there were investigations from time to time to see that this was done. In Normandy the duke had no safe check on the number of knights his vassals enfeoffed. The vassal might well find that his private interests and his private feuds made desirable a larger force than he was bound to produce in the duke's service. Nor could the duke summon the whole of his entitlement on every occasion. The whole host could be summoned for the defence of the duchy ; for lesser occasions or for service with the duke's own lord, the French king, only a fraction could be summoned. Finally, private warfare was forbidden in England, whereas it could only be held in check in Normandy. The difference in practice was not so great: even in England only the strongest of kings could hope to prevent it.

The Anglo-Norman hierarchy consisted, very roughly, of barons, lesser barons, and knights. The barons formed a remarkably homogeneous class of about 180 men. A few of them stood out : in particular, the Conqueror's brothers, Odo, Bishop of Bayeux and Earl of Kent, and Robert, Count of Mortain, both English landholders on a colossal scale. The barons of the Welsh frontier—the ' march ' of Wales—were given property sufficient for them to have the power to resist attack and even to carry out offensive operations on their own. Hence the large endowments of the Earl of Hereford, William FitzOsbern (forfeited by his son for rebellion in 1075) ; of the Earl of Chester, who had large estates in Cheshire and special rights there, as well as immense estates in other parts of England; and of the Montgomery earls of Shrewsbury. But even these were never so eminent among their fellows as the leading earls of Cnut and Edward the Confessor. And all these earldoms save Chester had left the families of their founders before the death of Henry I.

The word ' thegn ' had included every stratum of the Anglo-Saxon hierarchy, from men as well-to-do as the greatest Norman barons down to men poorer than most Norman knights. It originally meant a servant or follower, a member of a *comitatus*. The Anglo-Saxon upper class was differently constituted from the Norman ; it was more loosely knit. Before 1066 several thousand thegns, of every variety of standing, held their tenancies directly of the king. For the most part, only the great held of the king in Norman times ; lesser men were tenants or sub-tenants of the barons. On the whole, too, the Norman military class could be divided fairly easily into two, into barons and knights. There was no fixed line, and it was comparatively easy for a knight who won royal favour to become a baron or for the younger sons of barons to sink swiftly to the level of the poorest knights. But the baronial class was comparatively homogeneous. In Anglo-Saxon society the leading earls had powers and privileges and estates which set them apart from their successors. We have already seen how their power had unbalanced English politics.

In wealth and influence a considerable number of middling thegns came immediately below them, most of whom were comparable in standing to the lesser barons of the Norman period ; below the middling thegns came the large body of lesser thegns, predecessors of the Norman knights.

(2) THE NORMAN SETTLEMENT IN ENGLAND

The question is often asked, was feudalism introduced by William the Conqueror ? What traces were there of feudalism in the time of King Edward ? To these questions very various answers have been given, partly because historians have differed about the facts, partly because the question itself is ambiguous. Medieval men thought in concrete terms, of fees and fiefs ; the idea of feudalism is a rationalisation invented by modern lawyers and accepted by historians as a matter of convenience. ' Were an examiner to ask who introduced the feudal system into England ? one very good answer, if properly explained,' wrote Maitland, ' would be Henry Spelman [a distinguished seventeenth-century lawyer and antiquary], and if there followed the question, what was the feudal system ? a good answer to that would be, an early essay in comparative jurisprudence.' [1] Feudalism, as we have seen, was anything but systematic. It is easy to prove that there was no feudal system under the Confessor ; equally easy to prove that William's feudalism was as near systematic as any in Europe. If we must answer the question, then let us say : under William English feudalism was on the way to becoming the least unsystematic in Europe ; under Edward it had been present only in fragments.

The Normans were extremely adaptable. They could destroy, but they could also pick out from the ruins valuable materials, and make with them buildings more elaborate than those they had destroyed. The Norman Conquest was a catastrophe ; the Anglo-Saxon upper class was almost exterminated in twenty years. But it left behind it strong traces. In an earlier chapter we talked about hides and hundreds. The hide was an ancient unit of assessment ; in origin, it was the land which could support one family—and also, we may now

[1] *Constitutional History of England* (1908), p. 142

add, one fully equipped soldier. But as time passed, equipment became more elaborate and more expensive. St Oswald in the tenth century still reckoned that he could endow a warrior with two or three hides ; but he sometimes increased this number, and on the whole kings and great landowners of that period were tending to think of five hides as suitable support for a fully armed warrior. Needless to say, this was only a rough approximation ; the 'hide' was a very variable measure. But here and there about England, and most notably in the diocese of Worcester, we find traces of a 'five-hide unit', which supplied a fully armed warrior for the royal army.[1] Five hides provided Bishop Wulfstan of Worcester with a warrior and general factotum in 1062, when he became bishop ; the same five hides gave him a knight in 1095, when he died. What we shall never know is how widespread this type of continuity was. We may be sure that the 'five-hide unit' was in the Conqueror's mind when he set about fixing the quotas of knight service ; we may be sure that it did not always solve his problem ; we may be fairly sure that the situation in the diocese of Worcester was more coherent than was common before the Conquest ; and we may reasonably guess that a policy of gradualness would be more successful in the rare cases, as at Worcester, where the pre-Conquest lord survived until after Domesday. The Anglo-Saxon state had collected the materials ; the Normans knocked them into a rough building.

How was it done ? The feudal map of England is infinitely complicated. The holdings of most great barons were scattered about in many parts of the kingdom. The Earl of Chester held a reasonably compact estate in Cheshire, but his broad acres in other parts of the kingdom were widely scattered. Ingenious historians of a former age deduced from this that the Conqueror had cunningly spread his followers' estates, so that they should not have compact domains to form a basis for independent action. It is clear that the motive alleged had

[1] The services of the Worcester tenants were miscellaneous, often including riding on the king's errands, helping in the repair of *burhs* and bridges, and so forth. Some of the more particular services—helping in the lord's hunting expeditions, for instance—formed the basis for a special form of feudal tenure, known in Norman times as serjeanty. This literally meant 'service' : the tenant held his land in exchange for a specific service to the lord, such as looking after his hounds, acting as his steward, or the like.

little or nothing to do with the method of distribution : it is doubtful if such a scheme would have commended itself to the Conqueror, and certain that he could not have accomplished it if he had tried. As it was, in Sir Frank Stenton's words, ' the combination of several thousand small estates into less than two hundred major lordships must have been an administrative achievement comparable with the Domesday Inquest itself.' [1]

No doubt the Conqueror and his followers began with the idea of distributing the immense estates of the house of Godwin fairly widely, but of keeping the lands of lesser men intact. But the process of piecemeal distribution, piecemeal forfeiture, and constant dispute between new tenants about their rights made the pattern increasingly complex. Some of these disputes became *causes célèbres*. For three days the shire court of Kent sat patiently on Pennenden Heath while the Earl of Kent (Bishop Odo) and Archbishop Lanfranc disputed large portions of land. One of the great purposes, or at least achievements, of Domesday Book, was to sort out many outstanding claims.

For the most part, the only estates which passed without serious alteration through the Conquest were those of the greater churches. There were a few exceptions to this ; but to see the sort of thing which happened, let us take four examples from the single county of Wiltshire. Alfred of Marlborough held over 142 hides in the county in 1086, of which 112¾ had been held by Karl, an English thegn, probably of Danish origin, in 1066. William d'Eu held 86¼, of which 77 had been Aelfstan of Boscombe's—Aelfstan had also held most of the land in other shires which William acquired. The largest tenant-in-chief in the shire, Edward of Salisbury, was one of the unusual cases of an Anglo-Saxon thegn who had survived— he lived to found a great family, and his grandson became an earl. But Edward evidently owed his fortune to the Conquest. His holdings in 1086 contained remnants of 32 different estates, his own probably included. Milo Crispin, another large landowner, held much land in Wiltshire once Earl Harold's, much land once held by a middling thegn called Leofnoth, and the estates of five smaller men. [2]

Duke William's reign both in England and in Normandy

---

[1] *Anglo-Saxon England*, pp. 618–19
[2] See *Victoria County History of Wiltshire*, II, pp. 98-112 (R. R. Darlington)

provided many opportunities for social promotion. Many of the families in English history—Warennes, Montgomerys, Montforts, and the rest—who formed the backbone of the baronial class after the Conquest, had made their fortune in Normandy either in the service of William or of one of his immediate predecessors. Few of them can be traced before 1010 or 1020. And the opportunities for promotion did not cease to grow as the Norman dukes established themselves in Normandy and England, and Norman adventurers built kingdoms and principalities in Italy and Syria. Many new baronies were formed in the twelfth century. One of Henry I's new barons married Milo Crispin's heiress. William d'Eu's estate was forfeited for rebellion under Rufus, and so passed back into royal hands, to strengthen the royal demesne and free other lands to endow new baronies under Henry I. Of the estates I have listed, only Alfred of Marlborough's survived as a barony in the later Middle Ages. Social change continued, carrying with it the chance of promotion and aggrandisement.

(3) NORMAN GOVERNMENT

Another question which is often asked is : did feudalism conduce to strong government or to anarchy ? Such a question is not nonsensical. A governing class for whom warfare is a normal kind of exercise is not easy to control : a feudal society was never wholly peaceful. The country feudalised most early, what we call France, was the most anarchic in Europe in its day. Even in England, feudal anarchy flourished in the reign of Stephen (1135–54). But the question itself can never be answered. No king ever ruled by feudalism alone ; most of the problems of government cannot be answered in these terms. Anyone who wishes to understand the politics of this period must study feudalism in all its aspects ; but he must study other things as well. The Anglo-Saxon monarchy survived, developed and strengthened by the Norman kings. The Norman kings, notably Henry I and Henry II, have sometimes been described as anti-feudal. This they could not be ; they were feudal kings in a feudal age, accepting the whole range of values and aspirations of their class. But they were also the heirs of Alfred, Athelstan, Edgar, and Cnut.

This meant, first of all, a close liaison with the Church. William and Lanfranc were as close as Edgar and Dunstan. The partnership was not reproduced by their successors, owing to changes which we shall inspect later on. But the king remained king *Dei gratia*, as was emphasised by Henry II in his later years, when these words became a regular part of the royal style in all official documents. The Normans inherited the beginnings of literacy in government. They had been used to more primitive methods in the duchy. But they accepted what they found, and developed it. The writ was translated into Latin, since English was no longer the common language of the country. But it gained rather than lost in practical use. It rapidly became a normal instead of an occasional instrument of government. Its terseness was admirably suited to the Norman temper. ' Henry king of the English to Ranulph Meschin, Osbert the sheriff, Picot son of Colswein and Wigot of Lincoln, greeting. Go and view the boundaries between my manor of Torksey and my manor of Stow, and have the boundaries vouched for by approved men of the shire ; and if you do not believe them, let them confirm what they say by oath. For my will is that the bishop [of Lincoln] shall truly hold what his predecessors held there. Witnessed by Wigot of Lincoln, at Winchester.' Or even more succinctly : ' Henry king of the English to Almod the archdeacon, greeting. Give back to the abbot of Thorney his manor of Sawbridge (Warwickshire) in the condition in which you received it—and do not let me hear any complaint of injustice. Witnessed by Geoffrey son of Wimund. If you do not do what I say, Ralph Basset will. Witnessed by the same at Westminster.'

These writs were sent to individuals. But most writs were still addressed to sheriffs and shire courts, and there read out and interpreted to the people. The smaller hundred court lost something of its importance, but the Norman kings took stern measures to preserve the shire court as the essential point of contact between the king and the people. In the early days after the Conquest it had been necessary to appoint as sheriffs men of power, capable of handling a dissident population, capable of standing up to the most ruthless of their own colleagues and helping to organise the great redistribution of land. It is small wonder that some of them became bywords for force and greed. Sometimes the king had to intervene to curb their oppressions. But they were the only instruments capable of doing the job. They alone could manage the immense tasks which fell to royal officers and public courts.

In time their strength and their capacity became a serious danger to royal control. They wished their office to be hereditary ; they hoped to absorb more and more royal functions and perquisites into their family rights and inheritance. The Norman kings were slow to intervene. A few of the more unruly were removed, but the problem was not seriously taken in hand before the reign of Henry I. Henry himself tried various experiments. A cleric closely involved in royal administration, called Hugh of Buckland—a man with neither the family ties of a baron, nor the landed wealth which could make him independent, became sheriff of eight of the home counties early in the reign. Sheriffs were more often removed than hitherto. Finally, in the late eleven-twenties Henry felt strong enough to remove a large number of the sheriffs in one stroke. He appointed two trusted lay officers, Aubrey de Vere and Richard Basset, with a kind of roving commission as sheriffs of a large number of counties, whose administration they tidied up. After this the sheriffs were more tightly controlled ; but their opportunities for oppression were still great, and Henry II had to take similar measures in 1170, when he set up a commission to inquire into their doings, and removed most of them. In the long run, other royal officials were to weaken the hold of the sheriffs over the counties.

Henry I began the experiment which was to be enormously developed by Henry II and his successors, of sending itinerant justices on tour, on ' eyre ', to try cases in the shires. The court they sat in bore many superficial resemblances to the shire court ; but when the royal justice was present, the shire court became for a space the king's court, *curia regis*, and acted with royal authority. Thus were born the modern assize courts, and with them a closer liaison between king and shire.

Justices and sheriffs were the principal links between local and central government. The itinerant justice visited the shire, the sheriff reported at the royal court. These reports continued and increased in significance under the Norman kings. The audit of the royal Treasury became a more elaborate and literate affair, conducted in a new office called the Exchequer, set up at the turn of the eleventh and twelfth centuries, and developed under the guidance of Henry I's most distinguished administrator, Roger, Bishop of Salisbury, whose family held the royal treasurership on and off until the early thirteenth century.

The Exchequer took its name from the system of auditing, on a table resembling a chess-board or ' chequer ' (*scaccarium*). The table was divided into columns representing sums of money, and the accounts of each sheriff, and so the whole royal revenue, were worked out by moving counters about in these columns. The audit took place in the Exchequer chamber at Westminster twice a year, at Easter and Michaelmas. The new system of addition, brought in from the Arabs at about this time, not only speeded the arithmetic, but made it possible even for illiterate officials to follow what was being done by observing the movements of the counters. The clerks of the Treasury worked out the accounts meanwhile on great rolls, called Pipe Rolls, and the leading royal officers were present to settle disputes which might arise, to act as judges. The Public Records still contain a Pipe Roll from the year 1130, and something like a continuous set from 1156 until the early nineteenth century.

Treasury and Exchequer were the first more or less fixed departments of government—sometimes at Winchester, sometimes at Westminster. They were the only departments too cumbersome and regular in their activities to move with the king, as did the rest of the court. A description of all the court officials and their perquisites was drawn up just after Henry I's death in 1135, and shows us that the household was still quite a simple organisation. Sixty different types of official are named, from the Chancellor, Treasurer, and chamberlains down to the larderers, fruiterers, ushers, tent-keepers, and wolf-hunters (' 20d. a day for horses, men and hounds ; and they should have twenty-four running hounds and eight greyhounds, and £6 a year to buy horses ; but *they* say £8 '). Great men and small jostle each other in the list, and it has a homely look. Chancery and chapel are still one department though their head has the new style of ' Chancellor ', introduced by the Conqueror. Finance is kept within the province of the Chamber, which originally meant quite literally the king's bedchamber—even if royal treasure for centuries had been kept in separate treasuries. But some of this homeliness is deceptive. The dispensers, butlers, and sewers were great officers of state, leading barons ; so were the constables and marshals. From the larder to a bishop's throne might be only one step, as one of Henry I's clerks discovered. The household, furthermore, was often the scene of great ceremonies, the essential pageantry of medieval government. ' He kept a great state,' says the chronicler of William I. ' He wore his royal crown three times a year as often as he was in England : at Easter at Winchester, at Whitsuntide at Westminster, at Christmas at Gloucester. On these occasions all the great men of England were assembled about him : archbishops, bishops, abbots, earls, thanes, and knights.' In this way the Conqueror had attempted to prove to all his subjects, English as well as Norman, that he was king. The state he kept also emphasised the continuity of English government. He claimed to rule as Edward's rightful heir, and the Normans were very glib in their references to the laws and customs of King Edward, to which they claimed to adhere.

In course of time the Norman kings discovered another great predecessor to whom they could point. Alfred and his supporters had been inspired by lays of their heroic predecessors. In the late eleventh and twelfth centuries, the favourite entertainments in the royal and baronial courts of Europe were the *Chansons de Geste*, epics of feudal warriors and feudal heroes, centring in the court of Charlemagne. A version of the most famous of these, the *Song of Roland*, gave the Norman army heart as it went into action at Hastings. The court of Charlemagne became a direct political inspiration for his successors, the kings of Germany and France ; and it must have given great pleasure to the English kings when Charlemagne found a rival in the British King Arthur. The Arthurian legend only became really active in the second half of the twelfth century, but already in the eleven-thirties Geoffrey of Monmouth had put Arthur on the map in his fabulous history. Arthur appears here in the improbable guise of a twelfth-century Anglo-Norman king. In the central scene of his book

Geoffrey makes Arthur wear his crown at a Whitsun festivity. He describes the solemn ceremonial, the music, the festivities, the tournaments, and the business which occupied the court. If one subdues his exuberant detail and knocks a nought or two off his figures for the numbers present, one can accept Geoffrey's account as a picture of the crown-wearing ceremony in the Anglo-Norman court.

7 Manor, Village, and Town

(1) THE MANOR

IN THE last chapter we studied the king, barons, and knights, who comprised the ruling class. In all they numbered not much more than 5,000 ; in the next chapter we shall add to this the higher clergy. The English upper classes fill the pages of this book, because they controlled the country's destinies, and because 'those who worked' have left little memorial. But it is well to remember that the enormous majority of the million to a million and a half of eleventh- and twelfth-century Englishmen were peasants, farm labourers, or artisans.

Corresponding to the feudal organisation of the upper class was the manorial organisation of the peasantry, of the villages and 'manors'. England in the Middle Ages was a country of small and isolated farming communities. The unit was the village—and a much more self-contained unit it was than anything to which we are accustomed. But within many villages there was a legal, social, and economic institution which historians have reckoned typical of medieval England, and to which they have given the name 'the manor'. The manor was an organisation by which the English villages were fitted to the social structure of medieval England and its economic needs ; and it can be viewed in its social setting—its relation to the feudal hierarchy—and as an economic thing, the source of England's food. But the term itself is odd, and a word about its origin is necessary to make plain what follows. The manor in all essentials is ancient ; but the word itself came over with the Conqueror, and came of age, so to speak, in Domesday Book. The Domesday commissioners collected their description of England shire by shire, hundred by hundred, and village by village. Then their clerks set to work to rearrange the material within each shire into the holdings of each tenant-in-chief ; that is to say, by feudal holdings instead of geographically. All statisticians need units ; the men of Domesday Book expected lists and inventories to consist of concrete things—men and beasts and ploughs and pennies—not of abstract values or theoretical notions. But the ploughs and the stock had been recorded precisely because the commissioners wished to be able to compare the value of one holding with another ; and for this purpose not all ploughs and not all oxen are equal. And so the clerks and commissioners set to work to make their concrete terms just a little abstract. They boldly assumed, for example, that eight oxen made a plough-team, and bullied their statistics to fit the equation.[1] They failed to introduce real uniformity, but for their day they did an impressive task. Some of the results are confusing, some weird. At Stanford in Bedfordshire Alric held a tiny farm directly from the king. ' There is land for half an ox ; and half an ox is there : *ibi est semi-bos*.'

When the clerks rearranged the returns, which had been collected under hundreds and villages, into their feudal segments, a fundamental problem immediately arose. Many villages were wholly the property of one lord ; but many more were not. Villages were thus too variable to be treated as units, and the village had to be replaced by something which might be its equivalent in size, might be smaller, might even, in a few cases, be larger. This difficulty made the fortune of the Latin word *manerium*, which is a version of the French *manoir*. *Manerium* meets us on every page of Domesday Book.

From what we have just seen of the methods of the makers of Domesday, we should expect *manerium* to be at once concrete and abstract. Abstract it was, in that it represented the unit of feudal lordship within a village. But to the men who used the term it conjured up a definite image. *Manoir* in French probably represented *heall* in English—a hall, a strong building of wood or stone in which the lord might or might not reside, but which would at least contain offices, a bailiff, cellars, and storehouses ; a symbol of the lord's authority over the men of the village, or at least of his holding in it. Nor were the clerks disturbed by the fact that in many villages there was no

---

[1] It is unlikely that eight oxen were yoked to a plough at one time : perhaps four was a normal team, and eight allowed for two relays. But there was much variety.

hall. The manor was a concrete and an abstract notion at the same time. This is how we came by the word : the French call it *seigneurie*, that which pertains to a *seigneur*, a lord—a lordship, as we might say.

In the feudal societies of medieval Europe, the manor or *seigneurie* was the irreducible unit of lordship. A feudal society was a society organised for war ; a society whose landed resources were mobilised for the support of knights. The knights, being professional soldiers, had to be supported by the labour of peasants. The manor is the basis of the hierarchical society geared for war ; the sinews of the feudal army. Feudalism could not have existed without manorial or seignorial institutions ; and these in their turn existed at their most developed in just those parts of Europe where feudalism was most developed, that is, in northern France and in England. Nevertheless, the farming unit, the manor or *seigneurie*, was older than the military unit, the 'fief'. In England it was the word and not the substance of the manor which the Normans introduced. The villages of Anglo-Saxon England contained social arrangements and systems of tenure of an infinite variety ; and their history is exceedingly obscure. But so far as one can tell, something like manorial institutions may well have existed in many places as long as the Anglo-Saxons had been settled in the island, certainly as long as the period covered in this book. In many places, but not in all : throughout the Middle Ages there was great diversity in different parts of England.

Medieval villages were small and isolated communities ; their horizon was very limited. We should expect to find great variety among them—variety of methods of cultivation, of social customs, and of economic organisation. In the modern world, diversity is the product of economic specialisation ; our work and jobs, by medieval standards, are highly specialised ; but you meet much the same range in London as in Liverpool or Edinburgh. There was far more regional divergence then than now. One sometimes hears talk of ' the medieval village ' or ' the medieval peasant ' or ' the typical manor ', as if they were types. Eileen Power once said that ' the manor ' was a term about as descriptive as ' the mammal '. We now know that the ' classical ' manor described in the older textbooks was by no means so common or so characteristic of medieval England

Plate 7 (a) DOMESDAY BOOK (reduced). A page from Domesday Book, volume I. This is the last part of the survey for Bedfordshire, describing the land of small tenants. The passage quoted on p. 115 starts on l. 9 of the right-hand column. 'In Stanford tenet Alricus de rege IIII partem unius virgate. Terra est dimidio bovi, et ibi est semibos. Valet et valuit xii denarios. Isdem qui tenet tenuit T.R.E., et potuit dare cui voluit.' 'In Stanford Alric holds ¼ virgate; there is land for half an ox, and half an ox is there. It is and was worth 12d. (per year). The same man who holds it now held it in the time of King Edward, and he could grant it to whom he would.'

(b) A TALLY. After notches had been cut at the right-hand end, the stick or 'tally' was split down the middle; both pieces showed the identical notches, and so formed two halves of a receipt. This tally is of 1294, and is inscribed with the sheriff's name and the ground of payment; it has sixteen £1 notches below, two 1s. and four 1d. notches above. The penny notches are just visible at the right-hand end. (On tallies, see C. Johnson, *Dialogus de Scaccario*, pp. 22–4.)

Plate 8 (a) RIDGE AND FURROW. In 1795 a large area in Padbury (Bucks.) was enclosed by Act of Parliament. The fields in this picture became pasture and the hedges were planted; but the ridge and furrow of the old strips in the open field survive, and can be seen very clearly in this picture. Many of the strips can be identified on a map of 1591, so that it is likely that we are looking at the remains of a medieval open field (on Padbury see Beresford and St Joseph, *Medieval England*, pp. 30–3, 254–7).

Plate 8 (b) PLOUGHING IN THE EARLY ELEVENTH CENTURY. From the January page of a calendar (British Museum, Cotton MS. Julius A.vi, f.3). The team, of four oxen, and the heavy plough, with wheel and mould-board, are very clearly drawn.

as was once supposed. But it still provides the best starting-point from which to pursue the history of the manor.

One meets it in many parts of the Midlands and the north-east, where the land is rich and fertile, where the population was always fairly large, and especially on monastic estates, where the administration was fairly continuous.

In the centre of the village lay church and manor house ; and near them the little streets of peasant houses ; the crofts and tofts—small gardens and fields attached to the houses. The inhabitants of Burston (Plate 9) were evicted in 1488, and the shape of the village, still visible in the turf, remains clear. In the centre lie the vestiges of streets and houses, with tofts and crofts clearly marked ; outside these lay the fields. The rest of the village would be divided between open fields, on which the main crops were grown, meadow for sheep and cattle, and waste land, including woods and forests, which provided timber and game, and acorns and beechmast for the pigs of the lord and of the village community. The villagers lived by growing corn for bread and beer (ale, not milk or water, was their staple drink) ; sheep provided wool, cattle produced hides for clothing, both provided meat for the table. Thus the basic necessities were grown within the village, or at least a major part of them.

Before the days of modern scientific agriculture, the great difficulty was to prevent arable land from becoming stale, to ensure, that is, a reasonable harvest. Against occasional disaster—bad weather, floods, and war—the medieval farmer had little defence. But he developed a certain knowledge of methods of tillage. He knew the value of manure ; and he knew that land benefits from a change and a rest. Where the soil was reasonably fertile and the village population large, the arable fields had to be cultivated as intensively as possible, and so the whole area came to be divided either into two or into three fields. One of these in rotation was always ' fallow '—i.e. it had no crop ; it had a rest for one year in two or three. The other field in a two-field village bore all the year's crops—wheat, oats, barley, peas (such vegetables as they had, like leeks and onions, were grown with the herbs in the toft). In a three-field village, the rotation was slightly more elaborate. Each field was fallow one year ; bore ' winter ' corn (i.e. wheat or rye, sown in autumn) the next ; and spring corn (barley, oats, or peas) the third. The large open fields were elaborately sub-divided ; first into smaller irregular areas called furlongs, then into long narrow strips. The layout of a medieval village may still be vividly reconstructed in places like Laxton in Nottinghamshire, where something of its life still exists, or like Burston, where its outline is still clear in the turf. Outside the village proper (as in Plate 8a), one commonly sees the outline of long strips and furlongs in what was once its open fields. The corrugated turf, ' ridge and furrow ' as it is technically called, which marks the site of old strips, often shows us the plan of the open fields. Not all corrugations are ancient : the raised ridge between furrows dug for drainage was a common way of ploughing enclosed fields in many places down to the nineteenth century. But quite often, when strips continue across a more recent hedge or road, or when their layout can be compared with an early map, it is possible to prove that they represent ancient open fields. The fields in Padbury, for instance, shown in Plate 8a, can be compared with a map of 1591, which shows that the ridge and furrow exactly represent the open fields of Elizabethan times ; and there is no reason to doubt that they are in all essentials medieval.

The twelfth and thirteenth centuries saw more elaborate techniques in the administration of big estates, growing literacy in this as in other types of government. We have treatises on *Husbandry* by Walter of Henley (*c.* 1270) and others ; and we have, for the first time, large-scale, elaborate, and detailed surveys and descriptions of village fields. At this date we find that the strips in the open fields were minutely sub-divided between the various members of the village community. A number may have been held by the lord, though in some cases the land which the lord kept in his own hands, the lord's demesne as it was called, was concentrated ; in other cases there was no demesne. Each peasant's holding was widely scattered, sometimes according to a regular pattern, sometimes quite irregularly. The regular patterns, by which each peasant received a share of many different parts of the open fields, suggest that in an early distribution the land of the village was divided so that every peasant had his share of good and bad land ; or (on occasions) that each new furlong brought under cultivation was divided among the community. The strips originally allocated to each peasant seem often to have amounted approximately to thirty acres (a ' virgate ') or some fraction of this area. It has been suggested that in early days the strips were allocated in proportion to each peasant's contribution to the plough-team.

In many villages all over the country, however, the land was divided in a manner which seems to us wholly chaotic. We find this chaos even in the Midlands, in villages which may well have been originally divided into regular virgate holdings. It was the fruit of that constant debate between common and private interest which is the stuff of life in every moderately primitive agricultural community. The disorder seems often to have been due to prolonged small-scale transferences of land. In various parts of the country at various times the law was theoretically very strict in limiting the extent to which peasant lands could be divided or sold by the peasants of their own free will. How these laws operated is imperfectly known. What is certain is that innumerable minute transactions—gifts, sales, divided inheritances, marriage portions, and so forth—must lie behind the chaos we meet in many thirteenth-century surveys.

Every acre of land was held by a hierarchy of tenants, each of whom expected some return for it. To king, baron, and knight it was part of a knight's fee. To the knight himself, or to whoever was lord of the manor, it was also the source of money dues and labour services ; to the peasant who did the work it meant bread. All this helps to explain the very complex relations between lord and peasants in the manor. Peasant tenure varied as much as other forms of tenure ; but there was one broad distinction, that a peasant was either free or unfree. The freeholders were the aristocracy of the small farmers, and where they were plentiful, as in Lincolnshire or East Anglia, manorial institutions had a less tight control over individuals. The unfree were not slaves. Slaves existed in the time of Domesday, but they were rapidly disappearing, and their work came to be divided between peasant tenants and wage-labourers. The unfreedom of the villeins lay mainly in their being tied to their plots of land ; they were not free to move. Their money, cattle, implements, and other property, furthermore, were technically the chattels of their lord. The villeins were usually burdened with very heavy obligations—they had to work on the lord's demesne two or three days a week, and additional days at times of special stress, at ploughing time and harvest time especially. When we hear about villein tenure in detail in the thirteenth century, we are told of all manner of payments and restrictions. But the villeins had not always been so restricted, and some of the burdensome conditions of their tenure existed more on paper than in fact. We even hear tell of villeins who engaged in trade, and used their villein status as an excuse for not paying their debts. Since they had no property of their own, the argument ran, their goods could not be distrained.

The labour force which worked the lord's demesne was organised by the reeve, usually one of the peasants, under the lord's bailiff. The bailiff had at his disposal the labour force provided by peasant labour services, and on almost all manors a team of hired labourers, which might be small or large according to circumstances. This labour force was organised to do all the work of the lord's demesne, which was run as a large farm. Specialised jobs would tend to be done by hired labourers, the more exalted ones by those village aristocrats, the smith, carpenter, and miller ; but in the really big tasks, ploughing, harvesting, and carting, almost the whole village would do its share. The lord was a man of power, and the capacity of the villagers to stand up to him, to enforce their rights against him, was a very variable thing. Many factors of law, social organisation, and personality played their part ; but the most general factor was economic. When land was plentiful and labour scarce, the labourer and the peasant fared better at the lord's hands ; when there were more men requiring land and work—when land was scarce and labour plentiful—the lord had it more his own way.

The lord's demesne was a large farm run by communal enterprise ; and it was part of a larger communal farm, which comprised the whole village. When the peasants' strips were scattered broadcast over the fields and the lord's mingled among them, the farm work could not be done on an individual basis. Only a very prosperous peasant would own all the apparatus needed, or even plough and oxen. They were often shared ; hence the ' half-ox '. It is clear that the land was often cultivated in a fashion more reasonable than its tenurial divisions imply. Groups of strips, even whole furlongs, might be ploughed or reaped together. Thus a strong element of communal organisation combined with the strongly individual system of possession to make the ungainly manorial economy work.

One fact about the strips remained constant : they were always long and narrow. The reason for this seems to have been that the plough which tilled them was heavy and cumbersome—it was pulled by three or four oxen—and difficult to turn. The strip was designed to give the ploughman as few turns as possible in his day's work. Thus the heavy plough was designed to deal with heavy soils ; and we are immediately reminded that the kind of economy we have been describing was characteristic only of a certain part of England, where the country is open and reasonably flat, and the soil heavy ; in particular, of the claylands of the Midlands and of the vale of York. The layout of the fields in the thirteenth century, furthermore, was the result of centuries of change. The complex distribution of strips is a palimpsest of partition, re-partition, of piecemeal expansion, of a multitude of sales, leases, or exchanges. We return to where we started : in different parts of England there were different patterns, and some of these were profoundly altered by the passage of time. Place and time affected manor and village ; we must take their effects in order.

Open fields gathered round a large village centre were characteristic of the Midlands where the large village is still very common. Isolated farmsteads have always existed in every part of the country, but scattered farms and hamlets, with more compact holdings and small rectangular fields, have always been especially characteristic of Wales and Cornwall and the Lake District. In Wales in particular, this also reflected a radically different social system, but everywhere geography played its part. Hilly country and poor soil did not support large populations. The lighter soils were suitable for rough pasture for sheep and cattle. When crops were to be grown, there was no need for a heavy plough ; and a light plough could conveniently be manoeuvred round a rectangular field. The boundaries of these fields, sometimes great mounds of earth or stone walls, provided (and often still provide today) essential shelter for cattle or crops in the bleaker climate of the highland zone. Earth and stone walls have served the same purposes for many centuries—several millennia perhaps—and some are of immense antiquity.

In a similar way the poorer soils of many parts of England favoured less intensive types of agriculture ; and special conditions have favoured the growth of specialised tillage. Kent, for instance, has always been the orchard of England. These local peculiarities have often been enhanced by local customs and traditions, and historians have sometimes emphasised the identity of geographical and racial frontiers. The country of hamlets and scattered farmsteads is the country from which the Saxon never ousted the Celt. Kent was the home of a whole world of social and legal custom as eccentric as its economy.

When manor and village were coterminous, when the village was a large nucleated settlement, with the houses grouped together, when the bulk of the tenants were villeins, when the lord had the right to call on most of his tenants for labour services ; then the lord's control of his manor was strong, the manorial structure tightly riveted. Such manors were common in the thirteenth century, especially in the Midlands. In no county did they form a majority. On most manors, at least in practice, the lords drew more from rent than from labour. But in most villages of this area the rights of the lord were manifold and carefully maintained.

In strong contrast stand some manors in Devon and East Anglia. Heath Barton and West Town in Devon were two small manors in Domesday Book, but they were never villages. They were the centres of about ten isolated farmsteads. In such cases communal organisation, and the hold of the lord over the village economy, was slight. Similarly, two villages in Cambridgeshire contained between them no less than twenty-two manors. In these cases the manor had lost most of its significance ; it was merely a unit of lordship in a very divided village. Between the extremes of the closely organised and the loosely organised manor lay many varieties. Even in the manorialised Midlands, on the one hand, there lay villages of free peasants, like the village described in Dr Hoskins's *Midland Peasant*. Even in Devon and Cornwall, on the other hand, the lord was no cipher. West Town was held in 1086 by the formidable sheriff, Baldwin, one of the leading barons of the south-west. Personality and circumstance sometimes counted as much as geography and social tradition.

The simplest way to grasp the main outline of manorial chronology—to see the effect of time on the manor's organisation—is to watch the activities of the lord. It was the lord, by and large, who controlled the relations of the manor with the outside world ; and so he was the key to many changes, though not the only key. As soon as we ask, when did lordship start ? we are faced with the first of many insoluble problems, the problem of the origin of the manor. In the past, two fundamental answers were given to this question : either that we inherited the manor from the Roman villa, or that it came much later, because the early Saxon settlements were settlements of free men. Dependent tenure, on the second theory, was the product of time and depression. Both views still have their defenders ; most scholars would say that both were wrong. The first is wrong because Anglo-Saxon village settlements, with very few exceptions, are not on the sites of Roman villas ; they are new creations. The second is wrong because so far as we know there never was a time when most English peasants were free or independent of a lord. Hastings and Woking are well-known examples of a type of place-name which probably originated very soon after the Saxon conquest : they mean ' the settlement of Haesta and Wocca's folk '. Haesta, Wocca, and their like impressed their name on villages, most probably because they were lords of these villages.

To say this is virtually to say that the manor is as old as the Saxon settlement ; it is not to say that the sixth-century manor was identical in form with the manor of the later Middle Ages, nor that it was as ubiquitous as the manor of Domesday Book. We do not know how widespread the manor was in Saxon times. There were villages of free peasants in every century. We know very little about the early manor, save its existence, before the Norman Conquest. That little includes some inkling of the forces of change which were at work. First of all, we know that men were slowly changing and improving agricultural techniques through the centuries—especially by devising ways of increasing the acreage regularly under the plough in many villages, and so supporting a larger population, and in particular by experimenting with elementary methods of crop rotation. The three-field village of the thirteenth century is the product of long centuries of evolution, speeded up by a rapid growth in population between Domesday Book and the end of our period. The years between 1086 and 1272 witnessed a great expansion of the area under cultivation, the 'colonisation' of much land previously waste.

With the progress in technique went progress in other aspects of manorial economy. We sometimes think of our medieval ancestors as if they were in a state of subsistence agriculture—as if a village produced enough for its own support and no more, and was entirely dependent on its own resources. A medieval village was far more self-supporting than a modern one. But we must be careful not to over-estimate this self-sufficiency in the Middle Ages ; and the lord's demesne is a reminder of this. The demesne produce might be used in one of two ways : it might be carted direct to the lord's house and there consumed by the lord, his family and followers, his retinue, his servants, and hired labourers ; or it might be sold for money in a market. The produce of the medieval manor was used in both these ways ; predominantly in the first way, by direct consumption, in the early Middle Ages ; predominantly in the second way, by conversion into money, in the later centuries. In very early days the king let out his manors in return for ' a farm '—the produce sufficient to support the royal court for one day, the ' farm of one night ' ; and other lords did the same. Some part of this system survived for centuries. The manors of St Paul's Cathedral each had so many days or weeks in the year when their produce was supposed to be brought to the brewery and bakehouse of the cathedral to be converted into ale and bread for the support of the canons. The monks of Durham divided their broad acres into two groups ; the produce of those lying near at hand supplied the monastery and its many mouths ; the produce of more distant manors was sold in local markets.

England was on the silver standard from the eighth to the thirteenth century ; its currency was based on the silver penny.

There were halfpennies, farthings, and even for a time thirds of a penny ; it was only in the thirteenth century that rising prosperity and rising prices began to make possible a gold coinage. Thus there was coin throughout our period ; but its use changed considerably. Only gradually did coined money become a regular and essential part of the economy of every village and of every peasant. Only gradually were even the royal food farms converted into money ; by the twelfth century the process was complete.

Throughout the period of this book the change was taking place. More and more the economy of the manor came to depend on sale of its surplus, whether corn from the fields or wool from its flocks or meat from its herds. The permanent markets were in the towns. There were fairs, too, occasional large markets, held here and there for a few days each year. On the whole the buying of more permanent stores—spices and other lasting goods, and to some extent cloth and clothing, took place at fairs ; but the regular buying and selling of goods took place in the permanent town markets of the neighbour-hood. The growth of towns and the changes in manorial economy are thus intimately connected. The surplus corn of the manor went to feed the specialised population of the town, engaged in trade or elementary industry—or, from the eleventh century onwards, went to feed the large industrial population of the cloth-making towns of the Low Countries, along with the wool which provided much of the raw material of this industry. In return, the money provided by these commodities provided lord and tenants with their incomes. The lord could earn money in one of two ways. He could lease the land to a farmer, and so receive the profit indirectly, in the form of rent ; or he could farm it himself and market the produce. When the profits of agriculture were high, there was more money to be made by taking the produce to market oneself. But this was always difficult to organise, particularly on large estates ; and when profits were uncertain, or prices were falling, a steadier return could be ensured by letting the land out to a farmer and living on the rent.

What was involved in the lord's living on rent ? First, money and markets, where the tenants could earn the money to pay the rent. Nor was it only the produce of the manor which had to be translated into cash. The lord's wealth in a highly manorialised village included the labour services of his villeins, an important part of his capital. When the lord ceased direct exploitation through his bailiffs and reeves, he might dispose of labour either by passing it on to the farmer, or, more commonly, by turning it into money like the harvest itself—by demanding more rent instead of labour. Whichever was done, the lord would lose interest in his labour services, and they would tend to become merged into the general structure of rents. But if the lord wished to resume his demesne and to set up as a great farmer on his own account once more, he would need to revive the old labour force which he had allowed to disappear ; many an ancient claim to labour services would be unearthed and claimed once more ; and every effort made to enforce the lord's rights by legal and economic pressure. And this is precisely what happened in the thirteenth century. The population grew ; there were many mouths to feed, more men wanting land ; the price of corn and the value of land went up. For the landlord it meant a boom in demesne farming—a golden opportunity to revive every source of income and of labour to work his demesne. That is why the records of the thirteenth century are so full of references to the enforcement or re-enforcement of labour services. But even at the height of demesne farming, it was not solely by labour services that the demesne was worked—there was need for hired labourers, too, in almost every manor, and money was needed to pay them. All this means that the market played a crucial part in the history of the manor. Produce for market was only a small proportion of the whole produce of the manor, but sufficient to alter the manor's nature fundamentally—just as the sale of cocoa and ground-nuts by peasant-farmers very little removed from the subsistence level is fundamentally altering the economy of large parts of Nigeria today.

In detail, the chronology of the manor is very imperfectly known. Money and markets began to play a decisive part in the tenth and eleventh centuries. In the later twelfth century, when we first have records on any scale, many lords were living on rents, even though labour services were far from forgotten. In the thirteenth century, rising population made land and its produce increasingly valuable, and both market prices and rents rose. Where improved methods of administration made it possible, landlords, especially monastic landlords, farmed much of their land themselves. The manorial economy, in harness with local markets, was at its height.

(2) TOWNS AND COMMERCE

The intimate connection between town and manorial profits can still be seen in places like the port of Alnmouth, built some time in the twelfth century by the Vescy family, to provide a harbour for ships carrying goods to and from their headquarters at Alnwick ; or in the way the great lords of the East Riding of the late twelfth and thirteenth centuries founded ports round the Humber estuary to capture its trade and serve their manors—Hedon (now a village), Ravenserod (now submerged), and the king's town, Kingston-upon-Hull.

The borough in 1086, and even in the thirteenth century, was by our standards a very small affair ; a cluster of little houses often surrounded by imposing walls, perhaps dating originally from the time of Alfred or Edward the Elder, dominated by a great castle built by the Normans. A town of 2,000 souls was a large town in 1086 ; only London, Norwich, and Winchester had substantially more than 5,000 ; only London was a town by modern standards. All the boroughs of Domesday Book had fields and farms attached ; some were in fact small villages. But thirty or forty of the larger boroughs have an interest for us, and had a significance in their day greater than their size would suggest. They had permanent markets, which gave them the essential character of towns ; they had professional merchants, and some professional craftsmen ; they had walls to protect the market ; many of them contained the administrative headquarters of a shire ; they had from the first greater freedom from the close control of a lord than a purely rural manor could hope to have. The liberty of a borough began as a matter of circumstance, and acquired legal status only in the twelfth century. Circumstance usually took the form either of royal lordship, which was often generous to trading communities, or of so great a multiplicity of lordships that no single lord could acquire sufficient control to hamper the town's growth. In the twelfth century, growing pressure from lords and growing wealth in the towns led often to disputes ; in the end many towns acquired charters which guaranteed them the right to farm their own taxes, the right to a share in their own government and the right to manage their own market. The body which managed taxes and government ultimately grew into the town council ; the body which managed the market grew into a market gild, or ' gild merchant ' as it has been called.

The market gave the town its essential character ; walls and liberties were only aids to the market's growth. But now and then the walls came first. Alfred and Edward's *burhs* were sometimes placed where markets existed ; many of them for obvious reasons later became market towns. Every town has its own individual story. In some it even happened that market and traders came after the whole edifice of defence and government had been planned. King Richard I (1189–99) built a new town at Portsmouth ; and in the late thirteenth century Edward I laid out a series of new towns, and then enticed merchants and artisans to occupy them. Not all these new towns succeeded ; some faded away into insignificance. But most grew and flourished ; and the kings did not engage in town-building on this scale before it had become clear that towns were to play a large and growing part in national life.

Long before Domesday Book was compiled London had been the largest and most famous of English towns. At first sight it seems strange that a city which has played so dominant a part in English history should lie so near the south-east corner of the island. It owes its importance to the fact that it has been for long stretches of time the commercial and political capital of England. It first sprang to prominence when Britain was a distant province of the Roman Empire. Its position on the Thames made it a convenient port for visitors from the Continent ; as such it was an ideal base for military conquest, and the Romans made it the centre of their great network of military roads. After the Romans left, London fell into decay, but it was known at least as early as the eighth century as the foremost port in Britain. Though always important in later Saxon times, and always the main centre of commerce in the country, it was never the political capital of the country again until the twelfth century. Indeed, there was no capital, in the modern sense, before then ; the court moved with the king ; only the treasury remained stable, usually in Winchester. But as more offices of state became static, a headquarters had to be found which would suit a king constantly travelling between England and France, and at the same time be a suitable centre on which travellers from all over England could converge. Thus in the days of the Angevin kings some of the conditions of Roman times were re-established : London became once more the political as well as the commercial capital ; the greatest of the royal palaces was the palace of Westminster, a favourite residence since Edward the Confessor had built his great abbey there, conveniently sited only two miles upstream from the city. Even as early as the eleventh century the leading citizens had claimed to have a say in the election of a king.

'Among the noble cities of the world,' wrote William FitzStephen in the eleven-seventies, ' the city of London, seat of the English kingdom, is one which has scattered its fame as widely, carried its wealth and commerce as far, raised its head as high as any. It is happy in its climate, in its Christian observance, in the strength of its fortifications, in the nature of its site, in the honour of its citizens, in the modesty of its matrons ; happy too in its sports and fertile in noble men '— and he proceeds to enlarge on all these aspects of London's greatness, concluding his account of eminent persons born in London with a description of Thomas Becket, in whose honour the author had written his account of the city. He speaks of the churches and schools, of the sports of the citizens, and of many other fascinating aspects of London life. Most striking of all to the historian is the evidence of how much the royal court and mercantile prosperity already meant to the city. FitzStephen describes the royal castles, including the Tower of London in the city itself, and the palace of Westminster. ' Almost all the bishops, abbots and great men of England are, as it were, citizens of London ; they have their own fine houses there, where they stay, where they live expensively, when they are called by king or archbishop to councils, or come to transact their own business.' London, in the author's eyes, was almost perfect, save that there was

' too much drunkenness, and frequent fires ' owing to the compactness with which a great number of wood and wattle houses were crowded within its walls.

Two features of London which particularly impressed FitzStephen were the large public kitchen by the river (with supplies of fish ready to hand) and the weekly horse market just outside one of the gates. To this market came barons and knights in search of good mounts for war, for travel, and for the chase. There were horses there to suit every need, ' for ploughs, for sledges, for carts ' ; and this reminded him of the city's commerce. ' Merchants from every nation under heaven are happy to bring goods by ship to the city.'

The merchants who visited London in the first half of the twelfth century included an Englishman from Lincolnshire called Godric. No doubt he had visited London before, when plying his trade ; on the occasion of which we have information he came *en route* for Rome, where he was making the pilgrimage which was to be one of the early stages of his conversion to the religious life : he later became a monk at Durham and a hermit by the river Wear at Finchale. As a hermit he became famous. Another monk of Durham wrote his life ; and to this we owe one of the few surviving accounts of how an English merchant made his fortune in the early twelfth century.[1] Starting as a scavenger looking for wreckage on the seashore, he acquired enough money to become a pedlar for four years in Lincolnshire. Then he ventured farther afield, to Scotland and Italy ; and soon entered into a partnership, under which he owned a share in a boat, of which he himself acted as captain. Godric was evidently a fine sailor, and his pursuit of gold took him to Denmark and Flanders on many occasions, as well as to Scotland ; and his fondness for travel and the first stirrings of piety took him also to the great centres of pilgrimage, to Jerusalem, to the tomb of St James the Apostle at Compostella in north Spain, and to Rome.

Long-distance trade, from being a rare and occasional thing, was becoming a normal part of the European scene ; and with the growth of trade went a development of many other aspects of mercantile life. Godric and his associates

[1] Reginald, monk of Durham's *De vita et miraculis S. Godrici de Finchale* (Surtees Society, 1847)

were partners in their ship ; and more elaborate forms of joint-stock enterprise were beginning to be common. A wealthy financier would provide money for an enterprise and draw his share of the profits. Increasing use of money meant that money-lending and money-lenders became more common. The profession was particularly associated with the Jews, and Jewish merchants and money-lenders had settled in England under the protection of William I and William II. But not all money-lenders were Jews : if the most famous of twelfth-century money-lenders was Aaron the Jew of Lincoln (whose wealth passed into the royal exchequer at his death *c*. 1185 and whose affairs needed a special department to deal with them), a close competitor was William Cade, a Fleming, who died about 1166. Cade's loans helped the young Henry II to rebuild the shattered royal administration in the years following his accession in 1154.

Cade was a Christian, and therefore (nominally at least) subject to the strict rules of the Church concerning interest and usury. The Church had always set its face against avarice, against the pursuit of wealth for its own sake, and viewed with deep suspicion the progress in economic techniques which took place in the eleventh, twelfth, and thirteenth centuries. Money was the just reward of labour ; but this could not justify a man for letting out his money at interest and so enjoying the profits of a venture in which he had taken no active share. Money, it was felt, ought not to breed money. The effect of this view was partly to limit the financial activities of Christians—and so at first to leave much of the money-lending business in the hands of the Jews—and partly to encourage ingenious evasions. William Cade seems to have used two chief means of evading the rules against usury. Sometimes he pretended to have lent more money than he had parted with so that when the sum was repaid it was enlarged without the fact's being recorded in his bond ; sometimes the loan was secured by a pledge of a piece of land, whose profits Cade drew until the loan was repaid. These remained for centuries the favourite techniques of the Christian usurer ; though others—including various forms of partnership—were also devised. The Church meanwhile gradually realised that money-lending was not always vicious, and that the lender, even if engaged in no physical activity, was involved in the venture to which he lent his aid, and might well suffer if his money was not returned. Subtle distinctions came to be developed between lending upon usury and receiving some payment for the risk involved in lending. The Church ramified its teaching ; but the central doctrine of the wickedness of usury remained unaltered. Down to the eve of the third Crusade in 1189 the Jews were the chief money-lenders in England. In that year England was afflicted for the first time by a wave of anti-Semitism such as had commonly accompanied the preparations for a Crusade on the Continent, and widespread massacres started the decline of the English Jewish community.

The Norman kings had brought Jews with them, and also increased the number of Flemings in the country. Many of the merchants carrying English trade in the twelfth century were Flemings, though Scandinavians and Germans were also common. It was at this time that the close liaison between the Flemish and English economies which played so large a part in English history in the later Middle Ages was finally formed. There were large flocks of sheep in many parts of the country already in 1086 ; by the mid-twelfth century a large share of the wool of English sheep was going to Flanders to be woven into cloth. The export of wool was not new ; but the scale of it was far greater than in earlier centuries. English wool was already made into cloth in England itself, and the cloth industry grew in the twelfth and thirteenth centuries. But in the period covered by this book English prosperity depended above all on raw wool. The finer grades of English wool were the most sought-after in Europe.

In the twelfth century exports consisted mostly of wool, foodstuffs, and other raw materials ; and the towns, though growing, were not centres of large-scale industry. Even the cloth industry, centred in York, Beverley, Lincoln, Louth, Stamford, and Northampton, was to a great extent to move out of the towns in the thirteenth century and later, when the invention of the fulling mill [1] drove the fullers out into country

---

[1] Fulling was the process by which the woven cloth was beaten and compressed in water, and in the process shrunk and given a felt-like surface to make it more durable, with a smoother finish, and also cleaned. The

districts where fast-flowing streams would turn their mill-wheels. Apart from cloth, the most notable English industries were iron, tin, lead, and salt. The twelfth and thirteenth centuries saw rapid development of the resources of the iron-mines in Sussex, Gloucestershire, and Yorkshire. At St Briavels in the Forest of Dean in Gloucestershire all manner of iron implements were made ; they included 50,000 horseshoes ordered by Richard I for the third Crusade. Cornwall and parts of Devon throve on their tin-mines ; from the Yorkshire moors, from Derbyshire, and from the Mendip Hills in Somerset came lead ; and from the lead-mines of Devon the king also extracted much of the silver used by the royal mint. Already in the time of Domesday carts came from far and wide to collect salt from the salt towns in east Cheshire—Northwich, Middlewich, and Nantwich.

The activity of the merchants of the eleventh and twelfth centuries was an important part of the growing economic specialisation of the later Middle Ages. In earlier centuries the large majority of the population had lived near the sub-sistence level ; they could cease to do so only if they could market a perceptible proportion of their crops, especially of their crops in corn and wool. The corn and other food, and to a large extent the wool, too, went to market to provide for the feeding and clothing of men and women who did not grow what they needed : kings and their courtiers and retainers ; barons and knights and their large households of domestic servants ; bishops, monks, nuns, and all the higher clergy ; merchants and artisans—weavers, fullers, dyers, miners, smelters, moneyers, stonemasons, carpenters, and the rest ; shipbuilders and seamen. Royal and baronial courts were growing larger at this time ; and all the classes listed here were increasing. This was only possible because surpluses were being produced for sale in the market ; and because the elabo-rate machinery of commerce existed, or could be developed, to organise the distribution of these surpluses.

---

way in which fulling was mechanised by the discovery of the fulling mill is described by E. M. Carus-Wilson in ' An Industrial Revolution of the Thirteenth Century ', *Medieval Merchant Venturers* (London, 1954), pp. 183–210.

8   The Anglo-Norman Church

THE Normans invaded England under a banner blessed by
the pope.   One reason for papal favour was the contumacy
of Archbishop Stigand, who was finally removed in 1070 and
replaced by Lanfranc.   There could not be a more remarkable
contrast :   Stigand was the very image of old corruption,
Lanfranc one of the foremost monks and scholars of his day.
Lanfranc and William set to work to reform the English
Church.

The contrast between the two archbishops has sometimes
been taken as a symbol of the effect of the Norman Conquest
on the English Church.   The Normans, it is said, reformed a
corrupt, backward, isolated English Church.   But it is now
realised that the truth is more complex, more interesting, and
less flattering to the Normans.   The court of Edward the
Confessor had been one of the most cosmopolitan in Europe ;
it had contacts with France and Lorraine and Scandinavia,
and even with the Mediterranean world and with Hungary.
The English upper clergy were certainly not isolated before
the Conquest.   Nor were they corrupt by the standards of the
first half of the eleventh century—Stigand is no fair reflection
of the general state of the Church.   The monastic reformation
of Dunstan's day had not entirely lost its force ; here and there
—as at Worcester under the saintly Wulfstan II (1062–95)—
monastic reform was in full swing in 1066.   The English
Church was still strongly under monastic influence ; and even
the secular cathedral chapters had all been reformed so that
their canons should follow some kind of organised rule. English
architecture was mean by Norman standards ; but in religious
art, in painting, and probably in sculpture, England had the
mastery in western Europe.   The history of manuscript illumination is continuous from the age of Dunstan to the twelfth

century. Even before the Conquest English styles were penetrating Normandy ; after the Conquest the Norman monks in England adopted the superior techniques of the English ; in course of time a subtle blend of native traditions and new themes produced the Anglo-Norman schools of the twelfth century. In some fields of art the Norman Conquest was a disaster, as in sculpture ; in some it was the reverse of a conquest, as in illumination ; only in architecture did the Conquest bring real development.

The Normans profoundly altered the English Church. In some ways they may have made it better, in some ways worse ; they certainly made it different. If we look at Normandy and England together, and at the whole of the reign of William the Conqueror on both sides of the Channel, we immediately see that in church affairs, as in feudal organisation, the Normans changed themselves as much as they changed the English. There is a sense in which the Normans brought the English Church into line with continental fashions. It might have happened anyway in the late eleventh century, because the changes reflected two great movements which dominate the history of the Church at this time : the reform of the papacy, commonly known after its most dramatic figure, Pope Gregory VII (1073–85), as the Gregorian Reform, and the intellectual revival, which started in Italy and France in the eleventh century, and blossomed all over Europe into the Renaissance of the twelfth century. The papal reform was in part a general attack on clerical standards and clerical immorality. The reformers tried to enforce the rule against simony (the sale of church offices) and against the marriage of the clergy. There had been for centuries laws forbidding the clergy to marry, but they had never been strictly enforced over most of Europe. The papacy could claim that it was simply telling people to obey the law (a modest proposal) ; but in practice, in many places, it was putting into effect a social revolution. To make matters more difficult, the law was still very complicated. The case of Héloïse and Abelard in Paris at the turn of the eleventh and twelfth centuries helps to bring this home to us. After their baby had been born Abelard offered to marry Héloïse. But Abelard was in clerical orders. Héloïse realised that if he married he would be barred from promotion ; she was prepared to remain his mistress for the sake of his career. For once Abelard's affection and sense of honour got the better of his vanity ; he insisted and they were married. That should have destroyed his career in the Church, but there was a loop-hole. Such a marriage could be dissolved if both parties entered religious communities— and in the end, Héloïse became a nun and an abbess, Abelard a monk and (for a time) an abbot. Their story shows something of the tangle of the celibacy laws. It also gives us an insight into what they meant in terms of human suffering. Their passion and tragedy make Héloïse and Abelard unique, but their circumstances cannot have been so unusual. They, and others like them, were victims of the forces of change. Their story illustrates one aspect of the change in discipline for which the reformers were fighting.

Equally important was the attempt to establish papal supremacy on a new footing. It was not that the popes made new claims, so much as that they found new ways of putting their claims into effect. They created what we call the papal monarchy. The princes and bishops of France first felt the force of the new movement of reform at the dramatic synod of Rheims in 1049, presided over by Pope Leo IX in person. At this assembly, conducted in the presence of the relics of St Rémi, patron saint of the city, the pope ordered any of those present who had committed simony—that is, paid money for his office—to confess. Leo was committing a social gaffe, because his host, the Archbishop of Rheims, had won his preferment in this way ; so had a number of the other bishops, including Geoffrey, Bishop of Coutances. But Leo got his way : most of the bishops confessed. And though most of them were reinstated, European society suffered a shock from which the popes did not want it to recover.

Simony had been part of the normal process by which kings and princes appointed bishops, and behind the attack on simony lay the threat of an attack on royal control. Apart from their ecclesiastical duties the bishops were officials of the lay power—royal councillors, providers of contingents for the royal army. In countless ways bishops and abbots had always been pillars of royal authority. Many kings and princes had been extremely generous to the Church, and they expected a return—in two ways. They expected the Church to provide knights and they expected prayers. It suited them to have saintly monks and worldly bishops. But in the papal view bishops were spiritual leaders, pastors, shepherds of their flock —they must be spiritual men ; the Church must be free from lay control. In the last analysis, when pope and king fell out, their divergent views on the function of bishops nearly always lay at the heart of the quarrel. Was the bishop a royal official or a father in God ? The question was never answered : he had to be both.

The papacy claimed to be a spiritual monarchy ; and it claimed in particular to be the fount of justice in spiritual matters. In the twelfth century appeals in all sorts of important and trivial cases affecting ordinary people went to Rome. This was possible because of the development of canon law— the law of the Church—and the intensive activity in the law schools of Europe. Practising lawyers were being taught and textbooks compiled ; research was flourishing. This intellectual activity was affecting all sorts of subjects. Scholars were taking books on law, philosophy, theology, on the spiritual life, on history, and even on science from library shelves, blowing the dust off them and finding a world of new ideas in their pages. Schools sprang up ; students flocked to well-known teachers. A renaissance had begun. Some of this new learning raised difficulties for the Church ; from time to time teachers like Abelard were accused of heresy. But on the whole papal reform and the rise of learning were allies. At least we can say that the papal monarchy of the later Middle Ages is unthinkable without the sensational development in the study of law in this period.

At the time of the Council of Rheims in 1049, the Norman Conquest was only seventeen years away ; a vital coincidence. Even in that time Duke William and his churches felt and absorbed something of the new spirit. It is one thing to preach a reform ; another thing to have it enforced. William the Conqueror won golden opinions from contemporaries and has often been complimented since on his sincerity in the pursuit of church reform. There are many things in his career which make us believe in the reputation ; but there are also passages which lead another way. He looked to the great churches of his duchy (and later of his kingdom) for prayers and for knights ; and he sometimes appointed an abbot or a bishop notable for producing the one, sometimes for the other—sometimes for both. It is perhaps unfair to judge him by the two great warrior bishops, Geoffrey of Coutances and Odo of Bayeux, who fought at the battle of Hastings, since Geoffrey, a scion of the great house of Montbray or Mowbray and later founder of their fortunes in England, had bought his bishopric before the Council of Rheims, and Odo was William's brother. A more characteristic example perhaps was Gilbert Maminot, Bishop of Lisieux. He was the son of a baron and had been chaplain, head physician, and astrologer to the Conqueror. This is how Orderic Vitalis describes him : ' He was very skilled in the art of medicine, learned and eloquent, flowing in riches and good living, beyond measure inclined to have his will and pamper the flesh. He took his ease, and often indulged in gaming and dicing. In Divine Service he was idle and negligent, and always ready and eager—too eager—to hunt and hawk.' Then he passes to his better qualities—his generosity to the poor, his justice and rectitude, his kindness, and his good advice to the penitent ; and his close and friendly relations with his subordinates in the chapter. ' He instructed them in arithmetic, astronomy and physic, and other profound matters, and made them the confidants of his salon and boon companions in his revels.'

From the point of view of an ardent reformer, Bishop Gilbert was an untidy mixture of old corruption and the new learning. From our point of view he seems not a bad example of the material that the Church had to use throughout this period. But the churchman on whom the Conqueror most relied was of a very different stamp.

Lanfranc of Pavia had established his reputation as a master of dialectic and theology before he left Italy as a comparatively young man and settled in the newly founded abbey of Bec in Normandy. He soon gathered a school round him, so that Bec became one of the famous centres of learning north of the Alps. It was often in this sort of way—by students gathering quite informally round a great teacher—that important schools were formed. The organised university grew up only in the twelfth and thirteenth centuries.

As Archbishop of Canterbury Lanfranc found himself abbot of a leading English community of monks, leader of the English Church and first councillor to one of Europe's most powerful monarchs. He entered into all three tasks with great intelligence, energy, and persistence. We must not underestimate him as monk and theologian, nor yet as politician ; but he showed above all in his later years the qualities of a great administrator, and what interests us now is his work as head of the English Church.

Lanfranc's career is an epitome of the story of the Church in the eleventh century. He was born in Italy when new thoughts and new principles of reform were stirring ; as a monk he lived the life from which the inspiration for church reform ultimately sprang ; in Normandy and England he observed the dissemination of, and himself disseminated, the principles to which he had been brought up. He had belonged to a generation in Italy which was alive with new ideas ; but he had grown up none the less before the special direction of the papal reform could be discerned. He accepted the primacy of the Roman see, but not in the active, aggressive form in which it was proclaimed by Gregory VII. In this one respect, Lanfranc was conservative ; and that made him the ideal colleague for the masterful William the Conqueror. Lanfranc's successor, Anselm, had had a very similar career and had been his pupil at Bec ; but he was a generation younger, and was more sensitive to the possible dangers of too close links between Church and state. The result was that, though far from being cantankerous by disposition, he found it as difficult to collaborate with the Conqueror's sons as Lanfranc had found it easy to co-operate with the father.

Lanfranc came to England, not as a Norman reforming the decadent English by Norman standards, but as an Italian representing a new outlook in the Church, which had to struggle for a hearing on both sides of the Channel. In the long run, Lanfranc seems to have found the pulse of the Old English Church ; when he first arrived, he was far from sensitive to its special needs and special glories. He reformed the calendar, showing little respect for English saints. To replace the *Regularis Concordia*, he produced a new code of monastic customs and regulations aimed to bring English observance more into line with modern French customs. He did not try to enforce it outside his own community in Canterbury, but he clearly expected it to be widely used. Lanfranc was interested in making church law and its operation more efficient. He brought his own law-book with him from Bec, and had it circulated. In earlier times there had been no separate law-courts for the Church, and bishop and sheriff had both presided in the shire court. At one of his councils Lanfranc passed a decree establishing church courts separate from the shire—a decree made effective by a celebrated instruction from the king. This combination of conciliar decree and royal writ is characteristic of the close co-operation of king and archbishop. But in some respects Lanfranc's mastery in the Church was storing up trouble for future kings. His frequent ecclesiastical councils, in which the details of reform were planned, gave the leaders of the English Church a sense of community.

Lanfranc himself was only Archbishop of Canterbury; but he compelled the Archbishop of York to admit an entirely novel claim that Canterbury had primacy over York—a primacy of age and distinction it may have had before, but not the primacy Lanfranc claimed. A united Church under Lanfranc's guidance suited the king; and it may be that he found advantage, too, in Lanfranc's wider ambition. Lanfranc pursued his claim to be 'primate of all Britain' further than William pursued his efforts to assert suzerainty in Wales and Scotland. The Norman infiltration in Scotland and Wales was hardly under way in 1087, and Ireland was untouched. But Lanfranc asserted his leadership in parts of Scotland and in Dublin, though the conquest of the Welsh Church did not effectively begin before the early twelfth century; King William made a 'pilgrimage' to St David's over thirty years before a Norman was established there as bishop.

Lanfranc resisted papal intervention except in technical matters like the conferment of the 'pallium', the archbishop's scarf of office, and normal diplomatic exchanges. Simony and clerical marriage he attacked. In his handling of marriage, he was cautious and tactful; and it used to be said that this was owing to the special circumstances of the English Church.

But it was the Norman clergy, not the English, who had the reputation of being among the most uxorious in Europe : two reformers of the period who preached celibacy to the Norman clergy were nearly lynched—one by the clergy, the other by their wives. One of Lanfranc's councils decreed that married priests could retain their wives ; but no married men were to be ordained to higher orders in the future—and this decree seems to have been made to suit Norman as well as English churchmen. In the event it was a couple of generations before this was at all generally enforced among the upper clergy, much longer before it was enforced among the lower.

Lanfranc and his Norman associates, the archbishops of Rouen, with much help and some hindrance from their colleagues on the episcopal bench, and much cautious encouragement and some obstruction from their king and duke, were engaged in the common task of introducing the new European fashions of ecclesiastical life and thought both to the English and the Norman Churches.

(2) THE CATHEDRALS

The Normans altered the complexion of the English Church in two particularly obvious ways : they replaced most of the upper clergy with themselves, and they converted the bishoprics and larger abbeys into feudal baronies. Bishops and abbots always had been leading royal councillors ; now they became the suppliers—sometimes even the leaders—of feudal contingents. Some of them were appointed for their capacity to manage knights and plant them on the estates of suffering abbeys. Not many perhaps : William was too conscientious and Lanfranc too powerful for many cynical appointments to be allowed. But the feudal contingents were often extremely large—several abbeys had to produce forty or even sixty knights.

By the Conqueror's death most of the abbots, and all the bishops save St Wulfstan of Worcester (1062–95), were newcomers. So were a large proportion of the cathedral clergy. The cathedral chapters, indeed, were often completely remodelled. The English cathedrals had been peculiar in being served by two quite different kinds of community. Many were served by chapters of canons ; a few by monks, with the bishop as titular abbot, and a prior occupying the stall of the dean. Monastic chapters were an insular peculiarity, and some of the Normans looked askance at them. But the monastic chapters soon won Lanfranc's patronage, and more were founded not long after the Conquest. The chapters of canons were mostly in a weak state at the time of the Conqueror's accession ; such as they were, they were all under some form of a rule, binding them, in theory at least, to a communal, celibate life. They were not chapters of ' secular ' canons, living independent lives in houses in the cathedral close, such as those to which the Normans were accustomed.

The English cathedrals—Durham, Norwich, Winchester, and several others—are the greatest surviving monument to Norman energy. For their day the Norman cathedrals were immense structures, heavy and usually, before the time of Henry I, crude in construction ; but extremely impressive. They were in marked contrast to their Saxon predecessors. The Saxon cathedral at North Elmham in Norfolk was less than 140 feet long. A Norman cathedral was rarely less than twice this length. The size of North Elmham corresponded with that of churches built on the Continent two centuries before ; recent continental movements had increased the scale of church building tremendously. Sometimes the Normans rebuilt, as at Winchester or Canterbury. Often they moved the cathedral to a larger centre of population, and started afresh, as at Old Salisbury, Chichester, Norwich, and Bath. The last two were monastic chapters, the first two secular ; and at Salisbury Bishop Osmund (1078–99) founded the chapter which was to be the model for most English secular cathedrals, with a dean and dignitaries and a large body of canons, each with a separate income. The close link of bishop and chapter was emphasised by the presence of the bishop's chief officers, the archdeacons, among the canons. The secular chapter, the dignitaries, the archdeacons, were all Norman innovations—not based on any single Norman model, but an adapted version of what was normal in the north of France. In this respect their institutions and their architecture were of a piece. The Salisbury model is derivative, but not purely derivative ; Norman architecture was based on Norman and continental models, but new ideas and new techniques were added to the Norman or Romanesque style in buildings like Durham Cathedral.

Why did the Normans build so large ? The new continental fashions included a love of processions, growing ceremonial of every kind ; demanded, too, a supreme effort to build a stately home for the saint who lived in it. Winchester Cathedral was the highest effort of Norman building ; and it is a symptom of the rapidity with which Norman and English settled down together that it was built to house the shrine of a native English saint, St Swithun.

(3) THE MONASTERIES

Monasteries and monks played a very conspicuous part in the Norman Church ; not quite so conspicuous at court as in the days of Dunstan, but among the people at large, considerably more so. Between 1066 and 1154 the number of monastic houses in England rose from 48 to nearly 300 ; the number of monks from about 850 to well over 5,000—at a time when the total population was perhaps one-thirtieth of what it is today. Counting heads is a crude way of measuring changes in monastic life, but it tells us something. It reminds us that this was the golden age of medieval monasticism. The great religious movement of the eleventh century started in monasteries in different parts of Europe. From 1050 to 1150 a great number of the Church's leaders were monks ; many of the best minds of the day were being recruited into monasteries ; and this was so in England as on the Continent.

The housing of increasing numbers of monks is among the reasons why Norman monasteries and Norman cathedrals were built so large. To understand the kind of changes which were taking place, let us move forward to the middle of the twelfth century, and inspect the life in one of the great Cistercian monasteries being founded and built at that time. Then we can return to compare the Cistercians with the other leading Orders of the day.

The ruins of the abbey of Rievaulx, whose plan we reproduce, still dominate an almost unspoiled stretch of country near Helmsley in Yorkshire. They have been much altered since the twelfth century, but the plan is essentially what it always was—

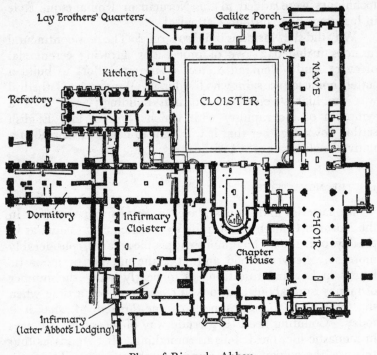

Plan of Rievaulx Abbey

that is, what all Cistercian plans were supposed to be. It lay isolated, surrounded by its own fields and sheep pastures; a large complex of buildings served within and without by its own community. The choir monks maintained divine service and formed the core of the monastic body; a large number of illiterate or semi-literate lay brothers tilled the fields and maintained the flocks. The buildings, like many Norman monasteries, were far larger than Saxon monasteries had usually been; but in the eleven-sixties they had to house 140 choir monks and 500 lay brothers. This was quite exceptional, even among the Cistercians, even at Rievaulx. But the church always had to be large, not only to house the monks, but also to provide chapels in which those choir monks who were priests—as most were—could celebrate daily mass. Next to the church, usually on the south side (as at Rievaulx) to catch the sun, lay the open square of the cloister, surrounded by a covered walk, at this date unprotected against the wind, where the monks could work or walk—an extraordinary and singularly unsuitable survival of the open courtyard of Mediterranean lands, where monastic customs had first been established in the West. Round the cloister lay the main offices and public rooms of the abbey. Above the east walk was the dormitory, where all the monks slept. About two o'clock every morning the community went down a staircase from the dormitory into the church for the first office of the day ; and then after a brief rest, there followed for them the main body of daily offices and masses lasting until about half past eight. Beside the church, beyond the sacristy, under the dormitory, and with its main door in the east walk of the cloister, lay the chapter house. To this room the monks came next, for the daily chapter, where matters of business and discipline and the like were discussed. Then followed a short period for reading in cloister, and a longer period of work in the fields. In the south walk of the cloister lay the door to the most imposing of the conventual buildings, the refectory, the monks' dining-room. They visited it only twice a day at most. After the midday meal (and in summer a siesta) they worked again and read ; then went to church for the evening offices of vespers and compline, and so to bed. Communal prayer, private prayer, spiritual reading, and work in the fields had each their share of the monks' waking hours.

In many respects the Cistercian life differed from that lived in other communities. It was based, like that of most monastic Orders, on the rule of St Benedict, which had grown steadily in prestige since the sixth century when it was written. In the early eighth century a centralising movement in the Frankish Empire had made St Benedict's rule, coupled with additional customs compiled by St Benedict of Aniane, the official rule of all Frankish monasteries. Although this movement rapidly lost its force, the reformers of the tenth century, whether of Cluny, Gorze, or Glastonbury, all looked to the combined works of the two Benedicts as the source of their way of life. This meant a very elaborate ritual filling an ever increasing part of the day ; it meant here and there a flourishing school within the monastery ; it meant that the monks did no manual work. One of the effects of the intellectual revival of the eleventh and twelfth centuries was that monastic leaders came to know more and more thoroughly the ancient books on the spiritual life, and above all, to read them freshly, without the accretions of tradition laid over them, as though they had just been discovered for the first time. The eleventh century saw many groups of hermits, or monks leading something like the life of hermits, formed in Italy and France, under the inspiration of the lives of the desert fathers, and of their great interpreter to the West, John Cassian (of the early fifth century). Some of these developed into real hermit Orders, like the Carthusians. The Carthusian Order has altered least of all religious Orders in the 850 years of its existence. The monks still live in their cells a life of total silence, only meeting occasionally in the church and for conferences. Some of the hermits, however, came to form more normal Benedictine communities. In their way of life the influence of both Benedict and Cassian is very evident. The English Carthusians were few in number, but they included St Hugh, especially famous for combining, in later life, the austerity of his Order with the office of Bishop of Lincoln (1186–1200).

The Cistercians, who first sought their vocation at Cîteaux in 1098, came to be the most famous of these new Orders. They owed their exceptional fame to the groundwork, both spiritual and constitutional, of the third abbot, the English Stephen Harding, and to the dynamic inspiration of St Bernard (died 1153), abbot of the daughter abbey of Clairvaux. Several of the most distinguished of the English houses, including Rievaulx and Fountains, were daughters of Clairvaux, founded under Bernard's own instruction.

It may well have been the founders of Rievaulx, passing through York early in 1132, who fired a number of the leading spirits in the Benedictine house of St Mary's, York, with a desire to follow the Cistercians into uninhabited places. St Mary's lay near the heart of a busy city ; the Cistercians looked for the silence and solitude of a deserted spot away from the cities. They looked for solitude for the community, and for space for fields which their own lay brothers could till. The Benedictine abbeys were often in cities, and they had no lay brothers, so that it did not matter to them if their estates were not compact and close. So vital, indeed, was solitude to the Cistercians, that on occasion they created it by moving villages, almost like an eighteenth-century landowner laying out a park.

The insurgent group in St Mary's, York, prepared to leave the abbey late in 1132. The abbot refused his permission—he did not wish to lose so many of his best monks. The monks appealed to the Archbishop of York, Thurstan, who was sympathetic. The archbishop visited St Mary's, but was mobbed by the abbot's party, and had to take refuge, with the monks who had appealed to him, in the abbey church. In the end he and they escaped, and the group of monks, now in touch with St Bernard, were established in a remote and wild spot near Ripon, given to them by Thurstan. To the modern visitor the ruins of Fountains, made more romantic by the skill of an eighteenth-century landscape gardener, have a unique enchantment. But they are the memorial of a very exacting life ; and before the great stone buildings went up, when the first community lived in temporary huts round the great elm which gave them their first shelter, life there must have been exceedingly austere.

The most distinguished of the English Cistercians was St Ailred, the third abbot of Rievaulx. We can get quite an intimate picture of this attractive, patriarchal abbot from the contemporary life written by his disciple, Walter Daniel. Ailred was a kindly, friendly superior—he gave his monks more opportunity for discussion, more spiritual conferences, than can have been common. One has the impression that human relations were more intimate and life less severe than in some communities ; but physical conditions were certainly austere, and Ailred himself gave a stern example of asceticism. His biographer, however, quotes him as saying that ' it is the singular and supreme glory of the house of Rievaulx that above all else it teaches tolerance of the infirm and compassion with others in their necessities.' This is a very attractive quality, and helps us to understand Walter's famous remark that on feast days you might see the church crowded with the brethren like bees in a hive, ' unable to move forward because of the multitude, clustered together, rather, and compacted into one angelical body '. Rievaulx was a haven of peace for the many rather than a home of strict vocation ; and this is a striking fact, because one of St Bernard's most telling charges against Cluny was that it let monks in without a strict noviciate. The Cistercians recruited over 1,400 choir monks and founded over fifty houses in their first twenty-five years in England, and this sensational growth can be paralleled in many parts of western Europe. It shows that they were never very strict in accepting candidates. To us the monastic vocation seems a very special one, suitable only for the few. In their first enthusiasm the Cistercians, like many other religious Orders and movements, felt themselves to have found the best path to heaven, and found it difficult to deny access to any man. In their early days they attracted a wide variety of character and talent, including many of the best minds of the age. They were in the forefront of several movements, and contemporaries felt them to be so. In one of his letters St Bernard compared the spiritual life to Jacob's ladder, on which the angels went up and down but did not stand still. So, he argues, in the spiritual life, ' you mount—or you fall : you cannot stay still '. There were bad monks and evil influences even then ; but down to the third quarter of the twelfth century many communities seemed to be mounting.

(4) THE SCHOOLS

One of the movements in which monks played a leading part in the late eleventh and early twelfth centuries was the revival of intellectual life. North of the Alps monastic libraries played a part only second to cathedral libraries in supplying the material for the revival. It is significant that three of the greatest names in Italian learning in the eleventh century, Peter Damian, Lanfranc, and Anselm, became monks. Two of these men became Archbishops of Canterbury. The upper clergy formed a thoroughly cosmopolitan society. The clergy had an international language, Latin ; they came and went freely in the schools of western Europe, especially in France and Italy. There was still much freedom in the organisation of these schools : the reputation of a great teacher could make a school, his disappearance mar it. It was only as the twelfth century went on that university organisation began to crystallise ; but already at the opening of the century Bologna

Plate 9 A LOST VILLAGE. Burston (Bucks.) was enclosed and depopulated in 1488: we are looking at the unaltered plan of a medieval village. This photograph gives a clear idea of the shape of the village, with streets running between rectangular plots, which represent the crofts (or gardens) of the villagers. The track running diagonally across the top of the village was evidently its main street. Outside the village centre lay the open fields. (See Beresford and St Joseph, *Medieval England*, pp. 115–16; see also p. 119 for a photograph in which the corrugations of an open field start where the streets and crofts of a lost village end.)

Plate 10 (*a*) KING EDGAR PRESENTS A CHARTER TO NEW MINSTER, WINCHESTER (British Museum, Cotton MS. Vespasian A.viii, f.2) (966), and

(*b*) KING CNUT AND QUEEN 'AELFGIFU' (EMMA) MAKE A PRESENT TO NEW MINSTER (British Museum, Stowe MS.944, f.6) (*c.*1031).

Among the most splendid fruits of the monastic reform of the tenth century was a wonderful series of illuminated manuscripts. Like the new monastic customs, this art owed much to Continental models, but had a special quality of its own. The new style first appeared in the early tenth century, but rose to its height under St Dunstan and St Ethelwold, who were both artists and patrons of artists.

The leaves winding over a heavy border in (*a*), the outline drawing in (*b*) —see also *Plate 8* (*b*)—and the sense of movement, especially visible in the draperies, are characteristic of the 'Winchester' school, as the artists who flourished under Ethelwold's patronage, and their successors in and out of Winchester, are called. New Minster (later Hyde Abbey) was dedicated in early days to Christ, St Mary and St Peter.

In (*a*) King Edgar, standing between the two saints, presents his charter to Christ in majesty, supported by four angels.

In (*b*) the saints are on either side of Christ; angels hold the Queen's veil and the King's crown; below are the monks of New Minster. Both pictures show the divine aura which surrounded late Anglo-Saxon kingship.

had achieved the pre-eminence for the study of law which it was to hold for centuries ; and Paris in Abelard's day was winning a special fame for philosophy and theology. England had her higher schools, mostly cathedral schools ; but it is not until the end of the twelfth century that Oxford begins to be in any sense eminent, and not until the thirteenth that Oxford and Cambridge grew into universities.

Anselm was the dominant figure in English learning at the turn of the eleventh and twelfth centuries. But in spite of his immense prestige, and although he gathered pupils and disciples round him at Canterbury, his intellectual influence was limited to a small circle, and confined by the circumstances of his office, and by his frequent absences from England. None the less, his distinction serves to remind us that monks still played an important role in English learning well into the middle of the twelfth century. This is especially true in theology, hagiography, and the writing of history, in which English monks, led by William of Malmesbury, excelled. But to get an impression of the scope of learning and the ways in which it spread at this time, and of the life of scholars, one must look at the careers of a few individuals. Here are three examples.

The chief studies of the higher schools were theology and law ; the foundation for these was broad, including almost every discipline known at the time (with special emphasis on Latin grammar—rhetoric and dialectic—or logic), but the summit of recognised sciences was comparatively narrow. This makes the exceptional career of Adelard of Bath all the more interesting. He was born before the eleventh century was out, and lived well into the middle of the twelfth. He studied at Tours and Laon—two French cathedral schools ; he travelled in Greece, Asia Minor, Sicily, south Italy, and probably Spain. He formed an extraordinary link between Moslem and Christian learning ; between the two great Norman states of England and Sicily ; between literacy and statecraft. He was probably one of the men learned in Arabic and Greek mathematics who had a hand in developing the accounting techniques in the English Exchequer. His main work lay in more academic fields, in translating Greek and Arab philosophical and scientific treatises—it was Adelard who first introduced Euclid to the West. But he was sufficient of a courtier to write a treatise on falconry for Henry II when Henry was a boy.

A contemporary of Adelard's, meanwhile, was making a more conventional career for himself as a theologian in the schools of Paris. What makes Robert Pullen's career remarkable is that, when already one of the foremost theologians in the French schools, he elected to teach in England—at Exeter and Oxford—in his middle years. In the eleven-forties he returned briefly to Paris, and was then swept into the papal curia, made a cardinal and papal chancellor ; he died in 1146.

One of the students who sat at Pullen's feet in Paris in the eleven-forties was a young Englishman called John of Salisbury. John had already heard most of the lecturers who were making the humanist studies of Chartres and the philosophical and theological studies of Paris celebrated at this time. At Chartres he acquired his immense classical learning, his love of *belles lettres*, his elegant Latin. At Paris he saw many of the great teachers of the day, starting with Abelard himself. He was twelve years a student, gathering one of the most substantial educations a man has ever had ; and then he had to search for employment. His time in France brought him in contact with two distinguished abbots, Peter of Celle, who gave him temporary employment and became his closest friend, and St Bernard of Clairvaux. To his friendship with Peter we owe one of the few really intimate correspondences which survive from the Middle Ages. But it was Bernard who helped him to employment in the household of Theobald, Archbishop of Canterbury. Canterbury was his headquarters from 1147 to Theobald's death in 1161. There he met many of the leading ecclesiastical administrators of his generation, and made friends with his patron's successor-to-be, Thomas Becket. Much of John's first years under Theobald were spent in journeys to the papal curia ; his fascinating book of reminiscences, the *Memoirs of the Papal Court* (*Historia Pontificalis*), is based on his experiences during these visits. It was also in this period that he made, or renewed, his friendship with an English cardinal, Nicholas Breakspear, later to be pope as Adrian IV (1154-9) —the only Englishman to have held the office ; a man who, as pope, began what was to prove a long and bitter conflict with the Emperor Frederick Barbarossa. In doing so Adrian worked out in his life principles of ecclesiastical liberty which were also strongly held by John. Unfortunately that part of the *Memoirs* which dealt with Adrian IV has been lost—if it was ever written. But what survives reveals John's skill in portraying his contemporaries in witty, though not usually malicious fashion. In Theobald's last years John was his personal secretary, writing many of his letters ; but John also had leisure to bring out his most substantial books, the *Policraticus* and the *Metalogicon*. The former is a vast rambling encyclopedia of learning and lore on political theory and related (often remotely related) themes ; it was dedicated to Thomas Becket, now royal Chancellor, and covered every topic in which John thought his friend ought to be concerned in his new office. At the same time he wrote a shorter book on contemporary logical theories and their sources, the *Metalogicon*, also dedicated to Thomas, to which we owe our knowledge of John's early career, and his famous description of the great teachers of his day. After Theobald's death and Becket's succession, John joined the latter's household, and he was mainly engaged in defending his friend's case and vindicating his memory until fortune brought him back, at the very end of his life, to the cathedral in whose shadow he had received the main intellectual inspiration of his life ; he was Bishop of Chartres from 1176 until his death in 1180.

In John of Salisbury several of the finest traditions of twelfth-century learning were represented. He is best remembered as one of the most learned scholars of his day, at least in the pagan classics ; and as a distinguished humanist. Humanism is an ambiguous and confusing word ; but whether we look in it for devotion to the classics or for a deep sense of human values, both are present in John—the latter perhaps not so powerfully as the former. In many respects he and a few others like him foreshadowed the humanism of the later Renaissance. He knew no Greek ; his passion for the great figures of the past was diffuse. Perhaps he differs most from scholars of the fifteenth century in the way he saw the classics through the spectacles of post-classical writers, especially of the pagan and Christian writers of the later Empire. John's outlook was entirely Christian.

Though not endowed with a high measure of physical courage, John held clear convictions and expressed them forcibly in his writings. Like many men who passed through the schools at this time, and came in contact with current theological and legal doctrine, he held clearly fixed in his mind the supremacy of the papacy in spiritual affairs and the ultimate supremacy of the spiritual over the temporal. Thus conviction as well as loyalty to friend and patron made him support Thomas Becket. It would be wrong to think of John as typical in this respect. It came as a great surprise to most contemporaries that Becket, after a normal clerical career in the schools, in the service of the archbishop and of the king, emerged when archbishop as a strong exponent of these views. The leading churchmen of the day were brought up in two worlds : in the world of lay custom of their parents and secular relations, and of the king whom most of the bishops had at one time served ; and also in the clerical world of the schools, in which they learned the theory of papal and clerical supremacy. In the minds of most of them custom held a stronger place than in John of Salisbury's or Thomas Becket's. But the conflict in which they became involved can be understood only as part of the story of English politics in the century after the Conqueror's death ; and to this we must now return.

9 William II, Henry I, and Stephen

(1) WILLIAM II, 1087–1100

IN THE last three chapters we have tried to give a broad sketch of Norman England. We have seen continuity in some parts of English life, rapid and catastrophic change in others. The Normans who settled in England were comparatively few in number ; they came as war-lords, royal servants, bishops, abbots, archdeacons, canons, and clerks. They did not come as peasants. Naturally they altered the feudal structure more fundamentally than the manorial, the cathedral more than the parish. By the Conqueror's death the main lines of change were clear. English and Norman were still distinct—the story of assimilation will come later. But there was no longer an English aristocracy to engineer an English restoration. Not that the English were negligible or their royalty extinct ; St Margaret, the Queen of Scotland, was descended from Alfred, Edgar, and Ethelred ; and her brother, Edgar Aetheling, had nearly become king for an hour in 1066. Henry I found it prudent to marry Queen Margaret's daughter immediately after his accession. But Henry I lacked even a clear Norman title at that stage. His queen was much loved by the English and helped her husband in many ways ; but we must not attribute too much political significance to the match.

The Conqueror had done his work thoroughly. Deep scars in the landscape of England still reminded men what it meant to resist the Norman will ; none of his children needed to be so ruthless in devastation as he had been. After his death his sons quarrelled and fought for his inheritance ; but when Henry, the youngest, finally won Normandy as well as England in 1106, he was able to build a state to all appearances even stronger than William's.

The quarrels began at the father's deathbed. The eldest

son, Robert, was in rebellion, and his father knew his incapacity. The old king reckoned that he could not pass his whole inheritance to William, his second surviving son, known as Rufus, and so gave his voice for Robert as Duke of Normandy, for William as King of England. William left his father's side even before his death, and within a little over a fortnight he had presented his credentials to Archbishop Lanfranc and been crowned in Westminster Abbey. It was the final act of the great partnership of Lanfranc and William I ; the crucial importance of having the old king's voice, and of taking rapid possession of throne and crown were never so clearly expressed. The Norman barons had never given their formal consent to the Conqueror's arrangements ; to many of them, with their estates divided between the two lands, a divided allegiance must have seemed exceedingly inconvenient. A party of them, headed by the new King's uncle, Odo of Bayeux, were more inclined to Robert than to William.

Early in 1088 William II faced the most dangerous rebellion of his reign. Most of his father's closest followers, the archbishop excepted, were against him. If Robert had acted with the same energy as William, he would probably have won the throne. But William kept a few great men on his side, a large number of lesser folk, and the bulk of the English who still counted—to whom Norman politics meant nothing. In the course of this campaign William's subjects were forcibly reminded that their King was a great warrior and a remarkable personality, and that the English king, whoever he might be, still counted for more in the country at large than any of the barons. In a few months the rebellion was crushed and only the Bishop of Durham still resisted. Under safe conduct he appeared before the King and claimed exemption, as a bishop, from trial in a royal court. He appealed to Rome. Already the force of the new canon law was a weapon which could be turned against the King. The bishop, however, had little support from his own colleagues. In 1082 Odo of Bayeux had been imprisoned, not as a bishop, but as Earl of Kent, as the Conqueror had neatly explained ; and Lanfranc and the English bishops seem to have accepted this view of the Bishop of Durham, too—it was as a baron, for his lay fiefs, that he was tried. The end of the case was a compromise ; nor was the bishop again to be found defending ultramontane principles.

William II's government was strict and severe, and in 1095 he again provoked some of the barons to rebel. With the suppression of the second rebellion—a more stringent suppression than had been possible in 1088–9—he was secure, as secure as ever his father had been, in his English kingdom, and could turn his attention to the conquest of Normandy.

By 1095 King William was thoroughly established in his reputation as king, Duke Robert thoroughly discredited in his reputation as duke. Both were fine soldiers. But in William the knightly qualities were only one aspect of a complex personality ; Robert was strong in nothing else. Robert enjoyed a battle too much to worry about its consequences ; he always forgave an enemy as soon as the enemy was beaten. He was incapable of controlling the Norman barons. But he was, though not a moral man, a pious one, and other events of the year 1095 gave him the opportunity for a far more promising adventure than petty war in Normandy provided. The pope was preaching the first Crusade, and found a ready listener in Duke Robert. Robert's only difficulty was money ; and this he found by the happy expedient of pawning his duchy to William. To the Crusade went Robert, and made a good name for himself, so to speak, as a brigade commander ; nor did he return until after William's death.

William was a splendid knight by the standard of the day, but no crusader. To his own knights he was lavish ; and he was never happier than when on campaign or in the hunting field. As a soldier he was loyal to his subordinates, in the way that he himself had been loyal to his father. He was a strict upholder of the soldier's code as he understood it. It was the only code he knew or cared for. He had nothing of chivalry in the modern sense ; cared not a rap for religion or the Church ; and knew no restraints save those of the camp. And so he was remembered in knightly circles as the greatest leader of his day ; by churchmen as a depraved tyrant. Granted the standards of the two communities, there is little to quarrel with in their judgments.

In fairness to Rufus, it must be acknowledged that his worst fault in the eyes of the Church was material : his rapacity.

His boundless generosity to his followers, and the expensive adventures of his last years, made money a constant and urgent need. Since he cared nothing for the Church he did what he could to mulct it. He left abbeys and bishoprics vacant, including the see of Canterbury itself, and took a substantial share of their revenues. He was thus provided with a plentiful store of silver, and was spared for the time the unwanted advice of another Lanfranc.

None the less, the chroniclers' portrait of Rufus is not inhuman. They hated him for his oppression, but they enjoyed telling stories about him ; he was an engaging ruffian. He lacked his father's dignity and presence ; he stammered and blustered when in difficulties. But he had a sharp sense of humour and a gay abandon in blasphemy which several chroniclers recorded. The London Jews brought him a present one day, and asked leave to hold a disputation with Christians in his presence. ' God's face,' said the King, with great delight, and announced that if they had the better of it, he would change his faith. A more serious tale was told against him by the historian Eadmer, that Rufus was once bribed by a Jew to compel his son, who had been converted, to abjure his Christianity, which the King—to his own intense annoyance— failed to do. These stories have given rise to a theory that Rufus was a thoroughgoing sceptic, but this is doubtful. He was what the Elizabethans called an atheist : not an un- believer, but a blasphemer. When secure from fear of death he scoffed at the Church and ignored it : he was also a wit, who kept no control of his tongue.

It is a strange irony that Rufus, of all English kings, should have invited one of the most attractive, distinguished, and saintly of possible candidates to occupy the see of Canterbury. In 1092–3 many of the leaders in Church and state were in a conspiracy to fill the see, vacant since Lanfranc's death in 1089. They were attracted by the immense prestige of the abbot of Bec, Anselm of Aosta, and he was invited to visit England. Anselm suspected what was afoot, and refused to come, although his abbey's possessions in England required his presence. Eventually the importunity of the savage old Earl of Chester, who swore he was on his deathbed, compelled Anselm to come. A sudden and violent illness made Rufus a party to the plot, and Anselm found himself, very much against his will, constrained to accept the archbishopric. ' You would yoke a weak old sheep to an untamed bull ', he said. Small wonder that he resisted : he was already an old man, and it needed no deep prescience to foresee that he would have to dedicate his last years to a fearful task. In the event he lived sixteen years, and spent them in resisting two of the most strong-willed and unscrupulous monarchs in the Europe of his day.

One cannot read either of Eadmer's books about him, nor any contemporary description, nor his own writings, without feeling the impact of Anselm's charm. The division of clerical and lay was never more sharply exemplified than in the contrast of Anselm and Rufus. Yet Anselm was no sheep. He did not fancy himself as a politician ; and he gives the impression of always striving to find some way out of the endless battles in which he was involved. But it was not for nothing that he was the finest philosopher whom Europe had seen for many centuries. He saw vital points of principle with extreme clarity and precision, and never wavered in defending what he regarded as essential. As a monk, spiritual director, thinker, and theologian, Anselm held and deserved an immense reputation. There seems at first sight something wasteful in the way he was pulled from his cloister and set in the militant theatre in which his last years were passed. But if we wish to understand the Middle Ages, Anselm's career is worth careful reflection. The Earl of Chester was not given to basing essential choices on sentiment. Nor were he and his like driven by fear alone, as was Rufus. It may be that Earl Hugh's chief wish was to stand before God's judgment seat and claim to have won for the English Church a saintly head. But in addition to this the story of Anselm shows that, however sharp the contrast between the two worlds of clergy and laity, men like Anselm and Earl Hugh could communicate.

The immediate result was a violent reaction by Rufus, who felt that he had been tricked into appointing Anselm, and used every trick he knew to be rid of him. There was trouble about the way Anselm should receive his pallium of office. There were two rival popes at the time, and the King claimed the right to choose which one should have the English allegiance. Anselm, however, had already accepted Urban II while abbot of Bec, as had the whole Norman church. This dispute was followed by other difficulties, until a number of bishops and a few barons reckoned that there would be no peace till Anselm had withdrawn from the archbishopric. In the end Anselm found his position untenable, and went abroad in 1097 to consult the pope. King and archbishop agreed to part ; Rufus was saved from excommunication by Anselm ; but it must have appeared that the English Church would be without an archbishop until either Rufus or Anselm died ; and since Rufus was barely forty and Anselm about sixty-five, the outcome seemed clearly predictable.

Rufus was himself so anti-clerical that historians for long ignored the evidence that his clerical supporters were extremely active in developing some of the literate aspects of government. It may even have been in his time that the new system of accounting came in at the Exchequer. What is certain is that it was in response to his urgent need for money that his notorious chaplain, Ranulph Flambard, developed and enforced the machinery for levying and manipulating taxes. Ranulph was as hardly treated by the chroniclers as was his master, and he was evidently unscrupulous ; but his long period of office in Chancery and Treasury marked an important stage in the development of royal government. What is uncertain is how much part the King played in these activities. Clearly his real interests lay elsewhere.

While Duke Robert was on Crusade, William set to work to restore order and expand the frontiers of his new principality in Normandy. He had only temporary possession of the duchy, but evidently intended to retain it altogether if he could. A series of campaigns against the heir to the French throne, the future Louis VI (1108–37) brought him the exercise that he and his followers loved, but no decisive advantage. Normandy became secure, however, and he was successful in reducing Maine to submission. England was secure as never before : in 1099 King Edgar of Scotland bore William's sword before him at the crown-wearing at Westminster, and the faithful Ranulph Flambard was rewarded with the frontier bishopric of Durham. There was talk of the Duke of Aquitaine following Duke Robert's example, and pawning his duchy to Rufus.

In the summer of 1100 Rufus boasted that he would spend Christmas in Poitiers. But on 2nd August he was shot by an arrow while hunting in the New Forest, and instantly died.

Contemporaries ascribed the event to an accident, but they saw in it God's judgment on his blasphemies and oppression. Some recent historians have suspected conspiracy. William and Robert had made each the other's heir, to the exclusion of their youngest brother Henry. Henry had no hope of William's nomination ; his only chance of the throne was to seize it by force when Robert was in no position to intervene. At the time of Rufus's death Robert's return from the Crusade was imminent, and he brought with him a bride who might bear him a son. Henry was a member of the fatal hunting party ; they were only a short distance from the royal treasure house at Winchester. The arrow was discharged by Walter Tirel, whose relations were treated by Henry with great favour. All the circumstances were singularly fortunate for Henry, and a suspicion attaches to him of conspiring to have his brother cut off. Of this we may probably acquit him. We might believe him capable of murdering to win the crown ; but to murder one's brother and liege lord was an act of treachery, the suspicion of which would have blasted his reputation. The stigma of quite a remote acquiescence in his brother's murder never left Ethelred II ; it is hard to believe that Henry could have been in a conspiracy and no wind of it reach us from contemporaries. If conspiracy there was, it was extraordinarily well concealed.

(2) HENRY I, 1100–35

Henry succeeded only just in time. Rufus died on the afternoon of 2nd August. By 5th August Henry had seized the Treasury at Winchester and had had himself elected and crowned at Westminster. Within a few weeks Robert was back in Normandy, and preparing to punish his upstart brother. Henry had still much to do to win sufficient support to face the threat. He made a bid for the barons and the Church by issuing an elaborate charter repudiating the notorious abuses of Rufus's régime ; like Rufus he made more promises than he had any hope or intention of keeping. He pursued his advantage with the Church by speeding the return of Anselm. He conciliated his English subjects by marrying Edith (alias Matilda), daughter of St Margaret of Scotland and niece of Edgar Aetheling. He won recognition from Louis of France, who was not sorry to see the Anglo-Norman Empire divided. But his position remained very insecure. Some of the great barons, with estates in both England and Normandy, feared that civil war between the two brothers would not be in their interest, and hoped that Robert would quickly unite kingdom and duchy again ; others saw advantage in civil war, and encouraged Robert to invade for a different reason ; others again felt that a crusader's rights should have been better respected.

At first the peacemakers had the better of the argument. Robert came, and at Alton peace was arranged between the brothers before the situation had come to a fight. Robert was to have Normandy and a large pension, Henry England and a Norman castle ; both were to forgive their rebels. Whether this was regarded as a lasting settlement is not clear. In any case Henry rapidly set to work to undermine it. Robert's fame as a crusader gave him a momentary return of prestige, which his incompetence soon dissipated. Henry meanwhile was proving himself a strong, capable, and just ruler. After his death he was known as the lion of justice. The title implies the nostalgia of men oppressed by the chaos of Stephen's reign which followed, and is in part a formal symbol. But the lion is not a kindly beast, and Henry succeeded, like his father, because he rapidly inspired fear and respect. He was capable, thorough, and ruthless. Like his father, he was also pious ; he liked to be on good terms with the Church—if the Church would respect and obey him in turn—and he took a real interest in endowing religious houses, a taste he shared with Queen Matilda. But his piety did not affect his morals ; though less systematic in destruction than his father, Henry was not a merciful man ; unlike his father, he was not a good husband. He acknowledged upward of twenty illegitimate children. Henry I was a constructive monarch in his way ; but as a person he is unattractive. It must be remembered to his credit that he kept men's allegiance ; after 1102 there were no more rebellions in England until his death. Partly this was because, unlike King Stephen, he was feared and respected, but partly too, because, unlike King John, he was trusted.

Duke Robert was no match for his brother. Henry quietly wove a fabric of alliances round Normandy, so as to ensure that his conquest of the duchy should be uninterrupted ; he also used every opportunity to prepare Normandy to accept him as duke. Rufus's old minister, Ranulph Flambard, was engaged in clerical intrigue on his own account and political intrigue on Henry's in Normandy in these years ; Henry's most distinguished lay supporter, Robert of Meulan, was sent to help Robert suppress disorder. In 1105 Henry openly invaded the duchy, and again in 1106. At the end of September Henry and Robert met at Tinchebrai, and the battle ended in Robert's capture and Henry's conquest of Normandy. Robert ended his days a prisoner in Britain ; Henry became Duke of Normandy ; the Anglo-Norman barons were freed from their divided allegiance ; and Ranulph Flambard returned to Durham to enjoy the novelty of being a respectable bishop. The nave of Durham Cathedral is a striking monument to the artistic unity of the Norman dominions, to the prosperity of Henry's kingdom, and to the ability and munificence of Bishop Ranulph.

Like his father in 1066, or William of Orange in 1688, Henry had achieved his conquest because of the temporary quiescence of neighbouring powers. Like them, he found himself in his triumph suddenly ringed with enemies. Some of his further schemes came to nothing, and he made no headway on the frontier between Normandy and the royal domain of France against the rising star of Louis VI. But he held his own in Maine, and continued to practise his diplomacy against the other powers of northern and central France. His diplomacy in Anjou was later to spoil his plans for the succession to his throne.

Meanwhile in England, Henry had made his peace with the Church. Anselm's return at the beginning of the reign had revealed a fundamental difference of principle between king and primate, which soon led the latter into exile again. Papal councils of the last decade of the eleventh century had been condemning with ever growing urgency the practice of lay investiture, first called in question by Gregory VII in 1075. It was the custom in most European kingdoms and many principalities for a new bishop or a new abbot to be granted his office by king or prince in a symbolic ceremony in which ring and pastoral staff were presented to the elect. Symbol and reality were felt in the Middle Ages to inhere in one another to a degree we find difficult to comprehend ; and staff and ring were the essential symbols of pastoral office. For those churchmen who were concerned to emphasise the distinction of lay and clerical, to free the Church (as they saw it) from lay control, this symbol was in every way offensive. Anselm had been present at two of the councils of the ten-nineties and could not ignore the problem. He refused to consecrate bishops who had been invested by the King. On the other side, many royal supporters thought the symbol as precious as the reality, and there was stout resistance to Anselm's demands. Many churchmen thought any kind of royal influence as offensive as its symbol, and the declared papal policy was to make the offices of bishop and abbot purely spiritual—to cut off the lay power from any say in the making of spiritual officials. To the King this was intolerable. He relied on the bishops for counsel and for knights as well as for prayers ; they were among his leading barons, usually his most faithful barons. It was essential to his government that he should choose them.

The impasse was solved by the desire of Anselm and Henry for peace. Anselm was weary of exile, anxious to return to his flock and perform his proper function as archbishop. Henry preferred to be on good terms with the Church, and needed all the support he could get for his attack on Normandy. And so in 1105 the basis for agreement was found. It was suggested to Henry that he give up investiture but retain the essential custom of receiving homage and fealty from the bishops. Anselm, after some hesitation, agreed to submit the proposal to the Pope, who accepted the condition, so long as it remained a personal grant to Henry alone. In 1107 Anselm was finally able to return to England, to consecrate the many bishops elected in his absence, to hold a last council and pass stringent decrees on clerical discipline (1108), before he died in 1109.

The compromise between Henry and Anselm later provided

a pattern for the compromise between the Pope and Henry's son-in-law, the Emperor Henry V, in 1122. In both a formal renunciation of investiture was made in exchange for a personal grant of the right of a symbol devoid of spiritual significance. In both cases the right survived, because the King's successors regarded it as the immemorial custom of their realms. Their actual influence on elections depended on political circumstances ; by and large the English kings had no difficulty in managing elections before the fourteenth century. But it rarely happened in the Middle Ages that a symbol was surrendered without cost. A profound movement was in progress ; clerical education was bringing men more and more to assume a measure of clerical independence. These new assumptions rarely came into the open except at times of conflict. But men about the English court must have noticed the disappearance of this well-known ceremony. It marked a stage in the process by which the king ceased to be undisputed master in the English Church. Henry I still got his way in later years ; but papal envoys—or legates, as they were called —and church councils became commoner.

Henry governed England by the fullest use of every traditional instrument. Like all the English kings of the twelfth century, he was a feudal king in a feudal age. His tastes lay in hunting, and preparing for war, like those of all his line. His natural associates were barons : Robert of Meulan and his family, and others like them, were constantly about him. Rebels he treated severely after his first two years ; he even broke the great house of Bellême-Montgomery, who had held semi-independent sway in the marches of Normandy and Wales under his father and brother. He broke them because they were rebels, not out of an 'anti-feudal' policy. If the greater baronage was weaker in 1135 than in 1100, the explanation lies in the fullness with which Henry used all the other instruments of government, not in any conscious effort to weaken his fellow feudatories.

The feudal aristocracy was certainly no caste. Henry himself was accused by Orderic of promoting men from the dust. But in practice his new barons were not yeomen or peasants ; they had all, by definition, to be trained to knightly pursuits, to be brought up in the traditions of the feudal classes. Henry undoubtedly added to the numbers of the barons, endowing them when possible by marrying them to heiresses ; when heiresses were lacking, he gave them portions of royal demesne. This was partly the fruit of necessity, partly of choice. The prestige of a usurper or of a newcomer to the throne was always liable to be weak if the great luminaries of the court in no way reflected his glory. It no doubt gave Henry strength in his own and other men's eyes that not all the great men of his court owed their place to his father or brother.

Henry's most important creations were able royal servants. The English royal council, be it Alfred's Witan or the Tudor Privy Council, has always contained an element freely chosen by the king and an element with something like an inherited claim to be invited. In a measure the English king always retained the right to consult and be counselled by whom he would. One of the most notable features of Henry I's court was the distinction of his councillors, both clerical and lay. We have already glanced at the achievement of Bishop Roger of Salisbury and his family in the Exchequer and elsewhere. Most English bishops of this time were recruited from the royal Chancery or some other office of state—with the singular exception of Canterbury, which always had a monk or canon regular before 1162. Greatest among Henry's lay officials were Aubrey de Vere and Richard Basset, who were given a roving commission in the late eleven-twenties to reform the sheriffdoms of much of England. Richard was a royal justice and perhaps for a time Chief Justiciar—a new office, carrying with it supremacy in judicial and administrative affairs in the king's absence ; Aubrey was made Master Chamberlain, that is, chief financial officer of the royal household, in 1133. In the next reign Aubrey's son acquired an earldom, and the Veres were earls of Oxford until 1604. The origins of Vere and Basset are an interesting commentary on Orderic's sneers. Aubrey's barony was not of Henry's creation. The founder of the family came from Ver near Coutances in western Normandy, and doubtless owed his promotion to the Bishop of Coutances ; by 1086 the first Aubrey was already established as a tenant-in-chief in his own right as well as tenant of the bishop in two counties. The Bassets held a small fee in southern

Plate 11 THE WEINGARTEN CRUCIFIXION. From a Gospel book illuminated in England, probably between 1051 and 1065, for Earl Tostig's wife, Judith of Flanders, who took it with her to Germany, where she later married Welf IV, Duke of Bavaria. The book was left to Weingarten Abbey in south Germany, where it stayed until the early nineteenth century. It is now in the Pierpont Morgan Library, New York (MS.709, f.1v). The jagged outline of the drapery is similar to *Plate 10* (*b*), but the technique has been adapted to give a moving impression of the human sufferings of Jesus and those about him.

Plate 12 VIRGIN AND CHILD, BY MATTHEW PARIS (British Museum, Royal MS. 14.C.vii, f.6). Since the days of the pictures in *Plates 8*, *10* and *11* many new influences had affected the style of English painting, especially, in the twelfth century, the Byzantine art of southern Italy and Sicily. But the older English tradition did not die : it can still be seen in the outline drawing here. The heavy black line is characteristic of Matthew Paris himself ; the subject and the grace of composition are characteristic of the thirteenth century. (On Matthew Paris as an artist, see R. Vaughan, *Matthew Paris* (1958), chap. xi ; on twelfth-century painting, O. Pächt, C. R. Dodwell, F. Wormald, *The St Albans Psalter* (1960).)

Normandy, and Richard's father had already attracted William II's notice before Henry came to the throne. Their sensational rise, and wide English possessions (with one very valuable marriage to an English heiress), they owed to Henry I. Henry did not choose his subordinates haphazardly; he selected men who had already proved themselves in a lower capacity. The man who owed most to him was his nephew Stephen, who can only be described as a favourite. Stephen was the son of Adela, Henry's sister, and Stephen, Count of Blois; his elder brother, Count Theobald, was a constant ally of Henry against the French king. Two large English fiefs, and two of the richest fiefs of Normandy came Stephen's way before 1118; and in 1125 he married the heiress of Boulogne, Matilda, niece of Henry's first queen, and so sprung from the Old English and the Scottish kings. Count Stephen was a magnate after the order of Earl Godwin or Earl Harold.

As Henry's nephew, Stephen had a place in the queue for his succession. It was not at first a very lofty place, since Stephen had an elder brother and Henry had children. But circumstances favoured him. In 1120 a boat carrying Henry's only legitimate son, William the Aetheling, and many leading men of his court, struck a rock in the Channel and sank. The wreck of the White Ship made a deep impression on contemporaries, and was a fearful shock to Henry. He married again, but had no children by his second wife; it was the pitiful irony of his later years that he should be surrounded by bastard sons, whom neither the custom of the land nor the Church would allow to succeed him. In spite of his evident affection for Stephen, he was very slow to think of him as a possible heir, and it is doubtful if Stephen took his own claims seriously before the very end of the reign.

There remained Matilda, Henry's only legitimate daughter. Matilda, at the tender age of eleven, had a taste of a higher office than any other member of her family; she was married to the Emperor Henry V. The marriage was childless, and on her husband's death in 1125 the Empress returned to her father's court, to be prepared for the English succession. On 1st January 1127 the English barons, including Stephen, swore to recognise her as Lady of England if Henry died without male heirs. Later in the year Henry betrothed her to Geoffrey,

Count of Anjou, and capped a year of triumph over enemies in France by marrying her to Count Geoffrey in June 1128.

For once Henry had overreached himself. The marriage was exceedingly unpopular. The terms allowed Geoffrey to become King of England and Duke of Normandy. To this the English barons had not given their consent. The Norman barons, many of them also English barons, reacted violently to the prospect of being ruled by their traditional enemy, the Count of Anjou. The French king naturally disapproved of an alliance between two leading powers of northern France. Finally, the Empress herself objected to an entanglement with a mere count ten years her junior. The English barons were threatening to repudiate their oath to Matilda when, in 1131, Henry found an opportunity for cajoling them to confirm it. Geoffrey repudiated his wife, and Matilda returned to England, apparently free of the Angevin yoke. The barons renewed their oath. But very shortly after, Matilda and Geoffrey were reunited, and on 5th March 1133 the future Henry II was born. The English barons had sworn to acknowledge Matilda, not her husband ; the King had promised the succession to Geoffrey, and Geoffrey was at first determined to have it. It is likely that Henry was beginning to repent of his offers to Geoffrey, and he certainly refused him an immediate share in government. The result was that Henry and Geoffrey were at war when the old King died (of a surfeit of lampreys) in December 1135.

(3) STEPHEN, 1135–54

Stephen won the throne by a rapid and forceful manoeuvre, comparable to the manoeuvres of 1087 and 1100. But he was never able to assert his supremacy in England as his uncles had done. From 1139 to 1148 the Empress Matilda was in the country, and never lacked supporters ; after her departure her eldest son was always plotting and executing dashing invasions. After 1144 Normandy was irrevocably lost : it had been conquered by Count Geoffrey. In England Stephen's reign was remembered, with some exaggeration, as nineteen years of chaos, anarchy, and suffering. In fact, the anarchy was intermittent and often local, and the later years of the reign were less severe than those which followed the Empress's invasion in 1139. But anarchy there was, such as England had not seen since the Conquest.

The anarchy has sometimes been viewed merely as a reflection of Stephen's weakness of character; sometimes as the inevitable outcome of the circumstances in which he took the throne, and of the disputed succession; sometimes as a natural reaction against the excessively autocratic rule of Henry I. Let us look at these aspects in turn.

' When the traitors saw that Stephen was a good-humoured, kindly, and easy-going man who inflicted no punishment,' wrote the Peterborough chronicler, ' then they committed all manner of horrible crimes. They had done him homage and sworn oaths of fealty to him, but not one of their oaths was kept. They were all forsworn and their oaths broken. For every great man built him castles and held them against the king; and they filled the whole land with these castles. They sorely burdened the unhappy people of the country with forced labour on the castles; and when the castles were built, they filled them with devils and wicked men. . . . Never did a country endure greater misery, and never did the heathen act more vilely than they did. Contrary to custom, they spared neither church nor churchyard, but seized everything of value that was in it, and afterwards burned the church and all it contained. . . . And men said openly that Christ and his saints slept. Such things and others more than we know how to relate we suffered nineteen years for our sins.' [1]

King Stephen was easy-going, though a good knight and in his way a pious man. In fact, he resembled his uncle Duke Robert, save that he had more than Robert's share of energy and determination. Indeed, he achieved more than Robert while lacking most of Robert's advantages. His right to the throne is not easily assessed. Matilda was nearer in blood to Henry than was Stephen; she had been designated by Henry and received the oaths of the barons. It is true she was a woman, and would not be expected to rule alone; and the barons had never accepted her husband as king. But Matilda and Geoffrey jointly had Henry's voice, and their children

---

[1] *Peterborough Chronicle*, under the year 1137 (*Anglo-Saxon Chronicle*, trans. G. N. Garmonsway, pp. 263–5)

would have a far better hereditary claim than Stephen. But Stephen's claim was not negligible. It was solemnly debated before the pope in 1139, and upheld. Hereditarily it was weak, but heredity was only one of the elements in king-making, and not the most important. Some of the Norman barons were for Count Theobald, who became duke for a day ; but when news came that Stephen had been crowned King of England, Theobald gave way to his younger brother, and for the time Stephen was accepted as *de facto* duke in Normandy as well as king in England.

In putting himself at the head of the English baronage in their rejection of the deep-seated plans of Henry I, Stephen stored up for himself future trouble. Henry I had been increasingly autocratic in later years ; his rule had grown harsh and oppressive. He had used his rights arbitrarily to extort money from the powerful, and they had come to resent his rule. The course of Stephen's reign shows that the English aristocracy saw little advantage to themselves in strong government ; and bitterly distrusted the financial organisation developed under Roger of Salisbury. Stephen was carried to success on the shoulders of a baronial reaction, and had to show the barons some return for their support, in the shape of a milder government. More important, perhaps, he had the prejudices of his class—the feudal hierarchy meant more to him than royal authority, and he had the layman's distrust of the literate clerical civil servants.

In 1138 Count Geoffrey had invaded Normandy and at the same time rebellion first showed in England, headed by Matilda's half-brother, Robert, Earl of Gloucester, and timed to coincide with an invasion by David, King of the Scots. But the two attacks were beaten off ; the Scots were defeated in the famous ' battle of the Standard ' ; and Stephen seemed secure. Rebellion had aroused his suspicions against Roger of Salisbury and his family, and he proceeded to throw his own administration into confusion, and embroil himself with the Church by picking a quarrel with Roger himself, with Roger's son, who had been royal Chancellor, and his two episcopal nephews of Ely and Lincoln. Roger only survived his arrest four months, to die in December 1139. Meanwhile Stephen's brother, Henry of Blois, Bishop of Winchester, at this time head of the English Church in virtue of his office of papal legate, had attempted unsuccessfully to rouse a Church council to condemn his brother's action ; and the Empress had landed in England.

From 1139 to 1145 there was anarchy in England. Fighting took place sporadically in many parts of the country, especially in the west and west Midlands, where the Empress's following was strong, and in East Anglia, where one of the most powerful of the robber barons, Geoffrey de Mandeville, Earl of Essex, was at large. In 1141 Stephen was captured at the battle of Lincoln ; for a moment the Empress was triumphant, and she marched to London to be crowned. But some of Matilda's difficulties were of her own making : by temperament she was self-willed and haughty, disinclined to make concessions to her subjects' demands or even to good manners. Within a week she was forced out of London, and a few months later, after a hazardous march, she was established once again in the western strongholds of her half-brother, Robert, Earl of Gloucester. A powerful counter-attack under forces organised by Stephen's queen led to Robert's capture late in 1141. Robert and Stephen were exchanged, and the Empress's brief triumph was at an end. But not the anarchy ; it continued unabated, and rose to its height in 1144. In that year Geoffrey de Mandeville died. He had played one side off against the other, exacting bribes and favours from each in turn, and so had won large estates, royal offices, and an earldom. The same game was played more subtly for even higher stakes by the Earl of Chester, who fancied himself as a king-maker. He remained a power to be reckoned with until his death in 1153, but after a brief arrest in 1146 his activities were somewhat curtailed. From 1145, indeed, the anarchy began to subside ; the arrest of the Earl of Chester in 1146 and the death of the Earl of Gloucester in 1147 marked important stages in its decline ; when the Empress finally abandoned the struggle in 1148 and returned to her husband, the way seemed clear for a return of peaceful government. But Stephen's difficulties were far from over.

The greater barons had tasted liberty and many of them were still disinclined for a stronger régime. They met threats to the peace of their own domains by organising pacts with their neighbours. By the end of the reign a generation was growing up which had forgotten both the peace and the oppressions of Henry I. Some were prepared to accept a stronger yoke and the security which went with it; others rejoiced in present opportunities for plunder and promotion. The anarchy was a rare interval when the strong government of Norman kings was relaxed, and some of the more violent potentialities of feudal society could come into the open. Many tendencies in twelfth-century society fought against such violence; but the great barons in whose hands lay the decision of the conflict needed to be convinced that it was not to their interests to let it continue.

As Stephen grew older he made more and more urgent efforts to settle the succession. Following a practice common on the Continent, he wished to have his elder son, Eustace, crowned in his own lifetime. To Stephen the deciding factor on this occasion was heredity and his own voice; he had decided, Eustace must be king. It was true that the nobles had tasted new opportunities for bargaining, had acquired a new sense of their own importance in king-making, as a result of the anarchy. Secret and open Angevins were now for the Empress's son, Henry, who made his existence known by raids in 1147 and 1149. But Angevins, for the moment, were few; and Stephen was able to win his barons' consent for the succession of Eustace. The only determined opposition came from the Church. The papacy had never withdrawn its acceptance of Stephen, and never agreed to reopen the case after 1139. But formal processes of king-making were not of major concern to the Church; its essential interest lay in the suitability of the candidate for his lofty office, especially suitability as the Church's protector, and the Church's own part in the business, the ceremonies of anointing and coronation. In 1152, acting on the Pope's specific prohibition, the Archbishop of Canterbury refused to crown Eustace, and fled the country.

Archbishop Theobald's refusal was the culmination of a remarkable effort to maintain a consistent front in the circumstances of the anarchy. When he first became archbishop, he was compelled to take orders from his subordinate, the Bishop of Winchester, because the Bishop was papal legate. Theobald had done homage to Stephen, and even in 1141, when Stephen was imprisoned, and the Church rallied round the Empress, Theobald refused to give up his allegiance without Stephen's permission. He remained throughout the reign a reluctant supporter of the King. At the same time, he attempted to maintain the unity of his province in a divided country and against the encroachments of rebellious bishops. After 1143 Henry of Blois was no longer legate, but he continued to strive for independence from Canterbury; so did the Bishop of St David's. To maintain his position, Theobald had to enter into correspondence with the Empress's supporters. Presumably for this reason, he became the object of violent suspicion to the King, and was forced into temporary exile two or three times and once took refuge in Angevin territory. Stephen's attempts to resume control of the Church became increasingly ineffective ; even episcopal elections took place behind his back. Meanwhile the Angevin cause, though weak in England, had prospered in Normandy, which was conquered by Count Geoffrey in the early eleven-forties. Prolonged war between Stephen and Geoffrey would in effect be civil war, since the leading barons held fiefs on both sides of the Channel. It is clear that at some date in the eleven-forties Theobald and his circle made up their minds to work for an Angevin succession. It can only have been at their instance that the pope forbade Eustace's coronation.

The factors which told against Eustace helped his rival in other ways as well. Henry returned to England in 1153 under very different circumstances from those of his earlier visits. He was now Duke of Normandy in his own right, and since his father's death in 1151, Count of Anjou ; he had recently married the ex-Queen of France, Eleanor, heiress of Aquitaine, whose marriage to King Louis VII had been annulled. Henry was lord of half France, and a mature warrior of nineteen. For those who wished for lasting peace, he offered some prospect of a return to the days of his grandfather. For those barons with extensive Norman domains, he held out a threat of blackmail. The solution was either the immediate defeat of Stephen or a compromise by which Henry should be recognised as Stephen's heir. But Stephen was not easy to defeat, and Eustace's ambition prevented a compromise. The impasse was solved by Eustace's sudden death. Stephen's younger son, like his father, was a great feudal baron at heart, and was satisfied with the many lordships which Henry I had granted to his father. Great trouble-makers like the Earl of Chester trembled for their Norman lands, and joined the Archbishop in negotiating peace. Stephen was to be king until his death, and Henry was then to succeed. Stephen died in the next year, and on 19th December 1154 Archbishop Theobald had the satisfaction of crowning Henry king.

10   Henry II, 1154-89

(1) HENRY II AND THOMAS BECKET

HENRY II was one of the most remarkable characters in English history. We know a great deal about him. He lived in an age when it was fashionable to comment on the activities of kings, when history and especially contemporary history was popular ; and Henry impressed his contemporaries so strongly that they could not refrain from saying what they thought of him. Most of them disliked him. His enemies found him too brilliant and mercurial, too overwhelming to be forgiven ; those close to him feared both his charm and his occasional outbursts of wild anger, and were exasperated by his unpredictable activity. But they all admired him. He was a great figure in European society, comparable in prestige to the Emperor Frederick Barbarossa. He married his daughters to kings of Sicily and Castile and to Henry the Lion, Duke of Saxony ; the Duke was father to the Emperor Otto IV, the King of Sicily cousin to Otto's famous rival and supplanter, the Emperor Frederick II. Henry's wife was Eleanor of Aquitaine, ' divorced ' wife of the King of France—Eleanor's children and grandchildren became kings or queens of most countries between England and the Holy Land.

Henry had been named after his grandfather, and in many ways resembled him. Both were ruthless and cunning, yet both were fundamentally trusted as well as feared by their followers. Both had an exceptional capacity for choosing men to serve them ; both had a ferocious eagerness to see justice done. Few men have done more for the peace and security of the English kingdom. The resemblance is in part increased by the younger Henry's admiration for his grandfather, whose reign provided a model for his own. Henry II had many friends, and some intimates. But he was not an easy man to live with. Like Henry I, he was unfaithful to his wife ;

nevertheless, he had seven children by her before they finally quarrelled. Eleanor was probably as difficult as Henry, but when the breach came the sons, on the whole, followed Eleanor. For ordinary courtiers Henry's behaviour could be a nightmare. Peter of Blois has left a vivid account of the horrors of living in a court always on the move—the constant uncertainty, the stale food, difficulties with the billeting officers, ' and if the king promises to spend the day anywhere, especially if a herald has published the royal will, you may be sure that the king will leave the place bright and early, and upset everyone's calculations in his haste. It frequently happens, that those who are having bloodletting, or receiving treatment, leave their cure and follow the prince, and chance their life, as it were, on the throw of a dice, risking to lose themselves rather than lose what they haven't got and are not going to get. You may see men rushing madly about, urging on the pack-horses, fitting the teams to their wagons ; everyone in utter confusion —a perfect portrait of hell. But if the prince has announced that he is setting off early to reach a particular place, beyond doubt he will change his mind and sleep till noon. You will see the pack-horses waiting loaded, the wagons silent, the runners asleep, the court merchants in a pother, everyone grumbling.' He goes on to describe the throng of camp followers waiting for news of the king's movements. Then word came [1] that the next night would be spent in such a place, and hopes rose, because shelter and food were to be found there. But as the day drew in, the King changed his mind, and ' turned aside to another place, where there was maybe a single house, and no food for anyone else. And I believe our plight added to the king's pleasure.' Peter had seen enough of court life : ' I shall dedicate the remainder of my days to study and peace.' But the King's perversity and sudden changes of plan were not the only qualities which had impressed Peter of Blois. Elsewhere he fills out the picture. The physical description is famous : the hair once reddish, now turning to grey, of middle height, round-headed, his eyes brilliant as lightning when roused, his face lion-like, surmounted by a fine mane, his deep chest, strong arms and bow legs.

[1] The change of tense is Peter's ; he switches from a generalised picture to a particular memory.

The legs were constantly sore because he was so often in the saddle, yet he never sat down, not even at mass or in council—he was tirelessly active. Peter attributes this partly to his many interests, partly to his desire not to grow fat—which also explained his comparatively simple and frugal manner of life. Peter then goes on to give a conventional, though doubtlessly sincere account of Henry's remarkable qualities as a leader and ruler, and of his special interests. ' He is an ardent lover of the woods : when he is not at war, he amuses himself with hawks and hounds. . . . As often as he has free time he occupies himself in private reading or expounds some knotty problem to his clerks.'

Henry I had been called ' Beauclerc ', because he could almost sign his name. Henry II was the first English king after the Conquest to be fully literate. He had been well tutored as a young man, and showed something of Alfred's mixture of kingliness and culture : he liked to have learned men about him, was passionately curious about history and literature as well as about war and hunting. There is a certain integration in his intellectual apparatus. His idea of history was a French epic on his forefathers and their great deeds—the *Roman de Rou*, which he commissioned ; his idea of science was a treatise on falconry. Many other treatises were dedicated to him ; a sign that his patronage was generously given. Thus he emerges a brilliant figure, fascinating, dangerous and yet somehow intensely human.

The King's energy, the size of his dominions, and the complexity of his tasks make it very difficult for us to get a comprehensive view of his reign. We must limit our vision drastically. Wales, Scotland, and Ireland belong to the next chapter ; leaving them aside, we may crudely divide Henry's reign into three segments—his attempt to reconstruct the England of his grandfather, which culminated in his quarrel with Thomas Becket ; his attempt to develop the legal machinery of his grandfather and lay new foundations for English government ; and his attempt to resolve the problem of governing an unwieldy empire and an unruly family by setting the family to rule the empire. Between each of the three there is a rough logical and chronological division, but they often overlap.

Henry had won the throne because many Englishmen wished to see a return to more settled government, and a few great ones saw specific advantage in supporting him. His first task was to convince the former that good government was to be restored, and to prevent the latter from repenting their choice. The great barons presented him with many tricky problems, but good fortune aided him to solve them. The Earl of Chester died late in 1153 ; the Earl of Hereford retired to a monastery to die in 1155. Henry did not try to abolish the earldoms granted under Stephen, but it was still necessary for him to destroy the new castles which were the most formidable weapon in twelfth-century warfare. In 1155 he seized the Bishop of Winchester's castles, his first overt attack on Stephen's family ; in 1157 he treated the castles of Stephen's son, Earl William, in the same fashion—and relations between Henry and William stayed uneasy until William's death in 1159. Castles fell ; faithful subjects found the new King prepared within limits to respect the *status quo* ; would-be rebels found him a terrible enemy. The financial machinery of the Exchequer, the old mechanism of local government, and the royal courts very rapidly returned to the efficiency of Henry I's day. Henry II was fortunate to succeed before the memory of the exercise of crown rights by his grandfather had died away. It was a number of years before Henry tried any striking innovations : what his grandfather had done was at first sufficient.

The most powerful man in England after the king was the old Archbishop of Canterbury, to whom Henry owed much. Relations between them were outwardly cordial, and Henry rarely refused an urgent request from Theobald. Most striking evidence of Theobald's influence was the presence of his favourite clerk and archdeacon, Thomas Becket, in the office of royal Chancellor and in the most intimate counsels of the king. But it is clear that Henry felt that the Church had acquired the habit of acting more independently than was fitting : and that he found the old man too assiduous a counsellor. Under these conditions was born the most disastrous of all Henry's schemes. When Theobald died he was to be replaced by a man who would fall in with Henry's plans, who would assist him to rule the Church as his grandfather had done, and would be a constant and welcome ornament of his court. In Thomas Becket Henry pictured a right-hand man after the pattern of Rainald of Dassel, Archbishop of Cologne, Arch-chancellor of Italy and confidant of the Emperor Frederick Barbarossa.

Becket as chancellor had revealed just that mixture of efficiency and glamour which made him a perfect servant for Henry ; someone who could maintain the pageantry, organise the detail of a great court, and yet be wholly subservient and wholly congenial to the King. His life was moral, but extremely worldly. There was nothing to indicate that he would not play the same role when he became archbishop in 1162. But in fact from that date he changed his way of life and tried to find an entirely new relation to the King. He became the ascetic monk ; the prophetic spiritual leader ; the King's father in God. Henry was bewildered and irritated. He had looked for secure co-operation from Becket ; the more Becket acted out of his character (as Henry knew it) the more insecure Henry felt. A series of minor disputes, which would normally have been settled by compromise, swiftly developed into a major quarrel. At last, in 1164, Henry determined to break him. In January, at Clarendon, he tried to secure the consent of the Archbishop and bishops to a catalogue of essential customs governing the relations of Church and state. The Constitutions of Clarendon describe themselves as ' this record or recognition of a certain part of the customs, privileges and dignities of the king's predecessors—to wit of his grandfather King Henry—and other things which ought to be observed in the kingdom '. They were no statement of new law, but a solemn affirmation of ancient practice, and Henry browbeat Thomas and his colleagues into assenting to them.

The constitutions covered many disputed points where the jurisdiction of Church and state overlapped. To take two crucial examples, they laid down the procedure by which clergy convicted of crime (' criminous clerks ') should be punished, and they affirmed that no appeal should go to Rome without royal assent—clearly implying that this was to be something exceptional. The constitutions were for the most part a fair statement of practice under Henry I ; many clauses indeed were not controversial. But the essential clauses, including these two, were far from being fair statements of practice in Stephen's later years, and were inconsistent with the Church's law. By publishing the constitutions, Henry made it certain that the area of conflict should become known to the pope, and so invited condemnation. Had the customs never been forced on the pope's attention in so lucid a form, the King might have been able to continue quietly to enforce them.

At Clarendon Becket submitted ; then repented of his submission, and put himself at the mercy of the Pope. In October the Archbishop went to Northampton, where he had been summoned to face trial before the king on several of the points at issue between them. But whatever the ostensible grounds of the Archbishop's trial, everyone knew that the real question was whether the Constitutions of Clarendon were binding and whether Becket was to continue in office. At Northampton Becket refused to submit to trial. He claimed as clerk and bishop total exemption from the jurisdiction of lay courts ; and his final answer to the King's persistent threats was to fly the country and appeal to the pope. By this act Becket symbolically breached two of the most critical of the Constitutions.

The rights and wrongs of this quarrel will be disputed to the end of time. In the point of law each side was right on its own assumptions. Henry was upholding royal custom ; Becket the law of the Church. Beyond question the two were incompatible, though it was no easy matter to decide how far. Clerks accused of anything, say the Constitutions, shall go to the royal court to answer what pertains to its jurisdiction, to the Church court for what belongs there. So far Lanfranc at least would have agreed. Nor need the rider that a royal justice should go to the Church court to keep an eye on proceedings be taken too seriously. More dangerous was the vague final sentence : ' If a clerk has confessed or been convicted, the Church shall protect him no further.' In practice this meant that a clerk would be unfrocked by a Church court for some crime, then punished in the lay courts as a layman for the same crime ; nor was it clear that this was contrary to canon law. But Becket maintained—and in the end the Pope settled the matter (for the time being) by accepting his interpretation

—that no man could be punished twice for the same offence. On this issue there was no question of right or wrong : the law of the Church was obscure.

Behind the law lay a whole world of ideas and assumptions in which the lay and the clerical view diverged. It affected most critically the office of a bishop or archbishop. He was a leading figure in the Church's hierarchy, a lord spiritual ; but he was also a leading figure in the hierarchy of the kingdom of which he was a member, a leading subject, and counsellor of his king. The dichotomy and the dilemma it created were neatly summarised by Becket himself when writing to King Henry : 'You are my lord, you are my king, you are my spiritual son.' Good order in the Church depended on good appointments to bishoprics, on the spirituality, strength of character, and independence of the bishops ; good order in the state depended only to a slightly lesser extent on the king's controlling his bishops, on their being sound, reliable statesmen, with a strong sense of loyalty to him. At every point the issues between Church and state touched deep convictions of the medieval mind : the theology of the Church, the sacred nature of kingship, the sacredness of the feudal bond tying bishops to their king, the inherited tradition of social prejudice which accompanied the deep cleavage between clergy and laity.

Beyond all this lay the personal clash between Thomas and Henry, and the tragedy of an intimate friendship translated into a bitter quarrel. Henry's view of the matter was comparatively straightforward. He had trusted Becket implicitly, and Becket had let him down ; the Archbishop had sworn fealty to the King, and broken his oath. He was 'the traitor'. But why had Becket changed ? What strange compulsion accounts for the new mode of life of 1162–3, for the alternating submission and resistance of 1164 ? How was the man who had dedicated his life to the service of the King from 1154 to 1162 able to spend his remaining years in resisting him—able to face exile from 1164 to 1170, and death in 1170 ? It is unlikely that these questions will ever be answered satisfactorily, because their answers must depend on reconstructing the logic of a world which is irrecoverable, and on fathoming the mysteries of a deep and complex character, one who puzzled his contemporaries as much as he puzzles us. Becket was only too well aware that, at the time when the King forced the monks of Canterbury to elect him archbishop, he was widely regarded as a time-serving royal minister, who would continue his old way of life even as Archbishop of Canterbury. Above all, he knew that the older bishops, led by Gilbert Foliot of London, one-time monk of Cluny, and Roger of York, a colleague of Becket in the circle of Archbishop Theobald, regarded him as a caricature of an archbishop, a royal toy. Circumstances counselled him to make some effort to convince the world that he was going to try to be a real archbishop, not too unworthy a successor of Lanfranc or Anselm, or his old master Theobald ; above all, he needed to dispel the illusions of the King. But it was not only circumstances, powerful as they were, which compelled Becket to act as he did ; in some way he was compelled by his own nature. Can we go further, and say that he felt the necessity to convince not only king, bishops and old associates, but also himself? No set of events in the twelfth century is better recorded than the dispute of Henry II and Thomas Becket ; we have twelve or so *Lives* and some 800 letters from which to reconstruct the story. But the central character remains an enigma.

At the end of 1164 the Archbishop laid his case before the Pope, Alexander III (1159–81), then in exile at Sens. Alexander was a fine theologian and canon lawyer and a diplomat of great distinction. Becket was a fearful embarrassment to him, since he already had an anti-pope and a war with the emperor on his hands. The Pope never let Becket down, yet managed to restrain the Archbishop's occasional outbursts of violence until 1170, when a much more favourable international situation enabled Alexander to take sterner measures. Behind the scenes the old rivalry of York and Canterbury played a significant part in embittering the struggle. By custom Canterbury alone might anoint and crown a new king ; and custom was supported by a papal mandate to protect Canterbury's rights while Thomas was in exile. But Henry II was impatient to have his eldest surviving son, another Henry, crowned king in his own lifetime—he wished to prevent his own path to the throne setting any precedents detrimental to royal authority or hereditary succession.

Impatiently he ordered York and his colleagues to crown the young Henry; and York complacently agreed. In June the son was crowned; Archbishop Thomas (supported by the Pope) instantly threatened an interdict—an order closing all the churches in the kingdom. The grave effects of an interdict on a medieval kingdom made this a threat too strong even for Henry II, who immediately patched up a reconciliation. Shortly afterwards Becket received authority from the Pope to excommunicate the bishops who had assisted at the coronation. At first Becket hesitated; then he decided to publish the anathemas, and the next day (1st December) he returned to England in an atmosphere no less charged than at the time of his departure six years before. The King was violently angry; and a host of difficulties awaited Thomas, made worse by the King's renewed hostility. But his troubles were soon over. On the evening of Tuesday, 29th December, four knights, incited by the furious anger of the King, broke into Canterbury Cathedral, and deliberately and brutally murdered the Archbishop before a crowd of witnesses.

Few events in medieval history shocked the conscience of Europe so profoundly or so immediately. Becket's death was followed by a whisper that miracles had been performed at his tomb; soon the reports became insistent and widespread, and in a very short time the Pope was moved to canonise the murdered Archbishop. Then even his enemies had to submit, and King Henry was compelled as an act of penance to walk barefoot through the streets of Canterbury and submit to a thorough flogging from a number of bishops and from the monks of Canterbury Cathedral. In due course churches were dedicated to Thomas's name in many remote corners of Europe.

The practical effects of the murder in the cathedral were less dramatic. The Constitutions of Clarendon were abrogated; but most of their clauses remained quietly in effect. On all crucial issues new compromises were found. The King could not stop appeals to Rome; but that had been a forlorn hope in 1164. Criminous clerks were saved from the gallows, but not long guaranteed from secular penalties. 'The Church holds the felonious clerk,' writes Professor Cheney, 'but the sheriff holds on to his chattels.' It was a long time before another English bishop came so near to secular condemnation as Becket in 1164. But the character of the episcopate was not altered. The long quarrel had left many sees vacant; when they were filled in 1173-4, one, Canterbury itself, went to a monk, most of the remainder went to royal servants—including one or two of Becket's particular enemies. As a young man Henry II had seen the affairs of the Church too exclusively in terms of his grandfather's customs. In his later years he learned to accept so much of the new canon law as had won general acceptance, while retaining in substance much of the influence held by his predecessors.

(2) LEGAL REFORM

Violent though this quarrel with Thomas Becket was, it did not hinder the steady reconstruction of royal government in England. Frequent outbreaks of crime and, in particular, the frequent usurpation of property by force or guile, remained as the heritage of the anarchy. It was against these two evils that royal justice was most powerfully mobilised under Henry II; and in the process of mobilising it he developed the structure of royal jurisdiction and laid the foundations for that co-operation between royal and local officials which was to be the hall-mark of English government.

The detection of crime was a rough and ready process; all that Henry could hope to do was to make life difficult for the notorious criminal. In the Assize [1] of Clarendon of 1166, elaborated by the Assize of Northampton ten years later, a procedure was laid down by which a committee, or jury, of twelve men from each hundred and four men from each township, should periodically denounce to sheriff or royal justice any notorious criminals of the neighbourhood, or

[1] The word 'assize', *assisa*, was used in a variety of senses in the Middle Ages. Its basic meaning was the sitting or session of a court, in which the members of the court joined with the judge to settle a case or a point of law, or to make an assessment for taxation. From these usages stem the words 'assize' and 'assessment' as we use them today. The most solemn *assisae* in the Middle Ages were the sessions of the king's court, and the word 'assize' came to be applied to a law or an edict promulgated in the king's court—hence the 'Assizes' of Clarendon and Northampton; and so, by deduction, to the legal procedure laid down in an 'assize'—hence the 'possessory assizes' and the 'Grand Assize', described below.

harbourers of criminals—who should then be put to the ordeal. The procedure was crude, but at least it was a procedure ; and it was supported by the strongest power in the land. ' Liberties ' and ' franchises '—areas normally exempt from royal jurisdiction—were ignored ; the sudden rounding-up of criminals became a regular event in the countryside.

This procedure was probably not new : like so many of Henry's expedients, it had been tried out by his grandfather. But it was enforced with a new energy, and from being a very occasional instrument to deal with a crime-wave it became a normal police measure. Similarly Henry's even more important measures for improving land-law were based on earlier precedents, but made effective in a new way.

Cases dealing with land-tenure had hitherto been dealt with in feudal courts—that is, in the courts of barons, not the royal courts ; land-tenure provided the most important business of the barons' courts. But disputes between tenants-in-chief, or disputes of unusual complexity between lesser men might come to the King's court. The power of the royal courts had been greatly enhanced by the Norman Conquest and the great prestige of the Domesday Inquest. Henry II began a process whereby more and more quite trivial disputes on tenure came to the King's court—once again, he was developing and making regular what his grandfather had done as an occasional act of power.

The procedure even of the royal court, however, was inclined to be slow. A case was started by the purchase of a writ from the royal Chancery. The plaintiff might have to pursue the King to a distant corner of his empire for writs and judgment ; procedural difficulties could delay a case for months. All this was an invitation to a strong man to seize his neighbour's land, and enjoy the fruits of it for many a long day until his neighbour could prove and enforce his right. Such acts had been common under Stephen, and were difficult to prevent even under Henry. What was needed was a swift and effective procedure for restoring possession to someone dispossessed without due process of law. To provide this, a number of ' possessory ' actions or ' assizes ', as they were called, were established. The most important of these actions was that of ' Novel Disseisin ', established at the same time as the criminal jury in 1166. A holder of free land who had been dispossessed could buy a writ of Novel Disseisin, which instructed the sheriff to summon a jury and ask the members whether in fact the plaintiff had been recently put out of possession. If they said yes, the sheriff had to restore him. Once again, a rough and ready measure ; but it was of unique importance in strengthening the idea that the royal court was the fount of justice *par excellence*, and a normal place in which to settle even quite minor disputes.

' Novel Disseisin ' had two sister writs. ' Mort d'Ancestor ' bade the sheriff ask the question whether the plaintiff's father was in possession when last a tenant died and an heir succeeded. If so, and if the plaintiff was the true heir, he was to be put in possession. ' Darrein Presentment ' dealt with a different kind of property—the right to present to a rectory or vicarage—and was intended to support the ' possession ' of the man who had presented on the last occasion. Some perquisites still attached to the right to present ; but its value lay mainly in the opportunity it gave a man to find employment for a relation, friend, or dependant.

Behind the question of possession or ' seisin ' lay the deeper question of right—not merely who *did* possess the land, but who *ought* to hold it ; who had the sounder title to it. Nor did Henry II leave this question undisturbed. Towards the end of his reign he introduced the ' Grand Assize '. A baron or knight in possession, if sued for his right to a piece of land, had hitherto usually had to defend it in the ordeal by battle— that is by fighting for it. Under the Grand Assize he had the option of laying his case before a jury of twelve local knights. These ' assizes ' for cases in land-tenure were of even greater importance than Henry's criminal assizes. They were popular and widely used ; they accustomed men to pleading in the King's court as a normal event ; they brought in much revenue and enhanced the court's importance.

The issuing of writs added to the work of the royal Chancery. In every sphere of administration and justice the second half of the twelfth century saw rapid growth. The over-powerful sheriff found himself more and more subject to checks and controls. In 1170 a swift investigation of all the sheriffs was undertaken, and the majority were relieved of their posts.

Furthermore, the audit at the Exchequer became more effective; more and more jurisdiction was taken over by specially appointed royal justices, who toured the country. The justices were not as yet trained lawyers, nor did they work to a system. Henry was for ever trying new expedients—now a larger number of itinerant justices who could travel farther or more swiftly ; now a small bench of more expert men who could work in Westminster for a longer period. Some of his judges were clerics, to whom no doubt he owed some ideas imported from canon law ; some were laymen, including the Chief Justice or Justiciar of his later years, Ranulph Glanville. It was under the aegis of Glanville that the first systematic treatise on English law was compiled. It is no very elaborate treatise —essentially it is a commentary on the writs which can be bought in the royal Chancery and the way they can be used ; a practical manual of procedure and of the law administered in the royal court. But its appearance was a portent. In a wholly new sense, the royal court was the centre of English litigation and justice ; and there was shortly going to be a new profession for educated men—the profession of trained lawyers —who would need a manual and a textbook for their guidance.

Justices had posted into the counties and met juries long before the accession of Henry II. But from now on such meetings were regular events ; and it was in the meetings of juries of local knights with royal justices that the idea of local responsibility—of the crucial link between royal government and the natural representatives of local society—was born.

(3) THE ANGEVIN EMPIRE

Henry II opened the last act of his quarrel with Thomas Becket by having his son Henry crowned king in Westminster Abbey on 14th June 1170. His family were growing up ; he had already quarrelled with his wife, and for the rest of his life he was seldom free for long from quarrels with one or other of his children. These quarrels neutralised the great potential strength of his empire. Under a harmonious family, the Angevin power would have been irresistible.[1] But Henry and

[1] Henry II and his successors are commonly known as the Angevin kings, because they were descended from Geoffrey, Count of Anjou,

his sons, heirs of two of the most violent dynasties in western Europe—Anjou and Normandy—were not made for peace or co-operation.

Of Henry's family it could be said that war was their pleasure, but marriage their business. It is true that Henry owed England, *de facto*, to the Norman Conquest; but he was also one of the few known descendants of the Anglo-Saxon royal line, through his grandmother, Matilda. His father had been hereditary Count of Anjou, and his mother heiress of England and Normandy and of claims in Maine and Brittany. It is doubtful if Geoffrey had envisaged the permanent union of the traditional rivals, Normandy and Anjou; but Henry was too ambitious to share his heritage with anyone else. His own marriage brought Aquitaine, and he constantly schemed and plotted for equally good matches for his children. At one moment it even seemed that he might marry his son, Henry, to the heiress of the kingdom of France. But in the end Louis had a son, and when Henry II died in 1189, he was already being outmatched by the most successful political intriguer of the day, the young King Philip II of France. Philip's speciality was to breed dissension among the Angevins; and in the end he destroyed the Angevin Empire by guile and by force.

Henry based his rule in the various parts of his empire on different claims and titles, and only slowly gave the various sections anything resembling a unified administration. In fact he was never equally secure in every part of the domains. In England, Normandy, and Anjou he was heir to a long tradition of strong government in which Stephen's reign was just an interlude; in Aquitaine he was heir to a tradition of anarchy. In a measure he and his wife and his son Richard overcame the separatism of parts of Aquitaine, but their government there was never wholly secure outside Poitou, the old centre of power of Eleanor's forbears. In the south-east of

---

Henry's father. Count Geoffrey used as his emblem a broom flower, in French, *plante genêt*; and on this account a fifteenth-century claimant of the English throne styled himself 'Plantagenet'. This surname, often attached by modern historians to earlier members of the family, was never so used, as far as we know, by their contemporaries.

THE ANGEVIN EMPIRE IN 1154

The shaded areas include all territories under Henry II's direct rule at the end of 1154. (The Count of Toulouse accepted his suzerainty in 1173) For his relations with Wales, Scotland and Ireland see chap. 11, sect. 2–4.

the duchy their control was utterly precarious. Henry tried unsuccessfully to subdue Toulouse in 1159, and only in 1173 acquired suzerainty over its count.

The events of the tenth and eleventh centuries had decided that England was to be henceforth a united kingdom ; but they had set no firm boundaries to an English king's claims and ambitions. One of the great questions in English politics in the twelfth and thirteenth centuries was where the frontiers of England would be laid : in the Welsh marches, at the Irish

Channel, or in Ireland ; in Cumberland, on the Forth, or at John o' Groats ; at the Channel, at the Channel Islands, in France, at the Pyrenees ? None of these questions was finally settled by 1272.

The ambitions and the interests of the monarchs were only one group of factors in settling these questions. So great was the play of personality and circumstance in medieval politics that it is often most misleading to talk of ' deep underlying forces '. It is for the most part true to say that no medieval empire which could not be comfortably ruled by one man could be lasting. This means that a monarch had to visit every corner of his empire and be personally known to all his leading subjects if his rule was to be effective. The empire of Henry II was made possible by the restless energy of the King ; even Henry did not quite know how one man could rule it all, and he tried to take his family into partnership.

As soon as his sons were old enough to help or hinder his government, Henry began to distribute the titles of his possessions among them. Richard was enthroned Duke of Aquitaine in 1167 ; Henry King of England in 1170 (he was also made Duke of Normandy and Count of Anjou) ; Geoffrey became Duke of Brittany in 1181 by marrying the heiress ; John was made Lord of Ireland in 1185. But these were not meant to be independent commands : Henry was to be kept firmly under his father's control, and the other sons were ultimately to do homage to Henry. Under this constraint they chafed, and no strong bond of family affection kept them at peace with their father : sooner or later each of them plotted rebellion. The most serious outbreak was in 1173-4, when Henry, Richard, and Geoffrey, encouraged by their mother, raised rebellions on both sides of the Channel, and were strongly supported by Louis VII and the leading powers of northern France. In the end the rebellion collapsed. Henry tried to improve his sons' humour by giving them more responsibility ; but there was little trust among them. The young Henry ended his troubled career in 1183 ; Geoffrey died, plotting, in 1186 ; and only Richard and John were left to conspire with the young French King, Philip II. The final rebellion bade fair to destroy the empire ; but Henry's death (1189) and Richard's rapid succession left it once more united in strong and capable hands.

11   The British Isles

(1) ENGLAND

IN RECENT chapters we have been studying the effect of the Norman Conquest on many aspects of English life. We have seen England as part of a Norman and Angevin Empire ; but England as a part of Britain has eluded us. The time has come to see England in its geographical context ; to leave the lowland zone ; to look towards the hills. Interesting as the history of these other lands is, our main theme must be the contrast between the way the Normans conquered and settled England and the way they failed to conquer Wales, Scotland, and Ireland. First, then, we must summarise the assimilation of the two peoples in England.

Eleventh-century Britain was a Babel of many tongues. In the north and west the various Celtic languages were spoken ; in England itself the chief languages were the Anglo-Saxon dialects. But scattered all over the island, and especially in the English Danelaw, were people still speaking a Viking language, Danish or Norwegian ; and equally scattered were the representatives of the educated clergy, who read and sang and often spoke Latin. Into this medley the Normans brought their own dialect of French, and for three centuries at least Norman French remained the language of the English court.

This may seem complicated enough ; yet it probably still gives the modern reader far too simple a picture. The Celtic languages are themselves diverse. Of the two main groups, Gaelic (Goidelic) and Brittonic (Brythonic), some version of the former was spoken throughout Ireland and northern Scotland ; some version of the latter in most of Cumberland, Wales, Cornwall, and Brittany. Here and there—as in Wales—the groups intermingled ; everywhere there were local dialects which might make communication with a Celt from another tribe far from easy. Although the differences between the Anglo-Saxon dialects were less profound, they might also make communication difficult between one region and another. There was no ' standard English '. In these conditions many folk knew two or three languages ; but interpreters were much in demand. Queen Margaret of Scotland (died 1093) had been brought up in Hungary and presumably Magyar and English were her native tongues. It is clear that she could read Latin. For Gaelic she had her husband as interpreter, as her biographer tells us when recounting how she disputed for three days to the discomfiture of a council of the Scottish clergy. The learning and ignorance of royalty have always been subject to special privileges. Monarchies, especially hereditary monarchies, tended in the past to be dynastic and international, however much they might pretend the contrary. As late as the eighteenth century England had two kings who could not speak English. The rest of the upper classes have had to accommodate themselves more promptly. It must have been normal for the Scottish nobles to talk French and Gaelic as it came to be normal for the English upper classes to talk French at court and English in the fields.

The stages by which this took place can never be precisely known ; but what we do know about the development of English in the two centuries after the Norman Conquest is especially interesting, because it reveals to us, as it were in a mirror, the assimilation of the English and Norman races. One may still occasionally hear the ancient boast, that this or that person's ancestors ' came over with the Conqueror '. It has long been an idle boast. All Englishmen are descended from a number of men who fought on each side at Hastings ; almost none of us can prove who our ancestors were. We are all ' Anglo-Normans ' in a sense ; and though the phrase had lost its meaning already before 1272, the process by which it lost it has left many vital traces in our history.

At first Norman French (or ' Anglo-Norman ') was the language of the new aristocracy—and so to a large extent of the upper clergy also ; English the language of the middle classes and the peasants. Both languages must have been spoken in every noble household ; and from the first the mingling was enhanced by the frequency of intermarriage. Gradually, as time passed, the French language became more artificial, less and less an affair of every day. Its death lies far outside our period. But already in the twelfth and thirteenth centuries it was beginning to affect the English language which was to supplant it. Modern English may be based first and foremost on Old English and Middle English (as its post-Conquest successor is called) ; but in structure and vocabulary it has an immense Romance element, mainly derived from French ; and the bulk of this came in from Anglo-Norman in the centuries following the Norman Conquest. Romance influence may have helped to save modern English from the complex inflexions which still flourish in most other Teutonic languages, and to give it the chance to develop the freedom and variety of construction so visible in Chaucer and Shakespeare ; but inflexions had already long been in decay. The fact that French was the language of the upper classes is still evident in our words tournament and jousting, lance and castle, forest and venison. But words are strange things, and if we pursue their origin too assiduously, they will play us many tricks. The Norman knight lived in his hall for many centuries ; but knight and hall are English words. The greatest barons were called earls, like Thorkell the Tall and Godwin, though their wives to this day are countesses. Words give us many hints ; but we must not expect too much of them.

It ought to be possible to trace the mingling of the races by observing the Christian names we meet in documents of the late eleventh and twelfth centuries. But this is particularly difficult, because the fashion soon arose for English parents to give their children French names ; and because other fashions were altering the type of name favoured. Names of the great heroes of romance, Arthur and Alexander, of Old Testament figures, Adam and David, of apostles, Peter, James, and Andrew, were coming in alongside the English Edward, Edgar, and Alfred, and the Norman William, Ralph, and Robert. But it was rare for a great baron to call his children by English names. It was not until the birth of an heir apparent in 1239 —to a king who revered Edward the Confessor—that the name Edward re-entered the English royal family. The mingling of names in native English families may lead us to ante-date the assimilation of the races.

Yet the Christian names are not wholly without significance.

A few great thegns survived the Conquest, married into the invaders, and founded 'Norman' baronial families. Still more Norman barons gave a shadow of legitimacy to their usurpations by marrying English heiresses. Most striking of these was Henry I of England—though he changed his wife's name from Edith to Matilda in the process. But in the middle region, below the barons but above the peasantry, intermarriage must have been common. Already at the turn of the eleventh and twelfth centuries we meet a canon of St Paul's with a French name and a French wife, but himself the son of an English father. Ralph, son of Algot, was not only a member of the upper clergy ; he was also an alderman in the City. In these regions assimilation moved fastest ; and since it was from canons and small knights that many bishops and new barons were later recruited, intermarriage at this level came to have a wide significance. The Angevin Empire preserved the French contacts and French interests of the very great ; a baron in the twelfth century noted in his writs that he was addressing his subjects both French and English ; a chronicler, even at the end of the century, will sometimes notice that an important man is of 'English' descent. By the thirteenth century the distinction, for the most part, was beyond research.

The same story is told by the changes in English and Anglo-Norman literature. One might suppose that English literature would have gradually disappeared, to be replaced by French. In fact the two proceeded hand in hand until the point at which English conquered or assimilated French as the language of the great. It is true that the Anglo-Saxon writ died shortly after the Conquest ; that the *Anglo-Saxon Chronicle* was only continued in a single copy after 1079—it came to a stop at Peterborough soon after 1154. But there is a thin stream of continuous tradition in the writing of sophisticated English verse and devotional literature. In *The Owl and the Nightingale*, of the late twelfth century, asceticism and gaiety debate according to a fashion met with elsewhere, but with a skill and freshness equal to anything in French. The chief source book for the Arthurian romances, Geoffrey of Monmouth's Latin *History*, was translated (or rather adapted, as plays and books are nowadays adapted for the cinema) both into French and

English. This is a particularly striking example. The Arthurian legend, the ' Matter of Britain ', was in a sense native to this island. But it owed its immense popularity to the way in which it was adapted to suit the tastes of courtly circles. The court of Arthur was made the centre of many cycles of courtly romances—of tales of knightly prowess performed to do honour to ladies. The chief cycles were written in French ; the courts in which they chiefly flourished were in France. Although one of these courts was the Angevin court, the romances are less associated with England than with Eleanor of Aquitaine and her court at Poitiers, with her son Richard I, crusader and troubadour, and her daughter (by Louis VII) Marie of Champagne. None the less they flourished throughout western Europe, and it was inevitable that Arthur should be especially celebrated in England. It is significant that Arthurian romances for English audiences were written in English as well as in French ; and as time went on the English versions became as widely known and as sophisticated as the French.

If we ask in the end, as we must, what was the impact on England and the English of the Norman Conquest, we ask a question to which we can expect no final or clear-cut answer. It is none the less worth asking. On numerous occasions in history we find evidence that a warrior aristocracy invaded and dominated a larger native population—it happened on more than one occasion in the earlier history of Britain. But it is very rare for us to be able to trace these settlements in detail. We know a great deal about the Norman Conquest, and it gives us a unique opportunity for studying such a movement. Furthermore, it was the central event of medieval English history, and our curiosity can never be satisfied until we have made some effort to grapple with the most fundamental problem which it invites us to face.

The Normans and their French allies came in comparatively small numbers. They settled as soldiers, knights, feudal warriors ; they brought their own social organisation ; their own idea of land-tenure ; but they grafted them on to the highly elaborate legal arrangements of the country they had conquered. They brought no new ideas of government ; they came from a duchy unprovided with elaborate administrative institutions. They took over and adapted what they found. What they brought, however, perhaps mattered more than institutions at that time : they brought a new dynasty of exceptional energy and ability, and they brought a capacity and a will to experiment and adapt. They took over the Old English institutions ; but within two generations they had developed them far beyond what could have been imagined by Cnut or the Confessor.

In part this was due to the Normans themselves, in part to the fashions of the day. New ideas of statecraft were abroad. The Norman kings were more cosmopolitan than their predecessors, not because they travelled more widely—several Anglo-Saxon kings had visited Rome, and none of the Norman kings, before Richard I, travelled far outside his dominions—but because that was the fashion of the age in which they lived.

The same is true of the Norman impact on the Church. The Normans brought the English Church up to date, they brought it into line with continental models. But it had not been old-fashioned in 1050, still less had it been out of touch. It was merely that the Norman Conquest coincided with great changes in the Church at large ; and that the Normans, brilliant adapters that they were, never hesitated to alter what they did not like. Many profound and ancient institutions were not affected. English spirituality seeped through to the invaders. The English taught the Normans how to paint. Meanwhile the Normans were transferring cathedrals to new sites, rebuilding cathedrals and abbeys on an immensely grandiose scale ; peopling the English Church at its apex— with bishops and abbots and monks and canons—as they peopled the apex of lay society. They thought the old English dioceses disorganised, and introduced archdeacons and rural deans. Their efforts were certainly not negligible or fruitless. No group of Englishmen built on so magnificent a scale before the eighteenth-century dukes and the nineteenth-century railway contractors. Recent study has done something to soften the impact of the Norman Conquest—to show that in many directions change was not so rapid or so radical as we had once supposed. It affected the peasant far less than the thegn, the merchant, and the monk. There is very much that we do not know about its effects in detail. But when all is said and done, it remains a dramatic episode, and such contemporaries felt it to be. Here, in conclusion, is the opinion of the Normans held by William of Malmesbury, one of the shrewdest observers of the second generation, and himself a man of mixed Anglo-Norman stock.

' The Normans . . . are exceedingly careful in their dress, nice beyond all conscience in their food ; a race given to warfare, utterly at a loss without it ; indefatigable in pursuit of an enemy, and where force is not sufficient, they use guile and money no less. They build enormous buildings as economically as possible, vie with their equals, strain to surpass their betters, carp at those beneath them while striving to protect them from everyone else. They are faithful to their lords—but swift to break faith for a slight occasion. A breath of ill-fortune and they are plotting treachery, a bag of money and their mind is changed. But they are the most friendly of races and treat strangers as honourably as themselves ; they intermarry with their subjects. They have raised the standard of religious observance, extinct in England at their arrival [this we need not take too seriously]. Everywhere you may see churches building, and monasteries both in town and country ; the land flourishes in a new way—every man of wealth thinks the day lost which he has not marked by some notable act of generosity.'

(2) WALES

For its day the English monarchy was the most centralised in Europe. This fact provides us with a great temptation to tell its story in isolation : to ignore both its intimate contacts with France and Europe, and its even more intimate contacts with Wales, Scotland, and Ireland. There is nothing more difficult in this period than to do justice to the other principalities and kingdoms of the British Isles. Their history is obscure and confused ; their native traditions were immensely tenacious ; yet their fate depended closely on the ambitions of the English king and the Anglo-Norman leaders. These conditions somehow created an extremely uneasy equilibrium, in which none of these lands was conquered or subdued and yet none was wholly independent of the English kings. The consequence of this is a contrast of deep importance in our history. The

Normans rapidly assimilated themselves to their English subjects, and a mixed people with a mixed culture emerged. Had they conquered the Celtic lands as thoroughly as they conquered England, the British Isles might have achieved the unity which has always evaded them. But no such conquest took place. To make clear why that was so, we must first tell, in rough outline, the story of the kingdoms ; then sketch the nature and extent of Norman penetration.

Alfred had had close contacts with his elder contemporary, Rhodri Mawr (the great), ruler of most of Wales, a man with a more cultivated court and apparently more stable power than a west Saxon king could expect to have had when threatened by the Danes. Welsh empires rarely survived their founder ; but Rhodri's grandson, Hywel the Good, built up a power more substantial than Rhodri's, worked in close liaison with his nominal overlord, Athelstan, and left a great name as a legislator. But the sole foundation for Hywel's power was personal prestige and his relation to the English quasi-emperor. No institutions bound the Welsh principalities together and only the flimsiest of traditions supported unity. Nor could the geography of so divided a country help a ruler of all Wales ; for nature has conspired to baffle and bewilder human communications.

The power of Hywel had been supported by his connection with the English court. The power of the next ruler of all Wales, Gruffyd ap Llywelyn, was won in spite of the English leaders. From this time forward princes who defied England and princes who knew how to manipulate an English alliance were often rivals for the first place among the Welsh leaders. The lords of the south, Rhys ap Tewdwr, a friend of William the Conqueror, and his grandson, Rhys ap Gruffydd (' the Lord Rhys '), owed their position partly to English favour, which helped them to retain their independence against the penetration of the English Marcher lords and their northern rivals. They were never mere satellites, nor would they have retained the respect of their subjects had they been so. The younger Rhys, indeed, had won much power at English expense early in Stephen's reign. More consistently anti-English were the leading rulers of the two northern principalities, Gwynedd and Powys. The first really distinguished ruler in the north

Plate 13 FOUNTAINS ABBEY (Yorkshire). The splendid trees on rising slopes either side remind us that the abbey grounds are now a specimen of eighteenth-century landscape gardening ; but they tend to hide the fact that the abbey was itself a splendid example of monastic engineering. On the left the church stands on dry flat ground in the middle of the valley ; on the right (from bottom to top) the guest house, the long white line of the lay-brothers' dormitory, the kitchen and refectory, the monks' dormitory and latrines, the abbot's lodging and (beyond the curve in the stream) the infirmary, were skilfully designed to use the river and a variety of artificial conduits for water-supply and drainage. The church tower is of the sixteenth century ; most of the rest dates from the twelfth or thirteenth. The lay-brothers' dormitory gives an idea of the size of the community in a large Cistercian abbey—it could hold at least 200 (compare the plan of Rievaulx, p. 144).

Plate 14 FRAMLINGHAM CASTLE (Suffolk). The greatest weapon in twelfth- and thirteenth-century war was the castle; when Roger Bigod, Earl of Norfolk (1189–1221) replaced the wooden keep at Framlingham (compare *Plate 1*), destroyed by Henry II, with a great stone castle he imitated the latest military design. A high stone wall, with a walk on top, surrounds the entire area; numerous towers project from it, from which archers could command stretches of wall on either side. Within the curtain walls was space for domestic buildings far more extensive than those even of a stone

after Harold had destroyed Gruffydd ap Llywelyn in 1063 was Gruffydd ap Cynan. Though imprisoned by the Normans from 1081 to 1093, he was able after his escape to organise a steady reconstruction of the power of Gwynedd until his death in 1137. He was succeeded by his distinguished son, Owain Gwynedd (1137–70), who started his career as leader of the northern wing of the great revolt made possible by the anarchy of Stephen's reign, and ended it in triumphant independence after twice successfully resisting a full-scale invasion by Henry II. Owain's grandson, Llywelyn the Great (died 1240), pursued a career blending the characteristics of Rhys and Owain. King John of England had had important possessions in the Welsh marches before his accession and knew something of Wales. When he came to the throne in 1199, he rapidly accepted Llywelyn, already the most powerful man in northern Wales, into his favour, and gave him his illegitimate daughter, Joan, in marriage. But Llywelyn became too powerful, and John had ambitions to annex Wales to the English crown. In the end his plans miscarried, and Llywelyn was able to take advantage of the chaos of John's last years to establish his position and clear large tracts of south Wales of English garrisons. He did homage to Henry III. In return he was allowed to live and die in undisturbed possession of his principalities. Once again it was left for a grandson of the old prince to revive his power ; but Llywelyn ap Gruffydd, the first ' Prince of Wales ' and the most powerful of all the Welsh princes, did not die in possession of his conquests. After a brilliant career of warfare in Wales and diplomacy in England, he was finally overthrown by Edward I in 1282, and the English ruled in his stead.

(3) SCOTLAND

The most widely known event in Scottish history before the late thirteenth century is the destruction of Macbeth and the accession of Malcolm III. These events have been wonderfully telescoped in Shakespeare's play—old Siward's victory took place in 1054, Macbeth held out until 1057, and not until 1058 was Malcolm hailed as King of Scotland. Our serious knowledge of Scottish history, the story of Norman infiltration and the effective unity of the Scottish kingdom all date from the accession of Malcolm ' Canmore ' (' big head ') in 1058. There had been a long preparation for this unity. By the tenth century most of northern and western Scotland was subject to the kings of the Scots and of Strathclyde. For a brief while King Edmund united the two kingdoms. More significant, in the late tenth or early eleventh century the English lands between the Forth and the Tweed, then known as Lothian, became part of the Scottish kingdom. These lands had anciently formed part of the kingdom of Northumbria, were thoroughly English, and quite distinct from the Norse and Celtic amalgams of Scotland and Strathclyde. Nor did the translation of Lothian immediately alter its character—the southern lowlands did not become fully ' Scottish ' until the days of Sir Walter Scott. But the attachment of a new province, reasonably prosperous and closely allied in culture and institutions to the English kingdom, permanently shifted the centres of power in Scotland and ultimately changed the character of the kingdom. Lothian provided a base such as the Welsh princes never possessed.

Lothian finally joined Scotland in 1018, in the reign of Malcolm II, who also won Strathclyde for his grandson, Shakespeare's Duncan, first king of all Scotland. But the dynasty and the union were both insecure before the accession of Malcolm III. Malcolm himself had the idea then traditional among Scottish rulers, that their profession was to raid England; but the Norman Conquest of England had the effect of filling the Scottish court with distinguished English leaders, the greatest of whom was Malcolm's second wife, Margaret, sister of Edgar the Aetheling, better known as St Margaret of Scotland. This dominant lady allowed her husband to amuse himself with warlike pursuits. Meanwhile she impressed on her court, her numerous children, and the people of southern Scotland, both her Christian principles and her English culture. She was a cosmopolitan lady ; though an English princess, she had been brought up in Hungary, and she found Scotland backward and cold. She brought to the north new standards of luxury in food and dress, as well as new standards in the practice of religion. But her deepest influence was felt after her death. Different as she and her husband were in every

ENGLAND, WALES & SCOTLAND
in the 12th and 13th centuries

+ English and Welsh cathedrals
× Abbeys founded by King David I of Scotland

Chester, Lichfield and Coventry formed
a single diocese, as did Bath and Wells.
Some earlier names of kingdoms, etc.
mentioned in this chapter have been included.

×Kinloss

SCOTLAND

•St Andrews

×Cambuskenneth
Firth of Forth
×Holyrood
Edinburgh
Newbattle
Berwick
Melrose
Roxburgh
Jedburgh ×
Alnwick
LOTHIAN
•Alnmouth
STRATHCLYDE
Tweed

•Newcastle

+Carlisle
•Whithorn
Durham

Rievaulx

Fountains
+York
Hull•
•Hedon
Ravenserod

+Lincoln

+Chester
Bangor
+St Asaph
GWYNEDD
Norwich
+
POWYS
+Lichfield
Strata•
Shrewsbury
Marcella
•Coventry
+Ely
WALES
Worcester
Cambridge•
Strata
+
Northampton
Florida
Hereford
•Evesham
St David's+
•Gloucester
Oxford
DEHEUBARTH
•Neath
LONDON+
Rochester+
Margam•
+Llandaff
+Bath
+Wells
Canterbury
+
Salisbury+
•Winchester
Clarendon
Chichester
Lewes

Exeter+

199

way, they were devoted to one another, and she died of grief very shortly after Malcolm's death in 1093. After an interval, three of her sons succeeded one after the other, and the reigns of Edgar, Alexander I and, above all, of David I (1124–53) witnessed a major change in the nature of Scottish government. In effect, it was David who engineered the Norman conquest of Scotland. It was not a violent conquest, and it was very far from complete ; but after 1124 the history of Scotland is inseparable from the history of its relations with the Anglo-Norman kingdom. The very names of its kings—David, Alexander, William, and Malcolm—bear witness to the cosmopolitan nature of the superstructure which Margaret and her successors had built over Celtic foundations that were still deep and vital.

(4) IRELAND

Complex as it is, the history of Wales and Scotland is simplicity itself compared with the history of Ireland over these centuries. The tenth century had seen very extensive Norse settlement ; in the eleventh the Norse built towns and some of them became peaceable merchants. Meanwhile the last king to enjoy suzerainty over all Ireland in the manner of the great Welsh princes was killed in battle in 1014. Nominally, all the Irish kings acknowledged the ' high-king ', but his power was normally as slight as the power of the French kings in Burgundy and Aquitaine. In politics and culture the eleventh and early twelfth centuries were a bleak epoch in Irish history. There are hints that the early Norman kings had thoughts of conquering the island ; and although, as in Wales, they would have had to create their own institutions, it is unlikely that they could have been very powerfully resisted. But a curious fatality attached to the few medieval Englishmen who thought seriously of settling the problems of Ireland— they included King John and King Richard II.

In fact Ireland plays a small part in our story, and that in itself is a significant fact. Edward I was able in large measure to redeem the failure of the Normans to conquer Wales ; the Scottish kingdom was ruled by Anglo-Norman barons throughout the later Middle Ages. These conquests only partially assimilated Angle and Celt : they came too late to give the peoples of the British Isles the sense of common domination by a Norman overlord—such as was felt by the far more diverse peoples of south Italy and Sicily—or the chance to assimilate and be assimilated together. To the Celt, the rulers of England have always been Saxons, Sassenachs. None the less, in the long run, Wales and Scotland became united to England as a part of Great Britain ; so for a time did the whole of Ireland, but the contrast in its history is obvious, and is reflected already in the conditions of the twelfth century.

In the mid twelfth century, by a concatenation of circumstances, the King of Connaught was high-king of Ireland. In 1156 he died, and the kings of Ireland fought for his place. The first round was won by the King of Tyrone, aided by Dermot, King of Leinster ; then Connaught's son and heir, aided by the King of Brefni, recaptured the evanescent prize. The King of Brefni had a feud against Dermot of Leinster, who had carried off his wife for a time many years before. This feud he now prosecuted with great vigour. So far the pattern was normal enough, and the story of Troy seemed about to be re-enacted. But in this crisis the King of Leinster fled to England, and Ireland entered the orbit of English politics.

(5) NORMAN INFILTRATION

Medieval kings had little sense of national frontiers. No English king would have regarded it as impossible that he should rule in Wales and Scotland ; few after the Norman Conquest had any sense of incongruity in ruling much of France as well as England ; several had large ambitions elsewhere. Richard I intervened in the affairs of all the kingdoms of Europe, Henry III's brother became (for a time) King of the Romans (i.e. of Germany), and his son was offered the kingdom of Sicily. But the fact that there was no strict limit to their ambitions meant that they often failed to concentrate on projects under their noses. The Norman kings were French by blood ; they spent much of their time out of England; they rapidly settled their headquarters at London, which lay, not in the centre of England and Britain, but midway between the English lowlands and the Continent. This orientation is the main general reason why they were so slow to become kings of Britain.

The Norman kings inherited a tradition of uncertain supremacy throughout the island. Many Welsh and Scottish princes had sworn fealty to leading English kings, like Athelstan and Edgar and Cnut. There are ample signs that the Normans assumed that this relation could be turned into something more definite. They settled great lords and established great lordships along the frontiers ; for a time they encouraged active conquest. In 1081 William I visited St David's, ' to say his prayers '—but also to meet Rhys ap Tewdwr and establish him as prince of south-western Wales. In spite of many vicissitudes, the English frontier was pushed west ; Marcher earldoms were established at Chester, Shrewsbury, and Hereford, and other lordships farther south ; and Anglo-Norman barons and knights built castles throughout Glamorgan and Pembrokeshire. Gradually the area under Welsh rule contracted, so that little more than half modern Wales was included in the ' Principality ' taken over by Edward I from the native princes. But even in the Marches settlement went ahead slowly, and the conquest of Wales did not take place in the period covered by this book.

The reasons for this are exceedingly interesting. In the first place, the Marcher lords, like their royal masters, had many other interests ; they had lands elsewhere in England and in Normandy. The first Earl of Hereford, William FitzOsbern, was killed fighting in Flanders. The great house of Bellême-Montgomery, Marchers in Normandy as well as in England, earls of Shrewsbury and conquerors (for a brief time) of much of south and central Wales, were caught up in Norman politics and broken by Henry I early in his reign. In the time of Stephen most of the Marchers followed the Earl of Gloucester in supporting the Empress, and became too deeply involved in English politics to stem the Welsh revival. These circumstances probably have more to do with the survival of Welsh independence than the power of the Welsh to resist. It is true that there were many heroic rebellions ; that even the most spectacular English invasions sometimes achieved very little. The feudal host marched into

Wales ; the princes withdrew into the hills ; no battle was fought ; the English went home at the end of the season, and the Welsh were left, poorer in sheep and food, to declare an uncertain victory. This pattern was repeated many times, especially under Rufus and Henry II. But these invasions were not usually intended to be conquests ; nor were the Normans foolish enough to imagine that this was the way to conquer Wales. When Edward I aimed at conquest a series of campaigns was only the prelude to building castles and towns and settling English soldiers and merchants. He was only repeating, on a very grandiose scale, what many Norman barons had done in earlier times. Political circumstances, and the chances of Welsh politics, gave the Normans more time and opportunity in the hundred years following the Norman Conquest of England to build castles in south Wales than in the north and centre.

There were also deeper reasons, both for the concentration on the south, and for the slow progress of Anglo-Norman infiltration. Wales was still a country of tribes and clans ; economically it was very poor, and (especially in the centre and north) utterly different from the rich agrarian lands of the nearby English Midlands. In culture, too, it was backward. We need not take seriously the taunt that Welsh and Scots were ' barbarians ' ; and we must not forget that the time was not so long past when Ireland and Wales had supplied teachers to England and the Continent. Nor was their learning entirely forgotten ; there were a few schools still remarkably active before the Normans came. But in standard of living, in economic organisation, and in mode of life the Welsh were still comparatively primitive. They had no coinage other than cows and precious ornaments. They had not yet benefited from the economic progress of recent centuries which had made England one of the richest countries in Europe. The Normans invaded England partly because it was rich ; and they were able to settle because social conditions provided them with a *milieu* not wholly uncongenial. Social conditions and the whole tradition of life were more deeply alien in the Celtic lands than in England ; and the poverty of Wales and the combativeness of its people made it less attractive. There must often have been occasions when the Marcher earls, lords of rich land in England and Normandy, were deterred from serious efforts at conquest by the thought :

> We go to gain a little patch of ground
> That hath in it no profit but the name.

And finally, there is a sense in which the feudal warrior, bred for war, but starved of activity in a comparatively peaceful kingdom, looked on the marches as his playground. For whatever reason, Wales was the playground of English warriors for two centuries after the Norman Conquest, and suffered fearfully for it. The Normans fought and hunted over Wales ; but they failed seriously to settle it or govern it.

There was, however, another Norman conquest of Wales whose story was very different, and that was the conquest of the Church. Down to 1066 the old Celtic institutions, though nominally subjected to Rome, had survived reasonably intact. Wealth and influence lay mainly with the abbots of the old *clas* or community churches, which retained a native life and tradition of their own, but resembled monasteries not at all. In later days the *clas* churches had declined, and the bishops seem comparatively more important than in other Celtic lands. But the bishops had no sees. So far as we can tell, their area of jurisdiction depended entirely on the power of the prince to whose court they were attached. The Welsh Church inevitably conformed its organisation to the secular arrangements of the Welsh principalities, cantrevs, and commotes. In the north, these arrangements were slow to change. On paper, there was an Anglo-Norman bishopric established at Bangor from 1092 and at St Asaph from 1143, and these sees corresponded roughly to the kingdoms of Gwynedd and Powys. But their tenure was uncertain and until the early thirteenth century there were long vacancies, and long periods in which the bishops, ground between Rome, Canterbury, and the Welsh princes, wandered in exile. In the south the story was very different. At first the bishops in Dyfed (west Pembrokeshire) and Glamorgan resisted Norman infiltration, and tried to assert their independence of Canterbury and of one another. But as south Wales fell into Norman hands, so the Normans granted its churches and their territories away to English monasteries and appointed Anglo-Normans to the bishoprics. The diocese of St David's was created by a clerk of Henry I called Bernard, who organised it on normal lines, with archdeacons and rural deans. Superficially, he was a typical Norman organiser ; but some freak in his ambitious make-up led him to accept the claims of his see to be an arch-bishopric independent of Canterbury, and so to win the favour of the Welsh princes. Bernard's effort to become archbishop failed of its ostensible object ; but his diocese never suffered the fate of Bangor and St Asaph. His chimera, carried on heroically, and somewhat absurdly, by the famous Gerald of Wales at the end of the twelfth century, helped to make his arrangements respectable. The other southern diocese was created, so far as we know, out of nothing, by the genius of Urban, a Welsh bishop educated in England. He was con-secrated at Canterbury in 1107 to serve the Church in Glamorgan, and left, like Bernard, to define his own diocese. In the end, quite logically, the diocese of Llandaff came to be roughly equivalent in size to Glamorgan, but not before Urban had attempted to include large portions of Hereford and St David's in it, had supported his case by brilliant invention and daring forgery, and spent many weary months trekking to Westminster and to Rome in its support. The result did not measure up to the effort. A Welshman created a Norman diocese in mainly Norman territory. His achievement does not compare with Bernard's, who created a Norman diocese in territory mainly Welsh. But the *Book of Llandaff*, compiled by his relations and followers shortly after his death, is a brilliant illustration of what could happen when Celtic fancy and Norman energy met and mingled.

The second stage in the Norman conquest of the Welsh Church is marked by the foundation of the Cistercian abbeys in the mid- and late twelfth century. Though never so rich or so distinguished as the leading houses of Yorkshire, Neath (1130), Margam (1147), Strata Florida (1164), Strata Marcella (1170), and the rest, played much the same role. The Cistercian monks were used to travel, had cosmopolitan connections. Not only did they bring the fervour of the new movement, the breath of Stephen Harding and Bernard of Clairvaux into the land of David and Gildas ; they brought merchants, new flocks of sheep, new ideas of how to market wool, an opportunity to Wales for peaceful economic progress. Wales had always been a largely pastoral country ; but it had not grown wool for export. The Cistercian settlement meant that there were men all over western Europe who had learned that Wales was more than a tilting ground.

I have dwelt at length on the fortunes of Wales, because it was the Celtic land most intimately connected with England, and because its story is repeated, with many significant differences, in Scotland and Ireland. The first and most obvious difference is that both these other countries were more remote from the centres of Norman power, and less economically dependent on England than was Wales. This affected even the Church. Archbishop Lanfranc, a figure more imperial even than his royal master, had consecrated a bishop for the Irish-Norse church in Dublin and exerted his primacy in Scotland as well as over York. But the English primacy depended largely on the strength of royal support—which normally carried little weight in Scotland, and none in Ireland. When the Irish Church came to be effectively reformed in the twelfth century it was as part of a wider movement, inspired by St Bernard and his friend, St Malachy of Armagh and Down. In the mid-twelfth century the Irish Church—which had a finer past and more undistinguished present than the Welsh— was brought into line by a great act of power exerted by a papal legate at the synod of Kells in 1152. Four provinces, with Armagh as primate, and thirty-six dioceses were created ; and although for a while much of this was a paper constitution, the reform of the Irish Church went steadily on. As in Wales the Cistercian invasion gave vital impetus to spiritual revival and economic change. It was a long time, however, before reformers in the two countries ceased to grumble about the strange customs of the people—about abbots who married and passed their abbeys by hereditary succession, and about princes who practised polygamy.

Although Ireland was more remote, geographically and in every other way, from England than were Wales and Scotland, it came the nearest to a regular conquest in the late twelfth and early thirteenth centuries. Its military techniques were more primitive, and it lacked the geographical defences of Wales and the political tradition which made a single monarchy possible in Scotland. Its conquest had been planned early in Henry II's reign, and the consent of the English Pope Adrian IV (1154–9) was granted in the famous bull *Laudabiliter*. But the scheme was soon abandoned. When Dermot of Leinster came to Henry II in 1166, he was allowed to recruit troops, though Henry II refused him direct support. Dermot was able to enlist a force led by Norman barons from south Wales, and in 1170 his army occupied Dublin. But it had already ceased to be an expedition for the reinstatement of Dermot, and even the pretence was dropped after Dermot's death in 1171. The small expedition held its own against great odds, and seriously disturbed both the native rulers and its own overlord. Later the same year Henry came in person, and made a swift and skilful settlement of the affairs of Church and state. The Irish princes submitted to him and were protected ; the leading English invaders were settled on large estates in eastern and central Ireland. But the settlement was very temporary. The Irish hoped to recover what they had lost ; the English were determined to win more. The most distinguished of the English leaders, John de Courcy, began his brilliant conquest of Ulster in 1177. He soon established himself as a semi-independent paladin in northern Ireland and married into the kingdom of Man. For a time he was made a respectable Justiciar of Ireland—that is, the king's lieutenant ; he was supplanted in the time of King John. This type of career, with its dazzling promise and strange vicissitudes, was followed in a more modest fashion by many other, lesser men in this period. Meanwhile the English kings tried to maintain some semblance of control. In 1185 Henry sent John to Ireland to govern in his name. The experiment was disastrous, and he had hastily to be recalled ; under John de Courcy a sounder administration was established. But Prince John had learned his lesson, and later as king he showed a special interest in his old lordship. In 1210 he visited the country again, and revealed his determination to keep and strengthen the existing system. Two-thirds of the country, ' the land of peace ', was in the control of the colonists, led by William Marshal, the shrewd and loyal Earl of Pembroke ; the rest still lay under its native kings, who acknowledged John's suzerainty and enjoyed his favour. Throughout the thirteenth century Ireland bade fair to become a settled sub-kingdom. The English conquest had been ruthlessly accomplished ; but the Normans could be quick settlers if they wished, and they showed this inclination in parts of Ireland. In spite of this, the land of peace was not quiet long enough for a stable settlement to be made.

Scotland was the only country in which a native dynasty consistently pursued the policy of resisting English pressure by imitating English strength. After his mother's death David I had been brought up at the court of Henry I ; he was endowed by Henry with the earldom of Huntingdon and one of the richest heiresses in England. When he succeeded to the Scottish throne in 1124, he came north a well-trained Anglo-Norman baron, with many like him in his following ; and although Scotland remained predominantly Celtic and Norse, the extensive settlement of Norman barons, especially in Lothian, and the contact with his English fiefs, enabled David to rule more like an Anglo-Norman king than any of his predecessors. He built castles at Roxburgh and Berwick, round which collected the beginnings of flourishing towns. His Norman vassals included the first Bruce to settle in Scotland, and his steward, Walter FitzAlan—of Breton origin, as we now know, since J. H. Round laid the ghost of Banquo [1]—was ancestor of the hereditary stewards, later more widely known as Stewarts or Stuarts. Celtic land-tenure began to give way to feudal arrangements ; ' mormaers ' became earls ; sheriffs and Norman justice made their début in Scotland.

New movements in the Church had deeply influenced Scotland in the days of St Margaret ; but profound changes in organisation did not take place before the reign of David. A see more akin to an English diocese than the old Welsh sees had long existed at St Andrews, and another was founded by David at Glasgow before he became king. But before his accession the north of Scotland was still organised on traditional lines, and the formation of territorial dioceses took place gradually during his long reign. Scottish clergy came into closer contact with the Church at large ; parishes were formed and parish churches built. Most important, as in Wales and

---

[1] Round disproved the legend of Stuart ancestry enshrined in Shakespeare's *Macbeth*, in his *Studies in Peerage and Family History* (1901), pp. 115ff.

Ireland, was the monastic revival. Many abbeys, including several of the most eminent in Scotland, honoured David I as their founder.

King David's household was Anglo-Norman; so were many of his leading barons. But most of the country was still only superficially Normanised, and the north remained so throughout the Middle Ages. The concentration of his power in the south of Scotland was an inevitable consequence of David's English connections. Not only were he and his son English earls, but he was constantly involved in the politics of the anarchy, from his abortive attack on Stephen in 1138, defeated in the ' battle of the Standard ', to his knighting of the young Henry in 1149. For most of his reign he was Lord of Cumbria, and his son, Earl Henry, was Earl of Huntingdon (1136–52) and Northumberland (1139–52). He died at Carlisle, which lay in his possession, in May 1153, shortly before his protégé's triumph.

David's successors continued his policies : they fostered the Church, they developed Norman institutions ; they intervened with varying success in England. In 1173 William the Lion joined the great rebellion against Henry II, but was captured, and compelled, like many of his predecessors, to do homage to his neighbour, and to accept something like tutelage. From then on the Scottish claim to Cumbria and Northumberland and the English earldom was never seriously revived, though often discussed. But the tutelage did not survive Henry's death. Richard I restored its more humiliating symbols to William for a large price, and although John and Henry III played a crucial part in Scottish affairs, they never tried to humiliate Alexander II (1214–49) or Alexander III (1249–86) as Henry II had humiliated William the Lion.

The Norman settlement of Lothian had provided the Scottish kings with a solid foundation for their power, which grew with the passage of time, the assimilation of the peoples, and the spread of new influences over other parts of the kingdom. For long the kings were least secure in the highlands, and they frequently had to deal with rebellions there. The great achievement of the thirteenth-century kings was the sub-jugation of north-western Scotland and the conquest of the Western Isles. The Hebrides had hitherto lain at the meeting-point of Scottish, Irish, and Norwegian influences ; and there were many indications in the thirteenth century that they might fall rather to the Norwegian than to the Scottish empire. But in 1263 the last Norwegian attempt to assert control of the islands failed, and thereafter the Hebrides were part and parcel of the Scottish kingdom.

Meanwhile the early years of Alexander III had been troubled by the first outbreak of serious faction within the ranks of the Norman-Scottish baronage—a type of faction which was to bedevil Scottish politics for many centuries to come. In 1255 Alexander was captured by an obscure official of large pretensions called the ' Doorward ', who was supported by the Steward and the English king ; in 1257 the opponents of English influence, led by Walter Comyn, carried him off in their turn. Comyn's death and the outbreak of trouble in England in 1258 simplified the situation for a time, and soon after Alexander himself took over the government. But faction within the kingdom with the threat of English intervention behind it had already given a presage of what was to come. For Alexander outlived his three children, and when his grand-daughter, the Maid of Norway, died in 1290, Edward I was called in to settle the claims of thirteen competitors for the Scottish throne.

12   Richard I and John

FEW English kings have played so small a part in the affairs
of England and so large a part in the affairs of Europe as
Richard I.   It may seem paradoxical to speak in this way of a
man who has entered so deeply into legend as Richard ' Cœur
de Lion '.   But he visited England only twice as king, once for
three months, later for two ; and his reign was spent wandering
restlessly about Europe and the Near East, disposing in grandiose
fashion of gold, marriages, fiefs, kingdoms, and empires which
had not the remotest connection with the English throne.
His viewpoint was cosmopolitan and dynastic, and in this he
resembled his brilliant enemy, the Emperor Henry VI.   Richard
disposed of England and half of France—his own inheritance ;
he went on Crusade and fought and arranged marriage
alliances with Saladin ; on the way he settled the affairs of
Sicily, Cyprus, and Syria.   Henry (King by inheritance of
Germany and Lombardy) revised the settlement of Sicily,
and won it for himself ; imprisoned Richard and made England
a fief of the Empire ; schemed to become Lord of France as well.
The reigns of the two powerful kings formed a fitting close
to the glories of the twelfth century ; but their dreams were
short-lived.   Both died young, Henry in 1197, Richard in 1199,
and their empires rapidly disintegrated.   Henry's fame soon
came to be overshadowed by his even more brilliant son,
Frederick II, the ' wonder of the world ' ; but Richard's
place in English legend is undisputed.   He is remembered as
the great soldier, the crusader, and troubadour ; and the legend
is substantially true.

Had he given his mind to it, Richard might have been a
very able and successful monarch : he combined his father's
shrewdness and strength with his mother's panache and sense
of grandeur.   But he made little effort to apply himself to

ruling England. Immediately after his coronation, he pillaged the country for money for the third Crusade, and left behind him a regency so complex as to be unworkable. Two brothers had to be provided for. John was loaded with secular honours, Geoffrey (an illegitimate son of Henry II) was made Archbishop of York; both were then sent into exile. The chief man in the kingdom was the Chancellor and papal legate, William Longchamp, Bishop of Ely, who found that royal favour in the absence of the King was insufficient to compensate for the unpopularity which attached to a conceited *parvenu*; nor were Richard's arrangements sufficiently straightforward to give his deputy a free hand. But Longchamp and Walter of Coutances, Archbishop of Rouen, whom Richard sent to support or replace Longchamp according to circumstance, were both devoted and capable royal servants, and it is possible that Richard's scheme might have worked if his brother, John, had not had friends in England and France, and made skilful use of his opportunities for intrigue. In the event Longchamp was removed from office, and John prepared to follow up his victory by intriguing with Philip II of France for the throne itself.

In 1189 Richard left England; in 1190 he set off for Sicily, whose government he reorganised. His brother-in-law, King William II of Sicily, had recently died; and Richard's interest in the kingdom was among the most striking of many links between the two islands which the Normans had won in the ten-sixties. In the mid-twelfth century an Englishman had been Chancellor to King Roger II; and one of the leading Exchequer officials of Henry II, Master Thomas Brown, had served his apprenticeship in Sicily. Exchange of men and ideas was frequent.

While in Sicily Richard married Berengaria, a princess from Navarre. It was not until 1191 that he arrived in the East—at the siege of Acre, in time to join in the capture of the city. Richard's arrival and the capture of Acre led to the departure of the King of France, Philip II, who was always a reluctant crusader, and who had urgent business at home. One piece of business was the opportunity offered by Richard's absence to intrigue in Angevin affairs. Once Acre was captured and Philip gone, Richard became the effective leader of the

Plate 15 DURHAM CATHEDRAL, NORTH TRANSEPT (*c.*1100). The choir and transepts were consecrated in 1104, the rest of the cathedral completed about 1140 ; and as the cathedral has been comparatively little altered, we can see in it the development of Norman techniques of engineering and decoration over two generations. The three storeys, main arcade, triforium and clerestory, and the alternating round piers and clusters of columns, are characteristic of early Norman style ; so also is the appearance of massive weight. But the bold spiral ornament on the piers was a novelty ; as were the stone vaults, for which the Durham masons devised new techniques while they were building the cathedral.

Plate 16 SALISBURY CATHEDRAL. After the move from Old Sarum, the new cathedral was planned and built in the thirty or forty years following 1220. Thus it has a unity of design unique among medieval English cathedrals. The pointed arches of very varied shapes, the clusters of Purbeck marble shafts round the columns and the deep mouldings of the arches are characteristic of 'Early English' style. This picture shows the north side of the choir and the opening of the north-eastern transept (built soon after 1225). The containing arch was added later, perhaps in the late-fourteenth century, to strengthen the building.

Crusade. The purpose of the third Crusade was to restore the shattered kingdom of Jerusalem and to recover the Holy City itself, which after being for nearly ninety years in Christian hands (since its capture in the first Crusade in 1099) had fallen again to the Turks in 1187. Richard set about these tasks energetically. In September 1191 he defeated Saladin at the battle of Arsuf. At Christmas he was within twelve miles of Jerusalem itself, but could not risk the dangers of a siege. In the spring of 1192 he took a leading part in the negotiations which gave the kingdom of Jerusalem to his nephew, the Count of Champagne, and himself compensated the disappointed candidate with Cyprus. Finally, after a last, ineffectual effort to reach the Holy City, he made peace for three years with Saladin—after an unsuccessful attempt to marry a sister or a niece into Saladin's family—and in October 1192 set sail for home.

News of his exploits travelled ahead of him, and Richard was regarded as a hero in many parts of Europe, in spite of the failure of the essential purpose of the Crusade. But in the courts of Europe he had many enemies. His brother, John, was plotting with Philip II to prevent his return. Learning of this, Richard made his way up the Adriatic, presumably aiming to by-pass France to the north-east. It was too late in the year to cross the Alps in comfort, so he skirted round them and came to Vienna. In Vienna he was captured and imprisoned by an old enemy, the Duke of Austria, who was shortly afterwards constrained to hand him over to the Emperor Henry VI. The conscience of Europe was disturbed by such treatment of an honoured crusader, and the Pope was outraged. But Henry had captured a rich prize, and needed the ransom ; he also wanted to use Richard to forward grandiose schemes against Philip of France ; and he badly needed a hostage for dealing with Welf enemies in Germany (Richard's nephews) and the King of Sicily (Richard's protégé). The price was colossal. Richard was to further schemes for reconciling the Emperor and the Welfs and to pay £100,000 in ransom. The Welfs were reconciled ; the money was paid and went to finance Henry's conquest of Sicily ; Richard surrendered his kingdom and received it back as a fief of the Empire, and he and Henry concerted plans for humbling the King of France. At last, early in 1194, Richard was released.

A month later he was back in England. In spite of all the confusion caused by his absence, he stayed for only two months. Then he returned to France to pursue his feud with Philip II ; and in France he lived for the remaining years of his life.

The most significant event of Richard's brief visit to England in 1194 was his re-coronation by the new Archbishop of Canterbury in Winchester Cathedral. It symbolised the establishment of a new régime. The stigma of imprisonment was washed off ; all men could see that Richard was king again in fact as well as in name ; and the event sealed an alliance between king and archbishop under which England was governed until the accession of John. When Richard had lain in captivity, John and Philip of France had entered into a plot for the capture of Richard's kingdom. In 1193 John had rebelled. But the English leaders remained loyal. Aided by the dowager Eleanor of Aquitaine, now long accustomed to dealing with family difficulties, they rapidly disposed of John's supporters and prepared to subdue his castles. On Richard's release, John made a desperate bid to let Philip into Richard's French possessions before his brother was back in the saddle. It failed of its object—though it left Philip in possession of much Angevin territory—and John was compelled to throw himself on his brother's mercy. Meanwhile Richard's chief agent in England was now the former Bishop of Salisbury, Hubert Walter, an old royal servant, whom Richard had made Archbishop of Canterbury while he was still in prison (1193). Hubert was rapidly advanced to fill the place of William Longchamp. In Richard's last years he was Justiciar and papal legate. He was a distinguished lawyer—perhaps the author of the treatise on law which passes under the name of his old master, Ranulph Glanville ; he was an administrator of unusual ability; he was evidently more tactful than Longchamp, and his own family was more distinguished. Hubert was a great man of the world ; pious in his way, but his way was that of a business man, a lay patron, not of a churchman. He has left a mixed memory behind him ; but for Richard he was ideal. Henry II's dream had come true ; the chief offices in Church and state were combined in the hands of a single, devoted, royal servant.

From 1194 to 1199 Richard was repairing the damaged structure of his French empire and preparing doom for Philip of France. He reconquered lost territory, built up alliances, constructed castles—especially the famous Château Gaillard, which guarded the Seine as it twisted into Normandy. As always, he planned grandiosely and spent beyond his means. Early in 1199 he learned that treasure had been found in the Limousin ; and it was treasure that he needed above all for his schemes. He rode south in great haste ; but while he was attacking the Viscount of Limoges, he was wounded in the shoulder by an arrow, and after a few days was dead.

(2) JOHN, 1199–1216

Richard had made no firm settlement for the succession ; and the customs of his various dominions allowed a claim both to his brother, John, and his nephew (son of John's elder brother, Geoffrey), Arthur of Brittany. The doyen of the Anglo-Norman baronage, William the Marshal, quoted Norman custom and declared for John ; so did the Archbishop of Canterbury ; both were echoing the dying voice of the late king. Thus John came to the throne with little difficulty, and after a tussle was able to make terms with Philip of France under which he received the whole inheritance ; in return he recognised that his French dominions were fiefs subject to feudal law in the court of the French king, accepted a number of other restrictions and made a small concession of land. For the time John appeared to have won his ambition at last, and to hold virtually all that his father had held.

One might have thought that the constant absence of Richard I would have made his reign a comparatively insignificant episode. But the absence of the King had given the larger departments of government—the Chancery and Exchequer—an opportunity to live a life of their own ; compelled them, indeed, to organise themselves more bureaucratically, more independently of royal control. This development was most conspicuous under the administrative genius of Hubert Walter, and so fully did John trust the Archbishop that Hubert's career suffered no check in 1199. 1199 was in fact a crucial year in the history of English administration. The first series of rolls on which copies were made of documents issued from the Chancery began in that year. These rolls—the equivalent of modern files—marked an epoch in record-keeping; the Chancery was beginning to take on the shape of a modern office. Nor was it solely a matter of book-keeping: the critical part which the Chancery played in thirteenth-century politics reflected in part the success of Hubert Walter's régime. The Chancery clerks had had a taste of semi-independence; the king was to become jealous of their independence; the magnates—having regard to the great diversity of legal and financial writs, which could affect their properties, rights, and finances, and which were to be bought in the Chancery—were increasingly anxious to keep a check on its activities.

No medieval English king save Richard III has been so much discussed in recent years as John, and many attempts have been made to salvage his reputation. They can hardly be said to have succeeded, but they have shown that the traditional picture of him as a monster of cruelty, alternating between fits of lethargy and outbreaks of wild activity, was overdrawn. This portrait was based almost entirely on the picture given in a single unreliable chronicle, that of the St Albans monk, Roger of Wendover, and repeated, with additions, by Matthew Paris. In recent years we have inclined to take a less favourable view of the personal characters of the rest of his line, and some have wondered whether John was really any worse than his father or brothers. To this it can only be answered that contemporaries clearly thought that he was. All the early Angevins were ruthless, despotic, and capable; none of them was particularly moral. But Henry and Richard were trusted by their followers; they respected the basic feudal code; they were true leaders in the field, trustworthy in success and adversity, and they repaid loyalty by loyalty. Precisely what was wrong with John is very hard to say. But men did not trust him; they refused to fight in his company; they sought to exact unusual promises from him. It may have been a freak in his nature, allied to his ghoulish sense of fun. But it may have lain deeper. The trouble was not merely that he had plotted against Richard and intrigued with Philip of France—many men had done that; to plot was a younger brother's birthright, and John had done little that Henry I had not done before acquiring the throne. John showed some deeper ground for distrust.

It would be unfair to blame John's flaws of character for all his failures. He was left a difficult legacy. Richard had spent far more than he could readily afford, and John was compelled to levy unpopular taxes to pay for his own wars. Nevertheless John's exactions were excessively arbitrary. His uncertain title to his lands enabled Philip to use Arthur as Philip had once used John; and the clauses of the treaty between John and Philip gave the latter an easy handle to revoke it. John had subjected his French lands to the feudal jurisdiction of the French King's court; and he soon gave that court a chance to act. The county of La Marche was disputed by a man and a lady; they arranged their differences by betrothal. In 1200 John put away his wife—their marriage had been technically illegal—and married the lady claimant to La Marche, who was also heiress of Angoulême. His rival rebelled, was suppressed, and given scant justice; he appealed to the French King. Philip was in no hurry to hear the appeal. He waited until his preparations were properly made, then heard the case; and his court gave judgment that John was to forfeit all his French fiefs. For half a century Capetian and Angevin had competed for power in north and central France, without either side gaining a decisive advantage. Suddenly, in 1202, the Angevins were condemned to lose all their lands; and, even more sensational, Philip was able to enforce a great part of the judgment. From the south of France neither he nor his successors could dislodge the English, though they could confine them to smaller territory than that of Eleanor's inheritance. The core of John's inheritance, Normandy and Anjou, was conquered by the French. The Angevin Empire had collapsed.

John never reconciled himself to the loss of Normandy and Anjou, and plotted and intrigued incessantly for their return. The *débâcle* continued. Anjou had gone in 1203; nor had the elimination of Arthur, who had plotted with Philip and been captured by John, helped John's cause. It is not certain how Arthur died, but it is generally thought now, and was generally thought at the time, that John was responsible for his death, and this belief led to the revolt of Brittany. In 1204 Normandy was lost, in 1205 the last castles in Anjou, in 1206 Brittany finally came into Philip's hands. John tried hard to raise an army in England for the recovery of his lost territories, and to raise enemies against Philip on the Continent. His difficulties were great. Once Normandy was lost, his English barons were unwilling to fight on the Continent. Most of them in any case no longer had Norman lands ; a few, including William Marshal himself, had acknowledged Philip as their Norman overlord, and were pledged not to fight against him. For these and other reasons John's various campaigns were abortive, and it was not until 1214 that he was able to mount a serious offensive.

Meanwhile the two other disputes which dominated the reign of John had come to a head. From 1206 to 1213 John was embroiled with the Pope. The occasion of this violent disagreement was the election of a new archbishop to succeed Hubert Walter. Hubert had quarrelled with the monks, and they were determined to avoid another King Stork ; the King was equally determined to replace him with a faithful royal officer ; the English bishops, wishing to assert their right to a voice in the election beside the monastic chapter, sided with the King. The monks made a secret election of one of their number, and sent him to the pope to be confirmed ; then under royal pressure they made a public election of the nominee of king and bishops, and sent again to Rome. By now a significant proportion of the monks was gathered in Rome. Pope Innocent declared both elections illegal and invalid, and set the monks to work again to elect a third candidate in his presence. Their choice was directed towards Stephen Langton, an English cardinal of great learning and prestige, but without recent experience of English affairs. In the end Langton proved himself a very effective primate. But for the time the King was outraged : his wishes had been totally disregarded. He refused the archbishop entry into England. The pope laid the kingdom under interdict, and subsequently excommunicated the King. This interdict meant that all the churches were closed : no masses sung, no marriages or funerals conducted. Only baptism and confession for the dying were permitted. For seven years the churches were silent, while pope and king and archbishop wrangled. In 1213 peace was arranged : the King surrendered. He was preparing for a final passage of arms with Philip Augustus, and needed all the support he could get. Furthermore, the pope was threatening him with deposition, and it was far from clear that the sentence might not prove effective. In 1213 John was absolved, in 1214 the interdict was lifted. From being the Church's enemy, John suddenly found himself in the unwonted role of its most faithful son. He even surrendered his kingdom to the pope and received it back as a papal fief : a gesture which did Innocent III little good, but strangely convinced him of John's sincerity. Stephen Langton was not so easily convinced, and no sooner was he established in England than he found himself falling out of favour with the pope.

In 1214 John made his last, supreme effort to recover his lost lands in France. He formed an alliance with his nephew, the 'Welf' Emperor Otto IV, who was still struggling to assert the Welf position in Germany against the rising star of the young Hohenstaufen, Frederick II.[1] Otto and his allies, with English reinforcements, were to invade France from the north-east, while John attacked through Poitou. But the great plan miscarried. John's campaign failed to achieve any serious penetration. He revived his power in Poitou and marched to Angers, but soon found that his Poitevin vassals would not fight against the French king. In July, at Bouvines, the Emperor's army was heavily defeated. Bouvines was that rare event in medieval warfare, a decisive battle. Philip was rid of his enemies. The Welf Emperor suffered fearfully in prestige, and the success of Frederick II was soon assured. John's hopes of recovering Normandy were gone, and he returned to England to face discontent with an empty treasury

---

[1] The Welfs (or Guelphs) and the Hohenstaufen were the two families who competed for mastery in Germany in the twelfth and early thirteenth centuries. They were the descendants, respectively, of Welf IV, Duke of Bavaria (died 1101), and of Frederick of Hohenstaufen, Duke of Swabia (died 1105) ; and their rivalry had its climax in the conflicts between Henry the Lion, Duke of Bavaria and Saxony (whose wife, Matilda, was daughter of Henry II of England) and the Emperor Frederick Barbarossa, and between Henry the Lion's son, Otto IV, and two Hohenstaufen— Frederick Barbarossa's younger son, Philip of Swabia, and Philip's nephew, the Emperor Frederick II.

and shattered prestige. An arbitrary king could not afford such a record of failure.

Already in 1213 the discontented barons had discussed the possibility of extracting from the King some guarantee that he would govern more moderately and predictably. In fact John was not much more despotic than his father and brother, but his manners and his misfortunes made him appear to be so, and the disasters of his reign encouraged men to resist him to his face. As yet they had little idea what they wanted. Something was wrong; the King, they argued, must have broken the customs of the kingdom. They looked into the past, and they found that Henry I had issued a charter at his coronation listing the abuses that he specifically wished to renounce. So the malcontents began to gloss Henry's charter and plan a new one of their own. The *débâcle* of 1214 gave them their chance, and early in 1215 rebellion broke out. In May the King knew he was beaten, and in June, in the meadow called Runnymede, John agreed that his seal should be set to Magna Carta.

The Charter was drawn up in the royal Chancery, and is a masterpiece of chancery drafting. It was drawn up after very elaborate consultations between the king, the rebel barons, and a few neutral figures of great prestige, such as the Earl Marshal and the Archbishop of Canterbury. Probably the swift solution of differences and some of the clauses in the Charter owed more to Stephen Langton than to the rebels. But the main choice of topics included in it must have been suggested by the barons themselves. It is a fascinating revelation of the views and horizons of the leading English barons of the day.

In form Magna Carta was a grant, in sixty-three clauses, of numerous rights and privileges and legal arrangements which the King guaranteed to observe. The Angevin monarchy at its height had been immensely powerful and arbitrary. John promised that it would accept the shackles of responsible custom. The assumption of the Charter was that there is or ought to be a recognisable body of law covering all essential operations of royal government and the relations of king and subjects; and that royal government was tolerable only if this body of law was known.

These laws were extracted by the barons, and they stood

to profit most from them; but other sections benefited too. As we read the Charter we are reminded how strongly the barons needed allies. In the years leading up to 1215 both sides had been looking for support; and the King had tried to make a name for himself for fair dealing and justice among lesser folk. Some members of all classes had suffered from his tyranny; but it is clear that the barons had to compete with the King for support outside their own class. The Archbishop and the Earl Marshal may have given them wise counsel, and seen to it that the Charter was not too narrow a document; but it is clear that self-interest also inclined the barons to be generous to other groups and interests. The English Church was to be free to obey the pope and canon law; the privileges of London and other boroughs were confirmed; merchants and all other travellers were to come and go freely; justice was to be done to Welshmen who had been dispossessed, and John's Welsh hostages were to be surrendered. The vaguest of all the clauses promised some measure of justice to the King of the Scots. Some clauses specifically, and many in practice, benefited all freemen. Many of Henry II's legal innovations were confirmed and (from the subject's point of view) improved; many unpopular taxes were abolished and arbitrary exactions by royal servants restrained. Substantial reductions were promised in the area of the royal hunting grounds, the much-hated ' forests ', which had been governed by special restrictions against anything liable to damage the game or reduce their breeding grounds, enforced by savage penalties.

One clause must be quoted in full. ' No free man may be arrested or imprisoned or disseised or outlawed or exiled, or in any way brought to ruin, nor shall we go against him nor send others in pursuit of him, save by the legal judgment of his peers or by the law of the land.' The Charter did not specify what the law of the land was; but it none the less succeeded in doing very much more than protest against John's arbitrary condemnations. It stated very firmly that there was a law—which meant that there were recognised procedures, and that these must be followed. ' The king should be under God and the law', wrote the great judge of the next generation, Henry Bracton. Magna Carta does not quite say that—

after all, in form these clauses are grants from the king, of his own free will. But the assumption is there. The great achievement of Bracton's age was to settle the main framework of an English legal system. In Bracton's day there were professional judges and something like a code, in marked contrast to the England of Henry II. The professional judge first appeared at the turn of the twelfth and thirteenth centuries; the code was Bracton's own work, *On the Laws and Customs of England*, ' the crown and flower of English medieval jurisprudence ' in Maitland's phrase, compiled in the twelve-fifties. Magna Carta helped to spread the idea that English law was reasonably fixed and knowable, and so to lay foundations on which men like Bracton could build.

It has often been discussed whether Magna Carta was the foundation of English liberties or a reactionary document extracted by a class or clique in its own interest. There is no simple answer. The majority of the clauses benefited the barons in some degree, and a number specifically detailed ways in which relations between king and tenants-in-chief were to be subjected to fixed custom. When a tenant-in chief died, the king could exact a ' relief '—a substantial sum of money—from his heir before the heir could succeed; this was to be limited to £100 for earl or baron. If the heir was under age, his lands were in ' wardship ', that is to say the king, or whoever was granted the wardship by the king, became the guardian of the heir and had possession of his property; the king furthermore had the right to dispose of heirs and heiresses in marriage. These rights were limited and defined by the Charter, to ensure that the heir was not cheated by his guardian, nor married beneath him. In these and other ways the barons saw to their own interests; but many other interests and privileges were also protected.

By a long-standing tradition a new king swore at his coronation to keep Church and people at peace, to put down iniquity, and to show justice and mercy in his judgments. From time to time the coronation oath was developed into a charter, such as that issued by Henry I, which was known to the barons of Magna Carta; and from time to time kings repeated or developed their oaths on solemn occasions. In 1213 John himself had sworn a slightly altered version of the oath, which laid emphasis on the revival of good laws and the abolition of bad. The novelty of Magna Carta lay not in the fact that the king bound himself to maintain good law, nor that he issued a charter of liberties ; but that the Charter should contain so elaborate and detailed a statement of important custom. We must not expect too much of it : it is a collection of clauses, not a rounded whole. But it was felt to serve a purpose ; to limit the monarchy by defining the law. The Charter included an elaborate clause providing machinery for its enforcement by a committee of twenty-five barons, to be called into existence if the king broke the Charter. But there was no suggestion yet that such a committee might be a normal thing ; that the duty of the king to consult his barons on important issues should or could be defined. Any such idea still lay in the future. The barons of Magna Carta felt they were dealing with an exceptional crisis ; and when John himself was dead, the Charter was re-issued without any reference to the committee of twenty-five. From then on the Charter was often re-issued as a reminder to king and people that the king was not free to break these fundamental customs. A few changes were made ; the forest clauses, for instance, were carried off into a separate charter. But what could make sense was preserved ; and after 1225 subsequent re-issues showed virtually no further change.

By 1225 the Charter was accepted by all parties ; but it had not been so in 1215. The Charter gave King John a breathing-space, which he used to obtain from the Pope a bull condemning it as contrary to moral law and reprimanding the Archbishop, and to gather forces to crush his enemies. There is little doubt that he would have succeeded, had not a fresh outbreak of rebellion attracted the support of the King of France. In an elaborate, if somewhat absurd manifesto, the French court announced that John was deposed ; and the French Dauphin was sent to replace him. John made rapid attempts to deal with his enemies, but after a summer and autumn of marching and counter-marching, and after losing his baggage-train (including all his jewels and valuable relics) in a quicksand at the head of the Wash, he succumbed to sickness and died at Newark in October 1216.

13 Henry III, 1216-72

WHEN his father died Henry was a boy of nine. His position was exceedingly weak, and it was bound to be a number of years before the new King could rule on his own. But from some points of view his father's early death benefited his cause. Henry had no personal enemies. The Pope found himself guardian of a small child, which strengthened his determination to support John's dynasty. The more chivalrous of the barons gathered round him. Under the shrewd guidance of the legate Cardinal Guala and the experienced regency of William the Marshal, Henry's affairs prospered beyond expectation. Within two years Louis the Dauphin was compelled to abandon his attempt on the English throne and leave the country. The King's supporters had been notably successful, and their efforts to restore order and sort out the confusion caused by civil war helped to make England reasonably peaceful and prosperous.

It is notoriously difficult, however, for a group of regents to act together without friction. The skill of Guala and the prestige of the Marshal kept them in control at first. But Guala left in 1218 and the Marshal died in 1219. In the early twelve-twenties the leading role was played by the Justiciar, Hubert de Burgh, a royal servant well rewarded by John, who had risen from the ranks of the country gentry and was now made Earl of Kent and married to a Scottish princess. But he was not trusted by the greater barons, and his position would have been untenable but for the steady support of Archbishop Stephen Langton. Hubert and Stephen were at this stage very much trusted by the King himself, and they took advantage of this fact gradually to release him from tutelage—thereby in effect strengthening their own position. In 1223 the Pope (acting as Henry's overlord) allowed him the personal use of his own seal, under certain restrictions; early in 1227 Henry declared himself of age and his personal rule effectively began. He was now nineteen and had been king for ten years.

Henry was lavish and artistic: he built palaces and castles and adorned them with the best ornaments, hangings, and furnishings that money could buy. He was also extremely devout. His extravagance, sense of beauty, and piety were especially concentrated on rebuilding and enlarging the Confessor's church at Westminster. He consciously modelled himself on the Confessor; he called his eldest son Edward; and in certain respects he resembled his distant predecessor. Both were devout; shrewd in their way, but lacking the strength and brutality for consistent success in politics or for winning renown on the battlefield. Henry was very self-conscious about his kingship, yet he was never able to throw himself into the essential exercises of kingship as his father and grandfather had done. He had serious weaknesses of character: he could be obstinate, petulant, and mercurial, was extremely sharp-tongued, rather ungenerous. Those whom he trusted, he trusted implicitly; but he was suspicious of most of the world and fearful of treachery. He was shrewd rather than subtle; his piety lacked depth. To compensate for all this, there was a certain quiet simplicity in his nature which prevented him from being embittered or warped by the miseries and failures of his reign. But he was not the sort of man whom the English barons instinctively admired or trusted.

Henry's adult reign falls into two parts. Down to 1258 he was, on the whole, in control of affairs; after 1258 government was often out of his hands, sometimes controlled by committees of barons, sometimes by the heir to the throne, the Lord Edward. But through it all runs a single theme— conflict between the efforts of Henry to maintain the near-absolutism of his predecessors, and the efforts of his barons to control the King, his council, and his ministers. There was never any question of abolishing the monarchy, even when the King himself was in prison and Simon de Montfort was acting in his name. Everyone assumed that government was the King's government. Indeed, the royal court was becoming increasingly the centre of English life, the key to power and wealth. Profound changes in society, and growing concern with the way in which the great power of the Crown was wielded, led to constant unrest ; failures in royal policy from time to time gave excuse and opportunity for unrest to express itself. But the unrest was political. With the exception of the brief periods of open civil war, the reign was a prosperous time for England at large.

From 1227 until 1232 Hubert de Burgh remained Justiciar, and his power was undisputed. But his position depended on royal favour, and when the King grew weary and jealous of him, his fall was assured. In 1232 he was removed from office and imprisoned, and his place taken by another old servant of John, Peter des Roches, Bishop of Winchester, whose son or nephew, Peter des Rivaux, became effective head of the royal administration. The new government was, so to say, purely bureaucratic : it consisted of trained civil servants. But the system was short-lived ; in 1234 the two Peters were disgraced, and a largely baronial council, of which Hubert de Burgh was again a member, was re-established. The civil servants and the baronial council represented the two elements from which the royal council was selected. The King's attempt to rule entirely by the counsel of officials of his own choice, and the reaction against it which established a council of barons, were portents of greater events to come.

The next twenty-four years, from the crisis of 1234 to the crisis of 1258, witnessed no serious outbreak of trouble, but a succession of minor crises which failed to mature. The relations of Henry and the barons at large were never free from suspicion. Henry's minority had taught the barons what it meant to have a government which regularly consulted them ; his later attempts to rule almost entirely through his own servants reminded the barons that they wished to be regularly consulted. The term ' royal council ', applied at any date in the Middle Ages, is ambiguous. In the period covered by this book it might mean two things : it might mean the body of immediate councillors, barons, and royal servants, who attended regularly on the King and advised him on day-to-day affairs ; or it might mean the Great Council, in which the leaders of the kingdom, lay and clerical—who regarded themselves as the King's natural advisers—met and advised the King on great issues of state. The composition of the Great Council was far from fixed ; the King always had a fairly free choice as to which of the barons should be summoned, and although its deliberations were a traditional part of English government, strictly speaking there had been no obligation on the King to consult the barons on affairs of state. Henry III tended to arrange royal marriages and transact important business without consultation ; and this was the more aggravating because the King's closest associates included several of the ' foreign ' relations of his wife, Eleanor of Provence, who were thought to encourage in Henry excessive concern for his claims in France, which threatened to commit the English kingdom to expensive adventures in which the English baronage had no interest.

Through the minor crises of Henry's middle years we can see developing something like a programme of reform, which the baronial leaders pressed on the King with growing insistence. Their first demand was usually for the re-issue of Magna Carta, which was quite readily granted. Their second demand was that they should be regularly consulted on important matters of state ; that is, that meetings of the Great Council should be frequent and effective. They had come to see that the Charter alone was not enough ; the baronial leaders never trusted Henry III, and they had slowly come to recognise the implication of this, that the King must be kept under constant surveillance. But the demand, in this precise form, was novel ; and it was not until 1258 that it was pressed by a large party among the barons with any consistency of purpose ; even then the demand was a temporary one, only intended to last for the lifetime of one impossible king.

The third demand of the barons was to have a say in the control of the great offices of state, the Chancery and Exchequer. Although the English monarchy had passed through several vicissitudes since the death of Henry II, the royal administration and the royal courts had developed steadily in authority and effectiveness. Government was a more elaborate thing, and the organs of state more powerful, than had been dreamed of even two generations before. The Chancery had followed the example of the Exchequer, and become a department with a fixed headquarters—it had gone

' out of court '. Developing power made the offices objects of suspicion to the baronage, and gave them many motives for wishing to have some say in their control ; and their growing independence gave the barons some excuse for intervening in their working. It was much more difficult to object to the king's managing the affairs of his own household ; and although the household itself was developing fast at this time, and an increasing share of royal revenue was being administered by the royal Wardrobe (a financial department which travelled with the king and was not under the control of the Exchequer), the barons attempted to interfere with household administration only in the major crises of 1258 and 1264. Thus the claim to a say in the appointment of Chancellor and Treasurer became a regular feature of baronial schemes for reform ; and the barons sometimes tried to interfere also in the appointment of the head of the judiciary, the Justiciar. But before 1258 Henry never submitted to such proposals. He would pay lip-service at least to the principle that the Great Council should be consulted on important issues ; but he insisted that he must be free to appoint his own officers.

A minor crisis in 1238 brought to the front of the stage two of the leading figures of Henry's later years : his brother, Richard, Earl of Cornwall, and a notable from the south of France called Simon de Montfort, who was trying to claim the earldom of Leicester as his inheritance. In this year Henry consented to the secret marriage of his sister to Simon ; and the protest against the secrecy of the proceedings was led by Earl Richard. Henry agreed to amend his ways, and from that date had in Richard a steadfast supporter of great value to him ; an able financier of immense wealth who on more than one occasion saved Henry's finances from disaster.

For a time, he also had a faithful supporter in Simon, who duly became Earl of Leicester in 1239 ; but a series of difficulties gradually alienated the brothers-in-law. Simon de Montfort was one of the most remarkable personalities of his day. He had many friends and many enemies in his lifetime, and he has had many of both since his death. There can be no doubt of his great ability and self-confidence, of his clear imagination, and of his skill as a soldier. He began as a foreign adventurer who won the liking of Henry III and married his sister. Like all the king's close associates, he found Henry an exasperating master. From 1248 to 1252 Simon was in charge of Gascony, which had been in a condition bordering on anarchy. He performed a difficult task with great energy and some success, and inevitably made enemies in the process. Henry expected (or claimed to expect) success more rapid and complete ; feared (not wholly without cause) that Simon's tendency to arrogance was increasing the number of his enemies ; and suspected Simon's semi-independent position. In due course Henry began to listen to Simon's enemies ; and finally, in 1252, Henry summoned Simon home to answer his accusers in a trial at Westminster lasting five weeks. Simon in return was exasperated by Henry's failure to stand by him in his difficulties, and regarded the trial as an act of treachery. The trial opened, after a preliminary accusation by the Gascon representatives, with a violent attack on Simon by Henry himself. In the end the King was compelled to admit that the evidence told in Simon's favour ; but he did not restore Simon to his command, nor could there be friendship between them again. Henry feared Simon, we are told, more than thunder and lightning ; and Simon could never trust the King to act with sense and consistency or to stand by his friends.

The differences between Henry and Simon were enhanced by the fact that Simon, like many foreign-born settlers, had a much sharper vision of the true state of England, and a natural dislike of the muddle and confusion of Henry's mind. Simon was Henry's brother-in-law ; he had no wish to see royal government abolished or even circumscribed ; he wished to see it effective. In this he resembled Henry's son, the Lord Edward : both wished to see government conducted in an orderly and rational way, on the basis of a harmonious understanding between king and notables. The difference was that Edward wished to keep the ultimate initiative in the King's hands, while Simon was prepared if necessary to imprison the King and act in his name. All this lay in the future in the early twelve-fifties : Edward was still a boy (he had been born in 1239), and Simon's views were only slowly forming. But it is clear that Simon was already one of the leading figures in a group of magnates who were seriously discussing methods of curbing the King's misgovernment. Simon's friends included Robert Grosseteste, the eminent and saintly Bishop of Lincoln ; and there are fascinating hints in the letters of their mutual friend, the Franciscan friar, Adam Marsh, that Simon was privy to some great scheme propounded by Grosseteste for the reformation of morals in England. Apparently the scheme had some bearing on secular as well as ecclesiastical affairs, though probably not, directly, on how government should be conducted. These glimpses of Simon's relations with Grosseteste show that Simon had a mind large enough for great schemes ; just as a wealth of other evidence shows how precise a grasp he had on the practical details of government and administration and how well calculated was his cool, firm, sardonic manner to rouse Henry's temper.

In 1250 the Emperor Frederick II died, and the intrigues which followed his death involved the English royal family in endeavours even more grandiose than those of Richard I. Frederick had been king both in Germany and in Sicily, and the popes were determined to prevent the two kingdoms from being united again ; they were equally determined to complete the destruction of the Hohenstaufen dynasty. Complicated manoeuvres by the Pope and by the leading subjects of the two kingdoms led Henry III in 1254 to accept the kingdom of Sicily for his younger son, Edmund, and Richard of Cornwall in 1257 to accept the kingdom of Germany for himself. Richard spent a number of years fruitlessly pursuing his phantom kingdom. Germany was relapsing into chaos, and a foreign potentate, however rich and able, had little hope of resolving its factions. Edmund amused himself for a while distributing titles and properties of his kingdom, but by the end of 1257 the whole of Sicily was in the hands of the Hohenstaufen Manfred, and Henry was left with nothing to show for the affair but an immense debt which was the pope's price for the kingdom. The Sicilian adventure, however, had two consequences of greater moment than itself : it persuaded Henry to prepare the way for a definitive peace with Louis IX of France, and it led to his surrender to a committee of barons in England in 1258.

The Treaty of Paris marked the formal end of the Angevin Empire. Henry renounced his rights in Normandy, Anjou, and Poitou ; Louis acknowledged Henry as his vassal in Gascony and other lands in the south. The treaty was on the whole generous to Henry ; but its terms were so complex as to leave room for future trouble. For the rest of Henry's reign, however, France and England were at peace.

In domestic affairs, the events of 1257–8 started a crisis which lasted until 1265. Seven years of strife were followed by seven years of peace and restored royal government, ending in the King's death in 1272.

When Henry surrendered to the baronial opposition in 1258, a new system of government was established by the famous Provisions of Oxford, which reduced the King to little more than a *primus inter pares*. A new Council of Fifteen was established, consisting of seven earls (Simon de Montfort included), five leading barons, the Archbishop of Canterbury, the Bishop of Worcester, and one royal clerk ; in all affairs of state the King had to consult the council. The three great officers of state, Justiciar, Chancellor, and Treasurer, were to be appointed by the Council and to be responsible to it ; a baron was made Justiciar. In addition, the Provisions included a number of administrative reforms, particularly designed to ensure the Council's control over sheriffs, castellans (i.e. governors of castles), and lesser officials, and to reform abuses. The leaders in 1258, as in 1215, were a group of powerful magnates, and as in 1215, they needed to win allies by providing benefits for other classes than their own. But the reforms outlined in the Provisions of Oxford showed a far more coherent notion of how government was to be conducted than John's barons ever attained.

The Provisions of Oxford, supplemented by the Provisions of Westminster of 1259, remained the basis of English government until 1262. But government by a Council was too novel and elaborate an idea to win easy acceptance or to work smoothly. The Provisions of Oxford had been the fruit of co-operation between a number of leading magnates; gradually, as the years passed, they fell out among themselves. Personal differences divided Simon de Montfort from the Earl of Gloucester, the other dominating figure ; Gloucester and others could not accustom themselves to ruling in evident disregard of the King's real wishes ; and some of the reforms

which had been instituted compelled the barons themselves
to submit to unwelcome investigations of their own subordinates'
abuses. In 1259 and early 1260 Henry was in France completing his settlement with Louis ; Earl Simon, meanwhile, was
coming to hold an increasingly dominant position in England.
He had even come to an arrangement with the Lord Edward,
who first appeared in 1259 as an important figure in English
politics. Edward had put himself at the head of a group of
young men, mostly of baronial family, who accepted his views
or his leadership, and who came to form a small but important
party. They were hardly a faction : they did not imagine
that government could lie wholly in the hands of this or that
group of barons—they knew it must be more widely spread ;
they respected the law and Magna Carta. In Edward they
had a leader who would one day be king, and who would
restore to the monarchy the kingly virtues, the prowess in
tournament and battle which Henry so patently lacked. Unlike
Henry, Edward would be trustworthy, competent, and a
soldier. It was possible at this time for Edward and Simon
to come to terms : both were prepared to maintain the Provisions of Oxford, even if Edward regarded the Council as
essentially an advisory body, while Simon wished it to control
the King.

The alliance between Edward and Simon aroused Henry's
deepest suspicions ; he seems to have suspected Edward of a
plot to betray him, perhaps even to usurp the throne. Henry
returned to England, asserted himself, and sent Edward into
exile ; and then set to work to undermine the Provisions.
Most of their makers were now lukewarm in their support,
and by the turn of 1261 and 1262 Richard of Cornwall and a
group of bishops were able to organise an arrangement between
the King and the leading barons. In 1262 the Pope absolved
Henry from his oath to the Provisions ; Earl Simon went into
exile ; and Henry was king again in fact as well as in name.

Henry's triumph was exceedingly short-lived. He failed
to re-establish order in England, and he failed to come to terms
with Simon. The barons who had welcomed a return to the
more normal régime quickly remembered the distrust of Henry
which had inspired the revolution of 1258. Discontent was
widespread, but as in 1640–2 men differed on the distance to

which it was possible or desirable to carry resistance to the King; and it was far from clear how many of the barons would support the King, how many oppose him if it came to war. The issue was decided by the prompt action of Simon de Montfort in 1263. He returned to England, put himself at the head of the insurgents, and forced the King to promise a return to the Provisions. Late in the year Earl Simon's supporters and the King agreed to submit their case to the arbitration of the King of France; and in January 1264 St Louis, who was every inch a king, declared for Henry on every count and condemned the Provisions root and branch. This judgment, known as the 'Mise of Amiens', left the opposition barons no alternative but to submit or to fight for their cause; its effect was civil war, with both sides well supported.

In 1263 the Lord Edward finally decided that Simon's paths were too extreme, and when civil war broke out in 1264, Edward commanded the King's forces. On 14th May Earl Simon's army fell on the King's at Lewes in Sussex, attacking down a long slope into the town. Simon's left, consisting mainly of the Londoners, was broken and pursued by the Lord Edward; but the rest of Simon's army quickly overwhelmed the bulk of the royal force. When Edward returned from his pursuit, he found the day lost. The King surrendered, and Edward became a hostage for Henry's good behaviour. From May 1264 till August 1265 Simon de Montfort was effective ruler of England.

Simon was in intention no dictator. He honestly believed that a return to the Provisions of Oxford was possible, and he strove to achieve it. Meanwhile, he and two colleagues, the young Earl of Gloucester (whose father had died in 1262) and the Bishop of Chichester, governed in the King's name, and chose to assist them a Council of Nine, with functions very similar to those of the Council of Fifteen of 1258–62, but more widely representative of the English upper classes. Simon had no wish to govern as the head of a clique, and for discussion of important matters of state he relied more than hitherto on the Great Council, at the same time trying to increase its solemnity and representative character.

The Great Council was reckoned to be a meeting of the

leaders of the kingdom, lay and clerical; but the King had always had a fairly free choice as to which of the barons should be summoned. In the first half of the thirteenth century groups of lesser men, representatives of the knights and burgesses who were becoming increasingly active in the management of shires and towns, might be called to attend a council for a special purpose. Their presence was exceptional before the fourteenth century. But three times in Henry's later years, in 1258, in 1264, and in 1265, knights were called to represent the shires, and on the last occasion burgesses also attended to represent the towns. The dates are significant: one of these was the council which issued the Provisions of Oxford, and the others were the councils in which Earl Simon and his colleagues tried to reconstruct the government of the realm. The notion of the 'community of the realm' was gathering force. It was the strength of Earl Simon's position that he had won a considerable following among the 'gentry'. The weakness of his position was that his following among the barons was dwindling.

From the middle of the thirteenth century it became common to refer to the more important sessions of the Great Council as 'parliaments'. It was precisely in the years 1258–65 that the word 'parliament' was first commonly used. Originally the word simply meant a 'parleying', a conference between king and notables. It was not an institution, but an occasion; an occasion when a meeting of a Great Council gave the king the opportunity to discuss with the magnates important affairs of state—the levying of taxation, the solution of tricky legal cases—or to receive petitions. Gradually men came to draw a distinction between Council and Parliament, to see Parliament as an institution, to know (or think they knew) who ought and who ought not to be summoned to it, how its procedure was to be organised, what kind of business it should transact, what powers it had. All this lay far in the future. In 1272 nobody knew or could have guessed that these conferences in Council were to grow into the central institution of English government. What Simon and his followers—and the Lord Edward—did know was that within the royal Council, and by broadly based discussion, vital aspects of royal government, jurisdiction, and administration could and had to be conducted.

Through the spring and summer of 1265 Earl Simon's position weakened. His chief associate, the Earl of Gloucester, had decided that royal government conducted by Simon could lead to no good result in the end. Late in May the Lord Edward escaped, was joined by Gloucester, and gathered an army in the Welsh march. On 4th August Simon's army was caught at Evesham in Worcestershire and quickly beaten. Simon himself was killed, and the King was once more restored to effective government.

Simon de Montfort's achievements were not buried with him. It is true that the idea of limited monarchy was a temporary expedient to deal with a crisis. But the idea that important affairs of state should be regularly discussed in Great Councils, and that there must be more continuous co-operation between the king and all the groups and interests among the English ruling classes had been firmly implanted in Edward himself, in his own followers, and in many others. The revolution of 1258 and the events of the following seven years had created precedents and started experiments which were not to be forgotten.

These seven years had also raised feuds and violent dissensions which it took many years to settle. Immediately after Evesham Simon's supporters were deprived of their lands, and the long guerrilla warfare against the 'Disinherited', as they were called, began. They took refuge where they could, in fen and forest. Some of them organised bands of outlaws, and one of these (with its headquarters in Sherwood Forest) may have given rise to the famous legend of Robin Hood ; but Robin more likely belongs to the early fourteenth century.[1] Eventually a fair settlement was devised and carried out on the basis of the firm but moderate document known as the Dictum of Kenilworth (1266) which was followed by the more elaborate Statute of Marlborough (1267). This settlement was a triumph above all for the papal legate, Cardinal Ottobuono ; but he found allies in Edward himself and in the Earl of Gloucester, neither of whom wished to see the positive achievements of the baronial plan of reform destroyed. Initiative in government was restored to the king ; he was to be free to choose his servants and councillors ; but Magna

[1] See Powicke, *King Henry III and the Lord Edward*, II, pp. 529–30

Carta was to be enforced and responsible government ensured by regular ' parliaments '.

The legate was not solely concerned to restore peace and good order to the kingdom ; he had also come to preach a Crusade. The Sultan of Egypt was engaged in the piecemeal conquest of the surviving Christian outposts and principalities in Syria and Palestine. Although the crusading movement had lost the popular appeal which it had had in the twelfth century, the great effort of papal propaganda of the late twelve-sixties had quite a substantial effect. The Crusade, however, got under way very slowly. Ottobuono left England in 1268 ; it was not until 1270 that the English contingent, led by the Lord Edward himself, set sail. In the same year St Louis of France also set out on Crusade, to meet his death in Tunis before he ever reached the Holy Land. Louis' death severely weakened the Crusade, and Edward had to content himself with leading some raids on the Syrian coast, and helping in negotiations for peace with the Egyptian sultan, under which the coastal settlements round Acre and elsewhere were preserved until the sixteenth century. Late in 1272 Edward set out on his return journey, and had only reached Sicily when he received news that his father had died on 16th November 1272.

Edward's journey home was extraordinarily slow : it took him nearly two years to travel from Sicily to England, a space of time occupied in formal visits to the Pope and the King of France, in taking part in his last tournament, and in settling the affairs of Gascony. England, meanwhile, was securely held by his friends. Edward had been accepted as king by hereditary right and by the will of the magnates immediately on his father's death. But it was not until 19th August 1274 that he was crowned in his father's choir in Westminster Abbey.

14   England in the Thirteenth Century

IT IS estimated that the population of England in 1086 was very roughly 1,500,000, in the late thirteenth century something over 3,000,000. These estimates are not very secure, but it is unlikely that they give a very false impression. The population had doubled, perhaps trebled. This was a substantial, even a sensational rise. The reasons for it are not entirely clear ; but it seems likely that it reflects both a rise in the birth-rate and a decline in the death-rate. Throughout the Middle Ages expectation of life was far shorter than today. Many children died at birth ; many more in the first year of life ; inadequate care and ignorance of nutrition prevented many children from surviving early childhood ; if they grew up, accident and disease might carry them off at any age. Medieval medicine was primitive ; neglect was often preferable to treatment, and supernatural cures—invocation of a favourite saint, touching by the king for scrofula (' the king's evil ')—were usually more beneficial than was medical attention ; at least they could involve no positive harm. The expectation of life was perhaps a quarter of what it is today ; but no figure would be of any significance. The important fact is that death was always near ; life always insecure. If a man survived childhood and escaped a fatal illness or a fatal accident in early manhood, he might live to be eighty or ninety ; but a man entered old age soon after fifty and by sixty-five would have buried most of his contemporaries.

Two circumstances might gravely increase the death-rate : hunger and plague. It was not until the fourteenth century that bubonic plague came to carry off perhaps a third of the total population in one visitation. In earlier centuries famine was a more serious danger. The nearer people are to the

subsistence level—the more they depend on what they themselves grow—the higher is the danger of famine : a bad
harvest finds them without reserves to draw on, and without
the money to buy food from more fortunate neighbours. The
progress of money economy between the eleventh and thirteenth
centuries reduced men's dependence on what they grew in
each particular year, and so reduced the danger of widespread
famine. This provided one of the conditions in which the
population could rise ; and increasing wealth, especially among
the upper classes, coupled with some improvement in living
conditions, no doubt enabled more of the population to survive
childhood, to grow up and have children, and so contribute
in their turn to the growth of population. But there was
probably also a rise in the number of children born within
the majority of families. The cause of this cannot be discovered now ; but we can guess that the invasion of the
Normans, already an extremely prolific people, had something
to do with it.

The population had grown : so had the area under
cultivation. The villages had spread : some had split into
two or three, others had increased their area under the plough.
In forest and fen, land had been cleared and drained and new
villages founded. The lands laid waste so thoroughly by
William the Conqueror had been resettled. The vale of
York was thick with corn again before the end of the twelfth
century. The small boroughs of Domesday Book had grown ;
many others had been founded to compete with them ; new
markets and new fairs had appeared, organised by merchants
English and foreign. Exports and imports were no longer a
tiny margin in an economy not far from the subsistence level.
English wool went to Flanders and came back as cloth ; English
cloth and corn went to Norway, and timber and furs and
many other supplies came back in their place ; corn and
herrings went to Gascony in exchange for many gallons of
wine ; from the Mediterranean came southern fruits, silks,
sweet wine, raisins, and currants (' raisins of Corinth ')—and
the precious stones and spices—rubies, emeralds, pepper,
ginger, cloves—which the merchants of Italy had brought
from the Middle and Far East. England was far richer and
more prosperous than it had been in 1086.

The wealth, however, was even more unevenly distributed than in the eleventh century. The large majority of the people were still peasants, and their standard of living had altered little. Indeed, rising population had increased the pressure on land ; and land-hunger increased the dependence of many peasants on the goodwill of their lords. Freedom and unfreedom and all the complex rights of the manorial lord were being more closely defined by the lawyers and estate bailiffs. The life of the peasant remained hard and comfortless. But increasing national wealth, though it might bring little relief to the mass of the peasantry, meant a great increase in the opportunities which the few could take who prospered and saved. An active peasant could add field to field. No doubt this had always been possible ; it was certainly easier and more common in the thirteenth century than before. A prosperous peasant could build up quite a substantial small property, endow his sons and give portions to his daughters from it, and still hope to leave a decent holding to support his widow and his heir.

Hand in hand with rising population went growing economic specialisation—still very small by our standards, but far beyond what the eleventh century could have dreamed. In particular, the fine wool produced by the English sheep tempted not only merchants from Flanders, but Italians in particular, who came to hold a preponderant place in English long-distance trade. The Italians owed their position in the first place to the large and growing papal taxes. The Italian merchants were the papal bankers. They collected taxes in money and in kind—and it was thus that they became accustomed to handling English wool on a large scale. The Italian merchants were often unpopular in England, but the country prospered in their hands. They taught English merchants their own more elaborate techniques, they provided capital and credit, they strengthened and simplified trade with the Mediterranean —especially in and after the late thirteenth century. It was papal taxation which brought capitalism and mercantile prosperity to England.

The Italians were not, however, the only merchants in England, nor must their initiative be exaggerated. The multiplication of fairs and markets meant a rapid growth in the number of English merchants. If much wool was exported, much was also manufactured into cloth in England itself; and weavers, fullers, and dyers were increasing in numbers. Cloth-making was only one of many industries : iron, tin, lead, salt, and even coal were providing increasing numbers with a livelihood. More than ever were engaged in building. The urban classes had come to be an important element in English society. Some old boroughs, like Bristol, had been in the forefront of rapid development, especially on account of the wine trade with Gascony. Many new towns, like Lynn, an outlet for the fenland abbeys, Hull, the port of York and Beverley, and Newcastle, centre of the Norwegian trade, and also of the only important coalfield then exploited, grew and throve between the Conquest and the death of Henry III. But London remained far and away the greatest city in England. Now that new life was stirring in many corners of the country, it might have been supposed that London would feel the pressure of new competitors. But it retained its situation as the centre of the English road system, as a vast sheltered port convenient for continental shipping ; and as royal government became more elaborate and more complex, more of its functions came to be performed in London and Westminster. In the days of Stephen, the Londoners had played an active part in national politics by expelling the empress and welcoming the queen. In 1191 the citizens formed a commune and claimed the right to a considerable measure of self-government ; and although the ' commune ' was never officially recognised by the king, the privileges of London slowly grew. By the thirteenth century the city oligarchy of mayor and aldermen was firmly established. London figured in Magna Carta ; it played a decisive part in the events leading up to the battle of Lewes. Barons and knights were no longer the only powers in the land.

In 1086 a baron valued his lands first and foremost for the knights they could supply. A man's prestige depended on the distinction of his retinue ; his power depended on the number of men who would fight for him ; his place at court and in royal favour depended on the behaviour of his contingent in war. By the thirteenth century the knights' fees had lost a great part of their importance. The cost of knightly armour had increased ; the knight's fee could no longer support a fully armed knight. The quota was in process of being reduced. Meanwhile the fees had come to be subdivided and sub-infeudated by all the changes and chances of 200 years. The exaction of the very elaborate and tiresome military service of early feudal days was no longer practical. Neither baron nor king could rely on the feudal levy any longer. From at least the early twelfth century the king had depended largely on mercenaries ; by the late thirteenth century the leading barons were no more than the officers of a mercenary army. King and barons had to tax their subjects to provide money to pay the royal host.

Other reasons also conspired to increase the barons' interest in cash. The wooden hall of eleventh-century days had given place to the great stone keep of the twelfth ; and in the thirteenth century military necessity and the quest for comfort were increasing still further the dimensions of castles. Knights and barons were more often living in unfortified or semi-fortified houses as private war became rarer ; large but simple, by our standards, with often no more than two rooms, but far more luxurious than the twelfth-century keep. The few pieces of solid furniture were beginning to be supplemented by more hangings and rugs, by glass for the windows and ornaments for the table. The great baron still had to have a castle, but usually reckoned to build a commodious house within large ' curtain ' walls (see Plate 14) rather than suffer the discomforts of a dark keep. Curtain walls with ever more elaborate fortifications were being developed to separate the garrison more effectively from the new siege engines and their missiles. The climax of these developments can be seen in Edward I's great castles in Wales.

Within the baronial hall the greatest expense of the lord was not in furnishing, but in the lavish hospitality he had to keep up and the generosity he was expected to show to followers and guests. The decline of the knights' fees did not reduce the need for a lord to be well followed : very much the reverse. As the Middle Ages went on, retinues grew larger, and the code of chivalry demanded ever more extravagant generosity. This reached its height perhaps in the fourteenth century, but chivalry was far from cheap in the thirteenth. The code demanded that a lord be brave (*preux*), loyal, and generous above all. A twelfth-century troubadour said that it was a disgrace for a man to live within his means. He ought to mortgage his estates and spend his substance entertaining and giving presents. The favourite form of entertainment for a rich man was to organise a tournament. This notable sport replaced private war as the favourite occupation of the warriors in the late twelfth and thirteenth centuries; though from private war it differed little, save that there were a few more rules to be obeyed. At first the tourney was a general mêlée, fought between two sides; only in the course of the thirteenth century did this begin to be replaced by jousting, by individual bouts between armed knights, which gradually acquired rules akin to those of modern boxing.

Two powerful social groups modified the nature of tournament and chivalry as time went on : the ladies and the Church. The status of women was still low. Under certain circumstances they could inherit land; a few great ladies, like the Empress Matilda and Queen Eleanor of Aquitaine, played a leading part in politics in their own right; but they were debarred from the two most respectable professions of the day —from the feudal host and from clerical Orders; only a few became nuns. A nobleman's sisters and daughters tended to be treated as pawns in the game of marriage alliances which he would be constantly playing. The lady's place was the home; her business child-bearing, which was probably at least as dangerous as war. Some wives were submissive; others were beaten; many, as in every age, dominated their husbands. But as long as marriage was a business, constant child-bearing the established custom, and education open only to the very few, the status of women could not be fundamentally altered.

New influences were at work to modify these traditions. The romantic ideal, incorporated into the courtly romances of the Arthurian and other cycles, was giving a new dimension to the code of chivalry. The romances were first written in the mid- and late twelfth century; they were at the height of their popularity in the thirteenth. Their commonest theme was the lonely quest of the knight, in pursuit of adventures which might do honour to his lady. As expressions of earthly love, the romances varied from the trivial to the sublime. They brought into current use an attitude to women entirely new in European history—an attitude which has given us the word ' romantic '. At their best they incorporated this idea into a lofty ideal of knightly chivalry, most fully shown in some of the German and French stories of Sir Perceval or Sir Galahad in pursuit of the Holy Grail ; and the romance made popular throughout western Europe some ancient stories, like that of Tristan and Iseult, hitherto confined to a single land. Tristan (Drystan) first meets us in Wales ; but his story was later sung in many parts of the Continent. The developed romance of Tristan was one of the few in which these tales rose to the height of romantic passion. The legend of Iseult was a constant protest against the actual status of medieval women.

The romantic ideal had its influence in the world of chivalry. Knights fought for their ladies' favour, and the ladies' gallery became an essential feature of a tournament. But the influence was slow to affect the married life of the ordinary world. Some of the men who sang that women were ethereal creatures, to be worshipped from afar, partially believed what they said ; and many of the women who heard themselves so described were disinclined to be treated as chattels and drudges. The presence of the ladies at tournaments helped to civilise the tournaments and, in the end, to civilise the world.

At first the Church condemned the tournament as it condemned private war ; and until the reign of Richard I the king officially forbade them too. But a baron could not win men's respect unless he conformed to the fashion. When told on his deathbed to repay all that he had taken, that model of chivalry and honour, William the Marshal, replied : ' The clerks are too hard on us. They shave us too closely. I have captured 500 knights and have appropriated their arms, horses, and their entire equipment. If for this reason the kingdom of God is closed to me, I can do nothing about it, for I cannot return my booty. . . . But their teaching is false —else no one could be saved.' [1] In course of time, as the tournament became less violent, the Church's opposition weakened. Chivalry slowly became respectable. Meanwhile, it was extremely expensive ; and the man who organised a tournament was liable to provide entertainment and gifts for an army.

[1] Quoted in S. Painter, *French Chivalry*, p. 89

To meet the royal taxes and the demands of his social position, the baron needed money. To some extent this could be provided by sound management of his estates. The thirteenth century was a great age of arable and sheep farming. Profits were high, techniques of estate management were developing, and by screwing higher rents out of his tenants and by exploiting some of his manors through his bailiffs a lord could hope to improve his income handsomely.

Some of the barons had immense estates. The baronage was no larger in the thirteenth than in the eleventh century— new blood had been compensated by the disappearance of old families. It was therefore, in general, much wealthier. But the increase in wealth had been modified by two circumstances : that the ' mesne ' vassals (barons' vassals) and the knights— what were later to be called the ' gentry '—had much increased in numbers and had absorbed some of the new wealth ; and that a large share of baronial wealth was concentrated in a few hands. Wealthiest of all was Richard of Cornwall, Henry III's brother, whose annual income would have been a fortune to a lesser man, who himself financed the currency reform of 1247, shored up the finances of the king and others by princely loans on many occasions, and was still a rich man after the costly attempt to establish himself in Germany. A few leading earls had incomes between £1,000 and £2,000 a year—incomes which, in modern terms, made them millionaires ; most of the barons had incomes from land varying from £100 to £500 a year. The average annual revenue of King Henry III has been estimated at £34,000 to £35,000.

But we must not think of the economic position of the great lords purely in terms of their income. We are often told that wealth is power ; and in a society in which armies were coming increasingly to consist of mercenaries this may seem on the way to being true. But in the thirteenth century it could equally well be said that power was wealth. The key to fortune lay as much in having influence at court as in good husbandry ; and this was to be true of the English aristocracy for many centuries to come. Richard of Cornwall's wealth was only to a limited extent derived from his inheritance ; royal favour showered properties and gifts on him—including the earldom of Cornwall, carrying with it much profit from the tin-mines, and the profits of the royal mint ; in return Richard saved the crown from bankruptcy.   The earls of Gloucester combined two of the best baronies of the Welsh march and substantial portions of other holdings.   In theory this was the fruit of prudent marriages ; but no lord could hope to acquire or keep fiefs on such a scale unless the king was behind him.   There was one way in which the barons were even more closely dependent on the king for their livelihood. Several of the clauses of Magna Carta regulate the arbitrary use of feudal incidents—the money the king could levy from his tenants under a variety of conditions, especially for ' relief ' when the baron died and his heir succeeded.   Hitherto, when the king exacted fine or relief, he named the sum arbitrarily ; and Henry I and John in particular—and all the English kings in some measure—had named fantastic sums.   No-one expected these to be paid in full ; the baron paid what he could from year to year, and was eventually forgiven the rest.   The amount the king actually received depended on the baron's capacity to pay and on political circumstances.   A powerful baron whose support the king needed might never pay more than a fraction of his fine.   Unless the baron was particularly offensive to the king, he was unlikely to be broken by a royal fine. There are cases of barons who impoverished themselves in this period and sank to be small gentry or farmers ; but in the main the tradition was already established that a baron should be helped to maintain his station.   The king rarely extracted more than the baron could afford ; barons in difficulties might hope to receive grants of offices, sheriffdoms, castles, and even lands or money to assist them.   It is estimated that sixty per cent of the barons owed money to the king in 1230 ; a number of them also owed money to merchants and money-lenders. The baronial class was not sinking under its debts.   It no longer had the monopoly of power which had once been in its hands.   But in reality it was richer and potentially more powerful than ever.   Nor did debt make the barons sycophants of the king—after all, the king was as much in debt as they were. But it did ensure that the court played a large and increasing part in men's calculations.   It was the chief source of wealth and social prestige for the upper classes.   The two were intimately connected.   Debt was a normal part of the evidence that a nobleman was leading a good life according to the code of chivalry.

One notable extravagance of the upper classes has still to be mentioned : their benefactions to the Church. The heroic days when barons founded new monastic houses on a grandiose scale were mostly past by 1200. But a few new foundations were made ; smaller institutions, hospitals, and the like were still endowed ; chantries were being established in the thirteenth century to ensure that a priest would sing mass for the founder's soul in perpetuity ; and large and frequent expense on charity to the poor, the sick, and the Friars was expected of every rich man. Most barons had inherited an interest in one or more monasteries, to which they looked for prayers, and which looked to them for economic and political aid when it should be required.

The Church was wealthier than ever before ; but its funds were almost as unevenly distributed as those of the laity. The basis of the Church's income lay in the revenues of parishes, de-rived from tithes and other ' gifts ' due from parishioners to the parish clergy. Beyond that, bishoprics, cathedrals, and abbeys had been given extensive lands ; the faithful contributed to the building and upkeep of churches and gave precious relics and ornaments to them. In efficient farming, Benedictine and Cistercian monasteries were often pioneers in the thirteenth century ; and most monasteries were reasonably well en-dowed and supported. The leading bishops were particularly well provided. The two archbishops and the bishops of Winchester, Ely, and Durham had incomes equal to those of the wealthiest of the barons. Like the barons, much was expected of them : a string of palaces, a large team of chaplains, and an immense household staff; open hospitality and princely generosity. Other bishops were not so well endowed ; nor had the practice yet arisen which compensated a Welsh bishop for the poverty of his see by allowing him to hold an English deanery as well and to live in hopes of translation to a wealthier diocese. Below the bishops the possibilities of pluralism were being extravagantly explored. It has never been worse : Henry III's leading clerks amassed immense fortunes out of royal office and large pluralities. Later in the century Bogo de Clare, son of the Earl of Gloucester, put together church offices and rectories with the avidity of a collector. Pluralism was shortly to be tamed, so that its worst abuses could be avoided and such function as it had be carried out more efficiently. It was reckoned that tithes and parish dues produced more than enough for many parish priests ; yet the Church had no source of income for many of its other officials. How were clerics in the service of the king and of the bishops to be supported ? The answer may seem obvious to us ; but it did not seem obvious either to the king or to his clerks that they should live on their wages. Moreover, those engaged in learning and teaching in the rising universities could often only be supported by taxing this or that parish on their behalf. For reasons good and ill, the Church's wealth was being redistributed, as yet haphazardly and most unevenly ; but there were not wanting men who wished to see this distribution more equitably and efficiently arranged, who cared first and foremost for the cure of souls.

The thirteenth century was a great age in the history of the medieval Church. The monastic Orders had lost much of their original fervour ; the papacy, though far from forgetful of the source of its inspiration, was losing something of its original prestige as it grew increasingly powerful, increasingly involved in law and politics. But the thirteenth century saw an unusually high number of really distinguished bishops ; saw Oxford and Cambridge grow and flourish and produce a number of the finest of the scholastics ; saw the arrival of the Friars and the spread of the ideals of St Francis and St Dominic in England ; and saw the development of Gothic architecture —the flowering of the Early English style and the beginnings of the Decorated—culminating in the choirs of Westminster Abbey and Lincoln Cathedral.

After the death of Stephen Langton (1228), the English episcopate included three men of outstanding character : St Edmund of Abingdon, the saintly and earnest Archbishop of Canterbury (1234–40) ; St Richard Wych, a graduate of Oxford, Paris, and Bologna and a protégé of St Edmund, who was Bishop of Chichester (1245–53) ; and Robert Grosseteste, Bishop of Lincoln (1235–53). Grosseteste had been the leading teacher at Oxford and first Chancellor of the University ; he was intimately associated with the early history of the Franciscan Friars in this country, though he never himself joined the Order. As bishop he was an ardent reformer. He attempted to enforce the methods and standards promulgated in the Fourth Lateran Council of 1215. Though always capable of taking an independent line, he was a faithful servant of the papacy. There was hardly an aspect of the Church's life which he did not touch ; and if in the end he impresses us as a man of somewhat overbearing temper, the Church would have been much the poorer without him.

Oxford had been the seat of a school for about a century before Grosseteste came to study and teach there. Its formal development as a university came in his time ; Cambridge was also beginning to emerge as a university in the first half of the century. Oxford had established its reputation as a centre for the study of law ; Grosseteste's teaching gave it special distinction as a school of theology, but his own academic interests were immensely wide, ranging from the translation of Greek treatises through the diverse concerns of the books he was translating—mainly philosophical and scientific—to the study of the Bible and of theology itself. Perhaps he is most widely known as one of the first Western scholars to do any original thinking on scientific problems. His mind was encyclopedic and his activity ubiquitous.

In 1221 Friars of the Order of Preachers, the Dominicans, first came to England. They were intended to be an Order of instructed preachers, who could raise the standard of learning and orthodoxy in the Church, make up for the deficiencies of the parochial clergy in preaching and teaching, and lead the counter-attack against heresy : it was in his tours among the heretics in northern Spain and southern France that St Dominic of Caleruega (c. 1171–1221) conceived the idea of his Order. Heresy was a very slight problem in England, but there was much work which an order of preachers might do ; and the Dominicans immediately looked for a university town in which to establish their chief school in the country. Oxford was already the obvious choice ; it was natural that the preachers should establish themselves there quickly, and that Grosseteste should be one of their earliest and most influential contacts.

Even closer was his friendship with the Order of Friars

Minor, the Franciscans, who first arrived in England three years later than the Dominicans, in 1224. These two were the oldest and most eminent of the Orders of Friars. The way of life of the two Orders was similar : both were bound by oaths to poverty, obedience, and chastity ; both lived by rules, but not by monastic rules. The Friars were not monks : they were not confined within the walls of a monastery ; they moved freely in the world and found their essential apostolate there ; neither of the two Orders could hold any property of its own. Dominic's ideal was based on mature reflection by an experienced man on the special needs of the Church of his day. These needs influenced Francis, too, and led to changes in his Order ; but its foundation was the result of an intense experience of conversion and illumination by an enthusiastic young Italian layman in his twenties. Francis was called to the life of the Gospel : his message was the message of Jesus to his disciples, to go out two by two, taking nothing for the way, ' neither gold, nor silver, nor brass in your purses . . . , neither shoes, nor yet staves : for the workman is worthy of his meat.' They were to do good, to preach, to work ; and to live on charity, if necessary by begging. They were to be poorer and humbler than the poor.

The infectious gaiety of St Francis of Assisi (c. 1181–1226) still captivates us after the lapse of seven centuries. Nor was this quality lacking among the early Friars in England. ' The brothers were at all times gay and happy among themselves,' writes their chronicler, Thomas of Eccleston, ' so that when they looked at one another they could scarcely refrain from a smile. And so because the young Friars at Oxford laughed too frequently, it was ordained that as often as one laughed in choir or at table he should receive so many strokes of the rod.' And he goes on to tell the pathetic tale of the Friar who had had eleven strokes and still could not keep a straight face.[1] The first two heads of the Franciscans in England—' ministers of the province of England '—Agnellus and Albert of Pisa, both seem to have been a nice mixture of sternness and good humour. Certainly they were men of distinction, and under their leader-

---

[1] Thomas of Eccleston, *De Adventu Fratrum Minorum in Angliam*, p. 26. The story ends with a disturbing dream of the Friar, which led the brothers to behave more soberly.

ship the English province acquired a very good name. In certain respects it followed the founder's ideal very closely ; but from the first, contrary to Francis's intention, the Friars included scholars who cultivated their learning. The schools of Paris and Oxford were the centres of the movement which transformed the Order and provided it with a strong nucleus of learned men. Leading figures in this transformation were Albert of Pisa himself, who left England to become head of the Order in 1239, and the English Haymo of Faversham, who succeeded Albert as Minister General in 1240. Many of the great names among English Franciscans—Adam Marsh, the friend of Grosseteste and Simon de Montfort, John Pecham (later Archbishop of Canterbury), and Roger Bacon—remind us that the Franciscan School at Oxford was a vital centre of learning in the great age of scholastic thought. The Order was transformed in two ways : it acquired this learned nucleus, and it declined from its original fervour. But in 1272 we are still far away from the days of Chaucer's Friar.

Robert Grosseteste had been himself a leading influence in the development of Oxford and in the formation of the English provinces of the Orders of Friars. That he played much part in the building of Lincoln Cathedral is less certain—though the nave at least may date from his time—but it remains one of the most remarkable monuments of thirteenth-century piety and art. The new Gothic forms, worked out in the twelfth century, were finding maturity in England as in France in the thirteenth. An austere and simple grace is as characteristic of Lincoln and the myriad churches which belong to its age, as the riot of line and ornament was characteristic of the early fourteenth century. These great churches are monuments to the wealth of English society : most strikingly Salisbury, where Bishop Richard Poore (1217–28) was able to conceive and in large measure execute the astonishing idea of moving cathedral, close, and the whole town bodily from its old hill fort to the banks of the Wiltshire Avon. These great churches were finely built, but not extravagant. Their height, their colour, their use of glass was restrained when compared with their contemporaries in France. To this the main exception was Westminster Abbey.

Westminster represents the personal taste of a king who

had more artistic flair than political sense. In it French and English motifs were nicely blended ; and the abbey choir, though hidden today by countless tombs, shorn of its colour by the Reformers and darkened by London's soot, can still make us see why it was reckoned in its day a masterpiece—to be imitated in the proportions and splendid sculpture of the Angel Choir at Lincoln and in many another English church. Westminster introduced a new idea of richness, of splendour in decoration into England.

'The new work at Westminster,' wrote Sir Maurice Powicke, 'was more than a royal tribute to a favourite saint, and much more than an embellishment of the London suburb where the king had his chief house and courts. It was the most strenuous and concentrated, as it was also the most gracious expression of a rich artistic life ; and this life, fanned into intensity by the king, was in its turn the outcome of a social activity which engaged the interests of thousands of people, and meant more to them than all the political and ecclesiastical issues of the day. At one period in the course of the work some 800 men were engaged upon it, but these 800 had behind them the quarrymen who dug out the stone in Caen and Purbeck and many other places, the sailors and wagoners who brought it to Westminster, the woodmen in the forests who felled the oaks for timbers, the merchants who collected the materials for work in cloth and jewellery, in mosaic and metal, the tilers at Chertsey and other places where men made tiles, the financiers who advanced money for wages. Nor was the work at Westminster isolated ; it was but part of a general activity.' [1]

Once again we are reminded of the critical importance of the court, as a centre of artistic influence, as a vast exchange and mart where money was taken and received, where offices and lands and marriages were granted out, where men were employed on a scale unequalled elsewhere. Men who counted and men who wished to count in English life—still an infinitesimal proportion of the total population—could meet and pursue their ambitions, their quarrels, and their friendships in the English court. But it was far as yet from monopolising English life. England was still a country of small communities,

[1] *King Henry III and the Lord Edward*, II, pp. 572-3

governed by intense local patriotisms. It is true that the natural leaders of local society, the great barons, the knights of the shire, and the more eminent burgesses, were frequently acting as royal representatives for the countless activities of royal justice and administration in shire and borough, and less frequently meeting in conference, parley, or Parliament under the shadow of the royal court. These local communities were beginning to learn ' self-government at the king's command '. But the idea that local communities and central government must meet regularly if government is to be conducted with the consent of the people, still lay mainly in the future. In this and in other ways we must beware of looking forward too far. We are separated from what follows by the massive achievement of Edward I. But England was already far more populous, more wealthy, and more civilised than it had been 200 years before. The twelfth and thirteenth centuries saw great and fundamental changes, even if the way of life of the majority of the people had altered little. We can never say whether men were better or happier. We can only say that the choices of occupation and ideal open to most of them had increased ; that they had larger opportunities. How they used them we can never hope, in detail, to know.

Appendix A

TABLE OF DATES

POLITICS (reigns of kings in italics)		THE CHURCH AND LITERATURE	
871–99	*Alfred*	871–99	Alfred's *Laws* and Translations
878	Alfred at Athelney, Battle of Edington, baptism of Guthrum	about 891	Oldest surviving copy of *Anglo-Saxon Chronicle*
		893	Asser's *Life of King Alfred*
899–925	*Edward the Elder*		
911–25	Re-conquest of Danelaw, first stage		
918	Death of Aethelflaeda, Lady of the Mercians		
919	Raegnald, King of York		
925–39	*Athelstan*		
937	Battle of Brunanburh		
939–46	*Edmund*	940	St Dunstan, Abbot of Glastonbury
946–55	*Eadred*		
949 or 950	Death of Hywel Dda		
955–9	*Eadwig*	957	St Dunstan, Bishop of Worcester (London, 959 ; Archbishop of Canterbury, 960–88)
959–75	*Edgar*		
		961	St Oswald, Bishop of Worcester (also Archbishop of York, 972–92)
		963–84	St Ethelwold, Bishop of Winchester
		about 970	*Regularis Concordia*

973 Coronation of Edgar

975–8	*Edward the Martyr*		
978–1016	*Ethelred Unræd*	1002–23	Wulfstan, Archbishop of York
991	Renewal of Danish attacks : Battle of Maldon		

1012 Murder of Archbishop Aelfheah

1013–14	King Swein in England (died 1014)
1016	Death of Ethelred and Edmund Ironside ; triumph of Cnut
1016–35	*Cnut*

POLITICS		THE CHURCH AND LITERATURE
	1027 Cnut's pilgrimage to Rome	
1035–40	Harold I	
1040–2	Harthacnut	
1042–66	*Edward the Confessor*	1049–54	Pope Leo IX
1051	Exile of Earl Godwin	1051–2	Robert of Jumièges,
1052	Return of Godwin (died 1053)		Archbishop of Canterbury
1053–66	Harold, Earl of Wessex	1062–95	St Wulfstan, Bishop of
1055–65	Tostig, Earl of Northumbria		Worcester
1063	Death of Gruffydd ap Llywelyn		
1066	*Harold :* Battles of Fulford (20 Sept.), Stamford Bridge (25 Sept.), and Hastings (14 Oct.)		
1066–87	*William I, the Conqueror*		
1068–70	Rebellion in the north	1070–89	Lanfranc, Archbishop of
1075	Rebellion of the earls ; execution of Earl Waltheof		Canterbury
		1073–85	Pope Gregory VII
1085	(Christmas) Planning of Domesday		
1086	Domesday Survey		
1087–1100	*William II, Rufus*	1093–1109	St Anselm, Archbishop of Canterbury
	1095–96 Preaching and start of the first Crusade		
		1097	Foundation of Cîteaux
		1099–1128	Ranulph Flambard, Bishop of Durham
1100–35	*Henry I*		
1106	Battle of Tinchebrai ; imprisonment of Robert, Duke of Normandy (died 1134)	1107	End of Investiture Dispute in England ; Anselm's return from exile
1120	Wreck of the White Ship ; death of William the Aetheling	1125	William of Malmesbury, *Acts of the Kings*
1128	Marriage of the Empress Matilda and Geoffrey, Count of Anjou (Henry II born, 1133)	1132	Foundation of Rievaulx and Fountains Abbeys
1135–54	*Stephen*	1138	Geoffrey of Monmouth,
1137	Death of Gruffydd ap Cynan		*History of the Kings of Britain*

POLITICS		THE CHURCH AND LITERATURE	
1137–70	Reign of Owain Gwynedd	1139–61	Theobald, Archbishop of Canterbury
1139	Matilda landed in England	1139–43	Henry of Blois (Bishop of Winchester), papal legate
1141	Battle of Lincoln and imprisonment of King Stephen ; imprisonment of Robert, Earl of Gloucester ; release of king and earl		
1144	Death of Geoffrey de Mandeville		
1144–5	Conquest of Normandy by Geoffrey, Count of Anjou		
1145–9	Geoffrey of Anjou, Duke of Normandy	1146	Death of Cardinal Robert Pullen

1147   Start of second Crusade

1147	Death of Robert, Earl of Gloucester	1147–67	St Ailred, Abbot of Rievaulx
1148	Matilda left England		
1149	Henry (later Henry II), Duke of Normandy (Count of Anjou, 1151 ; married Eleanor of Aquitaine, 1152 ; Duke of Aquitaine, 1153)		
1153	Duke Henry invaded England ; Treaty of Winchester	1153	Death of St Bernard of Clairvaux
		1154–9	Pope Adrian IV (Nicholas Breakspear)
1154–89	*Henry II*		
1155–62	Thomas Becket, royal Chancellor	1159	John of Salisbury, *Policraticus* and *Metalogicon*
		1159–81	Pope Alexander III
		1162–70	Thomas Becket, Archbishop of Canterbury

1164   Council and Constitutions of Clarendon (January). Council of Northampton ; flight of Becket (October)

1166	Assize of Clarendon		

1170   Coronation of young King Henry (14 June).   Murder of Thomas Becket (29 Dec.)

1176	Assize of Northampton	1173–4	William FitzStephen, *Life* of St Thomas Becket
1180–1223	Philip II ' Augustus ', King of France	1177	Richard FitzNeal, *Dialogus de Scaccario*
1183	Death of young King Henry	about 1187	' Glanville ', *De Legibus et Consuetudinibus Angliae*

POLITICS		THE CHURCH AND LITERATURE	
1189–99	*Richard I*		
1189–94	Richard I absent on third Crusade (capture of Acre, 1192) and in prison in Germany	1193–1205	Hubert Walter, Archbishop of Canterbury
1190–7	Henry VI, King of Germany and Western Emperor (crowned 1191)		
1197	Death of the Lord Rhys (ap Gruffydd)	1198–1216	Pope Innocent III
1199–1216	*John*		
1199	Beginning of Chancery rolls		
1204	Conquest of Normandy by Philip II		
		1207–28	Stephen Langton, Archbishop of Canterbury

1208–14   Interdict in England

1214	Battle of Bouvines		
1215 (June)	Magna Carta	1215	Fourth Lateran Council
1216–72	*Henry III*		
1227	End of Henry III's minority	1221	Arrival of Dominican Friars in England
		1224	Arrival of Franciscan Friars in England
		1226	Death of St Francis of Assisi
1240	Death of Llywelyn the Great	1234–40	St Edmund of Abingdon, Archbishop of Canterbury
		1235–53	Robert Grosseteste, Bishop of Lincoln
1254	Henry III accepted the crown of Sicily for his son, Edmund	1258	Thomas of Eccleston, *De Adventu Fratrum Minorum in Angliam*
1257	Richard, Earl of Cornwall, elected king of the Romans (i.e. of Germany)	1259	Death of Matthew Paris
1258	Provisions of Oxford (denounced 1262)		
1258	Llywelyn ap Gruffydd, Prince of Wales (died 1282)		
1259	Treaty of Paris ; Provisions of Westminster		
1264	Mise of Amiens (January) Battle of Lewes (May)		
1264–5	Government of Simon de Montfort		
1265	Battle of Evesham and death of Simon de Montfort (August)		
1272	Death of King Henry III		

Appendix B

GENEALOGICAL TABLES

TABLE I KINGS OF WESSEX AND ENGLAND, before 1066

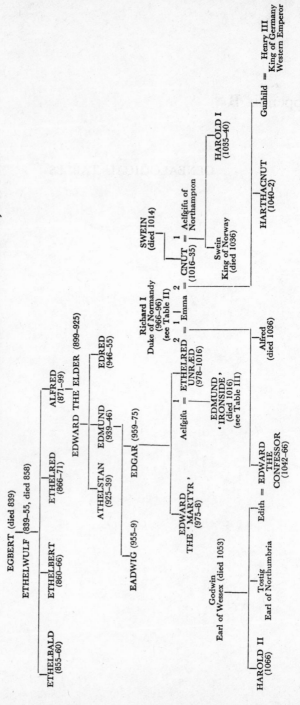

TABLE II THE NORMAN AND ANGEVIN KINGS

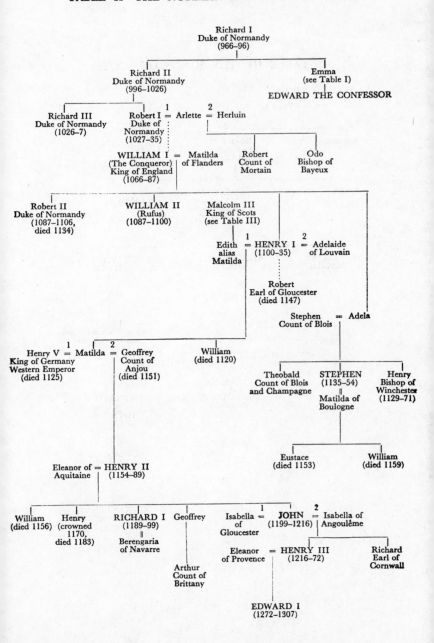

TABLE III   THE KINGS OF SCOTS

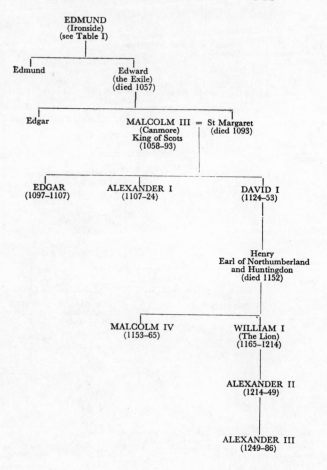

EDMUND
(Ironside)
(see Table I)

Edmund

Edward
(the Exile)
(died 1057)

Edgar

MALCOLM III = St Margaret
(Canmore)   (died 1093)
King of Scots
(1058–93)

EDGAR
(1097–1107)

ALEXANDER I
(1107–24)

DAVID I
(1124–53)

Henry
Earl of Northumberland
and Huntingdon
(died 1152)

MALCOLM IV
(1153–65)

WILLIAM I
(The Lion)
(1165–1214)

ALEXANDER II
(1214–49)

ALEXANDER III
(1249–86)

Books for Further Reading

Fuller bibliographies will be found in the volumes of the Oxford History of England by Sir Frank Stenton, A. L. Poole, and Sir Maurice Powicke, and in *English Historical Documents*, I and II, listed below.

Maps

Useful maps may be found in many historical atlases : e.g. in Muir's (ed. R. F. Treharne and H. Fullard, 1962), W. R. Shepherd's (1956 ed.), or *Cambridge Medieval History*, volume of maps. For religious houses, see the Ordnance Survey's *Map of Monastic Britain* (North and South sheets, ed. R. N. Hadcock, 1950).

Sources

(in translation, or provided with translations, unless otherwise stated)

English Historical Documents, I, ed. D. Whitelock (1955), selected documents, *c.* 500–1042

English Historical Documents, II, ed. D. C. Douglas and G. W. Greenaway (1953), 1042–1189

R. W. Chambers, *England before the Norman Conquest* (1926)

Regularis Concordia, ed. and trans. T. Symons (Nelson's Medieval Texts, 1953)

Anglo-Saxon Chronicle, trans. G. N. Garmonsway (Everyman's Library, 1960) or D. Whitelock *et al.* (1961)

The Bayeux Tapestry (Phaidon Press, 2nd ed., 1965), new photographs with full commentary by Sir Frank Stenton, F. Wormald, and others

Eadmer, *Life of Anselm*, ed. and trans. R. W. Southern (Nelson's Medieval Texts, 1963), and *History of Recent Events in England*, trans. C. Bosanquet (1964)

Ordericus Vitalis, *Ecclesiastical History*, trans. F. Forester (1853–6)

William of Malmesbury, *Gesta Regum*, trans. J. A. Giles (1889)

William of Malmesbury, *Historia Novella*, ed. and trans. K. Potter (Nelson's Medieval Texts, 1955)

John of Salisbury, *Historia Pontificalis*, ed. and trans. M. Chibnall (Nelson's Medieval Texts, 1956)

Walter Daniel, *Life of Ailred*, ed. and trans. Sir Maurice Powicke (Nelson's Medieval Texts, 1950)

Dialogus de Scaccario, ed. and trans. C. Johnson (Nelson's Medieval Texts, 1950)

Walter Map, *De Nugis Curialium*, trans. M. R. James (Cymmrodorion Record Series, 1923)

Autobiography of Gerald of Wales, trans. H. E. Butler (1937)

Jocelin of Brakelond, *Chronicle*, ed. and trans. H. E. Butler (Nelson's Medieval Texts, 1949)

M. A. Hennings, *England under Henry III* (1924), selected sources

Matthew Paris, *Chronica Maiora* (from 1235), trans. J. A. Giles (3 vols., 1852–4) (on this see R. Vaughan, *Matthew Paris* (1959) ; V. H. Galbraith, *Roger Wendover and Matthew Paris* (1944))

Thomas of Eccleston, *De Adventu Fratrum Minorum in Angliam* (Latin text ed. A. G. Little, 1951, Engl. trans. E. G. Salter, 1926)

W. Stubbs, *Select Charters* (9th ed., 1913). (Latin texts not translated ; on this book and its author see H. M. Cam, ' Stubbs Seventy Years After ', *Cambridge Historical Journal*, ix, ii (1948))

C. Stephenson and F. G. Marcham, *Sources of English Constitutional History* (1937)

G. G. Coulton, *Life in the Middle Ages* (2nd ed., 1954), selected documents

The European Setting

R. W. Southern, *The Making of the Middle Ages* (1953), a brilliant general survey from the tenth to the twelfth centuries

Z. N. Brooke, *History of Europe, 911–1198* (1938)

C. Petit-Dutaillis, *La monarchie féodale en France et en Angleterre* (1933, Engl. trans., 1936)

F. Kern, *Kingship and Law in the Middle Ages* (Engl. trans., 1939)

E. O. G. Turville-Petre, *The Heroic Age of Scandinavia* (1951)

P. H. Sawyer, *The Age of the Vikings* (1962)

J. Brøndsted, *The Vikings* (1965)

W. Ullmann, *The Growth of Papal Government* (1955)

C. H. Haskins, *The Renaissance of the Twelfth Century* (1927)

Cambridge Medieval History (8 vols., 1911–36), for reference

Cambridge Economic History of Europe (1941–   )

General and Political History

M. D. Knowles, ed., *The Heritage of Early Britain* (1952), a brief introduction, by a group of experts

P. Hunter Blair, *An Introduction to Anglo-Saxon England* (1956)

Sir Frank Stenton, *Anglo-Saxon England* (Oxford History of England, 1943)

D. J. A. Matthew, *The Norman Conquest* (1966)

E. A. Freeman, *History of the Norman Conquest* (6 vols., 1867–79), an elderly classic

A. L. Poole, *From Domesday Book to Magna Carta* (Oxford History of England, 1951)

F. Barlow, *The Feudal Kingdom of England, 1042–1216* (Longmans' History of England, 1955)

J. E. A. Jolliffe, *Angevin Kingship* (1955)

Sir Maurice Powicke, *The Loss of Normandy* (2nd ed., 1961)

Sir Maurice Powicke, *The Thirteenth Century* (Oxford History of England, 1953)

Sir Maurice Powicke, *King Henry III and the Lord Edward* (2 vols., 1947)

R. F. Treharne, *The Baronial Plan of Reform, 1258–1263* (1932)

R. F. Treharne, ' The Personal Role of Simon de Montfort in the period of Baronial Reform and Rebellion ', *Proceedings of the British Academy*, xl (1954)

Wales, Scotland, and Ireland

W. Croft Dickinson, *Scotland from the Earliest Times to 1603* (1961)

R. L. G. Ritchie, *The Normans in Scotland* (1954)

I. F. Grant, *The Social and Economic Development of Scotland before 1603* (1930)

A. J. Roderick (ed.), *Wales through the Ages*, I (1959), a series of short essays by various experts

J. E. Lloyd, *A History of Wales from the Earliest Times to the Edwardian Conquest* (3rd ed., 2 vols., 1939)

J. G. Edwards, ' The Normans and the Welsh March ', *Proceedings of the British Academy*, xlii (1956)

E. Curtis, *A History of Medieval Ireland* (4th ed., 1942)

The relevant chapters of G. W. S. Barrow, *Feudal Britain* (1956) are useful.

Constitutional and Legal

W. Stubbs, *Constitutional History of England* (3 vols., 1874–8), the starting point of modern study ; still a classic, though much of Stubbs's work has been revised, especially for the period before 1066

F. Pollock and F. W. Maitland, *History of English Law before the Time of Edward I* (2 vols., 2nd ed., 1898), Maitland's masterpiece

T. F. T. Plucknett, *A Concise History of the Common Law* (5th ed., 1956)

(Domesday Book and Feudalism)

F. W. Maitland, *Domesday Book and Beyond* (1897). (See p. 66)

J. H. Round, *Feudal England* (1895)

V. H. Galbraith, *The Making of Domesday Book* (Oxford, 1961), develops and corrects Round's *Feudal England* on the making of Domesday

V. H. Galbraith, *Studies in the Public Records* (1948), wider in scope than the title indicates

J. H. Round, *Geoffrey de Mandeville* (1892)

Sir Frank Stenton, *The First Century of English Feudalism, 1066–1166* (1932)

S. Painter, *Studies in the History of the English Feudal Barony* (1943)

(Magna Carta and the Thirteenth Century)

J. C. Holt, *The Northerners* (1961) and *Magna Carta* (1966)

G. B. Adams, *Origin of the English Constitution* (2nd ed., 1920), elderly, but a lively introduction to *Magna Carta*

S. Painter, *The Reign of King John* (1949)

F. Thompson, *The First Century of Magna Carta* (1925)

B. Wilkinson, *Constitutional History of England, 1216–1399* (3 vols., 1948–58)

(Administration)

S. B. Chrimes, *An Introduction to the Administrative History of Mediaeval England* (1952)

R. L. Poole, *The Exchequer in the Twelfth Century* (1912)

Social and Economic

E. Power, *Medieval People* (9th ed., 1950)

S. Painter, *William Marshall* (1933)

D. Whitelock, *The Beginnings of English Society* (Pelican History of England, 1952)

D. M. Stenton, *English Society in the Early Middle Ages* (Pelican History of England, 1951)

W. J. Ashley, *Introduction to English Economic History*, I (1909 ed.)

M. W. Beresford and J. K. S. St Joseph, *Medieval England, an Aerial Survey* (1958)

H. C. Darby (ed.), *Historical Geography of England before A.D. 1800* (1936)

C. S. and C. S. Orwin, *The Open Fields* (2nd ed., 1954)

P. Vinogradoff, *The Growth of the Manor* (2nd ed., 1911)

G. C. Homans, *English Villagers of the Thirteenth Century* (1942)

E. A. Kosminsky, *Studies in the Agrarian History of England in the Thirteenth Century* (Engl. trans. by R. Kisch, 1956), the work of an eminent Russian historian

E. Power, *The Wool Trade in English Medieval History* (1941)

E. M. Carus-Wilson, *Medieval Merchant Venturers* (1954)

Sir William Savage, *The Making of our Towns* (1952)

G. C. Brooke, *English Coins* (1932), for reference

A. L. Poole (ed.), *Medieval England* (1958), a collection of essays by various experts, on many aspects of English life

The Church

Dom David Knowles, *The Monastic Order in England, 943–1216* (1940)

Dom David Knowles, *The Religious Orders in England, I, 1216–c. 1340* (1948)

Dom David Knowles and R. N. Hadcock, *Medieval Religious Houses, England and Wales* (1953), a catalogue, with an admirable introduction on monastic history

D. E. Easson, *Medieval Religious Houses, Scotland* (1957)

J. Armitage Robinson, *The Times of St Dunstan* (1923)

F. Barlow, *The English Church, 1000–1066* (1963)

R. W. Southern, *St Anselm and his Biographer* (1963)

Z. N. Brooke, *The English Church and the Papacy from the Conquest to the Reign of John* (1931)

Dom David Knowles, *The Episcopal Colleagues of Archbishop Thomas Becket* (1951)

C. R. Cheney, *From Becket to Langton* (1956)

D. A. Callus (ed.), *Robert Grosseteste* (1955)

R. L. Poole, *Illustrations of the History of Medieval Thought and Learning* (2nd ed., 1920)

H. Rashdall, *The Universities of Europe in the Middle Ages* (ed. Powicke and Emden, 3 vols., 1936)

H. Waddell, *The Wandering Scholars* (1927)

Art and Literature

W. P. Ker, *Medieval English Literature* (1912)

R. M. Wilson, *Early Middle English Literature* (1939)

T. S. R. Boase, *English Art, 1100–1216* (Oxford History of English Art, 1953)

F. Saxl and R. Wittkower, *British Art and the Mediterranean* (1947)

P. Brieger, *English Art, 1216–1307* (Oxford History of English Art, 1957)

G. Webb, *Architecture in Britain, the Middle Ages* (Pelican History of Art, 1956)

J. and H. Taylor, *Anglo-Saxon Architecture* (2 vols., 1965)

A. W. Clapham, *English Romanesque Architecture* (2 vols., 1930–4)

R. A. Brown, *English Medieval Castles* (1954)

M. Rickert, *Painting in Britain : the Middle Ages* (Pelican History of Art, 1954)

F. Wormald, *English Drawings of the Tenth and Eleventh Centuries* (1952)

A. Gardner, *English Medieval Sculpture* (3rd ed., 1951)

L. Stone, *Sculpture in Britain : the Middle Ages* (Pelican History of Art, 1955)

New Oxford History of Music, II, *Early Medieval Music to 1300*, ed. A. Hughes (1954 ed.)

INDEX